The GLITTER and the GOLD

FRED MUSTARD STEWART

The GLITTER *and the* GOLD

NAL BOOKS

NEW AMERICAN LIBRARY

A DIVISION OF PENGUIN BOOKS USA INC., NEW YORK
PUBLISHED IN CANADA BY
PENGUIN BOOKS CANADA LIMITED, MARKHAM, ONTARIO

PUBLISHER'S NOTE

This book is a work of fiction. Names, characters, places, and incidents are either the product of the author's imagination or are used fictitiously, and any resemblance to actual persons, living or dead, events, or locales is entirely coincidental.

Published simultaneously in Canada by Penguin Books Canada Limited.

NAL BOOKS TRADEMARK REG. U.S. PAT. OFF. AND FOREIGN COUNTRIES
REGISTERED TRADEMARK—MARCA REGISTRADA
HECHO EN BRATTLEBORO, VT., U.S.A.

SIGNET, SIGNET CLASSIC, MENTOR, ONYX, PLUME, MERIDIAN and NAL BOOKS are published *in the United States* by New American Library, a division of Penguin Books USA Inc., 1633 Broadway, New York, New York, *in Canada* by Penguin Books Canada Limited, 2801 John Street, Markham, Ontario L3R 1B4

Designed by Julian Hamer

LIBRARY OF CONGRESS CATALOGING-IN-PUBLICATION DATA
Stewart, Fred Mustard, 1932–
The glitter and the gold / by Fred Mustard Stewart.
p. cm.
ISBN 0-453-00676-0
I. Title.
PS3569.T464G57   1989
813.'.54—dc20   89-33620
                                                                CIP

First Printing, October, 1989
3 4 5 6 7 8 9
PRINTED IN THE UNITED STATES OF AMERICA

F
STE

To my beloved wife, Joan, who never lost faith,
and to my great grandmother, Emma Busch,
who came from Germany to America
in the last century

ACKNOWLEDGMENT

I wish to thank the wonderful staff of the
New York Society Library, who were so helpful
to me during the research for this book.

Fools' Gold:
The Price of Everything

"THAT was the Passelthwaites on the phone, asking us to come to Marbella tomorrow," said Guy de Lambert as he came into the bathroom of his Paris Ritz suite. "I said we'd love to."

His American-born wife, Claudia Collingwood de Lambert, stared at him from the bathtub. "But you hate Marbella," she said. "And you're not exactly wild about the Passelthwaites. You've always said Rodney's a bore."

"I know, but you like Margot. Besides, you've been cooped up at the château for months and it's our anniversary. I thought it would be a nice vacation for a few days. Margot says there's a ten-o'clock flight from Orly to Málaga, and she'll pick us up at the airport."

"You might have asked me before you accepted." Claudia's normally pleasant voice had an edge.

Her husband checked his watch. "You'd better hurry. Our dinner reservation's at eight," he reminded her as he started out of the bathroom.

"Guy!"

"What?"

She was annoyed by his odd heartiness, but not enough to start a fight.

"Nothing," she sighed.

He smiled at her. "You know, you're still as beautiful as that first day I met you two years ago."

And you're still as handsome, damn you, she thought as he left the bathroom. He was manipulating her, and she didn't know why. His accepting the invitation to Marbella was as untypical as his bringing her to a thousand-dollar-a-night suite at the Ritz. Something strange was going on, and she didn't know what it was. She was even wondering if this second anniversary might not be their last. She was still wildly attracted to the handsome Frenchman, but in her heart she knew she was beginning to fall out of love with him almost as quickly as she had fallen in. She soaped her arms with the sponge soggy with Hermès *bain de détente* and remembered that magic day two years before.

3

She had been driving through that most undiscovered province of western France, la Charente-Maritime, photographing châteaux, when she came upon a tiny gem of a building overlooking the Charente River. It was a fairy-tale castle replete with a round tower topped by a witch's-hat roof. There was a walled courtyard in front with open gates. Pulling into the short drive, she parked her rented Peugeot under a chestnut tree, slung her Nikon over her shoulder, and walked to the gate. Inside the courtyard, a gardener was weeding a bed of marigolds, which blazed garishly in the August sun.

"Excuse me," she said in her not-bad French, coming up behind the man. "Could you tell me the name of this château?"

When the gardener stood up and turned, her pulse zigzagged. He had movie-star good looks.

"You're an American?" he asked in English, which surprised her. In this rural region, English-speaking Frenchmen were as rare as tourists.

"Yes . . ."

His tanned face broke into a smile. "I like Americans."

"And I like Frenchmen. Could you tell me the name of this château?"

"It is the Château de Soubise."

"Is the owner around? I'm taking pictures for a book on French architecture, and this is so charming I'd like his permission to photograph it."

The gardener, whose hair was jet black and thick, smiled. "*I* give you permission. I also ask you to lunch."

"That's very kind of you, but I really should ask the owner—"

"Permit me to introduce myself. I am Guy Octave de Lambert, comte de Soubise."

"Oh, my God. And I thought you were the gardener!"

"I am also the gardener. Now: about lunch? And pardon me for stating the obvious, but when I see a beautiful American blond, I think: Aha! She must be from Florida."

"Wrong. I'm from California."

"You see? I don't know what I'm talking about."

Claudia emerged from the bathtub and put on the white terry-cloth bathrobe to dry. It had all been so incredibly romantic: she had fallen for him like a swooning teenager. They had gone inside the château, where lunch was cooked and served by Marie-Claude, a fat old woman who had taken care of "Monsieur le comte" since he was a baby. It was simple and superb: a *mouclade*, a Charentais specialty— a bowl of mussels in a sweet, creamy sauce with shallots, saffron, and white wine; a mixed salad; and a bottle of Graves. They ate in the cool dining room with its high ceiling and period furniture, some of which, she noted, was rather shabby. French windows opened out onto the rear garden and the Charente River, bordered by willows and wild-flowers. He had talked about his cognac and his vineyard, of which he was extremely proud. She had listened to his soft voice with the curious French-English accent—he had spent a year at Rugby, he explained. She sipped the wine, feeling blissful and dreamy. When he asked her to spend a few days at the château to "get to know the region," she didn't even hesitate before accepting.

A week later, she telephoned her father, Spencer Collingwood, in California.

"Daddy, fasten your seat belt."

"What's happened?"

"I'm about to become a French countess."

"A *what*?"

"He's the most wonderful man! His name is Guy, comte de Sou-bise, and he owns a cognac distillery and I'm just crazy about him! We're getting married in a week, so you'll have to fly over right away—"

"Hold on!" Her father's voice blasted halfway around the globe. "Is he after your money?"

"He doesn't know I have any."

"What did you tell him you were?"

"A farmer's daughter."

"A farmer? Did you tell him that 'farm' is the Calafía Ranch, the biggest goddamn private ranch in California?"

"No, I didn't. For once in my life, someone has fallen in love with *me*, plain old Claudia, instead of Claudia de Meyer Collingwood."

"You're not just 'plain old Claudia,' any more than I'm 'plain old Spencer'! For Chrissakes, grow up! You have a responsibility to me and the ranch."

"Daddy!" She wanted to scream, but she told herself to keep calm. Spencer Collingwood was a recluse who lived alone on the hundred-square-mile Calafía Ranch in Orange County, his one passion in life being sports-car racing. He was a cranky, difficult man who dug in his heels when confronted with any new situation. His only child marrying a foreigner was definitely a new situation. "Daddy, you know I'm a responsible person who loves the ranch. But it's important to me to find a man who loves me, not the Collingwood inheritance. When the wedding's over, you can tell him anything you want."

"Claudia, honey, I love you, but you still think like a twelve-year-old. All right, marry your goddamn Frenchman. It's your life. But if he turns out to be a creep, don't come crying to me. How much land does he own?"

"About forty acres. It's some of the best land in Cognac."

"Forty lousy acres? Jesus Christ, you stand to inherit a kingdom in California and you marry some froggy jug-wine-maker with forty acres? My God, I don't understand you. My daughter's a goddamn hippie. Next thing, you'll start wearing crystals and bark at the moon."

"Daddy, it's very easy to understand: I'm in love."

"Love!" he snorted. "That's the trouble with this family: the women are always falling in goddamn love."

Love. She sat on the stool before the marble sink and began to blow-dry her hair. She remembered the wedding in the small stone chapel in Soubise. Then the honeymoon at the Voile d'Or at St. Jean Cap Ferrat on the Riviera, a week of swimming and boating and tennis and sex. Then, the first week of September, returning to the château to await the all-important *vendange*, or harvesting.

That was when the reality had begun to intrude on the fairy tale. Far from being impressed when he learned his young wife was heiress to millions, Guy resented it. Their first fight had been over money. Claudia had wanted to buy herself a Mercedes, but Guy had objected, saying they were too expensive. When Claudia persisted, he had blown up and called her a damned spoiled rich American—something she had never forgotten. Guy was also a card-carrying *phallocrate*, French for "male chauvinist pig." Claudia was no radical feminist, but she had grown up in California, was a bit of a tomboy, and was used to being treated as an equal. She quickly learned that in Guy's eyes, a wife was somehow definitely not equal. She had married a man with a nineteenth-century mind—perhaps fourteenth-century!

Worse, she began to suspect he loved his vines almost more than her. Viniculture was his passion, and life at the tiny château, with its centuries-old routine, was all-encompassing to Guy. To Claudia it became a bore. It might have been better if she had had children, but Guy had said he didn't want any for a while. The result was, she had no purpose. She began to wonder if her father hadn't been right after all. Had she given up a kingdom in California for forty acres in the backwaters of Bordeaux? She often thought about her family, whose history was so intertwined with the history of California, especially of her great-great-great-grandmother, the legendary Emma de Meyer. Emma had fallen as madly in love with Archer Collingwood as Claudia had with Guy, but Emma would never have played second fiddle to a grapevine.

Claudia shook her tousled curls, hating the ugly grimace reflected in the mirror. The week before, something had happened, something mysterious and rather frightening. Guy had come home from the distillery to tell her that vandals had broken in the night before and destroyed fifty cases of his cognac. Not stolen: destroyed. They had smashed the bottles on the concrete floor. The police had no idea who had committed such an act of senseless violence. Nor did Guy . . . or so he maintained. But she had seen the overnight change in his manner. His hands trembled at dinner. When she tried to talk to him, he changed the subject, but she felt certain he was frightened of something. Hard on this followed his suggestion that they celebrate their anniversary at the Ritz, which was so unlike Guy, who was a certifiable tightwad. And now this off-the-wall trip to Marbella . . .

"Darling, we have to hurry." He stuck his head in the bathroom. "I don't want to be late at Taillevent."

"Coming."

She got up to begin dressing. Something was happening behind the scenes, something sinister she didn't understand.

The beautiful blond heiress to California's greatest fortune suddenly felt threatened by an ominous shadow.

"Don't think Marbella's all sunshine and glitz," said Margot Passelthwaite. "There's a lot of sleaze and a big drug scene down here," she went on as she sped in her white Ferrari toward the resort town on the southern coast of Spain. "But overall, it's wonderful. Four million sex-crazed tourists squirming the night away in discos. Sex-crazed Euro-trash and billionaire Arabs all boozing it up. Rodney and I will take you to the Marbella Club tonight and you can see the whole scene. It makes the fall of the Roman Empire look like a Tupperware party."

Margot, who had been Claudia's roommate at Vassar, was a Central Park West princess, but four years with Rodney Passelthwaite had given her a Sloane Square accent—or at least enough of one to fool anyone but the English.

"Look at all the vile bodies!" she exclaimed that night as she and Rodney led Claudia and Guy through the crowd at the Marbella Club. The air was smoky and the noise level was ghetto-blaster loud as tanned blonds with gold chokers and men with gold chains over hairy chests maneuvered around tiny round tables loaded with bottles of Diet Coke and Scotch. "The place is packed with titles: it's Euro-trash heaven! Sorry, Claudia: I forgot you're Euro-trash by marriage."

"I don't think 'Euro-trash' is a particularly attractive way to describe either my wife or myself," said Guy, whose dislike of the Passelthwaites was becoming more evident by the minute.

"Guy, dear, I love you passionately," said Margot, "but you could never be accused of having a sense of humor. There's nothing wrong with titles. I adore titles!"

"A good title can get you discounts at boutiques," said Rodney, an overweight Oxonian with sandy hair and pink cheeks who represented one of the major London stockbrokerages in Marbella. "And a title looks smashing on your stationery."

"Rodney's so profound," said Margot. "He's always searching for the basic truths in life."

Across the room, two men watched them. One was tall and thin, with striking features and slicked-back silver hair. He wore a blazer with the burgee of his yacht on the breast pocket, an open-neck white pima-cotton sport shirt, white duck slacks, and white espadrilles with no socks. The man beside him had a Mephistophelian black beard with a sweeping, upturned mustache. He had a monocle in his right eye, two gold chains revealed by his open-necked shirt, and a red boutonnière in the lapel of his white suit. The latter was Don Jaime de Mora y Aragón, the brother of the Queen of the Belgians, and he knew all the gossip of Marbella.

"That's the comtesse de Soubise," he said, indicating Claudia. "She's the heiress to that huge ranch in California."

"Yes, I know," said Nigel Sinclair, first Viscount Northfield. To Don Jaime's surprise, Nigel started across the room. Was it possible Nigel was as well-informed as Don Jaime?

"There's Gunilla von Bismark," Margot was saying to Claudia, indicating a golden-haired beauty in a hip-hugging sequined gown who had just come in. "She's at every party worth talking about. Her brother, Prince Ferdinand, is developing the Marbella Hill Club—oh, my God, it's Lord Northfield, and he's coming our way."

"Who's Lord Northfield?"

"Darling, you've been buried too long in the backwoods. Lord Northfield just happens to be the third-richest man in the world, with the second-biggest yacht—or is it the other way around? I never can remember. More later," she whispered as Nigel approached the table. Rodney got to his feet and stuck out his hand, his smile revealing terrible teeth. "Nigel, old boy," he said, for they had known each other at Oxford. "Do you know the de Soubises?"

"Of course. Guy, how are you?"

To Claudia's surprise, her husband was shaking hands with the Englishman. Guy, forcing a smile, replied that he was fine. Then Lord Northfield was introduced to Claudia. The silver-haired viscount kissed her hand, his blue eyes piercing her green ones.

"I've wanted to meet you for years," he said. "I've heard you're the most beautiful countess in la Charente-Maritime, and I can now testify that it's the truth. Guy, would you mind if I dance with your wife?"

"Of course not."

"Claudia?"

"I'd be delighted."

He led her to the packed dance floor, then took her in his arms, holding her close by necessity because of the crowd. Dozens of eyes watched. He was a half-head taller than she, but their bodies fitted nicely. Claudia was wearing a short black dress by Martine Sitbon, a young Parisian designer she liked. Her blond hair brushed her bare back as they moved in slow, tight circles. Her only jewelry was shell-shaped gold ear clips.

"Did you know I grew up on the Calafía Ranch?" he said.

"Really? That's odd. I grew up there and never noticed you."

He smiled. "I grew up there in my imagination. When I was a boy, I bounced around a half-dozen countries with my father. He was always getting fired from jobs or going bankrupt. Anyway, I felt rather home-less, and when I started reading books about the American West—particularly California—it fascinated me so much I suppose I made it my home. Since your family was involved with so much of it—the Gold Rush, the Tong Wars, the Barbary Coast—I read all about the de Meyers and the Collingwoods. And here I am, dancing with Claudia de Meyer Collingwood. It's terribly exciting."

"I'm flattered. Where did you meet my husband?"

"Guy? I'm a fancier of fine cognacs. I also own a chain of resort hotels, and I personally select the wines for them—or I should say, the top-of-the-line wines. I've bought a lot of Soubise cognac and met Guy at his distillery."

"I'm sorry he's never asked you to the château."

"Yes, I'm sorry too, especially now that I've met you. But all this past neglect can be solved. Tomorrow I'm taking a three day cruise on my yacht. We're going over to Tangier, then sail along the African coast a bit. There'll be some interesting people aboard. Would you and Guy care to join us?"

A bell was ringing in her head: there was something rather odd about this. On the other hand, she liked his suave good looks, the firm strength of his hand on her back, the faint, tawny smell of his Penhaligon cologne. But she sensed Nigel was a tiger. Of course, one didn't get to be one of the richest men in the world being a lamb.

"Well, we're staying with the Passelthwaites . . ." she equivocated.

"Oh, Rodney and Margot will come too. Rodney's my stock-broker, you know. Or one of them. We're old school chums."

"If Guy wants to go, I'd be delighted."

"Good. Then it's settled. We'll have a smashing time."

"I said, if Guy wants to go."

"Yes, I heard you."

It struck her that he seemed terribly sure Guy would want to go.

Nigel's white Rolls Royce picked them up at the villa the next morning and drove them to Puerto Banus, the harbor next to Marbella. When it stopped by an enormous white yacht, Claudia climbed out of the car and looked up at the immense toy. She was certainly no stranger to wealth, but her father would never dream of owning such a screaming example of conspicuous consumption. Four crewmen hurried down the gangway to pick up their luggage. As the Mediterranean sun blazed down on them, they climbed to the immaculate teak main deck, where a blond officer in a white uniform saluted them. "Welcome aboard the *Calista*," the officer said with a pronounced German accent. "I'll show you to your staterooms."

He led them aft past the gleaming white bulkhead. The marina was filled with yachts, many of them well over one hundred feet in length, but the *Calista* was so much longer it seemed in a class by itself—almost two hundred feet, Claudia guessed. Above her, on the top deck, a helicopter was lashed. The superstructure bristled with the latest radar, loran, and ComSat navigational devices, all of which must have cost a fortune.

There was a distant roar, growing louder. Margot pointed to a man zooming across the water toward the yacht on jet skis.

"Our host, Mr. Jock," she said. "Nigel eats high-fiber competitive cereal for breakfast. He's also a tennis nut and once paid Bjorn Borg fifty thousand dollars to play him in a private game, donating another fifty thousand to charity."

"Did he win?" asked Claudia.

"Of course not, but he can brag that he was beaten by Bjorn Borg. These days it's who you play the game with that counts."

The jet skis roared by like a buzz saw, and Nigel waved.

"Tell me, how did he make his money?" Claudia asked.

"He calls himself an entrepreneur," said Rodney, looking a bit stunned despite himself at all the luxury. "Although others call him a pirate. He buys companies cheap—"

"And sells them expensive?"

"He did that at first. But then he began holding on to the companies and making them profitable. He's turned a lot of companies around. He has his share of critics, but I don't think anyone would deny that he's brilliant. He donates tons of money to the Tories, which is why Mrs. Thatcher arranged a title. But she also admires him."

"Is he married?"

"Three times," said Margot. "His current wife is Lady Calista Gascoigne, the daughter of the Marquess of Chalfont."

"And how did you meet him, Guy?" Claudia asked casually.

"We knew each other at Rugby," he replied.

He's lying! she thought. But why? They can't even get their stories straight: Nigel said they met at the distillery.

Why is he lying to me, his wife?

"What's going on?" Claudia asked her husband that evening as they walked along the deck toward the main saloon of the yacht. The ship had cast off after lunch, heading for the African coast; she could see the sleek bow slicing the water into curls of white foam.

"What do you mean, 'what's going on?' " countered Guy.

"Why are we here? It's obvious you hate Marbella, you can barely stand the Passelthwaites, and yet you bring us down here, suddenly Nigel appears out of nowhere and invites us on his yacht. I don't believe all of this is just 'happening.' What's going on?"

"I have no idea what you're talking about."

"But you do! You're lying to me, Guy—I feel it in my bones! And I'm getting damned fed up with these lies—"

She saw Nigel's other guests approaching them, and she shut up. They had met Billie Ching and his wife at lunch. Billie, a moon-faced man from Hong Kong, was the president of the Bank of South China. His wife, a beauty named Perfume, was one of China's leading film stars. At lunch, Perfume had casually announced that she spent a half-million dollars a year on clothes.

"As the Mediterranean gets more polluted," Nigel said after they had all seated themselves in the air-conditioned dining saloon, "it's becoming more difficult for the fishermen to catch *loup.* But in my opinion, it's worth the trouble. I think it's the best fish in the world."

"Best fish in world is shark," said Perfume, who was sitting at Nigel's left, if "sitting" was the applicable word, since the enormous black-and-red pouf skirt of her Christian Lacroix dress made her look slightly tilted. She wore a dazzling emerald-and-diamond necklace with matching chandelier earrings which flashed in the candlelight. Her black bangs slashed across her forehead above her almond eyes, which stared across the table at Claudia. Her English was somewhat idiosyncratic. "I like you dress," she said. "It Giorgio Armani, no?"

"Yes."

"It pretty. You pretty. How much you pay for dress?"

Claudia looked uncomfortable as Margot stifled a giggle.

"Let's just say it wasn't cheap."

"I bet you pay maybe three thousand," Perfume continued, undaunted. "You know how much I pay for this Christian Lacroix—and now *W* say pouf skirts is out? I pay twenty-five thousand bucks. I gotta be crazy, no?"

"You gotta be rich," said Margot.

"Oh sure, I plenty rich. Billie, he richest man in Hong Kong—and that's *big* rich."

Billie, who was sitting at Claudia's right, growled something in Chinese. Perfume just shrugged.

"Billie just tell me it vulgar to talk about money," she went on, unperturbed. "Billie gotta be real vulgar, 'cause that all he ever talk about—money. How much he worth, how much it cost, how much he make. Money make world go round, so why not talk about it? It most interesting thing in world except maybe sex. Maybe more interesting than sex, who know?"

The white-jacketed Cambodian waiters were passing the silver trays holding grilled fillets of *loup* with fennel. As Billie placed some of the exquisite fish on his plate, he frowned at his wife. "Perfume, you're becoming tedious."

At lunch Claudia had been surprised by his flawless upper-class English accent. She was also impressed by his perfect table manners, his immaculately cut dinner jacket, and his gold-and-lapis-lazuli cufflinks.

Perfume shrugged. "You say I boring, but I bet everybody fascinated. Fifty year ago, nobody talk about sex, now everybody let it all hang out. Why not do same thing with money? When I go to New York, that all they talk about."

"This conversation is reminding me of Oscar Wilde's definition of a cynic," said Claudia.

"Exactly," said Lady Calista, Nigel's wife. She was a tall, attractive blond in a black sequined dress that shimmered in the candlelight. "A cynic knows the price of everything and the value of nothing. I quite agree with you, Countess. If we can't keep *some* things private, we might as well all dance naked in the moonlight, like druids. Or did druids dance naked?"

"Well, they painted their bodies blue," said her husband as the sommelier refilled his glass with the Château Grillet.

"I suppose it sounds like a corny old song," Claudia went on, "but I believe the best things in life are free. Like the stars and the moon and the land."

"Ah," said Billie Ching, next to her, "do you think the land is free? Real estate is the most valuable thing on earth. Would you give away your Calafia Ranch for nothing?"

"Of course not. But I wasn't thinking of real estate—"

"But all land is real estate, isn't it? And as the United States becomes a second-class country, it will sell more and more things off to us foreigners just to keep afloat. The last thing it will sell will be its real estate, and then history will have come full circle. America, which started off as a colony, will end up a colony once again."

She looked at his smooth Buddha face, a half-moon in the chiaroscuro of candlelight. "In the first place," she said, "I don't think America is becoming a second-class country—"

"But you haven't been home lately. Something like twenty percent of Americans are functional illiterates. Over half your young people know nothing of history—they can't even date your Civil War within fifty years. Your average American brain has been reduced to jelly by continuous rock music, celebrity worship, and trivial game shows. Most Americans know more about Vanna White than they do about Abraham Lincoln. Consequently, you can't compete against us bettereducated foreigners, and your trade deficits will mount until you drown in them. That's the ugly truth your politicians are afraid to admit. And if that isn't a definition of a second-rate country, I don't know what is."

"America is *finito*!" said Perfume. "Pfft!" She waved her jeweled hand.

"I seem to recall that Europe would have been *finito* forty years ago if it hadn't been for us—not to mention China," Claudia said angrily.

"You won the war," Billie Ching said, "but you lost the peace. America is sliding down into the dustbin of history, and the irony is, you're doing it to yourselves."

"We're ganging up on our Americans," said Nigel, "which isn't fair."

"Can I smoke?" said Perfume. "I know everyone hate smokers, but I don't eat food so I can fit into this crazy dress for twenty-five thousand buck. Okay to smoke?"

She already had the cigarette in her mouth. Guy, next to her, pulled a slim gold lighter from his pocket and lit it.

"Bulgari," said Perfume, pointing at the lighter. "Solid gold. Cost you two thousand buck, I bet."

Even Claudia laughed. She had bought it for Guy the previous Christmas, and it had cost—two thousand buck.

"A penny for your thoughts," said Nigel, coming up to Claudia as she stood at the port rail, looking at the lights of Tangier in the African night. Shortly after dinner she had gone outside to get some air.

"Oh, I was wondering if it's true that America is washed up," she said. "And then I became terribly homesick."

"For the ranch?"

"Yes."

"Do you love it?"

"Naturally."

"Then why did you leave it to marry a French cognac maker?"

"I fell in love. Of course, my father thinks I'm avoiding my family responsibility."

"Which is?"

"Well, my family, as you said, has been tied up with so much of California's history that . . ." She shrugged. "I don't know. Perhaps I was running away from it a bit. Maybe I'm beginning to feel a little guilty."

"What if there were a way for you to get involved with your family's history again?"

"How do you mean?"

He took her arm. "Come. I'll show you." And he led her forward toward the bow of the yacht.

Nigel took her to his large paneled office. A silver ceiling was illuminated from a recessed coving, and there were several splendid paintings—she recognized an Odilon Redon. But everything else was a fleeting first impression, for on a large table in the center of the room lay a topographical model that grabbed her attention. Approaching it, she admired the three-dimensional skill of the construction. The ocean and rivers were painted blue, the land mostly purplish-brown, much like the Calafía Ranch. It was then she recognized her home.

"Yes, it's the ranch," said Nigel. "A modeling firm in Paris made this from drawings done by Gabriel Catroux, a young French architect who's something of a genius, in my opinion. Take a look."

Slowly she circumnavigated the table, looking at tiny model towns built along the coast—what towns? she thought. There were no towns on the ranch.

"Gabriel spent six months studying the ranch from aerial photographs and topographical maps," Nigel was saying. "He's thought of just about everything, including a system of reservoirs up in the hills— you see them there?"

"Yes . . ."

"Our studies and projections indicate that within five years we'd be bringing in a population of over two million, so obviously we'd need reservoirs, since the rainfall couldn't support anything near that many people."

She looked at him suspiciously. "So you want to develop the ranch? Who's 'we'?"

"Myself and Billie Ching. We own a company called the World Leisure Group. We've developed a very successful resort near Biarritz and a large housing development on the west coast of Florida. We also own the Excelsior Hotel chain with fifty-eight first-class hotels around the world, so we think we're amply qualified to develop the Calafía Ranch. It would be our largest and most exciting undertaking."

"Does my father know about this?"

Nigel leaned on his English Regency desk, folded his arms over his chest, and smiled.

"Oh, no. We know that Spencer Collingwood hates developers. That's why we're approaching you first. The Calafía Ranch is one of the choice pieces of real estate left in America, and it must be developed correctly, not only to maximize the use of the land, but also to protect the ecology. We don't want tacky shopping malls and fast-food chains, and neither do you. That's why I thought if I could get you here on the yacht, get to know you a bit, have the opportunity to show you that we're not just fast-buck operators but rather that we have a dream for the ranch, to preserve as much of its natural beauty as possible— well, that perhaps we could get you to join forces with us. We've already approached your cousin Jeffrey Brett, who controls the other fifty per-cent of the ranch, representing the rest of your family—or, more for-mally, the Class A shareholders of the Collingwood Corporation. Jeffrey is interested in our proposal, and if we had you on our side, I feel we would have a fairly formidable proposal to make to your father."

"But I'm telling you, Daddy would never sell the ranch."

"Perhaps. But everything has a price."

"You sound like Perfume."

"She may be right. Who knows? Money certainly seems to make the world go round. At any rate, our cash offer is two billion dollars."

Claudia hesitated. "Two billion?" she repeated softly.

"Yes. It's a lot of money."

"True, but it's a lot of land. I may have been away from California for two years, but I'm not totally out of touch. I know what's happening in Orange County. It's exploding with development. The ranch is easily worth two billion. What did my husband have to do with this?"

"Well, we asked him to help us get you down here."

"Why didn't you just come to me directly?"

"I was assured by many people, including Jeffrey Brett, that if we approached you cold, so to speak, you wouldn't talk to us. My hope was that this way we could open a dialogue. You see, Claudia, the ranch has to be developed eventually. There's no way that that much land that close to Los Angeles and San Diego can remain undeveloped. The question is, how to do it *right*. I hope to be able to convince you that we are the best people for the job. Does that strike you as unreasonable?"

"No, I suppose not. But you've rather thrown me with all this. You can't expect me to give an answer *now*?"

"Of course not. Take all the time you want. It's an important decision."

She looked at the model again.

"It may be one of the most important decisions of my life. And having said that, I think I'll go to bed. You've taken my breath away, and I have to sleep on it."

"Certainly." He went to the door and opened it, smiling at her. "Good night, Claudia."

"Good night."

She stepped into the cool night air, her mind reeling. Nigel was certainly a slick showman, a Ziegfeld of big business: she had been taken totally by surprise. She walked back to her stateroom and let herself in. The sitting room was empty, but she could hear the water running in the bathroom. She locked the door and went in the bedroom. Guy had already undressed for bed and was in the bathroom brushing his teeth.

"Well, the mystery is solved," she said. "Now I know why I'm here. I might add, it seems I'm the last one to know. I feel like a first-class pigeon."

He rinsed his mouth and put his toothbrush away. "Did Nigel show you the model?"

"Yes. And you knew about it all along?"

"Yes."

"And Margot and Rodney? I suppose they were in on it?"

"Of course. Rodney's Nigel's stockbroker. Nigel throws him a half-million pounds a year in commissions."

"But, Guy, why didn't you tell me? Why wasn't I told this whole elaborate charade was a setup? I happen to be your wife, you know."

"Nigel wanted it done this way. He told me to take you to the Ritz for our anniversary and he'd pick up the tab—"

"Damn you! You mean even that was a phony?"

"You know I don't have that kind of money. He said he wanted to put you in a good frame of mind to 'prepare you for the presentation,' as he put it. Then to bring you down here, and he'd do the rest."

"How could you have treated me this way? You betrayed me!"

He came to her and tried to put his arms around her, but she pushed him off and went into the bedroom.

"All right, it's natural you'd be angry," he said, following her.

"Angry? I'm furious! And how much did he pay you?"

"That's a helluva thing to say!"

She turned on him. "Why? Rodney, my best friend's husband,

sold me out for a half-million pounds in commissions. I'd be interested to see what my husband thinks I'm worth."

"Oh, for God's sake, Claudia, don't make such a drama out of it! Nigel didn't pay me anything. The point is, are you going to go along with him?"

"I don't know."

"A billion dollars is an incredible amount of money, and that's what you'd get for your half."

"Oh? Is that my price? You've always sneered at my money. You called me a spoiled, rich American—which I haven't forgotten—but a billion bucks suddenly makes me look a little less spoiled?"

"That's not true, and it's a rotten thing to say! You know, if anything, I hate your damned money!"

"Then why?" she almost screamed. "Why did you betray me— and believe me, Guy, that's how I view this: as a betrayal."

Even with his tan, she could see the color drain from his face. He sat on the bed and buried his face in his hands for a moment. Then he looked up at her and whispered, "I did it because I'm afraid of them."

"Afraid?" she repeated, knowing he was telling the truth. "Guy, was Nigel responsible for those men breaking into the distillery last week?"

"Yes. Claudia, for God's sake, do what they say. Give them what they want. These men are dangerous."

His fear was contagious.

"What do you think they might do?" she whispered.

He clenched his fists, then unclenched them. "It's Billie Ching," he whispered. "He's the dangerous one. I talked to my brother-in-law in Paris, who talked with some bankers he knows. The rumor is that Billie's Hong Kong bank launders money for the Triads—"

"The what?"

"The Hong Kong gangs. The Chinese are getting into crime all over the world, and Hong Kong is their home base—at least until the mainland Communists take it over from the British in eight years. Nigel wants to seduce you into joining with them against your father. But if that doesn't work . . ."

"Well? What?"

"Billie Ching sent a message by breaking into the distillery. The message being that they may use violence."

"Oh, my God, like what?"

"I don't know, and I don't want to find out."

She began pacing in tight little circles, trying to keep calm. "All right," she said. "We're not going to panic. No big scenes. I'm going to tell Nigel in the morning that I want to go to California and discuss this with Daddy. You go back to the château. We'll pretend we're going along with them just to get off this bloody boat." Suddenly she whirled around. "But, Guy, why didn't you tell me sooner? That's what I still can't understand. Why didn't you trust me?"

He jumped off the bed. "You, you, *you!*" he yelled. "Is that all you ever think of? What about me? What about my château, that's been in my family for three hundred years? Am I supposed to endanger that because of your bloody ranch in America that doesn't mean a damned thing to me?"

"What are you talking about?"

He crossed the bedroom to one of the built-in lacquer cabinets. Opening the top drawer, he took out his wallet and removed a folded piece of paper, which he brought back and shoved into her hand.

"The morning after they broke into the distillery," he whispered, "this was delivered to the château in the mail. This is Billie Ching's second message."

She unfolded the paper. On it were two crude ink drawings. One was of the Château de Soubise—unmistakable with its round tower and pointed roof. The château was in flames.

The other drawing was of a knife cutting off a pair of testicles.

Two mornings later, a Concorde lifted off the runway at Charles de Gaulle Airport and pierced a leaden sky with its long, sleek nose. Inside, strapped into one of the leather seats in the cramped cabin, Claudia looked out the port as Europe fluttered in and out between the clouds below. After two years she was going home, and in her heart she knew she would never come back to France, at least not as the comtesse de Soubise. True, the threat of arson and castration had terrified Guy, but if he had only told her, if he had trusted her! Instead he had crumpled before Nigel and Billie like a straw man and manipulated his duped wife into their well-manicured hands. Guy's betrayal had delivered the coup de grace to her love. The threat of his precious château being burned had shown his priorities: it was more important to him than his wife. Perhaps she was being unfair, even cruel, but she no longer could love him. She hadn't told him yet, but she was going to file for divorce.

She had thought divorce so commonplace, and yet, now that she faced the prospect herself, it hurt more than she had imagined. "I'm twenty-five, without a man, and confronted with a war." Was it possible? she thought for the hundredth time. Billie Ching, with his Oxford accent? Nigel, so suave, so rich, married into the very heart of the English establishment. Did they resort to violence like common crooks?

"Some call him a pirate." Rodney's words rang in her ears. The smashed cognac bottles, the crude threats of arson and castration. Yes, it was possible. She had left the yacht on a seemingly friendly basis, but she had no illusions that she had seen the last of Billie and Nigel. The yacht had been merely the first skirmish in a war for the Calafía Ranch, and with Billie's connection to the Hong Kong Triads, the war promised to be as bloody and lurid as the Tong Wars of the past century. Well, her ancestor, Emma, had survived the Tong Wars and worse. Claudia would survive this war.

But she knew she would have to be as strong and resourceful as Emma if she hoped to save what her family had built over so many generations.

·ONE·

A Passage to California

1

EMMA de Meyer had no way of knowing it was to be her last recital in the Old World.

It was a warm May Sunday in 1849, and as she sat at the rosewood Pleyel piano in her father's crowded ballroom, she was a dream of loveliness. The few gentiles present for the occasion found it rather shocking that someone so recently widowed would wear a white silk dress with fashionable puffed sleeves, but Emma had sat shiva for her husband and wasn't about to put on a black dress. Her jet-black hair was pulled back from her face and exploded in a cascade of bouncing curls in back. Her large amethyst eyes—eyes her mother boasted were the most beautiful in Germany—intently watched her fingers flying over the ivory keys. Though she was frowning in concentration, her nose was firm and straight, her mouth small with a hint of voluptuousness, and when she smiled, her teeth were white and even. Her one flaw— if it was that—was the small mole on her lower right cheek. But Emma called it her beauty mark, and few would have quibbled with that.

She's perfection, thought David Levin, Emma's twenty-two-year-old second cousin from London. He had been living in the de Meyer household for two years, polishing Emma's already excellent English. But, he reflected, she'll never love me. Me, with my bookish looks. Perhaps if I grew a beard . . . Emma's nice to me, she likes me, but could she ever love me? She does admire my mind, admires the fact that I want to be a writer.

How long had he wanted to hold her in his arms, to kiss her? David's chaste soul could hardly imagine actually making love to Emma, even though, of course, she was no virgin, having been married for two weeks to the ill-fated Anton Schwabe.

Emma concluded the Beethoven sonata and rose to curtsy to the applause of the tight little world of Frankfurt's Jewish elite. The tall French windows on the second floor admitted a welcome breeze, and outside, a small audience had gathered in the street to listen to the music. As Emma smiled at the thirty-odd people in the white-and-gold ballroom with its two crystal chandeliers, she made a point of smiling directly at Baron Henckel von Hellsdorf, one of the few goyim present. With thick blond hair and mustache, Henckel was a commanding figure, and Emma had a weakness for good-looking men.

That was why she had been so angry at her mother for forcing her to marry Anton Schwabe. She had shuddered every time he touched her, which he had done too often for her taste. She had dutifully gone through with the ceremony because she loved her mother, who wanted her daughter married to a Schwabe because Anton's uncle was the most respected rabbi in Germany. But God could be perverse. Despite the rabbi uncle, Anton was killed shortly thereafter in a carriage accident, and Emma was unexpectedly free to start looking for a good-looking new husband.

Emma liked to think of herself as a pure romantic, but secretly she suspected that she had inherited her mother's practical streak as well. So when she smiled at Henckel, she considered not only his good looks but also his rank as a baron.

Of course, he's only after Poppa's money, and he's dumb as a gourd besides, she thought as she sat back down and launched into her selection of Chopin waltzes. And Momma would never permit me to marry a gentile.

Look at him, thought Mathilde de Meyer, who was sitting in the front row wearing a taupe gown with black piping. Baron von Hellsdorf, indeed. You can see the greed in his eyes! All the goyim are interested in is money and titles, and they accuse us of being greedy! If only my Emma wasn't so willful and proud. She even insists on calling herself Emma de Meyer again, as if she never married! She has her eye on him, I can tell.

Sitting next to Mathilde was her husband. Whereas Frau de Meyer was tall and growing ever more stout, Felix de Meyer was a delicate, small-boned man. Everyone agreed Emma had inherited her striking looks from her father. Felix had a dreamy, almost effeminate face, with large, sad violet eyes belying the hirsute fierceness of his graying beard. He had tears in those eyes as he listened to his daughter play, for he adored his only child.

Even as he listened, though, his mind was filled with foreboding. As a Sephardic Jew, and Frankfurt's leading jeweler, he could never entirely forget the ominous events swirling all around him. An armed uprising in Dresden only a week before, following the revolutions in Berlin and Paris the past year. People had been starting to say things were calming down, and then it broke out in Dresden. More strife could only mean a resurgence of hatred toward Jews.

They had made great advances in Germany, although the German ghettos had been opened less than a half-century and Frankfurt's had been one of the worst. A century before, when Mayer Amschel Roths-child had begun his journey out of the Frankfurt ghetto, Jews had been forced by imperial decree to live in the Judengasse, a street twelve feet wide wedged between the city walls and a trench and sealed from the rest of Frankfurt by heavy iron doors—nominally for protection against the Christians. Jews had to wear a yellow patch on their coats, were forbidden to powder their wigs, and paid a Jew tax when they crossed the bridge over the River Main. But now much of that had been changed, and the de Meyers lived in one of the most elegant areas in the city, Westend, less than a block from the Rothschilds, many of whom were Felix de Meyer's best customers.

But only a fool would think anti-Semitism was dead in Germany. As revolutions erupted all over Europe, royalists and conservatives accused the Jews of financing revolutionaries in order to overturn the old regimes, while the liberals, communists, and many of the students tarred the Jews as greedy capitalists trying to control the world's money markets with their Judengelt. Europe was falling apart, and Felix was sharing what many German Jews were feeling: America fever. He was still young, forty-three . . . what an adventure America would be! The uncharted forests, the freedom from centuries of European anti-Semitism . . . and lately, the reports of gold discovered in California. It was heady stuff. Of course, he thought, Mathilde would never agree to go to such an uncultured place as America. She had once said she doubted if there were two pianos in the whole country. Yet America beckoned to Felix like a Lorelei.

Emma concluded a spirited rendition of the Minute Waltz and rose to curtsy to the applause of gloved hands. Then, as fans fluttered, her audience rose from their gilded chairs as Felix's footmen, looking very *dix-huitième* in powdered wigs, entered carrying silver trays with flutes of champagne and bowls of strawberries. The high-ceilinged room buzzed with gossip as, moments before, it had hummed with melody. The afternoon sun streamed through the windows with their gold bro-cade curtains. As Emma was encircled by her friends and relatives, all kissing and congratulating her for the recital, she thought she had never been happier.

"Fräulein!" It was handsome Henckel pushing his way through the crowd to her. As he took her hand and raised it to his lips, she gave him her most fetching smile. "Your playing was enchanting," he was saying. "And even though I find Czerny's music superficial—"

"It was Chopin, Baron."

"Ah, I knew it began with a C."

The girls, none of whom failed to appreciate Henckel's good looks, tittered. Henckel laughed at his own mistake. "Well, well, there's no point pretending I know anything about music, is there?" he said, taking a glass of champagne from a passing footman. "I always say music is for the ladies. Your instrument, my dear Emma, is a piano. Mine is a shotgun, eh? You fire the notes, I fire the bullets."

"If Napoleon had fired notes instead of bullets, think how many young men might still be alive." She smiled, amused at the shocked look on his face. "They might be tone-deaf, but they'd be alive." My God, he *is* thick! she thought.

Mathilde came to her daughter's side, taking her right arm. "I enjoyed your recital very much, my dear," she said, smiling at Henckel. "However, it seemed to me you played the last waltz rather too quickly. Facility of technique can never replace feeling and sentiment. Now, come, you must mingle with your guests. We cannot allow Baron von Hellsdorf to monopolize you."

She guided Emma through the guests. It was then that they heard the chanting. It began as a murmur, the buzz of distant locusts, but quickly it became louder and more distinct. A single word became distinguishable: *"Juden. Juden. Juden."*

The conversation of the guests died as the elegantly dressed people turned toward the three open French windows.

"Juden. Juden. Juden."

It was louder now, accompanied by a drum that rat-a-tat-tatted an ominous accompaniment.

"Juden. Juden. Juden."

It crackled with hate.

David Levin went to one of the windows and looked out. The cobblestone street had emptied, as if the people listening to Emma's music shortly before had scattered before the coming storm. And then he saw them: students, many of them with university caps on their blond heads, were marching down the Westendstrasse. It was a wild-looking bunch. Many of them carried beer steins and were obviously half-seas-over. One of them, who didn't look more than fifteen, carried the drum. Others carried banners: "Student Radical Union," "Union of Communists and Friends of Blanqui," "Down with Jewish Capitalists!", "Expose the Jewish Plot of World Domination!"

"Student radicals!" David cried to the guests.

"Juden. Juden. Juden."

Felix hurried to the middle window, stepping onto the narrow balcony. By now the students—and there seemed to be a hundred of them—were massed in front of the house. Mathilde joined her husband.

"It's that article!" she had to shout over the chanting. "I told you not to talk to that reporter. Now we have every maniac in Frankfurt!"

"All I said was that the economy couldn't survive if order wasn't restored—"

"You should have kept your mouth shut. Never talk to the press."

Felix and Mathilde had been spotted. Now the students started jeering at them.

"There they are!"

"The filthy Jew capitalist!"

"*Judenbengel, Judenbengel!* Jew-boor, Jew-boor!"

"You want order?" cried one, who had pried a paving stone from the square. "We'll give you order: the order of the streets!"

He hurled the stone up at the center window, and it struck Mathilde on the forehead.

"Mother!" screamed Emma, coming up beside her. Her mother slumped backward onto the parquet of the ballroom. Emma and Felix knelt beside her as other paving stones began flying through the windows. The stone had gashed a deep wound on Mathilde's forehead. Blood was oozing out, smearing Emma's white dress as she cradled her mother in her arms.

"Get a doctor!" yelled Felix.

David Levin ran toward the double doors as the other guests backed away from the three open windows. One paving stone hit one of the chandeliers, causing it to dance crazily and sending a shower of crystals tinkling to the floor. Another rock smashed a large and priceless *famille noire* K'ang Hsi jar. The guests began screaming, thronging toward the doors.

"I don't believe it," said Felix, holding his wife's left hand in both of his. There were tears in his eyes. "She's dead."

"Momma!" sobbed Emma. "Momma . . ."

As the rocks continued to crash into the gold-and-white ballroom, Emma de Meyer's elegant little world died.

Nineteen-year-old Archer Collingwood stood in the rain before the newly erected tombstone of his mother: "Martha Collingwood, 1811–1850." Thirty-nine years old, Archer thought as the rain streamed down his face. My sweet mother, dead at thirty-nine. "The fever," Doc Brixton had called it, but what the hell did he know? I could tell, looking at him, that he didn't know what was happening to Ma. Poor sweet Ma. Dead a week! A week in that cold grave. Oh, God, how I miss her!

He was six-foot-one and rangy, with blond hair that hung almost to his broad shoulders. He had blue eyes, clear skin, and clean-cut features—a face that never failed to elicit sighs from the neighbor women, who called it "the face of an angel."

He was wearing his only suit, a black one of homespun, to come to the country churchyard in northeastern Indiana. It was a chilly March day, and Archer wore his fringed buckskin coat over his suit. The rain formed puddles at his booted feet. "Joseph Collingwood, 1806–1846." His father's grave was next to his mother's. Joseph had been barely forty when he had been killed by a falling tree branch in a violent hailstorm.

I'm all alone, Archer thought.

He shuddered as a gust of wind wrapped him in rain. Kissing his mother's tombstone, he walked back to his horse and started for home— the forty-acre farm Joseph Collingwood had bought for forty dollars in gold when he came to Indiana in 1824 from New York State. There had been Indians then, and life had been hard as the land was cleared and the log cabin built along with the barn and the chicken coop. But slowly, as the seasons melted into one another, the farm began to sustain itself. And then, two bad years in a row, 1840–41, had forced his father to take out a mortgage, and the Collingwoods had been in debt ever since. As Archer rode home, he told himself he might be able to hang on if the bank would only help him through the next summer. If the weather were decent and he had a good crop, he could start meeting the mortgage payments. If, if, if—farming was all ifs.

He came around the bend and saw the horse and buggy parked in front of the cabin. Spotting a fat man tacking a sign on the front door, Archer spurred his horse to a gallop. Hooves splashed through mud puddles.

"Hey!" yelled Archer. He reined his horse and jumped off. "What the hell are you doing?"

It was Mr. Perkins from the bank. Mr. Perkins with his newfangled rubber raincoat and black hat. He turned as Archer ran up on the porch.

"Hello, Archer."

He looked at the sign. It was a notice of foreclosure from the Lima Bank and Trust Company.

"You can't do this, Mr. Perkins!" he yelled.

"Archer, there's nothing we can do at the bank. Your mother was five months behind in mortgage payments before she passed away. And with the funeral expenses, we know you're out of cash. We've given you every extension we can, Archer. Now we have no choice but to foreclose. I'm sorry."

Archer's rain-slicked face contorted with anger. "But this is my home. You can't take it away from me . . . I'll work . . . I'll slave. You know I'm a good worker. You've got to give me a chance!"

Mr. Perkins shook his head. "I'm sorry, boy. I'd like to help, but we have an obligation to our depositors. We'll give you to the end of the week to move out. I'm truly sorry, Archer."

He put his hand on Archer's sodden shoulder as he started off the porch. Archer angrily pushed it off.

"The hell you're sorry," he yelled. "You're glad. You know this is some of the best land in Indiana! What are you gonna do, Mr. Perkins? Buy it yourself for next to nothing? Do you think I'm stupid, Mr. Perkins? Don't you think I heard about the Waldo farm? And the Wharton farm? And the Tucker farm? Don't give me any of this shit about feeling sorry, Mr. Perkins. You're a goddamn crook who calls himself a banker!"

Mr. Perkins stabbed his finger at him. "You be out of this place by noon tomorrow, you bastard, or I'll have the sheriff throw you out. Understand?"

Archer was trembling with rage.

"Get off my land!" he yelled. "Get off!"

He lunged at Perkins and shoved him. The banker, whose waist had an inch for every one of his forty-six years, stumbled down the log steps, slipping and falling to his knees in a puddle. Furious, he struggled to his feet.

"It's your land now, Collingwood, but for only about twenty-four more hours." Wiping the mud off his pants, he strode to the buggy and climbed in. "Noon tomorrow," he yelled.

Then he flicked his whip and the buggy lurched into motion. Archer watched from the porch, rage on his face. Then, when the buggy rounded the bend, he sagged. Slowly he went to the door and looked at the sign. He bit his lip. Then he leaned against the plank door and cried his nineteen-year-old heart out.

"The land," he sobbed. "They've taken my land."

After a while he stopped crying and straightened. "It's not fair, dammit," he said, his anger returning. "Who's more important? Bankers or farmers? It's not fair."

A look of determination came over his face. Suddenly he knew what to do. Archer had a strong streak of the idealist in him. If the world was out of joint, well then, it was his responsibility to fix it.

At nine-fifteen the next morning, a tall man in a dusty black suit and a black hat entered the two-room Lima Bank and Trust Company across the state line in Ohio. He had a red bandanna tied over the lower half of his face, and he was holding a gun in his right hand.

"Hands up," he said as his left hand locked the bank door behind him, then pulled the green shade down over the door's window.

"Oh, my goodness," said an old woman making a twenty-dollar deposit. "I do believe it's a robber. Why, we never have robbers in Lima."

"Don't do anything, Mrs. Crawford," said Frank Pardee, the bald teller, raising his hands behind the iron bars of his cage. "Just keep calm."

The robber, whose thick blond hair hung almost to his shoulders, hurried to the cage. The gun in his right hand was shaking. "Excuse me, ma'am," he said to the tiny old thing in a black bonnet. She clutched her black purse with her two white-gloved hands. Gray curls peeped out of her bonnet as she stepped aside, watching the robber alertly.

"Gimme your cash," said the robber to Frank Pardee. His voice was quavering. "This gun's loaded!"

"I don't doubt that, sonny," said Pardee. "This is your first time?"

"Just . . . just gimme the money."

"Sure, sonny."

"Don't call me 'Sonny'! And . . ." He hesitated, unsure of what to say next. "And hurry up!"

"Goin' as fast as I can. Afraid I've only got seven hundred in the drawer."

"Seven hundred? I don't believe you! What kind of bank is this?"

"Well, it's a small bank. If you want more money, you'll have to talk to Mr. Perkins in the back room. He keeps most of the cash in the safe back there."

Pardee raised the bars and shoved a chamois bag across. The robber hesitated, then took it.

"You know, sonny, bank robbers can get themselves lynched," said Pardee gently. "Folks don't take kindly to having their money stole. I wouldn't make a career of this."

"Excuse me," said old Mrs. Crawford, tugging at the robber's coattail. "I know you. I recognize your hair. Why, Archer, your mother would be terrible ashamed if she saw you robbing a bank. Goodness gracious, you come from a nice family—"

"Mrs. Crawford, please shut up!" Archer almost screamed. He was panicking.

"Oh, my."

He ran from the room.

"Dear me, he's always seemed like a *nice* boy." Mrs. Crawford was shaking her head as Frank Pardee ran to the rear door. "And his mother not a week in her grave, poor dear."

Archer was running down a narrow hall to the back door of the building.

"Mr. Perkins," yelled Pardee. "There's a robber in the bank! He's running to the alley!"

Archer pushed open the door and ran into the alley, his heart pounding. He had tethered his horse loosely to a wooden hitching post. Now he untethered it, jumped on, dug his spurs into the horse's sides, and galloped down the back alley. My luck! he thought wildly. Mrs. Crawford had to be in the bank!

He had almost reached the main street of Lima when he heard an explosion behind him and a terrible pain bit his left shoulder. I've been hit! Oh, Jesus—

He looked back to see Mr. Perkins standing in the alley, reloading a shotgun. Just as he raised it to fire again, Archer galloped into the street and turned to the left, out of sight. The few pedestrians out that drizzly morning saw the man with the bandanna over his face galloping down the muddy street and wondered if there had been a robbery. How exciting if there had been, because nothing ever happened in Lima, Ohio.

Back in the bank, Mrs. Crawford was shaking her head. "Such a sweet boy," she was saying to Mr. Pardee, who was unlocking the front door on his way to the sheriff. "With the face of an angel. Best-looking young man I've ever seen. Why, it don't seem possible he could rob a bank. Of course, I did hear Mr. Perkins foreclosed on his farm, which don't seem quite fair . . . ."

She stopped as she realized she was all alone.

Dr. Parker H. Robertson was about to go to his kitchen for lunch when he saw through the window of his office a man on a horse galloping up to his house. The man was leaning forward in a curious way. Suddenly he slipped off the saddle and fell to the ground. Dr. Robertson had practiced medicine for ten years in Van Wirt, Ohio, but he needed no degree to know that something was terribly wrong.

He hurried to the front hall, threw a coat over his head, opened the door, and ran out into the rain. The young man was lying on his back next to the pawing horse. He was unconscious. Blood had stained his left shoulder. The doctor knelt and put his hand under the coat. When he pulled his hand out, it was smeared with blood.

With some difficulty Dr. Robertson picked Archer up in his arms and carried him into the house.

"Ah, you're awake."

Morning sunlight flooded the second-story bedroom. When Dr. Robertson, a tall man with a brown beard, came in, Archer was sitting up in the bed. His left shoulder was bandaged.

"How's the shoulder?" asked the doctor, coming over to the bed. Archer was staring at him nervously.

"Uh . . . excuse me, sir, but who are you?"

"I'm Dr. Parker Robertson. You fell off your horse in front of my house yesterday. You'd fainted from loss of blood."

"Yes, I remember now. I saw your doctor's sign—that was yesterday?"

"That's right. You've been unconscious a long time. I took a lot of buckshot out of your shoulder. You're a lucky man. Nothing was broken. You'll have to favor your shoulder for a few days, but it should be all right in a week or so. How did it happen?"

"I, uh . . . it was a hunting accident."

Dr. Robertson pulled up a wooden chair and sat down. "Archer, I know who you are," he said. Archer tensed. "I found the money in your saddlebag, and the sheriff has put up wanted posters for you all over the county."

Archer forced a grin, but he was terrified. "I guess I'm not a very good bank robber, am I?"

"Have you ever been in prison? I don't mean as an inmate: I know you've never broken the law before. But have you ever seen what a prison is like?"

"No, sir."

"Well, I have. My uncle was warden of the prison at Zanesville, and I was in that prison lots of times. My uncle was a decent man and ran the prison as well as a prison can be run, but it still was a terrible place filled with terrible men. Violent men. Murderers, thieves, rapists. Is that what you want, Archer? To spend the best years of your life behind bars? To be turned into a brute?"

"No, sir."

"Then why did you rob that bank?"

"Because it foreclosed on my farm. Because it took away the land my father paid for in gold. You don't have to scare me with talk about prisons, Doc. I'm already scared. But I don't regret doing it, no, sir. I may have broken the law, but the law that lets bankers like Mr. Perkins foreclose on a farm, then buy it back for ten cents on the dollar, is just as wrong."

The doctor looked at him a long moment before he finally said, "I agree with you. I know how Perkins operates. It's amazing to me his bank hasn't been robbed before. Hell, I'm surprised he hasn't been shot. I'll make a bargain with you, Archer."

"What do you mean?"

"I see no point in ruining a young life for seven hundred dollars. I'm willing to help you if you'll swear to me you'll never break the law again. Would you swear to that?"

Archer frowned. "You mean, you won't turn me in?"

"No. Where were you planning to go?"

"I had an idea to go to California."

"That's not a bad idea. You could start over there. I'll help you get there. You can use the bank's money—we'll call it a sort of loan. You'll need the money to get to California, and you can send it back

someday when you've made some honest money. You can send me ten
dollars for fixing your shoulder, by the way. Do you swear, Archer?"

"Yes, sir."

"Say: I swear to God that I will never break the law again as long
as I live."

"I swear to God that I will never break the law again as long as I
live."

The doctor stood up. "I'll be mighty hurt if you disappoint me,
Archer."

"I won't disappoint you, sir. I swear I'll make you proud of me
someday. And thank you, sir. I thank you from the bottom of my
heart."

"I put your things in the cupboard. By the way, your gun wasn't
loaded."

"I know."

Dr. Robertson smiled. "That's when I decided you weren't a very
dangerous criminal. You'd better buy some bullets for it. I hear California's pretty wild, and getting there's no picnic either. But they say
it's worth the trip. They're even talking about making it a state, now
that we took it away from the Mexicans. The great state of California.
Has a nice ring to it, doesn't it?"

"Yes, sir, it sure does."

"Well, my wife will bring you up some breakfast."

"I'd better get my shirt—"

"It's outside, drying. Sarah washed out the blood. And she's seen
naked flesh before. I expect she'll survive seeing yours."

After the doctor left the room, Archer thought a moment. Then
a smile came over his face. "California," he whispered.

It sounded a lot better than jail.

2

"ANYONE interesting aboard?" The man leaning on the starboard rail of the riverboat *City of Pittsburgh* was tall and nattily dressed in a well-cut black coat with slim checkered trousers, a bowstring tie, and a beaver hat. Smoking a cigarillo, he was watching the southern shore of Indiana pass as the big white sternwheeler descended the Ohio River bound for Louisville. The man, whose name was Ben Byrd, had come aboard an hour before at Cincinnati.

"Yes, in fact we have several interesting passengers," replied the ship's purser, Hans Friedrich Richter. A native of Hamburg, Richter had sailed the North Atlantic on German ships for ten years before deciding to become an American. He had moved to Pittsburgh and gotten a job on the river. "There's a family from Frankfurt who came aboard at Pittsburgh. They're traveling first class to New Orleans, where they've booked passage on the *Empress of China* for California."

"First class means money. So does sailing to California."

"I think there's plenty of money. They're in three cabins, seven, nine, and eleven. The father's name is de Meyer, Felix de Meyer. He was a prominent jeweler in Frankfurt, but his wife was murdered in some sort of political uproar last year and they've decided they've had enough of Germany. Then there's the daughter—a real beauty. Her name is Emma. And an English cousin with them named Levin. He's the one I talked to. The father keeps pretty much to himself."

"Why didn't they take the *Empress of China* from New York?"

"It isn't sailing till next week, and they decided to take the riverboat and see something of America. The father has a Yiddish accent, but the girl's German is refined. She speaks excellent English, too—the cousin is her tutor. Oh, there's money there, all right, though they haven't checked anything in the ship safe."

"Interesting. Perhaps you can arrange to seat me at their table tonight."

"I already have."

Ben Byrd, who was a part-time actor known as Shakespeare Ben for his windy declamations from the Bard, smiled and shook out his

34

long, greasy black hair. "Always thinking, Hans, you sauerkraut rogue."

"We haven't done bad these past two years. Then there's a young man who came on at Cincinnati this afternoon with you. His name is Alex Clark, in cabin ten. Told me he wanted to eat all his meals in his cabin because the rolling of the boat makes him sick. He struck me as rather odd."

"If the ship's rolling doesn't get him, your food will. But this German family sounds interesting. Well, well. As the immortal Will wrote, 'Look like the innocent flower/ But be the serpent under't.' *Macbeth*, Act One, scene five."

He flipped his cigarillo into the turbulent waters of the Ohio River.

Emma looked in the small mirror over the washbasin in her cabin and pinched her cheeks. The months of pain and sorrow over her mother's horrible death, the seven days of sitting shiva in sackcloth and ashes, were finally receding into the distance of time. The pain was still in her heart—it always would be, because she had deeply loved her mother. But slowly the wounds had begun to heal as the excitement of coming to the New World filled their lives. David Levin had begged to come along on the dangerous trek to California. Felix had been surprised, but Emma hadn't. She had sensed for some time that David held sentiments toward her that were much more passionate than cousinly; besides, his prospects of making a fortune were much brighter in California than in England, with its rigid class system. He had managed to save enough for his passage to New York, and Felix had agreed to lend him money for the rest of the journey. Emma was glad for David's company because he was bright and sweet. But even though she was enormously fond of him, she had never felt anything toward him remotely like love.

She quickly ran her brush over her smooth black hair one more time and adjusted the bolero jacket of the dark blue velvet dress she had bought in New York. Emma loved clothes and had been delighted to find that New York women were as smartly dressed as any in Hamburg or London. However, past the Hudson it had become a different story. Most of the women on the *City of Pittsburgh* were dowdily dressed, if not downright frumps, and Emma's smart wardrobe had attracted many looks—some of disapproval from the more straitlaced females, but most envious. Emma liked attracting stares. Her major fault was that she was not modest or shy and retiring the way proper young ladies were supposed to be, a fact that her mother had tirelessly drummed into her head. Emma was too full of life to be shy and retiring, which she thought rather boring.

There was a knock on the louvered door of her narrow cabin.

"Coming." She took a paisley shawl from the hook on her closet door and put it around her shoulders. It was the first day of spring, but the river still had a wintry chill after the sun went down. She opened her door and smiled at David Levin.

"They've just announced the first sitting," said David, offering his arm.

"I hope they don't serve that ghastly vegetable soup again," she said, locking her door, then taking his arm. "What the Americans do to soup should be made illegal." The English accent David had conveyed to her seemed almost foreign amid the nasal twangs of the Midwest. They were joined by Felix, whose cabin was next to his daughter's, then the three of them walked forward on the upper deck of the boat toward the first-class dining saloon. It was a chilly, clear night. On the Kentucky shore to port, an occasional light glimmered from the window of a farmhouse, but mostly the wooded shore looked dark and abandoned, and the riverboat seemed to move through an empty continent.

Her father's suggestion that they move to the New World had caught Emma by surprise, and her first reaction had been negative. Hadn't her mother said there were no pianos in America? But Felix had convinced her that California would be a grand adventure and that he was bringing enough money to buy a dozen pianos, so soon enough her reluctance had turned to enthusiasm. After all, she had been an eyewitness to the ugly anti-Semitism that had killed her mother, as well as the lackadaisical response of the Frankfurt police to the murder. She could share her father's pessimism about the future of Jews in Europe. California might be distant and perhaps crude, but theirs would be a new start with a fabulous potential, and that appealed to Emma as much as it did to her father.

They entered the dining saloon, a long, narrow room with white gingerbread corbels supporting the ceiling. White naperied tables marched down the middle, leaving a narrow space on each side for the black waiters to maneuver. The headwaiter took them to their table, where a man with a long face was already seated. Now Ben Byrd rose, his eyes fixed on Emma. Placing his left hand on his heart, he extended his right hand as he intoned in his rich stage baritone: " 'But soft! What light through yonder window breaks?/ It is the east, and Juliet is the sun.' " Leaning across the table and almost knocking over a water pitcher, he took Emma's hand and kissed it.

"Fair damsel, whoever you are, you have brought joy to this table. May I present myself? I am Ben Byrd—spelled with a Y—who has played all the major roles of the immortal Bard from Boston to Baltimore, happily to the applause of critics and groundlings alike. Might my ears be blessed by your name, as my eyes are dazzled by your radiance?"

Emma suppressed a giggle at his flamboyant hamminess.

"Indeed, sir. I am Emma de Meyer, and this is my father, Felix, and my cousin, Mr. Levin."

"Welcome, dear friends," exclaimed Ben, resuming his seat as the others took their places. "I hear the bill of fare on this vessel leaves something to be desired, but 'Tis not the food, but the content/ That makes the table's merriment.' Eh, dear friends?"

"We've found most of the food to be acceptable, Mr. Byrd-with-a-Y," said Emma, removing her napkin from its ring. "But tell me: are there many theaters in this part of America? From the little we've seen so far, this area seems barely settled."

" 'Tis true, alas: there are few theaters. But I feel it is my duty to bring the works of the immortal Bard to the rude farmers of the western states, and have been giving a series of readings in villages and hamlets throughout Ohio. I am now on my way to New Orleans to join a repertory company presenting three of the greatest tragedies throughout the South. I will have the honor of portraying Hamlet, among other roles." At which point, he couldn't resist declaiming:

> " 'I'll call thee Hamlet,
> King, father, royal Dane. O, answer me!
> Let me not burst in ignorance, but tell
> Why thy canoniz'd bones, hearsed in death,
> Have burst their cerements; why the sepulcher
> Hath op'd his ponderous and marble jaws
> to cast thee up again. What may this mean
> That thou, dead corse, again in complete steel
> Revisit'st thus the glimpses of the moon,
> Making night hideous?' "

He paused dramatically. The rapidly filling dining saloon had fallen silent, listening to his recitation. Now the passengers burst into applause.

"You're wonderful!" exclaimed Emma, smiling as she clapped.

Shakespeare Ben bowed his head low.

"I am but a humble thespian, dear lady."

The purser looked both ways. Seeing the dark upper deck empty—everyone was dining—he pulled a passkey from his pocket and unlocked cabin eleven. Letting himself in, he closed the door and lit the kerosene lamp hanging in a gimbal by the washstand. Quickly, expertly, Richter began searching Felix de Meyer's cabin, going through his two valises, then searching the wardrobe and under the mattresses of the double-decker bunk.

Finding nothing of interest, he put out the lamp, let himself out, and relocked the door. He repeated the same operation in Emma's cabin next door.

Watching this from the shadows of the bow section of the upper deck was a tall young man in a black suit with short black hair.

An hour later, Emma and her father returned to their cabins from the dining saloon. "Wasn't he amusing?" she asked.

"The actor? Something of a . . . what's the word?" Felix's English was not as fluent as Emma's. *"Ubertreibung?"*

"A ham."

"Ya, a ham. And I don't like David going with him to the bar."

"All he wants is to try some bourbon. Mr. Byrd said if we're going to become Americans, we have to learn to like bourbon."

"Ridiculous. I'll stay with wine and beer, and so should David. Better yet, he shouldn't drink at all. Well, I'm going to bed. Good night, Emma."

"Good night, Poppa."

He kissed her forehead, then went into cabin eleven and locked the louver door. Emma was unlocking her own door when she heard a "Psst!" Turning in the direction of the sound, she made out a man standing at the bow of the boat's upper deck. He was motioning to her. She hesitated, then walked toward him. Even as she approached, she could barely make him out in the darkness. All that the flickering light of two huge burning torches jutting from the starboard and port bows, providing illumination to the wheelhouse just above their heads, enabled her to see was that the stranger had dark hair.

"That is your cabin?" he whispered, pointing back to her door.

"Yes, number nine. Why? And who are you?"

"Mr. Clark, in cabin ten, on the other side. Who was the man you were just with?"

"My father."

"While you were eating dinner, the purser went into your cabin and your father's and the one on the other side of yours—I guess it's number seven."

"Mr. Richter? But why would he do that?"

"I got the feeling he was searching for something."

Emma turned around to look back at her cabin. She thought a moment. Herr Richter? The pleasant red-faced German purser who had been so friendly?

"There must be some mistake . . ." she said, turning back.

But Mr. Clark had vanished.

After another moment's thought she hurried down the deck to her father's door and knocked. She saw the light come on through the louvers. "Who is it?"

"Me, Poppa. Let me in."

He unbolted the door and she slipped into the narrow cabin. Felix was wearing a flannel nightshirt and slippers.

"Do you have the diamonds?" she whispered after he closed the door.

A look of surprise sparked his violet eyes as his hands felt the money belt around his waist beneath the nightshirt.

"Yes, of course. You know I never take the belt off. Why?"

"Because someone just told me the purser was searching our cabins during dinner."

Felix hesitated. "You see?" he said. "I was right not to put the jewels in the safe. We trust no one till we get to California. But how would he know . . . ?"

"He must have guessed we have money somewhere. I think we should report him to the captain."

Felix frowned. "No. If the purser is a thief, the captain may be too. Damn! Of course, we don't know for certain what the purser was doing . . . Who told you this?"

"A man on the deck, a Mr. Clark in cabin ten. I guess he must have seen the purser."

"You 'guess'? Didn't he tell you?"

"No. He just vanished like a phantom."

"Ach," Felix muttered. "This is crazy—phantoms, crooked pursers . . . crazy America! Well, we can't do anything tonight. Go back to bed. I'll think it over."

He let her out, then closed and locked the door. He reached under his nightshirt and unstrapped the leather money belt. Taking it to his bunk, he sat down and opened one of the pouches. He pulled out a handful of diamonds ranging in size from a half-carat to over two carats. As he held them up in his palm, they flashed in the lamplight.

When Felix had sold his jewelry business and house in Frankfurt, he had converted all his assets to diamonds to take to California. He was carrying more than three-quarters of a million dollars' worth around his thin waist—a fortune in 1850. He realized it was dangerous, but how else could he transport his wealth to a place halfway around the world that had no banks?

3

EMMA hurried around to the starboard side of the boat and knocked on number ten. After a moment a whispered voice came through the louver. "Yes?"

"Mr. Clark? It's Emma de Meyer, in cabin nine. Might I speak with you a moment?"

Such a long pause followed that she wondered if he'd gone to sleep. Then the light came on, the door opened, and she looked at the most handsome man she had ever seen. Archer Collingwood was also wearing a flannel nightshirt, but unlike her father, he was barefoot.

"Come in," he whispered, standing aside. She went into his cabin, which was small and narrow like hers. He closed the door. "What do you want?"

"You said the purser was searching for something in our cabins. What gave you that idea?"

"Why else would he have gone in?"

My God, he thought, she's gorgeous!

"He might have been checking out something about the boat."

"Not for five minutes in each cabin."

They were staring at each other.

"Yes, I suppose. Well, uh . . ." *Leave*, you goose! she thought. And yet she wanted to stay. "You didn't eat supper tonight?"

"I had it here, in my cabin. Boats make my stomach a little . . ."

Silence. Again they stared at each other. Her eyes, he was thinking, I've never seen such a beautiful color. Like violets . . .

"Yes, I know what you mean," she said, desperately trying to keep her mind on the stilted conversation when she was really thinking that his eyes were as blue as cornflowers. She had never felt such an intense physical attraction. She had a fierce desire to touch him. "I was terribly ill coming across the ocean."

"You're from England?"

"No, Germany. Are you going to New Orleans?"

"No, I'm changing boats at Cairo . . ." Her skin is like milk—no, cream . . .

40

"Egypt?"

"Uh, no, Illinois. I'll go up to St. Louis, then over to Independence, and join one of the wagon trains."

"You're going to California? So are we! Are you going to the gold fields?"

"No, ma'am. I'm a Bible salesman." Archer had not only dyed his hair black to avoid being spotted by the police, and dreamed up a phony name, he had also dreamed up a phony occupation.

"A Bible salesman?" She put her hand over her mouth, trying to hide her smile.

"Is there something wrong with that?" he asked, rather confused by her reaction.

"No, it's just . . . I don't know, it just seems a funny thing to sell. I can't imagine a Torah salesman."

"What's a Torah?"

She stared at him, this time in disbelief.

"You've never heard of a Torah?"

"No, ma'am."

"Well, it's sort of . . ." She hesitated, not sure how best to describe it. "Well, it's a scroll that's in the temple . . . It's sort of a Jewish Bible."

He blinked uncomprehendingly.

"I'm Jewish," she added, trying to help him out.

"You are?" He said it in wonderment, almost as if he were meeting some fabulous myth.

"Is there anything wrong with that?" she asked rather stiffly.

"Oh, no. It's just that we don't have any Jews in Indiana that I know of. Well, isn't that something? I've always wanted to meet one of you people."

"Why?"

"My ma used to read me out of the Bible, and it said that you people killed Jesus Christ and—"

"Good evening, Mr. Clark."

She went to the door.

"Hey, did I say something wrong?"

She turned, her amethyst eyes blazing.

"I was hoping there would be no anti-Semitism in America. I was obviously wrong."

"Anti-*what*?"

"Oh, you're as dumb as Henckel von Hellsdorf!"

"Who?"

She left the cabin, slamming the door. By the time she was halfway back to her own cabin, she wondered if perhaps she had been unfair.

He didn't seem to know anything at all about Jews, so how could he possibly be anti-Semitic? She started to go back to apologize, then changed her mind. It was obvious that hateful canard about the Jews being to blame en masse for the death of Jesus had reached America, seeping its almost two-thousand-year-old brand of poison into the collective mind, so maybe he *was* anti-Semitic. Maybe all the goyim were, whether they thought about it or not. *Juden, Juden, Juden* . . . The memory of the chanting students in Frankfurt thundered in her ears. It was hateful, horrible, and she would never let it conquer her.

But she had to be fair with Mr. Clark. Perhaps he hadn't meant to offend—and, my God, he was handsome! Although there was something odd about his hair.

She was about to unlock her door when she heard a retching sound. She looked down the deck and saw a young man leaning over the rail, vomiting.

"David!" She hurried toward him. "David, what's wrong?"

He straightened, wiping his mouth on his sleeve as his other hand hung on to the rail. He seemed in agony and he was trembling.

"The bourbon, it made me sick. I—"

"David, you're drunk," she whispered.

"Yes, I—hic!—drank too much. Feel horrible."

"I'll help you to your cabin. Put your arm around me."

He did, leaning heavily on her. She guided him toward his door, wrinkling her nose at the stench of vomit and whiskey.

"You reek," she said.

" 'O what a rogue and peasant slave am I.' "

"Sshh! You'll wake Poppa, and he'll be furious."

"Yes, you're right. . . . Sh-Shakespeare Ben was quoting that—hic! He's a funny man . . . terrible ham—hic! 'To be or not to be, that is the—' Hic! Oh, my God . . ."

He rushed to the rail and threw up again. As Emma waited patiently by his door, she suddenly realized what was odd about Mr. Clark. His hair was black. But he hadn't shaved, and his whiskers were blond.

He had dyed his hair. But why? And then she knew, remembering his rather furtive manner. He's hiding, she thought. Yes, I'm sure he's hiding. How bizarre!

But hiding from what?

"There are diamonds," Shakespeare Ben whispered to the purser. They were standing at the rear of the main deck. Behind them the huge sternwheel's dripping paddles swirled around with fierce regularity, biting savagely into the black waters of the Ohio as it propelled the riverboat downstream at a steady twelve knots. It was midnight and the decks were deserted except for the two men.

"How do you know?" asked Richter.

"I got the kid loaded on bourbon. He told me Jews never drink much, but he seemed to like the whiskey. He started talking about the de Meyerses and how wonderful they are—I think he's got a crush on the girl. Then he said the father had paid his way to America and how grateful he was to him, and I said that must have taken a lot of money, buying three first-class tickets across the Atlantic. And he laughed and said, 'Mr. de Meyer's got half the diamonds in Frankfurt.' Believe me, he wouldn't have said it sober."

"Well, there's nothing in the cabins. I searched all three."

"He must have them on him."

"A money belt?"

"Probably."

"How could we get it from him?"

Shakespeare Ben leaned over out of the wind to light a cigarillo. Then he straightened. "Well," he said, exhaling, "seems to me we'd have to arrange an accident. It's a big river."

The purser frowned. "That sounds like murder," he whispered.

"Doesn't it? But 'half the diamonds in Frankfurt' sounds like a retirement fund for both of us."

Hans Friedrich Richter thought a moment. "As you say," he whispered, "it's a big river. And what the hell, he's only a Jew."

Archer lay on the bunk in his cabin, staring at the ceiling and wondering what he had said that had so offended the beautiful Emma de Meyer. "Emma," he whispered. She had obviously taken offense at his remark about the Jews killing Jesus Christ, but hadn't they? And what in the world was anti . . . ? Whatever it was she had said. Semitism? If it meant being against Jews, well, he certainly wasn't that. Jesus Christ was a Jew, wasn't he? None of it made any sense, but he had certainly stung her. He remembered the look in her fabulous eyes, the way she had slammed the door of the cabin. He had never seen such an exciting girl, such a beautiful girl. He really hadn't seen many girls at all, growing up on a farm, but the few he had seen had never affected him like this one. Emma de Meyer was the girl of his dreams, and he had had dreams. Many of them. Dreams of violent passion that had awakened him in a sweat, his flat stomach covered with semen.

He sat up. He had to explain to her that he had meant no offense. He stood up and pulled the nightshirt over his head, flinging it on the bunk. Naked, he looked down at his young body. When he thought of Emma, he felt a strange sensation in his penis, that organ that was to him a source of embarrassment, since it had a tendency to get stiff at awkward moments—like now. Hurriedly he started getting dressed. *I have to see her, have to explain, and I don't dare leave this damned cabin during the day for fear someone may spot me. If we can just get to Louisville, I should be safe. If, if, if . . .*

Dressed, he let himself out of his cabin. The stars shimmered on the dark river as the huge paddle wheel shush-shush-shushed in the distance with deadening monotony. He hurried toward it, then around the upper deck to the other side, starting toward cabin nine. It was then that he saw the two men coming the other way. Quickly Archer stepped back against the bulkhead. The two men stopped in front of cabin eleven.

Archer recognized one of them as the purser.

Richter pulled the passkey from his pocket and inserted it in the lock. He turned it and opened the door. Shakespeare Ben, holding a gun in his right hand, slipped by him, went to the bunk, and smashed the butt down on Felix's skull. He grunted into unconsciousness.

"The lamp," Ben whispered.

Richter closed the door and lit the lamp. Shakespeare Ben was leaning over Felix, who was lying on his left side, blood beginning to mat his hair where the gun had struck.

"Yeah, he's got a belt."

Ben tugged up Felix's nightshirt and unstrapped the belt.

"Look at his skinny little ass."

Ben brought the belt to the lamp and opened one of the pouches. "Jesus Christ, look at this." He pulled out a handful of diamonds. They glittered in the lamplight.

"It's a goddamn fortune!"

"Let's get out of here," said Richter nervously. "No one's seen us, there's no need to kill him after all."

"And what happens in the morning? He'll tear the boat apart looking for these rocks. If we toss him over the side, it could be an accident or suicide, and who'll ever know the difference?"

The cabin door opened.

"Up with your hands."

The two men gaped at the young man in the door with the gun. Shakespeare Ben grabbed his gun and started to raise it when Archer fired.

"Yeow!"

Ben was hit in the right shoulder. Dropping his gun, he fell back against the bulkhead, holding his shoulder. Richter, his arms in the air, shouted, "Don't shoot!"

"Toss me the belt. You, Mr. Richter."

Trembling, the purser picked up the belt and tossed it. The diamonds in the open pouch spilled onto the deck as Archer caught it.

"Now slide the gun to me. Hurry!"

Richter shoved Ben's gun with his foot, and it slid through the diamonds. Still aiming his own gun, Archer knelt down and picked it up.

"Mr. Clark! Oh, my God, Poppa!"

He turned to see Emma in a bathrobe behind him. As he shouted, "Get away!" Shakespeare Ben lunged at him, pushing him against the bulkhead so hard Archer lost his balance. Ben grabbed the money belt and ran out of the cabin. As Emma screamed, Ben ran toward the rail.

"He's going to jump!"

Ben swung one leg over the port rail, then the other. Holding the belt over his wounded right arm and the rail behind him with his left, he poised to dive as he stared down at the black water thirty feet below.

The purser rushed up behind Archer, who had fallen on the deck, and wrenched one of the guns from his hand. He aimed at Ben's back and fired. The ham actor from Irvington, New York, who had already served three years in the Pennsylvania Penitentiary for armed robbery, was hit in the spine between his shoulder blades. Howling, he fell face-forward into the river, letting go of the money belt as he hit the water. The pull of the swiftly moving hull dragged him under the wake. Only half-conscious, he became aware of a giant marching toward him in the cold blackness of the river. Shush, shush, shush . . . Then one of the blades of the huge sternwheel crushed his skull, decapitating him as the rest of his body was thrown back into the maelstrom of the sternwash.

"Everything's all right!" shouted the purser to the dozens of frightened passengers who had heard the gunshots and come out of their cabins to see what was happening. "A thief broke into cabin eleven, but he's been killed."

"A thief?" shouted Archer, getting to his feet. "*You* let him in!"

Richter looked at him in surprise.

"Excuse me, sir, but I just killed him, as everyone saw. The truth is, he forced me at gunpoint to let him into this cabin, but I certainly was not his accomplice. Everyone please go back to your cabin," he shouted, turning his back on Archer. "Everything's all right. Go back to bed."

Emma rushed past Archer into the cabin and knelt beside her father, pulling down his nightshirt as she touched his face.

"Somebody get a doctor!" she cried to Archer. "Please, God," she whispered, recoiling slightly as she touched his matted blood, "don't take my father too."

After a moment Felix stirred slightly and moaned. Then he opened his eyes and looked at his daughter uncomprehendingly.

"Emma, what happened?" he asked in German. He started to sit up, then moaned and lay back down. "My head . . ."

"The diamonds," she whispered in German. "They've been stolen."

He gasped as he felt his waist. Fear came into his eyes. "It's gone," he whispered in English. "Everything is gone."

"Not everything, sir," said Archer, who had picked up the loose diamonds off the deck. He came to the bunk, holding out his cupped hands filled with stones. Felix sat up and looked at them.

"But that's not a tenth of what I had," he whispered.

Emma hugged him. "It doesn't matter, Poppa. You're alive, which is the important thing. And we have Mr. Clark to thank for that."

She smiled at Archer, who stared at her, struck dumb by her beauty. It was then that she saw the red slowly spreading over his white shirt under his black jacket.

"Mr. Clark," she said. "Your shoulder! You've been wounded."

Archer gave the diamonds to Felix, then straightened, feeling his left shoulder under his jacket. When Shakespeare Ben had shoved him against the bulkhead, the wound on the back of his shoulder had re-opened, soaking his shirt.

"Uh, no, I must have cut my shoulder against the door. Excuse me."

Holding his shoulder, he hurried past the purser, who was watching him intently. Back in his own cabin, he quickly removed his jacket and shirt and examined his shoulder in the mirror. The blood had already begun to coagulate, and it was obviously nothing serious. Archer wet a washcloth and began wiping the drying blood off his skin. When he had cleaned his shoulder, he pulled some of the cotton out of the box Dr. Robertson had given him back in Ohio. Rather awkwardly he began to put on a new dressing.

Five minutes later, he heard a light knock on his door. Throwing his shirt over his shoulders, he went to the door and whispered through the louver, "Miss de Meyer?"

"It's Mr. Richter, the purser."

Archer's heart started pounding. He opened the door angrily. "What do you want?"

"How is your shoulder?" the purser asked in his German accent, pushing the door shut. Without waiting for Archer to answer, he lifted his unbuttoned shirt and looked at the dressing. Then he let go of the shirt and looked at Archer.

"Did one of the bullets hit?" he asked.

"No, I banged it against the door."

Richter smiled, nodding toward the bloody shirt as he pulled something from his pocket.

"Lot of blood for a bang. Sure the bang wasn't from a gun, Archer Collingwood?"

Archer stiffened as the purser held up a Wanted poster.

This man, on March 15, held up the Lima Bank and Trust Company of Lima, Ohio, escaping with $700 in GOLD! He is 19 yrs. of age, about 6 ft. tall, of fair complexion with long fair hair. It is believed he was *wounded in the left shoulder* while fleeing.

He is considered DANGEROUS!

A reward of $1000 is offered for information
leading to his apprehension!

$1000!

In the center was a pen sketch that looked somewhat like Archer.

"I thought there was something odd about you when you came aboard," Richter said. "Hiding in your cabin. And then, just now, the wounded shoulder, and suddenly—ding-dong! A bell rings in my head. I go back down to my office and look at this poster and I'm saying, 'We have a celebrity aboard.' Hm?"

Archer was trembling. "What are you going to do?" he whispered.

"Now, Archer, we make a little deal, no? You back up my story that Shakespeare Ben forced me to open Herr de Meyer's cabin door this evening, and I'll not tell the police in Louisville about this poster. Doesn't that seem reasonable? Of course, if you don't back up my story, I'll be forced to do what any law-abiding citizen would do and turn you in to the police for the thousand-dollar reward. So what do you think?"

He smiled, waving the poster tauntingly in front of Archer's face. Then he folded the paper, put it back in his pocket, and pulled out his gold pocket watch.

"It's almost two-thirty," he said, returning his watch. "We dock in Louisville in five hours. I'll be in my office. You'll let me know your decision. Good night, Archer—excuse me, Mr. Clark."

4

"OH, Mr. Clark, I was just coming to your cabin."

Emma, looking beautiful in the early-morning light, had almost bumped into Archer on the upper deck. It was seven-forty-five the next morning, and the *City of Pittsburgh* had just finished tying up at the Louisville dock. She thought the tall young man coming up the ladder from the main deck seemed nervous and troubled.

"My father and I both want to thank you for last night," she said. "Your brave action saved at least some of our fortune, when we might have lost everything. We can't thank you enough, and I, for one, am eternally in your debt."

"Well, it really wasn't much. How is your father?"

"His head still aches, but I think he's going to be all right, thank heaven. But, Mr. Clark, now that we're docked in Louisville, don't you think we should go ashore and report to the police what happened?"

She was surprised at the look of fear that sprang into his eyes. "The captain's making the report," he said tersely.

"But"—she lowered her voice—"how do we know the captain isn't in partnership with Herr Richter? I'm not sure we can trust anyone on this boat."

"No, Mr. Richter wasn't involved. I mean, he *was*, but Shakespeare Ben forced him to open your father's cabin."

She frowned. "But you said last night—"

"I know, but I was mistaken. Excuse me, Miss de Meyer, but my stomach's a bit queasy this morning."

To her surprise, he hurried away in the direction of his cabin.

"David, I know something's wrong," she said an hour later as she walked on the plank sidewalk of Louisville's main street, looking in the shop windows. She carried a black lace parasol to protect her from the sun, which was warm for so early in the spring. But pretty and feminine though she looked, she was shopping for a gun.

"What do you mean?" asked David Levin, who as usual looked as sartorially unimpressive as Emma looked smart.

48

"Mr. Clark is hiding something. He's in some kind of trouble. I know the purser was involved in what happened last night, and Mr. Clark knew it too. Now he denies it. There's something extremely peculiar going on."

David, who had a miserable headache, was also feeling miserably guilty. "Emma, about last night . . . I think it may have been my fault. I think when I was drinking that ghastly bourbon—well, I may have mentioned the diamonds. I don't really remember, but—"

"Oh, David, I've already figured that out. They got you drunk on purpose. But never mind: you didn't mean any harm, and I'll never tell Poppa."

"Thank you, Emma. I can never forgive myself for what happened, but if your father ever thought it was I who had cost him so much, he'd never forgive me and I couldn't bear that. Mr. de Meyer is almost like a father to me, you know."

"I know." Emma was barely listening, for her thoughts were focused on the mysterious Mr. Clark. She couldn't get him out of her mind. He needs help, she thought. I'm sure of it. And I must help him, because we owe him so much. If he hadn't risked his life last night, we would have nothing. Yes, I'll go see him tonight after supper . . . in his cabin. He seems to be a man who prefers darkness.

"Isn't that pretty?" She stopped in front of a shop window and pointed at a white bonnet with a light blue silk ribbon. "That's the first pretty hat I've seen since New York."

"Do you really like it?" David asked.

"Yes, but look at the price. Thirty dollars is outrageous, and I can't afford it after last night. Besides, I'm in the market for guns, not hats. Once bitten, twice shy."

As she walked on, David stared sadly at the hat, thinking: It's my fault. If I hadn't gotten so stupidly drunk, they would never have known about the diamonds, and Emma could buy a hundred hats. Damn, what an ass I was! To hurt these people, of all people. The woman I love can't even buy herself a hat.

Taking a deep breath, he hurried into the hat shop.

Emma returned to the riverboat a few minutes before eleven, its scheduled hour of departure, and the crewmen were already manning the bollards, preparing to cast off the heavy hemp lines. She hurried up the gangway of the large white boat, noticing for no reason that its two iron stacks were flared at the top like peeled radishes. The main deck was crowded with passengers, most of whom began whispering about her when they spotted her. Emma knew now they were talking about the attack on her father instead of her flashy clothes. She was sure that knowledge of the money belt with the remaining diamonds had spread throughout the ship, which meant they were in danger of another attack. For this reason Felix had decided reluctantly to carry a gun. Neither he nor his daughter liked the idea of guns, but it was obvious in America, particularly as they neared the frontier, that people had to protect themselves. So Emma had bought a Smith & Wesson .32-caliber with ivory grips for her father and an elegant .45-caliber single-shot derringer for herself. The derringer, misspelled after its designer, Henry Deringer, was small enough to carry in her purse.

When she reached her cabin, she found a beautifully wrapped hat box on her bunk. A card tucked into its red bow read: "I will carry my guilt—and my love—to the grave. Yr. affectionate cousin, David." She opened the box and pulled out the bonnet she had admired. Frowning, she took off her own hat, went to the mirror, and tried on the new one. It was undeniably becoming.

"Do you like it?"

She turned to see David standing in the door, his big brown spaniel eyes on her.

"David, you shouldn't have bought it. We all have to watch our pennies now—you in particular—and the last thing I need is a new hat."

Seeing the stricken look on his face, she walked toward him and smiled. "But yes, of course I like it. Thank you. You're terrible with money, but you know you're my dearest friend."

And she kissed him on the cheek.

Friend, he thought. Damn, right now it's the ugliest word in the English language!

"Mr. Clark, it's Emma de Meyer."

She had left her cabin after supper and come to number ten, knocking on the door. After a moment she saw the light through the louvers and the door opened. As on the previous evening, he was in a flannel nightshirt and barefoot.

"May I come in?" When he hesitated, she smiled. "I know people may talk," she whispered, "but I don't care."

"Then neither do I."

She came into the room and he quickly closed the door.

"I wish I could offer you a chair," he said, "but I'm afraid all I can offer is the bunk."

"I know, these cabins are small."

She sat on the unmade bunk, her blue skirt billowing over the rumpled sheets like a great morning glory. Archer eyed her apprehensively. He had never met an elegant European woman, and he was overawed. At the same time, he wanted her, but he assumed that was out of the question. He spotted the thin gold wedding band on her finger.

"Are you married?" he asked.

"I was. Unhappily, it lasted only two weeks. My poor husband was killed in a carriage accident."

"You're awfully young to be a widow."

"Yes, I know. It was an arranged marriage, so it didn't have much to do with love. That's one reason I'm glad we've come to America, because I read that they don't have arranged marriages here. Here people marry for love, and I think that's so important, don't you, Mr. Clark?"

"I guess. I don't know much about love, or marriages, for that matter. Where I come from, folks just"—he shrugged—"get married. It seems to work out all right."

She found his innocence positively delicious. "You make it all sound very simple, and maybe it is. But no one is ever going to tell me whom to marry again. Once was enough. Mr. Clark, may I ask you a question that may seem rather rude? Why do you dye your hair?"

He blinked quickly. "I don't think that's any of your business—"

"Oh, please." She leaned forward. "Believe me, I want to help you. I sense you're in some sort of trouble. . . . I'm not blind: the hair on your legs is blond, but the hair on your head is black. A man doesn't dye his hair unless he's in some sort of trouble. You did such a wonderful thing for us last night, can't you understand I want to help you in any way I can? I know it's not my business, but I'm making it my business."

He had been leaning against the bulkhead beside the washstand, but now he slid down the wooden wall until he was sitting on the floor, his knees jackknifed in front of him. For a moment he covered his face with both hands. Then he looked up at her.

"I robbed a bank in Ohio," he whispered. "I'm wanted by the law. The purser knows. He told me if I didn't back up his story about last night, he'd turn me over to the police."

"You robbed a bank?" she whispered disbelievingly.

He nodded. "The bank stole my farm—they foreclosed on it after my mother died. So I figured I had a right to steal something from the bank. In a way, I'm glad you cornered me. I've been so alone here, I don't know if I can stand it much longer."

"Mr. Clark—"

"That's not my name. My real name is Archer Collingwood. And, needless to say, I'm not a Bible salesman."

"Archer." She rolled the name on her tongue, tasting it. "Like a bowman. I like that name. It's terribly romantic."

He smiled slightly. "Well, I don't know about that. But I guess it's more romantic than 'Zeke.' At any rate, my story isn't a very pretty one, but I'd appreciate it if you didn't tell anybody else."

"Believe me, your secret is safe with me. Besides, I know you're innocent. It's not only that you look innocent, which sounds silly, I suppose, but I just know in my heart you could never harm anyone without a reason."

She fell silent, staring at him. As he stared back, he felt himself stiffening below.

"So you're a widow-lady?" he finally said.

"Yes."

"What was your husband like?"

"His name was Anton, and he was twenty-two. He was tall and stoop-shouldered, like my cousin David."

"Do you have any suitors now?"

"No."

"You're so pretty, I don't think you'd have . . . much trouble . . ."

He could hardly speak, he wanted her so much. Slowly he got to his feet. The small cabin was filled with invisible vibrations as the two young people silently yearned for each other.

"I wanted to apologize for what I said about Jews," he said softly. "The fact is, I don't know much about them or your religion."

"Yes, I realized that. Our religion is really very simple, which is why I think it's so beautiful. Most of us don't believe in an afterlife. There's no hell to punish us if we're bad. Therefore, since we go through this life just once, we must—or at least I believe we must—grab things when they happen . . . like love."

His hands were resting on the bunk above her. He was leaning toward her. "Yes," he whispered. "Life is so full of uncertainties, we must grab . . . love. And I think I'm in love with you, Emma."

He bent toward her and their lips touched. She closed her eyes, feeling adrift, as in a dream. He brought his hands down and gently lifted the shawl off her head, putting it beside her on the bunk. Then he sat beside her, holding her in his arms, kissing her. It all happened so quickly and naturally. She put up no resistance, reveling in the warmth and strength of his young body. As he kissed her again and again, the kisses became more passionate. His hands began pressing her full breasts. For the first time in her life she was actually enjoying lovemaking. It was lyrical and beautiful beyond her most extravagant dreams. For a moment she thought of trying to stop him. But she couldn't. Besides, they had gone too far now. She wanted him, wanted him fiercely. It was too late for coyness or flirtation. She wanted rapture.

Stripping off her voluminous dress and entangling undergarments

was as difficult for her as it was easy for him to slip off his nightshirt.
Then they were both naked in the soft lamplight of the cabin, staring
at each other's beauty with the hunger of youth.

"Oh, God," she whispered, holding out her arms to him, "come
to me, my love."

He was on top of her, kissing her as she wrapped her legs around
his and felt the purest, most sensual happiness of her short life.

"Thank you," she whispered to him afterward, kissing him ten-
derly. "You have given me such a beautiful gift: the gift of joy. I'll
never forget this, even if I live to be a hundred. I'll never forget this
night. Oh, how can anything as beautiful as this be considered wicked?
Yet it is wicked, I suppose. And I'm a wicked woman."

He propped his head on one hand while he put his other on her
left breast. "If that's true, then I like wicked women."

"Archer?"

"Yes?"

"Was it your first time?"

"Yes. I expect I wasn't very good, was I?"

"Oh, you were marvelous. You were Romeo, the perfect lover.
'Lover.' What a wonderful word! But you know, my darling—and what
a wonderful word that is!—you know, you mustn't feel any obligation
to me. I know you said you love me, but you really don't have to say
it."

"But I do love you!"

Her face shone. It was what she had wanted to hear. "Do you?"
she whispered.

He leaned down and kissed her. "I've never been happier in my
life than right now, so that has to be love, doesn't it?"

"Oh, my darling, *darling* Archer!" She sat up and hugged him.
"You'll have to change your plans."

"What do you mean?"

"Come to California with us, on the *Empress of China*. It's much
easier and safer than going in one of the wagon trains, where I hear
people are dying like flies of cholera. Oh, yes, you must come with
us."

"I don't think going around the Strait of Magellan is exactly a
picnic."

She put her head against his chest, reveling in the clean smell of
his smooth skin. "Please say you'll come with us," she whispered. "I
don't think I could bear leaving you."

He stroked her hair. "You're right. I couldn't bear leaving you
either."

"Then it's settled." She put her hand on his thigh. "We're like

Adam and Eve, aren't we? Emma and Archer in our tiny little Garden of Eden."

He kissed her ear, then whispered, "You know what?"

"What?"

"I want to do it again."

"Archer, I expect you're almost as wicked as I am."

"Being wicked can probably get to be a habit."

5

"So you want to change your ticket to New Orleans?" said Hans Friedrich Richter the next morning as he sat in his office on the main deck looking at Archer.

"Any objections?"

"None at all. Of course, it will cost you some money."

"How much?"

The purser opened a drawer of his desk and pulled out the Wanted poster.

"Let's see now," he mused. "You stole seven hundred dollars from the bank, and your first-class ticket from Cincinnati to Cairo was forty dollars, so you have . . . let's say six hundred dollars left. So your ticket to New Orleans will cost you six hundred dollars."

"You rotten thief—"

"Ah, ah: temper, temper. You are the thief, Mr. Collingwood—excuse me, Clark. It says so right here on the poster. It also is costing me the thousand-dollar reward for not turning you in. So I think it's only fair you pay me six hundred—in gold. Otherwise"—he held up the poster—"our next stop is Cairo tomorrow, and I'm sure the Cairo police will be interested in this."

"We made a deal!"

"So we did, but deals can be broken. I might add that I don't think too many people would trust the word of a bank robber like you against the word of an honorable man like myself. There is, of course, another alternative."

"What?"

"One of my crewmen tells me he saw Fräulein de Meyer leave your cabin early this morning. I can't tell you how shocked I was to hear that fornication is occurring on this boat, but I will refrain from moralizing."

Archer was standing in front of his desk. Now he leaned his knuckles on the desk. "You say one word about Miss de Meyer," he said softly, "and I'll kill you, you rotten bastard."

"I doubt that. But I am touched by your chivalry. I can only assume that a sentimental attachment of a romantic nature has grown between you two."

"We're in love! Is there anything wrong with that?"

"As a native of Germany, the very birthplace of romance, I would hardly be against love, would I? The point is, her father still has a small fortune in diamonds. If you could bring me the diamonds, you could keep your gold."

Archer reached across the desk, grabbed his shirt, jerked him out of his chair, and plowed his fist into his nose. The purser "oofed" and fell back into his chair, which toppled. Richter flipped backward onto the floor, banging the back of his head against the bulkhead.

"I'll bring you my gold," said Archer, opening the door. "And you can stuff it up your ass."

He left the cabin, slamming the door.

Richter struggled to his feet. Blood was running from his nose. He pulled a handkerchief from his pocket and put it against his nose.

"That's going to cost you, Mr. Collingwood," he muttered, putting the poster back in the drawer. "That's going to cost you a lot."

She was one of those women the French call "of a certain age." Though she was forty, she could easily have passed for ten years younger. When she swept into the first-class dining saloon that evening, everyone turned to stare, and now it was Emma's turn to be envious. This woman would have stood out in the courts of Europe, much less a riverboat filled with frumps. Her maroon dress with black trim was simple but elegant. She wore a diamond star and feathers in her beautifully coiffed hair. Emma was convinced the blond color had been "helped" by a French maid. It was the way she carried herself, though, that gave her a natural elegance: the woman had style. She was led to their table by the headwaiter. As Felix, David, and Archer rose, she smiled and said, with a light accent Emma couldn't quite place, "Good evening. I am Countess Davidoff and I have been assigned to your table. May I join you?"

"Indeed, Countess," said Felix, raising her gloved hand to his lips. Archer watched, fascinated. He had never seen anyone kiss hands before, and he had certainly never seen a countess. He was rather surprised she didn't wear some sort of crown. "May I introduce myself?" Felix was saying. "I am Felix de Meyer, late of Frankfurt, and this is my daughter, Emma, my cousin Mr. Levin, and Mr. Clark."

"I am lucky to have such handsome gentlemen as my dinner companions," she said, sitting next to Felix. "But, Herr de Meyer, am I not correct in saying that you were the victim of the attack last evening?"

"You are, unfortunately, correct."

"It is scandalous," she said, unfolding her napkin. "I hear there are all sorts of criminals on these riverboats. Thieves, professional gamblers, and what I believe are called confidence men. In my country such things would not be allowed."

As Emma asked, "And what is your country, Countess?" Archer envied the easy way these Europeans made small talk. The lilt of their accented voices was musical compared to the twangs he had grown up with.

"Russia. I am from St. Petersburg. My late husband, Count Davidoff, was in the *corps diplomatique*. I am on my way to Buenos Aires to visit my daughter, who is married to an *estanciero* out in the pampas. My daughter herself has two daughters whom I have never seen, so you can perhaps imagine how I am looking forward to Argentina."

"It is a pleasure having a woman of your elegance aboard, Countess," said Felix, eyeing a handsome diamond-and-ruby brooch on her left shoulder. "And as a jeweler, may I compliment you on your brooch? It is a lovely piece, and that Burmese ruby is exquisite."

"Thank you. It was a gift from my husband."

"Might I guess that he bought it in Paris from M. Lemmonier?"

She smiled with delight. "Herr de Meyer, you are a wizard. I am terribly impressed."

Felix blushed. Poppa is interested in her, thought Emma, reaching for Archer's hand under the table. How bizarre! I've never seen him interested in any woman other than Mother.

David, sitting on Emma's left, saw her hand in Archer's and his heart filled with rage.

"Might I ask, Countess," said Emma, "why you did not sail directly to Buenos Aires?"

"Ah, but that would have been such a bore. I wanted to see this new America everyone is talking about. And also I have invested in some land in Kentucky that I wished to see. It's a horse farm. I came aboard at Louisville, and unfortunately had to take to my bed with a slight cold. But it's over now, and I'm looking forward to the trip to New Orleans."

"That's where we're going," said Felix. "We're catching the *Empress of China* there for California."

"But this is quite extraordinary! I'm taking the *Empress of China* to Buenos Aires." She smiled at Emma. "We must become friends."

But something tells me we won't, Emma thought.

Emma likes this Clark fellow because he's good-looking, David thought, stewing. If I only had his looks! Damn him!

"I should warn you, Countess," Archer said. "Don't leave your jewels with the purser. He's not to be trusted."

Countess Davidoff turned her green eyes on Archer, thinking he was an extraordinarily handsome young man. "Thank you, Mr. Clark. I shall certainly heed your advice."

This woman's an adventuress, thought Emma, bristling with dislike. A manhunter. Well, she'd better not go hunting for my Archer, or I'll claw her green eyes out!

Emma waited impatiently in her cabin until eleven-thirty, at which point she was reasonably certain the decks would be empty and most of the passengers in bed. Then she let herself out, quietly locking her door, and started down the windy deck toward cabin ten. A figure stepped out of the shadows and grabbed her arm.

"Emma, where are you going?"

It was David.

"I couldn't sleep. I thought I'd take a turn around the deck—"

"You're lying. You're going to *his* cabin, aren't you?"

"What do you mean? And let me go!"

"You know what I mean. Emma, how can you cheapen yourself like this? Clark is a lout, an uneducated, uncultured clod—hardly a gentleman."

She wrenched her arm free and slapped him, hard. "How dare you say that about a man who saved my father's life? Mr. Collingwood is a fine person! He's gentle, sincere, and—"

"Who's Mr. Collingwood?"

She hesitated. "I mean, Mr. Clark. And I will not have you or anybody else telling me what I can or cannot do."

David was holding his cheek. Her slap had stung, but her attitude wrenched his heart. "Do you love him?" he whispered.

"And if I do?"

"But he's one of the goyim."

She bit her lip, impatient to get away. "David, you're not only a snob, you're a bigot."

Again he grabbed her, realizing for the first time in his life that he had to act forcefully if he wanted any chance of winning this jewel. "I love you," he whispered. "And it kills me to see you throwing away your reputation and . . . and yourself on this stupid American."

"He's not stupid. And how am I 'throwing away' my reputation?"

"You've made love with him!" His whisper was of such envious intensity that it was almost a hiss.

Again she wrenched herself free of his hold. "For God's sake, I'm no virgin," she whispered angrily. "And this is none of your business. Now, stop following me!"

Turning defiantly, she walked down the deck.

Damn her, thought David, tears of rage and jealousy in his eyes. She's not worth breaking my heart over.

But his heart was breaking nevertheless.

When Emma reached Archer's door, she hesitated before knocking. She was enormously upset by what her cousin had said. Though she was angry with him for interfering, she also knew that much of what he said was right. In Emma's native Germany, the middle class to which she belonged had a strict code of morality, but the young Romantics, led by artists, poets, and writers, had rebelled against Biedermeier prudery and called for "free" love.

Emma did not want to become a wicked woman, though she might say it half-jokingly. On the other hand, the physical rapture she had experienced with Archer had been so sweet she couldn't believe it really was so wicked. And the farther they traveled from the strictures of European society and the closer they came to the mostly uninhabited frontier of America, the less wicked it seemed to be. Archer had aroused in her passions she had never experienced before. Yet she knew David would never understand her feelings; nor would her beloved father.

Still, with all her rationalizations, she knew if she knocked on Archer's door tonight, she was going to burn a lot of comfortable bridges behind her.

She knocked.

While she waited, her cousin's words rang in her ears: lout, uneducated, uncultured, clod, not a gentleman. She had to admit that the description of her lover was apt. A country with no pianos—wasn't that how her mother had described America? Chopin, Beethoven—suddenly she missed them and what they stood for in her mind: beauty, culture, the finest things in life. What am I doing? she thought. What have I done?

The door opened, and there stood her lover. She came into his cabin and he closed the door and took her in his arms, kissing her hungrily. After a moment he backed away.

"What's wrong?" he asked.

"It's . . . nothing."

"No, I can tell something's bothering you."

She turned slightly away. "Archer," she finally said, "have you ever heard of a man named Frédéric Chopin?"

Silence. She looked at his face. He's a god, she thought, not for the first time. His face is so beautiful. It's also so blank.

"Frédéric who?"

He's Henckel von Hellsdorf, she thought with a sinking feeling, beautiful but dumb. No, that's not fair. He's a tabula rasa. He's Rousseau's noble savage.

"It doesn't matter."

"No, it does matter. Who is this man? Is it someone you know?"

She stifled a laugh. "Frédéric Chopin is a famous composer who died last year."

He frowned. "I see. Well, I guess he's not that famous."

She reached over and took his hand. "It really doesn't matter," she said, smiling.

"You keep saying that. Okay, I've never heard of Chopin. Don't think I'm not aware of the differences between us. I saw it tonight, at dinner with that Russian lady. You foreigners know how to talk, your manners are polished, and I'm just a hick. Someone pointed this out to you, isn't that right? Who was it? Your father?"

"No, my cousin David. You see, he's jealous of you. He knows we've become lovers, and he wishes he were you. So he attacked you. And me. He told me I was throwing away my reputation, that I'm not acting like a lady. And he's right, I suppose."

"Is your reputation important to you?"

"Of course. . . . I guess."

He pulled his hand away from hers. "Then you'd better go. And I understand. By the way, I told your father that when I changed my ticket to New Orleans, the purser tried to get me to steal what's left of your diamonds."

She suddenly remembered what Archer had done for them, how much they owed him. He may be a rustic, she thought, and he may never have heard of Chopin, but by God, he *is* a gentleman. He's worth two of David, who got drunk and told Shakespeare Ben about the diamonds.

"I don't care about my cousin!" she blurted out, throwing her arms around him. "And I don't care about Chopin! Oh, Archer, I love you and I don't care if . . . if you think the world is flat."

He laughed as she covered his face with kisses. Then his laughter died away as he started kissing back.

In what seemed like only a moment, she was lying on the bunk, her eyes closed in ecstasy, as his tongue slowly licked her breasts. It darted playfully over her stiff nipples, then plunged into her cleavage, licking its way slowly up through the valley between her breasts toward her neck. She moaned with pleasure as he carefully straddled her, still licking. Her hands rubbed his strong, naked thighs as slowly he lowered himself on top of her. She felt his penis gorged with blood on her stomach. He was rubbing it up and down against her in a mesmerizing dance. His tongue licked her right ear, then her cheek.

"Archer," she whispered. "My love."

Then his mouth was against hers, his tongue forcing its way between her lips. As their tongues touched, she felt him inserting himself in her. Then ever so slowly—largo, as she thought of it in musical terms—he began pressing his midsection against hers.

Chopin's sweet E-flat Nocturne insinuated itself in her mind. Then, as the pulse quickened, a Valse Brillante. Then the surging excitement of Beethoven's Waldstein Sonata. And then as she gasped with passion, the mighty cymbal-clashing Choral Finale of the Ninth Symphony.

"*Freude*," she whispered as he lay beside her.

"What?"

"The German word for 'joy.' That's what the chorus sings in the last movement of Beethoven's Ninth Symphony. You *have* heard of Beethoven?"

"Yes, but I've never heard a symphony."

She turned on her side, took his face between her hands and kissed him. "Oh, my darling," she whispered, "someday I'll take you to a symphony, and we'll hold hands and listen to the Ninth and you'll be as thrilled as I was the first time I heard it with Herr Mendelssohn conducting!"

"Herr who?"

"Never mind. Darling Archer, you have given me the joy of love, for which I shall be eternally grateful. And someday I'll give you the joy of music."

Archer considered this a moment. Then he said: "You are my joy and you are my music."

She sighed. He was, in fact, the noble savage.

She had never slept so deeply or so peacefully. Now, as she was awakened by the knock on her cabin door, she was still filled with the sweetness of lovemaking. "Archer . . ." she murmured to herself, turning over on her right side, thinking of the strength of his hands on her breasts . . .

"Emma! Are you awake?"

It was her father. Yawning, she sat up. "Just a moment, Poppa."

Rubbing her eyes, she slid from the bunk and splashed some water from the washbasin on her face. Quickly drying herself, she put on her bathrobe and went to the door to unbolt it.

Felix was an elegant man—some people in Frankfurt had criticized him as being a fop, though there was nothing effeminate about Felix de Meyer. It was simply that as a jeweler to the rich, he had had to dress the part, and his natural good taste and slim good looks gave him an aristocratic elegance that Emma admired. This morning he looked natty as usual, with his gray beaver hat and gold-handled walking stick. But one look at his face and she knew something was wrong.

"Good morning, Poppa. What time is it?"

"Almost noon."

"Good heavens, I overslept."

"Perhaps that's because you were out of your cabin until after three this morning. May I come in?"

She stood aside, realizing what was wrong. Her father came in, removing his top hat. She closed the door.

"Please take the bunk, Poppa."

"Thank you, but I'll stand."

She smiled rather uncertainly and sat on the bunk herself.

"Emma, after your mother's tragic death," he began, "I took it upon myself to act as both father and mother to you, if that is possible. However, I fear I may have failed somewhat. Exactly what is your relationship with Mr. Clark?"

She took a deep breath. "I won't lie, Poppa. I am in love with Mr. Clark."

"I assume you were . . . with him last night?"

"Yes."

He frowned. "This is indelicate, but did you make love?"

"Yes."

"I see." He ran his index finger over his thin lips, a gesture she had often seen him make when he was thinking. "I have nothing against Mr. Clark," he continued. "In fact, we are all in his debt for saving at least a part of our fortune. By the way, since the incident the other night, I've been giving a great deal of thought as to whether we should continue to California in our reduced financial circumstances. I have concluded that we still have enough money to establish ourselves in California, though of course we won't be able to operate on as grand a scale as I had formerly envisioned. Does this decision meet with your approval?"

"Of course, Poppa. It never even occurred to me not to go to California."

"Well, it had occurred to me. But since we've already paid for the passage on the *Empress of China*, which was not an inconsiderable sum—"

He was interrupted by the mournful blast of the ship's whistle. Felix removed his gold pocket watch and checked the time. "Noon," he said. "Whatever deficiencies this boat has, it at least keeps to its schedule. We're supposed to leave Cairo at noon."

The boat shuddered as Emma heard the distant shush-shush-shush of the sternwheel. Felix returned the watch to his pocket. "Are you aware," he continued, "that Mr. Clark's name is a false one?"

"Yes, but how do you know?"

"The news is all over the boat. Apparently your young lover robbed a bank in Ohio."

She tensed with alarm. "Poppa, what's happened?"

"About two hours ago the police came aboard shortly after we docked at Cairo. They arrested Mr. Clark, whose real name seems to be Collingwood."

"Archer!" She stood up. "I must go to him. Where is he?"

"They took him ashore. He is to be returned to Ohio for trial—"

"Archer!"

As she bolted for the door, Felix raised his walking stick to bar her.

"It's too late. The boat has left."

She turned on him, a look of anguish on her face, her gorgeous amethyst eyes filling with tears.

"Why didn't you wake me?" she almost screamed.

"You must forget Mr. Collingwood, Emma. It will be painful at first, I know, but you must forget—"

"You did this on purpose. You let me sleep while they took him away." A look of panic came into her eyes "The purser must have turned him in."

She pushed the walking stick aside and ran to the door, throwing it open.

"Emma!"

She ran out, barefoot and in her negligee.

"Emma, come back!"

She ran toward the stern, shoving gaping passengers aside until she reached the rail. Shush-shush-shush—the huge paddles of the stern-wheel flew at her, dipping down, throwing their spray into the wind as they pushed the boat away from the Illinois shore, heading for the great Mississippi River. The wind blew her loose hair in writhing ebony curls as she stared at the tiny river town of Cairo receding into the distance.

"Archer," she sobbed.

Two middle-aged businessmen from Louisville hurried forward to catch her as she collapsed on the deck.

"My dear Mr. de Meyer," said Countess Davidoff, coming up beside Felix as the two men carried her into her cabin. "Whatever has happened to your beautiful daughter?"

"I fear," he said sadly, "her heart has just cracked."

6

BY the time she boarded the *Empress of China* in New Orleans, Emma knew she was pregnant. She had missed her "monthly," as she thought of her menstrual cycle; moreover, she felt the existence of something inside her. The realization that she was carrying Archer's child—there was no doubt of the father—left her with mixed emotions. On the one hand, she felt an inner joy that she had this living memento of the young man she had fallen so desperately in love with, and she began struggling out of the depression his arrest had plunged her into. On the other hand, she was faced with the enormous practical difficulties of becoming an unwed mother. Her father had said little about her confession of having made love with Archer, but his actions showed plainly where his thoughts lay. He had delayed awakening her until the riverboat was ready to leave Cairo, thus preventing her from making any foolish attempt to follow Archer. By this she knew he was saying, "Archer is a nice young man—for a bank robber—but he's better out of your life." She knew that Felix would hardly welcome the news that she was in the family way—with no family.

She desperately wanted someone to talk to, but who was there? Surely not David, who seemed delighted that Archer was out of her life. The three-masted clipper ship *Empress of China* carried fewer than a dozen passengers, being primarily a cargo ship, but obviously Emma could talk to none of these strangers about such an intimate subject.

Finally, on the second day out of New Orleans, as the ship flew across a hot Gulf of Mexico, bound for Havana and thence to Buenos Aires, she decided to approach Countess Davidoff. The elegant Russian noblewoman, who was traveling with a French maid named Cecile, had become increasingly friendly with all of them. And though Felix was attracted to her in a manner that was becoming more obviously romantic every day, rather to Emma's surprise the countess had behaved impeccably, doing nothing that would add fuel to Emma's first impression of her as an adventuress. Her charm had melted Emma's initial hostility, and so Emma decided to talk to her after her daily nap. She was on the main deck waiting for the countess to appear for a turn around the ship. Meanwhile, she watched with interest the activity aboard the graceful clipper that was going to be their home for at least the next four months.

The clipper ship was the pride of America and the fastest ship afloat. So far, Emma had been impressed by the efficiency of the crew and the cleanliness of the ship, whose home port was Boston, even though she intensely disliked the smallness of her cabin. Now she looked up to watch the crew climbing the rigging, the great white sails billowing before a brisk wind, heeling the ship to port as it sliced through the Gulf.

"Beautiful, isn't it?" said a voice beside her. She turned to see a giant of a man in the uniform of the ship's captain. In his early thirties, she judged, he was a commanding figure with broad shoulders and a narrow waist. His thick hair was a blazing copper color, and his face was almost as red, burned permanently by a thousand days at sea, she supposed.

"The ship," he added, tipping his tricorne. "I think a fine clipper ship is as beautiful as anything on earth, with the exception of a lovely woman like yourself. May I present myself? I'm Captain Scott Kinsolving, skipper of this ship and also its owner. You, I believe, are Miss de Meyer, of stateroom three?"

"That is correct, Captain."

She had the distinct impression that Captain Kinsolving, who was almost a foot taller than she, was entertaining ideas about her beyond his professional duties, and she decided to nip that in the bud with as cool and formal an attitude as she could muster.

"We're going to see a lot of each other the next hundred or so days," he said, "so we should get to know each other."

He smiled, rather insolently, she thought.

"I wasn't aware that buying passage on a ship obligated one to become friendly with the crew," she said, thinking that should shut him up.

He looked at her with blue-green eyes as insolent as his smile. "I'm not the crew, Miss de Meyer. While you're on my ship, I am God. Good afternoon." He started to leave, then hesitated, looking at her blazing amethyst eyes. "I do believe, Miss de Meyer, that if looks could kill, I'd be dead."

"Big redheaded ox!" she muttered as he vanished inside the ship. "Who does he think he is? 'God,' my foot!"

The ship continued to creak and groan as the wind blew it toward Havana.

"But, my dear Emma, he *is* God," said Countess Davidoff twenty minutes later as the two women strolled the deck. "It was not wise of you to tweak the nose of Captain Kinsolving. While we are at sea, he is the master of all our destinies."

"Maybe so, but he struck me as a conceited ape."

The countess laughed. "But you are very harsh on him. I am told he is one of the richest shipowners in Boston. I also hear he has a rather scandalous and mysterious love life."

"He does?" said Emma, her interest piqued despite herself. "What is it?"

"Ah, if we knew, it would not be a mystery, would it? And if there is anything more unsatisfying than an unsolved mystery, it is a solved mystery."

Emma smiled. Countess Davidoff's rather brittle humor was amusing, and her accented English gave it an elegant piquancy.

"But I can't tell you how pleased I am to see the color back in your cheeks," she went on. "In the last few days I have watched your spirits climb—which pleases your father, I might add. He was worried about your health, you know. But I told him, 'Time, my dear Felix. Give her time. Time heals all wounds, even wounds of the heart.' "

"Time will never heal this wound, Countess."

"You will see that even the dashing Mr. Collingwood will someday fade from your memory."

"That's not very likely, as"—she took a deep breath—"as I'm carrying his child."

Countess Davidoff looked at her. "Is this true?" she whispered.

"I'm afraid it is."

"You have not told your father?"

"No, and I'm afraid to, frankly. I love Poppa with all my heart, but I don't think he's going to look on what has happened quite the same way I do. I know I've sinned, and I'm ready to accept the responsibility for what I've done. But poor Poppa," she sighed, "I fear this may break his heart."

"Of course it will shock him, that's to be expected. On the other hand, your father is a reasonable man, which is why I'm so fond of him. . . . Perhaps you would like *me* to tell him? It might be better that way."

"Yes! Oh, I think it would be much better. Poppa likes you, I can tell, and . . . well, I was hoping you might be the intermediary. Isn't it odd? When I first met you, I thought I wouldn't like you. And here we are becoming friends. At least I hope we are."

The countess patted her arm. "I hope we are too," she said, smiling. Then she thought a moment. "I must tell your father soon. Your being *enceinte* presents certain problems, other than the obvious one of there being no father."

"What do you mean?"

"This ship will be going around the Horn in the months of the South American winter. It will undoubtedly encounter fierce gales. For a woman with child, it will not exactly be like lying on a chaise longue in Frankfurt, will it? It might even be dangerous."

"I hadn't thought of that."

"You weren't thinking of a lot of things. But that, alas, is what love is all about: the rapture of the moment, with little thought of the future. You are young, my dear. I was young once, and I know all about it, so I don't criticize you. Oh, no, I must help you."

"Dear Countess, how good you are."

"Not 'good' so much as practical. And you must call me Zita. 'Countess' is so stuffy. Isn't Zita a wonderful name? I made it up myself when I was five. My real name is Irina, like my dear daughter, but 'Zita' sounds much more fun, don't you think? Like Gypsies, some-how." She frowned. "Well, well, how to tell your father?" She shrugged. "Perhaps the best way is the most direct: tell him the truth. After a good meal and a glass of wine, of course. Perhaps even two glasses of wine."

"I have the feeling you know a lot about men."

"Oh, yes, I know a great deal about them. Someday I must tell you my life story. It's almost as scandalous as Captain Kinsolving's."

The image of the tall red-haired captain flashed through Emma's mind, and she suddenly found herself burning with curiosity to know his secrets.

"That de Meyer girl in stateroom three," said Kinsolving to his navigator, Mr. Roseberry. "She's a rare beauty."

"Aye, that she is, Captain."

The two men were standing on the poop deck behind the helms-man. Mr. Roseberry, a young former whaler from New Bedford, was waiting for the sun to set so he could attempt a star fix, though the wind was so strong he knew it would be difficult. Still, the sky was clear, and the first-magnitude stars—the great navigational bodies of the northern hemisphere, such as Vega and Aldebaran—would soon be blinking on as the sun sank below the horizon. He would have only a few precious minutes to shoot the stars with his sextant, when it was dark enough to see the stars but still light enough to view the horizon clearly. Perfect conditions would include a smooth sea to give the most accurate readings, but Mr. Roseberry knew that perfect conditions rarely obtained, and it was his professional duty to attempt to shoot the stars whenever he could. He loved his work because he was in love with the stars, whose mystery and beauty constantly awed him.

Scott Kinsolving's thoughts weren't on the stars. They were on Emma de Meyer's amethyst eyes, on her breasts, on her private parts, which floated so alluringly through his imagination. Scott, the son of a Gloucester fisherman, had made his fortune the hard way, and there was little romance in his soul.

"Carry on, Mr. Roseberry," he said aloud. "I'm laying below to my cabin."

"Aye, aye, Captain."

"Try to get a good fix. The glass is falling, and I suspect we'll get a bit of muck the next few days. I'd like to know where we are."

"I'll do my best, Captain."

As Scott left the deck and headed for the door leading below to his quarters, he automatically checked to make sure the running lights were on: red for port, green for starboard. Scott had been at sea since he was fourteen, and was generally considered to be one of the most able skippers on the China Run, which was how he had made his fortune. The China Trade, transporting the products of the great factories of New England to distant Cathay and returning with the silks, teas, spices, and porcelain from Hong Kong and Canton, had made millionaires of many enterprising men. The Kinsolving Shipping Company, with seven clipper ships, was well-run, and Scott was highly regarded by his peers, though the snootier among them bemoaned his lack of refinement.

He reached his cabin, which was at the stern just below the helm, and went inside, closing the door. Abner Peabody, his fourteen-year-old cabin boy, was lighting oil lamps. Through the ports the Gulf reflected the last lingering scarlet of the sun.

"Cookie's fixing you some shrimp gumbo for your supper, Captain."

"Good. I'll take my rum now, Abner."

"Aye, aye, Captain."

Despite his humble birth and his propensity for four-letter words with his shipmates, Scott had no intention of remaining an unrefined ignoramus all of his life. Five years before, he had donated twenty thousand dollars to Harvard, asking the president, Edward Edwards, to recommend fifty books he should read to become educated. President Edwards had gladly complied for such a handsome donation, and Scott had slogged through twenty of them already, finding, rather to his surprise, that the pagan Plato interested him much more than most of the Christian authors he tackled. He now went to the bookcase, which covered one entire bulkhead of his capacious cabin. The leather books, protected from the pitching of the ship by brass bars, looked impressive. He removed Conyers Middleton's *A Free Inquiry into the Miraculous Powers Which Are Supposed to Have Existed in the Christian Church*

Through Successive Ages, the heavy-going but fascinating tome written in 1748 that he was currently reading. Taking it to the long, cushioned window seat that curved around the stern bulkhead beneath the ports, he plumped some cushions and stretched out as Abner brought him a pewter mug filled with Jamaican rum. The cabin was handsomely furnished. Scott liked his creature comforts and saw no reason to deprive himself at sea.

There was a knock. Abner went around Scott's desk to open the door. It was Felix de Meyer.

"Might I see Captain Kinsolving? I am Mr. de Meyer, of stateroom five."

"Come in, Mr. de Meyer."

Scott jumped to his feet, propelled by visions of Emma. He came over to shake the hand of the well-dressed bearded jeweler from Frankfurt. "Would you like a shot of rum, Mr. de Meyer? Or perhaps some port?"

"No, thank you, Captain."

"Sit down, sir."

Scott signaled the cabin boy to leave as he offered a fringed red plush armchair to his guest. Felix sat down, resting his hands on his walking stick. "I believe, Captain, that you are empowered to perform marriage services at sea?" Felix asked.

"I am."

"Then could you marry my daughter to Mr. Levin, possibly tomorrow?"

Scott examined Felix's bearded face, smelling a definite rat. "Yes, I suppose. But—"

The door burst open and one of the most extraordinary sights Scott had ever seen appeared. It was Emma, in a green velvet dress, her eyes wide, her gloved hands outstretched as if she were exploding into the room.

"No," she cried, hurrying to her father. "Poppa, you can't make me marry David. I don't love him and I won't be forced a second time to marry someone I don't love. I won't do it!"

"Emma, go to your cabin."

"No!" She turned to Scott. "There must be some rule that says you can't marry a woman against her will, isn't there?"

Scott drank her in. The first time he had seen her, he had thought she was beautiful. Now he thought she was magnificent. Her anger seemed to heat her beauty, searing it to splendor. My God, he thought, I was wrong. This isn't just a woman. This is a goddess.

"In fact, Miss de Meyer, you are correct. There's no rule, but I certainly would not marry you, or anyone, against her will."

She smiled. "Thank you, Captain." Then she turned back to her father. "You see, Poppa? This isn't the tenth century, and I can't be ordered around like a slave. I married Anton Schwabe because Momma wanted it, but I will not marry David. I'm in love with someone else."

"A bank robber who by this time is probably in jail." Felix stood up. "When do we reach Havana, Captain?"

"If the wind holds, we should be there the day after tomorrow."

"I'll have David arrange the marriage there. I even believe there might be a synagogue in Havana, which of course will be preferable."

"Poppa—"

"I will hear no more about it!" he interrupted, raising his voice to almost a shout, something she had never heard before. "I love you, Emma, which you know. I would never force you to do something against your better interests. David is a fine young man who will make you an excellent husband. There is nothing more to be said on the subject."

He walked out of the cabin, closing the door behind him.

For a moment Emma didn't move, staring at the door as Scott stared at her. Finally she whispered, "I won't do it."

"If I were a betting man, I'd lay heavy odds you will."

She turned on him. Again he wore that insolent smile. She started to snap at him—she really didn't like him—but changed her mind. He's an ally, she thought, and right now I need all the help I can get.

"Is there a synagogue in Havana?" she asked.

"No. But there's plenty of Catholic churches. Do you think your father would settle for a Catholic ceremony?"

"He'd die first. Then maybe I'm safe—"

"There's a synagogue in Jamaica."

She looked at him suspiciously. "We're not stopping in Jamaica?"

"We could."

Again that insolent smile. Damn him, she thought. He's toying with me like a cat with a mouse. I could kick him! But I'd better be nice. . . . "You've been so gallant, Captain," she said softly, flashing her most alluring smile. "I mean, by refusing to marry me, which I certainly appreciate. I'm sure you have no intention of stopping in Jamaica, do you?"

He made a mocking bow. "Damsels in distress always bring out the best in me," he said. "We will not even go near Jamaica. Of course, I could clear up the whole mess, if you'd like."

"You could? How?"

"I can tell by the eager way you said that, you are deeply in love with this Mr. Levin."

Damn him! she thought. "David is my dearest friend, but I don't love him—which should be obvious. I'd appreciate it, Captain Kinsolving, if you would stop treating me like a nitwit."

"I see you have a sharp tongue as well as a temper. I wonder if Mr. Levin knows what he's letting himself in for? Something tells me twenty years from now you might turn out to be a real shrew."

"Never mind twenty years from now. You said you had a way out of this?"

"First, tell me why your father is so eager to get you married. Somehow I have a vision of a shotgun in mind."

She stiffened, but she didn't blush. Emma had never blushed in her life. "I'm not ashamed to admit the truth," she said. "I'm carrying a child."

He grinned. "I take it the happy father was this bank robber your father mentioned?"

"Yes, though it's none of your business."

"You've led a busy life for someone so young, Miss de Meyer. I don't suppose I could get you to fall in love with me if I robbed a bank?"

"Captain Kinsolving, if I were Eve and you were Adam, I'd die an old maid before I'd fall in love with you."

"That would have had serious consequences for the human race. Tell me about the bank robber."

"He's sweet and brave and handsome beyond belief and I will love him till the day I die and please tell me how you intend to help me."

What a fascinating little vixen, he thought. "When we get to Havana, Miss de Meyer," he said suavely, "I'll show you."

What an exasperating man! she thought. "Then I'll have to wait till Havana, won't I? Thank you, Captain Kinsolving. I appreciate all you're doing for me."

She started toward the door, but, quick as a cat, he sidled in front of it. "You might show me your appreciation," he said, grinning.

She stopped. "Captain Kinsolving—"

"Call me Scott."

"I prefer to keep our relationship on a formal basis, thank you. Please step aside."

"You don't seem to understand the situation. I don't do favors for nothing. If you want me to help you escape the foul clutches of Mr. Levin, you're going to have to pay me with—at the very least—a kiss."

She glared at him. "You're obviously no gentleman."

"Since you were rather loose with your handsome young bank robber, I'd say you're obviously no lady. Emma, you're magnificent when you're angry, but the blushing ex-virgin is not one of your better roles."

"You are the rudest man I've ever met. And I didn't give you permission to call me Emma."

"I know. Well, I have better things to do than argue with you."

He left the door and started across the cabin. "I hope you'll be happy with Mr. Levin."

As he went to his desk and unrolled a chart, she glared at him.

"Oh, all right, then. Kiss me."

She came to him and tilted her face toward him. He looked down at her a moment. Her eyes were turned to the extreme right, avoiding him.

"I'll wait," he finally said, "till you look at me. Really, Emma, I'm not that bad to look at."

Her eyes glared into his. "Oh, hurry up. I haven't got all night."

"You have a wonderful way of filling a man with romance. But someday, Emma, you'll beg me to kiss you."

"Someday pigs will fly. I'm waiting."

He took her in his arms and pressed his mouth against hers, hard. He held her for almost a minute. Then he released her. They looked at each other. Again the insolent smile came over his thin lips. "Well?" he said. "Did I light a bonfire?"

"You didn't even strike a spark."

She walked out of the cabin. In the narrow passageway she placed her hand on her heart and leaned against the bulkhead. Breathing deeply, she stared up at the lantern swaying above her. My God, she thought, I've never been kissed like that before. He made me feel indecent.

Then she straightened, a look of determination coming over her face. But I'll never let him know I liked it, she thought as she started toward her stateroom. The conceited ape.

7

FIVE years.

The words of the judge echoed in Archer's head like the thumping of funeral drums: "Archer Collingwood, you have been found guilty of armed robbery. I hereby sentence you to five years' imprisonment in the state penitentiary."

Now he sat with six other prisoners in a van pulled by four horses. There were iron leg chains, and their wrists were cuffed by iron bands. They had been ordered not to speak. Two armed guards sat in the rear, watching them with bored expressions. Two more armed guards rode in front with the driver.

The van stopped before the twenty-foot-high stone wall of the Ohio Penitentiary outside Columbus. The huge iron gates opened slowly inward. The van lumbered through a courtyard. Once the gates were closed, the van stopped. The rear door was opened and the two guards climbed out.

"Okay, you birds, get out," one of them said. "And welcome to your new home."

The new home was a huge stone edifice, recently built, that consisted of four great cellblocks constructed around an inner courtyard. There were crenellated guard towers at each corner, and the entire compound was surrounded by the great wall. The towers, in the currently fashionable Gothic Revival style, gave the ugly place the look of a fairy-tale castle, the home of a dragon perhaps.

Archer stared at the grim fortress and shuddered.

Five years.

"I am Warden Edward Ridley," said the mild-looking man wearing pince-nez on his sharp nose. "You are being incarcerated in one of the most modern penitentiaries in America. The purpose of your incarceration is not only to punish you for your crime but also to rehabilitate your moral character so that when you leave these walls you will take your place in society as a useful citizen."

He paused. Archer was standing at attention before the desk in

73

the warden's spacious office over the main entrance to the stone prison. Within the past two hours Archer had been stripped, deloused, issued two sets of horizontal-striped cotton uniforms and two striped pillbox hats, had his hair cropped within an inch of his skull, and been assigned a number: 4162. Then he had put on the baggy uniform and been brought to the warden's office. He no longer felt human. He was a number.

"This prison is run on a modified version of the Auburn System, named after the prison in Auburn, New York," the warden continued. "You will observe a rule of total silence during the day, at work and at all meals. You will march in lockstep with eyes cast downward. Only when you return to your cell at night may you talk, but only with your cellmate. Any rowdiness will be harshly dealt with. Any infraction of prison rules will earn you time in solitary confinement on a diet of bread and water. I can guarantee you this is extremely unpleasant. You will be well advised to avoid it.

"However, this is, I believe, a humane institution. You are young and a first offender. I have no desire to turn you into a hardened criminal. If you behave yourself, you can earn what we call 'good time.' For every ten days of your incarceration without infractions of the rules, you can earn one day off your sentence, thus reducing your sentence by one-tenth, or, in your case, six months. However, one infraction of the rules and your good time is totally erased. Is this understood? You may speak."

"Yes, sir."

"Good. A Bible is available to you should you desire divine guidance. You have been assigned to cell forty-one. I wish you good luck, 4162. Send in the next prisoner."

The guard grabbed Archer's right arm and led him out of the office. Then he was marched down a wide corridor hung with oil portraits of Ohio's governor and two senators, until he reached another iron door. Over it a sign read: "You are entering Cellblock A." The guard rang a bell. An eyehole opened. Then the door was unlocked and swung inward.

"Prisoner 4162, assigned to cell forty-one," announced the guard, pushing Archer through the door. His leg chains had been removed, but his wrists were still manacled. Now another guard frisked him. They were standing in a small vestibule. Before them, heavy iron bars rose from stone floor to stone ceiling. Beyond stretched an immensely long three-story-high room. On the right side rose three tiers of cells. From the walls jutted iron gas jets. Through the barred windows on the left, pale light seeped, almost unwillingly. The cellblock was empty and eerily silent.

"Prisoner 4162, assigned to cell forty-one," announced the second guard to a third guard on the other side of the bars. This guard unlocked the gate. Archer was pushed through. The guard relocked the gate, then grabbed Archer's left arm. His fingers dug into his flesh, hurting him. The guard walked him down the long cellblock toward an iron stair. The guard was young, with black hair and a pockmarked face.

"You're going to like your cellmate, 4162," he said softly. "He's an injun, and he hates us white men. You're real white, 4162, so you'd better watch your ass or you just might wake up dead one morning. What do you think of that?"

Archer started to say something, then remembered: silence. Good time. The guard grinned.

"I see you're smart, 4162. You didn't answer me. But one day you'll forget and speak, and then I'm gonna have to send you to the hole. I'd sure hate to do that to a nice boy like you. 'Course, you wouldn't be so nice after a few weeks in the hole."

And he started to giggle. Archer's flesh crawled. The guard smelled of stale tobacco.

"My name's Sergeant Woolridge, 4162," the guard went on as they started up the iron grate stairs. "I'm real popular with the cons. Real popular. We'll get to be good friends too, 4162. Not much else to do around here except be good friends and wait. And you've got a long wait, 4162. 'Course, we've given you a nice cell on the second tier. It's a cell with a view—sort of. Roomy, too, like all our cells. You and Joe Thunder gonna be real comfortable. That's your cellmate, Joe Thunder. He's a Shawnee injun and real mean. They say he scalped a five-year-old white boy once. Imagine that! So watch your step, 4162. Like I said, you're real white. Here we are. Home, sweet home."

They had reached the second tier and walked down the grated gallery past iron doors with small barred windows. Now they stopped before a door marked forty-one. Woolridge pulled a key ring from his belt and unlocked the door.

"The cons are all at supper now," said Woolridge. "You don't get any supper tonight, but you're not missing much. Frankly, the food here is shit." He chose another key and unlocked Archer's wrist bar. As Archer rubbed his raw skin, he finished, "Okay, 4162. This is your cell. Keep it clean: we make surprise inspections, and if your cell's dirty it can put you in the hole. And give my regards to Joe Thunder."

He shoved Archer into the cell, then slammed the iron door shut and locked it.

Alone, Archer sank onto the lower cot. It was iron covered with a thin mattress, and a blanket was neatly folded at the end. The stone cell was three and one-half feet wide, seven feet long, and seven feet high, a claustrophobic stone cage. The small window in the door was the only access to ventilation and light, for there was no exterior window or lighting fixture. A slop bucket on the floor was the toilet.

"Oh, Jesus," whispered Archer, putting his face in his hands. He was buried alive with a murderous Indian named Joe Thunder.

His body ached for Emma as his mind longed for freedom and California. He wondered if he'd ever see either of them.

He lay on his side on the cot, curled into the fetal position, and tried to blank out his horrible world with sleep.

He was jerked into wakefulness by a hand grabbing his arm and pulling him up.

"What are you doin' on my bunk, white boy?" whispered the most evil-looking man Archer had ever seen. The face bore a huge scar on the right cheek, fierce black eyes, the nose of a hawk, high cheekbones, red-brown skin, and thick black hair. The man bodily picked Archer up and threw him onto the stone floor. "I'm Joe Thunder, and no white boy lies on my bunk. You unnerstan that, white boy?"

The Indian, who was tall and muscular and looked to be in his twenties, leaned over Archer, glaring down at him. Archer, whose head had banged on the floor, was seeing stars.

"I didn't know it was yours," he blurted angrily, trying to sit up. Joe Thunder pushed him back down, then jumped feetfirst on his stomach, causing Archer to grunt with pain.

"Who the fuck did you think it belonged to? I been in this cell two fuckin' years, I boss-man in this cell, you unnerstan, white boy?"

Archer threw both arms around Joe Thunder's ankles and jerked them forward, throwing him into the air. The Indian did a backward somersault, banging his head against the iron door. Howling with pain and rage, the Indian charged at Archer, who was just getting to his feet. Archer leaned his head down and butted Joe Thunder's stomach like a ram. Joe Thunder howled, again becoming airborne, this time sailing over the crouched Archer. He barely managed to land on his feet, narrowly missing the slop bucket. Now the two men, confined by the narrowness of the cell, attacked each other, yelling and howling. The noise pierced the silence of the tomblike prison like a knife, electrifying the inmates in the other cells, who began howling, kicking, and banging their cell doors. The high cellblock raged with the pent-up noise of two hundred men subjected to the frustration of enforced silence, one of the stranger innovations of contemporary penology. Guard whistles shrilled. Guards swarmed up the iron stairs to cell forty-one. Sergeant Woolridge unlocked the door; then he and two others squeezed inside, banging their billy sticks on the two fighting prisoners.

"Take 'em both to the hole!" Woolridge yelled. One guard grabbed Joe Thunder, battered into semiconsciousness, and the other snatched Archer as he raised his hand to feel blood pouring out of a gash over his left eye. Both were dragged out of the cell. "Thirty days' solitary apiece!"

"Hey, white boy," yelled Joe Thunder. "You fight good! You okay!" Archer barely understood what he was saying. "See you next month," the Indian warbled almost maniacally. "We get along swell. You see."

"Silence!" howled Woolridge, bashing his stick down on Joe Thunder's skull. The Indian moaned and collapsed into oblivion.

8

"JAMAICA," Countess Davidoff said softly. "How utterly beautiful. It is like a dream."

The Russian lady was standing at the port rail as the clipper ship sailed along the coast of the Caribbean island. In the brilliant sunshine, ribbons of white beach fronted jungled slopes that rose and vanished in the misty peaks of interior mountains. Set in pellucid turquoise waters, Jamaica was a thing of magic. But to Emma, standing next to Zita, Jamaica looked ominous.

"Why did he change his mind?" she said, holding her white lace parasol that protected her complexion from the fierce sun. "Why aren't we going to Havana?"

"Captain Kinsolving said he was making the change for your sake," said Zita, who also held a parasol. "There is a synagogue in Kingston. I thought it was extremely considerate of him."

"Yes, but . . ." Emma bit her lip. She liked Zita, but she wasn't sure she dared trust her with the fact that Scott Kinsolving had promised to help her in some unspecified way in Havana. Suddenly the ship had changed course for Jamaica instead. He's betrayed me, she thought, almost desperate. But why? And dare I tell Zita? She's so close to Poppa, will she tell him? What can I do?

She turned as Scott walked across the deck toward her, his hands clasped behind his back, a smile on his tanned face. The big ape, she thought. Look at his smile. He *has* betrayed me. I could kill him!

"Good morning, ladies," he said, doffing his hat and making an elegant, if brief bow. "We could hardly ask for more glorious weather for a wedding, could we? And how is the bride-to-be?"

He grinned, and his white teeth seemed to flash his mockery in her face.

"The bride-to-be was under the impression the wedding was to take place in Havana." She almost spat the words in his face.

"Ah, but Jamaica is so much more romantic. Did you know the word 'Jamaica' comes from the Cuban Indian word 'Xaymaca,' and—"

"I couldn't care less what 'Jamaica' means," interrupted Emma, "but I know what 'Kinsolving' means. It means 'traitor.' "

Scott laughed. "Well, you never know. We'll be standing into Kingston harbor at noon. I'll be dropping anchor off Port Royal, and your fiancé will be going ashore in a boat to make the arrangements for your wedding."

"He's not my fiancé," she almost yelled, clenching her fists.

"Call him what you want, but he's marrying you tomorrow. Meanwhile"—again he tipped his hat—"ladies?"

He strolled on as Emma glared at him.

"Emma, dear, why are you so antagonistic to the captain?" Zita asked.

"There's something about him that I can't stand."

"That's fairly obvious."

What am I going to do? she thought. I don't want to marry David. I want Archer. Oh, Archer, where are you, my love?

Zita saw the tears in her eyes and understood. She reached over and squeezed her hand. "David is such a sweet young man," she said. "And he loves you. It's going to be fine, you'll see."

"It won't be fine," said Emma softly. "I don't love him. Oh, Zita," she said, turning to her sadly, "can a marriage possibly succeed without love?"

"Mine did." Zita smiled. "You confuse love with passion, which is normal for someone as young as yourself. You will find that passion doesn't last. But love, if it is true, can last to the grave, and even beyond, perhaps."

But at nineteen, Emma wasn't interested in the grave. To her, love without passion was meaningless.

The sails were furled and the anchor of the *Empress of China* dropped as the clipper ship came to rest in the magnificent Kingston harbor. To starboard stretched the long peninsula that protected the harbor; at the end of it was what was left of Port Royal, which in 1692 had vanished into the sea after a monstrous earthquake. To port was the city, rising gently to the northeast to Long Mountain and, beyond that, Dallas Mountain, named for a family whose number included the man who had just finished a term as U.S. Vice President and given his name to a Texas city.

David Levin, looking unusually well in his best suit and top hat, was standing on the main deck holding Emma's hands. "I'll be back this evening," he said, smiling, his bookish face transfigured by love. "Oh, dearest Emma, I do believe I'm the happiest man in the world. Are you as happy as I am?"

"Yes," said Emma, deadpan. Beside Zita and Felix at the rail stood a grinning Scott Kinsolving, his arms folded across his massive chest.

"Kiss the bride!" he boomed jovially. "Let's see a little lovey-dovey!"

Members of the crew snickered as Emma shot him a look to kill. "Captain Kinsolving, I'll thank you—yet again—to mind your own business."

"But, Miss de Meyer, we poor sailors are starved for romance. Our souls cry out for tenderness. Come, come, Mr. Levin, do your duty. Kiss your bride, sir!"

"With pleasure, Captain!"

David eagerly threw his arms around Emma and kissed her square on the mouth as the crew applauded and whistled.

After a moment Emma pushed him away. "That's enough, David," she muttered, adjusting her hat, which he had jostled. "Now, please go."

"She loves him," whooped Scott. "Did you ever see such passion? Damn, I could weep."

Emma, murder in her eyes, folded her white lace parasol, went over to Scott, and banged him over the head with it. The crew went wild, cheering and laughing. Scott, rubbing his head, grinned as Emma stormed away.

Her father chased her, looking outraged. "Emma!" he said, catching up with her. "I have never seen such an undignified exhibition."

"Well, you're going to see more," she said, reopening her parasol with a snap. "You're forcing me into this . . . this immoral marriage."

"Might I remind you it is you who have behaved immorally?" he said, reverting to German. "And you will remember that you have been raised a lady, not a tramp." The word he used, *Flittchen,* was so coarse that she gasped and came as close to blushing as she ever had.

"Poppa," she whispered, "that's cruel. I'm shocked!"

"And I'm shocked at you. Now, you will behave yourself henceforth."

Scott watched this spat with amusement. Then he turned to David. "Your boat is ready, sir."

"Thank you, Captain."

David began descending the accommodation ladder rigged against the white hull. Below, a small boat with two sailors bobbed in the water.

"Good-bye, Mr. Levin," Scott yelled down, waving pleasantly. David waved back as he awkwardly stepped in the boat. He plopped on one of the thwarts and the sailors shoved off. "As soon as the boat's back," Scott said, turning to Mr. Roseberry, his navigator, "we'll get under way. Lay course for Port of Spain, Trinidad. We'll lay in supplies there instead of Kingston."

As he started toward his cabin, Mr. Roseberry looked stunned. "But, Captain, what about Mr. Levin?"

"What about him?"

When Emma saw the men in the rigging unfurling the sails an hour later, she was confused at first. Then, as the great white sails flapped, filling with wind, and as the capstan raising the anchor chain made its final turn, she asked one of the crew, "What's happening?"

"Sailing for Trinidad, ma'am."

"But Mr. Levin . . . ?"

The sailor shrugged. A look of amazement came over Emma's face. As the ship turned, though, preparing to stand out of the harbor, she started laughing. She hurried across the deck and vanished through the door leading to Scott's cabin. Scampering down the ladder to the small passageway, she knocked on his door. It was opened by Abner Peabody, the freckle-faced cabin boy.

"Is Captain Kinsolving here?" she asked.

"No, ma'am, he's topside."

"Oh."

"But when we're out of Kingston harbor, he'll be back down for lunch. If you'd like to wait for him, I'll tell him you're here."

"Why, thank you."

Abner stood aside, allowing Emma to enter. After he closed the door behind her, Emma looked around. The paneled cabin with its low, beamed overhead, was handsome and immaculate. It was also, not surprisingly, a very masculine room. She went to the bookshelf and studied the titles on the leather spines. She ran her finger over the tops of several books: there was no dust. "He must actually read them," she said, impressed.

She edged around the red plush armchair, which was bolted to the deck against rough weather, and went to his desk. Behind it was a walnut chart cabinet, its thin drawers neatly labeled. She pulled one drawer out and looked at a chart of the South Atlantic. She ran her finger down the coast of South America, then across the Strait of Magellan. What Zita had said came back to her: they would be rounding South America during the winter, endangering her pregnancy. She shuddered and closed the drawer.

Then she looked at the desk. There was a rack of pipes, a handsome silver inkwell—when she tried to pick it up, she found it was screwed to the desk. So far the voyage to California had been relatively smooth, but the fact that something as ordinary as an inkwell might become a dangerous flying object again reminded her of the rough seas ahead. She placed her hand on her stomach. Inside her a child was forming, Archer's child. She must protect him at all costs.

The faint, queasy fluttering she felt jerked her back to the here and now. Her gaze fastened on the starboard side of the cabin and his bunk. Walking over to it, she was noting that it was immaculate like everything else on the ship when she spotted something peeping from beneath the pillow. She reached down and pulled out a small daguerreotype with an oval, elaborately chased gold frame. It was a portrait of an incredibly beautiful young woman dressed in a strange costume.

Emma's eyes widened as she realized that the woman was Chinese.

"Captain, I demand an explanation for this outrage!" Felix de Meyer, holding his top hat against the strong breeze, was shouting at Scott on the poop deck. Scott was holding a telescope to his right eye, looking at Port Royal off the port bow as the *Empress of China* sped out of the harbor.

"What outrage, Mr. de Meyer?" Scott asked casually.

"You have left Mr. Levin in Kingston, sir."

"Oh, that outrage. Yes, I'm terribly sorry about that, but the glass is falling quite precipitously, and for the safety of the ship, I thought it best to put to sea at once."

"But you will return for him, surely."

Scott lowered the telescope. "Well, no, I'm afraid I can't do that, Mr. de Meyer. We're on a tight schedule, you know."

Felix looked amazed. "But you can't just leave the boy. He has very little money—"

"You perhaps saw the other clipper ship in the harbor? It's the *Flying Cloud*, out of New Bedford. I sent word to Captain McKinney to pick Mr. Levin up and take him to San Francisco. The captain is an old friend, and he agreed. All things being equal, Mr. Levin will arrive in San Francisco a few days after us." Scott handed the telescope to Mr. Roseberry and smiled at Felix.

"Whatever you may take me for, sir, I am not a fool," Felix huffed. "This was all arranged, wasn't it? Did my daughter propose this mad scheme to you?"

"Your daughter knows nothing, Mr. de Meyer. I realize her heart will be broken, being deprived of Mr. Levin's company for another four months. However, something tells me she'll survive. Your daughter, while the very epitome of feminine charm, of course, is a very tough young lady. I suspect Emma would survive the end of the world. Now, if you will excuse me, sir, it's time for my lunch. Carry on, Mr. Roseberry."

Touching his fingers to his hat, he walked off the poop deck, leaving the normally suave Frankfurt jeweler totally nonplussed.

A few moments later, Scott opened the door to his cabin. He saw Emma dart her hand behind her back and look at him, rather startled. Standing by his bunk, she was wearing a white cotton dress trimmed in green, with a tight-fitting bodice that billowed below her black belt into a full skirt. He had seen her angry and thought she was magnificent. Now he saw the blood rouging her cheeks in guilt, and he found her ravishing. She really *does* take one's breath away, he thought.

"Welcome, Miss de Meyer," he said, closing the door. "My cabin boy told me you were paying a visit." He removed his hat and nodded toward a table in front of the window seat. "Perhaps you'd join me for lunch?"

"That's very kind of you, Captain, and I accept."

"On the other hand, it's possible you've lost your appetite, grieving over the loss of Mr. Levin?"

"You know perfectly well that's not true, Captain. Let's keep deception at a minimum, though I can see from the way you got rid of David that you have a sly, secretive nature that delights in playing games."

"Which is perfectly fine as long as the games benefit you?" he asked, hanging his hat on a peg.

"Oh, yes. I certainly didn't come here to criticize you, Captain. I came to thank you, and I want to apologize for the way I behaved earlier today."

Scott rubbed the top of his head. "Yes, you pack a mean wallop. Maybe I should wear a helmet when I'm around you."

"I swear I'll never do it again."

"Mmm. I just spoke to your father, who looked fit to be tied. I explained to him that I had arranged passage for Mr. Levin on another ship, but he looked no less fit to be tied."

"I still don't understand why you came to Jamaica instead of Havana."

"I knew the *Flying Cloud* would be in Kingston and that I could get rid of Mr. Levin with a minimum of inconvenience for him."

"Well, it was very sweet of you, and I'm forever in your debt."

"A debt I fully intend to collect one day. Might I ask what you're hiding behind your skirt?"

She hesitated, then held up the daguerreotype. "Who is this?" she said.

Shock registered in his blue-green eyes. Striding up to her, he snatched it out of her hand. "You witch!" he roared. "Who the hell gave you permission to snoop in my cabin?"

"I wasn't snooping—"

"I'd like to know what the hell you call it!"

He went to his desk, opened a drawer, put the daguerreotype in, and slammed the drawer shut. Then, just as quickly as his rage had erupted, she saw him bring it under control. His normal sardonic mask returned, complete with the slight smile. How fascinating, she thought. He's a play-actor. His facade is all composure and control, but underneath, he's a passionate man.

There was a knock, and the door was opened by the cabin boy. "May I set the table, Captain?" Abner asked.

"Yes. We'll be two. Miss de Meyer is joining me."

"Aye, aye."

After he had left, there was an awkward silence.

"Her name is Chingling," Scott said softly. "Her mother is a Manchu princess. Her father, Prince Kung, was the viceroy of the Two Kwangs, possibly the most powerful man in China after the emperor and chief eunuch."

"I don't believe 'eunuch' is a word to be said before a lady," said Emma rather primly.

"Pardon me. I keep forgetting how respectable you are. You do know what a eunuch is?"

"Yes. But what are the Two Kwangs?"

"Two provinces of China, Kwangtung and Kwangsi. Kwangsi borders the kingdom of Laos to the south, and Kwangtung is directly east. Both Canton and Hong Kong are in Kwangtung province, and they are extremely important cities to the emperor. But the Chinese don't know what they want. Their society has changed very little for centuries, and the emperor still thinks he is God—"

"Like you?"

"Oh, much more than I. At any rate, my company does an enormous amount of business with China, but the damned imperial officials keep changing the rules. There are four hundred million Chinese— think of it: four hundred million! What an incredible market that is for American and European factories. They have no manufactured goods—"

"But they also have no money," said Emma, more interested than she might have supposed.

"Yes, but the money could grow from trade. We buy their silks and porcelain, but it's the very devil to sell anything back because the emperor and his court are suspicious of foreigners and have put up all sorts of barriers to the 'round-eyes'—one of the more polite expressions they use to describe us whites. The point is, to get anything done, we are forced to bribe the Chinese officials. Prince Kung was taking huge bribes, and the emperor found out about it. He sent his Bannermen south from Peking to arrest Prince Kung, they brought him back to the

Forbidden City, and he was beheaded." Emma winced. "Sorry, Emma, but the Chinese play rough. At any rate, Prince Kung's wife and daughter fled into hiding when the Bannermen arrived—"

"What are Bannermen?"

"Are you really interested?"

"I wouldn't ask if I weren't. I keep reminding you, Captain, I'm not a nitwit."

"Yes, I see you're not. Well, let's go back a bit. In 1644 the Manchu cavalry swept down from Manchuria into Peking and conquered the city. The last emperor of the Ming dynasty hanged himself from a tree, and the Manchus set up a new dynasty called the Ching, which is the present dynasty. The Manchu army is organized into eight military companies called Banners, and the men are called Bannermen."

"In other words, they're soldiers?"

"Exactly. Princess Kung, whose name is Ah Toy, knew she and her daughter would be killed by the Bannermen, so she fled. I met them at a reception at the house of an English merchant in Canton, and Ah Toy brought her daughter to my ship and pleaded that I take them to America. I couldn't very well say no, so I did. They live in San Francisco today."

"That's all?"

He shrugged. "Isn't that enough?"

"It's not enough to explain why you became so angry when I found Chingling's daguerreotype under your pillow, or why people whisper about your secret love life. Isn't it the plain truth, Captain, that Chingling is your mistress?"

Again she saw rage light his eyes. "What if it is?" he said softly.

Emma started for the door. "Thank you for the luncheon invitation, Captain, but I just remembered I have a previous engagement."

"Damn you," he roared, coming around his desk. "Don't put on these prissy airs with me, you baggage. Speak plain. What's wrong? Is it because I bed a Chinese woman?"

"Yes," she cried, turning on him. "I knew the moment I met you there was something about you I disliked, and now I know what it is."

"Why, you beautiful bigot . . ." He grabbed her arms, pulling her to him, and kissed her. She tried to push away, but he did it for her. "Is that kiss any different from the last one?" he said.

She wiped her mouth on her sleeve. "Yes. I could taste Chingling, you terrible, revolting *immoral* man."

He put his fists on his hips and laughed.

"What's so damned funny?" she almost yelled.

"You! Talk about immoral. Who the hell went to bed with a good-looking bank robber and got herself pregnant?"

"Oh! You . . . you bastard!"

She slapped him, hard.

"You bitch!"

He slapped her, hard. Emma looked so amazed that, again, he laughed.

"Face the ugly truth, my dear Miss de Meyer: you have no right to look down your nose at my morals—or my lack of them, to be more precise. You're a smug little hypocrite who's in dire need of a good spanking, and if I weren't trying to be on my most gentlemanly behavior, I'd give it to you. Yes, Chingling is my mistress, or my concubine, to put a finer word on it. I don't flaunt the truth, but I'm not ashamed of it either. The fact is, Chingling knows more about love in her little finger than you do in your whole, quite delectable body. Moreover, she's not a hypocrite."

"Stop using that word. I'm not a hypocrite."

"Then what do you call it? And what really astonishes me is that you, a Jewess, could be bigoted about anybody when your people have been the victims of prejudice for centuries."

She frowned. *Juden, Juden, Juden*: the chanting of the Frankfurt students rang in her ears. *Juden, Juden, Juden* . . .

There was a knock on the door, and Abner stuck his head in. "May I set the table now, Captain?" he asked.

"Yes. Except Miss de Meyer won't be lunching after all."

Emma looked at him. Then she straightened in determination. "Oh, yes, I will," she said.

Scott's face slowly broke into a grin. "I think I'm beginning to like you, Miss de Meyer," he said. "And doesn't that beat all? In fact, it seems highly improbable."

She gave him a lofty smile. "You said the other day that someday I'd beg you to kiss me, Captain. Well, maybe someday you'll beg me."

Scott stared at her back as she went to the window seat to look out over the Caribbean.

9

"WHY have you helped me?" Emma asked a half-hour later as Abner cleared away the dishes. The lunch had been delicious. She had had two glasses of an excellent white wine and was sipping her third.

"You mean, why did I relieve you of the burden of Mr. Levin? When I think of what you would have done with that poor man if you'd married him—namely, chew him up and spit him out—you might say I was performing an act of charity."

Emma giggled, feeling giddy from the wine. "You really are a terrible man. You know, I have a confession to make: I love the color of your hair."

Abner held out a box of cigars and Scott took one.

"I'm glad I don't totally disgust you. Mind if I smoke?"

"Oh, no, I like cigars."

She watched with her chin in her hand, her elbow on the table, as Abner lit the cigar. Scott exhaled a cloud. Abner quietly left the cabin.

"To answer your question: I got rid of Mr. Levin because an evil scheme is hatching in my warped mind."

"What are you talking about?"

"Let me tell you something about myself, Emma. I'm not a romantic man. I'm interested in money and power, not sentiment. In the past few years I've witnessed a miracle: California has transformed itself from a sleepy Mexican backwater into the biggest, boommingest place on earth. I was told in New York that it will very likely become a state before the end of the year, but even if it doesn't, statehood is inevitable eventually. I think when you see California, you'll fall in love with it as I have. It has everything."

"I thought you were not romantic."

He smiled. "All right, I'm a *bit* of a romantic."

"You make it sound like a dirty word."

He shrugged. "Business has a certain romance. Empire building has a great deal of romance."

She looked up in surprise. "Are you building an empire?"

"Perhaps. Because of the gold rush, I've been able to make a

87

considerable fortune. No, that's being modest: I've made a pile. The cargo of this ship, for example: do you have any idea what we're carrying?"

"No."

"Shovels. Bricks. Nails. Hardware. This ship is a floating general store. Why? Because San Francisco needs shovels, bricks, and nails, and I can make a thousand-percent profit providing them. It's not as romantic, I suppose, as finding gold. But while fortunes are being made in the goldfields, they're being spent on the items in my warehouses. Then, too, there's not much romance in real estate, but the land I'm buying cheap now will be worth a fortune in a few years. Am I boring you?"

He sucked on his cigar, eyeing her.

"Not a bit."

"Good. My faith in California is so great that I'm moving there. I sold my house in Boston and am building a house in San Francisco. A big, showy house. As big as any in town."

"You really aren't a gentleman. You're a nouveau riche."

"They don't come any more nouveau, or any more riche. But the pleasant thing about San Francisco is that everybody is nouveau riche. It's quite exhilarating. I have every intention of becoming the most powerful man in the state, if I can. And perhaps, one day, even the governor."

"You're certainly ambitious. But don't you have a slight problem? I know that California is a wild place, but even Californians might hesitate before they voted for a man with a Chinese concubine."

He looked at her coolly. "That's where you come in."

Her mind suddenly became clear and alert. Her eyes narrowed. "I think I'm beginning to see your 'evil scheme.' "

He leaned forward and lowered his voice: "You and I are a lot alike, Emma. We're fighters and we're winners. I need a wife to make me respectable. You need a husband to make you respectable and make your baby legitimate. We can both win. Marry me and I'll make you queen of California. I'll give your child the world. We'd make a damned good team, Emma—an unbeatable team. What do you think?"

"I think you've left out one little thing: love."

"I told you I'm not a romantic."

"But I am. To me, love is the most important thing in the world."

"You talk a lot about love, but if you ask me, you're a shrewd baggage. Think about the practical side of my proposal, Emma, and you'll come around to my way of thinking."

He couldn't have said anything to make her more angry, since he had put his finger squarely on what she considered her Achilles' heel:

she *was* practical. She was as practical and shrewd as her mother, who had arranged the advantageous marriage to Anton Schwabe. She stood up and gave Scott her iciest look.

"I thank you for your warm and loving proposal, Captain, but I really must decline. You may be the richest man in California, but you'll never be as rich as I am because I'm in love. However, you obviously could never understand that."

As she edged around the table, he jumped up and grabbed her wrist.

"Dammit, Emma, don't be a fool. Your father's going to marry you off to someone, so forget all this twaddle about love. I'm offering you the world on a silver platter."

"Let go of me! I'm not interested in what you're offering. Don't you understand? I pity you. You have no love in your soul. All you have is a bunch of nails and bricks and hardware."

She jerked her hand away and walked to the cabin door.

"I thought you were smart," he said softly. "Maybe I was wrong. So marry your goddamned bank robber—if he ever gets out of jail."

Her hand closed on the latch and gripped it fiercely. She closed her eyes, trying to compose herself. "He'll get out someday," she whispered. "And I'll wait for him."

"You'd better hope he doesn't mind wrinkles."

Her eyes flew open. He was grinning again, the customary insolence back on his face. She looked around the cabin, then yelled at him: "I'd throw something at you if everything in this place wasn't nailed down—except the photograph of that damned Chingling." Then she swung open the door and left.

Scott picked up his cigar and drew heavily on it, then exhaled. After a moment a grin crept across his mouth. "There's more ways than one to skin a cat," he said. "And that one sure as hell is a cat."

Sergeant Woolridge and two guards named Patterson and Evans marched down the stone steps to the basement of Cellblock A in the Ohio Penitentiary. Unlocking a barred door, they entered a narrow, musty stone corridor barely illuminated by narrow barred cellar windows along one side of the low ceiling. Marching past a row of iron doors three feet high on the right, they stopped at one marked four. It was solid iron except for four square-inch holes and a narrow door rather like a letter slot.

"Open it," Woolridge said.

Patterson pulled out a key ring and selected a key as Evans held a bull's-eye lantern whose beam pierced the gloom. The corridor had a foul stench that made the guards wrinkle their noses. Patterson unlocked the door and swung it open. Its hinges screeched in the silence. Inside, all was black.

"Collingwood," the sergeant announced, "your thirty days are up. You can come out. But shield your eyes or you'll hurt them."

Silence.

"Collingwood?"

Silence.

"Shit," the sergeant whispered, "is the bastard dead?"

"Naw, he took his bread and water this morning. Come on out, Collingwood."

"Go in and pull him out."

"Jesus, Sarge, that place is a shithole. Don't make me go in there. Christ, he's been in there a month, and the last week it's been hot."

"Shine the light in . . . wait a minute. Here he comes."

A naked man slowly crawled out of the tiny five-foot-high solitary-confinement cell on his hands and knees. His blond hair was matted with filth and his blond beard hung four inches from his chin. He couldn't have weighed more than a hundred pounds. His ribs and every muscle showed beneath his pallid, filth-smeared skin. His eyes were shut. When he emerged from the cell, he started breathing hard, filling his lungs with the less-fetid air of the corridor. The stench that was pouring from the cell was sickening.

"Phew," said Patterson, making a face. "Christ, this one really stinks!"

"None of them smell like fucking roses," Woolridge said. "Take him to the infirmary for a checkup, then we'll release the injun."

"Bet he'll smell like the fucking apehouse at the zoo. Come on, Collingwood. Upsy-daisy."

The two junior guards grabbed him under his arms and jerked him to his feet.

"Pretty boy ain't so pretty anymore." Woolridge grinned. "Did you enjoy your stay, 4162?"

Archer's closed eyelids opened slowly. He looked at Woolridge, squinting even in the gloom of the corridor after thirty days of total darkness. His blue eyes blazed with hatred.

But he remained silent.

"I'll pay 'em back for that," Joe Thunder whispered that night as he lay on his bunk in cell forty-one. "I get drunk and rob a grocery store of three hundred bucks, and they stick me in here four years. Then they stick me in that stinkhole thirty day. I pay 'em back."

"Well, pay them back without me," said Archer, lying on the top bunk. Both had been bathed, shaved, and given a meal before being sent to their cell. "I'll never go back to the hole. Never. I thought I'd go crazy."

"Yeah, it's my fault. I know that. I owe you somethin', white boy. I apologize. We'll be friends from now on, you see."

"I'm going to start earning good time. I'm going to obey every goddamn rule. I'm going to get out of this place as soon as I can, and then I'm going to California and find Emma."

"That your squaw?"

"Maybe one day."

"So you goin' to California? I thought of that once. Thought I'd find gold. But it's too late now. The white man's probably already taken it all. Shit, they may have taken away your farm, but the white man's taken away the whole fuckin' country from us. I'd like to kill every white man in the world—except you. You're my friend."

Some friend, Archer thought, staring at the dark ceiling. Yet, what the hell, we're stuck together for a long time. He's a little crazy, but I think he means well.

"Hey, white boy. Maybe we go to California together someday?"

"Maybe. Sure, why not? Gotta get out of here first, though. And the only way to do that is play by their rules."

Even as he scowled and stared at the iron bunk overhead, Joe Thunder considered what the white farmboy had said. Maybe he's right, the proud Indian mused. Maybe we stick together and beat them at their own game.

The second day out of Kingston, Abner Peabody knocked on the door of stateroom five. It was three in the afternoon of another balmy day, and the *Empress of China*'s forty-man crew was swabbing decks, polishing the ship's brightwork, and inspecting ropes. After a moment the door opened and Felix de Meyer, wearing a dressing gown, looked out. "Yes?"

"Compliments of the captain, sir. He requests the honor of your company in his cabin for dinner this evening at seven o'clock."

"Oh, thank you. I accept with pleasure."

"Countess Davidoff is also invited."

The cabin boy saluted and sauntered off as Felix closed the door and turned to Zita, who was sitting up in his bunk, holding a sheet over her breasts.

"How did he know I was here?" she whispered.

Felix looked uncomfortable. "I have no idea."

Zita smiled. "I think perhaps our dashing Captain Kinsolving knows more than we think about what happens on this ship."

"He's no gentleman," Felix said, sitting beside her and kissing her bare shoulder. "He made a fool of Emma on the main deck the other day. Of course, I must confess Emma was no lady to hit him over the head with her parasol."

"I thought it was all very funny."

"You have an easy sense of humor."

"My dear Felix, if one didn't have a sense of humor in Russia, one would go quite mad. Now, quit being stuffy and come back to bed. It was just beginning to be fun."

"You know," Scott said that evening as he dipped into a fish stew, "the crews of different ships gossip. While we were in New Orleans, some of my men talked with crew members of the riverboat you came down the Mississippi on. They heard about the attack on you and how you were saved by a young man named Collingwood."

"That's true," said Felix, who was sitting with Zita at the small table in Scott's cabin.

"This same Collingwood was later arrested for bank robbery. I assume this is the young man that Emma is interested in?"

Felix spooned his stew a moment.

"Although my daughter has been married—very briefly—she has had very little intimacy with the opposite sex," he finally said in a tactful tone. "The truth is, she knows hardly anything at all about men. Collingwood was a nice-looking boy, though of course totally lacking in education or refinement, and I fear Emma developed for him what we call in German *Schwarmerei*"—he turned to Zita—"*Comment dit-on en anglais 'l'amour d'adolescent'?*"

"Puppy love," Zita replied. Like most upper-class Russians, she spoke little German, but was at home in French and English.

"Yes, puppy love. It was just a passing fancy, but Emma has a penchant for melodramatizing her emotions."

"I see." He signaled Abner to pass the wine decanter again, then said, "Might I ask, Mr. de Meyer, what your plans are when we reach San Francisco?"

"I can say, perhaps immodestly, that I was a successful jeweler in Frankfurt. San Francisco has millions in gold, but I suspect very little to spend it on. My intention is to start a jewelry business."

"Retailing is something I know practically nothing about," Scott said. "But you're certainly right about San Francisco having no jewelers. You should have no difficulty making a success, and a big one at that. However, I'm going to offer you an alternative suggestion I'd like you to consider."

"What's that, Captain?"

"I have three warehouses near the Embarcadero that I keep filled with merchandise my ships bring to San Francisco from all over the world, and the local merchants come to me to buy wholesale. This has worked well enough the past several years, but now it's becoming awkward, and I've been thinking: why should I let those wolves walk off with the retailing profit? However, I'm a sailor, not a merchant. I'd make a mess trying to retail all the stuff I bring in, and besides, I don't have the time or the inclination. You, on the other hand, might be just the man I've been looking for. What would you say, Mr. de Meyer, of becoming my partner and instead of a jewelry shop, opening a great general store like the emporiums in New York and Boston? A store that sells everything, including jewelry?"

Felix set down his spoon and was startled by the clang he made. He turned to look at Zita, then back to Scott. For long moments he said nothing. Then, quietly: "Captain, that is an intriguing idea."

"Isn't it?"

"I certainly will consider it. What kind of partnership are you thinking about?"

"I've bought a good deal of real estate in the past year or so, and I own a parcel of land on Portsmouth Square. That's in the very heart of the town, and it's a perfect site for an emporium, in my opinion. I'd donate the land if you built the store, then we could split the profits fifty-fifty. I might add that since I'm importing most of the building material, you could buy all the lumber you need from me wholesale. No, hell, since we'd be partners, I'd do even better than wholesale. You could build the store dirt cheap."

"I can hardly see how we could fail," Felix exclaimed.

Scott's grin was mischievous. "Don't fool yourself, Mr. de Meyer. San Francisco's full of rogues and thieves—nothing is surefire in that city. But I think you'll find you have a partner with a certain amount of muscle in Scott Kinsolving. Well," he said, waving his hand dismissively, "we'll have plenty of time to work out the details, Felix—if I may call you that?"

"Please do, Captain."

"We have a long voyage ahead of us, and I won't pretend it's going to be an easy one. We'll pick up fresh stores tomorrow in Trinidad, but the pickings will get lean before we reach Buenos Aires. As you know, this is not a passenger ship, which is why we make such good time. But there are few amenities, and since I want to make the voyage as pleasant as possible to the few passengers I have, I want you to feel free to borrow books from my library, if you're so inclined." He gestured to the bookcase.

"Your books look rather formidable, Captain," Zita said. "I don't suppose you have any French novels?"

"Afraid not, Countess," Scott said, giving her a guarded leer. "So you like spicy fiction?" She lives it, he thought, having gotten reports from the crew of her visits to Felix's stateroom.

Zita raised her eyebrows mockingly. "Only as long as the heroine remains virtuous," she said, smiling.

"Ah, of course. Heroines must always remain virtuous, at least until they get married. I suppose after that a heroine can do pretty well as she pleases."

"You have a rather casual concept of marriage, Captain."

"I notice it's a concept shared by others. Does your daughter enjoy books, Felix?"

"Very much. She's an avid reader. Of course, her first love is the pianoforte."

"Oh? She plays?"

"Very well. In fact, one of my greatest problems convincing her to come to California was that she was afraid there would be no pianos there."

"She's probably right," Scott said, choosing a cigar from the humidor Abner had presented.

Pianos, he thought.

Interesting.

10

DAVID Levin sat in the Good Queen Bess pub in Buenos Aires, ruminating about Emma as he drank rum and fingered his new beard. Did he hate Emma for stranding him in Jamaica? No, he sighed. He could never hate Emma. Besides, he was almost certain it was that damned Captain Kinsolving's fault. Well, he was about to round the Horn on the *Flying Cloud*, so Emma wasn't rid of him yet. He was going to San Francisco, and with his new beard—why hadn't he thought of that before?—perhaps he still might have a chance with Emma. If someone else hadn't caught her in the meantime—

"Good evenin', lovey. Lookin' for company?"

He whirled about at the cockney accent. The girl standing beside him was wearing a tight black blouse that showed a lot of her big breasts. She had a rather ratty white boa around her shoulders, and even with David's limited knowledge of the opposite sex, he spotted this cheap beauty as a whore.

"I—" He gulped. The pub, run by a former British seaman, was near the Buenos Aires docks and catered to British sailors. Over the years it had attracted British prostitutes to service its clientele, one of the seamier aspects of the flourishing British Empire.

"You're blushin'," she cooed. "Ain't that sweet. Gonna offer me a drink, lovey? Me name's Cora, and I could make your pecker stand up and sing 'Rule, Britannia.'"

David almost fell off his bar stool. His father, Isidor Levin, owned a bookshop in London and was a close friend of Isaac D'Israeli, the well-known author and father of Benjamin Disraeli. The latter was David's idol, one of the first Jews to be elected to Parliament. He was also author of three brilliant novels, one of which, *Sybil*, David had bought in Kingston and was in the process of reading. David dreamed of writing a great novel one day, perhaps a story of unrequited love— alas, like his own for Emma. But David's very literary, very correct background left him utterly unqualified to write scenes of passion, he realized. He had certainly never heard anyone mention his private parts before!

"Do you . . ." he began, gulping again. "Do you like rum?"

"Oh, lovey." She smiled, revealing rotten teeth. "It's muvver's milk to Cora. And if you buy me two rums, I'll finish you off with me mouth as an extra."

David Levin, aspiring writer seeking social realism, nearly swooned.

The eight horsemen galloped down the moonlit road of the pampas sixty miles southwest of Buenos Aires. The pampas was the heartland of Argentina, a richly fertile plain that rolled like a sea to the mountains in the west. It was a country with few towns or roads, and the distances from *estancia* to *estancia* were so vast that dogs barking on even the stillest night could not be heard by neighboring dogs.

The horsemen were gauchos and they had murder in their hearts. They approached the *estancia* of Don Jaime María Uribelarrea, a young, wealthy *estanciero* married to Irina Alexievna, the daughter of Countess Davidoff. Don Jaime and his wife were asleep in the bedroom of their two-story ranch house when the cowboys dismounted. Most of them were *mestizos*, men of mixed blood of Indian and Spanish descent. The Spaniards had brought the horse to the Americas three centuries before, the Indians had quickly become superb horsemen, and their *mestizo* descendants were the best in the world. They were stocky men wearing broad-brimmed black hats, tight-fitting shirts, hand-embroidered bolero jackets, knotted scarves, baggy trousers, and short leather boots. Some of them carried shotguns, and each carried a silver-edged gourd and silver straw for sipping *yerba mate* tea.

The tea-sipping cowboys came up on the porch. One of them blew the lock off the door with a shotgun. Pushing it open, the men went into the small entrance hall, illuminated by a kerosene lamp. One picked up the lamp and started climbing the stairs.

In the master bedroom on the second floor, Don Jaime and his wife had been awakened by the gun blast. Don Jaime was pulling his trousers up over his naked haunches. The scion of one of the twenty most powerful families in Argentina, known as "The Oligarchy," Don Jaime owned 150,000 acres and 30,000 head of cattle. Grabbing a pistol from his night table, he had started toward the door when it was pushed open. Don Jaime fired, killing the first gaucho, but the second fired a shotgun. The young man's chest exploded in gore. As Irina screamed, the gauchos poured into the room, riddling her with bullets. Then they threw the kerosene lamp at the foot of the four-poster bed. The bed linens caught fire, and the flames quickly encircled Irina's bloody body, turning the bed into a pyre. As the room filled with smoke, the gauchos hurried out, shooting in the face two Indian servants who had appeared in the upstairs hall. Going into the nursery, they gored Don Jaime's two infant daughters in their cribs, killing both of them instantly. Then they hurried down the stairs, their silver spurs jangling merrily as the *estancia* turned into an inferno.

Before they galloped away into the night, one of the gauchos tossed a piece of wood on the ground. On it had been carved: "Death to all enemies of the great Caudillo, Juan Manuel de Rosas!"

The murderous work of five minutes was soon to become notorious as the Massacre of the Pampas.

"A piano!" Emma exclaimed. She had been led into the small dining saloon of the *Empress of China* by Scott. Felix and Zita were behind them, and a few of the other passengers were also gathering, as it was near suppertime. "Where did it come from?"

"I bought it this morning in Port of Spain," Scott said. "It's a spinet, and Franz Liszt would spit on it, but I thought you might be able to entertain us."

Emma squeezed around the dining table and sat down at the tiny piano, which had been bolted to the deck against the port bulkhead. She began playing the Schubert Sonata in A major. The sweet melody filled the low-ceilinged room, charming the listeners even though the unending creak of the ship, bending before an increasing wind, provided an eerie obbligato in the background. When she finished, her small audience applauded.

Emma rose from the stool and turned to Scott. "Thank you," she said, smiling her prettiest.

Scott nodded. "Thank you. The music was lovely."

She squeezed past him, her full skirts pressing against his legs.

She may be no lady, he thought, but she's got good breeding. She'd make a spectacular governor's wife. And who the hell wants a lady, anyway? Ladies are bores in bed. But something tells me this one . . ."

"How thoughtful of Captain Kinsolving to buy the spinet," Zita said as she and Emma took a turn on the deck after supper. The sun was just setting. A mile off the starboard lay the coast of Venezuela.

"Yes, wasn't it?" Emma replied.

"He really is a rather nice man."

"He's about as 'nice' as a rattlesnake."

"Aren't you being a bit unfair?"

"Oh, Zita, I know the man. In the first place, the lurid secret of his love life is that he has a Chinese mistress. While I don't think I'm a prig, that strikes me as a bit *de trop*. In the second place, he asked me to marry him so he could have a respectable front in San Francisco.

It was the most cold-blooded, calculating proposal—at least David Levin truly loved me. But this Captain Kinsolving doesn't have a loving bone in his body. And while I'm glad he bought the piano—though it's out of tune—if he thinks that will sweeten my opinion of him, he's in for a surprise."

"Well, my dear, you know I've become extremely fond of you, but I must confess I think *you're* a little out of tune."

"Why?"

"I've lived longer than you and I believe I know a little more about this peculiar thing we call 'life.' There are beautiful things that can happen to us during our brief stay on this planet, and there are terrible things. But I think the most important thing is children—having them so life can continue, and of course taking care of them. I have my beautiful daughter, and she has her two daughters, whom I'm so looking forward to meeting. I've lived a full life and, I think, a rich one, but these are my true treasures, my offspring. You are carrying a child and someday it will be your treasure. But you have a responsibility to it, Emma. It is not enough for you to talk of love, important as love is. You have a responsibility to find a father for your child. A good man who will be able to give the child everything it will need in life—position, wealth, and, yes, love. You say Captain Kinsolving has no love in him, but how do you know? You're to be on this ship for a long time, and there aren't too many eligible men around. Perhaps it's time you, shall we say, 'got in tune'?"

The countess gave her a thoughtful glance, then moved away.

Alone, Emma leaned on the rail, staring at the ocean. Archer. . . . The thought of him surged through her mind, searing itself on her memory. Would she never see him again?

Yet she had to admit there was some truth to what Zita had said. Probably a lot of truth. The child was the important thing.

Sighing, she told herself that perhaps she should take a second look at the copper-haired captain. She had to admit he was a handsome figure of a man.

And he kissed like the very devil.

Scott was checking his daily log at his desk when he heard a knock on the door. "Who is it?"

"Miss de Meyer."

A grin crept over his face. He closed the log, got up, and went to open the door. Wearing a black dress, over which she had thrown the black-and-red flowered shawl she had bought in Trinidad, she looked like a sorceress in the soft light of the oil lamps. His eyes drank her in slowly, from head to hem, then back again.

"Are we in mourning for Mr. Levin?" he asked.

As usual, his sardonic manner exasperated her. "Of course not. May I come in?"

"Without a chaperon?"

"As you know full well, I am not only a widow but also an unwed-mother-to-be, so I think it's a bit late for chaperons."

"You have a point. Come in. To what do I owe this honor?"

He stepped aside. She came into the cabin, her skirts rustling, and went to the window seat. Looking out, she tried to compose herself. Pretend you like him, she ordered herself. Then she turned. "Well . . ." Smile! She smiled. "I wondered if you could tell me more about California."

"With pleasure. It's one of my favorite subjects." He closed the door. "You'd better sit down. It's gotten a bit choppy. Would you like a glass of port?"

Gratefully she sat on the window seat, for the boat's up-and-down, side-to-side motion was making her queasy. "Yes, thank you."

He took the wide-bottomed glass decanter from its bracket and poured two glasses of the blood-red port. "What would you like to know about California?" he said, bringing her the glass.

"Oh, everything. Where does the name come from?" She took a sip of the sweet port.

"A good place to start. There was a book that was very popular in Spain called *Las Sergas de Esplandán*. The hero, a knight called Esplandán, went to an island ruled by a Queen Calafía. The island was called California and it was inhabited by a tribe of Amazons who wore golden clothes and carried golden weapons. Gradually the *conquistadores* began referring to the west coast of North America as California because they didn't know much about it and they hoped gold was there. Next question."

"What are the women in San Francisco like?"

He laughed as he sat in the red plush armchair. "Well, that depends on whether you want pretty lies or the ugly truth."

"I'll take the latter."

"There aren't many women, and the few there are, are, shall we say, ladies of easy virtue?"

"Like Chingling?"

His face became stony. "I'd rather not discuss her."

"Why? Are you ashamed of her?"

He looked troubled. Hesitating, he tried to explain: "Chingling comes from another culture—much older than ours and in many ways more sophisticated. In Chingling's world, concubines are not evil or sordid women. They can even be highly respectable. For instance, the emperor's concubines can attain great power at the court."

"You haven't answered my question."

"Am I ashamed of her? Not at all. But I'm no fool, either. I know what other people—other white people—say about me behind my back. As a race, we whites may be taking over the world, but our great flaw is that we're two-faced as hell. You're to be complimented for being at least honest enough to tell me what you thought about Chingling to my face."

"I wish I hadn't said it now. You were right: we Jews are the last people in the world to be intolerant. Is she as beautiful as the daguerreotype?"

"She's a moonbeam."

"Is she—?"

As she bit her lip, he laughed.

"The eternal female! You're dying to know if she's more beautiful than you are. Could it be I've made you jealous?"

"You are the most conceited—"

Be nice! Besides, maybe I am jealous. . . . She looked at him more closely. "How old are you?" she asked.

"Thirty-four."

"Would you have married before if it hadn't been for Chingling?"

"I never gave much thought to it."

"Don't you want children?"

"Of course, but I'm in no great hurry."

She drank some more of the port. "You said that . . . if I married you, you'd take care of my child. Did you mean that?"

"Why? Are you having second thoughts about my proposal?"

She felt her belly heave as the ship sank into the trough of a wave, then swiftly rose again. Feeling herself blanch, she asked, "What if I am?"

"Well, don't. You rejected me in a rather high-handed fashion— mind you, you were probably right. Love is the most important thing, and you love another man, who is undoubtedly far nobler than I. So my suggestion of our getting married was simply a mistake. Besides, your father and I are going into business together, and business and romance don't mix well. So forget my proposal, Emma. You were right to reject me: I'm not good enough for you. Some more port?" he asked, grinning.

She got to her feet rather uncertainly. "You devil!" she almost spat. "I wouldn't marry you if—"

"If I were the last man on earth. Yes, I get the gist of your sentiments. So it looks as if we both are doomed to a passionate celibacy."

"The only passion I have is anger! Of all the rude insolence, to retract your proposal. You are a blackhearted cad, sir, and— Oh my God."

The ship plunged into another deep trough. She dropped the glass and fell back on the window seat, clutching her stomach. As the ship began to rise again, she moaned. "Oh . . . Ohhhh . . ."

Scott hurried to her and gently picked her up in his arms. "My dear Miss de Meyer," he said as he carried her across the cabin, "a little bird tells me you're getting seasick."

"Oh, Scott, I feel terrible."

"And the best cure for that is a little fresh air topside." He opened the door and carried her through. "I'll ask you not to throw up on me, if you can possibly avoid it."

"You're not funny—" She gagged.

He carried her to the main deck, then took her to the lee rail and set her on her feet. "Hold on to the rail and let 'er rip."

"Oh . . ."

She sank to her knees, holding the rail with both hands as the ship bucked wildly.

"Don't watch!" she cried angrily.

He laughed, yelling over the wind: "Fear not, fair damsel, I shall avert my eyes. And yet, could anything be more romantic?"

"Oh, you . . . you . . ."

She gagged and threw up over the rail as Scott laughed and spray from the mounting sea showered over them. Thoroughly drenched, Emma slowly got to her feet.

"Feel better?" he asked.

She nodded weakly.

"I'll help you to your stateroom."

He took her arm, but she wrenched free. "I don't need your help," she said. "And you did watch, which no gentleman would have— Oh my God . . ."

She ran back to the rail and threw up again.

Mr. Roseberry came to Scott and saluted. "Captain, the wind is shifting to the northwest."

"Yes, it's getting nasty. I'll go to the bridge. You take Miss de Meyer to her cabin."

"Aye, aye, Captain."

Scott walked to the poop deck as the navigator helped Emma to her feet. "Better hang on to me, miss," he yelled. "We're getting a bit of weather."

"Thank you. I feel . . . a little better."

In fact, she felt so weak she could barely stand. But with Roseberry's help she made it back to her stateroom, where she undressed, hanging her wet dress on a hook, then collapsed on her bunk.

He's toying with me again, she thought, grinding her teeth. I could kill him. And yet she remembered how strong his arms had felt when he carried her to the main deck. She had liked that strength.

Three hours later, she awoke from a troubled sleep to find that her nausea had disappeared, even though the ship was still bucking like a bronco. She sat up in the tiny cabin and pressed her nose to the cold glass of the lone port over the bunk. It was as dark out as in, but when her eyes became accustomed to the darkness, she saw the foam of the huge waves in which the clipper ship wallowed. The groaning of the ship as it rolled from side to side was terrifying, and now she understood why everything on the ship was either bolted to the deck or provided with restraining devices. Even her small shelf for toiletries over her washbasin had three lines of cord to hold the bottles of cologne and perfume in place, and a wooden lip projected six inches above her mattress to prevent her from rolling out. She, her father, and Zita had bought the most expensive cabins on the boat, but the accommodations were still primitive and uncomfortable.

Her mouth tasted awful. Getting out of her bunk, she lighted the single oil lamp, which swung crazily on gimbals attached to the bulk-head, went to the washbasin, and gargled with rosewater. How humiliating it had been to get sick in front of that grinning baboon! And yet . . . She smiled slightly. It was rather fun sparring with him. He had a devilish streak that appealed to her, exasperating as he was. And what was that remark he had made about going into business with her father?

As the ship crashed into another wave, she crawled back into her bunk, snuggling into the corner. So he was reneging on his proposal? She'd see about that.

She might not be in love with him, but no one reneged on Emma de Meyer.

Shortly after dawn, the wind began to abate and Scott, who had been by the helmsman all night, gave the watch over to Mr. Appleton, his second in command. Exhausted, he went below to his cabin, stripped off his sopping clothes, and got some sleep. He woke at ten and went to his washbasin to give himself a splash-bath. Then, pulling on clean drawers, he started to shave, glad that the sea had become sufficiently calm for him to carry out that operation without cutting his throat.

He was halfway through when there was a knock at his door.

"Come in."

Emma entered, wearing her white dress with the green trim. When she saw Scott, she looked startled.

"Oh, I didn't realize you were—"

"Good morning, Miss de Meyer. Feeling better today?" he asked as he went back to shaving.

"Yes, thank you. Though I thought we'd surely sink in that storm."

"That was a minor hiccup compared to what we'll get in the Strait of Magellan. Then you'll see a real belch of a storm."

"You have such an elegant way of expressing yourself, Captain. Someday you must write your memoirs: *Forty Years at Sea in a Belch*."

He grinned as he scraped his throat. "I like that title."

"I spoke to my father. He told me about the business you two are talking about. I just wanted you to know I think it's a splendid idea, and whatever differences you and I have had must not come between you and Poppa."

She found herself staring at his broad shoulders and muscular back, and she liked what she saw.

"Oh, absolutely. As I said last night, business and love don't mix. Not that there's much love lost between you and me. You know, I've tried my damnedest to be charming to you, but you really don't like me, do you?"

He finished shaving, rinsed his razor, then splashed water on his face.

"You've been so busy proposing," she said, "then reneging on your proposal, I haven't had much chance to get to know you."

"Oh? You think I reneged?"

"What else would you call it?"

"I have my pride to consider. I proposed to you in all sincerity, and you told me in so many words to stuff my proposal up my derriere."

"There's no need to be vulgar."

Throwing down his towel, he came to her and grabbed her wrist. "You could use a little vulgarity," he said softly.

Before she could reply, his mouth was against hers and he had pulled her into his arms. Her head swam as she began responding to his kiss. He smelled faintly of shaving soap. But it was the sheer brute strength of his body that was exciting her. At the same time her hands felt the softness of the skin on his back. She put up no resistance as he began unbuttoning the back of her dress. Then he removed his mouth.

"You damned women cover yourselves up with so much stuff you need a pickax to undress you," he said. "Take your clothes off while I lock the door."

For the first time in her life, she was at a loss for words. She stared at him as he went to the door and bolted it. Then he pulled down his drawers, standing on one leg as he tugged them off the other. Again she gasped.

"Well, now, madam, don't pretend you've never seen a naked man before," he said. "Unless Archer Collingwood impregnated you with his pants on, which I seriously doubt. Are you going to take your clothes off or am I going to have to rip them off?"

She quickly unbuckled her belt and put it on the red plush chair. Then she stepped out of her dress.

"You wouldn't have the nerve to ravish me," she said.

"The point is moot, since it's quite obvious that rape isn't going to be necessary."

"And I can't believe you could use that disgusting word in polite society."

"Our society is getting less polite every second."

His blue-green eyes did not miss a detail as he watched her. She removed her two petticoats, leaving nothing on but her chemise and her white frilled pantalets.

"Go on," he urged. "I'm waiting for the grand finale."

"You have the morals of a tomcat."

"Exactly. Just like you. Or are you going to tell me your maidenly modesty prevents you from disrobing in front of a member of the opposite sex? If so, you've gone a bit too far to be convincing."

"I find your attitude revolting, and your gross vulgarity proves beyond a doubt that you have no breeding at all," she said, stepping out of her pantalets.

He laughed. "How right you are, my dear. No breeding, but I love to breed. Well, now, I'd say your legs are about as shapely as any I've ever seen. What a shame to cover them up! You women are just plain stupid to wear all those skirts and petticoats. But I perceive that Mr. Collingwood's gift is beginning to show a bit, or is our food too fattening?"

She frowned, only too well aware that her skirts were beginning to feel tight. "If I were you, I wouldn't mention Archer Collingwood at a time like this," she said.

"The great bank robber. No doubt he was stealing from the rich to give to the poor?"

"That's exactly what he did—the poor being himself! And he had gentleness and sweetness, qualities sadly lacking in you."

"By God, Emma, I'll fuck you till you forget Archer Collingwood ever existed."

She knew what "fuck" meant, since it came from the German slang "*ficken*" or "*fucken*," but his use of it to her face had an overwhelming shock force.

"What a disgusting word!"

"Believe me, it wasn't a *word* that made you pregnant."

He picked her up in his arms, then carried her to his bunk, laying her down on her back. She stared up at him. When his penis was erect, it arched upward like a scimitar, and she was more than a little impressed by its size. Then he climbed on the bunk, straddling her.

"You're a witch," he whispered, "but you're a beautiful one."

"More beautiful than Chingling?"

"You're dying to know, aren't you? All I'll say is, if she's a moon-beam, you're a sunbeam. Does that satisfy you?"

"No."

"It will have to do for the moment. Right now I'm otherwise occupied."

And he lowered himself on her, his broad chest of red-gold hair pressing against her breasts. She was overwhelmed by his masculinity, engulfed by it. She had to admit there was something thrilling in Scott's enormous vitality, in his physical size and strength. Mean, sarcastic, vulgar—yes.

Afterward, she told herself she could very easily get used to his vulgarity.

"Did I light a bonfire this time?" he asked as he lay beside her.

"I'm smelling smoke," she purred.

He laughed. "Where there's smoke, there's fire. Now I know you want to hear me say that I can't get you out of my mind. Well, dammit, it's true: I can't. All last night, through that damned storm, I kept thinking about you."

"Did you really?"

"Yes, I did really. The point is, maybe I'm in love with you and am too stupid to realize it. Now, I know you don't love me: your heart's with Ohio's answer to Robin Hood. But I'm a man of my word. You hurt me, Emma, and I'll admit it: that's why I reneged. But my proposal still stands. I can't very well marry myself, but when we reach Buenos Aires we could get hitched in proper style and that kid in your belly will be legal. How about it?"

"Oh, Scott, I think maybe you really do love me," she said, de-lighted. "Now, admit it: doesn't it make you feel wonderful?"

He snickered. "My God, you never give up, do you? All right, it makes me feel 'wonderful.' " He crossed his eyes and stuck out his tongue.

She laughed and pinched him. "You awful man."

"This awful man has proposed a second time and is still waiting for an answer."

"If I say yes, may I move in here the rest of the trip? I hate my cabin. It's so small."

"Do I perceive the beginning of a trend? Yes, you may move in here. *After* you become Mrs. Scott Kinsolving. I'll force you to be respectable until then."

She made a face.

"When do we reach Buenos Aires?"

"Two weeks, if the winds hold."

She snuggled up to him, running her hand over his chest and flat stomach. It was like having a wonderful new teddy bear.

"May I come pay you visits till then?" she whispered.

"Yes," he whispered back. "You can come to my cabin when your father goes to Countess Davidoff's."

She bolted upright, gaping at him. "You can't be serious!" she whispered.

"Oh, but I am."

"Poppa and Zita? I knew they liked each other, but are they . . .?"

"They are indeed—like middle-aged rabbits. My cabin boy keeps me informed of everything."

"Poppa's been so lonely since Momma died. Oh, I'm so glad they've fallen in love!"

"They've fallen in bed. Don't jump to other conclusions."

She lowered herself back into his arms. "You awful man."

"You said that."

"Am I not allowed to repeat myself? You are awful. And vulgar."

"Am I doing the right thing?" Emma asked.

"Marrying Captain Kinsolving? Oh, yes, definitely," Zita said. They were standing at the rail as the ship headed for the dock in Buenos Aires. "I'm surprised you have any doubts."

"I have many doubts," she said sadly. "First, of course, is Archer. I know I'm betraying him—"

"My dear, how can you be so foolish?" interrupted the Russian countess. "If anything, you are doing the best thing possible for him by finding a responsible father for his child."

"I suppose."

"And Captain Kinsolving will make a splendid husband. Surely you find him attractive?"

"He's all right, I suppose." She was lying. Actually, she was beginning to think of him as excitingly handsome, though she wasn't about to admit it. "But he has no manners. He has a terrible habit of using profanity in front of me. He does it to shock me, I think, but it's extremely distasteful."

"Oh, well, men will be men. Half the noblemen in Russia beat their wives and curse like peasants. Captain Kinsolving may not be perfect—who is?—but he will make you happy. And if you want to, you can tame him. That's half the fun of marriage, taming that wild beast known as man. And he loves you, I'm sure."

"Oh, in his funny way, I think he loves me a little. But his heart is with Chingling, as mine is with Archer. So I suppose I can't be too critical of him." She sighed. "What an odd marriage it will be."

"Don't be too sure his heart is with the Chinese woman," Zita said, pulling her sable wrap around her more tightly to ward off the chill. "And don't be too sure your heart is with Archer."

Emma looked at her with surprise. "Oh, but I am sure!"

"Time plays funny tricks, my dear. Time and propinquity. I've never believed that absence makes the heart grow fonder. Quite the contrary: absence makes the heart forget. How odd: I don't see my daughter on the dock. Surely she got my letter?"

The sky above the Argentine capital was leaden, and a cold wind was blowing up whitecaps as the *Empress of China* nudged against the municipal dock, which, aside from the stevedores, was empty. Emma looked aft to the poop deck, where the man she was going to marry that afternoon was standing with several of his officers, supervising the docking. For the thousandth time she wondered about her true feelings for Scott. There was no question that she enjoyed his lovemaking—so much so that she shuddered at the thought of what her mother would think of her wantonness, which was an accurate description of her activities over the past two weeks. Of course, her mother would never have allowed her to marry a goyim, much less go to bed with one. But in matters of both morality and religion, Felix had turned out to be much more easygoing than his dead wife had been. Emma felt it was mainly because of his own liaison with Zita, who was a gentile. Felix was in no position to preach. Also, to her surprise, she had found that one of the more endearing things about Scott was his utter disinterest in religion, which was another way of describing his lack of prejudice. At a time when anti-Semitism was rampant in America, Scott was refreshingly free of it.

But as always with Scott, for every positive quality he had, there was a negative. Scott was not anti-Semitic, but he was also not anti-Chinese, as was painfully obvious from his relationship with Chingling. The rather shocking truth was that Scott didn't seem to be anti-anything; the disturbing corollary to this was that he would sleep with anything and any*one*. She could overlook his sarcasm, his crude profanity, but as much as she tried to overlook Chingling's race, she couldn't overlook the woman herself. The existence of the beautiful Chinese as a rival was a constant irritant. Even if Emma didn't love Scott, she hated the thought of sharing him. He exasperated her, but he amused her. He was coarse, but he had a first-rate mind. She was marrying him for the sake of expediency. But her true feelings about him were . . . confusing.

"That must be Irina," Zita exclaimed, pointing to an elegant carriage that had just appeared on the dock. "Her husband's quite dashing. They met in Paris four years ago and it was love at first sight—so romantic! He belongs to one of Argentina's oldest families. Irina wrote to me that he's gotten involved with politics. It seems they're trying to get rid of this terrible dictator, Juan Manuel de Rosas, who apparently will stop at . . . nothing."

Emma looked at her. Zita was frowning as she gazed at the dock. A portly man in a fur-lined coat and top hat had climbed out of the carriage. He was looking up at them.

"It's Count Sheremetieff," said Zita. "The Russian ambassador. Why is he here?"

"Do you know him?"

"Yes. He was a colleague of my husband's."

The ambassador boarded the ship, said something to Scott as he shook his hand, then came to Emma and Zita. Removing his hat, he kissed Zita's hand. He spoke to her briefly in French, then led her inside the ship.

A moment later, Emma heard a scream.

Scott came up to her.

"Scott, what is it?"

"The ambassador told me her entire family was murdered by the dictator, de Rosas."

"Oh, no! Oh, God, poor Zita! Oh, Scott! I must help her—" She started toward the door, but Scott took her hand.

"I sent for your father. Let him go to her."

Emma looked at him and realized he was right. It was, aside from the piano, the first time she had seen him display thoughtfulness.

Perhaps I could learn to love him, she thought. And if I'm going to be his wife, I certainly must try.

But, dear God, I still don't know: am I doing the right thing?

·TWO·

In the Land of the Golden Hills

11

THE *Empress of China* dropped anchor in San Francisco Bay September 12, 1850, after a five-month voyage during which it lost ten days battling a fierce storm in the Strait of Magellan. It was a warm, bright day, but Emma was disappointed by her first glimpse of the city that was to be her new home.

"It's not a city at all," she said to Scott, who was standing with his arm around her now-much-expanded waist. "It's a bunch of shacks."

"What did you expect—Paris? You have to remember that three years ago this was a Mexican village of about three hundred people called Yerba Buena. Now it's got thirty thousand people and is growing by leaps and bounds. You have to admit the bay is beautiful."

"Yes, it's magnificent. But what are all these ships doing here?"

Some fifty ships, their sails stowed, were anchored almost gunwale to gunwale. Some of them seemed to be rotting, and all looked deserted.

"Their crews jumped ship to go to the goldfields to get rich. Most of them are still out there, still trying to get rich. I've lost some of my men too. Anyway, welcome to your new home."

He turned to Mr. Appleton, instructing him to take the passengers ashore first, then the crew, giving them three days' liberty after the long and arduous voyage. Then he and Emma were joined by Felix and Zita. The countess had been told by Count Sheremetieff in Buenos Aires that he could not guarantee her safety if she went ashore, for Juan Manuel de Rosas, a bloodthirsty despot of the worst sort, had vowed to murder not only all his political enemies but also their relatives as well. Thus Zita had no choice but to continue on to San Francisco. For weeks she had been inconsolable. But gradually Felix had been able to restore her to a degree of emotional stability. Now, dressed in the mourning clothes she had sent her maid ashore to buy in Chile, she walked down the accommodation ladder. Her black veils floated eerily in the slight breeze, presenting an image of stark tragedy that moved Emma to tears.

"Poor Zita," she whispered to her husband. "She still can hardly believe it happened. It was sweet of you to offer to put her and Poppa up."

"I like Countess Davidoff. She's a brave woman. Besides, there's not a hotel in town that doesn't have bedbugs. Come on."

He helped his wife, who was now in the sixth month of her pregnancy, onto the ladder, and they climbed down to take their seats in the boat. As the sailors pushed off and began rowing, the deserted ships loomed above them like dark ghosts, creaking as they rolled in the slight swell.

"Can Do should be on the docks," Scott said.

"Who?"

"Can Do. He's my number-one houseboy. I brought him over from Canton five years ago."

"With Chingling?"

Scott shot her a look. He knew that his beautiful young bride was obsessed with the idea of his concubine.

"Yes, as a matter of fact, it was the same trip. Anyway, Can Do is bright as a penny. I put him in charge of finishing the new house, and I'm eager to see how it's turned out. As you can see, San Francisco is a city of hills—some of them quite steep. That one over there is called Telegraph Hill because they're talking about putting a semaphore on top of it. See those boats heading for us? They're filled with store-owners coming out to buy my cargo. But this time they'll be disappointed, right, Felix?"

"Absolutely."

"None of the Kinsolving Shipping Company's goods are moving out of my warehouses until de Meyer and Kinsolving's Emporium opens its doors—with a few exceptions. By that time the customers will be so hungry we can triple our prices."

"I do believe, Captain," Zita said through her veil, "that you and Felix are doomed to become very rich."

"Put a Jew and a Scot together, and you've got an unbeatable combination."

They all laughed.

"Ahoy there! Kinsolving!"

One of the small armada of boats had reached them, and a man in a stovepipe hat and black jacket was waving toward them.

"Did you bring Chicago's dresses?" the man was yelling.

"That I did," Scott yelled back. "Two trunks full, the fanciest in New York. Mr. Appleton will give them to you after you pay the balance."

"Four thousand in gold, right?"

"Wrong, you thief. Five thousand."

The man laughed. "Just checking your memory. Drop by the Bonanza tonight. Chicago's got three new girls from Chile who'll deep-fry your oysters right smart."

Scott's face turned a shade redder. "Uh, Slade, meet my new wife, Emma Kinsolving."

"Jesus Christ, you got married? Excuse me, ma'am. I really put my foot in it . . . Well, I'll be damned! Scott Kinsolving married! Hey, Scott, what'll they say when they hear about this on Dupont Street? Huh?"

He guffawed as the boat passed on. Scott scowled. Emma looked at him.

"What's Dupont Street?" she asked.

"That's Slade Dawson, one of San Francisco's more charming crooks. He owns a casino on Portsmouth Square called the Bonanza."

"What's Dupont Street?" Emma repeated.

"Chicago's his girlfriend. Not to shock you, Countess, but Chicago is San Francisco's most prominent madam."

"It's rather confusing geographically," Zita said, "but believe me, Captain, I am not shocked. At the last census, there were in St. Petersburg four hundred and twenty *maisons de passe*, making prostitution one of Russia's leading industries."

"What's Dupont Street?" Emma asked for the third time.

Scott sighed. "It's the heart of Little China," he said.

Emma's eyes narrowed. "Chingling?" she whispered.

"Yes" was his terse reply. "Ah, there's Can Do." He stood up and waved at a young Chinese standing on the dock by an elegant open carriage. Can Do was dressed in a smart red uniform with gold buttons.

"Why do you call him Can Do?" asked Felix.

"You'll see. He speaks pidgin, like most of the Celestials—that's what the Chinese are called here, because they come from the Celestial Kingdom. Can Do," he yelled again. "Catch the painter!"

"Can do!" yelled Can Do as one of the sailors threw him the boat's rope.

"Now I understand your name for him," Felix said, smiling.

Don't show your anger, Emma thought as she climbed up to the dock. Behave with dignity. Be a lady. All the same, she was seething. It was obvious that Chingling, far from being a secret in San Francisco, was something of a local joke. My God, she thought, the whole city will be laughing at me. I never expected *this!*

The dock was crowded—she was to discover that the arrival of any ship drew a crowd, since the San Franciscans, cut off from the world, were starving for news—and with one or two exceptions, the crowd was male, and rather seedy-looking males at that. When they spotted

Emma, who, despite her swollen belly, looked bewitching in a white dress with matching white plumed hat and parasol, they broke into applause and whistles.

"Captain Kinsolving," yelled one young man who looked well into his cups, "did you bring some new girls for Chicago?"

Emma gasped. Scott came up to the man, grabbed his shirt, and slugged him on the jaw, sending him sprawling back into the crowd. A shocked silence ensued.

"My friends," Scott announced, rubbing his hands on his pants, "we all know that ladies are in short supply in San Francisco. But I'd hate to think it's been so long since you saw a lady that you'd mistake a genuine Russian countess and my wife for anything but ladies of the utmost refinement who will bring the charm and grace of the fair sex to our town."

"Cap'n Boss," an amazed Can Do cried, "pretty missy you wife?"

"That's right."

"Oh, boy . . . oh, boy" was all Can Do said, but Emma had the definite feeling he looked frightened.

Scott shepherded them all into the landau, which had its roof down and was driven by yet another Celestial dressed in a snappy red jacket trimmed with gold, suede trousers, and shiny leather boots. A plumed red cap topped off the livery, which struck Emma as gaudy to the point of ridiculousness. As the four-wheeler pulled away from the dock, one of the men in the crowd yelled, "She's a beauty, Captain. Congratulations."

Scott smiled and tipped his hat.

"I'm beginning to understand what they mean when they call this the New World," Felix said. "These people treated us as if we were all equal."

"That's what they think," Scott said, who was sitting opposite his wife. "That's what America is supposed to be all about."

"You say 'supposed,' Captain," Felix said. "Do you have some doubts?"

"I certainly do. In Boston and New York and Philadelphia, if you have money, that's fine. But if you don't have money—especially in New York—you lead a dog's life. There's no more equality in America than there is anywhere else in the world. Money is god here, which some say is America's blessing and others say is its curse. The one advantage we have is that if you're born poor but are smart and energetic, you can get rich. You may end up making a fool of yourself, but you can be a rich fool instead of a poor one."

Emma was hardly listening. Rather, she was drinking in the town. "There's no paving," she said. "And the sidewalks are nothing but wooden planks. It must be terrible when it rains."

"It is terrible," Scott said. "But paving will come, and sidewalks will come, and someday these wooden 'shacks' will be replaced by brick and stone—if for no other reason than that the city keeps burning down. Last Christmas Eve the whole city burned in one night."

"So on top of everything else, it's a firetrap," Emma growled, feeling sulky.

"It's a little late to go back," Scott said.

"Emma," her father said, "we knew it was going to be a bit primitive."

Emma dropped the subject. Leaning back in her seat, she held her parasol to shield off the California sun as the carriage bumped through streets lined with two- or three-story wooden buildings festooned with large signs advertising pharmacies, hardware shops, blacksmiths, groceries, dry goods, and sundries. Most of the buildings weren't even painted, and the wood siding was graying from exposure. Emma saw no flowers or plantings, and noticed an unusual dearth of trees, giving the bare hills a depressing bald look. It was all extremely ugly. She felt like crying. Had she left her beautiful home in Frankfurt, undergone all the trials of crossing the Atlantic, then going around South America, for *this*?

As the carriage started up a hill, she saw above her an extraordinary sight: a huge white house crowning the top. Girdled by a covered porch, the square structure rose two more stories to a spindled white railing that resembled a widow's walk and lent the house a rather New England Colonial look. Above it, however, soared a central tower that looked Italianate with its arched windows. The house was an architectural hodgepodge—some might have said nightmare—but compared to the drab buildings she had been seeing, it looked almost enchanted.

Can Do, who was sitting next to the driver, turned around with a big grin on his face as he pointed. "That's it, pretty missy. That your new home. You like?"

"Oh yes." Emma smiled, sitting up. "It's very pretty. And there are *trees*."

"I told Can Do to plant them," Scott said, turning around to look. "Most of the trees got burned in the fire."

"Oh, and look: a reflecting pool. How lovely."

"It's also a fire pond."

The carriage passed through a wooden gate, and Emma saw that the grounds of the house had been planted with flowerbeds and grass. The driver continued on the gravel drive around the circular pond, pulling up in front of the mansion. Two more young Celestials in the same gaudy red-jacketed livery were waiting for them. One of them held the door as Zita and Emma climbed out, followed by Felix and Scott.

Zita took Emma's arm. "Look."

Emma turned around. Zita was pointing below at San Francisco Bay and the Pacific Ocean, seeming to stretch to infinity. Emma gazed at it for long, rapturous moments. Then she turned to Scott. "I take it all back," she said. "I don't care how ugly the town is. This is the most beautiful place in the world."

He smiled. "Good. I was hoping you'd love it as much as I do. And now, Mrs. Kinsolving, being a proper bridegroom, I intend to carry you across the threshold of your new home."

He swept her up in his arms, her huge white skirt almost drowning him, and carried her up the four stairs to the broad porch. As two more Celestials held open the double front doors with their stained-glass windows, he carried her inside the house and set her down.

"Welcome home, Emma," he said, taking her in his arms and kissing her.

"Oh, Scott," she said after he released her, "it's so big! And so wonderfully nouveau!"

She gazed eagerly about the immense entrance hall. It was dominated by a wide wooden staircase with a red runner that climbed to a palm-decked landing. Dividing, it climbed farther to a second-floor gallery with an elaborate wooden rail that went around three sides of the hall. On the third floor was yet another gallery. The ceiling soared almost fifty feet above and contained an immense stained-glass skylight set into the tower.

"Can Do will show you to your room. You take a bath, have a rest, and tonight we'll celebrate with a banquet."

He headed back for the front door.

"Where are you going?" she asked.

"I have to supervise the unloading of the ship," he called back. "I'll be home this evening."

She frowned, certain that he was lying. And she had an excellent idea where he was going.

The carriage, now closed, bumped its way down Dupont Gai, or Dupont Street, the main thoroughfare of the Chinese section of Gum San Ta Fow—Big City in the Land of the Golden Hills—or Fah-lan-sze-ko, as most Chinese pronounced "San Francisco." The wooden sidewalks were lined with shops, most of them with outside bins filled with food or Chinese delicacies or silks. Shop owners haggled with their customers, and above them fluttered gaily colored Chinese banners advertising the wares.

Scott's landau stopped before a wooden building that had no bins but instead sported a rather severe sign that read "KINSOLVING SHIP-

PING COMPANY—WAREHOUSE FOUR." There were no windows on the ground floor, but balconies lined with pots of pink geraniums graced the top two floors. Scott climbed out and went to a door beneath the sign. Unlocking it, he let himself in. As he climbed the dimly lit stair to the second floor, he reflected on the Chinese who were pouring into San Francisco from Canton and Hong Kong, pouring money into his bank account. Thousands of Celestials were immigrating to Ka-la-fo-ne-a, paying an average of forty dollars a head for passage across the Pacific on Scott's ships, half of which ended up in his pocket. But most of the Chinese immigrants fleeing destitution in China distrusted the *fan kwei* (foreign devils) and wanted only to earn enough money in America to return to China, set up a small business, and become a *Gum San Hock*, or returnee from the Golden Hills of San Francisco. Thus thousands were also returning to Canton each year, almost doubling Scott's profits. Conditions belowdecks on the long voyages were anything but deluxe, and Scott knew his ships inevitably became filthy, though he urged his captains to keep conditions as sanitary as possible. Still, the Chinese were not slaves, and the fare, which represented a fortune to them, allowed for nothing better.

At the top of the steps, Scott emerged into a dingy hallway. He frowned as he heard the rinky-tink sounds of an out-of-tune piano playing "Abide with Me." He walked down the hall and opened a door. Beyond it was China.

Or at least the decor was Chinese, mixed with a curious blend of mid-nineteenth-century American, like some exotic tea. Chinese lanterns hung from the ceiling, and most of the dark furniture and standing screens were Chinese. But against the far wall was a very American brass bed, and next to it an American spinet.

Standing beside the piano, facing Scott, was the Manchu princess Ah Toy. The woman was perhaps forty, with a beautiful, impassive face that had been powdered dead white. A tiny scarlet teardrop had been painted in the center of her lower lip, and small round circles of vermilion were painted on her cheeks. Her jet-black hair was elaborately coiffed in the Manchu court style with long ebony sticks. She wore a high-necked scarlet silk dress woven with intricate patterns in black and gold thread.

When Scott closed the door, the girl seated at the piano with her back to him stopped the ghastly rendition of "Abide with Me," which she had been singing in a high singsong voice. Now she turned. She was twenty years old and dressed in a silver gown in the Manchu style. Her exquisite features were enough like Ah Toy's to proclaim a relationship, but the younger face was sweeter and more delicate. It also lacked the hint of cruelty in Ah Toy's face.

"Scott!" she sang out, jumping from the piano stool and hurrying across the room into his arms. She covered his face with kisses. "Chingling so happy.see you my sweetheart!" she said in her own hashed pidgin. "Chingling make Scott happy time!"

Scott pushed her away gently, looking instead at the mother, still standing by the piano.

"Welcome home, Captain," Ah Toy said. "We have missed you."

"I told you not to teach her those damned hymns," Scott said.

"Why not? My daughter must become Christian. Then she become true American. But I perceive the captain is in a bad mood. Would he like some tea? Or perhaps a pipe of *ah pin yin*?"

"Leave us alone," Scott said in a peremptory tone.

Ah Toy's face was a painted mask as she bowed. Then she went to a blue curtain and raised it, revealing a door. She slipped through it, and the curtain dropped back into place.

Chingling, which in the casual Chinese language could mean either "Happy Mood" or "Glorious Life" (the "ling" could mean either "life" or "mood"), now unbuttoned her silver robe and removed it, revealing her superb nakedness. Scott drank it in with his eyes, then pulled her to him and buried his face between her small breasts.

"Oh, Chingling, my darling," he almost sobbed. "I love you so goddamned much!"

Chingling ran her fingers through his red-gold hair. "Chingling love Scott," she said softly. "Chingling's whole life to make Scott happy."

He ran his hands over her firm buttocks, then down her smooth thighs.

"You must know," he whispered, "that whatever I do to you, I'll always love you."

A hint of fear came into her almond eyes. "What Scott do to Chingling?"

He stood up and forced a smile. "We'll talk later. Now is happy time."

He picked her up and carried her to the brass bed next to the piano, remembering that less than an hour before, he had carried Emma across the threshold of his house on Rincon Hill. Jesus, he thought, I've got to tell her. I've got to! But she's so beautiful. Just one more time . . . just one more time.

He set her gently on the bed. Chingling watched him as he started to undress. He was about to pull off his pants when Ah Toy reappeared from beneath the blue curtain.

"Damn you, woman," bellowed Scott. "Can't you see—"

He was stopped by the look of cold rage on the Manchu woman's face. She hissed something to her daughter in Chinese. Chingling got out of the bed and threw on her dress.

"What's happening?" Scott asked.

Neither woman said a word as Chingling hurried through the blue curtain.

"So," Ah Toy said. "It has happened."

"What has happened? And why the hell are you interrupting us?"

"Word has just come. The news is all over the city: you have taken a bride."

Scott sat on the wooden bench. "It's true," he said quietly. "So what?"

Ah Toy crossed her hands over her breasts, her long fingernails like spikes. "And what happens to my daughter?"

Scott frowned. "I've treated you well so far. You live here rent-free and I pay all your bills. I'm prepared to make a handsome financial settlement on you and Chingling. You'll never have to worry about money."

"I'm afraid it's not quite so simple, Captain," Ah Toy said. From behind the blue curtain came a baby's wail. Ah Toy smiled slightly as the curtain billowed and Chingling appeared, carrying a baby in her arms.

"We named her Star," Ah Toy said, "because the stars are beautiful and the truth is in the stars. Star is a beautiful name, don't you agree, Captain? Chingling, take Star to her father."

Scott felt paralysis seeping into his limbs as Chingling carried the baby to him.

"Isn't she beautiful, Scott?" Chingling whispered proudly. "You hold baby in your arms? You kiss her? Go on, she no hurt you."

As in a dream, Scott slowly extended his arms. Chingling transferred the baby, who was wrapped in a white blanket, into his arms. He took the baby, staring at it as if it were a creature from another planet. The baby looked up at her father, gurgling slightly. Then she reached out one of her tiny hands and pulled the hair on his chest.

"You no like baby, Scott?" Chingling asked anxiously. "You no proud to be her daddy?"

"I . . ." Scott took a deep breath, staring in shame at his mistress. Then he looked down at the baby again. "This is a bit of a surprise," he said lamely. "But Star . . ." He whispered the name. "Yes, it is a beautiful name."

"It is her Christian name," Ah Toy said. "We will raise her as a Christian. The question is, what will her last name be?" Scott didn't take his eyes off the baby's adorable face, but his ears heard everything.

"You are a Christian, are you not, Captain?" Ah Toy continued. "What do you suggest?"

"I'm not much of a Christian," Scott muttered.

"That is no answer."

The baby started crying.

"She's got strong lungs," Scott said, trying desperately to say something light. He felt as light as lead.

Ah Toy spoke to Chingling in Chinese.

"I take baby now," said Chingling, extending her arms. "But first you must kiss her."

The infant started bawling as her father leaned over and kissed her forehead. Then he handed her to her mother, who looked pleadingly at Scott. "You do love her, Scott?" she asked.

"Yes."

Chingling smiled, then took the baby out of the room. Scott put his shirt on as Ah Toy advanced slowly toward him.

"So, Captain," she said, "I have not yet told Chingling of your wife, but when I do, it will break her heart. She is foolish enough to love you, and while you were gone she told me she knew you would do the right thing—the Christian thing—when you came home. I tried to unveil her eyes. I told her you round-eyes despise us, even though in our veins flows the blood of Genghis Khan. In China I was a princess, but here I am expected to take in laundry. And my daughter? Oh, yes, you make love to her with your hairy body, but you will not marry her because her eyes are not round like yours. And now Star, the innocent result of all of this, Star is to have no father. My granddaughter is to have no name. It is not good enough, Captain. She is your daughter too. What do you propose?"

Scott fumbled with his last button. "I don't want to hurt Chingling," he said, "although obviously I already have. But I want to be fair. I'll adopt the child, and my treasurer, Mr. Fontaine, will set up a fund for you and your daughter. There'll be enough money so that you'll both be comfortable for life."

"Money." She sneered. "You think money can make up for your insult to my daughter?" She reached her right hand up and dug her long nails down his left cheek. As the blood gushed, she said, "Every time your round-eye wife looks at those scars, let her think of Chingling."

As the blood dripped onto his white shirt, Ah Toy walked to the blue curtain and vanished.

12

"I'M afraid my husband has dreadful taste in furniture," Emma noted to Zita as they walked through the large drawing room. She waved a hand at the Chinese chairs and tables and vases and pink-and-white garden stools.

"I disagree," Zita said. "I think these Chinese things are stunning."

"Oh? Well, I suppose Chinese is an acquired taste. It's one that I just haven't acquired yet. But the house is not even one-third furnished—you saw the rooms upstairs, they have hardly any furniture at all, Chinese or otherwise. And Can Do tells me there are no furniture stores. They get everything from China or New York, even clothes."

"Such a situation almost assures the success of the new emporium, doesn't it?" Zita asked, sitting on a bamboo chair. "And as for your clothes, I'll make them for you, just as I altered that dress you have on."

"That's sweet of you, Zita, and you certainly are clever with a needle—"

"I should be," she interrupted. "I was St. Petersburg's leading dressmaker before I . . . shall we say 'legitimized' my relationship with Count Davidoff."

Emma looked surprised. "You were? How fascinating! Why didn't you tell me?"

Zita smiled. "It took me years to live it down in Russia, so I thought why should I air my humble origins in America? As long as I call myself 'Countess,' people assume I was wellborn. But actually my father was a tailor."

"A tailor?" She could hardly believe it.

"He of course was the palace tailor, but sewing's in my blood. At the age of fourteen I went to work for Madame Rosa, who makes hats for the court ladies, and it turned out I had a certain flair. So I set up my own dress shop and was quite successful. In fact, after I married the count and closed the shop, I missed it dreadfully. Now, after this terrible tragedy . . ." She paused a moment, controlling her emotions. "I've been thinking that I have no home anymore, no family. In fact, you and your father have become almost like family to me after all these months, if I may presume to say it."

"Of course you can," Emma said, hugging her. "You are family."

"I think it's no secret that your father and I have become intimate."

"It's no secret, and I'm delighted."

"So I've been thinking that this country really is different and it really isn't all that disgraceful to be a tailor's daughter—the palace tailor's daughter. So why shouldn't I stay here and become San Francisco's leading dressmaker?"

"What a splendid idea!"

"Your father says he will give me space in the store he and the captain are planning. And the rich and beautiful Mrs. Scott Kinsolving—who I'm sure is about to become San Francisco's most prominent hostess—can be my first customer."

"Oh, Zita," Emma said, hugging her again. "I think it's simply wonderful."

"Mind you, my prices are going to be outrageous."

"Oh, Zita, it's going to be such fun, and thank heaven you're staying. I'd be so lonely without you."

"Well, my dear, you do have your handsome husband."

Emma's smile vanished. "Oh, yes, him." She walked to the bay window at the corner of the room and looked out at the distant Pacific. "You know where Scott is now?" she asked quietly.

"No."

"I'd bet a thousand dollars he's with that Chinese woman. Can you imagine? My first day in this city and after ten minutes he takes off like some tomcat in heat to go see his damned concubine. I could kill him!"

Zita stood up and came to her, putting her arm around her. "Perhaps, my dear, you must learn to accept her."

Emma turned, and Zita had never seen her beautiful eyes so sad.

An hour later, Emma emerged from what Can Do had proudly informed her was the first "indoor privy" in California and sat down at her crude vanity table to brush her hair. She had had her first complete bath in more than a year, for bathing on the ships had been restricted to sponge baths. The small comfort that gave her, though, failed to combat her fierce depression. The beauty of the view notwithstanding, the house was a half-empty tomb. Despite Zita's future dress shop, for the present Emma had only two dresses she could fit into. California's future might be golden, but the reality of the present was that she was stuck in a shantytown with no society, no culture, and, worst of all, no love. That Scott had gone to see Chingling proved beyond a doubt that her marriage was a farce. In the weeks after their marriage in Buenos Aires, she had tried to convince herself that Scott really did love her and that Chingling was fading from his mind like a ghost. Now, she told herself bitterly, I've been a naive fool. First Anton Schwabe and now Scott: two empty, loveless marriages.

She put down her brush and crossed the bedroom to a window, wrapping her robe around her—the robe that barely fit anymore. The room was vast but nearly empty: there were a big bed, a curious porcelain Chinese dog on the floor beside it that served as a bed table, her vanity and mirror, and nothing else. Not even a rug or curtain. She looked out at the ocean and noticed the sky clouding up. Closing her eyes, she thought of Archer and burned with longing. How cruel of fate to deprive her of the one thing she wanted most in the world!

She opened her eyes and closed her fists. To hell with fate. She would be the mistress of her own destiny. There must be a way to get Archer back, and then she could tell this faithless redheaded husband of hers what she really thought of him. Except, what *did* she really think?

"Emma."

She turned and saw Scott standing in the door. He had changed out of his captain's uniform, and it was the first time she had ever seen him in a "civilian" suit. She was surprised to see he was a stylish dresser. She was also surprised by the bandage on his left cheek.

"I have some presents for you."

He came in the room, followed by Can Do and two other liveried Celestials carrying boxes that they deposited on the bed.

"What happened to your cheek?" Emma asked as he came to her across the room.

"A cat jumped me down on the docks." It was such a feeble lie that she almost laughed in his face. Quickly he changed the subject. "When we were in Santiago last month, I asked your father to buy this for me. I thought I'd save it for our first night in our new home."

He handed her a black box. When she opened it, she found inside a large emerald ring circled by diamonds.

"Let me put it on for you," he said. "It's your engagement ring— a little late, admittedly. But I give it to you with all my love."

He slipped the ring on her finger as she watched him silently. Then he tried to kiss her, but she turned, offering her cheek instead. He stepped back, giving her a wry look.

"I see you're overwhelmed by gratitude."

"The ring's lovely."

"Your father told me emeralds are the softest gemstones . . . they can be scratched. He recommended I buy a diamond, because they're hard, but I thought you'd prefer an emerald. Maybe I was wrong."

"Oh, no. What's in the boxes?"

She went to the bed. Can Do had opened the top box. Now he pulled out a bolt of beautiful green silk and held up several yards of the shimmering material.

"You like, Kinsolving Taitai?" he said, smiling.

" 'Taitai' is Chinese for 'Mrs.,' " Scott explained. "The silk comes from my warehouses. I have enough to make you ten new wardrobes. Zita told me she could have a few dresses ready in three days."

Emma ran her fingers over the silk. "It's lovely," she said flatly. "Thank you."

She went back to her vanity and sat down, resuming her brushing. Scott signaled Can Do, and the Celestials left the room, silently closing the door. Scott leaned against a wall, crossing his arms over his chest. "All right, what's wrong?"

"Nothing."

"Cat got your tongue?"

"It's undoubtedly the same cat that scratched your face."

He came up behind her, leaning over her, looking at her face in the mirror. "You want to know where I went," he said. "All right, I went to see Chingling to tell her about you."

"Oh? Just a tête-à-tête? I don't suppose you touched her? No, how silly of me. I'm sure your relationship is strictly platonic and you discussed metaphysics."

"We discussed our child."

She looked surprised. "Your child?"

"Yes." He straightened and went to the window, putting his hands in his pockets. "I hadn't even known about the pregnancy till I got there this afternoon. It's a girl named Star. But I swear to you, Emma, you'll have no reason to be jealous of Chingling from now on. I'm settling a large amount of money on her and her mother so that Star will have a safe future. But I'll never touch Chingling again."

"As if I believe that."

He turned on her. "It happens to be the truth."

"As if you knew what the truth is. Can you honestly tell me you don't love Chingling?"

"What difference does it make if I do?"

"It makes *all* the difference. Don't you understand how it makes me feel to have you dump me here like a load of dirty laundry and then run off to Dupont Street? I've been in San Francisco less than a day and already I'm probably the laughingstock of the town! And if you think you're going to buy me off with a lot of silk and jewels, you've sadly misjudged my character. But what is *most* infuriating is: how can you possibly love her and not me?"

"Love, love, love, love!" he shouted, coming back from the window. "You babble about love like some moonstruck convent girl. The point is, we made a deal. I'm willing to give up Chingling—Christ Almighty, it's costing me a hundred thousand dollars—"

"A hundred thousand?"

"One hundred thousand dollars, madam. You squawk about how I don't love you. Well, if there's a price tag on my affections, you've just heard it. Now I expect you to live up to your end of the deal. I expect you to be a loving, ladylike wife. You don't have to be too ladylike, but enough for appearances, and in this town you could pass for a grand duchess. I expect you to run this house in a proper fashion and be a proper mother to my child—"

"Your child?" she interrupted. "You seem to have forgotten one rather vital statistic: the father is Archer Collingwood."

As he leaned over her, she saw the mirror reflection of the hate in his eyes. "Archer Collingwood doesn't exist, do you understand? That child in your belly is mine, and no one is ever going to know it isn't."

"That wasn't part of the deal."

"That was understood. My God, woman, you don't think I want to advertise the fact that you slept with some hick-farmboy/bank-robber before I married you? Unless you want us both to be the laughingstock of San Francisco."

She started to argue, but was silenced as her baby kicked inside her. Emma didn't believe in miracles, but the timing of that kick—not the first, by any means—was almost miraculous. Was the baby listening?

"You're right," she sighed. "There's no point in our both looking like fools. All right, Scott, you stay away from Chingling, and the baby is yours. I'll agree to that. Except . . ."

"Except what?"

She turned away, biting her lip and fighting the tears in her eyes. I'm not going to beg for his love, damn him, she thought. But I do want him to love me. Me, not her. I don't even know why I care, but I do.

The baby kicked again.

"Except nothing." She got to her feet. "Thanks for the presents," she said. "I'm rather tired. I think I'll have a nap before dinner." She started toward the bed. "By the way, your child has been kicking, so I guess it's sending me a message: 'Find me a daddy!' "

Scott hurried to the bed to clear away the boxes. "Do the kicks hurt?"

"A little, but never mind. It means he—or she—is healthy. Is there a decent doctor here?" she asked as she settled heavily on the edge of the bed.

"There's old Doc Gray. They say he got his medical degree through the mail, but he's birthed a lot of babies."

"Then I suppose he'll have to do. I have only one condition to our deal, Scott. But it's one I'm going to insist on."

"Which is?"

She looked up at him, defiance in her eyes. "If the baby's a boy, his name is Archer."

He started to say something, but a knock on the door stopped him.

"Captain Boss," called Can Do. "Mister One Eye, he downstairs to see you."

"Coming, Can Do." He lowered his voice. "All right, call him Archer. Call him Andrew Jackson, I don't give a damn. But he's still my son." He stalked to the door.

"Scott!" she called, knowing she had hurt him.

"What?"

"Thank you for the ring. It really is beautiful."

"Maybe I should have bought a diamond after all. It would be more appropriate to your character."

"What a terrible thing to—"

But he was already out of the room. He walked down the gallery to the stairs. At the bottom, waiting in the entrance hall, was André Fontaine, the treasurer of the Kinsolving Shipping Company. Fontaine had been a clerk in a Paris bank who got caught in the crossfire of a street battle during the Revolution of 1848. A piece of shrapnel had put out his left eye, a wound that prompted him to leave France and try his luck in the New World. The black patch he wore over his eye had earned him the nickname One Eye.

"Welcome home, Captain," he said as he shook Scott's hand. "I've just been out to the ship. Mr. Appleton assures me everything is going smoothly with the transfer of the cargo to the warehouses. He also told me you're planning to build a new store on Portsmouth Square."

"That's right, One Eye. I want you to find me an architect, if such an exotic creature exists in California, because we're going to move fast on this. I want to start putting the building up next week, if possible. I'm also making a hefty financial settlement with Ah Toy, which I want you to negotiate for me. How much cash do we have on hand?"

"A little over seven hundred and eighty thousand dollars. We have another four million in accounts receivable."

Scott frowned. "According to my records, we should have well over two million cash."

"That's because you haven't heard. Warehouse Two was raided last week. A gang of Sydney Ducks—at least, we think that's what they were—broke in and stole the entire shipment the *Southern Cross* had brought from Hong Kong."

"What the hell happened to our watchmen?"

"Shot dead. Both of them. I've hired new ones, doubled the number, but still . . ." He shook his head. "San Francisco's a jungle."

"Jesus Christ, the entire shipment?"

"They cleaned out the warehouse."

"Any idea who's behind it?"

"I have no proof, but I think it's Slade Dawson. He's trying to take over the town, Captain, and you're not here much."

"Well, that's sure as hell changing, as of today. Can Do!" He started for the front door.

"Yes, Captain Boss?"

"Tell Kinsolving Taitai I won't be home for dinner."

"She be disappointed, Boss! This her first night in her house."

"She'll survive. Tell her I'm starting my campaign to be the first governor of California. God damn, the entire warehouse!" He opened the door and looked back at his treasurer. "One Eye, this is war."

In a bedroom down the hall from Scott and Emma's on the second floor, Zita was lying on the big four-poster, holding her lace handkerchief to her eyes. After a moment Felix came into the room. He softly closed the door and came to the bed. "You've been crying."

She nodded. "I'm sorry. I was thinking of my daughter and the fact that I'll never see her or my grandchildren."

"Ah, my dear, of course I understand. My wife was murdered too. There's nothing for you to apologize for. But come now, what do you think of San Francisco?"

"Well, I don't know yet. But this house is certainly pleasant, and it was kind of Scott to let us stay. He really is a nice man, but Emma doesn't seem ready to forget Archer."

Felix frowned as he took her hand. "It's possible that marriage is doomed."

"Oh, Felix, what a terrible thing to say."

"Scott is not a Jew. Of course, we had little choice, and Scott is better than no husband at all, but still . . ." He sighed. "I wish it had been David Levin."

"You didn't put up any objections on the ship?"

"I had no choice. I wanted Emma's child to be legitimate. But now I'm haunted by what her mother must be thinking. I wonder if I've failed her—and Emma and my people—by allowing this marriage."

Zita studied his face a moment. "What you're really trying to tell me," she said, "is that you don't want to marry me for the same reason. Because I'm not a Jew."

There were tears in his eyes as he brought her hand to his lips and kissed it. "You've been hurt so much already," he whispered. "I hate to hurt you again. But I can't marry out of my faith. As much as I love you, I just can't. First Emma, and then me . . . I would be insulting the memory of my poor wife, particularly in light of how she was killed back in Frankfurt."

Zita forced a smile. "I understand, my darling, and don't worry. We'll be San Francisco's most-talked-about couple. It will be much more exciting than being married."

"I will always take care of you, Zita. You'll never have to worry. And if the store's a success, we'll build ourselves a fine house. It will work out, my love, believe me."

"I do believe you, Felix. You're very dear to me, you know. In my mind, you are my husband, and that's all that matters to me."

He leaned down to kiss her. "My wife," he whispered. "You are my most beloved wife. We will be parted only by death."

13

THE waitresses at the Bonanza Café were naked from the waist up, and the clientele, which was one hundred percent male and not known for excessive interest in either decorum or sobriety, loved it.

"Hey, Bessie!" bellowed a drunk gold miner. He had just come to town after four months at Placerville and was on his way to squandering his four months' gold findings on one blowout of an evening. "Bring me another of them Queen Charlottes! Better make it four! God damn!"

The crowd in the big saloon, with its round-globed crystal gasoliers imported from Bohemia, whooped and cheered. Queen Charlottes were one of the city's favorite drinks, a potent mixture of claret and raspberry syrup, and Barney Taylor, the gold miner in question, had already consumed a quart. Bearded, sporting a mammoth belly, Barney was seated at his own table surrounded by plates of oysters that he was shoveling in with his bare hands. His companion, a Mexican whore named Guadalupe, was seated opposite him sipping champagne, her bare breasts dangling casually. She was charging Barney an ounce of gold to sit with him, but later on, if she went upstairs with him to one of the ten "love suites" run by Chicago, the resident madam, the fee was a flat five hundred dollars. Vice did not come cheap in San Francisco.

Bessie, the waitress, squeezed through the crowd to the ornately carved bar, where the customers were three deep.

"Four more Queen Charlottes!" she yelled over the din. It was a busy night at the Bonanza. The air was foul with cigar and cigarette smoke, and the language was even fouler. Emma was right to feel she was in a city devoid of culture: the art here consisted of three huge gold-framed paintings of plump nudes sprawled lecherously on chaises longues, the products of a Munich pornographer-cum-painter named Friedrich Ernst Schultow. Entertainment, aside from sex, gambling, and booze, was at the level of Dirty Tom McAlear at the Goat and Compass Saloon on the Barbary Coast: for a few cents you could hire him to eat garbage.

"How's the game going?" Chicago asked. She was smoking a sto-
gie, named for the Conestoga wagon drivers who favored the cheap
cigars.

"Which game?" asked Mack, the monte dealer, who had just come
off duty from the casino behind the bar.

"Slade's game, asshole," snorted the four-hundred-pound madam
in the blond curly wig. As usual, she was seated in her custom-built
eight-foot-high chair, rather like a throne on stilts, which gave her a
bird's-eye view of the action.

"Captain Kinsolving's ahead about two thousand," Mack answered, staring up at the mammoth woman in the red satin dress with
ostrich plumes cushioning her alpine breasts and bare shoulders. Chicago's size never failed to awe him. Her tiny feet, perched on a rung
of her peculiar chair, were squeezed into laced black leather boots, and
the stockings of her elephantine legs, clearly visible from below, were
green and silver, horizontally striped.

She scowled down at him. "Who's got the deal?"

"Slade."

"Is Kinsolving sober or drunk?"

"He's drinking up a storm, but he looks sober to me."

"Shit. Climb up here a minute."

Mack obediently went around to the side of the chair and climbed
its ladderlike rungs. When he reached Chicago's level, she whispered
to him: "Who's waitressin' Slade's table?"

"Big Tits."

"Tell her to double the booze in Kinsolving's drinks."

"She already done that, Chicago."

"Huh. Is Slade got on the Holdout?"

"Yeah, but he ain't used it yet. Think he's waitin' for a big pot."

"Huh. Okay, you runt. Go home to bed."

"Good night, Chicago."

Mack scrambled down the ladder as Chicago finished her drink.
Then she yelled to a passing waitress, whose rosy breasts were bouncing
merrily over her tray. "Tina, you whore, get me another gin fizz."

"Right away, Chicago."

Ten feet away, in a large room reached by double doors next to
the bar, the gambling action was heavy. There were six monte tables,
for the fast-moving Mexican card game was the favorite in California.
A wheel of fortune, two faro tables, two crap tables, a *vingt-et-un* and
a *lansquenet* table, and two poker tables completed the equipment
in the casino. The biggest crowd in the room was gathered around
Slade Dawson's game. The forty-year-old professional gambler, who
had worked Mississippi riverboats ten years before coming west, was

dealing a game of straight five-card stud. Slade, a darkly handsome man with a black mustache drooping on either side of a cruel mouth, was wanted by the police in three states back east for swindling, but then, it was estimated that ten percent of the population of California was wanted by the police back east. That was why they were in California.

Scott, seated opposite Slade at the round table, picked up his cards. He had two pairs: jacks and eights.

"I can't open," said the Frenchman sitting next to Slade.

"Bye me," said Gus Powell, a crony of Slade's who was considering a run for governor.

"I'll open for five hundred," Scott said, shoving a stack of hundred-dollar chips into the center of the green baize.

"Too rich for me," said a man with an Australian accent. He was a Sydney Duck, one of the escaped convicts from Botany Bay who lived at the foot of Telegraph Hill in Sydney Town, San Francisco's most dangerous slum.

Slade fanned his cards. Two fives, two aces, and a four.

"I'll raise you three thousand," Slade said, pushing out three piles of chips.

Whistles from the onlookers. The other two players threw in their cards, leaving Scott and Slade. The two men eyed each other with dislike.

"That's a big raise," Scott said.

"Isn't it?" Slade smiled.

"I think you're bluffing me."

"Possibly. Gonna pay to find out?"

Scott pushed in the chips. More whistles. There was now sixty-five hundred dollars on the baize.

"Cards?" Slade asked.

"One."

Scott discarded, drawing to his jacks and eights. As Slade dealt him a card, beneath the table his knees opened slightly. A third ace pushed out of his right sleeve into his palm. Slade swiftly slid the ace into his other cards and palmed the four.

"You're not drawing?" Scott asked.

"Nope. And I'm betting three thousand. You in?"

He pushed out more stacks of chips. Scott looked at the small city of chips. He had drawn a six.

"I'm in." He pushed his chips.

"What you got?" asked Slade.

"Two pairs. Jacks and eights."

Slade laughed. "And I thought you knew how to play poker," he said. "You stayed on that shit when you knew I had a pat hand? Full house, aces and fives. Read 'em and weep."

He laid down his hand and reached for the chips. Scott pulled his gun.

"Hold it, Slade."

Slade froze, staring at the gun.

"I don't think you've been playing fair, Slade. In fact, I think you're a cheating son of a bitch. Stand up and take off your clothes."

"Huh?"

"Do what I say. Strip."

An ominous silence settled over the once-noisy room. Slade slowly stood up. Then, quick as lightning, he pulled his gun. Scott fired, hitting Slade's pistol, sending it flying.

"Strip," he repeated.

Slade hesitated, then took off his black frock coat.

"Now the vest."

Slade unbuttoned his embroidered yellow vest and took it off.

"Now the shirt."

"What the hell—"

"The shirt!"

Slade unbuttoned his ruffled shirt and took it off. Against his body was a strange silver-plated steel contraption consisting of a series of pulleys, cords, and telescoping tubes that ran up from his trousers to his shoulders, then down the underside of his arms, terminating in a metal "sneak," or clamp, that could hold cards.

"Behold, gentlemen," Scott said, getting to his feet, "the latest device in fleecing suckers. I read about it back in New York. That steel contraption is called the Kepplinger Holdout. Show them the whole thing, Slade. Drop your pants."

"You go to hell."

"Ah, ah. Do as you're told, like a good boy."

"Fuck you."

Red in the face, Slade dropped his pants. The Kepplinger Holdout went down through his underwear to his knees.

"You see how ingenious it is?" Scott said. "Slade attaches an ace to the sneak by his wrist. Then he waits till he draws a pair as he did in this last hand. Then by merely spreading his knees, he activates this infernal machine, which extends the ace into his palm. Neat, isn't it?"

Scott took off his hat, swept all the chips into it, then stood on a chair to address the room.

"My friends," he announced, "I learned this afternoon that we are expecting a ship any day from the East, bringing us papers signed by President Fillmore granting statehood to the Territory of California.

We're all aware of what it's like here in San Francisco, with ten policemen for thirty-five thousand citizens, and I hear it's worse in other
towns, like Los Angeles. I say it's time all right-thinking men pray that
statehood comes, because statehood means a proper police force and
law and order. And law and order means that cheap crooks like Slade
Dawson"—he pointed at a glowering Slade, who looked more ridiculous than menacing in his drawers—"will have to go straight or go to
jail. My fellow citizens, I'm announcing tonight that I have made my
last voyage as captain of one of my ships. I'm staying in California full-
time to help build this city and state into something we all can be proud
of." He grinned "And, hardly to be ignored, a city that my new wife
won't complain to me about. My friends, I'm submitting my name for
your consideration as first governor of the proud state of California,
and my platform is dirt-simple: law and order, justice for all . . . and
getting rid of shit like Slade Dawson!"

Silence. It was obvious the idea of law and order was not going
over well in the casino of the Bonanza Café.

"Well, hell," yelled one spectator. "If Slade's a goddamn cheat,
I say he's cheated us all and I say let's string the bastard up!"

This brought a burst of applause.

"Call the Vigilance Committees!" another yelled. "We got our
own law an' order that works just fine!"

"Right! We'll be judge and jury and Slade can be swinging' in an
hour!"

Slade, a look of panic on his face, started running for the door,
his dash severely handicapped by the awkward Kepplinger Holdout.
He was grabbed by the crowd, who started beating him as others continued to yell: "Lynch him!" "String the bastard up!" "Call the Vigilance Committees!" The noise was deafening.

Scott pulled his gun and fired at the ceiling. The hubbub quickly
subsided.

"Let Slade go!" he yelled angrily. "And nobody's going to call
any goddamned Vigilance Committees. That's what's wrong with this
town—too many vigilantes, too many lynchings. You!" He pointed at
a grizzled half-drunk miner. "Ed Bates, what if I said you cheated me
and could convince everyone in this room to hang *you*? By the time
anyone found out it was a mistake, you'd be a goddamned corpse. Let
Slade go. If I want to bring charges against him for cheating me, I'll
see him in court. And, Slade, I know damned well you've cheated me
other ways than card games, so maybe I will see you in court, and soon.
But," he yelled to the entire room, "I repeat, the Vigilance Committees
and the lynchings have to stop. Otherwise San Francisco will never be
anything but a goddamned jungle."

This time he got applause. It was tepid at first, but it began to build.

"So he made a fool of you?" Chicago inquired an hour later as she chewed on a pork chop in her apartment, a temple of gaudy bad taste on the third floor above the Bonanza.

"He made me strip to my drawers in front of the whole damned casino. I'll kill him. I'll kill the bastard!"

"Oh, shut up, Slade. You sound like the villain in a bad roadshow. Besides, he saved your neck, didn't he? You might be swingin' outside that window at this very moment."

Slade gulped and ran his hand over his throat. The near-lynching had been a horrifying experience.

"So he wants to be governor?" Chicago continued. "Interesting."

The fat madam, who had tucked a tablecloth-size napkin into her Grand Canyon–size cleavage, picked up her sixth pork chop with her fingers and began consuming it, grease running down her multiple chins. Chicago was co-owner of the Bonanza with Slade, and they shared the five-room apartment on the top floor. But they didn't share a bed. Slade bedded the girls downstairs, and Chicago? She had her pork chops and gin. Chicago purveyed sex like a butcher, but personally she was a vegetarian.

"I think he knows we raided his warehouse," said Slade. "He said something about seeing me in court soon." He was looking out one of the windows at the recently installed gaslights on Portsmouth Square.

"Sure he knows. Scott's no fool," Chicago said, licking her fingers. "If this place becomes a state and he becomes governor, then we got big problems, sweetheart. So we got to make sure Scott Kinsolving don't become governor and that Gus Powell does."

"There's his Chink girlfriend."

"Yes, but hell, she's no secret. Besides, Scott's got himself a proper wife now and has gone respectable. The trick is, we gotta go respectable, Slade. And I think I got just the ticket for us."

"Yeah? What?"

"It's who. That Jew kid, David Levin, who came in on the *Flying Cloud* ten days ago. He's been hanging around the bar drinkin' more than he oughta, and I've talked to him. He knows Emma Kinsolving real good—he lived with her family in Frankfurt for two years, teachin' them English, and he's not their greatest fan. He hates Scott Kinsolving, who left him stranded in Jamaica. He wants to open a newspaper, and I think we oughta finance him."

Slade looked sourly at her. "Who the hell wants a newspaper?"

"We do. Get up-to-date, Slade. The power of the press. Think of the blistering editorials David can write about Scott."

"Words." Slade sneered. "Words are shit. I'll take a gun over words any day."

Chicago bit into her seventh pork chop.

"We'll use both. Now, go downstairs and get Gus. I think it's time we started gettin' serious about his campaign. We got to find an issue that'll rile the voters, and if we can't find one, we'll make one up."

"To be stood up once on one's first day in town is one thing," Emma said that night as Scott came into their bedroom. She was sitting up in bed, wearing a pink bed jacket. "But to be stood up twice is some sort of world's record. Might I be so bold as to inquire where you've been?"

Scott came to the bed and sat beside her. "Didn't Can Do tell you?"

"He said something ridiculous about your starting your campaign for governor."

"I didn't think starting my campaign was exactly ridiculous, but oh, well. Slade Dawson—the man who was in the other boat this morning—has engineered the theft of over two million dollars' worth of merchandise from one of my warehouses. If we can't get some sort of police protection in this state, we're all doomed to be wiped out—Why are you crying?"

She turned away. "I'm not."

"Well, tears are oozing out of your eyes. You're certainly giving a damned good imitation of crying."

"You don't understand anything about women," she sniffed, wiping her eyes with her sleeve.

"That is probably a great truth. In fact, women baffle me. But I suppose you're angry because I wasn't here for dinner."

"Oh, no, I enjoyed staring at your empty chair. Of course, you did say something about our having a celebration tonight, but who cares about celebrations? Oh, what's the use? It's a waste of time getting angry because I suppose I can't blame you for this farce of a marriage. I have nobody to blame but myself. What did you call me? A moonstruck girl?"

"I'm sorry—"

"No, you're not, and it's probably true. You also said, in your gallant fashion, that I'm hard as a diamond. I think I'm a bit of both, Scott. A hopeless romantic who's hard as nails." She sighed. "I suppose I'm not the perfect wife, but we have made this deal and we're stuck with each other. So I would appreciate it if you'd show me a little courtesy. I *am* your wife, you know, like it or not."

He looked at her a moment, then nodded. "You're right. I've behaved like a cad and a boor. What can I do to make it up to you?"

She shrugged.

"We can make this marriage work," he said, taking her hand. "Tell me what you want. I'll give you anything in the world."

She looked at him, and now her eyes were dry.

"What I want," she said softly, "you don't have to give."

His eyes grew cool. "Oh, yes, the dashing Mr. Collingwood." He released her hand and stood up. He walked to the foot of the bed, then turned to her. "There's a first-rate private detective on Market Street named Horatio Dobbs. I suggest you go to him and hire him to find out what has happened to Mr. Collingwood. It will be expensive and may take a month or so, but by the time you bear the child, you should have some news about the natural father. I think this should give you, if nothing else, some peace of mind. I know how precious the memory of Mr. Collingwood is to you."

She smiled her prettiest. "Oh, Scott, thank you. That's terribly decent of you."

He nodded curtly. "As your husband, I can't tell you how delighted I am to bring such a sweet smile to your face. And now, since your advanced state of pregnancy is making it rather awkward to, shall we say, make love to you, I shall retire to the library and sleep on the sofa. Good night, Emma."

The smile vanished from her face. "You expect me to be a lady, you can at least try to be a gentleman."

"Oh, I'm trying, Emma. If I weren't trying my damnedest to be a gentleman, I'd ram your pretty teeth down your pretty throat."

14

"So, what are we gonna call this newspaper?" Chicago asked as she popped chocolate bonbons into her mouth. She was stretched on a chaise longue in her apartment, eyeing David Levin, who was standing at the end of the chaise, soiled hat in hand.

"How about the San Francisco *Bulletin*?" said David, whose thick brown beard now hung almost to the second button of his shirt, covering his tie. That was a blessing, since he was down to his last tie.

"Sounds good to me. I own the house next door, and you can use the ground floor as your office rent-free. You can sleep in the back room and use our privies, so that'll take care of your rent to boot. And I told you I've located a second-hand press I can buy for eight hundred, gold. What else will you need?"

"Ink and paper, of course. A typesetter, if we can find one. And delivery boys."

"We can use Celestials for that. They're dirt cheap. What kind of a salary would you want? Don't try to hold me up just 'cause I'm rich."

"Well . . . a hundred a week?"

"Eighty. Take it or leave it."

David shrugged. "I'll take it."

He would have taken fifty. David was desperate. When he had arrived in San Francisco, he had been as appalled as Emma at the primitive conditions. But he was quick to perceive the opportunity for a writer in a town with no newspaper. He might not be getting anywhere with his novel, but if he could get backing for a paper, he might actually make some money doing what he loved.

"You know our editorial policy," Chicago went on. "It's to discredit Scott Kinsolving and get our guy elected governor."

"Believe me, it'll be a pleasure to discredit Kinsolving."

"Yeah, I know you hate him 'cause he stole your gal away from you. I like a good hater, and I think you'll fill the bill. But what about Mrs. Kinsolving? You told me when you was drunk the other night you still love her. Is that true?"

David squirmed. "No," he finally said. "When the *Empress of*

China docked and the crew started talking about what happened on the voyage around South America—how Emma had been sleeping with Kinsolving even before they got married . . ." He bit his lip. That news had devastated him. "When I learned that, whatever love I had for her died. Emma de Meyer is an opportunist and a slut, and I never thought I'd say that about her."

Chicago put another candy in her mouth. Raggedy kid, she thought. Scrawny and shabby. But he's got fire in his belly. He'll do.

"Mmm. Well, you just keep pushin' that line of thought in your editorials, Davy. Might as well discredit the whole damn bunch up there on Rincon Hill."

Am I really going to do this to Emma? he thought. He remembered his pain when he learned she had married Scott, the pain he had tried to drown with the nepenthe of alcohol. Emma had turned him down first for that bumpkin Archer, and now Scott. Yes, I do hate her, he thought.

"There's another thing," Chicago said, licking her sticky fingers. "I seen you eyein' my girls. Would you like one of them for free? That's one of the goodies that come with workin' for me and Slade, and you sure as hell can't afford my girls on your salary. Not that you ain't overpaid!"

"That would be . . . nice."

"Got one in mind?"

"That pretty one named Letty?"

Chicago chuckled. "You got good taste, kid, but you're aimin' sorta high. Letty is Slade's woman. Nobody else touches her. Pick another."

"Ah, that redhead, Betty?"

"Yeah, the one from St. Louis. Nice girl. She's busy, though: you'll have to work around her schedule. She's pullin' in a couple thousand a night. Hell, there's one preevert from Placerville that paid her three hundred bucks just to touch her damned underwear. Can you imagine?"

David could indeed imagine. After his introduction to the heady delights of sex in Buenos Aires, he had found himself in a state of constant ruttishness. And since "nice" women were in short supply, whores would have to do.

What would his respectable parents back in London think? he thought, shuddering. He forced himself to forget about them. San Francisco was half a world away from Victorian London, and sex was what would vanquish his longing for Emma.

"I've come to cheer you up," Zita announced as she entered Emma's bedroom.

"Don't bother," Emma said, sitting up in bed.

It was a cold December day, and through the windows she could see fog hanging over the city like a shroud. Emma had put handsome blue silk curtains over her windows and brought in some plants, but otherwise the room still seemed empty. The house was emptier, as well: the month before, Felix had bought a small house at the foot of Rincon Hill, and he and Zita had moved out of the big house. But Zita still came to see Emma at least once a day.

"Item one," Zita said, perching on the side of the bed. "Last October 18, a ship sails into San Francisco Bay with the wonderful news that California is now a state. Your husband throws an open house to celebrate, but where is his charming wife? The lovely Mrs. Kinsolving stays upstairs, here in her bedroom."

"Zita, I'm big as an elephant, and you know it's not decent to show yourself when you're with child."

"My dear Emma, this is San Francisco, not London or Paris. The rules of decorum are much less strict here—and thank God for that. Item two: three weeks ago, on November 14, your father and your husband open de Meyer and Kinsolving's Emporium to great fanfare, and you haven't even been to see it yet."

"I'm telling you, I won't go out looking like this."

"You're feeling sorry for yourself."

"Do you blame me? Stuck in this horrid town with a horrid husband who hates me—"

"I don't believe he hates you. You have hurt him, which is vastly different. He really is a kind and generous man. He's been extremely kind to me."

"Oh, Zita, I don't want to hear about him anymore. If he's so wonderful, why doesn't he pay more attention to me, instead of gallivanting all over the state?"

"Well, my dear, he is campaigning to be the governor."

"I can't imagine who in his right mind would vote for Scott."

"You're very cruel to Captain Kinsolving, which I don't understand. I met your Archer only one time, and while he was admittedly handsome, he didn't seem to me to have any of the qualities your husband has."

Emma looked at her sadly. "If I could explain why I love Archer so much, I would," she said. "But he's in my mind almost every moment—especially now that I'm about to have his child. The little time we had together on the boat was so tender—he was so tender and sweet and innocent." Her eyes brimmed with tears. "He was the first man to ever make me feel beautiful."

Zita sighed. "Well, I feel sorry for you. You are a victim of love."

She stood up. "But I *am* going to cheer you up. Since you won't come to see my boutique at the emporium—which, by the way, is doing very nicely—I've brought the emporium to you."

She clapped her hands. The door opened and an attractive blond girl entered. She wore a peach silk dress with the most enormous skirt Emma had ever seen. She sat up, her eyes rapidly drying.

"This is Elaine, one of my models," said Zita. "Do you like the dress?"

"Oh, Zita, it's gorgeous. But isn't the skirt too big?"

"It's the latest fashion from Paris. Underneath is a horsehair hoop they call a crinoline. Show her, Elaine."

The model, whose blond hair was arranged in massive curls, came to the side of the bed and raised the outer skirt. Suddenly Emma gasped and clutched her stomach.

"My dear, what's wrong?" Zita exclaimed.

"Get the doctor," Emma whispered. "I think the baby is about to—" She let out a shriek.

"Run!" Zita exclaimed to the model. "Tell one of the servants to get Dr. Gray!"

As Elaine hurried out of the room, Zita took Emma's hands. "Hold on to me," she said.

"The pain . . ."

"Yes, it's terrible, I know. But it will soon be over, and we will have your darling new child."

"I . . . Oh . . . Oh, my God." She let out another scream. "I think . . . it's starting now . . ."

"Keep calm. The doctor will be here soon."

"Where's Scott? Why isn't he here? Damn him . . . oh . . . oh, my God . . ."

"Hold on."

"I've never hurt so . . ."

She was shaking, sweating. Can Do appeared in the door with a china basin and towels.

"Pretty missy have baby." He grinned, hurrying toward the bed. "Doc Gray come soon. Baby time! Oh, boy . . . oh, boy, Can Do like babies. Have three of my own, make many more before I wear out."

"I think," Emma gasped, "Can Do Taitai may wear out first."

Three hours later, Zita took the bawling baby boy from the doctor and held him up for Emma to see.

"Look, isn't he handsome?" She smiled. "Eight pounds, three ounces, and perfectly healthy. How wonderful."

An exhausted Emma looked upon the red-faced baby and smiled weakly. "Archer," she whispered. "At last I have your son."

The last thing she thought of before drifting off to sleep was that the detective she had hired to find Archer might have news before Christmas.

"He's in the Ohio State Penitentiary at Columbus," said Horatio Dobbs, a bald detective in a houndstooth suit. "He's doing five years for armed robbery."

"I see," Scott said. The two men were in his office in Kinsolving Warehouse Number One near the Embarcadero. Scott leaned back in his seat and toyed with a pencil. "Is that a tough prison?"

"One of the toughest. No one's escaped since they built it about ten years ago."

"Who's the warden?"

"A man named Ridley. He's a former alderman from Cleveland. The governor appointed him as a payoff for political favors."

"Is Ridley corrupt?"

Horatio Dobbs grinned and shrugged. "I don't know many politicians who ain't. Gossip is that he was on the take when he was alderman."

"Mm." Scott leaned forward. "Now, this is what I want you to tell my wife. Tell her that Archer Collingwood was killed during an attempted breakout at the prison. You understand? He tried to escape and was shot by a guard."

"I understand."

"Don't tell her till after the first of the year. She's just had a baby, and I wouldn't want to upset her for the holidays."

"Is this Collingwood a relation of hers?"

"That, my friend, is none of your business."

Scott opened a drawer of his desk and pulled out a chamois bag, which he tossed to the detective.

"There's an extra thousand in gold for you, Dobbs. That's to help you forget that I hired you before my wife did."

Horatio Dobbs smiled as he stood up. "Captain, I can barely remember your name."

For its first holiday season, de Meyer and Kinsolving's Emporium put up the first Christmas tree ever seen in San Francisco. Felix, who was general manager of the department store, was well-acquainted with the old custom that Prince Albert, Queen Victoria's German husband, was popularizing in England. Overlooking the irony that a Jew was introducing California to this custom, Felix had the mammoth four-story building lavishly draped with pine boughs decorated with red bows and placed a twenty-foot-high white pine on the roof of the first-floor entrance loggia fronting Portsmouth Square. With the memory of the devastating Christmas Eve fire the year before fresh in his mind, Scott had insisted the store be built of brick, and the young Chilean architect One Eye had found had designed a handsome building with an elaborate tin cornice bordering the mansard roof.

De Meyer's, as the store name was soon abbreviated, was an almost instant success. Felix brought sophisticated Old World merchandising skills to a town bursting with frustrated men with money to spare. The handsome wood-and-glass vitrines he installed on the first floor were filled with watches, silver, clothes, knickknacks, specialty goods, and even food items—an innovation for the time—that lured the gold out of the miners' pockets. In one corner was Zita's Ladies' Boutique, which had suffered a shaky start thanks not only to the dearth of ladies but also to her astronomical prices. But her clothes were so elegant— especially in a town devoid of luxuries—that the customers began flocking in, led by several of Chicago's topless waitresses from across the square. Loaded with gold gained by wearing hardly anything at all during their working hours, they squandered their tainted money on Zita's marvelous dresses, hats, and furs. Zita was well aware how they earned their money, but she wasn't about to turn away her best customers. "Later," she told Felix, "when we get some real ladies, then we'll see. But meanwhile . . ." She shrugged knowingly.

Felix agreed. "All our customers are rough and dirty now. But we'll set the tone, and someday they'll live up to us. Then San Francisco will be something to see."

"They've got the gold," Zita said. "We'll sell them the glitter."

Though Felix was managing the entire store, overseeing fifty-two employees, his heart lay in a corner of the second floor, where his small jewelry shop was sited, not far from the furniture department. "F. de Meyer. Haute Joaillerie. Formerly of Frankfurt, Germany," boasted the brass plaque over the door. Felix, whose passion was magnificent stones, was already displaying brooches, rings, and even a diamond necklace, all of his own design, manufactured by two Chinese artisans he had discovered and personally trained. And it was here that Emma made her first public appearance ten days after the birth of little Archer.

It was a week before Christmas, and the store was thronged. As Scott helped Emma out of the landau in front of the store, passersby stopped to stare. Zita's pearl dress, with its gigantic crinoline skirt, was set off by a sable-trimmed otter coat and a lavishly plumed hat. Even though Emma was still wan, she was an imposing beauty. Scott, distinguished in a top hat and beaver-trimmed coat, led his wife into the store as the onlookers applauded. Emma was met by her father, who kissed her. Then he and Scott gave her a guided tour of the entire store, ending up in the second-floor jewelry shop.

"Poppa, it's marvelous," she said. "The whole place is so elegant. It's like being back in Europe. I'm absolutely overwhelmed."

"But, Emma, dear, you must congratulate Scott too," Felix said. "He has worked as hard as I. Remember, it is de Meyer and Kinsolving's."

She turned to her husband and forced a smile. "Of course. I didn't mean to ignore you, Scott. Congratulations."

"Heartfelt as always," he said. "By the way, I have a gift for you, Emma. Your father designed it."

Felix handed him a black felt box. On the lid was embossed in gold: "F. de Meyer. Haute Joaillerie. San Francisco."

Presenting it to his wife, Scott said quietly, "This is for giving me a fine son."

She opened the lid. Inside, glittering in the gaslight, was a beautiful flower brooch.

"Emeralds and diamonds!" she exclaimed. "Oh, it's beautiful! Thank you, darling."

"Emeralds and diamonds," he said, unable to avoid a certain wryness in his tone. "It's you."

On Christmas Eve Scott gave Emma yet another spectacular piece of jewelry, this time a magnificent emerald-and-diamond necklace, again created by Felix.

"Scott," she said, "this is entirely too much. Are you sure we can afford it?"

He lifted the sparkling stones from the black silk-lined box and put them around her neck, attaching the clasp. "Believe me," he said, "we can afford it."

"Scott was right," Felix said, standing with Zita in front of the Christmas tree in the entrance hall. "The real gold mine in this state has turned out to be de Meyer and Kinsolving's Emporium."

"And we don't even have to dig," Scott said. "Can Do, bring a mirror for Taitai."

"Can do."

A moment later he rolled in from the living room a wood-and-gilt "psyché," or cheval glass. Emma, who was wearing another of Zita's dresses—this one pale blue taffeta—hurried to the mirror and studied her reflection.

"Thank you," she said, turning. She saw that Scott was looking at the stairs where Madam Choy, the chubby Chinese *amah* he had hired, was carrying Archer down from his third-floor nursery.

"Here's Archer coming down to see his first Christmas tree," he exclaimed.

Madam Choy carried him to Scott, who tickled his chin and cooed in baby talk, "Archer want to see his Cwissmas pwesent?"

Emma loathed baby talk, but she kept it to herself. "Madam Choy, has he had his six-o'clock feeding?" she asked.

"Yes, Taitai." The *amah* was also the wet nurse.

"Here's baby's Cwissmas pwesent," Scott said. He put a silver rattle into Archer's tiny hand. The baby shook it and giggled.

"My God, he's cute." Scott smiled. "He's going to grow up to be a real lady-killer."

Like his father, thought Emma, but again she kept the dig to herself. Whatever her feelings for her husband, she had to admit that he was turning out to be an adoring father, for which she could only be thankful. Since the birth of Archer, he had been kindness itself to her; and though Emma refused to think that her affections could be bought, she had to grant that it was difficult to dislike a man who kept giving her such marvelous presents. Furthermore, after Archer's birth he had returned to her bed, and their lovemaking after so many weeks' abstinence had warmed their once-frosty relationship. Emma had to admit Scott was an ardent and tender lover. She even began to wonder if perhaps he did love her, at least a little. But whether he did or not, the important thing was to give her baby a loving father. And as long as Scott kept up his side of the bargain, she would keep up hers and be, if not a loving wife, a good one.

She was about to suggest they all go in to dinner, when a scream came from upstairs, echoing around the high hall. Then one of the Celestial housemaids appeared at the gallery rail and began babbling in Chinese to Can Do.

"Evil spirit upstairs!" Can Do exclaimed to Scott. "Girl say she go to turn down your bed and see evil spirit."

"She must be drunk."

"No, Boss, she good girl."

Scott started up the stairs and Emma followed, wondering what in the world the maid had seen. Whatever it was, the poor girl was sobbing as she pointed at their open bedroom door. Scott, followed by Emma and Can Do, hurried inside.

"The *ch'i ling!*" Can Do cried, pointing. The porcelain-dog table next to the bed had been shattered into a hundred pieces. "Evil spirit come to destroy *ch'i ling*. Very bad."

"Scott, what's happened?" Emma asked, totally confused.

"The Chinese believe these lion dogs, or Foo dogs, keep evil spirits away," he said.

"Very powerful evil spirit," Can Do babbled. "Very bad, Boss. Evil curse put on your bed."

"Can Do, shut up. Somebody must have gotten in the house. Or maybe somebody on the staff did this, but it sure as hell was no evil spirit."

"But, Boss, I tell you last year you no check *feng shui* before you build this house—very, very bad. Now evil spirits get inside."

"What's *feng shui*?" Emma interrupted.

"It's the spirit of wind and water. Chinese check the *feng shui* before they build a house. Of course, it's all rank superstition, but they believe in it. Can Do, you're just scaring Taitai, and I want you to stop, understand? And I want you to find out who's responsible for this. I personally will punish him."

Can Do shook his head as he left the room. "How you punish evil spirit, Boss? But I try."

When he was gone, Emma asked, "What do you think this means?"

Scott frowned. "I don't know," he said. "But I'm not going to let this ruin Christmas Eve. Let's go down to dinner."

Emma followed him out of the room. But before she left, she looked back at the smashed Foo dog. She shivered slightly, as though a cold wind had blown through the big house.

But there was no wind.

15

ON January 3, 1851, a howling Pacific storm broke over San Francisco. Emma was standing at her bedroom window watching the pelting rain when she heard the door open behind her. She turned to see Scott.

"Detective Dobbs is downstairs," he said. "He has news of Archer Collingwood."

She hurried across the room toward the door. Her husband took her hand.

"You know Collingwood is not my favorite person in the world," he said. "But for your sake, I hope the news is good."

She was genuinely touched. "Thank you, Scott. Under the circumstances, that's extremely kind of you." She nearly flew out of the room.

Alone, Scott wandered toward the bed, gazing at the place where, until ten days before, the Foo dog had sat. It had been replaced by a Western-style table, but Can Do had not been able to solve the mystery of who had destroyed the *ch'i ling*. If Ah Toy had been in town, Scott might have suspected her: even though One Eye had arranged a system of annual cash payments that made the Manchu princess the richest Celestial in the city, Ah Toy still barely concealed her hatred of the father of her granddaughter, a hatred that manifested itself in the still-visible scars she had inflicted on his cheek with her nails. But Ah Toy had returned to China to visit the tomb of her husband in the Western Hills outside Peking. (Scott wondered how safe the widow of the bribe-accepting Prince Kung might be in the Celestial Kingdom, but he assumed she now had enough money to bribe her way in and out of China without losing her head.) So he was totally mystified as to who had smashed the Foo dog. He might have shrugged it off if he hadn't known how seriously the Chinese took their superstitions: evil spirits were as real to Celestials as fog was to Westerners. Someone had meant to put a curse on his marriage. The only person besides Ah Toy who had a motive for this strange, symbolic act was Chingling, but he dismissed this as incompatible with her sweet character.

He heard a soft sobbing and turned as Emma came back in the room.

"He's dead," she said, holding a handkerchief to her face. "He tried to escape from prison, and they shot him. Oh, Scott . . ."

"I'm sorry."

She came to him and he took her in his arms, hugging her as she cried.

"We have little Archer," he soothed, reflecting that the detective had carried out his orders well.

"I know you hated him," she sobbed, "but he didn't deserve this. He only robbed the bank because they took his farm."

"I know."

She thought of the angel-faced young man who had made such passionate love to her on the riverboat, and burst into another torrent of sobs. As she wept on her husband's shoulder, Scott thought: Now she's mine.

A week later, Emma received the following letter printed in crude, almost childlike capital letters:

Jan. 10, 1851

Deer Mrs. Kinsolving:
   Now you have baby boy maybe you like meet his haff-sister who name Star. If so pleez come No. 2 Dupont Gai tomorrow at 4 for tee. Pleez not to tell Cap. Kinsolving if you come.
                                        Hopping to be you frend
                                                    Chingling

Chingling. Emma looked up from the letter. Chingling, the woman she thought she loathed, asking her to tea to see her baby? Hoping to be her friend? It was bizarre. What were they to talk about, diapers? Toilet training? Husband sharing?

And yet in a way she was glad the letter had come. Not only was she curious to meet her husband's former concubine, she felt sure the woman would not have invited her if Scott were still seeing her on the sly. She would always revere the memory of Archer. But now that he was dead and she had little Archer, a curious thing was happening.

Emma was falling in love with her husband.

Since the beginning of the year, Scott had stepped up his campaigning, traveling all over the enormous new state. He was currently in the tiny southern town of Los Angeles, which had the highest crime rate in California outside San Francisco.

Scott knew that most of the Californios, as the Mexican ranchers called themselves, were adamantly against statehood. Three years before, the Treaty of Guadalupe Hidalgo, which ended the Mexican War, had ceded California, Arizona, New Mexico, Texas—all of the ancient Spanish empire north of the Rio Grande—to the triumphant Americans. The coincidental discovery of gold at Sutter's Mill shortly thereafter had brought a flood of gringos from the East to California, and suddenly the Californios found themselves and their sleepy way of life inundated by a horde of brash foreigners.

Realizing he needed the backing of the rancheros in southern California, Scott had arranged a luncheon with one of the most powerful, Don Vicente López y Guzmán, owner of the enormous Calafía Ranch south of Los Angeles. As Scott and his assistant rode up to the mission-style ranch house, he marveled at the beauty of the rugged coastline.

"I've seen these cliffs from the sea many times," he said to Walter Hazard, his young secretary/campaign manager, "but this is the first time I've seen them from the land. If this isn't God's country, I don't know what is—and neither does God."

"Yes, it's beautiful," Walter replied. He had made the trek across the Great Plains from Tennessee in a Conestoga wagon with his parents in 1849. An extremely bright young man, he had worked for Scott for more than a year and had volunteered to manage his campaign. Since there was no such thing as professional managers in California, Scott had been glad to accept. Walter had reconnoitered southern California earlier, and had set up this lunch with Don Vicente. Now, as they approached the two-story stucco ranch house with its orange tile roof, they spotted a group of three emerging onto the front porch.

"The fat one's Don Vicente," Walter said. "And the woman in black is his wife, Doña Felicidad. She's a Sepúlveda from Mexico City, very aristocratic, a bit frosty."

"How big is the ranch?"

"About one hundred square miles."

"My God."

"It was a grant to Don Vicente's grandfather from King Charles III of Spain. Don Vicente has about five thousand head of shorthorn cattle and fifty vaqueros working for him. But as I told you, he's short of cash. All the ranchers are."

"And nervous?"

"Very nervous. They're afraid that if their land grants are challenged in American courts, the American judges may declare them invalid. So your best bet to get the Californio vote is to tell the ranchers you'll support the Spanish land grants."

"I'm putting on my most charming smile," Scott said as they pulled up in front. Dismounting, Scott thought: One hundred square miles. What a prize!

"Señor Kinsolving," Don Vicente said, removing his white hat and making a courtly bow. *"Bienvenidos. Mi casa es su casa."*

"My house is your house," Scott thought as he shook the pudgy rancher's hand. Yes, and don't I wish your ranch was my ranch.

"And this is my wife, Doña Felicidad," continued Don Vicente, who spoke with a pleasant Spanish accent. Scott kissed the hand of the dark, voluptuous beauty, who seemed half her husband's age. "My wife has just presented me with a precious gift: a baby daughter." The rancher was beaming. "It is my first child, at the age of fifty-three—not bad, eh?"

He chuckled as he introduced his ranch manager at his side. Then he led the group inside to lunch. The house was cool and handsomely furnished. Its site near a cliff overlooking the ocean afforded spectacular views. As Scott was seated next to his host in the dining room, he kept looking out the window at the Pacific, so gorgeously blue beneath the cloudless sky.

"My house in San Francisco," Scott said to his host, "has a wonderful view of the bay, but I'll concede that your view of the Pacific is even better." This ranch is magnificent, he thought. Damn, I want it.

"Yes, I spend hours riding every day," Don Vicente said as the servants filled the blue-green glasses with white wine. "I love the view. One of my ancestors in the sixteenth century, a man by the name of Don Luis López, fell off one of the galleons of the Manila *flota* during a storm—it was about a mile off the coast here." He pointed out the window. "He washed ashore in front of the house. He was made a slave by the Indians, but he escaped with the help of a beautiful Indian maiden named Nan-da, who had fallen in love with him. It's quite a romantic story. Don Luis and Nan-da walked all the way to Baja California, where they were picked up by a ship and taken to Acapulco. When they arrived in Mexico City, Don Luis became a hero because he knew more about California than any other Spaniard of the day. When King Carlos granted my grandfather this ranch in 1776—the same year as your independence—it was partially in recognition of Don Luis' walk and the information he gave the crown about California."

"You say 'your' independence, Don Vicente," Scott noted as the Mexican servants passed the *puchero*, or beef-knuckle stew. "Don't you mean 'our' independence? After all, you're now an American, sir."

Don Vicente raised his thick black eyebrows skeptically. "Ah, yes, so I've been told. You are my guest, Captain Kinsolving, and I do not mean to insult you. But we Californios do not consider ourselves Americans. You won a few battles in Mexico three years ago, and for that you took half the North American continent as your reward. This is not the spoils of war, sir. This is thievery!"

"Washington prefers to call it Manifest Destiny."

"Washington has a facile way with words. You gringos have poured into California and taken it over. We are all expected now to speak English instead of Spanish. Someone has waved a wand and two centuries of Spanish heritage are supposed to disappear. Am I to dye my hair blond so I can look like a gringo? Well, I won't do it, sir. If you become governor, how do you intend to finance your government? Why do I think you gringos will finance your new state with property taxes—which of course will fall most heavily on us rancheros, since we own the most land."

He had spoken with passion and ill-concealed bitterness.

"You're right, Don Vicente," Scott said. "They talk in San Francisco of property taxes. That's why you and the other Californios need someone to protect your interests upstate. I'm hoping that someone can be me."

"I'll be blunt, señor. You are a gringo, like your opponent, Mr. Powell. How can I trust any gringo?"

"Well, you'd be right not to trust Gus Powell, who's a horse thief if ever there was one." Scott said it half-jokingly, but only half. "But I think I can convince you to trust me. I've talked with ranchers. They tell me the cattle business is in trouble."

"It's true. The price of hides has fallen badly."

"As you know, my ships carry California hides to Boston, where we sell them to the shoe companies. I'm prepared to offer you, and any other ranchero who supports me, a thirty-percent rebate on the shipping costs."

Don Vicente looked up in surprise. "That's very handsome, sir."

"I'm also told that you ranchers in the south would be better off growing produce like lettuce and oranges."

"There's not enough rainfall."

"Wells could be dug for irrigation."

"Wells cost money."

"I'm willing to lend you money, Don Vicente, to put in irrigation on this ranch. If we can show that farming in southern California can be made profitable, it's going to be a boon to this state—and a boon to its governor."

"It could take fifty thousand dollars, maybe more."

"I'll lend you whatever it takes, at three-percent interest. Is your ranch mortgaged, Don Vicente?"

"No, sir," the Californio replied indignantly. "I own the Calafía Ranch free and clear."

"My security would be a first mortgage on the ranch."

Don Vicente frowned. "Then, señor, we have no deal."

His wife, who had followed the conversation, looked distressed. She murmured something to her husband in Spanish, but Don Vicente shook his head.

"No. My wife says I should accept your offer. She has often talked of converting the ranch to orchards, but I want no mortgage on my land."

Scott leaned forward. "They are talking about gringos putting in claims on the great Spanish ranches, testing the validity of the land grants like yours in American courts. I personally am against this because I think it opens the door to all sorts of judicial shenanigans. Judges can be bribed and, in my opinion, they will be. The opportunity to get land cheap will be too great a temptation for a lot of people. But, Don Vicente, if your land had a mortgage on it held by me—a gringo, and possibly the governor of the state—your title to the ranch would be guaranteed. Think about it."

As the servants passed another carafe of the delicate Mexican white wine, Don Vicente López y Guzmán thought about it. Then he said softly, "Perhaps, señor, I am wrong. Perhaps we have a deal after all. And yes, I will support you for governor and I will tell the other rancheros they have a friend and protector in Scott Kinsolving."

Scott looked pleased. A mortgage on this ranch gives me a toehold, he thought. And someday it will be mine.

He was acting on a fundamental American truth that he had known all along: politics and business build empires.

16

Number 2 Dupont Gai loomed out of the dense fog as Emma climbed its wooden steps. In the heart of Little China, the house was brand-new, thrown up in less than a month in boom-town fashion. By local standards the narrow three-story house was elegant, and it was one of the few in town that was painted: white with blue trim. As she rang the bell, she wondered what a Chinese tea was like.

The door was opened almost immediately by a Chinese teenager dressed in a black silk suit with black slippers and a black cap on his pigtailed black hair. Though his face was handsome, her first impression was that it somehow manifested a lack of innocence in one so young. He bowed sharply.

"Kinsolving Taitai is welcome," he said in rather stilted English. "Please to come in."

Emma, who was wearing her otter coat and a handsome blue hat, came into the house. The Chinese boy closed and locked the door, then led her down a narrow stair hall to a curtained door. Lifting the curtain, he opened a door behind it and went into what Emma assumed was the drawing room. Overlooking a small rear garden, the room was decorated with Chinese furniture, a style Emma was grudgingly coming to admire. She noticed incense sticks burning in the lap of a fat stone Buddha squatting beside the fireplace, the smoke curling lazily to the ceiling. Despite the Chinese furnishings, the mantel itself was Western in style. And above it hung a distinctly non-Chinese painting: a large dreamy-eyed portrait of a rather effeminate Jesus Christ.

"You are surprise Chinese girl be Christian?" a soft, high voice inquired. Emma turned to see Chingling standing beside a Chinese jardinière holding a gigantic fern. She was wearing a tight-fitting green silk dress up which writhed a silver dragon. Her face was painted white, her mouth scarlet, and her hair was set in an elaborate Chinese coiffure. Emma felt a stab of jealousy. Chingling was exquisite. She could understand Scott's attraction.

"Yes, I suppose I am surprised," Emma answered.

Chingling smiled as she came forward, extending her hand. "I want to be a good American, and all Americans are Christians. It very sweet religion. Jesus such a sweet man, forgiving all his enemies, even though I not quite understand Immaculate Conception. Do you?"

"No, I find that a bit difficult. But then, I'm not Christian. I'm Jewish."

"Ah, yes," Chingling said, looking a bit confused. "That nice religion too. I thank you for coming. I once thought you my enemy, but I talk to Jesus and he say, 'Be nice to Kinsolving Taitai.' So we be friend, I hope?"

Emma smiled. "Yes, why not?"

"Crane, take Taitai's coat. Very pretty coat, and I love you dress. Is from boutique in de Meyer's?"

"Yes. Countess Davidoff designed it."

"I love her clothes. I wear Western sometime, sometime Chinese. You like see baby now?"

"Please."

She addressed the boy in Chinese. Crane, who had taken Emma's coat, bowed and hurried out of the room. Chingling motioned for Emma to be seated in a wicker chair.

"Crane my servant. He name for bird called crane, crane being Chinese symbol of long life. He very talented boy. He train in martial arts, have beautiful body. He orphan boy, son of a Singsong Girl—"

"A what?"

"Girl who sell favors to men. She die when Crane nine year old. My mother hire Crane before she go to China so he can protect me. He very loyal boy, very good."

Emma heard a baby's wail. Crane reentered, carrying Star in his arms, and brought her to Emma.

"Oh, she's beautiful," she exclaimed.

"Handsome poppa, beautiful momma baby must be beautiful, no?"

"Yes, but she's really adorable."

"You like baby?"

"Very much."

She spoke to Crane again in Chinese, and he abruptly took the baby away. Chingling sat next to Emma.

"We have tea now, and special cakes I make. You like pipe *ah pin yin*?"

"What?"

"Opium. I have best: Patna variety from India. Leave no headache after, nothing but sweet dreams."

Emma was mildly shocked. Though she was aware that opium

smoking was rife among the Celestials, it had never occurred to her that Chingling might be a user.

"I, uh, think not."

"Scott, he still smoke?"

Now Emma looked more than mildly shocked. "My husband? Smoked opium?"

"Oh, sure. Not all time, but often enough."

"Well, he doesn't now."

Chingling smiled. "You look shocked. I tell you many things about Scott that shock you. But maybe you don't want to hear."

Emma squirmed, tempted. "Like what, for instance?" she finally said.

But Crane reentered the room carrying a silver tray with a silver tea service on it. He set the tray on an octagonal table in front of Chingling.

"I serve tea English-style," she said, pouring from one pot into a delicate cup, using a silver strainer, then hot water from another. "Milk or lemon?"

"Milk, please."

Chingling expertly complied; then Crane carried the cup to Emma. Chingling handed him a plate holding small white cakes. "You must try my rice cakes. Very good."

Emma took a bite of one. It had a strange, sweet flavor. "They're unusual," she said.

"You like?"

"Yes."

"Then take more, please."

Emma took a second. "Thank you."

"I hear *ch'i ling* in your bedroom exploded by evil spirit," Chingling said conversationally. "Did that cast bad spell on Scott's lovemaking?"

Again Emma looked shocked. "I beg your pardon?"

Chingling giggled. "I forget. Round-eye ladies no like talk 'bout happy time in bed."

"But how did you know about the Foo dog?"

"Oh, that easy. I send evil spirit to house to break it. Evil spirit in form of Crane, who disguise himself as chimney sweeper." Emma looked at the boy, who smiled slightly. Now she remembered the young chimney sweep who had done the fireplaces just before Christmas. Crane suddenly looked a bit familiar.

"You have your nerve," she exclaimed to Chingling.

"Oh, I very bad. I want to cast bad luck on you happy time with Scott because you take him away from me. Of course, now I realize how wicked I was. Jesus told me how bad I was. Chingling apologize. I hope we still friend?"

Emma stared at her, holding her cup. "Well, I don't know . . ."

Chingling leaned toward her, lowering her voice. "To make up for wickedness, Chingling tell Taitai all secret love things Scott like do in bed. You know 'bout secret love things?"

"I have no idea what you're talking about."

"Scott never try different things with you? He get bored real easy. I used to work hard, use imagination, with help of books."

"What books?"

"Books my mother give me. They written two thousand year ago by wise men. They called *The Manual of Lady Mystery, The Secret Codes of the Jade Room*, and *The Art of the Bedchamber*. They describe all different positions to keep man happy in bed. For instance, the White Tiger Leaps mean man take woman from behind."

Emma almost choked on her tea. "From behind?"

"Oh, yes. Scott do that several times. Then there are the Dragon Turns, when woman stick her tail in air. Approaching the Fragrant Bamboo, when man and woman do it standing up. And really fun is the Jade Girl Playing the Flute, when woman puts man's big thing in her mouth—"

"Stop!" Emma cried, standing up. "I have never heard such disgusting . . . You wicked woman! I can't believe my husband would ever do such revolting things!"

Chingling smiled. "Oh, you very wrong, Taitai. But I 'pologize for disturbing you. Please not to go. We still be friend, no? Jesus want us be friends. He told me so."

Emma stared at her, wondering if she were mad. Suddenly she glanced to her right. The mysterious houseboy was standing by the fireplace, watching her with an intent look that frightened her for some reason. As the smell of the incense in the Buddha's lap began to cloy inside her nostrils, she was overtaken by a wave of panic.

"I don't know what Jesus says to you," she said. "Jesus has never taken the trouble to speak to me, but then, I'm not a Christian. I think I'll go home now."

"Taitai angry," Chingling said, rising to her feet. "Chingling very, very sorry."

"Something tells me Chingling's not that sorry. It has been interesting meeting you. Good-bye." She turned to Crane. "My coat, please."

The boy bowed and hurried across the room with catlike grace. He opened the door, raising the curtain, and bowed again as Emma passed into the narrow hall. He squeezed by her, hurrying ahead to the coatrack. He held the coat for her, then opened the front door and bowed her out. After she left, Crane ran down the hall to the drawing room.

"She's gone?" Chingling asked.

"Yes."

"She'll be dead in a day."

Crane looked surprised. "What do you mean?"

Chingling walked to the portrait of Jesus over the mantel. Standing before it, she softly sang, " 'Jesus loves me, this I know, for the Bible tells me so.' " Then she took the picture off the hook, turned, and smashed it over the head of the stone Buddha.

"I hate Jesus!" she cried. "And I hate that woman who steal my Scott!"

She wrenched the ruined portrait off the Buddha and threw it in a corner. Then she buried her face in her hands, weeping. Crane watched, sorrow and confusion on his young face.

"What did you do?" he finally asked.

Chingling removed her hands from her face and wiped her tears. "I poisoned her rice cakes," she said coolly. "For this I know I must die. You will help me prepare myself, Crane."

"Why you do this?" Crane asked, fighting back tears, for he had come to love Chingling as an older sister.

"When Scott left me, I tire of life. You know this."

"I hate Captain Kinsolving," he whispered, his dark eyes flashing. "He round-eye bastard."

She shook her head. "It too late for hate. Scott did what he had to do, I suppose. I have paid him back by killing his Taitai, so you must not hate him. Besides, money he give to me now go to you. I have come to love you like a son, Crane. I have written you into my will. You will inherit everything I own."

Again the boy looked confused. "But what of Baby Star?" he asked.

"She will go live with her father. I have given it great thought: it will be better for Star if she grow up in the round-eye world. But I charge you with her safety, Crane. Always you will be watching her as if you were her brother. If she ever in danger, you protect her as you have protected me. Do you swear to this?"

Feeling something terrible was about to happen, tears in his eyes, he whispered, "I swear."

"I have written a letter to my mother, which you must give her when she come home. Now: help me. And do not cry for Chingling. She no fear death. Without love, death is preferable to life."

Crane's heart broke for her, but her bravery inspired him. To Crane, the greatest principle of life was contempt for death.

As Emma drove home in the carriage she had hired (she had decided not to let Can Do or any of the servants know where she was going), she thought about the strange tea in the strange house. Could it be possible the things Chingling had said about Scott were true? That he smoked opium and delighted in bizarre sexual practices? As she thought back over her history of lovemaking with her husband, it seemed conventional enough and, to judge from his ardor, Scott had enjoyed it. But what did she know was "conventional"? She might have conceived a child out of wedlock, but otherwise her amatory exploits were certainly tame by the standards of, say, Lola Montez, the fiery dancer whose liaison with the King of Bavaria had shocked all of Europe. In Emma's world, where knowledge of foreign countries was slight and laced with wild exaggerations, the Chinese were exotic barbarians; for all she knew, they might do it upside down in trees. Her old jealousy of Chingling was reignited by the thought that she knew how to "pleasure" Scott in ways Emma didn't know. And a new fear stirred her heart: was Scott's apparent satisfaction with the physical side of their marriage merely a facade? Was he actually bored silly? The idea made her squirm with embarrassment and a gnawing sense of being naive and stupid. With the tender passion she was beginning to feel for Scott, the last thing she wanted was to be a frump in bed who left her husband lusting for the rarefied delights of two-thousand-year-old Chinese sexual-instruction books.

The carriage had just started up Rincon Hill when the first stab of pain knifed her in the stomach. By the time the carriage stopped in front of the house, she could barely climb out. As Can Do helped her down, she was stooped over, holding her stomach and gasping with pain.

"Taitai sick?" he asked, alarmed.

"I think"—another stab pierced her intestines—"I think I've been poisoned."

"Where Taitai been?"

Emma couldn't answer. Crying with pain, she fell out of Can Do's arms onto the gravel. He yelled to the other Celestials on the porch and they hurried down.

"I took her to Number Two Dupont Gai," the carriage driver said.

"Aieee! Chingling! She give her Fang of Dragon! Hurry! We must give her cure! Hurry—aieee!"

The four young Chinese picked up the moaning Emma and carried her up the porch steps as the amazed carriage driver whipped his horses, racing back down Rincon Hill to spread the news to San Francisco.

17

"YOU call yourself a reporter?" Chicago yelled, bursting into the small office of the San Francisco *Bulletin*. "Emma Kinsolving's dying, and you're sitting here writing editorials about the need for goddamned sidewalks? Get your ass to Rincon Hill and get the story!"

David Levin stared up from his desk at the blizzard of white boa that had just stormed in. "Emma's dying?"

"Yes! They say Chingling slipped her a Mickey in a rice cake—some crazy Celestial poison. It's eatin' her guts out. Now, hurry!"

The Emma he had once worshiped flashed through David's mind as he rushed past Chicago and jumped on his horse. As he galloped toward Rincon Hill, all his former resentment and rage washed away at the thought of Emma dying. All he could picture was a beautiful girl in a white dress in a white-and-gold ballroom.

Emma dying? God, no, she was too beautiful to die.

"Scott," Emma whispered. "Where's Scott?"

She was lying on her bed, covered with sweat, and a frightened-looking Zita was sponging her face. Dr. Gray was taking her pulse for the tenth time as Felix stood at the end of the bed, looking ashen.

"Scott's coming home," Zita said, though she had no idea whether that was true. All she knew was that Scott had been in Los Angeles a week. "He'll be here soon."

"Scott . . ."

Her eyes were closed and the others in the room couldn't tell whether she was conscious or mumbling in delirium. "I don't want to die without Scott."

Felix moved around the bed and took her hand from Dr. Gray. "You're not going to die, *schätzchen*," he said, praying he was correct. Can Do had given her emetics, forcing her to vomit up the poisoned rice cakes. That had been two hours ago, and though the stabbing pains were apparently ebbing, she seemed to be getting weaker and weaker. Dr. Gray was, as usual, at a total loss.

"You're going to be all right," continued Felix, switching to Ger-

158

man. *"Es werd' alles gut gehen. Du hast nicht zu fürchten, schätzchen."*

"Scott," she whispered again, beginning to thrash back and forth. "Where are you? I love you, Scott . . . Please come before I die . . ."

Felix kissed her hand, then hurried out of the room, feeling helpless and terrified. He couldn't believe his daughter was dying. Was it his fault for bringing her to this godforsaken place halfway around the world, where Chinese concubines poisoned people at tea and the only doctor was an incompetent quack? Outside, on the second-floor gallery, he burst into tears, covering his face with his hands. Was his life crumbling? First Mathilde, and now Emma . . .

"Herr de Meyer!"

Felix perked up at the familiar voice. Wiping his eyes, he hurried to the railing. In the entrance hall below, a shabbily dressed young man was looking up at him. At first Felix didn't recognize him because of the beard. Then he exclaimed, "David!"

"How is Emma?"

Felix shook his head. David ran up the great staircase, his stained hat in his hand. When he reached Felix, he said, blanching, "Is she dead?"

"Not yet."

"What can I do?"

"Find Captain Kinsolving." David stiffened. "She wants to see him. Maybe it will help, I don't know."

"Where is he?"

"On the Camino Real, I suppose. He went to Los Angeles last week . . . Oh, God, don't let her die." Grabbing the balustrade with both hands, he started sobbing again.

David watched him for only a moment. Then he ran down the steps and out the front door. He mounted his horse and started down the hill for the old Royal Road of the Spanish missions, the spine of California connecting north and south. The fact that he hated Scott Kinsolving had to be overlooked. Emma was dying—the horrible things he had said about her, the horrible things he had insinuated in his editorials came back to haunt him. How she must hate him! And how wrong he had been to not even give her a chance to explain herself. Perhaps the baby had forced her to marry Scott. Of course, wasn't its name Archer? Oh, you fool! he told himself. How could I have hated the one woman I ever truly loved?

"I ended up liking Don Vicente," Scott said to Walter Hazard as they bounced in the carriage a few miles south of San Francisco. "I'd like him even if he weren't bringing us the Californio vote, but since he is, I like him all the more. I'm not the world's most altruistic man by a long shot, but if California's ever going to amount to anything, some sort of modus vivendi has to be set up between us gringos and the Californios—"

"A horseman's comin'!" the driver yelled from above them. Scott stuck his head out the window to see a young man galloping toward them, waving his tan hat.

"Captain Kinsolving!"

Scott recognized David Levin, whom he had seen coming in and out of the *Bulletin* office on Portsmouth Square. How many times had he read and fumed over his hostile editorials? David turned his horse as he pulled up alongside, yelling, "Your wife, sir! Emma is dying! You must hurry!"

Scott looked amazed. "Is this some sort of damned joke?"

"No! She's been poisoned by a woman named Chingling!"

"Jesus! Driver, whip the horses! *Move!*"

The carriage rattled even more violently as the four horses galloped north toward San Francisco.

It was nine in the evening by the time the carriage pulled up in front of the house on Rincon Hill. A large crowd had gathered, for Emma had become a local celebrity and the story of her poisoning had whipped through the Bay City like a brushfire. As Scott leapt from the carriage, one of the onlookers called: "Our prayers are with you, Captain! And if she dies, the damned Celestials will pay!"

"Yes, the heathens will pay!" someone else yelled, and others took up the cry.

Scott glanced at David as he dismounted, then ran up onto the porch and into the house with Walter Hazard and David on his heels. He raced up the great staircase onto the second-floor gallery, where he was met by a teary-eyed Can Do.

"How is she?" Scott asked.

Can Do shook his head. "Not good, Captain Boss. Maybe you can help."

"Is it true? Was it Chingling?"

"Yes. She gave Taitai Fang of Dragon cakes."

"Christ . . ." Scott hurried to his bedroom door and let himself in. When Zita saw him, she sprang from the bed and took his hand.

"Thank God you've come," she whispered. "She's been asking for you."

"Can Do gave her emetics," Felix said, joining them. "If she lives, it will be thanks to him."

"Yes, and meanwhile the crowd outside is ready to lynch every Chinese in San Francisco," Scott muttered, advancing to the bed. When he saw Emma, he winced. She looked so pale and still that for a moment he thought she might have slipped away in the few seconds they had talked. Then he saw her lips move slightly. He knelt beside her, motioning to the others to leave the room. He knew what the Dragon's Fang was: one of the numerous poisons in the Chinese pharmacopoeia, based on intestine-eating narcotics, that was popular in the emperor's court for getting rid of used or unwanted concubines, rivals in the harem, or even unwanted ministers of state. That Chingling could have used such a painful poison to murder Emma was numbing. How I have wronged her! he thought as he leaned over his wife. I've put Chingling on a pedestal because I felt guilty about leaving her, but if she's murdered Emma, by God, she'll pay.

He kissed her forehead. "Emma," he whispered.

She opened her eyes, swimming up from a sea of nepenthe. "Scott," she murmured. "You've come."

"Yes, and you're going to be all right, my darling."

She smiled weakly as he took her hand. "Wouldn't it be funny if I really was your darling."

"It isn't funny. It's true."

Tears formed in her eyes. "Oh, Scott, you play such games with me. But it's nice that you came. I wanted you beside me."

"I'm not playing games, Emma."

"You never loved me," she whispered, closing her eyes again. "Our whole marriage has been a farce."

"I didn't love you at first, I'll admit. I thought you were beautiful, but I was in love with Chingling."

Her eyes opened again. "And I know why. She did those disgusting things with you . . . the Jade Girl Playing the Flute . . ."

Scott's eyes widened. "She told you that?" he whispered.

"Yes. Did you really enjoy it? And did you really smoke opium?"

His face was red, but not from anger. "Yes, I smoked a few pipes. And yes, Chingling showed me all the positions, and I'll admit I enjoyed them. But then I met you—"

"Oh, Scott," she sighed, "you once said I wasn't a very convincing virgin. Well, you're not a very convincing Romeo. You don't have to pretend."

"I'm not pretending! I . . ." He raised her hand to his mouth and kissed it. "I'm such an idiot, Emma. I'm no good at romancing, but I swear to God you're the only woman in my life. I was so wrong about Chingling. And I was so damned jealous of Archer."

"Archer." She looked away, the tears running down her cheeks. "Poor Archer." She looked back at Scott. "Promise me you'll be good to little Archer after I'm gone. Promise me."

"Of course, I promise. But you're not going—"

"You *will* love him?"

"I already do."

"Scott . . ."

"Yes?"

"I love the jewels you gave me—they really are so beautiful—but when I'm gone, will you have Poppa sell them and use the money to build a hospital here in San Francisco? The town needs one so badly. I'd like to be remembered that way. Will you do that for me?"

"Yes, I'll do anything, but you're not going to die!"

She closed her eyes. "That's sweet. I think you really are a kind man, after all."

"I'm not sweet, but you're digging your own grave with all this self-pity. You have to fight to live."

"I don't mind dying. And you mustn't be angry at Chingling. She only did it because she still loves you. Love. All my life I wanted love, and now . . . now I guess I've been killed by love."

"You're being maudlin," he said, exasperated. "If you die of anything, it'll be drowning in your own tears. Now, stop this goddamned deathbed scene and start fighting to live."

She opened her eyes, and he saw fire flash in them. "What a terrible man you are," she snapped. "Cursing me when I'm dying—"

"You're not dying!" he shouted.

"How do you know?" she feebly shouted back.

He straightened, smiling. Now he knew how to save her. "That's more like it. Since you refuse to believe I love you, I'll make you so damned mad at me you'll be too angry to die. Your precious Archer isn't dead. I paid the detective to tell you that."

"What?" Her head snapped up. "Why?"

"Because I knew it was the only way to get him out of your life. Because I love you and I wanted you for my own. I sent One Eye to Ohio to bribe the warden of the penitentiary to keep Archer in jail."

"I don't believe it!" she gasped.

"Well, it's true. I figured if they kept Archer behind bars for another five years, you'd have forgotten him."

"You horrible man! Oh, my darling Archer . . . he's alive?" She started out of bed, but Scott held her back.

"As delighted as I am to see you recoiling from the brink of the grave, my love, I think you're pushing it a little to get out of bed so soon."

"Let me alone!" she said, jerking her hand from his. "Oh, I hate you! You're a beast, a liar, a rotten, no-good, selfish . . . Oh!" She grabbed one of her pillows and threw it at him. Scott caught it, laughing, and went to the door. He opened it, revealing Felix, Zita, David, and Can Do, all looking extremely mournful.

"Cancel the funeral," Scott said, grinning. "My beloved wife has just had a miraculous recovery."

Something banged him on the back of the head. Zita gasped as Scott lurched forward and the object bounced to the floor. It was Emma's silver hairbrush.

Then they heard a cry from the bedroom. Zita pushed by Scott to see Emma kneeling on the floor by her bed.

"Are you all right?" Zita asked, kneeling beside her.

"I may have been . . ." Emma panted, "a bit optimistic."

"You must get back in bed and stay there," Zita said firmly, helping her to her feet. "You have been very sick."

"He lied to me, Zita," she whispered, climbing back in the bed. "Archer is alive. He lied! I'll never forgive him. I married the most horrible man in the world."

"Perhaps," Zita said, pulling up the coverlet. "On the other hand, fifteen minutes ago you were dying, and now . . .?" She plumped the pillows. "Now I think you may be around with us a little longer. So even though Captain Kinsolving may be a horrible man, perhaps he is not such a bad doctor, hmm?"

18

As Scott galloped toward Dupont Gai, he tried to reconcile the Chingling who had tried to murder Emma with the sweet girl he had known. If Chingling was not innocent in the Western sense of the word, Scott had certainly never sensed violence in her nature. Ah Toy perhaps. The Manchu princess was capable of any cruelty. But her daughter? It didn't seem possible.

When he reached Number 2, it was late, but the main street of Little China was still teeming with dozens of shoppers and strollers. He tethered his horse and climbed the steps of Chingling's new house, which he knew from several previous visits to see Star. The house seemed dark. He rang the bell.

Silence.

He rang again. Then he tried the front door. It slowly opened.

He peered into the dark entrance hall. Remembering that an oil lamp was kept on the table at the bottom of the stairs, he groped forward, found it, and lit it. The light bloomed slowly in the gloom. Closing the front door, he started down the hall to the rear, wondering why the house was so silent. There was something eerie and rather frightening about the stillness.

At the end of the hall he lifted the curtain and opened the door. The drawing room was dimly lit by two candles that had burned low in their sticks and were sputtering in the draft from the hall. The candlesticks were set on the floor on either side of the stone Buddha by the fire.

Kneeling in front of it, her back to Scott, was Chingling.

"Chingling?" he said softly. There was no response. He set the oil lamp on a table. He knew she was dead even before he touched her shoulder. She fell forward onto her side. He saw the knife sticking out of her stomach and the drying pool of blood beneath.

"She killed herself," a voice announced. Scott whirled and saw Crane emerging from the shadows in the corner. "She knew that since she poisoned your wife, there would be a great outcry against us Celestials by the round-eyes and she would surely be killed, perhaps by the Vigilance Committees. Others might be killed also. To avoid this, she took her own life. She told me she had nothing to live for anyway."

"But why? And why did she poison Emma? I knew Chingling. There was no violence in her."

Crane came closer, his face illuminated by the oil lamp. "How well did you know Chingling?" he asked softly. "She loved you. She gave you great pleasure, she gave you a daughter, and then you left her for the round-eye woman. She cried for days. 'My Scott, he leaves me,' she said over and over. And slowly her love turn to hate. You are lucky she didn't try to kill you. You rejected her love because of the shape of her eyes and the color of her skin. You are a round-eye son of a bitch. Her death is because of you."

Scott winced, knowing in his heart that what Crane said was true. The young man was standing less than two feet in front of him, his hot eyes burning mercilessly into Scott's.

"And Star?" Scott whispered. "What happens to Star?"

"Star your daughter. You take her if you want. Everything else belong to me. I am the heir."

"You?"

"Yes. Chingling told me she write me into her will. You no believe me, go to office of Chingling's lawyer. He have will. All legal."

"And what of Ah Toy?"

"She in China. Maybe she come out alive, maybe not. Meanwhile, I am now richest Celestial in San Francisco. I become *Kai Yee* of Little China."

"*Kai Yee?*"

"The Big Boss, The Number One Celestial."

Scott smiled scornfully. "You have big ideas for a kid."

Crane's face froze. He turned sideways, raising his clenched fists. As swift as lightning he twirled his right foot up, delivering a kick to Scott's midsection that sent the husky sea captain flying halfway across the room, crashing into a wicker sofa. As Scott fell to the floor, holding his stomach and groaning, Crane smiled slightly. "Some 'kid.' "

"I feel so defeated," Emma said the next morning as she lay in her bed. "Scott has defeated me."

"You make it sound like a war," Zita said, sitting nearby knitting a baby blanket for little Archer.

"Perhaps it is. Perhaps marriage is a war. At any rate, Scott has won."

"Dear Emma, you're too melodramatic and much too hard on him."

"Oh, Zita, that's not fair. I've tried to love him. I even was beginning to think I did love him. But every time, he does some mean, vicious thing, like what he did to Archer. Scott has a cruel streak in him, and I don't see how I can possibly live with him anymore. I don't know what to do."

"Don't you think that possibly he was trying to save your life yesterday?"

"Even if he did, that could never excuse what he's done to Archer. He's destroyed his life—"

There was a knock on the door. Zita got up, putting down her knitting.

"If it's Scott, tell him to go away. I have nothing to say to him."

Zita went to the door and opened it. "Good morning, Captain."

"How's Emma?" he asked.

"Go away," she called from her bed.

Zita raised her eyebrows as if to say: This isn't a good time to see her.

"I'll just be a minute," Scott whispered. "I'd appreciate it if you left us alone."

"She's in a difficult mood."

"I can imagine."

Zita stood aside, letting Scott enter. Then she tactfully slipped out, closing the door. Scott stood by the door as Emma glared at him.

"I really have nothing to say to you," she declared.

"Then I'll do the talking. I know you're angry, and I don't blame you. I made a mistake, which I regret."

"You regret? What about Archer?"

"I'm trying to rectify what I did. Mr. Appleton sailed an hour ago for New York on the *Pacific Zephyr*. He's going to cross Panama on the new railroad they've just put in, so it's possible he can be in New York in six weeks and in Ohio in eight. One Eye will have already been at the penitentiary, which can't be changed now. But Appleton will talk with the warden and even bribe him more, if that's necessary to undo what One Eye did. And I'm putting ten thousand dollars in a Columbus bank for Archer when he gets out of jail. He'll still be young, and with that money he ought to be able to get a good start in life. It's the best I can think of."

He couldn't have possibly surprised—or pleased—her more.

"Well," she finally said, "I have to admit that sounds fair."

"Now, I have a present for you."

"Oh, Scott, I don't want any more jewels."

"This is a different kind of jewel."

He went to the door, opened it, and beckoned. Madam Choy came in, holding a baby, which she carried to the bed.

"Chingling committed suicide," Scott said.

"Good Lord, when?"

"Last night. I'm going to raise Star and eventually adopt her to make her my legitimate daughter. That is, if it's all right with you."

Rather nervously Madam Choy held the baby out to Emma, who looked at her.

"I hope," Scott said, "that you can come to love my daughter the way I've come to love your son."

The baby had been asleep. Now it woke up and burped. Star looked up at Emma.

"Let me have her," Emma whispered, taking the baby from the *amah*. She cradled Star in her arms, then rocked her back and forth gently, humming a lullaby.

"Will it be all right?" Scott asked, trying to mask his apprehension.

"Yes, of course. She's adorable."

Scott looked relieved.

"I'm sorry about Chingling," Emma went on, "despite what she did to me. Are you sure it was suicide?"

"Yes."

There was another knock on the door, and Zita looked in. "Captain, Mr. Levin is here. He says it's important he see you."

"I'll be right out."

As Scott started for the door, Emma said, "Wait! Bring him here. I want to see him."

"Why? You've read that garbage he's been writing about us."

"I know, but he's only writing those things because I hurt him. And you did too."

"He's writing those things because Slade and Chicago pay him."

"And maybe we can win him over to our side. At any rate, it's time I apologize to him and try to reestablish good feelings. Scott, go down and get him. Let Zita help me look halfway presentable—if that's possible."

Scott hesitated. "Well, perhaps you're right."

He left the room as Emma handed Star back to Madam Choy, and Zita brought the hairbrush and mirror to the bed.

"I'm so pale," Emma said, looking in the mirror. "And I want to look good, for Scott's sake. David used to be in love with me: he can be a friend instead of an enemy. Do you think I could use some of your rouge?"

Zita smiled as she went for her purse. "It's about time you asked," she said. "Nature can always use a little help. But I thought you'd given up on your husband."

Emma ran the brush through her hair. "Maybe I was wrong about him," was all she said.

When David entered the bedroom five minutes later, he took one look at Emma and fell in love all over again. Even Scott was startled at how radiant she suddenly looked, until he realized the color wasn't quite natural.

"Dearest David," Emma said, smiling at him. "You've grown a beard. You look quite dashing."

"I . . ." he said, fumbling, staring at her. "I'm a writer. I suppose I should look the part."

"You haven't come to see me, David."

He was wringing his hands nervously. "It was . . . well, dammit, Emma, I didn't feel you'd want to see me. I mean, after the things I've been writing in the *Bulletin*."

"I've been hoping we could be friends again. Can you ever forgive Scott and me?"

He wanted to throw himself on his knees and beg her forgiveness. He wanted to make a fool of himself. Instead, his knees wobbling, he came to the bed and kissed her proffered hand. "You know I could never be your enemy," he said. "What has happened is forgotten. The question is, can you and Captain Kinsolving forgive me?"

"Of course. You may say whatever you want about us in your newspaper, and we'll understand. As long as we know that in private we still are friends."

"That's why I came," he said, releasing her hand and turning to Scott. "I've quit the *Bulletin*."

"Why?"

"It's no secret that Slade Dawson and Gus Powell are lowlifes, and God knows Chicago is no saint. I knew that, and, right or wrong, I was willing to close my eyes to a certain amount of dirt just to get the paper on its feet. But I found out this afternoon what they're planning to do at Chingling's funeral, and I want no part of it."

"What?"

"They're hiring a gang of Sydney Ducks to attack the funeral procession, and you know how important funerals are to the Celestials."

"But why would they do that?" Emma asked.

"The whole town knows Chingling poisoned you, and they think neither you nor Captain Kinsolving is going to do anything about it. Slade and Chicago want Gus to come out hard on the Celestials, to fire up prejudice against them as a campaign issue to get white votes. And what better way for Gus Powell to look strong and make you look weak than by his attacking Chingling's funeral to protect your honor? The Celestials don't have the vote, and Slade and Chicago figure that for every fair-minded white, there are three whites who hate the Chinese. It's brilliant politics, particularly since Gus Powell's first rally is tomorrow night in Portsmouth Square, but as far as I'm concerned, it's rotten morals. That's why I quit the *Bulletin* and came to warn you."

"And I thank you for it, David," Scott said, heading for the door. "Slade Dawson wants war? Fine. I've got my own troops."

He left the room. David turned to Emma.

"What does he mean?" he asked.

"I don't know. But, David, I want to thank you too. And now that you need a newspaper, perhaps Scott and I can find you a new one."

Her luminous smile worked its old magic with him. But he was also intrigued. So far he had been a loser in life. Was his luck starting to change?

19

CHINGLING'S funeral brought out more than half the Celestials in San Francisco. Crane had placed himself in charge of the obsequies, and although many wondered how a teenager who was no blood relation could be so presumptuous, no one tried to stop him. He consulted astrologers to choose a propitious date for the funeral, but when they told him the earliest was four months off, he decided to hold it the second day after Chingling's death. He realized the funeral must be held soon, while Chingling's suicide was still on everyone's lips, to spread his name throughout the city. He was truly stricken by her loss, and he would honor his vow to protect Star. But his boast to Scott that he would become the *Kai Yee* of Little China was not an idle one, and he had decided to use Chingling's funeral as a vehicle to thrust himself into the limelight.

The great procession down Dupont Gai started at noon on a beautiful, windy day. Dressed in the white robes of mourning, Crane led the pallbearers out of Chingling's house, carrying her body in a simple pine coffin. It was placed on a raised litter, perching rather precariously on a flat, rectangular bier raised on poles and swathed in white draperies; the coffin itself was shaded by a white panoply held by four plume-topped poles. The elaborate bier was lifted by the twelve bearers, six on a side, as Crane and the other pallbearers took their positions in front. Before them were six musicians, who began playing an Oriental dirge, and leading the procession were a dozen professional mourners dressed in white, who carried the things Chingling would need in the next world: money, food, clothes, and servants (though the Chinese, being more practical than the ancient Egyptians, who put real money, food, and living servants in the tombs of the pharaohs, made their tomb offerings of paper that was burned into the spirit world). The procession moved slowly down Dupont Gai, accompanied by the eerie, whining music, the clashing cymbals and drums, making a great show for the people thronging the wooden sidewalks. All agreed that Crane had done well by Chingling.

The cortege had gone less than two blocks when a crowd of white men appeared around a corner. They were shouting, "Death to the Pigtails!" and many carried crudely lettered signs: "Heathen Chinese Must Go!" "Send Celestials Back to the Celestial Kingdom!" "All Slant-Eyes Are Thieves and Whores!"

When Crane saw the gang, he immediately recognized them as Sydney Ducks, but was astounded all the same that they would attack a funeral procession. Hurling stones and mud, the Ducks charged the cortege, fouling the white robes of the mourners. They in turn started running, throwing their paper funerary gifts into the air as the crowd on the sidewalk screamed and ran. Some of the Ducks had wooden bats that they used to beat the marchers' heads and shoulders.

Crane, despite his illegitimate birth, had a deep feeling for ceremony and ritual. He was enraged at this blasphemy, but he didn't know whether to abandon his place as head of the procession and fight back, or to uphold Chingling's posthumous dignity by guarding her coffin. His immobility was abruptly shattered by a blob of mud hitting him in the face. As he tried to clean the muck from his eyes, he heard the shouts as the Ducks charged the heart of the procession. A bat slugged him on the side of the face, sending him sprawling to the dusty street; then more bats began beating him. By the time he cleared his eyes, he was surrounded by four burly ex-cons who were shouting as they battered him.

"Here's the chief pigtail!" yelled one, a cross-eyed slob with four days' beard.

"He was the boyfriend!" howled another, cracking his stick on Crane's upheld arms.

A volley of shots rang out. Crane saw his assailants freeze and look around. As more shots followed, Crane crawled quickly through the legs of one of the Ducks and sprang to his feet. He saw some three dozen men dressed in the uniforms of the Kinsolving Line charging up Dupont Gai, firing their rifles just above the heads of the attacking Ducks. Crane was amazed to discover that the sailors were led by none other than the round-eye he hated most: Scott Kinsolving.

The Ducks had no stomach for bullets. They took off on the run, leaving behind them a scene of filth and devastation. Celestials watched from behind screens and shutters as the crewmen from Scott's clipper ships in the harbor took command of the litter-strewn street.

"Are you all right?" Scott asked, coming up beside Crane, who was bleeding from a head wound. The young Celestial, his dignity miraculously unimpaired despite the mud and blood, looked coolly at Scott. "Of course," he lied. "But don't expect me to thank you, Captain Kinsolving. I know why you are here, and it has nothing to do with memory of Chingling or protecting us Celestials. It is all dirty round-eye politics."

As he brushed some dirt from his sleeve, he noticed a horrifying sight behind him. "Aieee!" he whispered.

"Chingling!" Scott gasped.

The funeral bier had been dropped by its twelve bearers when the Ducks attacked. The pine coffin had fallen on its side in the street, and the lid was open. Sprawling halfway out of her coffin, wrapped in her burial robes, was the corpse of Chingling, her lifeless eyes staring at the sun.

"What kind of man is this Captain Kinsolving?" yelled Gus Powell as he stood on the steps of the Bonanza Café addressing the crowd in Portsmouth Square. "What kind of man would attack those very men who were trying to avenge his wife's honor? The Chingling creature poisoned Emma Kinsolving, and what does her husband do? He protects Chingling's funeral procession. I tell you, Scott Kinsolving is a traitor to his race!"

The crowd, some of whom were carrying torchlights that flickered in the strong wind, murmured agreement, though Chicago, who was standing next to Slade on the Bonanza's porch, noted that the enthusiasm was limp and the assent anything but universal. She decided she would inject some excitement into the proceedings: so far, this political rally was a flop.

"Hell, Gus," she yelled, "Scott Kinsolving's not only a Celestial-lover, he's a Jew-lover. Look at that store across the square. What's that sign read? 'De Meyer and Kinsolving.' Who's his wife? Emma de Meyer Kinsolving! Ain't the de Meyerses Jews? You bet your ass!"

The Jew-baiting went over even less well than the Chinese-baiting.

"You may be right, Chicago," yelled one man in the crowd, "but what would we have if it weren't for de Meyer's? It's the best store west of the Rockies."

"Besides," another yelled, "Emma Kinsolving's bringin' some class to this town. And she's gorgeous—a helluva lot better-lookin' than those cows you overcharge us for!"

This brought a roar of laughter. Chicago's fat face scowled.

"And what about attackin' a funeral?" yelled a third man. "Even if it was a Celestial funeral. What the hell kind of people would attack a goddamn funeral?"

"I'll tell you what kind!" yelled the first man. "Sydney Ducks, those goddamn cons from Australia! Scott Kinsolving is talkin' law and order, and he's backin' it up with his own men. I say more power to him if he can stop the Ducks and the crime in this town!"

This brought a wild roar of approval, the first excitement the crowd had manifested.

"Shit," Chicago growled to Slade, "that Gus stinks as a speaker. Are we backing a loser?"

Slade looked at Gus, who was waving his arms, vainly trying to shout down the now-rowdy crowd. This had been the first Powell-for-Governor rally, well-advertised by posters and announcements in the *Bulletin*, timed to milk the attack on Chingling's funeral for all it was worth. But it was becoming painfully evident that the plan was back-firing. Gus—skinny, balding, unprepossessing—was one of the few men in town with a lawyer's degree, albeit one from a dubious law school in Missouri, which was why Slade and Chicago had decided to back him for governor. Besides, Gus was involved with enough crooked deals that Slade knew he could control him.

But suddenly Slade was seeing not only that Gus had zero political sex appeal but also that Scott's popularity, and the popularity of the law-and-order issue, was much greater than either he or Chicago had imagined. Were the rough-and-tumble, hard-drinking, whoring men of California beginning to look for some political maturity?

"I told you words were worth shit," Slade said. "There's a better way to win elections than playing whore to the voters."

He went back into the Bonanza Café as the crowd began chanting: "Kinsolving! Kinsolving! Kinsolving!"

"I'm so proud of you," Emma whispered as she lay in her husband's arms. "And I owe you such an apology."

Scott ran his hand slowly over her breasts. "You owe me nothing," he said, kissing her.

"I owe you my life, to begin with. You did make me so mad I wanted to fight to live. And I owe you for Archer—both Archers. And now I owe you for Star. What an unusual family we're building."

"It's going to be more than 'unusual.' It's going to be a great family. It's going to be the royal family of California."

She turned and kissed his shoulder. "David said Gus Powell's rally was a disaster tonight, so maybe we will be the royal family. Governor Scott Kinsolving. What a nice ring that has."

"Do you know you have the most beautiful eyes on the planet Earth?"

She smiled and kissed him. "And you're going to be the most handsome governor in California's history."

"Considering the fact there haven't been any, I accept the compliment with a huge grain of salt."

"Scott, I have a terrible confession to make."

"What?"

"I think I've been in love with you all along and didn't realize it."

"You mean all our fights have really been lovers' quarrels?"

She kissed him again. "Yes. Isn't it wonderful? And I believe you love me. I really do, now. It just took me a long time to . . . well, understand you. You're not every woman's idea of the ideal husband, you know."

"What's wrong with me?"

"Well, you are a bit devious. And I'd hate to be your enemy, because you have a long memory and like to settle scores."

"Mmm. That's probably true."

"And you're ambitious and a bit power-mad."

"Terribly power-mad. Royal family, remember?"

"But there's one thing I'll grant you."

"What?"

"You've given up using those filthy words."

"At least in front of you."

"But you know, all in all, you're really rather wonderful."

"Now, that's what I like to hear."

He leaned over and hungrily kissed her. She sighed with pleasure as she felt the warmth and strength of his body close over her like some magical blanket.

"I do love you," she whispered. "You've made me the happiest woman in the world."

As they began to make love, she marveled how she had fallen in love with her husband. It was not the rapture of her brief love with Archer, but a deeper, richer love based on character, friendship, and admiration rather than the heat lightning of physical attraction.

How strange the ways of the human heart, she thought. How strange the ways of *my* heart.

The cold wind blowing down from Alaska gripped its icy fingers around the tiny city on the bay, creeping in through leaky windows and forcing San Franciscans to shiver under their blankets. The two men climbing Rincon Hill at three that morning weren't shivering, though: they were used to extremes of climate. Named Barker and Farnsworth, they had been convicted of twenty-three counts of manslaughter and arson in England seventeen years before. They had been transported to Australia and had spent ten years on the tiny island of Norfolk, six hundred miles east of Australia in the Pacific Ocean, a living hell so horrible that convicts pleaded for execution rather than incarceration there. Both Barker and Farnsworth had been flogged numerous times— Barker had once received two hundred lashes in one afternoon—but flogging was but one of the fiendish horrors on Norfolk Island. Barker had been subjected to the "tube-gag," a wooden plug forced into his mouth with only a tiny hole to allow air, as well as the "spread-eagle," a form of crucifixion that left him paralyzed for days. Farnsworth had endured six days in the "water pit," standing waist-deep in brine, unable to sleep lest he drown. The dark, sadistic side of the British penal system had reached its most evil bloom on Norfolk Island, from which no one ever escaped.

Having finally served their time, the two were sent to Van Diemen's Land (Tasmania), where eventually they became ticket-of-leave men, the Australian version of parolees. Once free of guards, they quickly arranged their escape and, like so many other Australian cons, headed for the goldfields of California. Brutalized by the British penal system, they had joined the eleven thousand other Australians in San Francisco and become Sydney Ducks, two words that struck fear into the hearts of the toughest Californians.

As they neared the top of the hill, they looked up at the dark windows of the Kinsolvings' house looming above them.

Farnsworth was carrying a gallon can of lamp oil. "This is going to be easy, mate."

"Aye, but with this bloody wind, we may take the town too."

"Won't be the first time. Slade says it just increases real-estate prices."

Barker chuckled, and in the roaring north wind they continued to the top of the hill.

Can Do lived with his wife and children in a four-room cottage Scott had built a hundred feet behind the main house. Can Do was using the chamber pot when he saw the flickering through his bedroom window.

"Fire," he whispered. Then, jumping off the chamber pot, he cried: "Fire!"

Rushing out of the house on his bare feet, he ran for the fire bell Scott had foresightedly put up. Fire was a terrifying event in the almost totally wooden town, and one of the reasons the great Christmas Eve fire of 1849 had wreaked such devastation was that there had been only two hand-pumped fire engines available to fight it. To correct this, volunteer fire companies had been formed, each providing its own rope-pulled engine, each with its own esprit de corps, each in a friendly rivalry with the others to get to the frequent fires first. Whenever a fire broke out, the companies were alerted by the clanging of the great city bell, the location of the blaze pinpointed by coded strokes of the clapper.

As the gale winds whipped the flames, Can Do grabbed the rope of Scott's private bell to alert the rest of the alarm system. He could see that flames had already engulfed much of the engirdling porch and were licking their way up toward the Italianate tower. He gave the rope a strong jerk.

To his horror, the rope snapped and fell to the ground. Someone had frayed the bell rope so that it would part at the first tug. The bell, ten feet above him, was too high to reach without a ladder.

"Arson!" he cried, running up the hill toward the big house. He called at the top of his voice: "Captain Boss! Kinsolving Taitai! Fire! Get out! *Fire!*"

At first Emma thought she was dreaming: she was in a kitchen with the stove smoking. Then she woke up and realized the smoke she was smelling was no dream. She sat up, rubbing her eyes. She looked at the windows and saw the flickering firelight coming from below.

"Scott." She shook his shoulder. "Scott, wake up!"

"Huh . . . ?"

"There's a fire."

She was out of bed, running to the windows. She threw one open. The wind roared inside, flapping her nightgown and her hair. When she tried to look out, her face was blasted by the heat of the burning porch just below.

"Close the window!" Scott was shouting. He had run to the door of the bedroom and opened it. Great clouds of smoke from the entrance hall poured into the room. Emma slammed the window shut, telling herself not to panic. Archer . . . Star . . .

Scott had thrown a robe on. "Get out of the house!" he yelled to Emma. "I'll get the children."

"No, no, I'll go with you—"

"Get out!" he roared. "And hurry, before the stairs go."

He pushed her through the door, then followed her out. The fifty-foot-high entrance hall was thick with smoke, and the fire on the porch cast an eerie light through the windows. Emma ran down the gallery toward the stairs, looking up as Scott bellowed: "Madam Choy! Fire! Bring the babies! Fire!"

He started up the stairs toward the third floor, when a beam of light pierced the gloom as the nursery door opened. Madam Choy, in a frilly nightgown and matching cap, came out, holding the two babies.

"Madam Choy, thank God!" Scott yelled, bounding up the stairs. "I'll take one of them."

The *amah* was coughing as she started down the stairs, and one of the babies was wailing. Emma had reached the top of the main stairs.

Now she heard the front doorbell ringing. She also saw smoke and light pouring through the double doors to the dining room and realized with sinking fear that that part of the house must be burning also. She had started down the stairs when Can Do broke the glass window of one of the front doors, reached through, and unbolted it. As he pushed the doors open, the wind roared into the house.

"Taitai!" he yelled, spotting Emma on the staircase. "Thank goodness you okay—"

"Can Do, close the doors!" yelled Scott, who was racing around the second-floor gallery with Madam Choy and the two babies. "The wind is making it worse!"

In fact, the wind had stoked the fire in the dining room into an inferno. Flames shot into the great hall, slithering up the wooden walls like orange rats, rapidly shooting up the three stories to the skylight.

Madam Choy, who was coughing ceaselessly from the increasingly thick smoke, now screamed and stumbled. She fell forward on her knees, barely avoiding dropping Archer.

"Jesus Christ!"

Scott, who was holding Star, had just started down the stairs when he saw what had happened.

"Emma!" he cried. "Take Star!"

Emma, halfway down the great stair, now hurried back up and took the baby from her husband's arms. Then Scott started back up the stairs to the gallery, running toward Madam Choy, who was picking herself up.

Emma started down the stairs holding Star. The smoke and flames were now so intense that she too was coughing and having trouble seeing. "Can Do!" she called. "Help Captain Boss!"

Holding a handkerchief over his nose, Can Do passed Emma the other way, bounding the steps two at a time. Scott, holding Archer, was running around the gallery. Seeing Can Do, he yelled, "Take the baby. I'll go back to get Madam Choy!"

"Can do!"

They met at the top of the stairs and Can Do took Archer in his arms. Scott hurried back toward the *amah*, who was screaming in terror, holding on to the balustrade, obviously too panic-stricken to move. Can Do ran down the stairs. He saw that Emma had reached the front door and was going out on the porch. The heat was unbearable, the walls now burning, licking toward the ceiling. Suddenly the stained-glass skylight burst. Emma screamed as knife-sharp shards of glass rained down, one barely missing Can Do as he rushed for the bottom step. The broken skylight was the finale: the wind rushed up to the hole above and created a firestorm.

"Outside, Taitai!" Can Do howled, running to the door. "Onto porch!"

"Scott!" she screamed. "Where are you?"

"Outside!"

He pushed her through the front doors and past the inferno on the porch. They had raced onto the gravel drive when they heard a terrific crash behind them. Emma turned to see flames shooting from all the windows of the house.

"Scott!" she cried again, backing away from the blistering heat. "Scott!"

In the distance, the great city bell was clanging as the town saw the inferno on top of the hill. The wind was blowing the sparks and burning bits over the roofs of the houses below, and already some of them were starting to burn. Every fire company in San Francisco was coming to life. Torch boys ran ahead of the engines, providing light as the firemen pulled their cumbersome machines by rope through the streets toward Rincon Hill.

"Looks like this one's going to be bad," yelled one fireman over the wind.

"Scott!"

Emma was becoming hysterical. The house was a pillar of flame, but there was still no sign of either Madam Choy or her husband. Can Do had taken both babies to the far side of the reflecting pool.

"Taitai!" he yelled. "Get back!"

A part of the tower roof that had peeled from the heat was now torn off by the wind. The flaming sheet sailed toward Emma, but went over her head and crashed into the pool instead.

She couldn't believe what was happening. As she stared at the inferno, the horrible realization seeped into her consciousness that the man she had finally come to love was trapped for eternity in the furnace that had been their home.

She heard the fire bells in the distance. She heard the rattle of her father's carriage coming up the hill from his house. She felt Felix hugging her, then Zita putting a coat around her to protect her from the wind. Finally, the arrival of the fire trucks, the paying out of the hoses, the shouts of the firemen, the hiss of the steam as the geysers from the hoses spat into the flaming house. She heard people shouting, "The whole city's going!"

But none of it registered. "I lost him," she numbly whispered to Zita. "I lost Scott. Just when I was beginning to love him—"

She leaned on Zita's shoulder and began sobbing. As the older woman took her in her arms, she remembered how Emma's heart had broken on the riverboat when Archer Collingwood was torn out of her life. Now she heard it crack again over this new tragedy.

"Poor darling," she said. "Come down the hill to our house. You must be put to bed before you catch cold."

"Would it matter?" Emma cried, tears streaming down her face. "Does anything matter now? Scott, my darling Scott . . ."

She turned, as in a dream, and started toward the carriage, helped by Zita and Felix. Can Do came to her with the two babies, both of whom had miraculously fallen asleep amid all the noise and confusion. The lowering flames from the house cast flickering light on their sleeping faces as Emma looked at them.

"I was wrong," she said, coming out of her trancelike state. She held out her arms for the children. "They matter. The future matters. Give them to me, please, Can Do."

In silence the babies were transferred to her arms. Emma hugged and kissed them. Then she turned back to the gutted house.

"Scott," she whispered, a look of fierce determination coming into her reddened eyes, "you'll continue to live in these children, and in my heart. You'll be proud of your family, my darling. I'll make sure of that. It will be what you wanted: the royal family of California."

She kissed her babies again as, below her, half of San Francisco blazed, splashing the night sky with blood.

"It's going! God damn!" said Rick Birdwell, one of the four night watchmen at de Meyer and Kinsolving's Emporium. He and the three other guards were standing before the big store, watching the city burn.

"Well, hell, we'll just build San Francisco again," said Stu Amory, another guard. "We're getting damned good at building new towns."

"Yeah, practice makes perfect."

The wind had kept the flames away from Portsmouth Square, which was dark and empty except for a few lights at the Bonanza Café. Most of the townspeople not actually fighting the fires were watching them, leaving the rest of San Francisco virtually empty.

A shot rang out, hitting Rick Birdwell in the back. Then a volley of shots. The other guards were mowed down before they could even pull their guns. As they fell, dead and dying, in front of de Meyer's, twelve Sydney Ducks galloped up on horseback and dismounted quickly. One of them said, "We got an hour to clean out the store. Make sure them assholes is dead. Come on, mates, we got work to do."

As the others ran inside the dark store, one remained behind, delivering coups de grace with his pistol into the heads of the watchmen.

When he was done, he ran into the store, where already the others had smashed half the vitrines and trashed Zita's boutique.

"Ruined," Felix said. "Everything ruined."

It was the next morning. Houses everywhere were still smoldering, and a stench of burnt wood hung over the city. Felix was standing in the middle of the ground floor of the ransacked department store. Tears misted his eyes as he looked around the store he had filled with so many beautiful things. It was now a mess of shattered display cases, ripped clothing thrown everywhere, piles of trash.

"All we worked for," he said. "Gone."

"And the watchmen," said Zita, who had taken one look at her boutique and burst into tears, "all dead. I can't believe such wanton violence—"

"I can believe it," Emma said, holding her father's arm, her eyes red from crying. "It's a violent world. I used to believe in romance and Chopin waltzes, but then they killed my mother—and your children, Zita. Archer's gone, Chingling tried to kill me, and Scott was killed. This is a violent world, and only the strong survive. Well, by God, I'm going to be strong. Poppa, do we have insurance?"

Felix squeezed her in a hug. "Dear Emma," he said, "you have your own burden to carry. Don't worry about the business."

"I do worry. Half this store is mine now. Is there insurance?"

As Felix regarded his daughter, he saw not tears but a shrewdness in her eyes that reminded him strongly of his late wife, Mathilde. "No," he said finally. "There are no insurance companies in California, and we haven't been able to get insurers from the East to come out yet."

"No insurance," Emma repeated softly. "Then all that's left are the ships and what's in the warehouses. But that ought to be enough."

"Enough for what?"

"To rebuild all this." She gestured around at the destruction. "To rebuild de Meyer and Kinsolving's, and maybe start an insurance company too. We're not the only ones who've been wiped out. Half of San Francisco got burned last night. It's happened too often. People will want insurance, and we'll provide it for them."

Felix looked at her. "What do you mean, 'we'?"

"Just that. My husband wanted to build an empire in California. Well, he's been taken from me, and I have a strong suspicion the person responsible for his death is also the one behind the looting of this store." She was staring through the open doors at the Bonanza Café across the square. "A certain gentleman who is going to pay for what he's done."

"Emma, if you're suggesting that you take a personal part in Scott's business affairs—"

"I'm not suggesting, it's settled," she said, turning back. "Poppa, Can Do found the jewels Scott gave me. They were in a strongbox and weren't destroyed. Can you sell them for me? We'll need all the capital we can get."

"Well, I suppose . . ."

"Zita, you figure how much you'll need to get the boutique going again. We'll have this store open in a month. No, two weeks."

"But, Emma, you are a lady," her father exclaimed.

"Scott was never too sure about that. Besides, I can be a lady—whatever that is—at night. Scott wanted an empire and he's going to have one, even if I have to build it for him." She caught herself. Is this *Emma* speaking? she wondered. I've never cared about anything but good-looking men and love and pretty clothes. At that moment she realized the real Emma *was* emerging, the Emma who was as practical as her mother, the Emma she had always feared. But why should I be afraid? she thought, her determination building. What's wrong with being strong? What's wrong with getting things done? Just because I'm a woman doesn't mean I have to sit around having babies and doing petit point the rest of my life. "And the more I think of the insurance-company idea," she said aloud, "the more I like it. Insurance against . . . this." She forced a smile. "Scott," she said softly, "I'm going to make you proud."

Zita hugged her. "We'll all make him proud."

Emma squeezed her hand and then her father's. "Yes, we'll all make him proud."

Chicago sat in her elevated chair watching the action at the Bonanza Café. Two nights had passed since the fire, and business was back to normal. She took a sip of her gin and reflected on the resilience of San Franciscans. "Hell, I wonder what it would take to knock this town for a loop," she said to herself, smoothing the feathers of her emerald satin dress. She surveyed the scene: the topless waitresses, the drunken miners destroying their livers with booze and their lungs with cigars and cigarettes. It's a good business, she thought, but it could stand some professional entertainment. Maybe we should put in a stage show—

Suddenly the noise in the café subsided. All eyes turned to the doors. Chicago's eyes also turned. What she saw astounded her.

Standing in the doors, looking gorgeous in an elegant black dress, was Emma Kinsolving. The veils of her black hat were folded back to reveal her chalk-white face, and her black-gloved hands clutched a black beaded bag.

Total silence as she moved into the room. She came up to one of the frozen topless waitresses.

"Is Slade Dawson here?" she asked quietly.

The waitress gulped, feeling somehow that she was standing naked in front of the Queen of England. "Yes, ma'am. He's upstairs with Letty."

"Who's Letty?"

"She's his girlfriend, ma'am. One of Chicago's whores."

There was a titter from the men at the bar. But as Emma turned regally toward them, the laughter instantly died.

"I see," she said. "Would you be so kind as to tell me how to get to Letty's room?"

The waitress pointed to the stairs. "Up there, ma'am. Parlor A. It's got the best view of the square."

"Thank you."

The dirty, sweat-stained miners watched with fascination as the elegant widow crossed to the stairs and started for the second floor. They were seeing a new kind of entertainment: class.

What the hell is she up to? Chicago wondered nervously.

Slade thrust his naked haunches faster, with an almost misogynistic fierceness as he fucked Letty Brown, the pretty plump whore from Nebraska. And with Slade, it was fucking, not making love. He prided himself on his looks and his way with women, but deep down he disliked the female sex. They weren't good for much except bed and babies. Slade was, in short, a hard-core man's man.

Letty groaned as they both achieved orgasms. Then Slade pulled out and lit a cigarette. "You weren't bad tonight, baby," he said, exhaling.

"Thanks a lot," she said, sitting up. "You're such a Prince Charming, your flattery could go to a girl's head."

"What do you want, medals?"

"Maybe." She got out of the brass bed and picked a filmy negligee off a chair. She was blond and had a richly rounded figure. Slade scratched his hairy chest and watched her from the bed.

"You got great tits, baby," he finally said. "And your ass would give George Washington a hard-on."

"Gee, don't tell Martha."

She piled her hair on top of her head and tied it with a pink ribbon. Parlor A, the best of Chicago's "love suites," had three windows overlooking the square and was decorated with cheap chintz-covered furniture. Tiny roses crawled the wallpaper like roaches.

Letty turned to the gambler. "Slade, I don't think you love me. I ain't no fool. As far as that goes, I don't think you'll ever love any woman, because there's not much love in you, if you ask me. But anyhow, you'd better start doin' some serious thinkin' about the future, 'cause I'm carryin' your baby.''

Slade's thick black eyebrows met in a frown. "You're shitting me.''

"No, I'm not. And there ain't no question he's yours, as you well know.''

He knew she was telling the truth. As co-owner of the Bonanza, he kept the best room for himself and had installed Letty in Parlor A six weeks before as his personal "guest," telling Chicago she was off-bounds to the customers.

He sucked the cigarette, then grinned. "It might be fun having a kid," he said.

"It won't be much fun if he don't have a proper daddy.''

"If you're angling for me to propose, forget it. I wouldn't marry no whore.''

She shrugged. "Then the kid's gonna be a bastard, 'cause I won't go to no abortion mill—" She stopped as the door opened. "I beg your pardon!" she exclaimed.

Emma swept into the room, closing the door behind her. Slade quickly pulled the sheet up over his waist. He stared at her amethyst eyes, which were boring into his. He stubbed out his cigarette as she came to the bed.

"Excuse me, Mrs. Kinsolving," he said, "if you'd knocked, I'd have put on my drawers.''

She pulled her derringer from her purse and pointed it at his face. "If my husband had lived," she said, "and become governor, he would have set up a proper police force to deal with scum like you. But since you killed him, I have to take the law into my own hands.''

"Get the hell out of here.''

She jammed the muzzle against his forehead. "Don't think this isn't loaded.''

He froze, beginning to feel terror for the first time in his life. "Wait a minute," he whispered.

"Why? Did you let us wait two nights ago when you sent the arsonists to burn our house and kill my husband? Did you give those four watchmen a chance to wait before you killed them?''

"I don't know what you're talking about.''

"Yes, you do. I'm pulling the trigger, Slade Dawson. I am your executioner.''

"Jesus." He was shaking "Letty, call for help.''

"It's too late. Good-bye, you bastard.''

She pulled the trigger. Click. Letty screamed.

Nothing had happened.

Emma removed the gun and stepped back. Slade Dawson's body was covered with sweat.

"You bitch!" he roared. "You goddamn bitch! You scared the shit out of me!"

"That was the point. I wouldn't kill you. But I know what you've done, and you won't get away with it. I'm stronger than you are, Slade Dawson. You'll never be anything in this town but what you are: a cheap, vulgar, murdering crook. Garbage. San Francisco's going to be either your kind of town or mine, and I'm pretty certain that someday it'll be you who's run out of this town."

She put the gun back in her purse and opened the door. She gave Letty a quick, scornful look and Slade a final, lethal one. Then she left, closing the door with a click.

"What was that all about?" Letty asked.

"Garbage," he whispered, turning his gaze from the door to Letty. "She called me garbage."

"Well, let's be honest, honey. The pope ain't about to ask you to join the College of Cardinals."

With a roar of rage Slade jumped out of the bed, rushed her, grabbed her, and raised his fist to hit her.

"The baby!" she shrieked.

Slade hesitated, then slowly lowered his fist.

The baby. His baby.

Garbage.

We got to get respectable, Chicago had said.

"I'm sorry," he said, smoothing her arm with his hand.

Respectable. A son.

He looked at the door again, thinking of Emma. She was respectable, damn her. Maybe that *was* the future of California.

"What are you thinkin', honey?" Letty asked, putting her hand on his chest.

He looked at her again. Jesus Christ, I sure as hell have the money, he thought. But could I pass this whore off as a lady if I married her? God knows, in San Francisco, anything is possible.

20

"I BELIEVE you have an inmate named Archer Collingwood in this penitentiary," said the one-eyed man.

Warden Edward Ridley leaned forward, adjusting the pince-nez on his nose. "Yes. Number four-one-six-two. I'm pleased to say that after a very bad beginning here, during which he was sent to solitary, he has become a model prisoner. He has earned almost a month good time, and I will be pleased to recommend him for parole. His influence on the other prisoners has been exemplary too. He had a difficult cellmate—an Indian named Joe Thunder—but the guards tell me Collingwood prevailed on him to cooperate with the system, and I'm delighted to report that Joe Thunder was paroled two weeks ago." He cleared his throat. "As a warden, nothing pleases me more than to see our correctional system actually work."

One Eye's one eye was glazed with boredom. "Yes, I'm sure. However, Collingwood is known in certain high quarters in California. His moral character is known to be very bad, and he is suspected of a number of crimes that he has never been tried for. Unfortunately, the nature of these crimes makes them difficult to prove in a court of law. Consequently, it is in the interests of these persons in California—and in the interests of justice—that Collingwood be kept incarcerated for at least another five years."

The warden looked startled. "My dear Mr. Fontaine, that would be impossible."

One Eye pulled from his jacket pocket the bag of gold he had brought to Ohio all the way from California. Silently he placed it on the desk. The warden took it and peered in. Then he looked again at the one-eyed man sitting on the other side of his desk. The warden took a deep breath.

"Of course," he said, "there are sometimes extraordinary circumstances where the normal channels of justice are blocked . . ." He took the bag off his desk and stuffed it in one of his drawers. "Tell your friends in California, Mr. Fontaine, that Archer Collingwood will be punished for his"—he cleared his throat again—"his, ah, crimes."

One Eye had the grace not to comment. The former alderman from Cleveland had sold out without even a blush.

To survive the horror of his life in prison, Archer had dug into the rich resources of his imagination to create a romantic dream world he could inhabit, one in which beautiful Emma dominated his every thought. The reality of the so-called model prison was unbelievably ugly, riddled with sodomy and corruption. Violence was always simmering in the enforced silence and lockstep marching through the dismal corridors. The guards, most of whom relished their power, could and did make life miserable for those who didn't pay them off. It was well-known among the convicts that the prison staff, from the lowest guard all the way up to the pious-talking Warden Ridley, could be bought.

Archer had no money to pay off the guards, and for the first few months after his release from solitary they had taunted and bullied him relentlessly, particularly the pockmarked Sergeant Woolridge, who had taken a particularly sadistic hatred toward the good-looking farmboy. But Archer refused to be goaded into breaking the rules. He was earning good time, and each day he earned was one day nearer liberty and Emma. As the days inched by with their numbing routine, rotten food, and crushing boredom, only thoughts of Emma kept him sane.

Because of the rule of silence, it was difficult to get to know any of the other inmates except one's cellmate, which was one of the points of the rule. But cruel as it was, some of the more hardened prisoners preferred it to the other system of penology current in America, the Philadelphia System, in which prisoners were kept in separate cells, and neither their names nor crimes were known to the warders who brought them food. Worst of all, some swore, were the black hoods put over their heads whenever they were taken from their cells for exercise. Still, Ohio's Auburn System was little better. Convicts felt totally isolated and suffered severe depression because of the almost permanent silence.

One positive result was that Archer and Joe Thunder became soulmates as well as cellmates. As the months dragged by, they whispered to each other of their pasts and of their hopes for the future. It was an unlikely friendship, but nonetheless profound because of the disparity of their backgrounds and the bleakness of their lives. Archer shared his dreams of Emma with Joe, who shared his dreams of an Indian girl named Pink Dawn. Together they marked off the trickle of days on their calendar and complained incessantly about the food. Joe knew the grimmer details about the prison kitchen because he had worked there at his former civilian occupation of dishwasher.

Thus, when Joe was granted parole, Archer received the news with mixed emotions. He was glad for his friend's freedom, but his own loss plunged him into despair.

"That okay, you be out soon," Joe said on the night before his release. "Then we all go to California and have double wedding: me with Pink Dawn, you with Emma."

"Sure," Archer said, forcing a smile.

"How much good time you got now?"

"Eighteen days."

"Shit, Archer, you'll be eligible for parole in fifteen months. That's nothing."

"Yeah, I know."

"And I owe you a lot, old buddy. I was a crazy Indian till you talked me into doing my time. I appreciate it. Joe Thunder don't forget. I'll come see you every month."

After Joe had left, Archer lay on the top bunk and stared at the stone ceiling. Fifteen months. I'll make it, he told himself. There's no way they can break me. But it's going to be hard without Joe.

Three days after Joe's release, Archer was assigned a new cellmate, a meek-looking bookkeeper who had embezzled fifteen thousand dollars from one of his clients. This dolorous little man, named Simmonds, wept himself to sleep every night after mumbling prayers to his wife and three daughters, none of which was calculated to cheer up Archer.

The routine of the prison day varied only on Sunday, when a one-hour chapel service at least broke the monotony. There Sergeant Woolridge, known throughout the prison for taking bribes, donned the robes of hypocrisy, read interminably from the Bible, and played hymns on the organ—which was more than a bit peculiar, since the rule of silence forbade the convicts from singing. The six other days of the week were as inflexible as sidereal time: wake-up at six, breakfast at six-thirty. Then the silent lockstep marches to the various workshops, where from seven till noon Archer toiled in the steamy prison laundry. Noon to one, silent lunch. One to two, silent exercise in the prison yards. Two to six, more work. Seven, silent supper. Lights out at eight. Prisoners were shaved and bathed three times a week, no personal razors being allowed, and they were issued clean uniforms and linen twice a month.

Archer was involved in the latter function, and one day as he churned prison uniforms in a big vat of lye, he saw Sergeant Woolridge and two other guards enter the laundry and head his way.

"Four-one-six-two," Woolridge barked, "you're wanted in the warden's office. Manacle him."

To Archer's surprise, a guard grabbed his wrists and clamped a steel bar on them. He wanted to cry out, "What's happening?" but the training of a year and a half forced him to hold his tongue. He was marched out of the laundry through the endless corridors to the warden's office. There, the guards halted him in front of the warden's desk. Simmonds was standing in the corner of the office, shaking violently. His right wrist was bandaged.

"Collingwood," Ridley said, removing his pince-nez. "Simmonds claims you attacked him with a knife." Archer's eyes widened. The warden held up a crude-looking knife. "Sergeant Woolridge found this under your mattress. Did you make it in the laundry? You may speak."

"No, sir. And this is a damned lie."

"Are you accusing Sergeant Woolridge of a falsehood?"

"Yes, sir."

"Simmonds, is it true Collingwood attacked you in your cell? You may speak."

"Yes, sir," Simmonds said from the corner.

"You lie!" Archer yelled. "I did no such thing."

"Silence! I have not given you permission to speak! Collingwood, you are a dangerous troublemaker. Your good time is hereby canceled, and you can forget any hope of parole. Furthermore, I have discussed your case with the Department of Correction. They agree with my recommendation and have added an additional five years to your term."

"No . . . !"

"Silence! You will serve a full term of ten years with no hope of parole. And for breaking the rule of silence, you can begin the rest of your sentence with one month in solitary confinement. Take him away."

He almost vomited as the two guards grabbed his arms. The reality of what had just happened sank in: his dream of early release, the goal he had slaved for, the only thing he was living for, had suddenly been wrenched from him.

"It's a lie!" he yelled. "You set this up—you and Woolridge! You made a deal with Simmonds—"

"Two months solitary!" Ridley yelled, standing up. "Get him out of my office!"

"It's a lie!" he screamed, wrestling with the guards.

"Three months—"

"I'm innocent—"

"Four months! Four months' solitary confinement, and by God, if you say one more word, I'll give you a year!"

Archer stared at him as a grinning Sergeant Woolridge plowed his fist into his stomach, then smashed his billy club over his head.

He awoke in a beautiful gold-and-white corridor. Fog swirled up from an invisible floor. The corridor was lined with open windows through which a breeze was blowing, fluttering white gauze curtains. He seemed to be floating down the room toward a distant door. From somewhere an orchestra was playing a soft waltz.

As he neared the door, the music grew louder. The curtains wrapped themselves around him, caressing him. The door slowly opened, and he saw Emma standing in it, as beautiful as a dream.

He stretched out his arms, aching for her. She was wearing a beautiful silver gown. Now she opened her arms. Just as he was about to embrace her, he fell into a whirlpool of black water. Around and around he was swept, ever sinking, trying to claw at something to save him from drowning. He heard laughter now, the laughter of Sergeant Woolridge. He saw the face of Warden Ridley flash by him in the black vortex, then meek little Simmonds. They were both laughing too. He sank farther and farther into the whirlpool, becoming wetter and wetter . . .

He woke up in the pen. Blackness. Totally naked, he was lying on his side on the stone floor. The wetness was the sweat seeping from his body, for the solitary-confinement cell, known as a "pen," was searingly hot. His head ached from the blow of the billy club. As he started to sit up, the ache stabbed his brain. Memories of the month he had spent in the same stinking cell assaulted him: the horror of the loneliness, of the claustrophobia, the silence, the loss of knowing day from night . . .

Four months. The memory hit him like Woolridge's club.

"I can't," he whispered.

Ten years. No parole.

"I can't. I won't."

He started crawling on all fours around the tiny cell, which was too low for him to stand in, only crouch like an animal in a cage. His eyes became aware of the pinpoints of light from the air holes in the steel door. He reached out his right hand and touched the door. The steel was hot.

Four months. Ten years. No parole. No good time.

"I won't!" he cried out, banging his fists on the steel. "To hell with all of you! I won't eat! I'll die! I don't care anymore. Life's not worth living like this . . ."

He lowered himself back onto the floor, burying his face in his arms as he started sobbing.

Emma.

He heard the waltz music again, faintly, in the distance. Now he was waltzing with Emma through clouds of mist. She was so beautiful, her amethyst eyes so warm and loving. Emma.

The darkness and heat of the pen.

Waltzing to romantic music.

He didn't know where he was anymore. He didn't care. He wanted to die and go to heaven and be with Emma.

Emma was heaven.

21

JOE Thunder thought of himself as an Indian only in the sense that a Swede or Italian thought of himself as a European. Joe was a member of the Shawnee tribe, or Sha-wa-no, as he pronounced it, one of the tribes of the Algonquin Nation like the Kickapoo, Potawatomic, and the mighty Chippewa. His native language was a dialect of Algonquian, but he thought of himself as a Shawnee. His grandfather had fought a half-century before with the legendary Shawnee Chief Tecumsch, who had formed a confederacy of midwestern and southern tribes to protect their lands—what would become the states of Ohio, Indiana, and Kentucky—from the invading white men. Tecumseh had been as great a warrior as his brother Ten-squa-ta-way had been a great medicine man. But Tecumseh was doomed, like all the two hundred and fifty tribes populating the North American continent. He sided with the British in the War of 1812, figuring they were natural allies against the white Americans, but he was killed in battle.

He didn't know it, but his cause was already lost. In the year of his death, the Sauk and the Fox were fleeing west across the Great Water, the Mississippi, as the whites poured into the Midwest. During his career as a soldier, Andrew Jackson, known to the Indians with some justification as Sharp Knife, had caused thousands of Cherokee, Choctaw, Creek, and Seminole to be slaughtered. But when he became president, Sharp Knife passed a law declaring that all land west of the Mississippi would be Indian country. Most of the northern tribes—the Shawnee, Miami, Ottawa, Huron, and Delaware—were rounded up and moved west, taking their few belongings with them. But already white men were pouring across the Mississippi, and the discovery of gold in California made a farce of the law. Thousands of forty-niners thronged into the new home of the Indians, not giving a damn for their fate. The once-proud Shawnee tribe was reduced by disease, displacement, violent death, and drunkenness to fewer than twelve hundred. Where once they had roamed the rich valleys and plains of Ohio in harmony with nature, now even their burial mounds were desecrated.

Joe Thunder was one of the few Shawnee left in Ohio, and he and

his Shawnee "buddies," a newly popular word, were sinking into al-
coholism, the curse of the red man. Before his imprisonment, Joe had
worked as a dishwasher in a sleazy Columbus hotel and hung out at
night at Columbus' seediest bar, the Railroad Saloon. After his release
from the penitentiary, Joe found out that Pink Dawn had died of consumption, that he could get no work at all as an Indian ex-con, and
that his only living relation, his uncle, had disappeared, probably to
the West.

It was not long before Joe returned to the Railroad Saloon. He
favored it not only because the owner, a kindly former slave named
Tucker who had been manumitted by his Kentucky master, extended
him credit, but also because Indians, like blacks, had no other place
to go. Bars, restaurants, libraries, hotels, and theaters were for whites
only.

"News about Archer," Tucker said one morning as he poured Joe
his first drink of the day. "And it ain't good."

"Yeah? What?"

"He was put in solitary for four months and given another five
years on his sentence. They say he attacked his cellmate with a knife."

A look of fury came into Joe's eyes. "That big lie! Archer a gentle
man, he no attack nobody!"

"The word is that a one-eyed man from California paid off the
warden."

Joe started to pick up his glass of rotgut. Then he set it down again.
Today he would not get drunk. "I gotta save Archer," he muttered.

"Brothers, the white man has piled shit on our people," he said
in Algonquian that night, "but this doesn't mean all white men are bad.
I grew to know and love my cellmate, Archer, and I would give my
life for him."

"Why?" Charlie Red Cloud asked as he poured a mug of coffee
from a beat-up tin pot. He and three other Shawnees were sitting around
the wooden table in Charlie's one-room shack in a squatters' town on
the outskirts of Columbus. Charlie, Joe's best Shawnee friend, had lent
him fifty dollars, which was what he was living on. Charlie and Tom
Lone Wolf, both in their twenties, were the only men present who had
jobs.

"Because Archer taught me to play by the prison rules," Joe Thunder said, "which is why I'm out. But Archer has been rattlesnaked by
the warden. That white boy is young and tough, but no one can live
four months in solitary—I know because I spent one month and about
went crazy. So I'm going to get him out, and I need your help. Will
you help me?"

Charlie Red Cloud put the coffeepot back on the stove. "How can we get anyone out of the penitentiary? No one's ever escaped, and there's seventy guards in there, all armed."

"I know that damned prison like the back of my hand, and there's a way to get him out. Believe me, I've got it all planned. But I need your help."

The four Shawnee exchanged looks. Normally by this late in the evening they all would have been drunk, but Joe had insisted on the coffee until they heard him out.

"I don't know," said Tom Lone Wolf, whose Indian name was Guipago. "You may have the best plan in the world, but it still sounds dangerous to me."

"Sure, it's dangerous. All our grandfathers fought with Tecumseh and that was dangerous."

"Yeah, and they lost," said White Horse, another of the four.

"Why should I risk my neck for a white boy?" asked Kicking Bird, the fourth.

"Because," Joe said, "the white man isn't afraid of us anymore. He thinks he's beaten us."

"Maybe he has," White Horse interrupted.

"He has if we think he has!" Joe Thunder shouted. "He's taken everything from us. Sure, I played the white man's rules inside prison to survive, but outside prison, even if we play his rules, we lose. Look how many tribes have disappeared: the Pequot, the Narragansett, the Mohican—we're disappearing. The white man hates nature. Look how he's turning our beautiful land into dirty factories and dumps. We've been here thousands of years and never hurt the land. The white man's been here a hundred years and is making it ugly. He tells us to go west, the west is ours   we go west, and what happens? The white man comes and tells us to go farther west. What happens when we get to the great western sea? Do we jump in and drown? I'm telling you, our only hope is to make the white man fear us again, and a first step is to attack his great ugly prison and free one of his own right from under his damn nose. We'll make the white men look like fools. And maybe our brothers all over the country will hear how five Shawnee braves invaded the Ohio Penitentiary, and maybe they'll start feeling proud again. Maybe they'll even start fighting back."

His words had an electrifying effect.

"Yeah, maybe you're right, Joe," White Horse said. "Maybe it's time we fight back. Kick the bastard white man in the balls, go on the warpath again."

"Yeah, I like it," Tom Lone Wolf said. "What's your plan?"

"First, we need guns."

22

AT four that morning, five Shawnee galloped down a moonlit road past woods and log-cabin farmhouses into the sleepy hamlet of Bexley, which consisted of a dirt street two blocks long lined with dark wooden stores. The Indians had dressed in their native deerskin and put on their traditional war paint. Now they dismounted and advanced on a store whose window proclaimed "McGurdy's Hunting Emporium." Joe Thunder smashed the window with a rock. The Shawnee reached through, grabbed the hunting rifles on display and four boxes of ammunition, then remounted and rode off again into the night.

The great iron gates of the penitentiary swung slowly inward, and the white wagon with "H. Normamby & Sons, Purveyors of Fine Meat" painted on its sides rumbled into the prison yard and stopped. Two guards greeted the driver, Lex Turner, then went to the rear and opened the doors. It was a hot morning, but the immense slabs of ice in the wagon sent out a blast of chill. The guards gave a peremptory look at the sides of meat hanging from hooks over the ice, then reclosed the doors.

"Okay, Lex," one of them said. As the four-horse wagon rattled into motion, heading for the kitchen wing, the guards reshut the gates, not giving the wagon another thought. After all, the meat wagon arrived twice a week, every week. Two hawks circled lazily in the hot blue sky above the crenellated stone walls. In the eight guard towers sixteen guards surveyed the prison with "Mississippi" .54-caliber rifles. Dating from 1841, these rifles, which had been used extensively during the Mexican War, were already obsolete. The Sharps .52-caliber carbines the Shawnee had stolen four hours previously were, ironically, more up-to-date, their patents being brand new.

The meat wagon pulled up to the supply doors next to the kitchen. Two prisoners opened the rear doors and stared at a most improbable sight: four rifles held in their faces by four Shawnee braves covered with war paint. The prisoners backed into the kitchen as the Indians piled silently out of the wagon. Kicking Bird remained behind, pointing his rifle through a small window in the front panel at Lex Turner's head. Having hidden crouched behind the blocks of ice, the Shawnee were still trembling from the chill, but the heat of the kitchen quickly corrected that.

Joe Thunder, who had washed dishes here for three years, knew that the policy of convict silence would work in their favor. Moving like clockwork, White Horse and Tom Lone Wolf covered the only guard and the frightened prison comptroller as Charlie Red Cloud and Joe Thunder ran down the steps to the basement. Joe counted on the element of surprise: he knew the prison was designed to prevent inmates getting out. The authorities had never envisioned someone coming in.

The two Shawnee ran silently down the basement corridor to the guards' lounge, which had lockers for their uniforms. Joe Thunder knew that Sergeant Woolridge would be there alone, because each time a shipment of meat arrived in the prison, five percent of the best cuts were brought to the basement by the comptroller to be distributed to the guards through Woolridge, their representative—this was one of the many illicit perks that had sprung up over the years. Joe Thunder also knew that Woolridge had the keys to the solitary-confinement pens.

Woolridge, his blue tunic unbuttoned at the neck, was sitting on a sofa reading the newspaper and drinking coffee when he looked up to see the two Shawnee pointing their rifles at his head.

"You make one noise," Joe Thunder whispered, "and your skull's gonna be on other side of the moon. Nod yes if you understand."

Woolridge nodded yes. There was no one else in the lounge, for the biweekly meetings with the comptroller were a strict secret.

"Give me the key to Archer's pen," Joe said.

Woolridge shakily pulled a key chain from his pants. He trembled so much with fear that he had difficulty selecting one. Finally he held it up.

"Which key opens solitary corridor?"

He held up another. Joe grabbed the keys.

"You come with us, you pockmarked bastard," Joe whispered, jerking Woolridge to his feet. "And remember: now *you* under rule of silence."

He and Charlie Red Cloud shoved Woolridge toward the door. So far everything had gone smoothly, but now Joe knew he needed some luck. He had to get from the basement beneath the kitchen wing to the basement under Cellblock A, where the solitary cells were, without being seen. The basements usually were deserted, but he couldn't count on it. As the three men hurried down the long stone corridor, Joe's heart pounded with fear, but also with exhilaration. They were in fact making the white men look like fools.

Luck was still with them. They reached the barred entrance to the solitary-confinement cells without encountering anyone. Joe quickly unlocked the gate and pushed Woolridge through into the gloomy, smelly corridor lined on one side with the low steel doors to the pens.

"Where's Archer?" Joe whispered.

Woolridge pointed at one of the doors. Joe ran to it, unlocked it, and flung it open.

"Archer, it's Joe. Come out. Hurry!" He turned to Woolridge. "Take your uniform off."

The guard started to say something, but Charlie Red Cloud jammed the muzzle of his rifle into his neck. "Do what he says, white man."

With quivering fingers Woolridge started unbuttoning his tunic.

"Archer, where the hell are you? We're gettin' you outta this hole."

Archer, his eyes shut against the light, crawled out on his hands and knees.

"Give him your uniform," Joe said to Woolridge, "then you crawl in the fuckin' pen."

Woolridge, in his underwear, gasped. Joe was helping Archer to his feet. Now he grabbed Woolridge's uniform and thrust it into Archer's arms.

"Get these clothes on, fast."

Charlie Red Cloud pushed Woolridge to the floor, then kicked him hard in the behind. "Get in, white man. You got to the count of three or we throw keys in the river."

Woolridge scurried inside the pen. Charlie Red Cloud slammed the door shut and locked it. Archer, his eyes still squinting, was pulling on Woolridge's trousers.

"There's two others," he whispered. "Three and five."

"Shit, Archer, we can't free whole goddamn prison," Joe said, running to cell five and unlocking it. He opened the door and threw the keys in. "Free yourselves!" he whispered into the black, stinking hole. Then, motioning to Archer and Charlie Red Cloud, he ran back down the corridor to the barred gate. Archer, unable to believe his luck as he put on Woolridge's tunic, stumbled after him. Freedom!

"God bless you, Joe Thunder," he whispered.

"Forget the fuckin' blessings till later. We ain't out yet. Hurry!"

"Wonder what's taking so long with the meat wagon?" asked guard Pete Wainwright as he leaned on the parapet of East Tower A overlooking the prison yard. Twenty-five feet below, H. Normamby & Sons' white wagon was still backed up to the kitchen supply doors. One of the horses snorted in the heat.

"Maybe there ain't enough maggots in the beef," the second guard said, waving away a fly.

"Aw, come on. The meat ain't bad. My wife says it's as good as the stuff she buys in town, and what the hell, it's free."

"Yeah, the stuff they give us ain't bad. What they leave for the cons I wouldn't feed to a dog—there they go."

The two guards watched the wagon start up, heading across the outer prison yard toward the gates. The two gate guards came out of their house and walked toward the gates to open them.

The hawks continued circling in the cloudless sky.

Guard Armand Whitney, coming into the kitchen for a doughnut, found the huge room empty. "Hello?" He looked around. In three years at the prison, he had never seen the kitchen empty. Then he heard a muffled thumping on the big wooden doors to the walk-in ice room. Hurrying around the coal stoves, he opened the doors. Mr. Leverett, the comptroller, stumbled out.

"Sound the alarm! Stop the meat truck! Indians!"

"Indians?"

The kitchen guard was running across the room to ring the alarm bell.

"Indians!" Leverett shouted. "They took the whole damn kitchen staff with 'em!"

Grabbing the chain, the guard started clanging the bell.

"Jesus Christ, Indians?"

In the meat wagon, the seven kitchen convicts, Archer, and the Indians heard the alarm bell. Kicking Bird, crouched by the front panel, yelled through the small window to the driver: "Get through that gate or you're dead, white man."

Lex Turner, who had been shaking in a state of terror since seven that morning when the Shawnee confiscated his wagon at gunpoint, whipped his horses. They started galloping toward the gates. The steam siren was shrilling, signaling an escape.

On East Tower A, Pete Wainwright aimed his "Mississippi" rifle at the speeding wagon below and fired. His companion guard also opened fire.

"Try for the horses!" Wainwright yelled.

The two gate guards began pushing the mammoth gates shut as the meat wagon barreled toward them. All the guard towers began firing as the guards, confronted by the first mass escape in the prison's history, snapped out of their boredom.

Lex Turner, sweat pouring down his face, prayed to God as he whipped his horses harder, waiting for one of the bullets to kill him. The big gates were halfway closed. He heard gunfire from his wagon as the Indians fired back at the guard towers from the rear doors.

The meat wagon roared through the tall gates.

"We made it!" Joe Thunder yelled. "God damn, we made it!"

The Shawnee, Archer, and the convicts were yelling and hugging each other as the wagon continued careening down the prison road.

"California!" Joe Thunder cried as the high, grim walls receded in the distance. "Archer, we go to California, forget all this shit!"

"California!" Archer whooped. "You bet your ass we're going to California!"

Emma! he thought. He had been so close to death, and now his most cherished dream was miraculously coming true. He was free— free! He was laughing and crying as he hugged Joe Thunder.

"You know, when I first saw you, you scared the shit out of me," he said. "But right now, you're looking mighty like an angel."

Joe Thunder laughed. "An angel in war paint."

The wagonload of convicts and Indians went wild all over again as Lex Turner whipped his horses, heading, as per instructions, for the open countryside and the West.

23

THE knife inched across the white wrist, the blade just nicking the skin, causing blood to ooze.

"We be blood brothers now," Joe Thunder said as he put his own cut wrist against Archer's. "Your blood and mine mix. We protect each other always. You become part Shawnee, I become part white man—but just a little part."

The two were squatting beside a low-burning fire in a pine forest in western Ohio. They had abandoned the meat wagon outside Columbus and taken their own horses, leaving the other escaped convicts to scatter and fend for themselves. The other Shawnee had decided to go west with Archer and Joe Thunder, if not as far as California, at least across the Mississippi. As Charlie Red Cloud had said, "We sure as hell got no future in Columbus, Ohio."

Now Charlie stomped out the fire. "We sleep now," he said. "But only a few hours. We have to keep movin'. Every pig in America is gonna be after us."

The slang expression for policeman he used had become current in the past decade.

"Let 'em come," Joe Thunder said as he lay on the needles beneath a white pine, looking up through its boughs at the panoply of stars. "They'll never catch us now. We're free." He pointed at Archer. "Little Brother, you part Shawnee now. Tomorrow we'll kill a deer and make you a Shawnee suit. We'll turn you into a real brave."

Kicking Bird laughed. "A brave with white hair."

"Then we teach you ways of the forest and birch trees, how to make a canoe like the Chippewa. We teach you how to live off land and run fast as the hare. We teach you how to be smart and tricky like Glooscap."

"Like who?" Archer asked, sitting against a tree holding a piece of cloth to his bleeding wrist.

"Glooscap was first man on earth," Joe Thunder said. "Great Spirit gave Glooscap whole world, because he had conquered Kewawkqu', a race of giants and magicians, and the Medecolin, who was wicked sorcerers."

"Don't forget Pamola." White Horse yawned.

"Oh, sure. Pamola wicked spirit of the night. Glooscap kill her too, and lots of evil spirits and demons. So Glooscap is first man and great hero. But Great Spirit tell him there is one who still remains unconquered, and his name is Wasis."

"Was Wasis evil?" Archer asked.

The Indians laughed.

"Wasis was a little baby," Joe Thunder said. "But Glooscap had never seen a baby. So he go into tepee and there is Wasis, and he tell Wasis to move. But Wasis just smile and don't do nothing except suck his maple sugar. This gets Glooscap real mad because he first man and big hero and he used to people jumpin' when he say jump. He make so much noise, poor Wasis start crying and drown Glooscap out. Now Glooscap himself start cryin' and run out of tepee because little baby Wasis had conquered him. And so, that how world began. And every time you hear a baby go 'goo goo,' he reminding world how first baby defeated mighty hero Glooscap."

"I like that story," Archer said, smiling. "That's better than Adam and Eve any day."

"Oh, Indians got lots of stories." Joe Thunder yawned. "We been here thousands of years and Great Spirit tell us all secrets of nature. You'll like being an Indian, you'll see. Beats hell out of being a white man."

A moment later, he was snoring. Archer looked up at the stars and thought that maybe Joe Thunder was right. He liked being an Indian.

He felt reborn.

"Sergeant Woolridge," Warden Ridley said, "I have talked to the governor. He has agreed to your request. You are now appointed in charge of a posse to track down the escaped convict Collingwood, the Indian Joe Thunder, and the other unknown Indians."

Woolridge was standing at attention in front of the warden's desk. His lunar-landscape face was grim. "My informants tell me one is named Charlie Red Cloud, sir," he said. "He worked as a janitor in the high school."

"Well, they're all savages and none of them has a decent Christian name. I've been authorized to give you three thousand dollars' expense money, and here's a letter of credit for ten thousand more. The governor is as determined as I to capture these men and bring them to justice. If the red man gets the notion that he can make a mockery of the white legal system, there'll be hell to pay."

"If I may say so, sir, when they're caught, they should be made an example to the whole prison system."

"The governor has already agreed to life sentences."

"In my opinion, sir, that's not enough. Collingwood and the Indian should hang."

"Well, you may be right. But the first job is to catch them. God-speed, Woolridge. And I might add that if you succeed, there'll be a handsome promotion in it for you."

"Thank you, sir. But I'm not volunteering for any promotion. I'm a God-fearing, Bible-reading Christian, and my greatest reward will be to watch Collingwood and that heathen Indian drop through the trap-door of the gallows and twitch in the wind."

"May I say I share your Christian sentiment one hundred percent."

"What a crazy laugh," Joe Thunder said as he, Archer, and Charlie Red Cloud sat on their horses overlooking the meadow in which a small wagon train was preparing to move west. They were on the outskirts of Independence, Missouri, the launching point for most of the wagon trains onto the Great Plains. "This is all supposed to be Indian country, but the only Indians here is me and Charlie."

"And me," Archer said, who was wearing the deerskin suit Charlie and Kicking Bird had sewn for him back in Ohio ten days before.

"That right, Little Brother," Joe said, grinning. "I forgot about you. You not much Indian, but you some." He turned to Charlie. "You change your mind?"

"No. Too much cholera on the plains. Why should I die of a white man's disease? Besides, it's too late to start. Most wagons left five weeks ago on first May. You won't make it through the white mountains of the west."

"We'll make it," Joe said. "These white families carry all their junk, they go slow. Little Brother and I will fly like the eagle to California because we carry nothing except our brains."

"Then may the Great Spirit go with you, Joe."

They clasped each other's forearms.

"Good-bye, brother. When I get some money, I'll pay you back what you loaned me."

"Good-bye, Charlie," Archer said, leaning over to shake his hand. "I owe you my life. I'll never forget it."

Charlie grinned. "It was fun. We covered the white pigs with shit. I hope Great White Father back in Washington hears about our prison escape. Maybe he get scared, say to all white men, 'Hey, let's go back to Europe, give this stinkin' country back to the Indians.'"

They laughed. Then Charlie turned his horse and headed back to Independence.

"Let's go, Little Brother," Joe cried, digging his heels into his horse's flanks. The two galloped down into the meadow, which was strewn with litter left by the thousands and thousands of gold seekers of the past three years. It had been as curious a mixture as the world had ever seen: thieves, confidence men, upper-class English remittance men sent to the wilderness by exasperated parents; doctors, lawyers, merchants, workingmen, farmers; Whigs, Democrats, Know-Nothings, Abolitionists; Baptists, Transcendentalists, Mormons; white men, black men, Germans, Russians, Poles, and Frenchmen fleeing the European revolutions as the de Meyers had done . . . the lame, squint-eyed, pockmarked, bearded, beardless, the witty and the witless with their pet cats, canaries, dogs, their banjos, fiddles, accordions, pots, pans, dishes, family silver, family Bibles, what furniture they could carry, books, chamber pots, knickknacks, clothes, bonnets, shoes and shirts— all dreaming of California gold, if not the actual metal, the gold of the wonderful climate and rich earth, stories of which had drifted back east, transforming into legends.

A boy named Mark Crawford was one of the Wheeler Party, the name given to the eight-wagon train beginning its long journey west that hot June day. As Mark saw the two men galloping past his wagon, he pointed to one of them and said to his mother: "Look, Ma! A blond Indian!"

His mother looked at Archer, then climbed up onto her wagon. "My stars," she said, "a blond Indian! What'll they think of next?"

"A blond Indian?" Sergeant Woolridge asked the next day. "It must be Collingwood."

He and his ten-man posse had come to Independence on the assumption that Archer and the Shawnee would go west. Simmonds, Archer's cellmate, had told Woolridge that Archer had talked of his dream of going to California. Woolridge and his men hadn't been in Independence twenty minutes before they heard stories of the blond Indian.

"Did they go to California?" he asked the bartender in the Gold Rush Saloon.

"Well, I think two of them did. I hear the others got jobs in town. One of them's working at Brady's sawmill down the street."

Woolridge gave him a dollar. "Thanks for the help."

He started out, saying to the others, "Come on. Before the sun sets, those Indians are going to wish they'd never been born."

At five that afternoon, Charlie Red Cloud was offered a prayer from the Bible by Woolridge. Charlie Red Cloud spat on the Bible. "To hell with your white god," he said. "And to hell with your white justice. Where's our trial?"

Woolridge pulled a kerchief from his pocket and cleaned the spittle off his small black Bible, given to him by his mother when he was six. "You had your trial in my head," he said, leering with hatred. Then he raised his hand and waved the kerchief.

Charlie Red Cloud, Tom Lone Wolf, Kicking Bird, and White Horse had been rounded up and taken to a bluff overlooking the Missouri River. There, their hands had been tied behind their backs and four nooses tied around their necks. The four ropes were swung over the branches of a big oak and the other ends tied to the saddles of four horses. Now members of the posse took the horses' bridles and began walking them away from the tree.

Slowly.

The four Shawnee were slowly raised into the air by their necks. As they kicked and jerked, they were slowly strangled. Only Kicking Bird, who was the heaviest, was granted the luxury of a broken neck and quick oblivion.

The strongest Shawnee, Charlie Red Cloud, took seven minutes to die.

Sergeant Woolridge, who was timing it with his gold pocket watch, said, "Those are seven minutes he'll be talking about for a long time in hell, or wherever dead Indians go. Cut 'em down."

His men, hired guns and drifters whom he had easily recruited with the handsome hundred-dollar-a-week salary, went about the gruesome task of cutting down the four dead Shawnee. Woolridge sat under the oak tree and began reading from his Bible.

"Excuse me, sir," said one of the posse, a huge bearded man named Ezra Surtees who came up to Woolridge and knelt beside him. "I just wanted to tell you how much I admire your reading the Good Book at a time like this, which seems especially appropriate." He indicated the corpses of the Indians being piled in a cart. "As I mentioned once to you, sir, I'm a Mormon."

"Yes, I remember," Woolridge said, looking up from his Bible.

"Since you're obviously a God-fearing man, sir, I think it would be in your interest to hear something about the great Mormon Church. Especially since in our pursuit of these two outlaws, we may end up in the Mormon Empire out Utah way. Help from the Mormons could come in mighty handy. I'd sure be glad to fellowship with you about the Mormons, sir."

A look of interest came into Woolridge's eyes. "I'd be glad to listen, Surtees."

24

ALL through the summer, Woolridge and his posse chased Archer and Joe Thunder across the continental United States. The fugitives followed the basic route of the wagon trains: leaving the Missouri River, they headed into the Nebraska Territory and followed the south bank of the Platte River west to the Sweetwater River in Wyoming, thence to the South Pass. Woolridge followed them, guided not only by the trail of litter, garbage, and graves that three years of gold seekers had left behind them on their way west, trashing the Great Plains, but also by stories they heard about the blond Indian from members of the wagon trains they overtook. Archer and Joe had been spotted frequently, and stories of the two were building into legends. The blond Indian had been seen killing a buffalo at a hundred yards—with a bow and arrow. It was said that he had become a great hunter and could outrun the wind. It was said that the Shawnee had taught him how to live off the land and speak with the Great Spirit.

Woolridge took all this with a grain of salt, for it was obvious the members of the wagon trains, bored to distraction by their slow trek to California, had used their imaginations to turn the blond Indian into some sort of superhero with the same American love of exaggeration that could turn the admittedly murderous mosquitoes of the Great Plains into turkeys or buzzards. But whatever the reality behind the hyperbole, Woolridge had to admit that Archer Collingwood had caught the imagination of the pioneers.

But if Woolridge greeted the blond-Indian legend with skepticism, he swallowed hook, line, and sinker the story of the Mormon Church, which, in terms of flights of fancy, made shooting a buffalo at a hundred yards seem like child's play. As described breathlessly by Ezra Surtees, the Mormon religion had been founded some twenty years earlier by a young man from Vermont named Joseph Smith, Jr. Joe was the son of a farmer turned flimflam man whose specialty was finding buried treasure, including Captain Kidd's pirate gold. Of course, he never found anything, but Joe, sensing a good thing in buried treasure, bought himself a "stone," or crystal ball, and convinced a farmer in upstate

New York that he could find a lost Spanish silver mine on his land. Unhappily, Joe was arrested for being an impostor.

America was experiencing an epidemic of religious fervor, and Joe decided to turn his talents to the potentially more profitable field of religion. He announced he had a vision in which he was visited by an angel named Moroni, who told him he would lead him to an unknown Bible, written twelve centuries before on plates of gold. The angel said this new kind of buried treasure had been placed with two "stones," or "spectacles," called the Urim and the Thimmin, which would enable Joe to translate the everlasting Gospel as revealed by the Savior himself on a surprise visit to upper New York State in the seventh century. Joe claimed he dug up the Bible, translated it with the Urim and the Thimmin, and published all this in 1830 as *The Book of Mormon*. Despite the fact that the plates of gold and the Urim and Thimmin were never seen by anyone except Joe Smith, Jr., *The Book of Mormon* became a huge best-seller.

"I'll loan you my copy," Ezra said to wide-eyed Woolridge. "You read it and you'll be inspired. It will change your life."

"I can hardly wait," Woolridge said truthfully. The organ-playing, Bible-reading prison guard had a passion for religion. He read *The Book of Mormon* and became converted.

He too began dreaming of the angel Moroni.

"Hear that?" Joe Thunder whispered as he and Archer lay on their stomachs in the tall Nebraska grass. Ten feet ahead of them, a herd of buffalo were grazing. Archer strained to listen.

"I don't hear anything, Joe."

A look of disgust came over the Indian's face. "You still too much white man. The animals is talking to each other. You hear little click sounds?"

Again Archer listened. "No."

Joe sighed. "You hopeless."

"I'm trying."

Joe and Archer were racing their horses across the prairie. Joe's horse, Tecumseh, was a magnificent animal and Joe was a magnificent horseman. Archer had never raced in his life, but he was learning. The two galloped furiously toward a tree. Joe Thunder got there first, but Archer was a close second.

As they reined their horses, Joe grinned back at the blond Indian. "You getting pretty good, Little Brother," he puffed. "You almost beat me. Maybe there's hope for you yet. Maybe you become Indian someday."

Archer, who was panting so hard he almost fell off his horse, liked that. He was having the time of his life. After the horrors of the penitentiary, the freedom of the great prairies, with the mountains ahead towering into the arching blue sky, was like wine.

Archer squatted ankle-deep along the shore of the muddy Platte River, holding a stick he had sharpened with his knife. He remained frozen until a fat fish wriggled lazily toward him. As it passed between his feet, he struck, piercing the fish with his stick.

"Hey, Joe," he yelled, holding the wriggling fish in the air. "I did it! Here's supper!"

Joe, standing on the shore, nodded. "Pretty good, Little Brother. I'm impressed. I think it time to give you Indian name. I name you An-no-je-naje."

"What does that mean?"

" 'He Who Stands on Both Sides.' You on both sides: Shawnee and white man."

"Yeah, I like that."

He waded back to shore and began cleaning the fish. Joe watched him for a while before he said, "Tell me something, An-no-je-naje. You say you go to jail because you rob bank. Reason that you rob bank is that bank take your farm. Right?"

"Right."

"And you thought you was doing correct thing?"

"Absolutely. The law didn't see it my way, though." He shrugged.

"Yeah, you kind of idealistic person, I think," Joe went on. "You want to do right thing for all people. That why I don't understand why you so wrong."

Archer looked up from his fish. "Huh?"

"You don't own your farm, any more than the bank own farm. How can anyone own land? Land belong to everyone, like the sky and sun and stars. We Indians been here thousands of years, we never own anything. We just use land. That one thing I never understand about you, Little Brother. How you could think you own forty acres which was made by Great Spirit for everybody."

The idea struck Archer as so odd that he just stared at his Indian friend.

Two mornings later, they were sitting on their horses on a bluff overlooking a wagon train when the lookouts below spotted them and began firing.

"Let's go," Joe said, abruptly turning his horse and kicking it to a gallop. Archer followed him, burning with embarrassment at the hostility of his fellow whites. He might be He Who Stands on Both Sides, learning the ways of the Indian, but he knew he would never be an Indian. Still, he was witnessing the great drama of the taming of the West from the Indian viewpoint. During his childhood on the Ohio farm, the Indians had always been the enemy, looked down on as inferior, dangerous heathens. Now Archer was beginning to wonder if the Indian way of life were not infinitely better than the white man's. The nomadic idea of nonownership had stunned him. It was so totally alien to the white man's way, and yet it struck Archer as having a certain beauty to it that was lacking in the white man's world. He was not so idealistic as to think the white man could ever be converted to the Indian way of life, but he was seeing firsthand the injustice being done to the Indians and he yearned to do something to correct that injustice. But he didn't have the faintest idea what that something might be.

There were tears of rage in his eyes as he galloped away from the wagon train. The shots of the rifles grew ever fainter, but they were no less full of hatred.

"Woolridge hang four Shawnee back in Independence," said Half Moon, the Paiute brave, to Joe Thunder. "They named Charlie Red Cloud, White Horse, Tom Lone Wolf, and Kicking Bird. They get no trial, nothing. You know these men?"

Joe closed his eyes a moment. "Yes," he said, turning to Archer. The three mounted men were stopped along the Sweetwater River in southern Wyoming. "Hanged with no trial," Joe repeated. "White man justice. Woolridge pay for this."

"He's a butcher," Archer said, remembering the glee in the prison guard's eyes when Warden Ridley condemned him to four months' solitary.

"Woolridge is hunting you two," Half Moon continued. "He and his men not five mile from here. They stay last night with the Pemberton wagon train. That why I seek you out, brother. The Pemberton guide is old hunting friend of mine, a French trapper name Girard. He ask me if I know blond Indian and his friend, tell me about Shawnee, and that you in danger. This Woolridge real crazy man. He hire Girard away from Pemberton to guide his posse through mountains. Girard tell me Woolridge become a Mormon, and that bad for you, 'cause you about to enter Mormon Empire." He pointed to the southwest.

"What's a Mormon?" Joe asked.

"It's a new religion," Archer said. "I know all about them, because one of my cousins back in Ohio lost all his money in a Mormon bank that failed. The prophet, Joseph Smith, Jr., was murdered in a jail in

Illinois about eight years ago. The new prophet's a man named Brigham Young."

"He bad man, even for a white man," Half Moon said. "He want start his own Mormon country, claim God give him Utah Territory. Great White Father in Washington say to hell with that, Utah belong to him. 'Course, Utah belong to us, but nobody give a damn about us."

"They say Brigham Young's got seventeen wives," Archer said. "You can have as many wives as you want, which may be why the religion's so popular."

"Maybe that what this Woolridge want. He become a Mormon," Half Moon said. "He tell everybody he dream of seein' an angel named Moroni. He sound crazy to me. But Girard say, 'Tell your friends to run, 'cause Woolridge mean to kill them like he kill the Shawnee.' "

"We kill him first," Joe Thunder pronounced softly. "We pay back for death of Charlie Red Cloud and my brothers."

"There's ten of them. Won't be easy."

"How far are the Sierra Nevada Mountains?" Archer asked.

"About a month," Half Moon said. "You have to cross the great salt desert after great salt sea. That where prophet live with his many squaws."

Archer looked west at the mountains of the Utah Territory. It was already mid-September. "I've got an idea," he said quietly. "We're going to be as clever as Glooscap. Would this Girard help us?"

"He old friend," Half Moon said. "Sure, he help."

"We'll have to find a church."

"Out here?" Joe asked, surprised.

Archer pointed toward the Utah Territory. "Mormons," he said.

"Hey, *qu'est-ce que c'est?*" Girard Petitjean asked, looking through his binoculars. In the past month he had led Woolridge and his posse across the great salt flats of Utah and they were now halfway up into the Sierra Nevada Mountains. "Eet look like a goddamn angel or somezing."

Woolridge was sitting on his horse next to the bearded trapper-guide. "An angel? What do you mean?"

"You take a look. God damn."

Girard handed the binoculars to him. They had arrived at the head of a sharp ravine in the snow-covered mountains. Two early storms higher up in the mountains had dumped more than two feet of snow. The scenery was breathtaking on this cold, windy morning. Woolridge had never seen anything so beautiful as these towering white mountains on the eastern edge of California.

But now, through the binoculars, he saw something even more beautiful. Standing on a high bluff at the other end of the ravine was a man in a long white robe. A man with golden hair and great golden wings.

"It *is* an angel," Woolridge whispered, focusing the lenses. "It must be the angel Moroni."

The others in the posse stared at their leader, whose behavior had become increasingly erratic as they endured the hardships of the long journey.

"Look, Ezra," he said, turning to Surtees and handing him the binoculars. The Mormon put them to his eyes.

"It's a miracle," he said in awed tones. "It is the angel Moroni. And he's beckoning to us. He wants to talk to us, just the way he talked to the prophet!"

Girard lit a cigar, blowing the smoke into the wind.

"Les Mormons, zay say zay see lotsa angels all zee time," he remarked casually. "Zees Mormon Empire, eet full of *anges. C'est le pays des miracles*, zee country of miracles. *Bizarre, n'est-ce pas?* But you never know."

Woolridge had taken the binoculars back and was again focusing on the distant angel. Moroni, if it was he, was beckoning as the wind whipped his white robe.

"He wants to show us something," Woolridge said.

"Perhaps there are other buried plates of gold," exclaimed Surtees, his excitement mounting. "Maybe the Savior buried gospels here in Utah, just like he did in New York."

"Do you suppose that's possible?"

"Why not? Brigham Young said God gave us Mormons this country to settle in. Why wouldn't he have put gospels here too?"

"Come on, let's go."

Woolridge handed the binoculars back to Girard.

"Excuse me, monsieur," the guide said, "but I wouldn't go in zat ravine. Eet's not on our route, you know."

"Yes, yes, but we won't be long. You wait here, we'll come back. Come on, men," he shouted to the others. "We may be witnessing a bona fide miracle. Praise the Lord, praise the Lord!"

Woolridge spurred his horse and galloped into the snowy ravine, Surtees behind him.

"Fuckin' guy's a lunatic," said one of the posse. "But what the hell, he's payin' good money. Let's go."

The others spurred their horses and rode into the ravine, leaving Girard behind on his horse.

The guide puffed on his cigar, a slight smile on his face.

When the posse was halfway through the ravine, Joe Thunder, who had positioned himself behind a huge pine tree atop the right-hand cliff, fired his rifle. He fired twice more. The posse stopped, looking up. Girard, hearing the crack of the rifle shots, fired his rifle. Now the posse, spotting Joe high above them, started firing back at him. The ravine echoed with gunshots.

Suddenly a great cliff of snow dislodged itself from atop the left side of the ravine and began crashing down the sharp face of the mountain, picking up more snow as it fell. Veils of snow swirled gracefully into the air as the white blanket of death cascaded down the slope.

"It's a trap!" Sergeant Woolridge screamed just before he was buried by tons of snow.

For almost a minute the ravine echoed with the boom of the avalanche. Then, silence.

Girard tossed away his cigar. "I told zem not to go in zair," he said, shrugging.

A half-mile away, on the bluff above the ravine, Archer took off the papier-mâché angel wings they had stolen from the Mormon church basement in Salt Lake City and tossed them in the snow. Then he pulled the white robe over his deerskin suit. The wind snatched it from his hand and carried it away, a writhing ghost in the clear blue sky.

Twenty minutes later, Joe Thunder joined him with the horses. The two looked down at the white ravine.

"It's beautiful," Archer said.

"That only thing wrong with your idea, Little Brother," said Joe Thunder, "is that it too beautiful for that son bitch. We shoulda given that bastard an ugly death."

"But he's dead—that's the important thing. And our brothers are avenged. Glooscap works in mysterious ways, just like God."

"Yeah, you're right, Little Brother. So, shall we go to California?"

Joe Thunder fired his rifle in the air twice, a prearranged signal to the guide meaning: Thank you, Girard, for your help.

Then the two mounted their horses and started toward Donner Pass. The great cut through the mountains above Lake Tahoe, Girard had assured them, was still the best route to California, despite the terrible tragedy that had happened there six years before.

Archer, holding a bow and arrow, squatted on the bough of a tree and listened to the deer talking below him. He had finally begun to understand what Joe Thunder had been trying to teach him: the language of the animals. They did indeed talk to each other, with little clicking noises and soft snorts, especially the deer. It took time to understand their language, but Archer had finally begun to, and it had revealed to the white man a whole new magical world. Even though he had been raised on a farm, Archer had never experienced the sense of being part of nature that Joe Thunder imparted to him. Now it was as if scales had been removed from his ears and eyes. Now when he looked at birds in the trees, he saw them differently, as creatures possessing what Joe Thunder called "a little bit of the Great Spirit."

Drawing his bow, he released an arrow that flew into the heart of a doe beneath him. As the other deer scattered into the twilit forest, Archer jumped to the ground. He used his knife to cut off a haunch, leaving the rest of the deer behind, knowing she would be eaten by other animals and the forest would be left clean. They had traversed the Donner Pass without incident and descended into California. They had followed the setting sun, encountering a few farmers and miners who were initially hostile until they realized Archer was a white man, at which point they grudgingly gave directions to San Francisco. This night they were a few miles north of the town of Sonoma, and they judged they were within two days of the city by the bay. Archer's excitement had mounted as he realized he was coming closer to his dream of seeing the beautiful Emma again. But Joe's spirits seemed to be the reverse of Archer's. As the latter's soared, Joe became increasingly moody and silent. Confused, Archer kept asking why, but the Indian would not say a word.

Archer found Joe sitting cross-legged before a fire. The two skewered the venison on a stick and began turning it over the flame. It was early November, and chilly, but their bearskin coats kept them warm. Forty minutes after they started cooking the meat, they heard twigs snapping. They turned and saw a tall farmer approaching, pointing a rifle at them.

"What you two goddamn Injuns doin' on my land?" he demanded.

Archer stood up, but Joe remained where he was. "We didn't realize this was anybody's land," Archer said.

"Well, it's mine. I seen your fire goin', and—" He squinted at Archer's gold beard. "You're no Injun," he said. "You're white. What you doin' with this heathen?"

"He happens to be my friend," said Archer, restraining an impulse to hit the farmer.

The man's lip curled contemptuously. "Don't see how no white man could be friendly with an Injun, but I've heard of people back east bein' friendly with niggers, so I guess anything's possible."

"We'll leave in the morning," said Archer. "We won't be any trouble. We're on our way to San Francisco."

The farmer put down his rifle. "Well, I guess it's all right for one night, since you're white. Why do you dress like an Injun, son?"

Archer shrugged. "Can't afford regular clothes," he said.

Joe Thunder was watching, his black eyes gleaming, his legs crossed.

"Well, I wouldn't advise wearin' them clothes in San Francisco. Folks there don't cotton to Indians. Got enough problems with the damn Celestials. If you're smart, you'll earn enough money to go to de Meyer's and buy some white man's clothes—"

"De Meyer's?" interrupted Archer. "Did you say de Meyer's?"

"Yessir. Biggest store in California. De Meyer and Kinsolving's Emporium on Portsmouth Square."

"Is there a . . . an Emma de Meyer?"

The farmer frowned. "Well, of course. She owns the place, she and her pa. I expect she's the richest lady in San Francisco. Why do you ask, son?"

"She's my sweetheart."

The farmer gaped. Then he started laughing, slapping his knee. Archer looked at Joe, then back to the farmer.

"What's so funny?" he asked.

"You!" guffawed the man. "A ragtag tramp in Injun clothes sayin' you're the boyfriend of Emma de Meyer Kinsolving, the most elegant lady west of the Rockies. . . ."

"Kinsolving? Who's that?"

"Her husband," wheezed the farmer, wiping his eyes. "Except he's dead. Burnt to a cinder when their house burnt down. Oh, my God, a paleface Injun and Emma Kinsolving! That's one for the books. Well, so long, sonny, and good luck with your girlfriend. You'll need it."

Still hee-hawing, the farmer walked off into the night. Archer stood by the fire, watching him go, a pained expression on his face. Then he turned back to Joe, who was still sitting crosslegged by the fire.

"Emma married . . ." said Archer, slowly sitting down on the ground. "I guess I shouldn't be surprised, but . . . married. . . ."

"Her husband dead," said Joe in a flat tone. "You still got a chance. 'Course, the man's right. You'll have to get some 'regular' clothes, as you called them. I didn't understand all these months you been wearin' Shawnee suit you didn't think of it as 'regular.' "

Archer realized with a jolt that he had inadvertently hurt his friend. "Joe, I didn't mean that . . ."

"What *did* you mean?"

"Well, I . . . I guess I . . . I didn't *mean* it! Honest. I love this suit. I'm proud of being part Shawnee, you know that. My God, you're my blood brother, my best friend. These past five months have been the happiest time of my life."

Joe looked at him and smiled sadly. "I know," he said. "You

didn't mean to hurt me. But you not gonna have much chance with the elegant Mrs. Kinsolving if you go in her tepee with an Injun, are you?"

"It doesn't sound as if I have much chance anyway. And if she's gotten that grand and fancy, I don't know if I want her."

"You no answer my question. If she saw you with me, she'd run away like a deer."

"That's not true—"

"Come on, Little Brother, let's not fool ourselves. You know, I called you Little Brother because that how I thought of you when we was in the forest. I knew way of forest and you didn't, so when I teach you Shawnee way I thought of you as my little brother. But now we leave the forest and go to city, where life is white man way. So now maybe I become little brother to you."

"That's crazy, Joe. Do you think I know anything about cities? I'm just a farmboy, a hick."

"Ah, but you a white hick."

They sat in silence for a moment as the fat from the venison began dropping on the fire, making it sizzle. Archer felt miserably uncomfortable, but now he was beginning to understand Joe's recent moodiness.

"It funny," Joe finally said, leaning forward to turn the meat. "We use to talk back in prison 'bout goin' to California, startin' all over, maybe havin' double wedding—remember?"

"Of course."

"And I used to think, sure, California. Maybe I find a home there. Maybe there so much room out there Indian can live like he want, not be a dishwasher or janitor. But I think I was wrong. Or maybe I got here too late."

"Too late for what, Joe?"

"You heard that farmer. We're on his land. He owns this land. I told you Indians never owned land, we never owned America. So I guess maybe now I can't complain 'cause white man's taken it away from us. That what I'm too late for, Little Brother. There's no place left for me in America, not even California."

"Dammit, Joe, you're wrong. There's land"—he gestured around—"everywhere! I understand that you think it's wrong to own land, but maybe we'll have to do it the white man's way. We can earn money and buy land. We can start farming—"

"I don't want to be a farmer," Joe interrupted angrily. "I want to be what I am: a Shawnee."

He glared at Archer with that magnificent hawk face, and for the first time the blond farmboy from Ohio realized the enormity of the horrible crime the white man had committed against the red man.

But he didn't know what to say.

In the distance, an owl hooted. The fierce look on Joe's face softened. "Remember I teach you how animals and birds talk?" he said.

"Sure."

"That owl, he part of Great Spirit. He just say, 'Keep goin' west, Joe Thunder. You no find your home yet.' "

"But there isn't any more west, Joe. We're almost to the Pacific."

"Yeah, I know." Abruptly he glanced at the venison. "I think this about ready to eat, Little Brother. Then Joe Thunder go to sleep. It been a long journey, and Joe sorta tired."

Archer slept fitfully that night, his sleep haunted by dreams. He dreamed he saw Joe Thunder galloping on his horse, Tecumseh, across the Great Plains, just as Archer had seen him so many times: horse and man as one, magnificently swift and proud. Archer was riding beside him when suddenly Joe Thunder turned to him and waved. His horse galloped into the air. Joe and Tecumseh flew across the blood-red heavens toward the setting sun as Archer watched in awe. A great flock of birds appeared in the sky, also flying west: eagles, geese, hawks, ducks, even owls. And as they blackened the sky, a hideous witch on a giant goose flew overhead, and Archer knew that she was Pamola, the evil spirit of the night, the sorceress that the mighty hunter Glooscap had conquered at the beginning of time.

Pamola was white.

"Joe?"

Archer sat up, having just wakened. Despite the cold of the dawn, he was lathered in sweat from the dream. He looked around. The fire had died; the pine forest was still.

Joe was gone. So was Tecumseh.

"Joe?"

He jumped to his feet. He ran down the hill to the stream they had spotted the night before. Joe wasn't there.

It was a gorgeous dawn, the sky clear and pink. Archer ran back up the hill and climbed on his horse. He rode to the west.

It took him forty minutes to reach the Pacific Ocean. He spent another ten minutes riding down the beach until he spotted Tecumseh.

"Oh, Jesus . . ."

He spurred his horse. He had seen something bobbing in the surf near Tecumseh. He galloped up and dismounted. He ran down the beach to the water and knelt.

"Joe . . ." he whispered.

Joe Thunder was floating faceup. He looked at peace. He had finally found a home in California.

Archer picked the sodden corpse up in both arms and carried him up on the beach, hugging him. Tears trickled from his eyes as he kissed Joe Thunder's forehead. Then he looked up at the clear California sky.

"Great Spirit," he said softly, "or God, or whatever you call yourself: help me avenge Joe Thunder's death. There must be something I can do to stop this injustice. Help me, God, because I loved Joe Thunder and he helped me escape jail and he taught me the way of nature. Don't let Joe Thunder die in vain."

Tears streamed down his cheeks as the light ocean breeze swirled around him and the dead Shawnee.

25

THE rinky-tink piano music emanating from the Bella Union Saloon on Portsmouth Square clashed with the piano-violin-accordion-trumpet combo Chicago had hired at the Bonanza Café around the corner. It was early evening and the square was crowded with San Franciscans. The boomtown was becoming so cosmopolitan so quickly that a dozen languages could be heard, and the crowd was so colorful and gaudy that even Archer in his deerskin Shawnee suit didn't attract too many stares, though his blond hair and beard and dirty white skin caused some sidelong looks. Though Portsmouth Square was still the center of town, it was rapidly sliding downhill, becoming honky-tonk, if not seedy. Still, the gaslit square was thronged, and under normal circumstances Archer would have been pop-eyed. The brassy whores and bare-breasted waitresses he saw through the windows of the Bonanza excited his young flesh, for he was randy after his long months in prison. But otherwise, everything left him flat.

The suicide of Joe Thunder had devastated him. Now, in retrospect, he could see the signs that led up to it: the increasing moodiness, the contemptuous looks and remarks of the whites they met. But the act had taken him totally by surprise, and the blame he was putting on himself was twofold: he felt a collective guilt as a white man, but he also felt a personal guilt for not having foreseen the tragedy and in some way prevented it. To lose the one true friend he had ever had—the one who had saved his sanity and, probably, his life by freeing him from the penitentiary—threw him into the very depths of depression.

It was then that he saw the sign: "DE MEYER AND KINSOLVING'S EMPORIUM."

Emma. What would she think of him now? The farmer at Sonoma had laughed at the idea of his being the elegant Mrs. Kinsolving's lover, and he supposed it was laughable. He was dirty. He had no money. He was a convicted felon and an escaped convict. He walked around the square to the store and looked at the illuminated display windows: fur coats, elegant dresses, beautiful furniture, fine jewelry, housewares. It was all so utterly the obverse of his life with Joe Thunder. He had

lived without money for so long that the world of material things seemed
unreal to him. But did he want that world? And if Emma had become
such an entrenched part of that world, did he want Emma? They had
been separated almost two years. For all that time he had dreamed of
the Emma he had known on the riverboat. But would the new Emma
be the same?

He wandered to the window next to the front door. In a special
display case was a large nugget of gold on a black velvet mount. In
florid letters a sign read: "Have a Golden Christmas!" Small gaslamps
illuminated the display, and the gold glittered sensuously in the light.

The more Archer stared at the nugget, the more anger welled inside
him. The gold, the beautiful things in the windows, the store—it struck
him that these were the trappings of the civilization that had made him
an outcast and stolen Joe Thunder's heritage. Suddenly he hated the
gold.

He ran across the street to the park and picked up a rock.

"Hey! What the hell . . . ?"

One of the store guards standing inside the front door saw a young
man in Indian attire throw a rock. It smashed the glass window and
toppled the gold nugget.

Since the death of Scott Kinsolving, Emma had worked day and
night to build his empire for young Archer and Star. Although to call
it an "empire" was rather an overstatement as yet, still she was spreading into such a variety of enterprises that San Franciscans were beginning to compare her to the tycoons and moguls back east. The Golden
State Insurance Company she had started with two salesmen and a
secretary had by now quintupled in size. The San Francisco *Times-
Dispatch*, the daily newspaper she had financed for David Levin, was
beginning to compete with the rival *Bulletin*. And then there was the
store. After the vandalizing by the Sydney Ducks on the night of the
great fire, she had thrown herself into getting it reopened with such
demonic energy that the few ladies in the city had a field day clucking
about the impropriety and indelicacy of a woman—and a recent widow,
at that!—doing men's work with such unseemly vigor. Emma couldn't
care less what the hens of San Francisco clucked about her, and she
had the store open again in an amazing three weeks.

She had placed a partners' desk in her father's office on the second
floor, and here Felix and Emma, sitting opposite each other, became
the first father-daughter business team in the West. Felix was in charge
of managing the store, which included dreaming up the themes of the
various window displays: the gold nugget had been his idea. Emma was
in charge of the books, since figures bored Felix to distraction. That

evening she was going over accounts receivable. The store had been closed for over an hour when there was a knock at the door.

"Come in."

Paul Clark, the hulking black-bearded chief night watchman, came in. "Excuse me, Mrs. Kinsolving, but we've had a little trouble downstairs. A man threw a rock through the window of the nugget display."

"Did he steal it?" she asked, concerned. The nugget was insured for five thousand dollars.

"No, ma'am. He just broke the window."

"Why? Is he drunk?"

"No, ma'am. 'Least, I don't think so, though he's acting a little crazy. Dressed like an Indian even though he's white. He says he knows you, which I sorta doubt. His name's Collingwood. Archer Collingwood."

Emma put down her pen. "Archer," she whispered.

Paul Clark stared at his employer, wondering if she were having a stroke. "You all right, ma'am?"

"Yes, I . . . Is he blond?"

"Yes, ma'am."

She was getting to her feet. "Is he handsome?"

"Well, now, ma'am, that's kinda hard for me to say . . ."

"Where is he?"

"Downstairs. We're holding him until—"

As she ran past him, he was amazed to see she was crying. Emma de Meyer Kinsolving, the smartest, richest, toughest woman in San Francisco, crying? He couldn't believe it. She threw open the office door and ran out, going through the empty reception room, then into the second-floor furniture section. As she ran to the stair past the mattress section, she remembered the last time she had seen him, the last ecstatic lovemaking on board the riverboat. How much he had suffered since then!

Mr. Appleton had recently returned from Ohio with the report that Archer had been freed from prison by a party of Indians. She had been thrilled by that news, but she also learned of the horrors of the solitary-confinement pens. But it's all over now, my darling, she thought as she ran down the central stair of the store. You're free and you're mine—not tomorrow, but now . . . *tonight!*

She reached the bottom of the stairs and saw him leaning over one of the display cases holding watches. Two burly night watchmen flanked him.

"Archer . . ."

He straightened and turned. His face was dirty and his beard hung to his chest. "Emma . . ."

She ran past the many display cases into his arms, kissing him. The night watchmen exchanged incredulous looks.

"Why . . ?" She had so many questions to ask him, but she was so overjoyed, laughing and crying at the same time, she could only think of the most obvious. "Why did you break our window?"

He stared at her, struck dumb by her beauty, unable to believe they were together again. He hesitated to answer her question because he realized that by throwing a stone at de Meyer and Kinsolving's window, he had also thrown a stone at her. "Because," he said finally, "I was so angry."

She perceived that the innocent farmboy she had fallen in love with on the Ohio River had lost his innocence the hard way.

"This is my son?" he said wonderingly as he leaned over the bed.

"This is Archer Junior," Emma said, holding an oil lamp. They were in the second-floor nursery of a new brick house she had built on Russian Hill. Her old property on Rincon Hill she had donated for the site of the new Sailors' Home. "He'll be one year old next month, December 7. Isn't he beautiful? Look at his blond hair, just like yours."

"I didn't even know I was a father. What's his last name?"

"Kinsolving. Scott adopted him. It was a sort of deal I made with him."

"A deal? About a baby?"

"It's complicated. And over here is Star, Archer's adopted sister." She led him across the room to another bed, where Star was sleeping on her back.

"Is she yours too?" Archer asked.

"I adopted her, which was part of the deal. Scott was her father. Her mother was Scott's Chinese mistress."

"Chinese mistress?" he repeated, dumbstruck.

"Life is a bit more exotic in San Francisco than in Ohio."

"I see what you mean."

She put out the lamp and led him from the room. In the upstairs hall she pointed out to him the gilt-framed paintings she was beginning to collect. She stopped at a paneled door and opened it.

"This is your room, darling," she said, smiling.

"My room?"

"Yes. Can Do, my butler, has prepared it."

Archer walked in the big bedroom, gaping at its size. The opulence of the Tudor-style twenty-room house had stunned him almost as much as the news that he was a father.

"And these are your clothes." She pointed to the ornately carved walnut bed. On the counterpane, Can Do had laid out fawn-colored trousers, an elegant ruffled shirt with a scarlet cravat, a tailcoat, black silk socks with gold clocks, and underwear. On the floor were patent-leather shoes. "I guessed your size and had them brought over from the store. Over here is your bathroom. Can Do put in shaving equipment so you can get rid of that ghastly beard. Bathe and get dressed and we'll have dinner. We have so much to discuss—"

"Aren't you taking a lot for granted?" he interrupted. "In the first place, I can't pay for any of these things. I have no money at all."

"They're gifts, darling. You don't have to pay for anything."

"In the second place, how do you know I want to stay in this house?"

She stiffened slightly. "Well, I assumed—"

"Yes, you assumed, like your late husband assumed I wouldn't mind spending an extra five years in that stinking hole so he could make love to you. Well, I did mind. I lived through hell, Emma. And all right, maybe your husband changed his mind and sent someone else to get me out, but meanwhile I was *in*, Emma, and let me tell you, lying naked in a cell too low to stand up in for weeks on end is no goddamn picnic."

"Don't you think I know that? Why do you think I'm trying to make up to you for what my husband did?"

"And while we're on the subject: you asked why I threw that rock into your store window tonight. I said because I was angry. Do you know why I'm angry, Emma? Because this country has cheated me since the day I was born, and it's also cheated my friend, Joe Thunder. It cheated him so much he gave up and walked into the damned Pacific Ocean! But it hasn't cheated you, has it? God, no! Look at this house. Look at your clothes, your jewels. You've done very nicely, haven't you, Emma? I loved that beautiful girl I met on the riverboat, but I'm not sure I can love what you've become. Joe Thunder taught me the Indian way of life, which is beautiful and natural. So if you don't mind, I'll leave my Indian clothes on, at least until I decide whether I want to be a white man again or not—and right now I'm thinking being a red man has a lot to be said for it."

His attack angered her, but she told herself to hold her tongue, at least for now. "It's up to you," she said, going to the door. "But I'll point out that your beloved Indian costume, or whatever you call it, stinks to high heaven, and your beard looks like it has fleas. *I'm* going to change for what I hoped would be a romantic reunion for two people who once loved each other. However, if you want to look like the last of the Mohicans, that's your business. I'll await you in the dining room in an hour."

When she had left the room, he looked at the clothes on the bed.

Then he raised his arm and sniffed. He supposed to her he stank, though he'd grown used to his smell.

"Damn," he muttered. None of it was turning out the way he had dreamed.

She was furious at his behavior, but perversely, it made her all the more determined to have him. Irrationally as she thought he was behaving, his physical presence had reawakened all her old passion for him. Even his outburst had made her tingle. She had made love to no one since Scott's death—she hadn't even gone to a party, so fierce had been her devotion to her business—but now she was on fire. She wanted him, and she wasn't about to let his talk of the Indian way of life prevent her from having him.

She decided she would seduce him with the white man's way of life.

An influx of French nationals to San Francisco had brought French restaurants to town, but it had also provided Emma with a pretty French maid named Adele. As she entered her bedroom, she spotted Adele through the bathroom door, running the tub. She went into the marble bathroom, which was the wonder of San Francisco, and said, "Adele, you have one hour to make me irresistible."

Adele straightened from the tub. "I saw your Monsieur Collingwood," she said. "He is very handsome, but he look like a trapper or something."

"He thinks he's an Indian," Emma said as Adele unbuttoned her dress. "So tonight is going to be the French-Indian Wars all over again. You have to do something sensational with my hair and absolutely douse me with Nuit d'Amour. And I'll wear the red velvet dress with my diamonds. No man can withstand red."

"If I may make a suggestion, Madame? Red is too unsubtle. The pale green makes Madame look so much more *ravissante*."

Emma stepped out of her pantalets into the tub. "You're right," she sighed. "Oh, Adele, he was terrible to me, absolutely terrible! After all this time he started lecturing me. I wanted him to lift me in his arms and carry me to bed, and what did he do? Talked about his damned Indians."

Adele began soaping Emma's shoulders with a huge sponge. "Men, they are crazy," she said. "But we'll fix him. One look at Madame and he'll forget his Indians and think of nothing but making love to you."

"I so hope you're right. Oh, God, I'm a nervous wreck. Indians! But, Adele . . . ?"

"Yes, Madame?"

"I'm still mad for him."

"Then Madame will have him. No man can resist a beautiful woman in love."

The dining room had been done in linen-fold paneling Emma had imported from England, and the ceiling was a copy of one in Hampton Court. But romance had won out over period authenticity, and she had hung an eighteenth-century crystal chandelier over the nineteenth-century dining table, which could extend to seat twenty. Can Do had lit the candles not only in the chandelier but also in the two eight-branch silver candelabra on the table, imparting a soft glow to the room.

The door opened, and Emma swept in.

"Taitai look very beautiful tonight," Can Do said truthfully. Adele had set her hair in the sausage curls that were still the fashion, and her shimmering pale green satin dress revealed her shoulders and a sensational portion of her tempting bosom. She hadn't had to sell the jewelry Scott had given her after all, and the diamonds and emeralds glittered.

"Thank you, Can Do," she said, going to the Jacobean sideboard and looking at her reflection in the gilt mirror above it. Suddenly she knew she had made a mistake.

"The jewels," she muttered nervously, starting to unclasp the necklace. "They're wrong. He'll start lecturing me again." Hurriedly she put the necklace and brooch in a sideboard drawer and shut it as, in the mirror, she saw Archer come into the room.

He had bathed, shaved off his beard, and put on the new clothes.

As she turned to smile at him, she knew she had won the first skirmish.

"I'm drunk," he said two hours later as he took off the clothes she had seduced him into and then out of again. "I've never had champagne. I'm seeing two of you, but that's twice as wonderful. Oh, Emma, Emma, I've dreamed of you so many nights."

She was lying on her bed, her superb nakedness softly illuminated by the pink-shaded bedlamp. She opened her arms to him. "Come to me, my love," she whispered.

He knelt beside her on the edge of the bed, leaning down to kiss her. Then he slowly lay on top of her and their bodies began blending. His tongue was in her mouth as his hands rubbed her breasts and hers rubbed his back and she felt his stomach press against hers.

"I love you," she whispered as he started making love, the floodgates of his long-pent-up sexuality bursting. "I love you. Thank God you've come back to me, my darling, sweet love . . ."

He was beyond words as pure animal lust gripped him. Their bodies took control and brought them closer and closer to climax.

"Oh, my God . . . oh, my God . . ."

He came with such force that they both were panting, sweating, and moaning. She thought her heart would explode.

After they had rested in each other's arms awhile, he rose from the bed and walked to a window to stare out at the starlit bay. She watched him hungrily. "Are you happy?"

He didn't answer for a while, and when he did turn to look at her, she was surprised to see a tear rolling down his cheek.

"Yes, I'm happy," he said. "But I miss Joe Thunder. And the worst thing is . . ." He hesitated, a look of disgust coming over his face. "I've betrayed him. I became ashamed of my Shawnee suit. I chose to be a goddamn white man." He looked back out at the Pacific Ocean. "I know it probably strikes you as amusing, but it's important to me. I wonder if I'll ever forgive myself."

"Archer, it's sweet that you feel sorry for the Indians—"

"You don't understand. I admire them."

"How could you admire savages? The Indians are relics of the past. America is becoming a white man's country, and I say more power to it. We'll build a much richer society."

"But will it be any better?"

"Of course it will be better. Someday there'll be an opera house here, and art museums, theaters, schools—"

"I still say, is that any better? Is art better than living with nature?"

"Well, if we didn't believe that, what would be the point of five thousand years of civilization? Isn't Beethoven better than a tomtom? But come, we've been apart so long, it's madness for us to argue. We have to discuss your future."

"What kind of future do I have?" he said sourly. "An escaped convict, a farmer without a farm, an Indian without a tribe, and a white man with no money. I'm no good for anything. I might as well be a politician."

Her face lighted up. "Don't laugh. Scott would probably have been governor if he hadn't died. Maybe you should go into politics. Slade Dawson is dominating local politics because he hasn't had any opposition since Scott died . . . That's a wonderful idea."

"You seem to forget I'm a convicted felon."

"We'll buy you a pardon. Anything can be bought."

"But don't you see? I don't want to be part of anything so cynical. Oh, hell, I suppose I've become some sort of freak. They called me the 'blond Indian' back on the plains. Maybe I should get a job in a circus as a freak: Archer Collingwood, the blond Indian who talks to animals."

"Darling, I can understand why you've become bitter. But I think you should reconsider the idea of politics. Besides, you do have some money. Scott sent ten thousand dollars to be deposited in your name. Of course, when we found you'd escaped, we kept it. But now it's yours. And I have so much money—the businesses are doing terribly well. I want to share what I have with you."

"The general idea is that the *man* is the breadwinner."

"Who says you can't make money? If you don't want to try politics, then join me in one of the businesses—God knows, I need help. The insurance company is growing by leaps and bounds. You could go to work there and someday run it."

He rolled his eyes. "Insurance. I'd rather be in a circus."

"You're in no position to be so damned picky," she blurted, immediately regretting it.

He turned on her. "You're absolutely right. I'm nobody—a bum. And you're the great Mrs. Kinsolving, the fanciest lady in the West. What are you doing with me? Slumming? You should have better taste."

"Archer, please."

He picked his pants off the floor and tossed them onto a chair. "You can keep your fancy duds, Emma, and thanks for the dinner. I'll take my smelly Injun clothes and not bother you anymore—though I will take the ten thousand dollars, because I think that bastard you married owes it to me."

"Stop it!" she shouted, jumping out of bed. "In the first place, he wasn't a bastard. He was a fine man who adopted your son and intended to give him everything—"

"Except my name!"

"Yes, except your name! And if you had any guts, you'd stop whining and moaning about the Indians and give your son his rightful name!"

He looked confused. "What do you mean?"

"Do I have to spell it out? Do I have to get on my knees and propose? Marry me!"

"But . . ."

She ran to him and threw her arms around him. "I love you so much and I've been so lonely. . . . I have all this responsibility, and I want the children to have a father. Don't let's talk about money or jobs. We'll work out your future later. Please, Archer, stay with me . . . be my husband and my lover. You broke my heart once—I couldn't stand losing you again."

As he gazed into her amethyst eyes and felt the warmth of her flesh against his, his bitterness started to melt. "It broke my heart too," he whispered.

"Does that mean you'll marry me? Does that mean you'll be the father the children so desperately need?"

He nodded. "Yes."

She hugged him fiercely. After a moment he responded by tightening his arms around her.

"Everybody in California will say I married you for your money," he sighed.

"I don't care what everybody in California says. After all, if you hadn't saved my father's diamonds on the riverboat, where would we be? I'll tell them *that* if they say you're after my money. Besides, it's going to be our money now. You've had so much misery, my darling, but that's all behind you now. I'm going to devote the rest of my life to making you happy."

Archer looked at her, realizing that perhaps politics wouldn't be such a bad idea, after all. As Little Brother he was powerless. But Senator Collingwood might be able to do something for the Indians. Of course! It struck him like a thunderbolt: he had asked God to send him someone to help avenge Joe Thunder, and God had sent him Emma.

"You really think I could become a senator?" he asked, staring at her.

"It would take years to do—it would take lots of time and lots of money—but, yes, anything is possible."

"Maybe that is the way I could help Joe," he said softly. "I kept thinking there must be some way to help what's being done to the Indians, but I could never think of a way for me to do anything. I mean, who was I? A nobody. But if it were possible to become a senator, maybe I could do something."

"Archer, I swear I'll do everything in my power to make you a senator. I know it sounds cynical, but money *can* buy just about anything, and time fixes the rest. So let's use our money to do something good."

He began to smile. A great load of guilt and confusion and frustration was beginning to lift from his shoulders. He opened his arms and hugged her again.

"Maybe we can make a difference," he whispered. "I think it will be good, you and me . . ."

"Oh, darling. But you've forgotten something."

"What?"

"You haven't told me you love me."

"You know I love you. I fell in love with you that first time I saw you on the boat. No, that's wrong. It wasn't love so much as that I wanted you. And I still want you, but now . . . Emma, for the first time in my life, the future looks really exciting."

·THREE·

Nob Hill and the Tong Wars

26

THE young man in white tie and tails whipped the two horses of his victoria as they strained up the steep slope of California Street toward the summit of Nob Hill.

"Pull, you bastards!" roared Archer Collingwood Jr. "Pull!" It was an April night in 1877, and Archer was wildly, crazily drunk. At twenty-six, he was the richest, best-looking young man in San Francisco, "Crown Prince of the City" as Sydney Tolliver, the gossip columnist of the *Times-Dispatch*, called him. "Public Nuisance No. 1" was what he was called in the rival newspapers, as well as "Playbrat of the West."

The victoria finally groaned to a halt under the porte cochere of the great limestone mansion on top of the hill, diagonally across from the brooding James Flood mansion at the corner of California and Mason Streets. Archer stumbled off the driver's seat, almost falling on his face as he jumped to the cobblestone drive. As the Celestial groom took charge of the carriage, he weaved his way to the front door of the palace built by his parents four years before. Senator and Mrs. Archer Collingwood had bought an entire half-block atop the 338-foot hill that had become the Fifth Avenue of San Francisco and built a château in a style vaguely termed "French Renaissance." As Archer Jr. rang the bell beside the elaborate wrought-iron-and-glass front doors, he giggled and burped, recalling the breathless descriptions of the house that had appeared in the local papers. Even the *Bulletin*, owned by the rival Dawson clan, had gushed, though Slade Dawson never lost an opportunity to flail the Collingwoods in his paper. "The house," burbled the *Bulletin* reporter, obviously mesmerized by statistics, "has almost as many towers as the Château de Chambord in France, which inspired Mrs. Collingwood's architect. It has seventy-two rooms, more bathrooms than the White House, and its ballroom is said to be almost as big as the throne room in Buckingham Palace."

"Mr. Junior, you drunk again!" exclaimed a white-haired Can Do as he opened the door. "You very bad boy!"

"Shh!" hissed Archer, wobbling through the door with his white-gloved finger to his lips. "Mustn't let the Duchess know. Where is she?"

"Taitai at her office—"

"Counting her millions. Well, why not? She's got 'em to count. Anyway, I gotta go see my father. How is he?"

"Doctor say his fever down, he think he gonna be okay. But you better sober up chop-chop or Taitai gonna be plenty mad."

"Oh, she'll survive, Can Do. My mother survives everything. Fires, recessions, depression: I can't imagine what it would take to kill Mother—not that I want her dead. Oh, no. Remember how sweet she used to be, Can Do? How beautiful she was when she played those Chopin waltzes?" He twirled around in a little waltz step.

"Taitai still sweet, still beautiful. Now, you come to kitchen, sober up. For shame! And it not even dinnertime yet."

Archer grinned and hugged the rotund Chinese barely half his height. "Can Do, are you going to spank me like you used to when I was a kid?"

"You too big to spank now, but I should."

Archer straightened, still weaving.

"What do you think of this family, huh? Isn't this a crazy family? My father a senator? My mother should have been spanked for *that*. Buying a pardon as if she were buying a goddamn French sofa. Oh, well, what the hell, she's bought everything else in life, why not the Senate?" He burped and headed toward the three-story-high entrance hall and its great double staircase laced with an exquisitely delicate wrought-iron balustrade. Between the stairs, which swooped down opposite each other in a giant V, hung a life-size portrait of Emma in the slick style of a royal portrait by Winterhalter. Emma at the height of her dazzling beauty, standing on some imaginary terrace overlooking San Francisco Bay in the background. Emma magnificently regal in a Prussian-blue velvet ballgown, its great skirts swirling around her feet in rich folds. Emma, her chestnut hair piled high in a crown of curls held by a diamond star, her long neck draped with pearls, her bare shoulders made even more sensuously creamy by the creamy oils.

"Mother!" Archer cried, taking off his top hat and making a sweeping bow before the gilt-framed portrait. "The Grand Duchess of San Francisco." He burped, imitating baby talk. "Mommy build big, big house to show how rich she is to all the neighbors. Mommy has lots of jewels, lots of money, lots of everything. Mommy's the goddamned San Francisco mint."

"Mr. Junior, you stop talkin' that way," Can Do said, hurrying up and taking his hand. "Come on, we goin' to kitchen—"

"Let me alone, Can Do! I want to see my father."

He jerked his hand away and stumbled across the floor of black and white marble diamonds to the right-hand stair. He started climbing, leaning on the balustrade.

"Archer!"

He looked up. As his blurry vision focused, he saw standing at the top of the stair the woman who was, in his opinion, the most beautiful female in the West, if not the world: his adopted sister.

"Star," he whispered, almost stumbling to his knees.

Star was hurrying down the stairs. "Oh, Can Do, he's drunk again. Mother will have a fit."

"I try to take him to kitchen, Missy Star."

"Get some coffee. Maybe we can sober him up before Mother gets home . . . Archer, where have you been? At the club, I suppose?"

She referred to the Olympic Club on Post Street, one of the oldest amateur athletic clubs in the world, having been founded seventeen years before. She knew her brother spent most of his afternoons there, swimming, fencing, working out with barbells, and drinking.

He was leaning on the balustrade, top hat in hand, smiling up at her with bleary adoration. "You know," he said, "you're so beautiful."

She took his arm. "And you're so drunk. Honestly, Archer, are you trying to kill yourself? Now, come upstairs and I'll get you in a hot tub."

"Will you take my clothes off?"

"I'll help you—"

"More to the point, will you take your clothes off?"

"Archer, be quiet!"

"There's nothing wrong with that," he slurred as they crawled up the stairs. "We're not really brother and sister. We don't share any blood at all, so what's wrong when I want to kiss you? Hell, what's wrong when I want to make love to you? There'd be something wrong if I didn't!"

"It *is* wrong, we *are* brother and sister even if we share no blood, and if Clayton heard you talk that way, it would be all over San Francisco in ten minutes."

"Clayton Delamere, that blithering idiot. You shouldn't marry him, Star. You're too good for him. You should marry me."

She winced. "Don't say those things!" she whispered.

He grinned and leaned close to her, lowering his voice. "I could blackmail you, you know," he said, breathing whiskey in her face. "I know your secret."

She tensed. "There's no secret."

"Yes, there is. But if you kiss me, I promise I won't tell anyone, not even the Duchess."

Her amber eyes, with their hint of her Manchu blood, flickered with fear. "You wouldn't," she whispered.

"Kiss me and I won't."

She looked over the balustrade. Below her, the hall with its tapestries and suits of armor was empty. Then she turned her eyes to the adopted brother she adored but also feared.

"All right, but hurry."

He put his arms around her and pressed her to him, kissing her with a passion that was anything but fraternal. After a moment she pushed him away and slapped his face.

"You devil!" she hissed.

As she ran up the stairs, Archer's drunken laughter echoed around the limestone walls. Then he began singing as he continued climbing:

> "Oh, the miners came in forty-nine,
> The whores in fifty-one;
> And when they got together
> They produced the native son."

When he reached the top of the stairs, he paused as the two great crystal chandeliers depending from the coffered ceiling twirled like pinwheels.

"Mr. Junior," Can Do called from below. "I got coffee here."

"Later, Can Do. Wanna see my father. My father, the senator. Poor man. He told me once all he ever wanted to be was a Shawnee Indian. Can you imagine? Senator Archer Collingwood, the richest man in California. Only person who came to California not looking for gold, and he ended up with it all. Isn't that crazy?"

Can Do was hurrying up the stairs with a tray holding a coffeepot and cup, but Archer left the banister and headed down the upstairs corridor toward his father's bedroom. The wide corridor was lined with paintings good and bad: masterpieces by Titian, Watteau, and de la Tour were flanked by sentimental nineteenth-century schlock. Emma, who had picked them all, had a good eye but not an infallible one.

Archer weaved to a pedimented walnut door at the end of the gallery and knocked. His father had taken severely ill six weeks before with typhoid fever. During a particularly severe week of intermittent bouts of delirium coupled with acute intestinal hemorrhaging, the family had feared for his life, but the doctor now believed the crisis had passed, much to everyone's relief, for the senator was well-loved in California. It was no secret that Emma Collingwood was the driving force in the family: she was the business genius who had built a fortune to match the Vanderbilts'. But it was gentle, dreamy Archer Sr. that Mr. Junior adored.

Can Do hurried forward. "Drink coffee, Mr. Junior, please—"

"Sshhh. I think he's asleep," Archer said, turning the gold-plated knob.

He opened the door and went in. The great bedroom, with its

twenty-foot ceiling and globed crystal gasolier, was rather stuffy, and Archer's first instinct was to open one of the windows. He had started across the flowered Axminster carpet when he noticed the nurse dozing beside the distant walnut bed. She woke up at that moment, and he signaled her to silence as he tiptoed toward her, Can Do right behind.

A thousand memories assaulted him: of fishing and hunting like an Indian with his father, who had tried to teach him to listen to deer talking.

But Mr. Junior had never understood the Indian ways. In 1863, when Archer Sr. was chosen to serve out deceased Senator Brooking's term, his son was only thirteen. As he grew older, he became tremendously proud not only that his father was one of the few white men in America who had lived like an Indian, but also that he, almost alone in Washington, fought for the rights of the Indians. Archer Jr.'s classmates at Princeton had ragged him mercilessly about the "bank-robber, Indian-loving Senator Collingwood," whose wife had had to pay twenty thousand dollars to buy him a pardon just so he could vote, much less be elected to public office, and who had contributed money to Governor Stanford's campaign to grease the wheels for Archer's Senate nomination. But because of his father, Mr. Junior was sympathetic to the Indians, even if he had never learned to talk to the animals.

Two years before, in 1875, had come the Battle of Little Bighorn and the death of General George Armstrong Custer at the hands of the Indians. The nation had erupted in a frenzy of hatred against the red man they had stolen America away from. This had been the final straw for the "Indian-loving" Senator Collingwood, who had never liked Washington in the first place because he missed his family. He resigned his Senate seat and returned to California a broken man. He knew he had failed to avenge Joe Thunder, which had been the one great crusade of his life. The fact that no one person—not even a senator—could stop the tide of history made no difference: Archer Sr. believed himself a failure. Surrounded by the incredible wealth of his wife, he sank into lethargy, dreaming of days a quarter-century before when he had ridden with Joe Thunder. He had often told his son they were the best days of his life, and though Mr. Junior tried to understand, he couldn't. He liked too well the material luxuries his mother's money provided. Which was why, when he was drunk, he tended to attack Emma and apotheosize his father.

"Father?" Archer whispered, smiling down at the still-handsome man.

"Come, Mr. Junior," Can Do whispered. "Don't bother him."

"Father?"

A look of drunken horror came over Arthur Jr's. face as he reached for his father's wrist on the eiderdown quilt. The skin was cold, and there was no pulse.

"Oh, Jesus . . . oh, no . . ."

Archer sank to his knees beside the bed. The nurse hurried around the end.

"He's dead," the son whispered disbelievingly. "The sweetest man that ever lived. He's dead . . ."

He buried his face in his arms and began sobbing. The thought seeped into his awareness that he was no longer crown prince. He was now king.

But then, there was the queen, the all-powerful Emma.

He might be king, but he was not yet head of the family.

The nineteen-year-old Chinese youth took off his shirt and handed it to one of the two soldiers of the Suey Sing Tong, which translated as the Society of the Hall of Auspicious Victory. The boy, whose name was Fong Ah Sing, had a look of fear as well as excitement on his sallow face; this was the greatest moment of his life. The tong soldier folded the shirt and placed it carefully on a wooden chest as the second soldier opened an iron door. The two older tongmen were *boo how doy*, or hatchet sons, for the Suey Sing Tong was a killer tong, like most of the dozens of secret societies that were becoming notorious for dominating crime in San Francisco. Once the iron door was open, the two Suey Sings motioned to Fong Ah Sing to go through. The outer rooms of the Suey Sing hideout had been as hot and smelly as Spofford Alley, the filthy lane in Chinatown where the Suey Sing Tong was located. But as the boy passed through the iron door into the low-ceilinged room beyond, he felt a damp coolness and he smelled incense. The room was lighted by dim Chinese lanterns. The iron door was locked, and the Suey Sings led the boy down a narrow brick stair to a basement room.

It was empty and dark, but the boy could barely make out two wooden doors. Somewhere a distant gong was struck, and the two doors opened inward. The boy's arms were grasped by the Suey Sings and he was pushed into yet another room, this much bigger and well-lighted by candles and lanterns. A group of Chinese dressed in white sashed robes with piratelike bandannas and bands on their heads squatted on their heels watching Fong Ah Sing and his two sponsors. The initiation rite to the tong was taken with deadly solemnity, and the two sponsors were Fong's "godfather" and "godmother" for the occasion. The rite, which varied from tong to tong, was based on rituals dating back two centuries to the period when the first Chinese tongs were formed in Peking to resist the Manchu invaders.

Opposite the doors, a sheeted altar had been set up beneath a huge scroll covered with Chinese calligraphy. On the altar were arranged ears of corn and blue willow bowls, some filled with incense. In front of the altar, sitting cross-legged on a straw mat on the floor, was a man dressed in vermilion robes. In his thirties, he had a cruelly handsome face with a knife scar zigzagging down his left cheek like a bolt of lightning striking the corner of his thin, tight mouth. His dark eyes seemed to bore through Fong's skull, scrutinizing his secret thoughts.

Fong was led to the man by his sponsors.

"This is the *Kai Yee*," said one in Cantonese.

"Strip off your clothes," the *Kai Yee* said.

Fong obeyed.

"Examine him for birthmarks or other evil signs."

The two sponsors walked around Fong, scrutinizing his thin body. "He seems to be clean," the men reported in unison.

"Pull up your pants."

Fong obeyed.

"Have you carefully considered the step you are about to take?"

"Yes, *Kai Yee*," the boy said.

"Are you ready to storm the Great Wall?"

"Quite ready, *Kai Yee*."

"Have you been prepared with weapons?"

"Not yet, *Kai Yee*."

"How can a child be born without a mother?"

"My revered mother accompanies me, *Kai Yee*," Fong said, indicating the murderous-looking *boo how doy* to his left. "She stands upon my left, and my godfather stands upon my right."

"Are you ready to become a blood brother?"

"I am ready, *Kai Yee*."

"Then let thy mother shed the blood of maternity."

Fong was led to the altar.

"On the altar," the *Kai Yee* said, "you will see the symbols of our tong. They include dishes of sugar to remove bitterness from hearts, ears of corn to symbolize plenty, a dish of oil to light the future, and a bowl of vinegar into which we shall mix our blood."

The godmother sponsor grabbed Fong's right hand and pricked his index finger with a needle. Then he plunged the finger into a bowl of stinging vinegar, watching as the blood incarnadined the liquid, then stirring it into a swirl of color. The godmother pricked his own finger and stirred his blood into the darkening vinegar, as did the other sponsor. Then every man in the room advanced to the altar to mix his blood into the bowl as the others watched in silence. Finally the bowl was brought to the *Kai Yee*, who, still sitting on the mat, pricked his own finger and immersed it in the bowl. Pulling it out, he stuck the dripping, bloody finger in his mouth and sucked it dry.

"Now," he cried, "thou art my blood brother."

"Ho!" shouted the tong members, meaning "Good!"

The bowl was passed to each member, who likewise stuck his finger in the bowl, then sucked it dry, and shouted, "Thou art my blood brother."

"Ho!" roared the tong each time.

Finally the bowl was brought to Fong, who repeated the ritual.

"Now," the *Kai Yee* said, "for the test of courage. You must walk the Path of the Swords."

The tong soldiers quickly formed a double line, pulling swords, dirks, and daggers from their sashes. Fong, looking nervous, was pushed into the gauntlet formed by the swordsmen. Each man raised his sword or dirk and then brought it swiftly down, only at the last second turning the blade or diverting the point so that harmless steel smacked Fong's naked shoulders. Still, it was an unnerving experience. When the teenager reached the end of the Path of Swords, he was bathed in sweat.

He was then returned to the *Kai Yee*, who was standing holding the bowl with the vinegar and blood. "You have passed the test of courage," he said. "Now drink the blood of your brothers, swearing never to betray them. Wherever your steps take you, you will find your brothers in every corner of the globe. They will protect you to the death. But bear in mind that while the Suey Sing protects, it also punishes. Should you prove to be a traitor, we will seek you out mercilessly and the earth will drink your blood. Do you understand?"

"Yes, *Kai Yee*."

"Then swear the vow and drink the blood."

Fong took the bowl. "I swear fealty to the Suey Sing," he intoned, raising the bowl with both hands above his head. "And should I prove unfaithful, may the life be dashed from my miserable body."

"Ho!" roared the tong as the boy drained the disgusting contents of the bowl in one gulp.

The *Kai Yee* reached for a sword. "You are now a blood brother," he said, holding the sword upright before him. "But word has reached me that you are a spy from the Hop Sing Tong."

The boy's eyes widened. "No, *Kai Yee*, it isn't true!"

"You have betrayed our tong by falsely swearing fealty. You must now pay the price for your betrayal."

The *Kai Yee* swung the sword down, half-decapitating Fong. The teenager fell to his knees, blood spurting from the hacked gash in his neck. Then he collapsed in his own blood, dead at nineteen.

The *Kai Yee* raised the bloody sword and swung it three times in a circle above his head, sending fresh blood spraying around the room, spattering the walls and ceiling.

"Thus shall come death to all spies and traitors of the mighty Suey Sing!" he cried.

"Ho!" roared the tongmen.

The *Kai Yee* handed his sword to one of Fong's sponsors, then walked out of the room as the tongmen began to remove the body.

The *Kai Yee* was Crane Kung, the heir of Star Kinsolving Collingwood's mother, Chingling.

"My dear countess," Mrs. Leland Stanford said, "there is no doubt in my mind that you are a genius with a needle, but you're wasting your talents on me. I'm fat as a cow."

The wife of the former governor and co-organizer of the transcontinental railroad that had linked California to the rest of America eight years earlier was standing before a triple mirror in Countess Davidoff's temple of haute couture. Zita was rearranging the magenta bustle of the dress as two seamstresses stood by, watching. Jane Stanford might be one of the richest women in America, mistress of a two-million-dollar mansion at the corner of California and Powell streets on Nob Hill, owner of one of the greatest jewel collections in the world, with sixty pairs of diamond earrings, but she was undeniably fat. The bustle didn't help.

"My dear Mrs. Stanford," Zita said, smiling, "I have a wonderful new diet: grapefruit salads and tea. I lost three pounds in a week. You must try it."

"I have no time for diets. Leland and I are always going to political banquets, and one can't diet at banquets. Eating is the only thing that gets you through the boring speeches. And speaking of politics, how is poor Senator Collingwood?"

"Much better, I believe."

"I'm relieved to hear it. He's such a sweet man—and so dashing. Well, Zita, you've done it again. The dress is superb—all of them are. I'll take all six."

The new de Meyer's, six stories of exuberant French Second Empire architecture that took up one whole side of Union Square at Geary and Stockton streets, had opened five years before and was the talk of the West. The shifting tides of real-estate fashion had seen Portsmouth Square ebb as Union Square, named for a pro-Union rally held there during the Civil War, began to flood. Emma took the plunge, and the flag-bedecked department store with its system of pneumatic tubes and its terrifying new hydraulic elevators had been an instant success. Zita, in her Salon de Bon Ton on the second floor, was now dressing the wives of all the Big Four railroad kings: besides Mrs. Stanford, Mrs. Mark Hopkins (whose three-million-dollar Nob Hill mansion had stables with crystal chandeliers and rosewood horse stalls), the socially ambitious Mrs. Charles Crocker (whose mansion covered an entire block on Nob Hill), and Mrs. Collis P. Huntington (who, it was whispered, had once been a prostitute). San Francisco was a born-again boomtown. In 1859, just as the gold rush had slowed to a crawl, the Comstock Lode was discovered in Nevada and a new flood of silver had poured into the city on the bay, bringing a second boom bigger than the first. And all those newly rich wives lusted for clothes.

And jewels. Ten minutes after buying six thousand dollars' worth of Zita's custom-made dresses, Jane Stanford was in Felix de Meyer's jewelry boutique staring with hungry eyes at a magnificent pearl-and-diamond choker with a $300,000 price tag.

"Felix," she said, "it's beautiful. Breathtaking! But Leland says I'm spending far too much on jewelry. He says I'm in danger of becoming frivolous."

"Ah, but you are not just investing in jewelry," Felix said, clasping the choker around her pudgy neck. "You are investing in poetry. These pearls are the tears of mermaids."

Felix, still dapper but increasingly frail as he neared seventy, had floated to immense wealth servicing one of the greatest buying sprees in history. His customers with their itchy millions didn't need much of a sales pitch, but they loved listening to his mellifluous words anyway.

"You wizard," she sighed, looking at the jewels in a mirror. "You know my sales resistance melts before you. It is magnificent. But Leland says we must think of the poor, the wretched of this earth . . . Ah, but it is lovely. 'The tears of mermaids.' How can one resist?"

"I have just sold Mrs. Hearst a magnificent sapphire-and-diamond necklace, which she is wearing to my granddaughter's engagement ball next month."

Jane Stanford flashed him a look. "Phoebe Hearst is getting a little too uppity, if you ask me. You'd think she owned Nob Hill, the way she flaunts her money."

"Zita tells me the Czarina of Russia has a choker very much like this," Felix went on, knowing the key to sales success was persistence.

Jane Stanford's eyes returned to the mirror. She sighed. "I must have it. I—"

"Poppa!"

They all turned to the doorway of the heavily gilt Louis XIV-style boutique. Emma, in a sable-trimmed dress, was leaning against the door, tears streaming down her cheeks.

"Emma! What's wrong?"

"Oh, Poppa, Archer is dead."

Zita, who had accompanied Jane Stanford, hurried to Emma's side. Emma fell into her arms and gave way to hysterical sobs.

"Dead?" Felix exclaimed. "But the doctors said the crisis was over."

"Those horrid, stupid doctors, what do they know? They didn't even know it was typhoid fever till two weeks ago. I should have taken him to Boston, where they have decent hospitals . . . Oh, my darling husband, gone, gone, forever gone . . ."

"Dearest Emma, sit down," Zita said, helping her to a sofa. "I have some smelling salts—"

"No, no, I'll be all right. The sweetest man that was ever born, an angel . . . I'll *never* find another like him!"

Jane Stanford thought: Never find another so easy to boss around is more like it.

The next morning at breakfast, Emma suddenly remarked to her father, "A hospital."

"A what?"

"A hospital. I'll build a hospital and name it after Archer. The city needs a first-rate hospital and I'll build the best in the country. The Archer Collingwood Memorial Hospital. Poppa, isn't that a good idea?"

"Yes, darling," Felix said, taking her hand. "It's a wonderful idea."

"And that way the world will never forget him."

27

"So she's buried husband number two," Slade Dawson mused as he sat at the breakfast table of his Nob Hill mansion, perusing the morning editions. Emma's *Times-Dispatch* had, naturally, blared a headline: "DISTINGUISHED SENATOR COLLINGWOOD SUCCUMBS TO TYPHOID!" while Slade's *Bulletin* had buried the story on page two: "POLITICO DIES OF FEVER."

"You recall the first one," said his wife, who had changed her name from Letty to Loretta and become an Episcopalian in an attempt to mask her past as a hooker. "There wasn't anything left to bury except an ounce of ashes. Remember when she came in my room at the Bonanza and stuck a pistol to your head?"

Slade was still lean, but his black hair and mustache had turned gray. As he sipped his orange juice, he growled, "I'll never forget it. That bitch scared twenty years out of me."

"That bitch hasn't invited us to her daughter's engagement ball," Loretta said, slabbing a piece of toast with butter and marmalade. After bearing Slade two children, she had loosened her girdle and gone to fat. "She never invites us to anything, the stuck-up snob. Not that I'd go if we were invited, although I wouldn't mind seeing the inside of her house."

"My society editor's been there, and she tells me it's no better than ours." Slade finished his orange juice, then lit a cigarillo to smoke with his coffee. One day in 1858 a miner who had run up gambling debts of five thousand dollars at the Bonanza casino had settled by signing over his shares in a Nevada silver mine to Slade. Six months later, the former Mississippi gambler woke up to find himself part owner of the Comstock Lode, a silver baron worth fifty million dollars. After this catapult to fabulous riches, Slade put a big distance between himself and the Sydney Duck gangs. Emma's "garbage" epithet rang in his ears, and he decided to go respectable, or as respectable as he could be with an ex-whore for a wife. As he often said to Loretta, "If Collis P. Huntington can do it, why can't I?" He sold his share of the Bonanza Café to Chicago and, aside from publishing the *Bulletin*, began developing real estate. His greatest coup was building a fantastic hotel on what was becoming one of the most fashionable streets in the city, New Montgomery Street. Modestly named the Grand, the hotel covered two acres, had seven thousand bay windows, and its dining room boasted a one-hundred-piece service of solid gold. Slade Dawson had come a long way from his days as a con man and riverboat gambler.

He tapped his cigarillo in a silver ashtray. "Besides," he said, "there may not be any engagement ball for Miss Star Collingwood and Mr. Clayton Fancy-Pants Delamere."

"Why?" Loretta asked, her mouth full of toast.

"I've been waiting twenty-five years to get something on Emma Collingwood—"

"Honey, you certainly printed enough about her buyin' a pardon for that bank robber she married."

"Yes, but hell, it didn't seem to bother the public. They thought it was sort of funny. And I can't get much more out of the crown prince's drunken antics: they think that's funny too. But I've put one of my reporters on the lovely Miss Star, and he's come up with something that's going to blow the Collingwoods right out of the water."

Loretta leaned forward, her eyes bright. "Tell me!"

Slade smiled slightly. "Star Collingwood's got a Celestial boyfriend."

Loretta Dawson, the former Letty Brown of Parlor A, gasped. "You're kidding."

"Nope. And it gets better. There's been a murder in Chinatown. The police found the body of a decapitated boy. Rumor has it that the boy was a spy for a rival tong and that the Suey Sing murdered him. More specifically, the leader of the Suey Sing Tong, who calls himself the *Kai Yee*, or Godfather, of Chinatown, is a man named Crane Kung. Crane inherited all the money from Scott Kinsolving's Chinese mistress, and the police think he controls the opium and singsong-girl rackets. Star Collingwood's Celestial lover is this same Crane Kung."

"Jesus Christ, Slade, can you prove it?"

"Not only can I prove it, I'm going to publish it on the morning of Star Collingwood's engagement ball. And that night, the great Emma de Meyer Kinsolving Collingwood, who's spending a hundred thousand bucks on this blowout, is going to hold court at her big fancy mansion to an empty house."

Loretta Dawson purred. "Slade, sweetheart, I'm just tinglin' all over. Revenge is even better than sex."

Slade gave his pudgy wife a wry look. "I'm surprised you can remember."

* * *

With the rapid development of San Francisco, names had changed with bewildering speed. What had once been the Spanish Calle de la Fundación was renamed after a certain Captain Samuel F. Dupont, and this became the principal street running through Little China, known for years as Dupont Gai. But after the Civil War it was renamed again for Ulysses S. Grant, and the main thoroughfare of what was now called Chinatown became Grant Avenue. In a similar vein, when Crane had inherited Chingling's estate, he assumed the name of her Chinese father, Kung, since Ah Toy had died in China of natural causes.

As Crane rose to power in Chinatown, enriching himself with the rent rolls of the Chinatown real estate he had inherited, he built himself a stucco mansion in the Chinese style on Grant Avenue and surrounded his garden with a high stucco wall pierced by three moon gates. Here he installed himself as a Chinese warlord, though he was careful to maintain a respectable facade. The Suey Sing guards stationed around the house twenty-four hours a day hinted that the mansion was not exactly a stronghold of "law and order," but the San Francisco police tended to avert their eyes from what they considered the inherently criminal tendencies of the "heathen Chinee." Ten thousand Cantonese peasants had been imported from China at forty dollars a head (making a tidy profit for the Kinsolving Lines) to build the transcontinental railroad across the Sierra Nevada Mountains; and after the railroad's completion in 1869, they had returned to swell the population of Chinatown. Despised by most whites, the poor coolies (a word derived from the Chinese words for "dirty work") swarmed the narrow alleys of Chinatown looking for work, women, and fan-tan parlors. Since the ratio of Chinese men to Chinese women was woefully lopsided, the importation of singsong girls was the obvious answer to the problem. And with the Celestial whores had come opium. Thus, to the round-eyes, Chinatown was considered a moral sewer. And the Chinese, struggling to keep afloat in an alien culture, wrestling to learn a difficult language, began gravitating to the tongs as organizations that could help them survive in hostile America.

Even as a teenager, Crane had perceived that the tongs were the pathway to power. With his money, his black belt in tae kwon do, and his fierce will, he soon became head of the powerful Suey Sings.

But there were others in Chinatown plotting to destroy the warlord of San Francisco.

"*Kai Yee*, this note has just been delivered from Nob Hill," said Li Wang Yu, Crane's second in command and martial-arts sparring partner. Crane had been meditating in the gymnasium of his mansion, for he also practiced yoga. Taking the letter from Li, he opened it and read:

My only love:
My heart is so full of sorrow. Not only have I lost my beloved father, but now a new plague has come. Mother is convinced you are responsible for the murder of the young Hop Sing. Oh, my sweet love, I know she is wrong, but I can't convince her of your innocence. Alas, in the past few years she has turned more and more against you. Now she has forbidden me even to see you or come to you, and I don't know what to do.
When you came to my mother ten years ago and told her you had made a pledge to my natural mother, Chingling, to teach me the Chinese culture that is part of my heritage, you changed my life. Mother was reluctant, but I came to you eager and full of joy. Your teaching me the beauties of Chinese culture was like the sweetest rain that nourished flowers of thought in my mind as your own dear self nourished the flower of love in my heart. But also, perhaps inevitably, you sowed the seeds of confusion within me. How I have agonized over the differences between my parents' world and yours, for which do I belong to?
Now Father is gone and Mother is pushing me into the marriage with Clayton. Oh, dear one, I have told you I don't love Clayton, I have told you marrying him is the last thing I desire. But I simply cannot bring myself to deny Mother what she wants, as she has been such a dear, loving parent. And yet, the thought of losing you tears me asunder! Oh, Crane, my heart is yours and always will be. But what in God's name can we do? I cannot live in both worlds, and if I go into yours I will have to sever my ties with my family forever. So, after giving it my deepest thoughts, I have come to the conclusion that there is no future for us.
I can barely bring myself to write the word "farewell" to someone whom I love more than life itself. I love you forever, my true heart, but . . . Dear God, can I write this?
Farewell.

                                                        Star

Crane read the letter twice. The look on his scarred face was murderous.

When it came to death, Emma was very much a woman of her generation: she believed in all the lugubrious pomp of the Victorians, for whom death scenes held the fascination that sex scenes would for their descendants. Since Archer was not Jewish, there was no question of her sitting shiva for him. But she draped the limestone mansion in yards of black crepe and received for two full days. Archer's open bronze casket sat in the great entrance hall, banked by masses of flowers as the Episcopalian organist played on the pipe organ Emma had had installed under the right stair. She stood beside the coffin as the rich and famous of California came to pay their final respects to the man who had gone from prison to the U.S. Senate to champion the unpopular cause of the red man.

The funeral, by contrast, was kept small. David Levin arrived early in his carriage and was greeted at the door of the Nob Hill palace by a subdued Can Do. David, wearing formal mourning clothes with a black ribbon tied around his silk hat, looked properly gloomy, though Archer had never been one of his favorites. The years had treated David well: his gray beard was now trimmed in the currently fashionable Imperial style, and good living had put some twenty pounds on his scrawny body, giving him a dignity he had lacked as a youth. As he handed his coat and hat to Can Do, the latter indicated Emma at the other side of the hall, standing alone beside the open coffin. David went over to her. She was looking at the face of her dead husband. She gave no indication of being aware of David's presence for almost a minute. Then she said, "It's odd. He disapproved of me, you know."

"In what way?"

"My success. Archer really was an idealist. He never was comfortable with all our wealth. Oh, he loved me, but I think he would have been happier if I'd been a . . . I don't know, a washerwoman or something. His son disapproves of me too, although he's quite content being rich, thank you." She sighed, then turned to David and took his hand. "I miss him so," she went on. "I loved Scott, but Archer was the one true passion in my life. I don't think I'll ever marry again."

David gave her gloved hand a compassionate squeeze. "Don't be too sure," he said, and the remark was not without a certain self-serving element. In his heart, he still had hopes.

"Dear David," Emma said, smiling. "How much we've gone through together. But the irony is, I don't believe I'm successful at all—at least as a mother. My son is becoming a drunkard and my daughter . . . well, you know my fears about her relationship with Crane, which is all my fault, in a way. Although I think I've put an end to that. . . . David, might I ask you a favor?"

"Of course."

"I have to find something for Archer to do. The only thing he's ever shown any interest in is the newspaper. I know you disapprove of his wildness, but do you think you could find him a job at the *Times-Dispatch*? I don't want any favoritism shown—let him start at the bottom, I don't care. Would you do that for me?"

"Of course." My God, he thought, that spoiled brat on my hands?

Emma smiled, put her arms around him, and gave him a hug. "Dearest David," she whispered. "My truest friend."

That word! Thirty years a goddamned friend.

"Let's not let Archer know we had this conversation," she added, releasing him. "I want him to choose which business to go into, but I think he'll pick the newspaper. I want him to think he's making the choice himself. But I also wanted to check with you first."

She gave him a smile, and though it was sad, it still worked its magic. What an old fool I am, he thought. I still can't get this woman out of my heart.

"Archer, please don't get drunk," Star said, coming into the paneled library. Her brother was pouring himself a whiskey from the crystal decanter. "Not tonight, of all nights. They're just carrying out Poppa's casket."

"Why shouldn't I get drunk?" Archer asked, taking a big gulp of the bourbon. "That godawful organ music, all this crepe, poor Father lying in that ugly casket—"

"I don't think it's ugly."

"All caskets are ugly. Death is ugly. But this funeral was all wrong. It should have been held outdoors somewhere, in the woods he loved. He hated this house, which Mother never understood. Father was a free spirit who got trapped by Mrs. Moneybags."

"You don't seem to mind spending Mrs. Moneybags' money," said a voice behind him. Archer almost choked on his whiskey. His mother, dressed in black with three strands of pearls around her neck, stood in the pedimented door.

"Why have you been so cruel to me?" she asked, coming to her son. "Ever since your father's death, you've hardly said a word to me when I needed your love and support. And now, this cheap, contemptuous 'Mrs. Moneybags' slur—"

"You don't need my support," he said angrily. "You've never needed anybody's support. You're strong—stronger than most men! You were certainly stronger than my father, God rest his soul."

"Is it a crime to be strong?"

"It's unnatural. You're a woman. You should be doing womanly things like . . . like—"

"Needlepoint?" Emma interrupted, her magnificent eyes blazing.

"Yes! Or playing the piano. When I was a kid, I used to love listening to you play, but you haven't touched the piano in years. Now all you think of is business and money. Most women never see an office in their entire lives, but your office is your home! Your bank, your insurance company, the store, the shipping company—that's where your heart lies."

"My heart lies buried with your father, so don't tell me about my heart. But I'm quick to admit—as was your father—that although he had many fine qualities, a head for business wasn't one of them. I'm proud of what I've accomplished. I certainly don't have to defend myself to my son, whose main accomplishment in life so far seems to be a record-breaking capacity for alcohol."

"Yes, I drink, and you want to know why? Most sons have to compete with their fathers, which is bad enough. But I have to compete with my mother, which is totally unfair! Do you have any idea how hard it is for me?"

Emma looked at her son. She loved him so possessively that she had forced herself to keep an emotional distance over the years so as not to smother him, something she had seen other Nob Hill mothers do to their sons with disastrous results. But she didn't love him blindly. Now, as she studied his face—one that combined his father's Anglo-Saxon handsomeness with a hint of her own Jewish beauty—she detected the first signs of dissipation: tiny wrinkles around the blue eyes, incipient puffiness in the strong jawline. Even the rich, straight blond hair was beginning to thin a bit at the temples, and he was only twenty-six. But she could easily guess how hard it was for him to compete with her.

"We're not going to fight," she said, hugging him. "Especially right after your father's funeral. But the last thing I want is to be your competition, my darling." She released him. "I suppose a lot of what you say is true. Don't think I'm not aware of what people say behind my back—they say it to my face, as far as that goes. 'A woman's place is in the home,' 'she wears the pants in the family,' and so on, ad nauseam. A lot of them even say I'm good in business because I'm Jewish."

"Then they're not worth bothering about," Archer said.

"Of course they're not, but they say it. This country is all about becoming rich—for better or for worse—but God help you if you do, because then they'll say anything and everything about you. At any rate, Archer, I hope you and I can make a new beginning. I've let you go your merry way up to now because . . . well, I suppose because I've spoiled you. Probably a lot of your resentment is my fault. But the point is, your father is gone now, and whatever our differences, we're a family, and family is the important thing. Especially since you're the head of it now."

"Am I?" he asked. There was more than a hint of skepticism in his voice, which she didn't fail to notice.

"You are if you put that drink down."

He looked surprised. He glanced from the glass in his hand to his mother and back at the glass. He took a deep breath, walked to a potted palm, and poured in the whiskey.

Emma smiled. "That, my darling son, is your first step toward manhood. Now, I'm offering you a job. You can be the head of the family, but I'm still running the businesses until we see if you're any good and until you know what's what. You can start in any of the businesses you wish. In the past, you used to ask me questions about the newspaper. Would you like to start there?"

"Yes!" he said, so fast it left no doubt where his heart was.

"Good. Report to David Levin in the morning. You can learn the business from the bottom up. Now, my darlings, shall we go to dinner?"

All things considered, Emma thought, I handled that pretty well.

Star studied her naked reflection in the full-length mirror. Though she was normally vain, she sometimes wished she didn't look quite so different. The mixture of Scott Kinsolving's genes with Chingling's had produced an exotic creature who never failed to leave men gaping and women envious. Though few Californians had heard of an Austrian monk named Gregor Mendel, who was perfecting the science of genetics half a world away, nature knew, and Scott's genes had dominated. Thus Star's hair was a soft dark red, almost auburn, and her skin was white. But her amber eyes were almond-shaped, her face slightly round, and this hint of the Orient made her beauty spectacular. She was tall and slender, with small breasts and delicately rounded hips.

She was made for love, and she was in love. The object of her affections just didn't happen to be Clayton Delamere.

She went to her four-poster bed with the white canopy and took the white lace nightgown with pretty pink bows off the duvet. Zita had designed it, as she did all of Star's lingerie. Slipping it over her head, Star climbed into bed. Being the daughter and granddaughter of the owners of de Meyer's, she had an open account at the store, and her three enormous closets bulged with clothes and shoes and hats, gloves, accessories. Star adored clothes and she adored her mother for indulging her, but tonight she was nervous about those bulging closets, and it wasn't for the first time. If Emma was a problem for Archer, she was also one for Star, though in a different way. Star had admired the way her mother had handled Archer that night, and she was thrilled that her adopted brother seemed to be turning over a new leaf (if he in fact gave up his drinking, perhaps that would end his drunken advances on her). Family, her mother had said. Family was the most important thing.

Crane Kung was definitely not family.

She turned down her bed lamp, watching the shadows filter through the pink silk curtains and onto the dusky-rose wallpaper. She had to rip Crane out of her soul, uproot him like a dangerous weed. She had turned down so many eligible bachelors that she had finally run out of excuses. When her mother had pointed out that she was twenty-six and it was time, she finally gave in to the inevitable and accepted the proposal of Clayton Delamere. Clayton was not exactly a consolation prize. The handsome, kind son of one of the silver barons was certainly a catch. Moreover, he was madly in love with her and it was impossible for her even to consider not marrying him. It would destroy her mother. Her family.

But as she closed her eyes, she still burned for the fierce, muscular *Kai Yee* of Chinatown who had set her body and soul aflame.

She was awakened by a clinking sound.

Hurriedly sitting up and raising the bed lamp, she looked at one of the open windows. Beneath it a strange three-pronged iron hook was tearing the rose wallpaper. A rope was attached to the grappling iron, and someone was climbing the rope toward her window. She was starting to panic when she saw Crane's scarred face appear over the sill. Quickly he climbed in, pulling the rope up after him. Then he turned to look at Star. As usual, he wore his blue-black pajama suit with black sandals, and his black hair was pulled tightly back into a pigtail.

"You madman," she whispered. "What do you think you are, some Chinese pirate? If Mother finds out—"

"To hell with your mother."

He pulled his silk shirt over his head and threw it onto a chair. She looked at his hairless torso: after years of tae kwon do, every ligament was defined. He came to the bed and put his left knee on it, taking her face in his hands and pulling it to him. He kissed her with raw passion. She didn't even pretend to resist. She was like an addict who had tried to abstain from the drug she craved but was now giving in again to the hunger. Her hands rubbed his muscular back as he pressed down on her, his mouth still on hers.

He pulled her nightgown up and he moved his mouth down to her pointed nipples, first licking them, then sucking them, then biting them as his hand rubbed her *mons pubis*. As usual, the direct fierceness of his lovemaking drove her wild.

"Crane," she moaned, after pulling the nightgown over her head. She closed her eyes and repeated: "Crane."

He stood up and pulled his pants down, throwing them on the floor. He wore nothing underneath.

"I got your damned letter," he said as he climbed back on top of her. The heat, strength, and smell of his body enveloped her. "It was a pack of lies. You can't say farewell to me. Our souls are like one. Leave Nob Hill and all these stupid round-eyes. Marry me, Star, not that lapdog round-eye, who probably has a pickle for a penis."

Now she tried to resist. Family. She pushed against his steellike chest. "Crane, stop it—"

"You want me the way I want you. Say it!"

"It's true I . . . Oh, God, don't make it so difficult. I . . ."

His finger was inside her, softly massaging her. She couldn't speak, she was so overwhelmed by sheer animal lust. Then he licked his way down her body and she felt his mouth at her vagina and his hot breath was on her flat belly and his tongue was inside her.

"Oh, God . . ."

After what seemed an eternity, he pulled away from her and climbed up her body again, kissing her with abandon as his hands kneaded her buttocks. He seemed to commandeer her body, to own her. There was no part of her he didn't dominate, physically and mentally.

No, no, she thought, I have to fight him.

She pushed him as hard as she could.

"What's wrong?" he said, stopping his lovemaking.

"You know what's wrong." She was on the verge of tears. "I said it in the letter: we have no future."

"Why? Don't you love me?"

"Of course! You know I'm crazy about you, but I can't marry you."

"Because I'm Chinese?"

"Crane, I'm half Chinese. It's not that. Nor is Mother prejudiced that way. It's . . ." She hesitated.

"What is it? What has she said about me?"

"She thinks you're a criminal."

"And you? What do you think?"

"I know you're not . . ." Again she hesitated. Looking at the anger blazing in his eyes, she wondered for the first time if her mother might not be right after all. "You're not, are you?" she whispered.

"A criminal is someone who breaks laws he recognizes. Since I don't recognize the white man's laws, I don't consider myself a criminal." He got off the bed and put on his trousers. "You're right after all, Star. We have no future. You stay here in your Nob Hill mansion and pretend you're a round-eye. I'm going back to Chinatown and my people."

"Wait . . ."

"For what? You obviously don't love me."

"I do, but . . ."

"Not enough. If you loved me enough, you'd come with me."

"Crane, it's not that simple. What do you mean, you don't recognize the white man's laws?"

"Just that."

"Then did you kill the Hop Sing?"

"You sound like a round-eye prosecutor. Maybe you won't have to pretend to be a round-eye—"

"Stop it!" she screamed, jumping off the bed and running to him. She was crying now. She began beating his chest with her fists. For a moment he looked surprised. Then he grabbed her wrists.

"Why are you doing this to me?" she sobbed. "Why are you making me feel so dirty? Can't you see how I'm being torn apart? I love you, Crane! I want you, I want to be your wife, but I can't . . ." She broke down. Burying her face on his chest, she sobbed hysterically. He held her, smoothing her hair.

The door opened. It was Archer, in his pajamas and a bathrobe. He looked at his naked foster sister in the arms of the half-naked Celestial.

"You bastard!"

With a roar of rage, he ran into the room. Star screamed as Crane pushed her away, then turned halfway to confront her charging rescuer. Archer had been middleweight boxing champion at Princeton, but he didn't have a prayer. Crane's left leg shot up and out, plowing into Archer's gut. Then Crane shot out his left arm and smashed his fist into his face. The one-two *kata*, executed with ritualistic economy and grace, sent Archer crumpling to the floor in a semiconscious heap.

Crane took his shirt, went to the window, and threw out the rope. Then he looked at Star.

"I have come to Nob Hill," he said. "The next move is yours. If you want me, come to Chinatown."

It had all happened so fast, she was still in shock. Then, agile as a monkey, he climbed over the windowsill and lowered himself out of sight.

Across the street, in the shadows of the Flood mansion, one of Slade Dawson's *Bulletin* reporters took notes. Digby Lee knew this story was going to sell a lot of newspapers.

28

"LISTEN to this headline!" Slade crowed the next morning as he held up the *Bulletin*. " 'CHINATOWN VICE LORD ENTERS NOB HILL HEIRESS'S BEDROOM WINDOW! What Is Star Collingwood's Tie to Godfather of Chinatown?' "

"I love it, Slade!" Loretta said, sitting opposite him at the breakfast table. "But I thought you were going to wait till the engagement ball."

"What engagement ball? You don't think Clayton Delamere will marry her now? Not on your life. Besides, when they drop a whopper like this in your lap, you don't wait. Can you beat it? He climbed up a rope right into her window, then twenty minutes later climbs back out with his shirt off. If that doesn't take the all-time prize for nerve!"

"Oh, I can just imagine what Emma Collingwood must be going through. She must be furious. The whole town will be laughing at her."

Her husband leaned forward. "That's just what I'm thinking, Loretta. And I'm also thinking that this may be our big chance."

"For what?"

"Well, we've finally finished this house, which has got to be as fancy as any other house on Nob Hill. But we've never invited anyone in."

Loretta frowned. "You know why, honey. We've always laid sort of low socially, because of . . . you know, the past."

"To hell with the past. That was all twenty-five years ago. We're as good as anyone else in this town."

"Do you think so?" Loretta asked rather wistfully.

"Hell, yes! Now, here's what we're going to do: I've got a list from my society editor of everyone Emma invited to her daughter's engagement ball. You're going to send an invitation to everyone on that list to a ball here that same night. 'Mr. and Mrs. Slade Dawson request the honor of your presence at a reception, or open house, or whatever you call it . . . Come see our fancy new home.' I'll tell Alicia Beaumont to help you with the invites—she knows all that fancy stuff. It's time you and I took our place in this town as the important people we are."

Excitement was banking in her eyes. "Do you think people really would come?"

"Sure they'll come. I'm getting the swellest people in San Francisco at my hotel. If they go there, they'll come here. And I can tell you one thing: there won't be a respectable couple in California that would step foot in the Collingwood house after this headline, even if she does go ahead with the ball. And with the Collingwood reputation ruined, people may stop doing business with them too. We might just be able to buy them out one day, ten cents on the dollar."

His wife looked at him admiringly. "So that's what's behind all this. You're not only after revenge, you want to gobble them up."

"Anything wrong with that?" He smiled as he lit a cigarillo.

"How could you?" Emma cried a few blocks away as she crumpled the *Bulletin*. "On the very night of your father's funeral, you let this criminal into your bedroom and make love to him. You humiliate your family. After all the love you father and I have given you, I can't believe you would pay us back this way, with shame and ridicule."

"Mother, please . . ."

Star was sitting at the breakfast table, her face swollen from crying. Archer sat opposite her, a bandage over his left cheek where Crane had slugged him. Emma was pacing around the table in a towering rage.

" 'Mother please'? Please what? Please forgive you? Of course I forgive you: you're my daughter. But how could you have been so thoughtless? I assume this was not the first time he made love to you?"

"No, it wasn't. But I love him—"

"You desire him. That's something else entirely. I can't believe you could love a murderer—"

"We don't know that!"

"We know it! Don't fool yourself. My reporters are uncovering the same facts Slade Dawson's reporters are. Crane Kung is running most of the crime in Chinatown—opium and singsong girls, as well as owning a dozen fan-tan parlors. This is the man you desire. This is the man you let in your bedroom last night—"

"I didn't let him in! He crawled in the window—what was I supposed to do, push him out?"

"You didn't even push him out of your bed! I can't believe it. I'm trying to bring grand opera to San Francisco, and my daughter acts out a scene from opéra bouffe in her bedroom. Oh, I'm not going to preach or be holier-than-thou. I've always been honest with you two about my own past, and God knows I was no lily. But this lurid romance, if you can call it that, this throwing out of all common sense . . ."

She paused as she saw Can Do appear in the doorway.

"Excuse me, Taitai. A note just been delivered from Mr. Clayton."

Emma closed her eyes in resignation. "Well, I was expecting this. Give it to me, please."

Can Do brought her the envelope on a silver salver, then retired as she read it. She placed the note on the table.

"You can guess what it says. Clayton is sorry, he loves you, but under the circumstances his father has insisted he withdraw his proposal of marriage. Well, that does it."

"Oh, Momma!" Star rose, sobbing, and ran out of the room.

Emma sank into her chair to finish her coffee. "The one man I get her to accept, and now he cancels." She sighed. "I wonder if she'll ever get a husband now. Oh, I can't believe this has happened." She looked at her son. "Do you think I was too hard on her?"

"Not at all. She deserved it. I can't understand what Star sees in him."

"I can. He's exotic, he's dangerous, and he's Chinese. Star has always been confused by her heritage, which is natural. My mistake was letting Crane teach her, but when he came to me ten years ago I thought it was reasonable that she learn Chinese. Of course, I should have guessed there'd be trouble. Slade Dawson must be dancing in the street."

"I have a confession to make."

"What?"

"I've known for some time that Star was involved with Crane."

His mother shot him a look. "Why didn't you tell me?"

"I wanted to stay out of it. No, it's more than that. I . . ." He toyed with his fork. "I had mixed feelings about Star myself. I always have."

"What kind of mixed feelings?"

"She's very beautiful."

Emma frowned. "Yes, I sensed there was a certain tension between you two. I pray to God I don't have to worry about that."

He shook his head. "No, you don't."

"If Slade Dawson suspected that, it would really be the end. God, I hate that man. He caused the death of my first husband, and now he's covered us with shame and ridicule."

She turned away, clenching and unclenching her fist. As Archer watched her, he detected for the first time in his life a chink in his formidable mother's armor.

"Couldn't we attack him back?" he asked. "After all, everyone knows his wife was a prostitute."

"That's the problem: everyone knows. Loretta Dawson's nothing but a joke, what with her changing her name and becoming a devout churchgoer, buying her way into heaven." She hesitated, thinking. "On the other hand, maybe you're right. I know they're terribly sensitive about Loretta's past, as well they might be. And maybe it would sell some papers, which would be a blessing."

"What do you mean?"

She sighed. "You might as well know the truth now that you're going to start work at the paper. The *Times-Dispatch* is losing circulation. David Levin is a fine editor, but he's too principled, too classy. The public wants scandal and crime, they want excitement. The *Bulletin* gives it to them—it must have sold out this morning's edition!—and it's leaving the *Times-Dispatch* in the dust. Slade even made me an offer to buy it three years ago at a ridiculous price, but I turned him down, naturally."

"I wish you'd told me that."

"You were drunk three years ago."

"I might not have been if I'd known this."

He stood up.

"Where are you going?"

"To work. Remember? You gave me a job last night." He came around and kissed her. "And don't worry about Slade Dawson. I have an idea how to handle him."

She looked up at him. "What do you mean?"

He grinned as he left the room. "You'll see."

Alone, Emma fought back tears. For so many years she had tried to make the Collingwood name stand for class, culture, and integrity as well as power and wealth, and it had all been destroyed by this one incredibly stupid incident. She knew San Franciscans: if they weren't shocked by what had happened, they would be howling with laughter, which was almost worse.

She pushed away from the table. To be the laughingstock of California was, for a woman of her pride, excruciating. She walked to one of the high windows, nervously rubbing her hands as she looked through the lace curtains at the Flood mansion across the street. Was he laughing at her? Were all of them laughing at her, the Crockers, the Stanfords, the Hopkinses, the Hearsts? Scandal. And not the least galling aspect was that Slade Dawson's newspaper had scooped her own. The lead article in that morning's *Times-Dispatch* had been the need for more cultural institutions in San Francisco, including opera. What wonderful timing.

She had to do something, but what could she do? She paced about the table, frowning for a moment at the magnificent hand-painted wallpaper. As furious as she was at her daughter, she knew she had to protect her—if it wasn't already too late. In one appallingly catastrophic evening Star had plummeted from being San Francisco's most-sought-after debutante to a girl no eligible male would touch with a ten-foot pole. Her beauty, her family, and her wealth had overcome whatever racial objections society might have had about her mixed blood, but Emma knew that her going to bed with a tong lord would make her an instant pariah. Of course, she might try to picture it as a case of rape, but what San Francisco mother would buy that?

I have to get her out of town, she thought. Find her another husband somewhere else. But where?

Suddenly she knew. Yes, she thought, he's perfect. And he's in love with her, I'd swear. That one time he saw her six months ago, his jaw dropped. If only he's still available . . . there aren't many women down there . . .

She hurried to the petit-point bell cord and rang for Can Do.

There's no time to lose. If I can make a deal with his mother . . . And why can't I? They're practically penniless, and I hold the mortgage. Thank God for Scott's foresight. He always said that ranch was a good investment, and if it turns out to save Star, it will be a godsend.

"Taitai rang?" Can Do was standing in the door.

"Yes. Tell the coachman to get the carriage ready—the big one. And tell Adele to pack me enough things for two nights, and Miss Star too. And tell Cook to pack us a hamper. We'll be gone several days."

"Yes, Taitai. Where I tell coachman you going?"

"South. To the Calafía Ranch."

As she hurried out of the baronial dining room, she thought, maybe we'll bring some Spanish blood into the family. Why not? We've got practically everything else.

29

THE six hatchet sons walking down Ross Alley were dressed like all the other Celestials swarming in the narrow lane known as the Street of Gamblers. The Chinese were passionate gamblers, and Ross Alley was lined with murky fan-tan and pak-kop parlors, all advertising hock shops or laundries to fool the police, though they weren't fooled. The six young members of the Hop Sing Tong (The Society of Associated Conquerors) were led by a hulking man with a drooping black mustache and cruel slanted eyes. His name was Wong Yem Yen, and he intended to be the next *Kai Yee* of Chinatown.

They stopped before a two-story wooden building with a sagging porch. It was near midnight and the ground floor looked dark. But Wong Yem Yen and his second in command, Charlie Kong, knew that the Chinese characters "Hall of Celestial Chance" painted on black curtains meant "fan-tan parlor." If Ross Alley—dark, crowded, stinking—looked dangerous, the Hall of Celestial Chance looked downright menacing. Wong opened the door and led his hatchet sons inside.

The cigarette smoke mingling with the sweet smell of opium was as heavy as fog. The dirty room, beneath a filthy tin ceiling, was lined with wooden cots on which reclined the opium smokers, some young, some old with white beards, all with glazed eyes. There were four gambling tables, two for fan-tan, two for pak-kop, and they were surrounded by Celestials. On the fringe of the crowd hovered a few singsong girls, waiting for the winners. The room was hot and badly lit by gas jets. At one fan-tan table the dealer, or *Tan Kun* ("ruler of spreading out"), took a number of tokens from a dish, placed them on the table, and immediately clapped over them an inverted metal bowl. The players then began betting what remainder would be left when the tokens were divided by four.

"Three dollars on zero!" yelled one player in Cantonese.

"Three dollars on three!" yelled another.

Wong pulled a gun from his shirt, as did Charlie Kong beside him. One of the singsong girls saw the guns and screamed.

"Everybody out!" Wong yelled. "Except the *Tan Kuns*! The dealers stay, everyone else out!"

The Celestials thronged toward the door, some helping the groggy opium smokers off their cots and onto their feet. When the parlor was empty of all but the four terrified dealers, Charlie Kong closed and locked the door,

"This joint is owned by Crane Kung," Wong said, advancing on the cowering dealers. "That. Suey Sing bastard murdered one of our men. For every Hop Sing killed, we will take retribution of four Suey Sing minions."

"No!" one of them cried, falling to his knees. "I'm not a member of the tong—"

"For lying, you'll be the first to die."

Wong signaled. Charlie Kong and another hatchet son pulled knives from their shirts and lunged at the dealer, stabbing repeatedly as he screamed. Charlie Kong, who weighed over three hundred pounds, giggled as the hot blood spurted over his enormous belly.

Two of the other dealers bolted for the window. Wong turned and shot them both, though one managed to dive through the plate glass, adding to the racket.

The hatchet sons converged on the fourth dealer, who was backing into a corner of the blood-spattered room. As he squealed like a pig, Charlie Kong and the others stuck him like a pig, stabbing him in a dozen places, Charlie plunging his knife into the man's left eye, going into the brain. Blood gushed. The dingy room was becoming a scarlet pool.

"These fuckers are dead." Charlie grinned, his round face dripping with squirted blood.

"I'll tack up the sign, then let's go," Wong said, going to a wall and pinning up a scroll. It read, in Chinese:

The Hop Sing Tong Declares War on the Suey Sing Tong! The Hop Sings Will Be Victorious! Death and Dishonor to All Suey Sings!

Then Wong and the hatchet sons let themselves out a back door of the Hall of Celestial Chance and vanished.

"Excuse me, Miss Dawson, but I wouldn't recommend that book. I've read it, and it contains certain passages that are a bit highly charged—one might even say passionate—for a young lady of your delicacy and refinement."

Arabella Dawson turned and looked coolly at Archer Collingwood, who had come up behind her in the small bookstore near Montgomery Street.

"Mr. Collingwood," the pretty nineteen-year-old brunette replied, "I hardly need you or any of your family to monitor the morality of my reading matter. However, perhaps your charming sister might suggest some interesting Chinese novels."

Oh, you cool, nasty bitch, Archer thought. He forced a smile. "Touché, Miss Dawson. But perhaps when it comes to romantic literature, your mother might be a better guide. I understand she had extensive experience in the field."

"You cad," she whispered, her face turning red. "Don't you dare speak to me that way. My mother is an upstanding member of the Episcopal Church, and whatever scurrilous, revolting rumors you might have heard about her are filthy lies."

He smiled as he tipped his bowler. "In that case, I retract every word I said. That is, if you will join me for lunch."

"I'd rather lunch with a rattlesnake. My father has told me many times to stay clear of you, and in this instance it is a pleasure to obey him."

Archer sighed. "Ah, well. Then it seems I'll have to do my research elsewhere."

"What research?"

"Well, you see, I've begun working for the *Times-Dispatch*. And it occurred to me that since your father's newspaper has given my family such interesting publicity, it would be only fair for my mother's newspaper to return the favor. Thus, my first assignment has been to write a series of articles about that prominent San Francisco family the Dawsons—particularly their interesting and colorful origins. I thought I could combine work with pleasure by taking you to lunch to interview you about your mother. But since you prefer the company of reptiles, I suppose my next move is to go to Portsmouth Square and interview a certain rotund lady with the interesting name of Chicago." His face lit with a dazzling, shrewd smile.

As Arabella bit her lip, he took in her smart green-and-white-striped bustled dress with a matching hat and parasol. Her hair had been frizzed *à l'africaine*, which, along with poodle-dog fringes and *crève-coeur* curls, was one of the latest crazes in fashion-crazed San Francisco. She had tied a silk ribbon around her long neck (which San Franciscans called "tempration bows" or, in their mania for the French language, "*n'y-touchez-pas*"), two shoo-fly bows in her hair, and her lace stockings were embroidered with strawberries, which was considered about the most daring thing any decent girl could wear. Arabella Dawson was decent with a vengeance, having grown up in the malodorous shadow of her mother's iffy reputation. Archer couldn't have found a better way to terrify this tall, pretty girl with the bottle-green eyes and the ripe figure.

"Very well, Mr. Collingwood," she said. "I will accept your invitation on the condition that we both understand that this is blackmail of the rankest sort, and that you, sir, are no gentleman."

"Oh, I'm worse than that." He smiled and offered her his arm. "I'm a spoiled brat and a drunk. Which is why the ladies find me so devastatingly charming."

"This lady fails to appreciate your devastating charm, sir. Where are we lunching? Chinatown?"

"How about the Bonanza Café?"

He smiled. Again she bit her lip.

"Whatever you may say about my parents," she remarked a half-hour later as they were seated in the elegant restaurant of the recently opened Palace Hotel on New Montgomery Street (not far from Slade Dawson's Grand Hotel, a snub Arabella did not fail to catch), "your late and I am sure lamented father started life as a bank robber."

"This is true. And since your father began his spectacular career as a Mississippi riverboat gambler, I suggest that neither of our families is going to win the Bible Society Award for civic virtue."

She glared at him. René, the tall maître d' who had started his professional career as a dishwasher at Tortoni's in Paris, bowed to the well-dressed, handsome young couple.

"*Monsieur Collingvood, comment ça va?*" he asked, smiling. Archer was one of his best customers and biggest tippers.

"*Ça va bien*, René, you rascal, and you know better than to pull that wretched language of yours on me. Speak English."

"But the tips are better when I speak French," he countered, and Archer laughed.

"*Monsieur Collingwood n'est pas bien élevé*," Arabella said. "*Ou peut-etre il est stupide.*"

"*Oo la la!* Miss Dawson, she just say something terrible about you."

"I caught it. I'm too dumb to speak French."

"Well? Aren't you?" Arabella smiled smugly.

"I can see this is going to be a romantic lunch. René, bring us two champagne cocktails—"

"Pardon me. I will order for myself, thank you. I do not touch alcohol in any form. *Une tasse de thé, s'il vous plaît.*"

"One tea. *Oui, mademoiselle.* And Monsieur Collingvood? *Du champagne?*"

Archer frowned, remembering his pledge to his mother. He hadn't included wine in the pledge. He sighed. "A glass of water."

René looked shocked. "Water? What has happened to you? Fish die in water. Water is unclean."

"I got religion."

Muttering and shaking his head, René signaled to one of his waiters, then handed Arabella one of the enormous menus.

"Je vous recommand les huitres, mademoiselle. Elles sont superbes aujourd'hui. Et aussi le thon."

"He's recommending the oysters and tuna," Arabella said across the table.

"Thanks for the translation," Archer growled. "Perhaps you'll favor us with a can-can after dessert?"

"You not only lack refinement, Mr. Collingwood, you are gross." He's also terribly good-looking, damn him, she thought.

"It would be interesting to have my morals improved by a Dawson," he replied. Her mother may be a whore and her father a scoundrel, he thought, but they produced an interesting daughter. She's got a good head on her shoulders. Of course, she's an impossible snob and no great beauty, but all the same, it will be fun to knock her up.

And then will Slade Dawson howl.

"His full name is Don Juan Ramón José Vicente Santísima Trinidad López y Sepúlveda, but everyone calls him Juanito," Emma said to her daughter as their coach bumped down the Camino Real, sending up clouds of dust. "He's twenty-two, terribly shy, and stutters. His father and older brother are both dead, and he runs the ranch with his mother, Doña Felicidad. Are you listening to me?"

Star was gazing out the window at the brown, barren hills of Southern California. They had entered the Calafía Ranch three miles back; a vaquero at the border had been dispatched ahead of them to announce their arrival at the ranch house, another seventeen miles before them.

"Yes, Mother."

"What did I say?"

"His name is Juanito, he's shy, and he stutters."

"You realize this trip isn't simply an excursion?"

Star sighed. "Mother, I know exactly why we're down here. You want to marry me off, fast."

"I want to arrange a marriage for your own good, darling."

"Which is saying the same thing more politely."

"If you're not going to cooperate, Star, we're just wasting our time. I'm not going to force you into marrying anyone, but—"

"I'll cooperate."

Emma looked at her with compassion. "Darling, I know this is difficult for you—it's difficult for me too—but you do realize this is best for you?"

"I realize."

She turned her gaze back to the coach window. There were no more tears in her eyes: she had cried herself dry. Now she was simply numb. She still burned for Crane, but she was resigned to the fact that she could never see him again. If this Juanito wanted to marry her, fine. She didn't care anymore. Without Crane, her life was over.

She would marry Don Juan Whatever-his-name-was even if he had two heads.

He had only one, and it was far more striking than she remembered. As she stepped from the coach before the white stucco ranch house, he was standing with his mother in the shade of the small porch. A crowd of a dozen vaqueros were leaning on a fence nearby, watching the coach's arrival, for news had quickly spread that Mrs. Collingwood and her daughter were coming. Now Doña Felicidad, an imposing gray-haired woman dressed in black, stepped forward as Emma climbed down.

"Señora Collingwood," she said, extending her hand. "*Bienvenidos. Mi casa es su casa.* We are honored by your visit."

Emma, dressed in a brown traveling suit with a veiled Empress Eugénie hat, smiled as she shook her hand. "Thank you, Doña Felicidad. May I present my daughter, Star?"

Star, wearing a khaki-colored dress, curtsied as Doña Felicidad examined her.

"My son spoke of your beauty after visiting you in San Francisco last fall," she said. "Now I can see that he did not exaggerate. You are exquisite, my child."

"Thank you, Doña Felicidad."

The matron motioned behind her back to her son. "I trust you remember Juan?" she said. "Your mother was kind enough to receive him."

Star looked at the tall young man advancing toward her. She vaguely remembered being introduced to him, but at the time her thoughts had been exclusively on Crane. "Of course I remember," she lied. However, she was pleasantly surprised. Unlike his mother, whose skin was purest white (for Doña Felicidad, like all aristocratic ladies, never exposed her skin to the sun for more than a few minutes), Don Juan was tanned. Six feet tall and lean, he had jet-black hair, dark brown eyes, and thin features with an aquiline nose. He wore a black sombrero with a band of silver tinsel cord almost an inch thick; a *chaqueta,* or jacket, of cloth gaudily embroidered with braid and fancy barrel buttons; and pants called *calzoneras* with the outer part of the leg opened from hip to ankle. The borders were set with filigree buttons, and the whole was fantastically trimmed with tinsel lace. His leather boots had silver Spanish spurs. He stared at Star as if in a trance.

"Juanito," his annoyed mother prompted.

Nervously he glanced at her, then back to Star. He stuck out a trembling hand. "Huh-huh-huh-how do you do?"

Star shook his hand and curtsied. Then she turned to her mother as Juanito continued to gawk at her.

"Shall we go inside out of the sun?" Doña Felicidad inquired. "You've arrived just in time for lunch. Then perhaps Juanito can show the *señorita* some of the ranch, if she'd be interested."

"I'd be very interested," Star said with notable lack of enthusiasm.

"It's aw-aw-aw-awfully b-b-big," Juanito said.

Dear God, Star thought, if this is the man I have to marry, I'm really being punished for my sins.

"Th-th-th-this is a la-la-lariat," Juanito said an hour later. He had been stone silent through the excellent lunch of guacamole and enchiladas—two dishes new to Star. The conversation had been carried by the two older women, consisting principally of ranch business, the pith of which was that a persistent drought was slowly destroying them despite the irrigation system Scott Kinsolving had put in twenty-five years before. After lunch, Juanito had led Star outside to one of the branding pens and begun an impressive demonstration of rope twirling.

" 'La-la-lariat' c-c-comes from the Sp-Sp-Spanish word '*la riata,*' which m-m-means 'r-r-r-rope.' "

The loop he was twirling over his head he now brought down over his body. Expertly he jumped in and out of the twirling circle. Star was as impressed by his agility and grace as she was put off by his miserable stammer, though she noticed that when he spoke Spanish to the watching vaqueros, the stammer vanished. Now he shouted an order in Spanish, and two vaqueros shooed a young bull into the fenced enclosure.

" 'Vaquero' c-c-comes from '*vaca,*' which is Sp-Sp-Sp-Spanish for 'c-c-c-cow,' " he said as he expertly folded his lariat. "Am-American c-c-c-cowboys have ch-changed it to 'b-b-buckeroo.' Now wa-wa-watch, p-p-please."

He mounted a white horse with a handsome tooled-leather saddle. "This s-s-saddle is n-new," he said to Star. "It's c-c-called a Ca-Ca-California s-saddle and it's t-t-ten p-p-pounds lighter than the old Den-Den-Denver s-saddle. I loop the la-lariat around the s-saddle horn. In Sp-Spanish that's called '*dar la vuelta,*' 'to m-make the t-turn', but Am-

Am-American c-c-cowboys ch-changed that to 'dally.' O-ka-ka-kay?"

He dug his silver spurs into the horse and galloped around the enclosure, then through the gate. Star watched, thrilled, as he twirled his lariat, then threw it out, expertly looping it over the bull's neck. Then Juanito jumped off his horse, ran to the bucking animal, grabbed its horns, and twisted its neck until it crashed to the ground on its side. Swiftly he tied the bull's four hooves. As Star clapped and the vaqueros cheered, he remounted his horse and galloped back to her.

"Th-th-that's how we r-r-rope the c-c-cattle," he said.

"I'm very impressed," she said, smiling at him for the first time. And she meant it. She knew that Juanito had wanted to show her that the only thing crippled in his body was his tongue.

"Star's dowry will be one hundred thousand dollars cash," Emma was saying to Doña Felicidad in the rather shabby drawing room of the ranch house. "Plus I will retire the hundred-and-eighty-thousand-dollar mortgage I hold on this ranch as a gift. Of course, Star will also inherit part of my estate. I have recently written a new will and in it I leave her ten million dollars, so if your son marries her you will not only own the ranch free and clear, but Juanito will be a multimillionaire. By marriage, of course."

Doña Felicidad had sat silently in a Spanish-style leather-and-wood chair as Emma spoke. Now she said, "*Señora*, your daughter is very beautiful as well as being very rich. My son is handsome and in his veins flows some of the noblest blood in New Spain. However, we are poor in cash. I assume your daughter could have almost any man in the West. Yet you arrive here unexpectedly and present me with this extraordinary offer. Pardon me, *señora*, but I can't help but feel suspicious. What is wrong? Is your daughter not pure?"

Emma was ready for this. "She is pure in heart. Star is a sweet girl of education and refinement. I have tried to raise her carefully while at the same time offering her the greater freedom that young people in San Francisco seem to want these days. However, I will not lie to you, Doña Felicidad. My daughter is not a virgin. She was violated by a man who presented himself as a teacher of Chinese culture, but who in reality was a criminal."

"Then I assume she was deflowered against her will?"

"Unhappily, that is correct." God forgive me for this lie, Emma thought.

Doña Felicidad rose from her chair and went to a window. She looked out to see Star and Juanito walking toward the irrigated orange grove to the north of the ranch. As the cattle business had become less and less profitable because of drought and the huge cattle ranches that had sprung up in Texas after the Civil War, Scott's prediction that the Calafía Ranch's future lay in citrus fruit and farming had become true. Even so, the cattle losses were still crippling them. Only the infusion of capital from Scott and Emma had kept the ranch together. And now the promise of millions, a bolt from the blue.

She turned back to Emma. "I would of course prefer it if she were pure. But if Juanito wants her, and she agrees to raise their children in the Catholic faith, I will not stand in their way."

For the first time in the three days since the disaster had occurred, Emma felt a wave of relief.

"Well?" Emma asked as she entered her daughter's bedroom that night and sat on the side of the bed. "What do you think of Juanito?"

They had both been given guest rooms on the second floor of the ranch house and, though the furnishings were spare and worn, the architecture of the old house was gracious and the thick walls kept it cool inside. Star's room had two doors that led to a balcony overlooking the rear kitchen garden. She had opened them, and a cool evening breeze fluttered the curtains. To the east, the hills loomed black against a star-strewn sky. To the west lay the Pacific.

"He's very sweet," said Star, who was in a white lace nightgown. "Of course, he has that terrible stammer, but he tried so hard to be polite this afternoon and show me as much of the ranch as he could that I think I rather like him. And, Momma, the ranch is beautiful."

"You like it, then?"

"Oh, very much. Juanito told me he could teach me how to ride astride if I wanted to learn. Naturally I told him no lady would dream of not riding sidesaddle, but I think if I stayed here I'd take him up on it. The distances are so enormous, sidesaddle isn't very practical. The ranch is so huge, it's like a kingdom."

"It may be your kingdom, dear. I spoke to Doña Felicidad. She says if you are willing to raise the children as Catholics, she has no objection to the marriage."

"Juanito hasn't proposed yet."

"He will. Very soon. And if everything goes well, we'll have the wedding Saturday. There's a chapel in the mission at San Juan Capistrano."

"You certainly don't waste time, do you?"

"In this case, no. Then we can bring you and Juanito back up to San Francisco, and the engagement ball that I've ordered all the decorations for we'll turn into your wedding reception."

"I see you've thought everything out. Waste not, want not. Why waste those two hundred cases of French champagne you ordered, just because I scared away my fiancé?"

"I'm practical, yes. And your bitter tone is very unattractive."

Star sighed. "I'm sorry. It doesn't matter, though. I'll do whatever you want. Who cares about love, anyway?"

"I didn't love your father when I married him, but I came to love him very deeply."

"Then maybe I'll come to love Juanito. Who knows? He might even come to love me. But it doesn't matter if he doesn't."

Emma squeezed her hand. "You may be surprised, darling. You may end up happier than you would have been with Clayton." Emma got off the bed and kissed her. "Good night, Star. And I'm delighted you like Juanito."

"Good night, Mother."

Left alone, Star sat in bed staring at the room's slanting ceiling with the exposed wooden beams painted with faded flowers. That's me, she thought. A faded flower. Oh, Crane . . . She closed her eyes and clenched her fists. *No.* Crane was out of her life. Crane was a murderer, a Chinatown vice lord. There could be no question of that now.

Then she remembered his lovemaking and she burned.

She had just turned down the bed lamp when she heard the soft guitar beneath her balcony. Surprised, she got out of bed and went to the open doors. There was no moon and the sky was a breathtakingly lovely purple velvet. She stood for a moment, transfixed by the beauty of the night and the soft strumming of the guitar.

She went out on the balcony and looked down, but it was too dark to see anyone. Then a clear tenor voice began singing *"La Paloma."* It was Juanito's.

In Spanish, he didn't stammer.

30

ALTHOUGH there had been little anti-Chinese feeling in California in the first years after the gold rush, when thousands of Chinese were imported after the Civil War to build the transcontinental railroad, bigotry began to spread, particularly among the lower classes competing for jobs with coolies who would work for practically nothing. By the 1870's anti-Chinese feeling in San Francisco had risen to dangerous levels, fanned by tales of Chinatown crime, of singsong-girl slavery, and the debauchery of the gambling "hells" and opium dens. A so-called "pigtail" ordinance was passed, requiring all jailed criminals to have their hair cut to one inch from the scalp. Although this was ostensibly a sanitary measure to get rid of fleas, the Chinese took it as a way to humiliate them by depriving them of their beloved pigtails. (Though the Manchus had ordered the wearing of pigtails as a badge of inferiority, the Chinese in California had turned it into an object of native pride.) A Cubic Air Ordinance was passed, aimed at the over-crowded tenements in Chinatown, and a fifteen-dollar license fee was slapped on Chinese laundries, a mainstay of the coolie economy. The Six Companies were law-abiding Chinese organizations that the press kept confusing with the tongs, though the Six Companies were about as sinister as the Elks. Their leaders protested these laws as nothing more than legalized prejudice and sent a memorandum to President Grant insisting on the thrift and industry of Chinese-Americans. But they were helpless to stem the rising tide of anti-Chinese prejudice, which now was taking the form of a call not only to prohibit further Chinese immigration but also to repatriate resident Chinese to Asia. Anti-coolie secret societies formed, and the threats of violence against the Chinese were so rife that there was a run on handguns, dirks, and bowie knives in Chinese pawnshops. Chinatown had become a time bomb that the Suey Sing Tong War was to set off.

The day after the fan-tan murders, Wong Yem Yen, the leader of the Hop Sing Tong, walked with his two bodyguards to Waverly Place, known to the Chinese in San Francisco as Ho Boon Gai—Fifteen Cent Street—because that was the cost of haircuts on this street lined with barbershops. Wong went into the shop of his favorite barber, Chin Poy, while his two bodyguards, fat Charlie Kong and Ernie Wu, took positions outside the door, guns in hand.

Wong had had his pigtail cut off during a two-year stay at Leavenworth and decided against growing it back because he liked to advertise his criminal record. Now he settled in the one barber chair in the tiny shop, and Chin Poy put a hot towel over his face. Chin Poy picked up his razor and began honing it on a leather strop, watching through the window the backs of the two Hop Sing guards. When the razor was sharp, Chin Poy went to the chair, reached under the hot towel, and slit Wong Yem Yen's throat so swiftly that Wong didn't even cry out. He merely gurgled, then twitched slightly into eternity. Chin Poy replaced the hot towel over his face, quickly dropped the razor in a basin, then slipped out the back of the shop.

Seven minutes passed before Charlie Kong looked behind him and noticed that the shop was empty except for Wong, who was stretched out rather oddly in the barber chair.

Then he noticed that the towel on his face had turned red.

"Shit!" he yelled in Cantonese. He rushed into the shop, Ernie Wu behind him, and raised the towel. The gory gash on Wong's throat was so deep, his head had been half cut off. Blood was pouring onto the floor.

Charlie Kong erupted with rage. He ran to the back of the shop, then out the rear door onto the narrow, crowded alley.

But Chin Poy had disappeared.

"David, I can't believe this," Archer exclaimed as he barged into Levin's office on the second floor of the Times-Dispatch Building at 15 Montgomery Street. "You've buried the barbershop murder story on page six."

The white-haired, middle-aged editor, who was wearing a green eye shade and garters on his sleeve, looked up from the galleys he was reading. He was still in love with Emma, but he was definitely not in love with her son. "Archer, I know you've been working here less than a week, but I think it's time you learned I prefer my employees knocking on my door before coming in."

Archer frowned at the middle-aged man who had such a special relationship with his mother. " 'Employee'?" he said. "I think I'm a little something more than an 'employee.' "

"You can think what you like. To me, you're an employee, nothing more, nothing less. Now, what's your complaint?"

Archer came to his desk, holding up the morning edition.

"You buried the barbershop murder. This stuff's dynamite. The *Bulletin* slapped it all over the front page."

"The *Bulletin* is a trashy newspaper and the so-called 'barbershop murder' is a trashy story. I put it on page six, like the 'fan-tan murder,' and I'll continue to put trash where it should be put: buried."

Archer stared at the elder man. " 'Trash'?" he repeated disbelievingly.

"Trash. I've been managing editor of this newspaper for twenty-five years, and lurid murders are not what I choose to publish for my readers."

"Do you have any readers left? These lurid murders happen to be news, and this happens to be a newspaper. Don't you realize there's a tong war going on in Chinatown? It may be a trashy war, but it's a war and it should be covered by our paper."

"Close the door."

Confused, Archer went back to the door. In closing it, he glanced out the glass top half into the city room and its two dozen desks for reporters and editors. Then he returned to David's paper-piled desk.

"I'll be frank with you, Archer," he said. "I wasn't happy when your mother told me you were coming to work for the paper, even though she assured me you had turned over a new leaf. You say you're more than an employee: yes, of course you are. Someday you'll own this paper. I know that. But while you're here—for your own good, I might add—I can't show you any favoritism because the other employees are going to resent it. The morale of a newspaper is extremely important. We all are a team, and you right now are the most junior member of that team. You may have your own ideas about running this paper, but, Archer, while I'm managing editor, I run this paper. I hope I've made myself clear?"

"Oh, perfectly clear. Meanwhile my mother's losing a fortune on this rag, our circulation is less than fifteen thousand, and the *Times-Dispatch* is a bore—a b-o-r-e. This tong war's the hottest thing since the gold rush. The other papers are selling out, and you talk about trash—do you know what people do with our paper? They don't read it, that's for certain. They use it to wrap their garbage in, so don't talk to me about trash!"

David looked at him coolly. "You're fired," he said.

Archer blinked. "You can't fire me."

"I just did. You're fired. Get out of my office."

Archer put his fists on the desk and leaned close. "You hate me," he said softly. "You've always hated me, because Mother fell in love with my father instead of you. You're a big nothing, David. You always have been, with your crappy little garden down on Jackson Street, your mangy cats, and your whores. Oh, don't think I don't know about your girlfriends, your—shall we call them clandestine?—visits to some of the murkier cathouses on Pacific Street. Is that why you don't want to print trash? Because you're trash?"

"My love life is my business," David said, biting off each word. He could barely contain his rage. Archer had stumbled on his dirty little secret. "I might add, you are hardly anyone to preach morality. Now, get the hell out, Archer, before I throw you out. Which I am perfectly willing, and able, to do."

Archer straightened, rather surprised at David's spunky attitude. "Okay, I'll leave. But when Mother gets back from downstate, you'll be the one packing your bags. It takes juice to run a newspaper, David, and you haven't had any juice for years. I've got the juice, and I'm going to turn this paper into the biggest and best in the West." He walked to the door, opened it, and started to leave. Then he jerked his finger at David and added: "Make that the world."

David watched him through the window. He didn't regret what he'd done. Emma might have enslaved him for thirty years, but he'd be damned if he'd let her son walk all over him. He reached for his pen to write his letter of resignation.

He had no intention of being fired.

Can Do crossed the cavernous entrance hall of the Nob Hill mansion and opened the front door. Outside, a pretty but rather nervous girl in a lovely blue satin evening dress was waiting.

"I'm Miss Dawson," she said. "Mr. Collingwood is expecting me."

"Yes, come in, please."

Inside, she removed the chinchilla capelet protecting against the chilly May evening and gave it to Can Do along with the chiffon scarf she had over her hair.

"This way, please, pretty missy."

Can Do led her across the marble floor to the double staircase with the huge portrait of Emma. Arabella furtively glanced around, not wanting the butler to notice her curiosity but unable not to inspect this house that had been the talk of San Francisco and had consumed her mother with envy. Of course, she could never tell her mother she had been there. Neither of her parents knew where she was: she had told them she was visiting Clara Flood, one of the Flood cousins across the street. Her father had a bad temper, and though he had rarely struck her in her life, if he found out she had accepted Archer Collingwood's invitation to dinner, he might not be responsible for his actions.

"Mr. Archer, he waiting for you upstairs in picture gallery," Can Do said, leading her up the right-hand staircase. "He say he thought you might like see Taitai's pictures before dinner."

"That would be charming," Arabella said, trying to conceal her eagerness. During the lunch at the Palace Hotel, she had dropped not-so-subtle hints that she would like to see Emma's paintings. Like many wealthy San Francisco girls, Arabella had been sent abroad to be educated, in her case at a select school for young ladies of refinement in Paris, and her interest, which quickly bloomed into a passion, was art. She had been graduated the year before, and since college for women was still a novelty, she proceeded on a ten-month tour of the major museums and cathedrals of Europe. She had only recently returned when Archer had accosted her.

Emma's architect had placed the picture gallery on the top floor of the mansion in order to provide daytime illumination for the paintings through a skylight. Reaching the third floor, Can Do opened two mahogany doors.

"Miss Dawson here," he announced.

As he stood aside to let Arabella pass in, she found herself standing at the end of a long gallery illuminated by globed gas jets. Down the center ran a red velvet banquette for picture viewing. Shaped like a race track, it had potted palms leafing out of its center. The walls were lined with paintings, and their elaborate gilt frames glowed magically in the gaslight.

Archer, looking startlingly handsome in white tie and a clawhammer coat, came up to her and kissed her gloved hand.

"Good evening, Miss Dawson," he said. "Since I understand you're something of an expert on art, why don't you look at Mother's pictures in any way you prefer? If you have any questions, I'll try to answer them."

"Thank you, Mr. Collingwood."

She walked to the left wall of the gallery, and the first painting took her breath away. "Watteau!" she exclaimed. "I adore Watteau!"

"Yes, I like that myself," Archer said, following her, his hands clasped behind his back. "I like the clowns."

Glancing in embarrassment at him, Arabella opened her small silver purse. "Do you mind, Mr. Collingwood? I'm a trifle astigmatic." She pulled a gold-framed lorgnette from the purse and unfolded the lenses. "It's not a fact I advertise, but with such an exceptional painting . . ." She held up the lorgnette and peered hungrily at the canvas. "Yes," she finally said, more to herself than Archer, "the technique, the sublime colors . . . It's extraordinary."

After she studied the canvas for almost five minutes, Archer finally cleared his throat. "The next painting is a Rubens," he said. "If we don't go a bit faster, I'm afraid dinner will become a midnight supper."

Arabella lowered her lorgnette. "I'm sorry. But this is such a treat, I could go without dinner entirely."

"It's true that in the presence of such pristine beauty—and I include yourself, Miss Dawson—one would be a gross vulgarian to think of food. However, since I am a gross vulgarian . . . Besides, Mother would kill me if I upset her cook."

Her look became disdainful. "I'll try to move faster, Mr. Collingwood. However, fine art should be savored, not gobbled, a fact a vulgarian like yourself may not appreciate."

She moved on to the next painting, an enormous Rubens depicting leering, muscular satyrs running across the canvas carrying overweight, pink-hued nudes with dimpled buttocks and bulging breasts.

"This is *The Rape of the Sabine Women*," Archer said, deadpan. " 'Rape' in this instance of course meaning 'The taking away' or 'the capture.' "

Arabella shot him another cool look. "You really are a vulgarian and a rather poor comedian. Art is a religion that should be treated with respect." Her eyes returned to the picture.

"And what do you suppose Rubens was thinking of when he painted all this skin?" Archer asked. "Religion?"

Arabella looked at the canvas, a lascivious paean to human flesh. After a moment she snickered. Then she looked guiltily at Archer, trying to keep a stern face. Then she looked back at the painting.

After another moment she burst into laughter. "You terrible man!" she snorted.

Archer smiled.

Forty-five minutes later, her eyes gorged with some of the finest art she had seen in America, Arabella accompanied Archer down the great stairwell to the ground floor, where her ears began to feast on Beethoven.

"What's that?" she asked.

"A surprise," Archer said, offering his arm and leading her across the marble floor to a pair of doors in a classic, columned surround. The doors were opened inward by two Celestials and Archer led her into the dining room. Its gold Chinese wallpaper, depicting a fabulous pavilioned garden, shimmered in the candlelight. At the other end of the room, past the long polished table set with Emma's famous vermeil dinner service of a towering, fruit-laden epergne and four huge candelabra, a blue velvet curtain had been pulled across an alcove. It was from behind the curtain that the lovely music was emanating.

"A little chamber music always helps the digestion," Archer noted as he led her to a chair halfway down one side of the table. As Can Do seated her, Archer went around the table to sit opposite.

"It's the first Beethoven trio," he said, unfolding his damask napkin as one of the servants filled the Venetian goblets with ice water. "Do you like Beethoven?"

272 FRED MUSTARD STEWART

"Of course. I also like this wallpaper. What is it?"

"It's quite rare. It's a depiction made in the last century of the Yuan Ming Yuan, or the 'Round Bright Garden' built in 1709 by the K'ang-hsi emperor of China. It was a sort of pleasure dome outside Peking with pavilions and lakes and gardens. There were all sorts of animals and birds. The place was totally destroyed by the English and French seventeen years ago, which I consider one of the most despicable acts the so-called 'civilized' white man has ever perpetrated."

"Why?"

"Why? Look at it!" He gestured around him at the wallpaper. "It was a thing of incredible beauty! There can never be an excuse for destroying beauty."

Arabella looked at him with new interest. "Why, Mr. Collingwood," she said, "I actually believe you're a romantic posing as a vulgarian."

He turned back to her. "Maybe I'm a little of both."

As the Celestial servants ladled the mock-turtle soup into the delicate Chinese bowls, she studied him across the table. The brash young playboy with the wild reputation was turning out to be more complex— and interesting—than she had ever imagined. After the servants had left, she picked up her vermeil spoon.

"Mr. Collingwood," she said, "just what is it you're after?"

He smiled. "Can't you guess? You."

She felt a slight shiver. She didn't know whether it was dread or anticipation.

Perhaps it was simply excitement.

An hour later, he opened another pair of doors and led her into the ballroom. The *Bulletin* reporter's description of this being as big as Buckingham Palace's was rank hyperbole, but the room was undeniably impressive. Twenty feet high and sixty feet long, one wall was a series of French doors giving out to a narrow balcony over California Street, while the other three walls were auburn-and-white Sienna marble hung with three superb seventeenth-century Gobelin tapestries representing the Wedding at Cana. Two great crystal gasoliers softly illuminated the room, gleaming off the parquet. But most surprising to Arabella was the presence at the opposite end of an entire orchestra, which she recognized as San Francisco's favorite, Ballenberg's Society Band. The moment Archer opened the doors, the conductor raised his baton and the orchestra slid into the opening strains of "*Geschichten aus dem Wienerwald*," or, as the new hit Strauss waltz had been translated when it came to America, "Tales from the Vienna Woods."

"Waltz, Miss Dawson?" Archer asked.

"You didn't tell me you were giving a dance!"

"I'm not. At least, there's no one else invited."

She gaped at the empty dance floor. "You mean, it's just us?"

"Exactly. Waltz?" He extended his arms.

"You're a madman!" she exclaimed as they twirled onto the parquet. "You're totally insane!"

"Madly in love," he said, smiling. "And insane about you."

As they waltzed around the spectacular room, she wondered if he were leading her on, or if it might possibly be true. In her wildly pounding heart she hoped it was the latter, for Arabella Dawson, who had been taught all her life to hate the Collingwoods, was falling in love.

"Ice water, women, and song," Archer said. "Isn't it wonderful?"

"Yes," she sighed as the tapestries and windows twirled vertiginously by. "It's quite, quite wonderful."

31

CRANE KUNG and Li Wang Yu faced each other, their fists raised in combat readiness. Both men were barefoot and stripped to the waist. "Hai!" Crane yelled, kicking his left foot up and out. Li quickly countered with his right foot. Moving in, he executed a classic *kata*, which was turned aside by Crane. They were in the second-floor gym of Crane's Grant Avenue mansion, going through their daily tae kwon do practice session.

There was an explosion outside, followed by gunfire. Crane and Li ran to the window and looked out onto the garden. A hole had been blown in the street wall and men were pouring through, firing as Crane's guards fired back.

"Hop Sings!" Crane yelled. He ran from the window across the spartan gym to a door, yelling to Li, "Come on!"

The door opened on a narrow stairway leading to the roof, and the two men ran up it. Crane quickly unbolted a steel door and emerged on the narrow parapet that ran around the top of the house, the tiled roof sloping gently up behind it to the crest. It was just past sunset. Smoke was still billowing from the breach in the wall, and two dozen Hop Sings were shooting it out with Crane's guards. Shots and cries from the wounded filled the air, along with gunsmoke.

"The Gatling gun!" Crane said, running down the parapet and yanking the tarpaulin cover off one of the two Civil War-surplus guns he had bought from a used-arms dealer. Li was behind him, pulling from under the roof eave a wooden crate of ammunition, whose belts he began feeding into the gun, the first rapid-fire gun in history.

Below, in the dark garden, Charlie Kong was standing behind a tree firing at the house. After the explosion the guards had run inside and were firing back from the ground-floor windows. Ernie Wu ran from a clump of rhododendron bushes, ducking to avoid the intense fire.

"Is it time to storm the house?" he panted in Cantonese as he reached Charlie. It had been Charlie Kong's idea to steal the explosives and attack the house as retribution for the barbershop murder of Wong

274

Yem Yen. They had stolen the explosives the night before from the warehouse of the Southern Pacific Railroad: the Chinese, who had invented gunpowder, had learned the most up-to-date methods of blasting during the construction of the railroad tunnels through the Sierra Nevada Mountains.

"Let's do it," Charlie said, reloading his gun. "Pass the word: when I shoot twice in the air, we go in."

Ernie ran back to the bushes, where seven Hop Sings were firing into the house. Outside the wall on Grant Avenue, a crowd of Chinese had gathered, drawn by the withering gunfire. But even though word was passing swiftly through the city that a fierce tong-war battle had broken out, the round-eye police were keeping their distance on the theory that it was better to let the "bad Chinks" kill themselves off. However, Digby Lee, the *Bulletin*'s intrepid reporter, was speeding to the scene.

"We're storming the house," Ernie said. "The signal is two shots in the air—"

"Aieee!" one Hop Sing screamed, clapping his hand to his right cheek, then pitching face-forward into a rhododendron.

"Kill the Suey Sings!" Ernie screamed, firing at the house. "Kill, kill, kill!"

Charlie Kong fired his gun twice in the air.

"The signal! Let's go!"

The Hop Sings charged out of the bushes, firing as they raced for the house. Other Hop Sings emerged from behind a small stone pagoda overlooking a reflecting pool and charged the east side of the house.

Up on the parapet, Crane opened fire, cranking the Gatling gun's wheel that turned the barrel. The eight muzzles spun, spitting out fifty bullets a minute. A hailstorm of steel sprayed the garden. Hop Sings danced into death and collapsed on the lawn, blood gushing from dozens of wounds. Bullets tore up the grass, blasted early-spring blossoms, sprayed rhododendron buds about to burst into bloom.

"What the hell?" Charlie Kong gasped from behind his tree. He stared at the roof, where the Gatling gun was spitting fire. Ernie Wu ran up beside him, holding his bleeding left arm.

"They got a Gatling gun!" he shouted. "Let's get the hell out!"

Charlie Kong needed no prompting. The new leader of the Hop Sing Tong and his second in command ran for the hole in the wall and dived through just as Crane turned his gun on them. Bullets bit a corn row in the stucco.

Charlie and Ernie pushed their way through the crowd, heading for the safety of the tong headquarters.

* * *

"How many did we lose?" Charlie asked a half-hour later as he wrapped a bandage around Ernie's bloody arm.

"I don't know yet, but it was too many."

Five other Hop Sings were standing around them in the basement headquarters on Murderers' Alley. "We didn't have a chance against the Gatling gun," one said. "It was like a dragon on the roof."

"It was my idea to attack the house, and I take responsibility for its going wrong," Charlie said. "Do you want me to resign as the new leader?"

The Hop Sings looked at each other, then shook their heads.

"No, Charlie," one of them said. "We're still with you. Crane Kung is pulling in five million dollars a year from his rackets, and if we can destroy him, that money can be ours."

"Plus free opium and singsong girls!" said a third.

"All right," Charlie said, tying Ernie's bandage. "I messed up, but I won't the next time. We tried to attack Crane's house, but he was too smart for us. Next time, we must get him out of his house."

"How? He hardly ever leaves."

"There's a way," Charlie Kong said quietly. "There's a way."

Archer climbed out of the carriage and looked up at the seven stories of the Pacific Bank and Trust Building on Montgomery Street in the heart of San Francisco's financial district. It was the tallest building in the West, an elaborate brick-and-stone structure in the so-called neo-Florentine style, though Archer had never seen anything remotely like it in Florence when he had taken his grand tour of Europe after Princeton. Walking into the dark green marble lobby, he climbed the impressive stairs to the second floor. He had an appointment with his mother, and he knew it was going to be stormy.

Emma had become rich by having the right idea at the right time. The time had been eighteen years before, when the great silver discoveries were made in Nevada. Unlike the gold rush, where you could get rich with a pick, a pan, and some luck, the silver had been lodged in a mountain. Huge amounts of capital were needed to dig the shafts to the precious metal, and the miners had come to San Francisco looking for investments. It was then that Emma had the right idea: her insurance company was accumulating a huge pool of capital with its premiums. Why not open a bank?

The Pacific Bank and Trust Company opened its doors on October 1, 1859, and soon had issued millions of dollars in low-interest loans to the silver miners, taking their mining stock as collateral. When they defaulted, as many did, it had collected their stock, thus acquiring even greater ownership in the mines her bank was financing. Emma had the

Midas touch: the bank was a success from the start. Within five years, as the Civil War raged in the East, Emma built the Pacific Bank and Trust Building to consolidate her empire: the bank, insurance company, shipping company, and central accounting offices for the newspaper and department store. As Archer entered her reception room and was greeted by her male secretary, Mr. Quartermain, he reflected, not for the first time, that his mother had to be one of the most powerful women in America. It was indeed, as he had said, a tough act to follow. But Archer had every intention of following it.

He was led into the inner sanctum. His mother's office was meant to impress with a masculine sense of power: dark paneling like an English club, eighteenth-century English furniture, and, on the walls, paintings of the Kinsolving Line's now-defunct clipper ships, notably the *Empress of China* that had brought Emma to California so many years before.

Seated behind her formidable desk was Emma. As always, she was beautifully groomed, her hair swept up in a mass of curls on top of her head in the current poodle-dog fashion. Her stunning dress was of gray silk piped with scarlet. The Duchess of San Francisco, as he often thought of her.

As usual when angry, she dispensed with formalities. "David Levin has sent me a letter of resignation," she said crisply. "What do you know about this?"

Archer shrugged as he sat in a chair before her desk. "What does he say in the letter?"

"Not much. Reasons of health, which is ridiculous, because he's in excellent health. I checked with his doctor. But I suspect you. Five days after you go to work there, David resigns. Did you have a fight?"

"Yes. I told him I thought he was running the paper badly, and he fired me. And he is running it badly. He refuses to put the tong war on the front page where it belongs because he thinks it's trashy. Did you read this morning's paper? The Hop Sings invaded Crane Kung's house last night, blew a hole in his wall with stolen explosives, nine Hop Sings and four Suey Sings were killed, and he puts it on page eight! What's the lead story? There's a forest fire near the Russian River. It's ridiculous. It's like Columbus returning to Spain to report the good fishing in the Atlantic and then saying, 'Oh, yes, and I discovered America.' "

"You're right, of course. I know he's bad for the paper. I sometimes even think it's his way of getting back at me."

"For not being Mrs. David Levin?"

"Yes. But, Archer, couldn't you have waited? Five days! You might have waited a whole week before taking on the editor. Were you rude to him?"

"What makes you think that?"

"Because he says so little in the letter."

Archer hesitated. "I suppose I was rude, yes."

"Then I want you to apologize to him. David is a sweet man I've known almost all my life, and I will not have my son hurt him, no matter what he's done to the paper."

Again he shrugged. "I'll write him a letter," he said.

"And I'll pay him a handsome pension. But the question is, whom can I get to replace him?"

Archer leaned forward in his chair. "Why not me?" he said softly.

"Don't be ridiculous. You haven't even been there a week. I have to get someone with experience—"

He leapt from his chair. "Mom, give it to me, please! I've never wanted anything so much in my life! I can make it work! I've got ideas—"

"Archer, be serious."

"I am serious! You're losing money on the paper already, so why not give me a chance to turn it around? The worst I could do would be no worse than what David's done, but I believe I can make it work."

"Don't you understand? If I give you the paper, everyone's going to say, 'He couldn't have made it without his mother.' "

"I don't give a damn what they say. Look, I've been out of college four years and for three years I did nothing but get drunk and make a fool of myself—mainly because I was afraid of you. All right, I've taken the pledge. But I want to make up for lost time. The *Times-Dispatch* can be an exciting paper and a big money-maker—I know it. And I can do it. Give me this chance to prove myself, please."

She studied his face. "Well," she finally said, "you're certainly not afraid of me now, are you?"

He hesitated; the thought hadn't occurred to him. "No, I guess I'm not."

She drummed her fingers. "All right, it's yours. I'll pay you the same salary as David: ten thousand a year."

"Ya-hoo!" he yelled, running around the desk to hug her. "Thanks, Mom. You'll never regret it."

"Don't disappoint me," she said. "I have great faith in you, darling. Make me proud."

"I will! You'll see."

He almost ran to the door.

"Archer."

"Yes?"

"You haven't told me whom you're bringing to Star's reception ball tomorrow night."

He hesitated, his hand on the brass doorknob.

"Also," she continued, "I have received a bill for eight hundred dollars from Mr. Ballenberg. It seems that while I was away, you entertained a lady at the house and hired his entire orchestra for just the two of you. Can Do tells me the lady in question was Arabella Dawson. Is this true?"

He smiled. "You don't miss much, do you? Yes, it's true. And I've asked Arabella to the ball tomorrow night."

"Did she accept?"

"Yes."

Emma frowned. "What's going on? Loretta Dawson is giving a ball at her house tomorrow night and has stolen half my guest list— the silly cow is trying to upstage me, as if I care. But why in the world would her daughter come to our house?"

"Because she's in love with me. I told you I'd take care of Slade Dawson."

Before she could ask him anything further, he had bolted out of her office.

"Mrs. Leland Stanford, Mary Crocker, Phoebe Hearst. They're all coming tomorrow night, Nellie!" Loretta Dawson crowed as she stood before the mirror in her overfurnished bedroom. Her Australian maid was on her hands and knees pinning the skirt of her ivory ball gown. "What a triumph! The best hostesses of San Francisco standing up Emma Collingwood for me. Oh, it's heaven, sheer heaven. Ouch! You stuck a pin in me, you clumsy bitch."

"Sorry."

"At any rate, what a night it will be! Caviar, champagne—and my champagne will be as good as Emma Collingwood's. Perrier-Jouët, seventy-one, five dollars the bottle. Oh, they'll talk about tomorrow night for years to come. The night Loretta Dawson became queen of Nob Hill."

"Mother."

Loretta saw her daughter's reflection in the mirror. "Yes, dear?"

"May I talk to you a moment?"

"Of course. I was just telling Nellie how exciting tomorrow night's going to be. And Arabella's escort is going to be an English lord— imagine that!"

"I hate the English," Nellie growled.

"Oh, well, you Australians are all a bunch of convicts. It's natural you'd dislike the English. But these two charming Englishmen are visiting the British consul here, Lord Avondale and Lord Mandeville, and I sent them invitations and they accepted. Not only accepted, but Lord Avondale requested the honor of being Arabella's escort, which I of course accepted immediately. Just think, dear: you might be Lady Avondale someday, related by marriage to some of the best families in England. And, Nellie, he's so handsome—"

"Lord Avondale is not going to be my escort tomorrow night, Mother. And everyone knows he and Lord Mandeville are nothing but remittance men and fortune hunters."

Loretta turned to stare at her daughter. "He's not? What's happened? Is Lord Avondale ill?"

"As far as I know, he's in the peak of health. The fact is, I'm going to Mrs. Collingwood's reception for her daughter."

Loretta exploded in a coughing fit. When she finally caught her breath, she turned on her daughter. "You're what?"

"Archer Collingwood asked me to the reception and I accepted."

"Nellie, get out."

"But, Mrs. Dawson—"

"Get out, you Australian toad!" she screamed. Nellie scrambled to her feet and ran to the door. When she was gone, Loretta demanded, "What's going on? Have you been seeing Archer Collingwood behind my back?"

"Yes. Oh, and, Mother, he's really a fine, sweet young man—"

" 'Fine'? 'Sweet'? He's a drunk and a lecher. Has he put his hands on you?"

"He's been a perfect gentleman."

"I don't believe it. I don't believe that my own daughter, against the express wishes of her parents, would have secret trysts with a Collingwood."

"Momma, you have it all wrong, really. Archer's taken the pledge, he drinks nothing but water and orange juice."

Loretta, holding her hand to her ample breasts, limped to a chair and lunged into it. "This can't be true," she wheezed. "I can't believe my own daughter could be a viper at my breast."

"I'm not being a viper!" Arabella exclaimed hotly. "But I'm going with Archer tomorrow night."

Loretta pointed an accusatory finger. "I'll lock you in your room first."

"I wouldn't try any threats, Mother," her daughter said coolly. "One reason I'm going with Archer is to stop him from publishing a series of articles about you and Father and the Bonanza Café."

Silence. Loretta wrestled with her emotions as her face went red. Finally she whispered, "You know those stories are all lies."

"I used to think so, because you told me they were lies and I believed you. But today I decided it was time I went to Portsmouth Square and found out for myself. I went there this morning and talked to that horrible, drunken woman, Chicago." She paused and bit her lip. "Oh, Momma," she whispered, "how could you have?"

"I'll admit I was a waitress, but nothing else. Do you understand? Nothing! Dear God, the night before your father and I are inviting all of San Francisco to this house, do you want to ruin me?"

"Of course I don't want to ruin you. If nothing else, it would ruin me too. But, Momma, after all these years of lies and deception, I want the truth. You weren't just a waitress—Chicago told me that. You were what people politely call a 'soiled dove.' You were a"—she took a deep breath, for it was killing her to say the word—"prostitute!"

The two women stared at each other. Finally Loretta straightened in her chair.

"All right, it's true, I was," she said, defiance creeping into her voice. "You want to know the truth? My parents died of cholera on the way west, like hundreds of others, and when I arrived in San Francisco I had nothing but my youth and my looks. You can have no idea what it was like here then. Now this is a cosmopolitan city, people are calling it the 'Paris of the West.' But then it was a hole. There were no women, and the men had this great . . . hunger. They'd do anything, pay anything. I remember one man offered me three hundred dollars in gold if he could just look at my undergarments. I was earning a thousand dollars an hour—"

"Oh!" Arabella cried, putting her hand to her mouth.

"Oh, yes, you're shocked. You, who've never known what it's like to be poor, you, who've had everything given to you on a silver platter— clothes, toys, a Paris education, jewels, whatever you've wanted I've bought for you because I wanted you to be better than I was. And you are. You're a lady, which I know I'll never be if I live to a hundred. But don't look down your nose at me just because I had to make my living on my back. Your father made me respectable when I became in the family way with your poor sister—God rest her soul in heaven. Maybe it was God's way of punishing me that she was stillborn, I don't know. But at any rate, I've done everything in my power to make up for the past, and if you hate me for it, well, it can't be helped."

Arabella lowered her eyes: all these years her mother had lied to her. Almost to herself she said, "Who am I to judge? Under those circumstances, maybe I might have done the same thing."

"Oh, thank you, my darling." Loretta burst from her chair and hugged her stiff daughter. "Thank you. What a load off my mind this is. And promise me you'll stay away from Archer Collingwood?"

Arabella pulled away. "But why?"

"Can't you see? If my own daughter goes to the Collingwoods' house tomorrow night, I'll be the laughingstock of San Francisco."

"Oh, Mother, that's so silly—"

"It's not silly! To be accepted in society is important, and tomorrow night your father and I are going to be accepted. Besides, I hate Emma Collingwood. She's so high-and-mighty. I pass her in the street and she looks right through me, as if I didn't exist. Who the hell does she think she is?"

"Mother, if what Archer told me is true, she has a perfectly good reason for looking through you."

Loretta lit a cigarette.

"Oh, yes, she blames Scott Kinsolving's death on your father. She's been saying it for years, but she's never proved it and she never will. She's a mean, vindictive woman—and her son is worse. Promise me you'll stay away from him. Promise!"

"No. I'm going with Archer tomorrow night."

"You can't! You know what tomorrow night means to your father and me—you have to be here. It would be too humiliating for you to be . . . to be there!"

"Mother, I can forgive you for having been a 'soiled dove.' But what I can't forgive you for is being a social-climbing snob. I want to have no part of this silly war you're having with Mrs. Collingwood. All I'm interested in is Archer and myself. Good night."

Alone, Loretta clenched her fists. "Damn," she muttered. "Damn!"

Getting to her feet, she grabbed a hideous German porcelain vase and threw it with all her strength at the mirror, which shattered into a thousand shards.

32

ALICIA BEAUMONT was the society editor of the *Bulletin*. On May 18, 1877, she wrote the following article, excerpted, which filled the entire front page under the headline:

NEW STAR IN NOB HILL FIRMAMENT! GRAND BALL TONIGHT AT SLADE DAWSON MANSION!

Complete Description of House!

Wines from France, Caviar from Russia!

Bay City Bon Ton Prepares for
Social Event of the Decade!

Tonight, social history will be made in our fair city. All San Franciscans will watch with interest as a new leader of our dynamic social scene emerges to set the tone of the West: Mrs. Slade Dawson will hold a ball at her magnificent mansion on Nob Hill. The theme of the ball is "A Night in Old California," and for the occasion the foremost leaders of society have spent weeks having clever costumes made for themselves in the style of the old Mexican-Californio society. Mantillas, lace fans, and darkly flashing eyes are to be *de rigueur*, and surely many of our fairest young maidens may cause many a manly heart to flutter.

Of no little interest will be the mansion itself, completed four months ago at a cost of $3,000,000 and surely one of the most imposing homes in San Francisco. Built in the Parisian style, it has a grand entrance with a wide tessellated pavement of white and gray marble extending to the sidewalk. The inner staircase is of walnut, with elaborate lower newel posts, each supporting a bronze Ceres, while the great newel posts on the upper landing sport two Roman soldiers of fine bronze. Among the many dazzling features of the house is a hydraulic elevator, an immense drawing room with draperies of gold satin lined with yellow satin (it is said that the cost of decorating each window was $2,000, or about the price of a cozy house in Oakland), curtains of fabulous Alençon lace, and one of the largest Axminster rugs ever woven in England.

There is a billiard room, the bathrooms have faucets for dip, plunge, and spray ablutions; Mrs. Dawson's bedroom has rose satin curtains lined with white silk, furniture of curled maple trimmed with amaranth wood, and its own crystal chandelier. On her richly garlanded bed are embroidered pillowcases worth $140 the pair.

The finest French wines will be served, and the midnight supper will include *consommé de volaille*, stewed terrapin, *pâté de foie de canard*, snipe and quail, as well as dozens of other entrées. The decoration includes baskets of violets, heliotropes, roses, tuberoses, jessamine, mignonette, and other flowers.

The smartest people in town will be in attendance, and it is said that a former leader of society, whose family has so recently been seriously tainted by scandal, will henceforth languish in permanent social eclipse.

The previous day, when Archer had taken over editorship of the *Times-Dispatch* in a whirlwind of energy, he had called his society editor and gossip columnist, Sydney Tolliver, to David Levin's former office and laid out the following front-page spread:

TWO ENTIRE PAGES DEVOTED TO THE WEDDING OF THE DECADE! A BRILLIANT MATRIMONIAL DAZZLE! SPLENDID CELEBRATION OF THE COLLINGWOOD-LÓPEZ Y SEPÚLVEDA NUPTIALS!

A Description of the Collingwood Mansion!

How a Millionairess Surrounds Herself with Luxury!

The Most Elegantly Appointed Residence on the Coast!

Love in a Palace! Elegant Toilets of the Queens of Society!

The name Emma de Meyer Kinsolving Collingwood has become synonymous with all that is cultivated and refined in our fair city. Recently her name has come to stand for philanthropy as well, with her generous donation of a new hospital for San Francisco. Tonight this extraordinary lady is giving a ball at her palatial mansion on Nob Hill to celebrate the recent nuptials of her daughter, Star, whose radiant beauty has for several seasons graced the local social scene, with the son of one of California's oldest and most distinguished families, Don Juan López y Sepúlveda. For the occasion, Mrs. Collingwood has decorated her mansion with five thousand white tulips, grown in her greenhouses at her Palo Alto farm, and Ballenberg's Society Band of thirty-six pieces will provide the music. Mr. Archer Collingwood, recently appointed editor in chief of this newspaper, will attend his sister's reception with

Miss Arabella Dawson, whose mother is also holding a small entertainment tonight.

Though Loretta Dawson had managed to lure away some of the biggest names in town for her "small entertainment," Emma still attracted half the four hundred people she had invited. Carriage after carriage pulled into the porte cochere of the brilliantly illuminated Nob Hill mansion to disgorge their befurred and bejeweled passengers while across the street a crowd of gawkers gawked.

Inside the entrance hall, the pipe organ played transcriptions of popular arias from grand opera while Can Do shepherded the guests past the bins of white tulips toward the receiving line at the foot of the double staircase. At its head was Emma in an emerald silk bustled evening gown with black feathers surrounding the décolletage. Setting off the green was a dazzling ruby-and-diamond necklace and matching earrings. The dress had been designed by Zita, of course, and few women had the beauty or the figure to carry it off. Though the widow Collingwood was on the green side of fifty, which for most of Emma's contemporaries meant the beginning of old age, Emma was determined to hang on to her youth. So well had regular diet and exercise maintained her figure that not a few of the men felt a pleasant jolt of adrenaline at the sight of her. "She looks so young," whispered one envious dowager. "Do you suppose she might marry again?"

"Why not?" whispered her dowdy companion. "But who?"

At Emma's right, Star wore a pale peach satin gown with a diamond necklace that was a wedding gift from her mother. Then Juanito, looking dashingly handsome in his clawhammer coat. Then Arabella, radiant in a yellow plush dress with a huge skirt. And finally Archer.

Viewing all this from above on the landing of the left stairway was a thin little man with a mustache, a monocle in his right eye, an orchid in his lapel, and a notebook in his gloved hand. Sydney Tolliver, the only son of a Kentucky bourbon distiller, worshiped Emma and the Collingwoods as gods. A born minion, he now groped for a fresh word to describe what was undoubtedly the most lavish, glittering social event he had ever seen. I've used "breathtaking" to death, he thought. And "dazzling" and "glamorous" and "brilliant." I'll make up a word! And his gold pencil scribbled the following deathless opening sentence in his notebook: "Last night, Emma Collingwood gave a ball at her Nob Hill mansion that was absolutely swellelegant."

The English language reeled slightly, but survived.

"I want to thank you for not blasting Mother," Arabella said a half-hour later as she and Archer executed a fast galop on the crowded ballroom floor. "After the terribly snide things they printed in the *Bulletin*, I thought Sydney Tolliver was quite restrained."

"I told him to go easy on her," Archer said. "After all, I was to have the honor of your company tonight. It would have been stupid of me to insult your mother, wouldn't it?"

"I thank you for it anyway. Oh, Archer, your sister is so beautiful!"

Archer looked across the ballroom to where Star was dancing with Juanito. "Yes, isn't she?" he said almost wistfully. Then he turned back to Arabella and smiled. "But not as beautiful as you."

"I don't believe that for a moment." She hesitated, then smiled. "But I love hearing it."

"Are you huh-huh-happy?" Juanito asked as he waltzed with Star.

"Oh, yes, very," she said, and meant it.

"I luh-luh-love you."

"And I love you."

It was true. The tall, thin Juanito might stammer maddeningly, but in bed he had turned out to be as ardent a lover as Crane, a Don Juan in fact as well as name. The few short days since their San Juan de Capistrano wedding had been blissful, and now the shock and shame of Crane seemed to be fading in the distance of time.

"I luh-luh-like Archer a luh-luh-lot. Do you think he's in luh-luh-love with Arab-bella?"

"Oh, I don't know and I don't care. Tonight is our night, darling. We're going to waltz and drink champagne and get ever so tiddly, and then you're going to carry me upstairs to our bedroom and give me ten thousand kisses."

"That's a luh-luh-lot of kisses."

"Not from your sweet lips. A million wouldn't be too many."

"We're going to have a luh-luh-lot of children," he said, looking at his gorgeous bride with pride. "Fuh-five boys and fuh-five girls."

"I'm worn out just thinking about it," she laughed.

Ever so briefly she wondered what Crane was doing that night. Then she forced the thought out of her mind.

"She's quite magnificent," said Lord Radcliff Willoughby de Vere Mandeville, the second son of the Marquess of Thornfield, as he watched Emma waltz with her new son-in-law, Juanito. "Is it possible that anyone could be that rich and that beautiful?"

His companion, the British consul in San Francisco, Sir Percival Gore, smiled. "In America, anything is possible."

"This house must have cost millions. How rich is she?"

"They say if she cashed everything in, it might bring eighty million."

"Eighty million! Good Lord, that should be illegal. And there are no suitors?"

"None in sight, Radcliff. Getting ideas? Eighty million could restore Thornfield Abbey and the family fortune."

"And pay off my father's gambling debts. Well, it's certainly worth a go, isn't it? Since I came too late for the receiving line, perhaps you could introduce me?"

"With pleasure."

"She's a bit long in the tooth for me, but they say women, like beef, improve with age."

"Don't be swept away with romance, old boy."

"This won't be romance. This will be business, pure and simple."

"My dear Radcliff, business is never pure and rarely simple."

"Neither is romance."

"I see Sydney Tolliver lurking around taking copious notes," Emma said as she waltzed with her son. "I hope you're not planning to print more bilge like that vulgar junk on this morning's front page?"

"That 'vulgar junk' this morning sold us five thousand extra copies," Archer said. "Not bad for my first day on the job, would you say?"

"Yes, but really, Archer! You had practically everything in that article except my bathtub."

"You didn't read it carefully. It mentioned your bathtub and its solid silver faucet. People love to read things like that. Americans claim they're democrats, but at heart they want royalty. And since we can't have royalty, they'll take the next best thing: rich people. That's you, my cherished mater, and everyone else up here on Nob Hill. If you sneeze, I'll print it and it will sell papers."

"I still say it's vulgar."

"Of course it's vulgar."

"I didn't give you the *Times-Dispatch* to turn it into something as trashy as the *Bulletin*."

"Trashy! There's that word again. But the fact is, you gave it to me. It's mine now, to run as I see fit. Crime, scandal, gossip, and political corruption are what the newspaper business is all about, and happily San Francisco's got plenty of all four. By the way, I'm having lunch with Digby Lee tomorrow. I'm going to offer him five thousand a year more than Slade Dawson pays him to work for me."

Emma looked shocked. "Five thousand more? That's a fortune for a reporter."

"And he's worth every penny. He's the best reporter in California, and he's going to work for me, no matter how much I have to pay him. And I'm trying to contact Mark Twain to have him write some humorous pieces for the paper. Oh, I'm shaking things up on Montgomery Street."

"I think I probably should disapprove of you," his mother said rather sternly. Then she smiled. "But actually, I'll admit what you're doing sounds rather exciting even if it is vulgar."

"Do you know you have the most beautiful smile on earth? If you weren't my mother, I think I'd fall madly in love with you."

"And what about Miss Dawson? Are you madly in love with her?"

Archer frowned. "I'd rather not discuss that," he said, lapsing into a sulky silence that left his mother intrigued.

Gustave Corbeau & Sons had been hired to cater the reception, and thirty round tables seating eight apiece had been set up in the dining room, drawing room, library, and third-floor picture gallery. Promptly at ten, an announcement was made in the ballroom that dinner was served, and the 230 guests began milling through the mansion to find their seats for a feast featuring *galantin de dinde à la parisienne, langue de buffalo à l'echalote, civet de lièvre*, broiled quail on toast, canvasback duck, pies, almond cake, and citron macaroons. At each table M. Corbeau's bakers had constructed spun-sugar-and-confection models of famous architecture, including the Arc de Triomphe, the Vendôme Column, the White House, and the still-a-building Washington Monument.

Star and Juanito were crossing the entrance hall when one of the French waiters came up and presented her with an envelope. "This was just delivered at the front door, madam."

She took the envelope and opened it. Inside, on a dirty piece of paper, was written the following:

> If you want to see Crane Kung alive ever again, be at your mother's stables in one hour. Tell no one, and come alone, or Crane Kung will die.

There was no signature, only a crudely sketched snake, which Star knew was the sign of the Hop Sing Tong.

"Wha-wha-what is it?" Juanito asked.

Star forced a nervous smile, sticking the note back in its envelope. "It's from Clara Flood across the street," she said. "She has a cold and couldn't come tonight, but she sent her love and wishes us luck."

Mainly because of his stammer, Juanito seemed to be a shy and retiring young man. But he had inherited a hot Spanish temper, the fierce pride of an hidalgo, and more than his share of jealousy. This temper began to sizzle as he realized his young bride had, for the first time in their brief marriage, lied to him. He reached out for the letter. "Gi-give me that!" he whispered.

"No!" She jerked it away and thrust it into the bosom of her dress. She was terrified for Crane's safety. But from the murderous look in her husband's eyes, she was momentarily terrified for her own safety as well. The situation was relieved by the arrival of Emma.

"You two are upstairs in the picture gallery," she said, smiling. "I let the young people climb the stairs. We old folks will eat down here." She noticed the strained look on Star's face. "Is anything wrong?"

"No, Mother, everything is beautiful. It's a wonderful evening." She kissed Emma's cheek. "And I love you very much," she whispered.

Then she hurried toward the stairs. Juanito started to say something to his mother-in-law, then changed his mind and hurried after his wife. Emma watched them narrowly, certain something had happened. She loved entertaining and took her duties as hostess seriously. Now the fact that the very couple this lavish reception was honoring were experiencing some sort of difficulty bothered her, even more so since she had arranged Star's marriage to Juanito. Star had appeared to be happy so far, which gave her mother a not inconsiderable sense of relief. But was it possible she had read their apparent happiness incorrectly?

"Mrs. Collingwood?"

She turned to see Sir Percival Gore standing behind her with a very tall young man in white tie and tails.

"Ah, Sir Percival." She smiled, extending her hand. "I'm so glad you could come. I was afraid you might have deserted me for that other entertainment down the street."

The British consul kissed her hand. "That other hostess down the street is merely a shooting star," the diplomat said suavely. "You, dear lady, are like the moon in comparison: radiant, lovely, and a permanent fixture in the San Francisco heavens."

She laughed, eyeing the young man next to him. "You're flattering me, Sir Percival, and I adore it."

"May I present my guest, whom I took the liberty of bringing? This is my cousin, Viscount Mandeville, son of the Marquess of Thornfield."

Radcliff's blue eyes fixed on Emma's as he raised her hand to his lips. "I came to California to see the wild west," he said. "But I never expected to see anything as elegant as this house or as beautiful as yourself. Obviously we in Europe have received a mistaken impression of the American west. I expected cowboys and Indians and have gotten champagne and Venus instead."

"I hope you're not disappointed, my lord?" She smiled, thinking: He's absolutely gorgeous!

"Not at all. I've seen cowboys and Indians. They're amusing, but once the novelty wears off, they become boring. I couldn't imagine you becoming boring in a thousand years."

What a line, she thought. He certainly lays it on thick. All the same, it's rather pleasant to hear. . . . "I should be angry with you, Sir Percival," she said, her eyes still on the young Englishman. "You should have told me you were bringing Lord Mandeville so I could include him in the *placement*. Now he has no seat, and what will the English think of our American hospitality? But you can sit next to me, Lord Mandeville. I'll squeeze in an extra chair. That way, everyone will be insulted because I've given the place of honor to a perfect stranger."

"I may be a stranger, Mrs. Collingwood, but I'm far from perfect."

"Good. That leaves room for improvement, and I think all young men should need improvement. It makes them so much more interesting."

He offered his arm. "In that case, I must be exceedingly interesting," he said.

"Oh," she said, "you are."

They started toward the great double staircase. He's flirting with me, she thought. How amusing! No one's seriously flirted with me for years, because they knew it was a waste of time. Of course, it's all silly. He's half my age, and I could never be interested in any other man after my darling husband.

But it is amusing. He even looks a little like my sweet Archer.

"It must have been terribly romantic growing up at Thornfield Abbey," Emma said twenty minutes later as the waiters ladled the consommé. She had squeezed Lord Mandeville in to her right, somewhat to the annoyance of her father, who was now almost in Zita's lap to *his* right.

"If one considers freezing in the winter romantic, I suppose it was," Radcliff said. "It has none of the modern conveniences—including plumbing—and the kitchen is fairly much the way it was in the tenth century when the place was owned by the Church."

"Ah, but the history. Not only the monks, but your family. The Mandevilles have been there since Henry VIII, am I right?"

"Yes. He gave the Abbey and its lands to my ancestor when he took over the Church properties in the sixteenth century. I—"

"She's guh-guh-gone!" Juanito exclaimed, rushing up to Emma's table.

"Who?"

"Star! She luh-left our table a half-hour ago to puh-powder her nose, and now she's v-vanished!"

"But that's impossible—"

"I found the waiter," Archer said, hurrying up to his brother-in-law. "The one that gave Star the note. He said it was brought to the house by a Celestial."

"What note?" Emma exclaimed. "What are you talking about?"

"Star got a note a while ago. Juanito says she claimed it was from Clara Flood, but he thinks she was lying. I've called the police."

A cold terror began seeping through Emma's veins. "Do you think . . . ?"

"I don't know what to think."

Conversation at the five tables in the dining room was ceasing as everyone turned toward the center table.

"I'll tell you what I think," Juanito said, his face taut with fear and anger. "M-my wife's been kuh-kuh kuh kidnapped."

33

HIS tongue slowly licked her nipple. Green Jade was Crane's chief concubine and the most gorgeous of his thirty-nine singsong girls. They were both naked in Crane's dragon bed, as he called it. Occupying a substantial portion of his master bedroom, the bed was the talk of Chinatown. Crane had designed it himself and hired three Celestial woodcarvers to make the headboard: a coiling, vicious black-and-gold dragon whose scaly tail swept around the bottom of the black-sheeted bed to form the footboard. Incense from tripod braziers at either side sweetened the air as he proceeded to lick Green Jade's entire body. Then, his penis extended to its full, uncircumcised eight inches, he mounted the Cantonese singsong girl and slithered into her.

"*Kai Yee!*" cried a voice as someone pounded on the door. "*Kai Yee!*"

"Go away, dammit!"

"There is a note from Charlic Kong. It's important. They have taken Star Collingwood!"

"Star!" Crane whispered, pulling out of Green Jade. He climbed off the dragon bed, threw a red silk robe over his nakedness, and hurried to unbolt the door. Outside was Li Wang Yu. He thrust a letter into Crane's hand. It read:

> Despised Son of a Thousand Whores:
> We have Star Collingwood. If you wish her to live, you will come to the headquarters of the Hop Sing Tong, alone and without any weapons. If you pass our examination, you will be allowed to see her, and she will be allowed to leave. But if you disobey our conditions, she dies a slow death.

There was no signature, only a sketched snake.

Crane reread the note, then folded it and closed his eyes.

"What is it, *Kai Yee?*" Green Jade asked, coming to him and slipping her hands under his robe. "Who has taken Star?"

"Charlie Kong. Shit, I never thought of Star."

292

"What will they do to her?" Her cool hands rubbed his stomach.

"They'll kill her, unless I go to them. And of course, if I go to them, they'll kill me."

"Then you must not go. Let them kill Star—what is she to you?"

Crane leaned against the wall, pressing his head against the black silk with which he had lined the walls. Tears appeared in the corners of his eyes.

"She's everything to me," he whispered.

Star's disappearance caused the party on Nob Hill to flounder. When the police arrived, word had already swept through the mansion, and sight of Captain Tom Browder of the San Francisco police caused some of the more nervous guests to leave, even though the dinner was not half over.

"Do you think it was Crane Kung?" Browder was asking Archer in the music room, where they had gone for privacy. "Do you think he still has enough hold over your sister to lure her out of the house with a note?"

"Absolutely not," Emma said.

"Wait a minute, Mother," Archer said. "Crane's involved with this somehow. Whether he sent in the note or not is another question. But, Captain, I think your men should scour Chinatown."

"I agree. We'll go to Kung's place on Grant Avenue first."

"May I come?" Archer asked.

"Sure, if you want."

Another policeman entered the room. "Excuse me, Captain," he said. "We've just got word that George Coleman's called a meeting of the Anti-Coolie Society on Kearny Street. He's really riled up about the Celestials kidnapping a white woman."

"If that's what happened," Emma said.

Captain Browder was frowning. "Coleman could mean trouble. I'll send a detachment of men to watch him. Meanwhile, Mr. Collingwood, let's go to Chinatown."

The policemen started out of the room as Archer whispered to his mother: "The paper's going to have one helluva front page in the morning."

"Archer, you can't," Emma exclaimed. "It's your own sister."

"She also is news. Don't you think this will be all over the *Bulletin* tomorrow? For once our paper's not going to be scooped by Slade Dawson."

He headed for the door, leaving Emma almost as shocked by her son's reportorial zeal as she was by her daughter's disappearance.

* * *

As word swept the city that Star Collingwood López y Sepúlveda had been kidnapped by the Chinese, long-simmering anti-Celestial prejudice came to a boil. No one in the hastily gathered crowd on Kearny Street thought to question the truth of the assertion, but listened agog to one of the leading anti-Celestial demagogues and head of the semi-secret Anti-Coolie Society.

"What is a Chinaman?" yelled beefy George Coleman, a Baptist preacher from Alabama. "He's a foreigner who's come to America and brought his own laws with him. He's a slanty-eyed, pigtailed yellow man who refuses to obey the laws and customs of us white men. He's a worm in the apple of America, who makes prostitutes out of his own women, who smokes opium, and whose bloodthirsty tong soldiers murder and kill. Is Chinatown America? No! Chinatown is Chinese! I say to you, my fellow Americans, it's one thing when the Celestial slanty-eyes murder each other in Chinatown, but when they export their evil into white San Francisco, it's something else. They've sent their scum to the very heart of San Francisco—to Nob Hill—and have kidnapped the daughter of one of our fair city's leading families. And I ask you, are we going to allow this to happen?"

"No!" roared the mob.

"Then what are we going to do about it?"

"Burn Chinatown!" yelled one man in the crowd, and others quickly took it up: "Burn Chinatown! Burn Chinatown!"

"Then let's go!" Coleman yelled, and several hundred white San Franciscans, many of them armed, surged toward Chinatown.

Throughout Chinatown, in Sullivan's Alley, Murderer's Alley, Butcher's Alley—tension mounted as the Chinese heard the distant roars of a mob draw ever closer. Even though it was now past midnight, *Chun hungs*, or posters, started appearing on walls all over the Chinese quarter, calling on law-abiding Chinese to work against the tongs who were bringing this disaster down on their heads. And yet, many counterargued, weren't the tongs, with all their faults, at least Chinese? Could any Chinese trust the law of the *fan kwei*, the white foreign devil? And thus prejudice bred prejudice, and the city on the bay braced itself for an explosion.

"*Kai Yee*, we must do something!" Li Wang Yu insisted. Almost all the members of the Suey Sing Tong had jammed into the basement headquarters on Spofford Alley. Crane, in his vermilion robes, sat as still as a Buddha on his mat before the altar table with the willow bowls and ears of corn. "If we don't act," Li continued, "we'll lose control of Chinatown."

"He's right, *Kai Yee*," said Kwong Si, another young tong soldier.

"Our people are frightened of the anti-Coolie round-eyes. If we don't protect our people, who will?"

Silence reigned as the tong soldiers watched their leader, waiting for him to speak. Crane's face was stony, and his tensed eyes stared straight ahead, unblinking. Then he rose to his feet. He turned to the altar table behind him and picked up the sword he had used to decapitate the teenage Hop Sing spy. He held the sword up a moment with both hands. Then he turned and handed it to Li Wang Yu. As Li watched with confusion, Crane took off his vermilion robe and placed it on the altar. Naked from the waist up, he faced the tong.

"My brothers," he said, "you know that I place the Sucy Sing above my life. But there is one thing more precious to me, and that is Star Collingwood. As you know, Charlie Kong has taken Star and will release her only when I give myself up to him. He was more clever than I, for it never occurred to me that he might use Star to capture me. Therefore, I have no choice but to put myself in the hands of the Hop Sings. When I have done so, and when Star is returned to her family, then the danger from the round-eyes will be over and peace will return once again to Chinatown.

"But since it is my death that Charlie Kong desires, I reserve for myself the option of dying among my friends rather than my enemies. Therefore I ask you, my beloved blood brother Li, to whom I have given the tong sword, to carry out my execution."

There was a shocked murmur from the tong soldiers. Li started to protest, but Crane raised his hand to silence him.

"Send my severed head to the Hop Sings. That will satisfy them. Then, when they have released Star, you, my brothers, under the leadership of Li Wang Yu, will fight to retain your power in Chinatown. Good-bye, my brothers. I have tried to serve you well. But now the greatest service I can render is to leave you."

He sank to his knees before Li and bowed his head. "Strike hard," he said. "Do it clean and well. Do not cause me needless pain."

Stunned, Li looked at Kwong Si, who looked equally stunned. Then they both looked at the other tong soldiers in the room.

"Do it," Crane insisted, his bowed neck exposed.

"*Kai Yee*," Li said imploringly, "I cannot do this terrible thing. You cannot ask this of me."

"I don't ask," Crane said. "I order. Do it."

Li, trembling violently, grasped the sword with both hands and slowly raised it over his head. Staring at Crane's neck, he started to bring the sword down.

Then, abruptly, he stopped.

"No!" he cried. "I refuse responsibility of taking your life. Someone else do it." He turned to the others. "Does anyone volunteer to execute the *Kai Yee?*"

Silence. Crane looked up and around. Finally he got to his feet.

"Then," he said, starting toward the door, "you condemn me to a cruel and horrible death. Farewell, my brothers. I go alone to the Hop Sings." He stopped at the door and looked back at them. "For the first time in my life," he added softly, "I am afraid."

Drawn by two horses, the police van roared down Nob Hill as Archer hung on for dear life. At the bottom, Captain Browder spotted a line of policemen a block away on Pine Street. "Over there!" he cried.

The van turned and drew up to the corner of Grant Avenue and Pine. A large crowd of Celestials had gathered, watching the police, but here everything seemed peaceful. One cop came up to the van and saluted. "The Anti-Coolies were here a little while ago, Captain," he said. "But we blocked them from going into Chinatown, so they took off."

"Which way did they go?"

"Toward the docks."

"The docks?" Browder looked puzzled. "Why the docks?"

"Well, if they can't get into Chinatown," said Archer, who was sitting next to him, "they might try to burn a few ships of the companies that employ Celestials, like the *Pacific Mail.*"

"Send someone to the mayor," Browder said. "Tell him to wire the naval base on Mare Island to send a warship to protect the docks."

"Right, Captain."

"And let us through. We're going to Crane Kung's house."

The cop signaled his men, who made an opening in the line. The van galloped through.

But when they reached the mansion on Grant Avenue, it was empty.

The peephole in the door on Murderers' Alley was opened and a man in a white hood with eyehole slits peered through. Outside in the fog stood Crane Kung. The hooded Hop Sing unbolted the door. Holding a drawn gun, he opened it and looked out.

"I'm alone," Crane said.

Once satisfied he was telling the truth, the Hop Sing guard stood back. Crane, wearing a black pajama suit, came in. Beneath an oil lantern hanging from a beam in the low ceiling stood four hooded Hop Sings: two wielded machetes, one a hatchet, the other a gun. As the first closed and bolted the door, the man with the gun stepped up to Crane.

"Raise your arms."

Crane obeyed. Quickly the Hop Sing frisked him.

"He's clean."

"Where is Star?" Crane asked.

"We ask the questions," snapped the man with the gun, poking his finger hard into Crane's chest. "Now that you're here, you do one thing: obey. Otherwise, shut up. Take him below."

Two of the guards grabbed his arms and led him down a narrow hall to a door. Down a set of wooden steps they marched to a basement room with damp stone walls. Two more hooded Hop Sings stood guard before another door. They opened it and Crane was pushed into a large cellar room filled with hooded men squatting on the floor.

A fat man came up to him and removed his hood. It was Charlie Kong. He smiled cruelly. "We've been expecting you. Welcome to the Society of Associated Conquerors," he said, using the formal name of the Hop Sing Tong. "The mighty *Kai Yee* of Chinatown has been humbled a bit perhaps, hmm?"

Laughter from the hooded Hop Sings.

"Where is Star?" Crane asked. "I've obeyed your instructions. I've come here alone and unarmed. Now you must release Star, if you are a man of honor."

"Oh, I am. You'll see your sweetheart—one last time. But if you try to tell her who we are, she'll not leave here alive. She was brought here blindfolded, and she goes back the same way. Don't try anything stupid."

"I won't."

Charlie Kong put his hood back on and clapped his hands. At the other end of the room two Hop Sings opened a door. A moment later, Star entered the room. She was still wearing her peach ball gown, though she had left her diamonds on Nob Hill. Crane's heart raced at her beauty.

"Crane!" she cried, spotting him. "You're alive!"

She hurried around the seated Hop Sings toward him. Charlie Kong signaled the guards, who released his arms so that he could put them around her.

"I was so afraid," she said as he held her tightly. "They wouldn't tell me anything. I've been here three hours praying you were all right."

"Was it that important to you?" he whispered.

She looked up into his face. "More important than anything else. You know that."

"No, I don't. You married someone else."

"Only because I had no choice."

"But you love your husband?"

She hesitated. "Yes, but not the way I love you. You were right: we are one. I came to Chinatown for you."

He closed his eyes a moment. That was what he had wanted to hear. "Did they hurt you?"

"No."

"Then kiss me, and they'll take you back to Nob Hill."

She started to kiss him, then hesitated again. "What will happen to you?" she whispered, glancing nervously around at the hooded men.

"I'll be all right." He smiled. "I know it looks a bit ominous, but it's all part of an old ritual."

She looked back at him. "Are you sure?"

"These are my friends. We have some business to discuss, then I'm going home. I'm safe. Don't worry."

She looked relieved.

"Well, then . . ."

She lifted her face to his. He kissed her with all the passion in his soul. Then he whispered, "There was never anyone but you, Star."

There were tears in her eyes. "Oh, my darling, half of me may love my husband, but the other half will always love you. And I think perhaps it's the better half."

He smiled. "That's beautiful to hear. Now, you go home. We'll meet again someday. Somewhere."

A brief frown of doubt flickered across her beautiful face, but he touched his finger to her lips in a sign of reassurance. One of the guards took her hand and led her away. Just before she went through the door, they stopped her to put on a blindfold. She turned to take another look at Crane, who was watching her.

Suddenly she knew.

"Crane!" she cried.

"Go!" he yelled. "For God's sake, go!"

She was trembling as they put the blindfold over her eyes. "I love you!" she cried. "You're my heart!"

Then she was pushed through the door.

When it had been slammed shut, Charlie Kong removed his hood. "A touching scene." He smiled. "And I congratulate you. You played your part well. The noble lover sacrificing his own life for his sweetheart's safety. I'm moved."

"I thank you for letting me see her, and for not hurting her."

"As you said, I am a man of honor." He signaled the others. "Prepare him."

Three tong soldiers came up to Crane and began to rip off his clothes.

"What are you going to do?" Crane asked. "Just kill me and get it over with."

"Ah, but then we wouldn't have any fun."

The crowd pressing against the barbed-wire gates of the *Pacific Mail* dock was in a frenzy.

"Throw your torches!" George Coleman yelled. "Set the warehouse on fire and the flames'll spread to the ships on the other side!"

A barrage of torches sailed over the fence.

"Burn, burn, burn!" the mob yelled.

Most of the torches sputtered out on the ground, but some struck the wooden walls of the warehouse with a barrage of sparks. Falling to the ground, they began smoldering. Two terrified Celestial night watchmen ran out the door of the warehouse carrying buckets of water.

"Slanty-eyes!" the mob screamed. One of them raised a gun and fired. The trailing Celestial screamed and fell facefirst to the ground, spilling his bucket as he clasped his arm where he had been hit. The other had managed to drown one of the torches when a volley of shots riddled him with bullets. He fell to the ground, dead. The other watchman crawled back toward the door, but the crowd, smelling blood, fired again and killed him too.

By now two torches had ignited the warehouse wall and flames were licking toward the roof. The crowd began cheering as the fire pierced the patchy fog.

"Police!" George Coleman yelled as he saw two vans, their bells clanging, bearing down on the docks.

"I was right," Archer yelled from the first van. "The warehouse is burning. Damn, if I only had a sketch artist."

"Fire over their heads!" Browder barked.

The cops in both vans began shooting. The crowd, howling like banshees, began dispersing in all directions. But it was too late for the two dead Celestials.

And too late for the warehouse. Half of it was ablaze and fire alarms were ringing all over the city. Archer watched, as fascinated by the flames as he was appalled by the ugliness of the crowd. Something has to stop this anti-Celestial hatred, he thought, or there's not much future for San Francisco. Maybe I should run an editorial about the positive qualities of the Chinese, even in the midst of all this hysteria. At any rate—he paused to smile—editorial or no, we'll sell *ten* thousand extra copies tomorrow with this story. For the first time in his brief newspaper career, he was experiencing the excitement of a scoop.

It was then they heard a distant "Boom!" and a rocket shot into the sky above the bay, lighting in a fiercely burning star above the fog.

"The warships from Mare Island," Browder grunted. "They're a bit late, but what the hell . . ."

"Star," Archer muttered, looking up at the rocket. Here he was thinking about selling newspapers when, for all he knew, his sister might be dead. After they had found Crane's house empty, Browder had decided he had no choice but to go to the docks and try to contain the crowd of Anti-Coolies.

"Captain," Archer asked, "what about my sister?"

"Dammit, Collingwood," the mustached policeman exploded, "I can't do everything at once. In case you hadn't noticed, it's a fairly busy night in this town, and I'll remind you that it was your sister who started the whole damned mess."

"I know, but the fact remains, she's in danger."

"Well, sir, what do you want me to do? Where shall we look?"

"Isn't it possible the Hop Sings may have her? Shouldn't we try their headquarters?"

"On Murderers' Alley? I'm not going into that pesthole unless I have at least three dozen men. The Hop Sings are a killer tong."

"Can't you get three dozen men?"

"Mr. Collingwood, if you'd read your own newspaper, you'd know that the San Francisco police force is woefully undermanned. Now, sir, I've got every man available out on the streets tonight trying to protect this city from a bunch of maniacs wanting to kill Celestials, and much as I want to help your sister, my first obligation is to the citizens of this city—"

"Captain," Archer interrupted, "the mob's gone home now. You go to the Hop Sing Tong, and I'll promise you an editorial crusade in the *Times-Dispatch* that'll get you as many policemen as you want— and a raise in their salaries to boot."

Browder stared at him a moment. "You give your word?" he whispered.

"I do, sir."

"God damn!" He turned to his driver. "Head back to Pine Street. We'll pick those men up, then we're going to Murderers' Alley. Hurry!"

As the driver whipped the horses, Archer's blood surged. He was experiencing not only the excitement of the press, but its power as well.

He tilted the jar of honey and slowly poured its contents over Crane's genitals.

"I have a friend from Peru who works on the docks," Charlie Kong said, standing beside the table they had strapped Crane on. "He told me about the Indians in Ecuador. Apparently they're a bloodthirsty lot who spend a lot of time dreaming up exotic ways to kill people.

This is the way they dreamed up to punish rapists. You didn't exactly rape Star Collingwood, but we'll stretch a point. It should be an interesting way to go."

Crane, who had been gagged, stared down his stomach as the warm honey dripped over him, causing an eerie, faintly erotic sensation. He had no idea what the Hop Sings were up to, but he was covered with sweat, filled with terror, and feeling anything but erotic.

When the honey jar was empty, Charlie Kong, his arms crossed over his fat chest, said, "I think he's ready. Bring the bees."

Crane stared at him, twitching and gurgling.

"That's right, *Kai Yee.*" Charlie smiled. "Twitch. We have three dozen yellow jackets in a jar. We're going to put that jar over your prick and balls. Those yellow jackets are mean, *Kai Yee.* My Peruvian friend tells me they go crazy with all that honey. They're going to sting you, *Kai Yee,* in what I think you'll agree is a very sensitive spot. My Peruvian friend tells me that everything swells up and the pain becomes so intense that in the end they give the rapist a knife and he cuts everything off himself—which, of course, kills him. Ah, here's the jar."

One of the guards brought up a big glass jar with a piece of cardboard over the mouth. Inside, huge black-and-yellow bees were crawling up the walls. Crane, his face wet with sweat, stared at the insects.

"We'll watch you for a while, *Kai Yee,*" Charlie said. "It should be instructive as well as entertaining. All right, put it on. Get everything in. We'd heard you're hung like a horse, *Kai Yee,* so we got an extra-large jar."

Crane was spread-eagled on a table that had been tilted at a forty-five-degree angle. The Hop Sing slowly carried the jar toward his midsection, holding the cardboard cover in place with one hand. The tong soldiers watched with fascination. The cellar room was totally silent except for the faint buzzing of the bees.

Then the Hop Sing swiftly removed the cover and slammed the mouth of the jar over Crane's private parts, holding it firmly in place.

The bees did not move for a moment, as if stunned by the jerking of the jar against Crane's body.

Then they smelled the honey. They began swarming over the organs until they became an angry, crawling black mass.

Charlie Kong watched, mesmerized, as Crane began grunting with pain. The grunts became gasps. His body began twitching so violently that the Hop Sing guard had trouble holding the jar in place.

Then Crane bit through his gag. The scream that came out of his mouth was so horrible that even Charlie Kong's blood ran cold.

Within fifteen minutes his organs had swollen to half again their size and were turning purple. It was then that the door to the cellar room burst open and the Hop Sing guards ran in yelling, "Police!" Captain Browder and his men poured in after them, firing at the ceiling first, then into the Hop Sings as Charlie Kong pulled his gun and fired back. Charlie was killed, along with six other tong soldiers. Then the others gave up.

When Archer came into the room, the Hop Sings, their arms in front of them, were being handcuffed by the police. At the end of the room, Captain Browder and four other cops were standing around a tilted table. Archer crossed the room and looked.

"Jesus Christ," he muttered, staring at the ghastly sight. "Is he dead?"

"He sure as hell ain't alive," Browder said.

One young policeman took a look, then stumbled to a corner of the room and vomited.

A minute before the police arrived, one of the Hop Sings had cut off Crane's genitals and put him out of his misery.

34

"ANTI-COOLIE RIOTS DISPERSED!" the *Times-Dispatch* headline
screamed the next morning.

"NAVY CALLED OUT! PACIFIC MAIL DOCK FIRE CONTAINED!
POLICE RAID TONG HEADQUARTERS!

Your Editor's Eyewitness Account of Bloody Tong War Finale!

Ghastly Torture-Death of Suey Sing Lord as Hop Sing Tong
Smashed by Police!

Nob Hill Heiress Released Unharmed!"

"My father's furious!" Arabella Dawson cried as the maître d' at
the Palace Hotel Restaurant seated her and Archer the next day at
lunch. "I heard him yelling at Mother this morning that the *Times-
Dispatch* scooped the *Bulletin*."

"That's right," Archer said, grinning. "We went through four extra
press runs and sold the most papers in our history."

"What *was* the 'ghastly torture-death' of Crane Kung?" she asked,
lowering her voice. "I didn't quite understand from the article. Exactly
where did the bees sting him?"

"My dear Miss Dawson, I couldn't print the truth, nor will I
relate it to a refined young lady like yourself. Suffice it to say that,
whatever Crane Kung's sins, he paid for them dearly in the last
minutes of his life. My sister, by the way, is devastated, which is
not making my brother-in-law very happy. What do you recommend
today, René? In English, please, not that unpronounceable French of
yours."

"The abalone, *monsieur*. It is superb. We also have mutton chops
cooked with anise and sweet garlic."

He handed them menus. The elegant restaurant was packed, and

303

all eyes were on Archer and Arabella. Everyone had devoured the *Times-Dispatch* that morning.

After they had ordered and René had disdainfully poured the ice water, Archer reached across the table and took Arabella's hands.

"I saw things last night I'll never forget as long as I live," he said softly. "But the other part of the story I didn't print was as wonderful in its way as Crane's death was horrible. If what my sister tells me is true—and I have no reason to believe it isn't—Crane gave his own life to save hers, and he did it because he loved her, for which I admire him extravagantly. That's what I call the supreme test of courage and I guess it's the supreme test of love too. I don't know if I'd have that kind of courage, but I do know I love you."

Arabella blushed. "Please, Archer, everyone's looking."

"Let them, I don't care. Now, Arabella, I'm going to be very honest with you. I started out to entrap you."

She stiffened. "What do you mean?"

"I was furious at your father for what he printed about my sister in his paper, and I thought, 'How can I get back at him? What can I do to Slade Dawson that will really hurt him?' And then I thought of you. I thought that if I could seduce you—"

"Oh!" She wrenched her hands from his. "You horrible man!" She lowered her voice to a whisper. "I suppose you think that because my mother was what she was, you can have your way with me, that it's in my blood. Well, you're wrong."

"I know it, but hear me out. My idea was—right or wrong—to seduce you and then walk away, leaving you a 'fallen woman,' as they say in the dime novels. But something happened I didn't count on: I fell in love with you."

"You don't expect me to believe that?"

"Yes, I do, because it's true. You are a dear, sweet, highly intelligent, and very beautiful—"

"I'm not beautiful!" she interrupted. "Don't try to sweet-talk me. I know what I am. I'm attractive, period."

"If you'd quit interrupting me, what I'm trying to do is ask you to marry me."

She glared at him. "Well, you're doing it in a terribly clumsy way, is all I can say."

"You're probably right."

"Even if I could overlook your gross and insulting motives, my father would never allow me to marry a Collingwood. He'd disinherit me first."

"Good. Then you'd know I'm not after your money. By the way, my mother would probably disinherit me for marrying Slade Dawson's daughter, so we both might end up poor as church mice. Then we could find out if it's true you can live on love."

"You, sir, are not in your right mind if you think I'd consider for one minute giving up my inheritance to marry an impossible, deceitful . . ."

"Don't forget 'vulgar.' I'm a vulgarian, remember?"

"I certainly do remember! A deceitful, impossible vulgarian like yourself!"

"Well, that probably sums me up pretty well. But, Arabella, this newspaper business . . . it's in my blood. It's truly exciting. I can really do things for this city. Did you read my editorial this morning about the Chinese?"

"Yes."

"What did you think?"

"It was badly written."

"Probably. I wrote it at four this morning, half-asleep. But what did you think of what I said?"

She hesitated. "I . . . admired it. You wrote that prejudice against the Chinese is wrong. I'll also grant you it took a great deal of courage to run that editorial right now, with so much ill feeling against the Chinese in this city."

"So do you see what I mean? The newspaper can be a powerful weapon for good. I want to use that weapon, and I need a wife who'll help me use it. I need you, Arabella. Will you please at least consider what I've asked? I do love you so very much."

She continued to glare at him as a waiter holding a large silver tray with a salmon on it came up behind Archer.

"I've considered," Arabella said abruptly.

"Already?"

"Yes. I accept."

"You mean—?"

"I'll be your wife. I'll overlook all your terrible qualities because"—her stern look melted into a smile—"I love you too."

"Ya-hoo!"

He jumped out of his chair, throwing both arms into the air and in so doing banging the salmon tray, which flew out of the waiter's arms into the air. The salmon flipped and landed on Archer's head, its tail dangling merrily in front of his nose.

Arabella—and everyone else in the restaurant—broke into gales of laughter.

* * *

"You luh-luh-lied to me!" Juanito shouted as he stuffed his shirts into his leather valise. "And your muh-muh-mother lied too! You were in luh-love with that Crane K-K-Kung!"

Star was standing beside him in their bedroom. "Yes, I was, I'll admit it. And I suppose Mother did lie a little—"

"A little?"

"But, Juanito, he gave his life for me and of course I'm upset. No, more than upset. Crane was very dear to me, which doesn't mean I don't love you too."

"A wo-woman can't love two men at the s-same time."

"That's not true!"

He snapped his valise shut and turned on her. "Look, Star, I luh-love you. I fell in luh-love with you the first time I s-saw you. But I was s-sold a bill of goods. You weren't any fr-fragile virgin who was defl-flowered by an evil Chinese: you loved it! You luh-loved it so much that all it takes is one n-note—which you wouldn't sh-show me, your husband!—and you run out of the house!"

"I was trying to save his life, which he gave for me—someone who married another man. And I think it's vile and mean of you to throw him up in my face after the noble sacrifice he made."

" 'Noble sacrifice' my f-foot! Anyway, I'm through. I'm going back to the ranch."

As he snatched the valise from the bed and started for the door, she ran after him.

"Juanito, you can't leave me. I'm your wife!"

"You don't act like it. My idea of a w-w-wife is a w-woman who loves only one man: her husband. And y-you don't qualify."

He opened the door and went out into the upstairs hall. She followed him, grabbing his sleeve.

"You're not being fair," she cried. "I do love you. I'd never met you when I loved Crane—"

He turned and with his free hand slapped her so hard that she fell back against a marble-topped console table, knocking off a Chinese vase and sending it crashing to the floor.

"*Puta!*" he snarled as she burst into tears.

Then he stormed down the corridor, down the stairs, and out of the house.

"You poor darling," Emma said that night in the library as she hugged Star.

"He called me a whore and hit me!" she sobbed.

"Yes, and broke a Ming vase too. Our Juanito has a bit more temper than I supposed. Well, maybe it's just as well it didn't work out. Perhaps it never had a chance."

She released Star and sat on a sofa.

"What do you mean?"

"I did lie to his mother about you, so he's not being entirely unreasonable. But I don't like men who hit women, and that stammer is enough to drive you crazy."

Star hurried to the sofa and sat beside her mother. "Oh, but, Momma, I love him," she exclaimed.

Emma looked confused. "Darling, you have to make up your mind—"

"I do love him. I can't help it that I loved Crane too, but he's dead now and I want Juanito."

"Even after he slapped you and called you a whore?"

"Maybe I deserve it. I caused all the trouble. I was wildly passionate about Crane, so Juanito has reason to be angry. Momma, you have to get him back for me. Juanito's my last chance. If he leaves me, no other man in the world will ever want me . . ." She started sobbing again.

Emma put her arm around her and hugged her. "There's a way I can force him back if you really want him. But I have to warn you, he'll probably resent it and resent you, and I wouldn't give a marriage like that much chance of succeeding."

"It doesn't matter. I don't want to be alone the rest of my life."

"Being alone may be better than being married to someone who hates you."

"Are you happy alone?"

Emma bit her lip. "No," she admitted. "Being alone is hell." She looked at the eagerness in her daughter's tear-filled eyes and sighed. She knew any chance for Star's happiness had been lost. "All right, I'll get him back for you."

"How are you going to get him back?"

"Just be thankful I have a smart lawyer."

There was a knock on the door and Can Do appeared. "Taitai, Lord Mandeville is here."

Star looked at her mother, whose hand went automatically up to her coiffure.

"Oh?" Emma asked. "And what brings him?"

"He say he come pay his respects and see if everything okay after last night."

"How very thoughtful. Please show him in. And, Can Do?"

"Yes, Taitai?"

"Set another place for dinner. If Lord Mandeville is free, I'll ask him to dine. After all, his dinner last night was rather nerve-racking."

"Can do, Taitai."

After he left, Star said, "Momma, who is this Lord Mandeville?"

"A very charming young Englishman who's visiting with Sir Percival Gore. His father, the Marquess of Thornfield, owns Thornfield Abbey."

She got up from the sofa and went to the mirror over the mantel to check her reflection.

Good heavens, Star thought, watching her. Momma's interested in him.

"Lord Mandeville," Can Do announced at the door.

Star turned to see a tall, blond, impeccably tailored young man come into the room.

And I can see why Momma's interested!

"Hey, Juanito!" yelled the vaquero, galloping beneath the blazing sun across the field. "Your momma wants you! Juanito!"

In Levi's and chaps, Juanito was chasing a pony that had escaped from one of the corrals. He twirled his lariat, sent it sailing. With fabulous accuracy it landed around the pony's neck.

"Juanito!"

The vaquero reined his horse alongside as Juanito tied the lariat to the pommel of his saddle.

"What's up, Diego?"

"Your momma sent me to find you. There's a man at the ranch. He works for Señora Collingwood."

A scowl came over Juanito's tanned face. "I'll run him off the ranch," he spat in Spanish. "I don't want anything more to do with that damned family."

"Yeah, well, tell that to your momma. I sure as hell won't. And she says hurry!" He turned his horse and started back.

"Shit," Juanito muttered. Then he dug his spurs in and followed him.

Twenty minutes later, he walked into the drawing room of the ranch house to find his mother alone. Standing by a window, she was in tears.

"Momma, what's wrong?" he asked in Spanish. "Where's the man?"

Doña Felicidad wiped her eyes and turned from the window. "He left. Oh, Juanito, we are in terrible, terrible trouble."

Juanito hurried across the room to take his mother's hand. "What is it? Who was this man?"

"His name is Palmer and he is your mother-in-law's lawyer."

"Yes, I met him in San Francisco last week when I signed the marriage agreement."

"Did you read the marriage agreement?"

"Of course."

"All of it?"

"Well, not all. It was thirty pages long and boring—"

She threw up her hands and moaned. "Then we are ruined!" she cried. "Ruined!"

"Why? What is it?"

"Here! Read it now—now that it's too late!"

She went to a table and picked up a document that had been written on the recently invented miracle of the office world, the typewriter.

"Page ten, paragraph fifteen, subclause B."

Juanito flipped through to page ten and read the clause in question:

If at any time during the first five years of the marriage the groom, Mr. López y Sepúlveda, abandons for any reason the bride, Miss Collingwood, then the mortgage on the Calafía Ranch presently held by Mrs. Collingwood will revert in full force and the dowry of $100,000 will be returned as a penalty.

He looked up. "What does this mean?" he asked.

"What do you think it means? It means if you don't go back to your wife, we lose the ranch."

"Not necessarily. We return her dowry—I don't want her damned money now anyway—and the mortgage goes back in effect. We're back where we were before I got into this mess."

"Oh, Juanito, you're so naive. You don't understand how clever these Yanquis are. She's foreclosing the mortgage. We're three months behind in our payments, we have no money if we return the dowry, and she's foreclosing. We lose the ranch—lose everything!"

"That bitch!" Juanito whispered, his dark eyes filling with rage.

"But she has the money," sobbed his mother. "She has the power. This Señor Palmer says if we try to borrow more money from a bank, Señora Collingwood's bank will buy up what he called our 'paper,' so what can we do? We're helpless! Lawyers, bankers, what do we Californios know of lawyers and bankers? We are people of the soil."

Juanito's thin, handsome face looked determined. "It's time we learned something about lawyers and bankers," he said softly. "These Yanquis have come and destroyed our paradise. All right, so be it: Star yearns for my body. I'll keep her pregnant for the next twenty years so she'll never have a chance to look at a damned Chinaman or anyone else. And either I or one of my sons will learn about lawyers and bankers and money and power. We'll learn the Yanqui tricks, and we'll beat the blond bastards at their own game."

Then he hurled the copy of the marriage contract across the room. It hit the wall and fell to the floor like a dead bug.

But the power in the typed page was very much alive.

Lord Mandeville's blue eyes drank in the splendor of Emma's diamond-and-emerald necklace glittering in the candlelight of the gold candlesticks. Magnificent, he thought. And the breast is magnificent too. Not a wrinkle in the skin, and she must be near fifty.

"A penny for your thoughts, my lord," Emma said, raising her glass of champagne to her lips. "Although I have the odd feeling your thoughts are worth dollars rather than pennies. Perhaps even pounds sterling."

Radcliff smiled. "Was I so terribly obvious?" he asked. "I confess I was admiring your necklace. The stones are magnificent. I've never seen emeralds with such deep intensity. They're mesmerizing."

"My father bought them in Paris three years ago from an Indian maharajah."

"They must have cost a fortune."

"Enough to install indoor plumbing at Thornfield Abbey."

Radcliff almost choked on his vichyssoise. "Emma, you're a witch," he laughed. "That's exactly what I was thinking. I'm caught."

Emma smiled. "Radcliff—and I believe after dining with you four evenings in a row I may call you Radcliff, though you haven't offered it—when a young man of your obvious charms starts paying attention to a woman old enough to be his mother, it's fairly certain the young man is thinking real estate as well as romance."

"And what is the older woman thinking?"

"Ah, that's a fair question," she said, suddenly rather sad. "She's thinking many, many things. She's thinking she's no longer young, and that is a difficult thing to accept. Except it must be accepted. She's thinking of the two husbands she lost, both of whom she loved with devotion—I should really say 'passion.' She's thinking that she's very lonely now. She's thinking that she must not lose her dignity and do something foolish. But"—she turned her magnificent amethyst eyes on him—"she's thinking that perhaps life isn't *quite* over."

"I believe for a woman of your beauty and passion for living, life will never be over until you're quite dead. And perhaps not even then."

"Oh, I have no interest in being a ghost. Ghosts do such silly things, like rapping on tables at séances and moving Ouija boards. No, when I'm dead I shall stay dead, thank you. Once through this crazy world is enough. But meanwhile, I'm living. And another of my thoughts is that it might be a wonderful challenge to help you restore something as beautiful as Thornfield Abbey. That is, if I happened by some wild chance to become the Marchioness of Thornfield."

Again she smiled. My God, he thought, she gets straight to the point. Well, here goes. "I must remind you that my elder brother will succeed to the title."

"Yes, but I asked Sir Percival—behind your back, of course—and he tells me your elder brother has consumption and is not expected to live out the year. Furthermore, he has never exhibited the slightest romantic interest in anything but horses and dogs."

"This is true."

"So when your father dies—and he is eighty—the probability is that you will inherit one of the oldest titles in England, fourteen thousand acres of Yorkshire moors under which used to be rich seams of coal, one of the great stately homes of England, which is falling down, and something like one million pounds in gambling debts. It's a future with some pros, but quite a few cons."

"You've summed up the situation pithily."

"Now, my situation has pros and cons also," she said, cutting into her asparagus. "I have saved my daughter's marriage in a rather unpleasant way, one I think may not have been wise in the long run, but . . ." She shrugged. "Star wanted it saved, and she is precious to me. My son has told me this morning that he is going to marry the daughter of the man I loathe most in this world, which has come as a shock. I told him I'd have to think this over, which is why I'm being so blunt with you, dear Radcliff. Is your asparagus tender?"

"Yes, quite." More tender than your heart, old girl, but go on.

"Good. Now, if a certain charming young Englishman asked a certain rich but quite lonely American widow to be his wife, the widow's son and heir would undoubtedly be furious and cause all sorts of trouble. But if the widow agreed to his marrying the daughter of the man she loathes, then a quid pro quo would exist and a peaceful settlement could probably be reached on both sides. If you see what I mean?"

"Yes, I think I'm following you."

"Of course, the marriage would be at best an arrangement, probably without love on the Englishman's side."

"And what about the American's side?"

She looked at him sadly. "The American is tired of waking up alone," she sighed. "Is that so terrible of me?"

Radcliff put down his knife and fork and picked up his napkin. "Of course not," he said. "It's perfectly natural. I, too, dislike waking up alone."

"Dear Radcliff," she said, smiling, "I suspect you rarely wake up alone."

"Yes, um. Well." He wiped his mouth with his napkin. "Ahem. Since you have put things so succinctly, perhaps it would not be amiss of me to further a relationship that is becoming increasingly tender to me by the moment. Dearest Emma, since I first saw you last week, I have felt a burning sensation in my breast that has fired my most tender sentiments—"

"You used 'tender' twice."

He put down his napkin. "Dammit, Emma, I'm rotten at this sort of thing. I love you. Will you be my wife?"

She gazed dreamily at him for almost a full minute. Then she picked up her knife and fork and went back to her asparagus.

"I'll have to think about it," she said.

He almost, but not quite, pounded his fist on the table.

"Emma, could this rumor possibly be true?" David Levin demanded three evenings later as he confronted her in her library. For almost thirty years his heart had caught at her beauty, and tonight was no exception. In the soft glow of the gaslight she looked almost ethereally beautiful. She wore a dress of soft lime silk trimmed with delicate point lace. She wore around her neck her famous pearls and a few rings on her fingers, and this simple elegance took David's breath away. At a time when girls were using bismuth and preparations of lead to whiten their skin, tea and dye to lighten their hair, were dabbing India ink under their eyes, were dilating their pupils with sulfate of atropine and putting false eyelashes over those dilated eyes; at a time of such rampant artificiality in a scramble for physical attractiveness, Emma could still afford to rely on what nature had given her (with a little rouge).

"What rumor?" she asked, pouring her former tutor and editor a glass of his beloved sherry.

"Everyone in town is saying you're going to marry this Lord Mandeville."

"Are they? And why would they say that?"

"Because he's been here every night for a week. And he stays later every night." This last came out ominously.

Emma laughed as she handed him the sherry. "I'll bet that Alicia Beaumont and Sydney Tolliver are both dying to write about the wild orgies on Nob Hill, but they can't now that Archer and Arabella are getting married."

"You can make light of it, but Archer's terribly upset. He came to me this morning, and even though I swore I'd never talk to him again after the way he treated me, he was in such a state that I listened to him. He begged me, as your oldest friend, to try to talk some sense into you."

"We made a deal!" Emma said hotly. "I told him I'd agree to his marrying Arabella, which I did *not* want to do, if he'd agree to my marrying Radcliff. And now he's reneging? We'll see about that." She started for the bell cord.

"Wait! What are you going to do?"

"Call Archer down here."

"Emma, please, leave him out of it for the moment. Let me talk as . . . well, as almost a part of this family for so many years."

She took her hand away from the cord. "You *are* family, David. You know that." She smiled. "You might have been my husband if Scott hadn't stranded you in Jamaica."

"I'm all too aware of that. At any rate, Lord Mandeville is half your age—"

"Really, David, I'm no fool."

"And he's so obviously after your money—"

"That's hardly a secret either."

"Well, it just . . . it just seems wrong! You're an institution in this city. You've given this wonderful gift of a hospital, and I know people hope you'll give other things later, perhaps a museum—"

"I may indeed. But aren't they being a bit premature? I'm not dead yet—far from it. An institution? You make me feel like the orphans' home, or a Civil War monument."

"You know what I mean. People here love you. You've been here practically from the beginning—you're part of San Francisco's history, if you will. And for you to leave and go to England—"

"David, really, there's a railroad now. There are steamships. It's not as if California's the end of the world anymore. And besides, I"— she nervously twisted a rose diamond ring—"I feel sort of *over* here. Archer's the future of this family, and I think he's going to be a very strong future—and I know you disagree."

"No, actually, I don't. Archer has injected a vitality into the paper that I lacked. I'll admit that."

"Well, there you have it. Perhaps it's time for me to get offstage, so to speak. Clear the way for Archer. Besides, the idea of being a marchioness is rather exciting. It would be a whole new life for me, a new challenge. Besides," she said, smiling slightly, "Radcliff is young and so terribly dashing. And you know my weakness has always been for good-looking men."

David drank the rest of his sherry in one gulp, then stood up. "Yes, and you've been wrong!" he almost shouted. "Scott Kinsolving was a mean bastard who stole you away from me with a dirty trick. And your beloved Archer was just a pretty face with not much of a brain behind it. All he wanted was to go be an Indian."

"Don't you dare speak of my beloved that way."

"Your beloved what? You henpecked that poor man for twenty-five years, and everyone knows it. Now, for the third time in your life, you're running off after another pretty face, this time one who's half your age. You're going to make a fool of yourself and embarrass your family just because you don't have any common sense when it comes to men."

Emma could hardly believe her ears. "You've never talked like this to me in thirty years, David!"

"I know, and it's been my mistake. You're a wonderful woman, Emma, but you're far from perfect when it comes to the opposite sex."

"I resent that. And tell me about your great success with women? I've heard the stories, David—"

"Oh, yes, my fancy ladies. I don't deny it. I'm a man, with all a man's failings. And I'll admit that what Archer accused me of is true: I did try to keep the paper respectable because I wanted to be more respectable myself, and in the process I made the *Times-Dispatch* a bore. Oh, I have no illusions about myself, Emma. I'm a failure in life. I failed as a writer, I failed as an editor, and I failed as a lover. But I'm not going to fail you as a friend."

She was watching him with fascination. She had never seen him so forceful, so honest. "Archer was a failure," she said softly. "And yet I loved him more than any other man. There's nothing wrong with failure, David. Most people are failures, I suppose. Now you're telling me I'm a failure, and maybe I am, I don't know. At least, a failure with men."

"And there's another thing—and your father would agree with me on this, and so would your poor dead mother. Isn't it time you married one of your own kind? You've married two of the goyim. Now, instead of marrying this Anglican fortune hunter, don't you think it's time you thought of marrying a Jew?"

"But who?" she exclaimed.

To her absolute amazement, he knelt in front of her and took her hand. "Me," he said. "The man who's loved you for thirty years and who's never been more to you than a pet dog. Emma, I know I'm not glamorous like this Lord Mandeville, and I'm not young, and God knows, I'm not handsome—"

"No, David," she interrupted. "Tonight, for the first time, you are looking handsome."

"Well, I thank you, though I know you're just trying to be nice. But if love means anything to you, then I beg you to consider my proposal—absurd and crazy as it is. I love you with all my heart and soul, and that's all I have to offer you. But, Emma, if the poets are right, my love has to be worth something."

She stared at him. For one of the few times in her life, she was speechless. She remembered her mother, that Frankfurt ballroom so many years before, the shouts of the students: *Juden! Juden! Juden!*

"David, you've taken me so by surprise! I don't know what to say, except that I'm terribly flattered."

"Then give me an answer. Please. Yes or no?"

Lord Mandeville and David Levin. What an incredible choice!

"I'll have to think about it," she said.

·FOUR·

The Water and the Word

35

ONE March morning in 1906, young Cherise Wheeler was walking the beach in Santa Monica when she saw a black form bobbing in the surf ahead of her. When she came closer, she screamed.

It was the body of a man in a dark suit.

The tall, thin man descending the curving stair of the Spanish-style mansion in Pasadena had a reputation even at the age of twenty-eight of being one of the most aggressive businessmen in the West.

"Send a cable to my father in London," he was saying to the attractive secretary accompanying him down the stairs, almost running to keep up. " 'Have completed negotiations with Dallas people. Stop. They agree to sell us *Courier-Journal* for two million. Stop. Chester working out financing with our bank. Stop. Have initiated talks with Des Moines *Herald*. Stop. Last Sunday *Clarion* circulation topped half-million. Stop. Hope you're enjoying London. Stop. Love to Mother. Curtis.' Got that?"

"Yes, Mr. Collingwood," said Rose Markham, scribbling shorthand in her dictation pad.

"Don't I have a dental appointment this morning?"

"Yes. Ten o'clock."

"Cancel it."

"Mr. Collingwood, you've canceled two appointments. Dr. Simmons says if you don't get your teeth cleaned soon, they'll fall out."

"Let 'em fall. I haven't got time for dentists today. Good morning, Mary. How's the son and heir?"

A plump white-uniformed Irish nanny was coming up the stairs.

"He's got gas, poor thing. Cryin' his head off, he is."

"What do you do for babies with gas?" Curtis asked, checking his gold pocket watch as he passed the nanny the other way.

"Let 'em cry till they blow it out their rears and stink up the nursery."

Curtis grinned. "And lo, another Collingwood enters the world to stink it up."

"Mr. Collingwood, I'm not canceling the dentist. I'm not going to let your teeth drop out."

"Oh, all right. Rose, you're a damned bully."

They had reached the white marble floor of the entrance hall. Martin, the English butler, was standing beside the front door, holding it open. Outside, on the gravel drive, Curtis' new red-and-black Great Arrow automobile stood, his chauffeur holding the rear door. The Great Arrow was "*the* motorcar for the discriminating,". as some of the ads read, which meant "for the rich." Curtis Collingwood, Archer and Arabella's eldest son, was certainly rich. He had also inherited the Collingwood good looks—or, more accurately, the de Meyer good looks, because most people thought his slim face and black hair were throwbacks to his gorgeous grandmother, Emma. Rose Markham thought her boss of four years was the most dashing man she had ever seen. She was more than a little in love with him, but if Curtis Collingwood played around—and she had no idea whether he did or not— it certainly wasn't with any of the five thousand employees of the Collingwood Corporation.

"You haven't signed the contracts yet," she was saying as she hurried across the hall behind her boss.

"I'll sign them in the car. Good morning, Martin. Tell Mrs. Collingwood that Rose has abducted me for a breakfast meeting in town with the lawyers."

"Yes, Mr. Collingwood."

"Mr. Collingwood! Telephone!"

A maid had appeared in a doorway under the staircase. Curtis turned.

"Damn. Who is it?"

"Mr. Lee. He says it's important."

"Get in the car, Rose."

Curtis hurried back in the house and went to the service hall under the stair, where the nearest phone was. "Yes, Digby?"

He listened to the editor in chief of the Los Angeles *Clarion*, the city's second-largest newspaper and one of the Collingwood Corporation's fourteen papers nationwide.

"Murdered?" he asked, stunned. "Jesus Christ. I'll be in the office in twenty minutes."

He hung up, then ran out of the house.

"Get me to the office—*fast*!" he said to the chauffeur as he climbed into the back seat next to Rose.

"Somebody," he said to his secretary as the car took off, "has murdered Carl Klein."

Rose Markham gasped.

* * *

Detective Cliff Parker of the Los Angeles Police Department looked up at the new twelve-story Clarion Building on Hill Street. Parker, a native Angelino, got a thrill looking at the skyscrapers going up in his town: it was proof that Los Angeles was entering the big time. Forty years earlier, it had been a "vile little dump," in the words of Parker's father. Now it was a city of over a quarter-million, growing at a dizzying speed, rivaling San Francisco in size and importance. Skyscrapers! thought the rugged thirty-year-old detective, scratching his sandy mane. And murder.

He walked into the green-marble lobby and to the elevator bank with its six sculptured bronze doors. On the vaulted ceiling was a handsome mural representing the history of California, commissioned by the wife of the building's owner, Archer Collingwood. Here was Fray Junípero Serra converting Indians to Christianity, there were the missions, the Camino Real—all as pretty and brightly colored as a picture book, leaving out the murder, disease, and near-enslavement of the Indians by the Spanish missionaries. Oh, well, Parker thought as the elevator doors opened, it looks nice, and where are the Indians now?

"I've been put in charge of this case," he said a few minutes later in Curtis' office on the top floor. "Carl Klein's body was found in the surf at Santa Monica this morning. He'd been shot through the head around midnight last night. Does either of you gentlemen have any idea who might have killed your reporter?"

Curtis, who was sitting at his desk, exchanged looks with Digby Lee, who was slumped in a leather armchair. "No," Curtis said. "I wish I did. Carl Klein was a first-rate reporter and one of our finest employees. By the way, I'll offer a ten-thousand-dollar reward for information leading to the capture of his murderer."

"Was Klein working on any particular story?" Parker asked.

"Yes," said Digby Lee, whose successful reporting career at the San Francisco *Times-Dispatch* Archer had rewarded by putting him in charge of the L.A. paper. "He was working on a series of articles about the Owens Valley project."

"The plan to bring water down to L.A. from upstate?"

"That's right."

"That seems peaceful enough. I looked him up: Klein had no police record. Did he have any bad habits you know of? Women? Gambling? Booze?"

"Carl Klein was one of the most clean-living young men I know," Curtis said. "He didn't smoke and I don't think he'd ever even had a beer. He dated our receptionist, Miss Gwynn, and I suppose there were other girls he went out with, but I've never heard one whisper about anything immoral in his conduct."

"He sounds perfect."

"He practically was."

Cliff Parker looked at the two men. "Well," he finally said, "who would want to murder a perfect reporter writing about water projects?"

"I have no idea," said Curtis.

For some reason, Cliff Parker thought he was lying.

"We have one good lead," he went on. "There was a note on the body we think was written by the killer. It's signed 'J.' Does that mean anything to you?"

" 'J'? No, I'm afraid not."

'J' thought Curtis. Jesus Christ, he's done it!

"This pulpit, Mr. Collingwood, was carved in the mid-fourteenth century for a church just outside Siena. The carving is some of the finest of the period I've ever seen. I think the face of the archangel holding the lectern is particularly moving."

Archer and Arabella Collingwood walked slowly around the wooden pulpit with its spiral stair. They were in an antique shop on New Bond Street in London, although "shop" was a misleading description of the premises of one of the most famous dealers in the world, Lord Redfern. Redfern himself was showing Archer around the big showroom filled with the plunder of the ages. The fabulous Californian, as Lord Redfern thought of Archer, never failed to spend at least $100,000 during his annual visits, so Archer got the red-carpet treatment. So far he had bought a $20,000 medieval altar screen and a $50,000 seventeenth-century chest, and was now eyeing the $15,000 pulpit hungrily. All this at a time when Cliff Parker's annual salary on the LAPD was $1800.

"It's beautiful," murmured Archer, who was now fifty-four. Since the showroom was chilly, he had kept on his overcoat with its mink collar as Arabella had kept on her sables. Like her late mother, Loretta, Arabella had put on weight with the years, but Archer had retained his youthful figure, though his blond hair was graying at the temples. "I'll take it," he said abruptly.

"A wise choice, Mr. Collingwood," purred Lord Redfern, who never failed to be amazed by the fabulous Californian's lack of interest in haggling.

But then, when you had an annual income of $3 million, why haggle?

"It's very curious," said Arabella, examining the canvas through her lorgnette. "Very. But the artist has talent. Who is he?"

She and Archer had gone from Lord Redfern's to a picture gallery in Pimlico where an astute young man named Edward Lacey dealt in "adventurous" art of the "modern" school.

"He's a young Spaniard from Barcelona," said Lacey. "He's now working in Paris. His name is Picasso."

Arabella's trained eyes devoured the canvas called "Harlequin en Rose avec Femme Assise."

"Most interesting," she said as her husband read for the second time the cablegram he had received that morning. Archer's passion was antiques, his wife's art. Antiques bored Arabella as much as Arabella's paintings bored Archer. But the cablegram was anything but boring:

MR. ARCHER COLLINGWOOD   HOTEL SAVOY   THE STRAND LON-DON   REPORTER KLEIN MURDERED   STOP   REQUEST PERMIS-SION TO PUBLISH WHOLE STORY   STOP   WILL SCOOP OTHER PAPERS AND ADD 30,000 TO OUR CIRCULATION   STOP   WHAT ABOUT J   STOP   CURTIS

"How much?" asked Arabella, still examining the Picasso through her lorgnette.

"One thousand pounds," said Lacey.

"That's a fortune." Lacey remained silent. He knew she was hooked. "But I'll take it."

"Why in the world did you buy that hideous painting?" asked Archer twenty minutes later as he and Arabella drove in their Daimler back to their hotel.

"Why in the world did you buy that hideous pulpit?" countered his wife. "I hope you're not planning to put a private chapel in the new house?"

"It's a beautiful piece of wood carving. That painting could be done by a child."

"Perhaps that's the point of it. Really, darling, what happened to our truce? You buy what you like, and I buy what I like. And what was in that cable you got this morning?"

"Oh, just business." He smiled and put his hand on hers. "Say, you know, the weather's really rotten here and I read that it's raining and chilly in Rome. I'm having second thoughts about going to Italy."

Arabella sighed. "In other words, you want to go home."

When they got to the hotel, Archer sent the following cablegram:

MR. CURTIS COLLINGWOOD % LOS ANGELES *CLARION* LOS ANGELES CALIFORNIA   PERMISSION TO PUBLISH DENIED TILL I GET HOME   STOP   SAILING TOMORROW ON *KRONPRINZESSEN CECILIE*   STOP   FATHER

The man raised the riding crop, then brought it down hard on the Mexican girl's bare buttocks. Leaning over a sawhorse in a tack room off a stable, she writhed in agony. The crop had hit hard enough to raise an ugly welt on her firm brown skin. Her small breasts with their pointed brown nipples jiggled as she tried to shake off the pain.

"Ready?" whispered the man, who was sweating with excitement. His shirt was open, revealing a chest matted with black hair. He raised the crop and brought it down again, hard.

The girl started sobbing.

He hit her again, then again, then again. By the time he had given her twelve strokes, she was bleeding and starting to scream.

"Sssh! Don't make noise, you bitch, or I won't pay you," he whispered in Spanish.

"I don't want any more! It hurts!"

"All right, all right, I'm putting it away. Now, get off the sawhorse and crawl to me."

"But the floor's dirty, *señor*."

"I'm paying you enough to buy the best soap in Tijuana. Crawl."

The girl painfully straightened from the sawhorse, then got down on her hands and knees on the floor. As the young man watched, she crawled toward him. He was good-looking in a cruel sort of way, and his eyes were slightly slanted, hinting at a trace of Oriental blood. His thick hair was jet black and the skin was almost swarthy.

"Kiss my feet," he whispered, looking down at her.

She obeyed, kissing his bare feet.

"Now take down my pants."

She straightened and opened the fly of his Levi's snap by snap. The pants slid down. Then she pulled down his underwear.

"Now do what you do best, you whore," whispered Don Jaime Vicente Juan Ramón López, the eldest child of Star and Juanito and heir to the Calafía Ranch.

Twenty minutes later, he emerged from the stable, buttoning his shirt. His ranch manager was standing by the door, smoking a Sweet Caporal.

"Raul, pay her fifty bucks and send her home," said Jimmie Lopez. When his father had died in a train accident five years before, Jimmie had dropped the formally Spanish "y Collingwood" from his now-unaccented surname because it sounded ridiculous, and Anglicized "Jaime" to "Jimmie." Juanito had insisted his son be called Jaime because he had been a fanatic about retaining his Spanish heritage and insisted his four children be raised bilingual. Jimmie Lopez respected his Spanish heritage, but he was a quarter Anglo, it was the twentieth century, and he was a graduate of Harvard. Enough was enough.

It was a gray, chilly day and the Pacific was slate-colored, with occasional whitecaps. The cattle had long since been sold off as impossibly uneconomical and the ranch had been turned over to orange and lemon growing, but Jimmie retained a half-dozen wranglers to handle the horses and do odd jobs, and he still called them "vaqueros." Two of them were repairing a fence as he passed on his way to the ranch house. They tipped their hats and said "*Buenas tardes, señor.*" Jimmie might have anglicized his name, but he was still very much *el patrón*.

Juanito and Star had modernized the old ranch house with plumbing and electricity in the 1880's, but an earthquake in 1901 had broken the primitive wiring and caused a fire. The old house burned to the ground, killing two servants. After this tragedy Jimmie's parents had had one of their most spectacular fights. Juanito wanted to rebuild in the Spanish style, and Star—by now thoroughly fed up with everything even remotely Spanish, including her husband—wanted to build something modern. Because she controlled the purse strings, she won, and the new Calafía ranch house was a great shingled structure with wide covered porches, a round tower on one corner, and curved windows overlooking the ocean. Juanito had hated it so much that on the day his wife moved in, he moved out and took the Union Pacific from L.A. to New York to see the latest Broadway shows and sulk. Twenty miles outside St. Louis his train plowed into a freight, killing thirty-three people, including Don Juan. But his personality had been so forceful, and his hatred of his beautiful wife so vicious, that the servants whispered that his ghost haunted the house he had loathed.

Jimmie climbed the wooden steps to the big porch with its white swings and wicker furniture and pots of flowers. He was met at the door by one of his three sisters, Alicia.

"Mother's calling for you," she said as Jimmie came in the house. "She's run out again."

"That's hardly news. Let her wait awhile. I have to bathe."

He walked across the tile floor of the dark entrance hall and climbed the wooden stairs. A half-hour later, after bathing and putting on a white linen suit, he returned downstairs and went to the kitchen. Chinina, Raul's wife, was stirring a pot on the eight-burner coal stove.

"*Buenas tardes, señor,*" she said as he walked to the crank phone. She knew Señor Jimmie had spent an hour in the tack room with the *puta* doing unspeakable things. Her round face showed her severe disapproval, but Señor Jimmie didn't notice, and if he had, wouldn't have cared. He gave a number to the operator, then waited for the call to be put through. "Hello? Is Reverend Wonder there? . . . Yes, I'll hold." After a few moments he said, "Wanda? It's Jimmie. I'm leaving for Los Angeles in about ten minutes. See you at the prayer meeting.

Good-bye." Then he hung up and went into the butler's pantry with its stainless-steel counters and pulled a key ring from his pocket. Choosing a key, he unlocked a door in the wall and opened it, revealing a cupboard filled with gin bottles. He took a bottle, relocked the cupboard, then went back through the dining room to the entrance hall.

Alicia was at the foot of the stairs. When she spotted the gin, she frowned. "I thought you were going to wait awhile," she said nervously. "She'll be through that by lunch tomorrow."

"No, she won't. I'm going up to San Francisco for a few days. I'm going to tell her this will have to last her till I get back."

"Jimmie, she'll never make it. She'll go crazy again!"

He started up the stairs. "Maybe dearest Mommy already is crazy," he said. "And we're too afraid to admit it."

On April 3, 1906, the following column appeared in the San Francisco *Times-Dispatch*, which had merged with the San Francisco *Bulletin* when Arabella Collingwood inherited the latter on the death of her father.

THE TALK OF THE TOWN
Society News by Sydney Tolliver

Tomorrow, one of San Francisco's most prominent society matrons, Mrs. Sebastian Brett, will entertain a group of devotees of the arts at a luncheon at the exclusive Burlingame Country Club on the Peninsula. Mrs. Brett, who devotes much of her time to the arts in our fair city, is herself an accomplished sculptress and maintains a studio on her estate outside Burlingame, where her current project is a heroic Monument to the Pioneer Women, commissioned by the Nebraska Historical Society.

It was four in the afternoon when Alma Brett unlocked the door to her studio and let herself in. It was rainy and miserable outside, and she was glad to be through with the interminable, boring lunch she had hostessed at the country club. The two-story studio she had designed two years before was her private hideaway in a distant corner of her eighty-acre estate on a knoll overlooking San Francisco Bay, far removed from the mansion she inhabited with her husband, Sebastian, her two children, and twelve servants. At twenty-six, Alma was a stunning blond, one of San Francisco's best-known beauties.

She shook out her umbrella and stuck it in the porcelain stand. Removing the pins from her big hat, she walked down the short hall into the main room, a two-story space illuminated by a north-facing window that ran up one wall and followed the roof line almost to the peak. Dominating the room was a twelve-foot marble statue of a woman in a poke bonnet. Her head held high, she clutched a baby in her arms as she walked west across the Great Plains to California, a marble wind whipping her marble skirts against her marble thighs. It was the Monument to the Pioneer Women. Alma was a professional sculptress, and a good one.

She just wasn't very inspired.

She put her hat on a stand and shed her raincoat. The studio was utilitarian and comfortable, with plain wooden furniture and a big iron stove. Palms and flowers were everywhere.

After turning on several lamps, Alma walked slowly around her pioneer woman, examining the nearly completed statue. Once or twice she ran her finger over the marble, testing the finish. She had made a full circuit when she felt a hand on her side.

"Oh!"

"Alma." She felt two arms encircle her waist and the rough cheek of a man on her own smooth cheek. She smelled the after-shave lotion she adored.

"Jimmie! You scared me to death, damn you." She turned around to confront Jimmie López. Then she smiled. "But what a delicious surprise," she whispered.

He started kissing her as her fingernails slowly dug into his back.

He was stark naked.

"And how's the cutest baby in the whole wide world?" Curtis Collingwood asked, holding up his two-year-old son, Joel, and bouncing him as Joel tugged his father's thick black hair.

"Dada," the chubby towhead laughed.

"Has he been stinking up the nursery again, Mary?" he asked the nanny, who was standing nearby.

"No, he's over his gas, thank the Lord."

"Oh-oh, I think he's wet."

"Sweet Joseph and Mary, and I just changed him an hour ago. Here, I'll take the little darlin', Mr. Collingwood. You go down to the missus."

"Thanks, Mary. Good night, you rascal."

The adoring father kissed his son, then handed him to Mary and left the nursery. Curtis was in black tie and dinner jacket and more than ready for the cocktail hour. He was fully aware that the murder of Carl Klein might expose the Collingwood family to its worst scandal since Star's Nob Hill abduction almost thirty years before.

Curtis and his San Francisco-based brother, Chester, the heirs to the immense Collingwood fortune, definitely did not want a scandal.

"It's that damned cousin of mine, Jimmie López," he said to his wife a few minutes later as he poured a gin and French in their library. "Creepy Jimmie. I've hated him since we were kids."

"Darling, slow down," said Betty Collingwood, an attractive blond in a black dress. "What has Jimmie done now? And don't gulp down your drink."

"Cousin Jimmie would drive Carrie Nation to drink, just as his father drove Aunt Star to it."

"Because of Aunt Star's torrid romance with the villainous Chinese?"

"Exactly. Jimmie hates us Collingwoods because that stammering father of his poisoned his mind when he was young. Somewhere in Jimmie's murky brain is the idea that he's out to get us some way or other because we are the blond gringos who destroyed his Spanish heritage—despite the fact that Jimmie went to Harvard and Anglicized his name. Anyway, you know that one of our reporters was murdered. Well, I'm convinced the reason he was murdered is that he had linked Cousin Jimmie with one of the smelliest municipal scandals in the history of California, the Owens Valley project."

"Wait a minute," Betty said, fitting a cigarette into a black lacquer holder. "We all know Cousin Jimmie is—to put it pleasantly—a bad apple, but surely he's not capable of murder. After all, he did go to Harvard."

Her husband lighted her cigarette. "Whether Jimmie himself fired the bullet through Carl Klein's head, I don't know. But I'm almost positive he's involved with it."

"Do the police know this?"

"No, and I don't want them to know yet because this is the biggest scandal ever, a newspaper publisher's dream. The *Clarion* has done a lot of investigative reporting over the past six months, digging up the dirt on this thing, and some of the most powerful men in L.A. are involved in it, including the publisher of the *Express*."

"General J. J. Channing?"

"Yes. Needless to say, the *Express* is keeping mum, and when we publish, we'll scoop them *and* the police."

"Then why don't you publish?"

"Because of Father. I got a cable from him in London. We can't do anything till he gets back. Remember, he feels very protective of Aunt Star, and Cousin Jimmie's her son."

"Whom she hates. You have some prize relatives, darling. Doesn't Jimmie hang around that crazy church—what's it called?"

"The Church of Divine Meditation, led by that wacky evangelist, Reverend Wanda Wonder."

"That couldn't be her real name."

"No, her real name's Irma Dimbaugh, but she packs them in her church. Why Jimmie hangs around her, I'm not quite sure, except there's a lot of talk that Wanda is General Channing's mistress."

"It gets murkier and murkier."

"Jimmie's motivation isn't murky. It's plain old human greed."

36

THE hatchet had sliced through the paneling of the cupboard door and destroyed the lock.

"I couldn't stop her," Alicia Lopez said. "I was afraid she'd attack anyone who came near her."

Jimmie was counting the gin bottles. "She took three."

"She's been drunk since you left for San Francisco. Jimmie, what are we going to do?"

"It's time dearest Mommy was given a lesson," Jimmie pronounced. He paced through the dining room to the entrance hall and started up the stairs.

Following him, his sister said anxiously, "You won't hurt her?"

"She's hurt me. She's hurt all of us."

"But, Jimmie, Mother was terribly hurt! She loved Crane and he loved her, and Father could never forgive her. Be a little tolerant. She's led a terrible life."

"So have I," he said, climbing the stairs. "And I'm fed up with my life being ruined by an old drunk."

At the top of the stairs he headed down the hall to the corner tower room. Turning the brass knob, he opened the door slowly.

"I heard your auto," a raspy voice said. "I knew you were back. Welcome home, dearest Jimmie. Welcome home, *son*."

The last word dripped venom. Jimmie came into the room and closed the door behind him. The tower room was surrounded on three sides by large windows overlooking the Pacific. The furniture was all reproduction Louis XVI, painted white, the newest decorating rage spawned by Elsie de Wolfe. Star was sitting up in bed, propped against four huge pillows. Her white hair, which hadn't been brushed in days, lay against the dirty pillowcases, haloing her head like seaweed. Her face, once so radiantly beautiful, was now hideously wrinkled. She held a half-empty glass of gin in her claw. On the bed table were a half-empty bottle and an ashtray filled with butts. Two empty bottles were on the floor beside her bed.

"This room smells like a saloon," Jimmie remarked.

330

"This room is a saloon," his mother said, cackling.

"Mommy was very naughty while I was away. Mommy took a hatchet and broke into the gin cupboard."

" 'Lizzie Borden took an ax,' " she warbled, " 'and gave her mother forty whacks.' Jimmie would like to give his mother forty whacks, wouldn't he?" Again she cackled, but this time the laugh ended in a wheezing cough. As Jimmie advanced toward the bed, she grinned at him, revealing teeth brown with nicotine and rotting gums. Then the grin vanished. "You scorpion," she rasped. "How did I give birth to a scorpion? What horrible thing did I do to deserve you?"

"Maybe it's because you're a whore," her son said softly. "Father always said you were. He always said that if it hadn't been for Grandmother and all her stinking Jewish money, he wouldn't have touched you with a ten-foot pole."

"Ah, but he did touch me. Over and over again, making babies, babies, and more babies. That's all I've accomplished in my life, making babies. And my sweetest baby, my first and loveliest, is *you*, dear Jimmie. Jimmie the scorpion, who I see has started making disgusting anti-Semitic remarks. That's something new, isn't it? Where'd you catch that from? Your buddy, the so-called Reverend Wanda Wonder? Alicia tells me she's anti-Semitic."

"Alicia doesn't know anything about Wanda."

"Perhaps. Anyway, when are *you* going to start making babies, son? Or are you too busy beating those Mexican whores out in the stable? What a sick, twisted mind you must have. How you must hate women!"

"If I hate women, it's because I have a drunken whore for a mother!" he roared, grabbing the glass from her hand and throwing it across the room. It smashed against the mantel. *"Puta! Puta!"* he screeched as he climbed on the bed. *"Puta! Puta!"* He took her scrawny neck between his hands. As she gurgled, he started choking her. "My fuh-fuh-father hated you!" he yelled. "And I huh-huh-hate you. I've tuh-tuh-taken all I can st-stand—"

"Jimmie!" his sister screamed at the door. "Oh, God—Chinina! Raul! He's killing her! Jimmie, stop!"

She ran across the room, grabbed his arm, and tried to pull him off their mother. "Stop it, stop it!"

"Luh-luh-let go, Alicia! Luh-luh-let go!"

"He's stammering like Daddy! Oh, God, Daddy's come back!"

Raul ran into the room and rushed to the bed. Grabbing Jimmie's other arm, he and Alicia managed to pull him off. He stumbled to the floor, panting like an animal, animal rage in his eyes.

"I'll get you, old woman!" Jimmie yelled. "I'll get Doc Brewster to put you in the goddamn asylum! I'll commit you, you crazy buh-buh-bitch!"

Star was wheezing, rubbing her neck, which was red where his hands had choked her. Now she reached over to the bed table and picked up a piece of paper. "No, you won't," she rasped. "You won't do anything because my brother won't let you. Read this cable, scorpion. Read it."

She threw it at him, and it drifted to the floor. He picked it up. Still panting, he read:

"Mrs. Star Lopez. Calafía Ranch. Orange County, California. Darling am arriving L.A. private car tomorrow morning eight a.m. Stop Tell Jimmie to be there Stop This is an order Stop I love you Stop Archer."

Jimmie slowly crumpled the telegram into a ball as his mother lit a cigarette. She grinned at him.

"You'll be there, won't you?" she said, exhaling. "Jimmie doesn't dare disobey Uncle Archer, because Uncle Archer wields all the power. Now, get me a new glass. Mommy needs a drink bad."

For five decades after 1890, no status symbol in the world—with the possible exception of the private yacht—glittered more refulgently than the private railroad car. When all else had been achieved—château on Fifth Avenue or Nob Hill, gold dinner service, armies of servants, old masters on the walls—one crowning cachet of elegance remained: a sleek, private car fitted to one's own specifications by Pullman and attached to the rear of one of the great "name" trains. As one rolled across America, through small farm towns and great cities, people gawked at these wheeled monuments of money and wondered at the glaring inequalities of life in the land where men were created equal. For throwing your money in the teeth of the poor and inciting socialist riots, there was no handier method than forking over $100,000 or more for a private "varnish," as they were called.

Archer Collingwood was no more or less showy than his fellow millionaires, and he had an understandable loathing of socialism, but he considered a private car the only way to travel, and his *Arabella* was one of the prime examples of the breed. Dark green varnished steel on the outside, on the inside it was filled with rich paneling, crystal sconces and ceiling lights, red velvet draperies, and upholstered swivel chairs and sofas. The *Arabella* had its own commodious kitchen, two bedrooms and baths, a staff quarter consisting of two tiny bedrooms and connecting bath, a small dining room, and a large parlor. There was a wine cellar well-stocked with vintage labels for the guests of the teetotaling Archer and Arabella. The call buttons for the three-man staff were mother-of-pearl, and the faucets in the principal bathrooms were—what else?—solid gold.

In six days Archer and Arabella had steamed across the Atlantic. After leaving Arabella in New York to shop, Archer had crossed the country on the Union Pacific tracks in another six days—a remarkable improvement, he reflected, from fifty years before, when it had taken his mother six months to make the same journey from Europe to California. Now, as his white-jacketed steward, Claud, poured him a fresh cup of coffee, he looked through the double-pane window at the tracks of the Los Angeles station, across which his nephew, Jimmie Lopez, was making his way.

"Claud," said Archer, "go into the station and buy the morning papers—except that rag the *Express*. They'll be shunting us to track eight to put us on the *San Francisco Limited*, leaving at nine, so meet me there."

"Yes, sir, Mr. Collingwood."

Claud returned the coffee to the kitchen, then left the car from the rear while Jimmie climbed aboard at the other end.

"Uncle Archer," Jimmie cried, flashing a hearty smile as he entered the car. "Welcome to Los Angeles."

He looked dapper in a trim double-breasted gray suit with a jaunty panama hat. Approaching his uncle, who was sitting in an armchair, he extended his hand. His uncle didn't extend his.

"Sit down, Jimmie. This isn't going to be pleasant."

"So unpleasant you won't shake hands?"

His uncle peered up at him. "I'm not sure I want to shake hands with a murderer."

Startled, Jimmie laughed nervously. "Well, that's a provocative remark. Whom have I murdered? I'd like to know, just for the record."

He sat down in the chair opposite his uncle, placing his hat on the table beside him.

"One of my reporters, Carl Klein."

"How could I murder someone I've never heard of?"

Archer leaned forward. "I take it you've heard of the Owens Valley project?"

"Of course. It's a great idea that'll save the future of Los Angeles. I've never understood why your papers have been against it."

"Because Bill Mulholland and the Los Angeles City Council have stolen a whole damned lake and river from a bunch of unsuspecting farmers up north, that's why. Because Mulholland—who I'll grant you is, in his way, a brilliant water commissioner—sent his men up and started buying land and water rights before the farmers in the Owens Valley knew what hit them. And now they're going to build this gigantic aqueduct to bring all that water two hundred and fifty miles down to Los Angeles, which is going to cost the taxpayers millions, turn the Owens Valley into a desert, and fill the pockets of a number of insiders with fortunes. It's one of the worst swindles ever dreamed up by a bunch of greedy bureaucrats and hoggish businessmen—"

"Wait a minute!" interrupted his nephew. "You know L.A. has been having its worst drought in years. The artesian wells are running dry, and if the city can't get new sources of water, it'll stop growing. What alternative is there to the Owens Valley project?"

"Did it ever occur to you that Los Angeles is basically a desert and maybe there shouldn't be a city here?"

"That's ridiculous. There is a city here, and it's growing like crazy and it needs water. The same thing's happening in San Francisco with the Hetch Hetchy reservoir."

"Yes, but we're doing it legally."

"Dammit, Uncle Archer, I didn't get up at dawn to come here and argue water systems with you. What the hell does all this have to do with my supposedly murdering one of your reporters?"

His uncle sat back and pulled a notebook from his pocket. Flipping it open, he checked some figures.

"Two years ago, you applied to Chester at the bank for a loan of two hundred thousand dollars, putting up some of your mother's shares in the Collingwood Corporation as collateral. You told Chester you wanted the money to invest in a land-development company called the Valley Fund, which was buying up land in the San Fernando Valley cheap."

"So? How does this make me a murderer? Pardon me, Uncle Archer, but I'm not going to take much more of this without a lawyer present."

"You're not going to drag lawyers into this and ruin our family's name," his uncle said hotly. "I'm giving you fair warning, Jimmie: if you sell your Valley Fund stock and get out of the country—"

"Sell it? To hell with that. It's going to make me a fortune."

"It won't if I publish the secret deal your partners have made—the deal that Carl Klein found out about and that cost him his life."

"What deal? What the hell are you talking about?" He jumped up. "This is all crazy. I don't know any of your goddamned reporters, I sure as hell didn't murder one of them, and I'm not leaving the country. And I'll tell you something else." He fumbled in his pocket. "Your papers write all these crappy editorials about motherhood and family and the home and the flag, while your headlines are nothing but murders, rapes, and scandal because you know that's what sells papers.

Let me read you something from one of your own family and then tell me about the sanctity of your home!" He had pulled out a piece of pink stationery. Now he read: " 'My dearest, darling Jimmie: here is the key to the studio. Wear it over your heart, my love. Please, darling, come to San Francisco as often as possible. I hunger for your kisses and live for your love. Your devoted slave' "—he looked up into his uncle's eyes—" 'Alma.' Alma Collingwood Brett, your daughter. Recognize the stationery?" He held the letter in front of Archer, whose face had turned red. "Now, dearest uncle, if you try to implicate me in this lurid scandal of yours—whatever the hell it is—I'll take this letter to J. J. Channing. He'd be more than delighted to publish it in the L.A. *Express*. I can see the headline: 'CHAMPION OF FAMILY VALUES FINDS LOVE NEST IN HIS OWN BACKYARD!' That lacks zip, maybe, but you get the general idea."

Archer Collingwood, the Fabulous Californian, owner of fourteen newspapers across America, chairman of the board of the Collingwood Corporation, which controlled the Pacific Bank and Trust, the de Meyer and Kinsolving chain of six department stores, the Golden State Insurance Company, and the Kinsolving Shipping Line, stared at his nephew.

"Alma?" he whispered. "My sweet Alma is your mistress?"

"Your 'sweet Alma' is one hot pistol, Uncle Archer, and don't think I'm the first. And dear Cousin Chester, who gave me the bank loans? Do you know about his little love nest on Russian Hill?"

"Yes, I know, you bastard. But Alma!"

"Known among the young sports of San Francisco society as 'the Bitch of Burlingame.' There's a lot of hot blood in our family, Uncle Archer. I'm beginning to think your Anglo blood is as hot as my Spanish blood." He folded Alma's note and put it back in his jacket. "Anyway, this has all been very enlightening, I'm sure. But since you don't have one shred of proof to link me up with that murder—"

"Oh yes, we do."

Jimmie froze. The quiet menace in his uncle's voice sent a wave of fear through him.

"I'll admit when the police first told Curtis about the murder, he and Digby suspected you might be involved. Then they were told there was a note found on the body. Digby and Curtis went to the morgue to see it." He checked his notebook. "The note was dated March 28 and reads: 'Mr. Klein: If you want to know more about the Valley Fund, I'm ready to talk. Meet me at the Santa Monica Amusement Pier at midnight.' And it was signed with the initial 'J.' "

Jimmie stuck his hands in his pockets and tried to shrug nonchalantly. "So what? There are ten million 'J's' in the world."

"Curtis recognized the handwriting as yours. Which we haven't told the police—yet. We're trying to protect you, Jimmie, though I'm beginning to wonder why."

"You still have no proof!"

"Do you have an alibi for the night of the twenty-eighth?"

"Yes. I was at a prayer meeting at the Church of Divine Meditation on Oregon Avenue. Reverend Wanda Wonder will testify I was with her the entire evening."

"The anti-Semitic crackpot?"

"She happens to talk to Jesus! She was talking to Jesus the night of the twenty-eighth! Jesus will back my alibi!"

"Have you gone crazy?"

"Maybe it's you who are crazy, trying to pin this crappy murder on your own nephew. Well, you've come up with a big zero. What's your next move, Uncle Archer?"

Archer glared at him a moment. Then he said, "All right, Jimmie. Maybe we've been wrong. Maybe you weren't involved with the actual murder. But you're still involved with the Valley Fund, and you're still scum."

"Alma thinks otherwise. Alma would marry me if I asked her. This 'scum' you're talking to may become your son-in-law."

"If that ghastly event ever occurs, then Alma's judgment is infinitely worse than I imagined, and it will be much to my sorrow to learn of it. You ask me where I'm going next? I'm going to San Francisco to talk to my mother. I'm going to convince her to write you out of her will, which is going to cost you a lot of money, Jimmie."

"She won't do it," he hissed. "Granny loves me."

"Oh, yes, she will, when I get through with you. Now, get the hell out of my railroad car so I can fumigate it."

"I'll turn Alma against you."

"Goddammit, Jimmie, you're blowing smoke with your threats. Do your damnedest. If Alma's so mixed up as to fall for you, then she deserves what she gets. Now, go! I never want to see you again. Get out."

Trembling with rage, Jimmie snatched his panama hat off the table and walked to the end of the car. Then he turned. "If Granny writes me out of her will," he said, "I'll make Mother pay for it the rest of her miserable drunken life."

Leaving the car, he jumped down onto the railroad tracks. For all the brave show he had put up, he was panic-stricken. The note! he thought as he crossed the tracks to the platform. How could I have been so stupid as to leave the note on the goddamned body? He had never seen his uncle so angry. To have Uncle Archer turn against him was not good. Granny's money, all that wonderful Jewish money. She couldn't disinherit him . . .

He stopped as he saw a puffing steam engine back up to his uncle's private car and start to transfer it to the *San Francisco Limited*. San Francisco, maybe that's where *I* should go, Jimmie thought. Yes, talk to Granny, make peace. Maybe even see Alma and let *her* work on her father.

He ran into the station to buy a first-class ticket for San Francisco.

37

THE following column ran in the San Francisco *Times-Dispatch* on April 17, 1906:

THE TALK OF THE TOWN
Social Notes by Sydney Tolliver

Tonight, Mr. and Mrs. David Levin will entertain a gathering of notables at their Nob Hill mansion. Present at the dinner will be His Honor, Mayor Eugene Schmitz, to whom Mrs. Levin is to make a presentation for the benefit of the city. Mrs. Levin, known to all San Franciscans as Emma, is of course our fair city's leading benefactress. Among her many magnificent gifts in the past are the Archer Collingwood Memorial Hospital, her $10,000,000 endowment gift to the University of California, her $5,000,000 gift to our opera house, her chairmanship of the Symphony League, as well as other, anonymous gifts too numerous to mention. There is speculation that tonight's announcement will be the gift to the city of a museum of fine arts. If any one San Franciscan can be said to represent everything that is finest in our town, surely it is our own beloved Emma.

Alma Collingwood Brett was choosing the jewelry she would wear to her grandmother's dinner when the telephone in her Burlingame bedroom rang.

"Can you get it, sweetie pie?" her husband called from the bathroom. "I'm still shaving."

Alma took two of the ten diamond bracelets from the Florentine leather jewel box, then crossed the big bedroom to pick up the ivory-and-gold French phone. "Yes?"

"Alma, it's Jimmie."

She tensed, glancing behind her at the distant bathroom, where Sebastian was standing at his washbasin.

"No, I don't want a subscription to the *Saturday Evening Post*,"

338

she said, using their prearranged code, which meant "the husband's here."

"I have to see you. I just got in to San Francisco."

"We're coming into town to Granny's dinner," she whispered. "We'll be staying overnight at the Grand."

"I'll be there too. Ask at the desk for my room number."

"I wish you'd stop pestering me," she said aloud. "I hate the *Saturday Evening Post*."

She slammed down the phone.

"Who was that, sweetie pie?" called Sebastian, a strapping six-footer who had played tackle at Yale and was heir to a silver fortune.

"Oh, that idiot trying to sell me a subscription to the *Saturday Evening Post*."

"Again? God, he doesn't give up, does he? He must be the most persistent magazine salesman in America."

Alma raised her eyebrows slightly, amused by her husband's stupidity. "Maybe I should buy a subscription just to shut him up."

Alma's maid, Lily, came into the room. "Have you chosen your jewels yet, Miss Alma?"

"Yes. Pack these two bracelets"—she tossed them to Lily—"and the sapphire necklace and earrings."

"Oh, the sapphires'll be divine with the silver dress."

"I have to look good for Granny. Tell Anthony to bring the car around in twenty minutes."

"Yes, ma'am."

Jimmie, Alma thought, her flesh tingling. I wonder what's wrong? He sounded scared.

She glanced at the bathroom again. Sebastian had finished shaving and was leaning over the basin, examining his face for nicks. The big ox, she thought. Maybe if he gets drunk tonight, as usual, I can sneak to Jimmie's room. Her heart beat faster as she thought of his fierce lovemaking. Her husband, by contrast, was a flopping fish. She was convinced he thought about the stock market when he made love to her. The only saving grace was that it was becoming less frequent with every month of their dreary marriage.

"I don't see why I'm not invited to your grandmother's dinner." Ellie Donovan pouted as she bit into a chocolate candy. She was sprawled on the sofa of her bedroom on Russian Hill. "You'd think I had some disease."

"You'd be bored anyway," replied her lover, Chester Collingwood, who was tying his white tie in front of her bureau mirror.

"Oh, stop lying, Chester. I know why I'm not invited. I'm the piece of fluff you keep on Russian Hill, the cheap actress. I can just hear your family talking about me. 'Oh, my de-ah, she's so horribleh cheap, she uses makeup.' Well, I've read about your family. Your grandmother was a goddamned whore at the Bonanza Café."

"We try to overlook that," said Chester, the youngest of Archer and Arabella's three children. He and Alma had inherited the fabulous good looks of their paternal grandparents.

"You're all a bunch of Nob Hill snobs looking down your noses at everybody else in this city. Sometimes I feel like telling you to go to hell. You'd miss me if you didn't have me to keep you happy in bed. All your la-di-da society virgins think sex is something for dogs to do."

"I think you're a bit mistaken there."

"Then why don't you marry me?"

Chester put on his tailcoat and brushed his shoulders. "That, my sweet Ellie, is a total non sequitur, but like almost everything about you, it was charming."

"Baloney."

He came to her and kissed her. "Now, if you'll look in that envelope on the mantel," he said, pointing to the brick fireplace, "you'll find a ticket to the John Barrymore play at the Tivoli. The curtain goes up in an hour, so you'd better get dressed."

A smile brightened her beautiful face. "John Barrymore! He's the dreamiest actor in America!"

"And you're the dreamiest actress. I'll be back at midnight to tell you all about my snooty grandmother's boring dinner. Then we can fuck till dawn."

Ellie giggled. "That sounds fun."

"My favorite sport."

"And you're pretty good at it, handsome. Thanks for the ticket. And I'm sorry I was mean. You know I really do love you."

Chester kissed her again, then hurried down the stairs of the house he rented for Ellie. It was a foggy night outside. The vice-president of the Pacific Bank and Trust and the Collingwood son destined someday to run the family businesses, as Curtis was being groomed to run the family newspapers, got into his snappy Welch touring car that had set him back the not inconsiderable sum of $5,500 and drove off through the fog toward Nob Hill.

The automobile, like the private railroad car, was a plaything of the rich, but people were already commenting that its exhaust fumes were much less offensive to the nose than horse manure. Manure, on the other hand, smelled for only a few feet, while the exhaust fumes of the automobile rose into the air to poison the atmosphere of the entire planet.

"But you have to give me a room," Jimmie Lopez was saying at the reception desk of the Grand Hotel.

"I'm terribly sorry, sir, but the hotel is full," the manager said. "Signor Caruso is singing Don José in *Carmen* tonight, and every opera lover in the West is in town."

"You're new here, aren't you?"

"Yes, sir."

"Then perhaps you don't know who I am. I'm Archer Collingwood's nephew, and I'll remind you that Archer Collingwood's father-in-law built this hotel. Now, get me a room, goddammit."

The manager hesitated. "We have a suite on the top floor I can make available, Suite 6-A."

"That's more like it. And I believe Mr. and Mrs. Sebastian Brett have a reservation here tonight?"

"Yes, sir, they are in the suite directly below yours."

Jimmie took a twenty-dollar bill from his wallet and placed it in the manager's palm. "You'll make sure Mrs. Brett knows where I am."

Two miles away, on the bottom of San Francisco Bay, dozens of hermit crabs were scuttling across the ocean floor. They shared it with millions of the *Crago franciscorum*, the bay's unique form of shrimp. An octopus hiding nearby in a deep rock crevice was one of the shiest of the bay's inhabitants, although it inflicted a lethal bite in a fight. Sailing overhead was a bat stingray with a wingspread of four feet and a stinging spine four inches long. It was searching for oysters, its favorite food.

Far below the bay floor, pressures were building along the San Andreas Fault, titanic pressures with the potential of twelve million tons of TNT that would explode the delicate marine ecology.

Something huge was about to move: the city of San Francisco.

38

THE great mansion on Nob Hill was ablaze with light, as on so many other festive occasions in the past thirty years. Emma's domestic staff of twenty were executing their duties with their accustomed efficiency. In the basement kitchens, below which lay a half-million-gallon fresh-water reservoir for the house alone, the French chef was putting the final touches on the gala that would, ironically, mark the wrenching passage of San Francisco into the twentieth century far more than the New Year's Eve six years before. The classic nineteenth-century menu for Emma's dinner, getting a last-minute once-over by the gray-haired Can Do, was, to say the least, elaborate:

Huitres
Chablis
·
Consommé Royale
Sherry Isabella
·
Saumon Glacé au Four à la Chambord
Sauterne
·
Boudin Blanc à la Richelieu
Château la Tour
·
Filet de Boeuf à la Providence
Champagne
·
Pâté de Foie Gras
Château d'Yquem
·
Timbale de Volaille Américaine au Sénateur
Clos Vougeot
·
Cotelettes d'Agneau Sauté au Pointes d'Asperges
Sorbet

•

Becassines au Cresson
Château Margaux

•

Salade à la Française
Les Desserts

The young chef, who had trained with Escoffier at the Paris Ritz, was considered San Francisco's finest and, like all the French flocking to the "Paris of the West," was called a "Kesskydee," a local rendition of the Frenchman's continual query, *"Qu'est-ce qu'il dit?"* or "What's he saying?" He was hovering over one of the eight burners of the huge coal stove, whisking his sauce for the *timbale* with a *fouet.*

Upstairs, in the third-floor picture gallery, Margaret Gilliam, Emma's social secretary, was making a last-minute check of the *placement* at the long oval table that had been set up for the occasion. Emma's famous silver-gilt state dinner service—made by Thomire in Paris in the 1820's and similar to the set bought by President James Madison for the White House—had been brought out. This was complemented by the white-and-gold Limoges service, made originally for Catherine the Great, and the vermeil plate, once belonging to King Louis Philippe of France. The six huge vermeil candelabra, each holding twelve candles, the four-foot-high epergne, and the *surtout de table* set an appropriately regal tone for the evening. Between the candelabra, great explosions of white tulips, Emma's favorite flower, mingled with stephanotis and masses of orange blossoms, burst from six-foot gilt vases. At each place setting an engraved menu for the evening reposed on a porcelain stand, surrounded by six crystal goblets hand-blown on the island of Murano for an eighteenth-century doge. Emma had given away millions in the past quarter-century, but she still entertained in the style of a Rothschild.

Since she had been one of the first San Franciscans to install electricity ten years after her marriage to David Levin, the forty-odd paintings on the gallery walls were illuminated by picture lights. And what pictures! The old masters were well represented: Watteau, Rubens, Rembrandt, de la Tour, Copley, Ingres, Fra Angelico, Fra Lippo Lippi, two Titians, and three Gainsboroughs. In the past ten years, Emma had begun buying some of the new French painters as well: Degas, Monet, two Manets, and two swirling van Goghs. The new paintings had attracted howls of derision when Emma first hung them, but now people were beginning to admire them. Conservative San Francisco was sticking a nervous toe into the murky waters of what people were beginning to call "modern art."

In front of the mansion, a Great Arrow town car turned into the porte cochere. Seated behind the chauffeur was Zita, looking quite spry for a woman in her eighties. Around her neck was the brilliant diamond necklace Felix de Meyer had given her in 1890, studded with the eight huge "pigeon's-blood" rubies from the Mogok Stone Track in Upper Burma. The necklace was one of the many treasures Felix had given his beloved over the years, and when he had died in 1894, he had left Zita ten million dollars. (The rest of his estate—his half of the de Meyer and Kinsolving stores—had gone to Emma.) On his deathbed, as Zita held his hand, he whispered, "I've always loved you." To Zita, who believed in love, this was more precious than the jewels or the money.

She climbed out of her car and walked to the wrought-iron-and-glass front door held by an aging Can Do.

"Good evening, Can Do." She smiled. "Is Taitai in her room?"

"Oh yes, Missee Zita, and she very upset."

"She is? What now?"

"She don't like color of her new dress you make for her."

Zita sighed. "I feel an argument coming on."

She crossed the marble foyer and started up the great stone stair, casting a glance at the huge portrait of Emma. How much time has flowed by since we all came to California, she thought. Mounting the stairs, she wondered, as she often did these days, to whom she should leave her fortune. She had not only the money Felix had left her but also the money she had made on her own from her dress business. To have so much, and no blood relative to leave it to. She reflected sadly on her child butchered a half-century before by a raving South American dictator. As she reached the landing, she marveled at how her life had intertwined with Felix's family. Maybe I should leave everything to one of them, she thought, heading for Emma's room. Perhaps Curtis' baby, Joel, the youngest of us all. That way I would be remembered well into this century.

Yes, perhaps Joel.

When she reached the bedroom, Emma was standing before a full-length mirror scowling at her new dress.

"Can Do tells me you don't like your dress," Zita said, coming into the room.

"It's violet," Emma said. "Violet is an old lady's color."

"Nonsense. Violet is very becoming to you."

"I still say it's an old lady's color. I may be seventy-four, but I don't feel old. This dress makes me look like I should be in a wheelchair."

"I've been designing your clothes for longer than either of us wants to remember, and have I ever gone wrong?"

"No, except tonight—of all nights! The dress is beautiful, but I just don't like this color."

"Here's David. Let him be the judge."

David had just entered, wearing white tie and tails. Despite the fact that he was four years older than Emma, he still looked surprisingly spry. His hair and beard had turned a beautiful snow-white.

"Emma's complaining about this dress," Zita said. "Do you like it?"

David came up to the two old ladies. "I think it's stunning," he said. "Darling, you've never looked better."

"Which is a lie, but at my age you take whatever flattery you can get. All right, violet isn't an old lady's color. I'll wear it."

"Archer's downstairs," David said. "He just got in from Los Angeles and wants to know if he can spend the night here, since Arabella's in New York."

"Of course. He can have his old room."

"He wants to see you. He seems upset about something."

"Tell him to come up."

"I'll tell him," Zita said, going to the door. "I'm going downstairs. You two lovebirds stay here."

" 'Lovebirds'?" Emma asked after she'd left. "At our age? Zita's definitely becoming gaga."

David put his arm around her and kissed her. "Oh, I don't know. You look so beautiful tonight, I almost feel sixty again. I might do something foolish."

She laughed as she put her hand on his cheek. "Doing something foolish at our age might land us both in the hospital. Now, I've given you the senator's wife tonight, so you're going to have to do most of the talking."

"Thanks a lot. The last time I got her, all she talked about was Alice Roosevelt's wardrobe."

"I know she's a bore, but most politicians' wives are, and you just have to put up with it."

"I'm very proud of what you're doing tonight, Emma. The museum's a magnificent gift. And all your paintings!"

A little-girl look of excitement came in her eyes. "Do you think they'll like it?"

"Like it? Of course they'll like it. They'd be fools if they didn't. It's the most wonderful thing you've ever done."

"Oh, no," she said softly. "The most wonderful thing I've ever done was marry you. I love you so very, very much, my darling. You've made me the happiest woman in America."

She kissed him, and they gazed at each other, holding hands. They looked very much like what Zita had called them: lovebirds.

There was a knock at the door and Archer came in. Emma saw at once that something was indeed the matter. Archer, usually so buoyant, so full of energy and drive, now seemed to sag. He came to his mother and kissed her, then shook hands with David.

"How was London?" Emma asked as she went to her wall safe, hidden behind a movable panel.

"Foggy and rainy. I had a terrible meeting with Jimmie this morning. Terrible." He sank onto the end of his mother's chintz chaise longue. "It's upset me so much that, well, for once in my life, I'm not sure what to do."

"Then you're convinced he did murder Carl Klein?" Emma asked, turning the dial. Her grandson, Curtis, had kept her informed of the case, as she was kept informed about everything in the huge business empire she still controlled, if not actually ran.

"No, I'm not sure he killed him. He says he has an alibi because he was with that crazy evangelist, Reverend Wanda Wonder."

"The anti-Semite."

"That's right."

"Curious company for one of my family," she remarked dryly as she opened the safe and pulled out two large leather boxes stamped "Felix de Meyer, Haute Joaillerie, San Francisco." She carried them to her dressing table.

"Yes, isn't it?" Archer said.

"And what about the Valley Fund?" continued his mother, opening the large case and lifting out the diamond necklace with the eight egg-size cabochon emeralds her late father had bought from an Indian maharajah. Her husband helped clasp the piece around her neck. "Do we have proof that Channing's going to use the Los Angeles aqueduct to bring water to the San Fernando Valley?"

"Carl Klein had the proof in his head, which is why they put the bullet through it."

"I don't understand," David said. "What about the San Fernando Valley?"

"General Channing and his partners, including Jimmie, have bought up hundreds of acres dirt cheap," Emma said, attaching her earrings. "It's desert now, but if they can bring in the water from the new aqueduct, they can develop the valley and make a fortune. Of course, the catch is that the Los Angeles taxpayers will be footing the bill for the water and not make a penny profit from it. It's a very sophisticated form of highway robbery, though I suppose you'd call it high water robbery." She turned to her son. "But if you don't think Jimmie killed Carl, what happened this morning that got you so upset?"

"It's Alma," Archer said. "Jimmie's her lover."

"My God, since when?"

"I don't know. It's devastated me. You know how I've doted on her. I was foolish enough even to think she was happy with Sebastian and the kids, but now . . . And Jimmie, of all people. That dirty, rotten . . ."

Emma came over and sat beside him on the chaise. Taking his hand, she noticed tears in his eyes. "Darling, are you sure?"

He nodded. "He showed me a note she'd written him. She sent him the key to her studio. God, I feel like such a total failure."

"Don't be ridiculous. You're anything but a failure. We're all terribly proud of what you've done with the newspapers. Even David admits you've done wonders, and it's no secret he's not one of your greatest fans."

"Oh, I've done wonders. I've turned them into a circus. Jimmie really put it to me this morning. He said I write editorials about motherhood and the flag and print headlines about murder and rape to sell papers. And he's right, damn him. I know he's right. If you could have seen the smug look on his ugly face when he showed me Alma's note—"

"Archer, you can call Jimmie a lot of things, but he's far from ugly."

"He's ugly to me. It's even occurred to me that he went after Alma just to have a weapon to use against me in case I started bringing heat on him and Channing about the Valley Fund. At any rate, he's here tonight, in San Francisco. I saw him in the train station. You didn't invite him to your dinner, did you?"

"No."

"Then he's come up to stop me."

"From what?"

"From talking you into writing him out of your will."

His mother looked jolted. The phone rang.

"I'll get it," David said, going to the bed table and picking up the intrahouse phone. "Yes?" He listened a moment, then hung up. "It's Can Do. The senator's arriving with Mayor Schmitz."

"Then we must go down." Emma stood up and smoothed her son's hair. "I'm so sorry about Alma," she said. "But maybe things will work out."

"How? That sort of thing never works out."

"She's your daughter. It's natural you'd think of her as a saint, but there aren't many saints in this world."

Archer stood up. "My father always said he failed the Indians, but at least he was a noble failure. I'm just a failure, period."

Emma turned on him, her amethyst eyes flashing their old fire. "Now, that's enough!" she said. "I'll have no more maudlin self-pity out of you, Archer. You've made mistakes—we've all made mistakes—

but you're far from a failure. There are no failures in this family: not you, or me, or . . ." She turned to David and held out her hand, remembering the night he had proposed to her. "Or especially my beloved husband. We all fail in some ways, but we succeed in others, and that's what life's all about. Now, let's go downstairs and greet the guests." She held out her other hand for her son, and they started toward the door. "But I can see that Jimmie has to be punished. Maybe you're right. Maybe I should disinherit him in favor of his sisters. They're sweet, particularly Alicia. I'll have to think about it. Meanwhile, this is an evening I've been looking forward to for a long time. Let's have a good time."

"I wish to thank all of you for coming here tonight," Emma said two and a half hours later after the final dishes of the elaborate dinner had been cleared. "And now you'll have to pay for Alain's cooking by listening to my speech, though I promise to keep it short. David was going to make the speech, but he has a slight cold—which is a lie. All of you know I always make the speeches."

Laughter went around the long oval table. Jewels flashed in the candlelight. The very cream of San Francisco was there in force, tycoons, power brokers, society leaders, as well as San Francisco's mayor and one of California's senators. Emma was standing at one end, her white hair piled on top of her head in the poodle-dog look that had become her trademark.

"I came to San Francisco fifty-six years ago," she continued. "I came around South America with my dear late father on a ship owned by my first husband, Scott Kinsolving. San Francisco wasn't much of a town then, and I remember that my first impression of the place was that it was ugly. Scott said, 'Give it a chance to grow,' and he was right: it certainly has grown. We're almost half a million people now, which is hard to believe. They say California is the state of the future, and I guess maybe they're right." She paused to take a sip of water. "At any rate, we didn't have anything but dreams in those days," she went on. "We dreamed of a great city with hospitals and fine schools and thriving businesses and opera, and we have all those things today. But the one thing we don't have is a fine museum." She smiled slyly. "I intend to remedy that lack."

A murmur of excitement ran around the table as all eyes focused on the magnificent paintings.

During the early hours of April 18, the city was still shrouded in fog and mist. The ten-story Golden State Insurance Company Building on "Insurance Alley"—Montgomery Street between California and

Sutter—was dark. Farther down Montgomery Street, the Pacific Bank and Trust Company Building had a few windows lighted, for the paperwork of the bank's many accounts and stock transactions, both on the San Francisco Exchange and the New York Exchange, required around-the-clock attention. Even farther down Montgomery Street, at Number 15, the Times-Dispatch Building was fully lit, putting out its Wednesday-morning edition, the headline of which screamed: "EMMA GIVES CITY HER PICTURES AND A MUSEUM!"

Elsewhere, the theaters were empty but the hotel bars were full as the party-loving San Franciscans celebrated the presence in their town of Caruso and the young John Barrymore. On Nob Hill the fabulously rich James Ben Ali Haggin was giving an after-theater supper that was almost as glittering as Emma's.

In June 1836, a great earthquake had shaken the San Francisco Bay area. Though it had caused much destruction, few lives had been lost, since the population was so tiny. Two years later, another quake hit the San Francisco Peninsula. A great fissure that had opened had reached southward to Santa Clara, and the shock had cracked walls in the Presidio and Mission Dolores. In 1857, 1865, and 1890, there had been shocks along the San Andreas Fault, and in 1868 an earthquake along the Hayward Fault on the eastern side of the bay.

The San Andreas Fault is an old fracture of the earth's crust, running from Cape Mendocino in northern California to the Colorado Desert, east of Los Angeles. In the San Francisco area it passes under the Pacific Ocean at the Golden Gate. As Mayor Eugene Schmitz was enjoying the sumptuous pleasures of Emma's table on Nob Hill, he was thinking more of the food and wine than the city's water supply. Though the location of the San Andreas Fault was well-known and its dangers well recorded, the thirty-inch water mains supplying the entire city of San Francisco in several places crossed over the fault. If the mains were broken, there would be no water to put out fires.

It was a recipe for disaster, and although no one knew it, the disaster was about to strike.

39

JIMMIE was awakened by a knock on the door. Getting out of bed, he put a bathrobe over his red silk pajamas, went into the living room of the suite, turned on the lights, and unbolted the door.

Clad in a pink peignoir, Alma stood outside in the wide hallway.

"Let me in," she whispered.

He stood aside and she hurried in. He closed and bolted the door, then took her in his arms and began kissing her.

"Sebastian passed out, finally," she whispered. "I came up the fire stairs absolutely terrified one of the house detectives would see me."

"What time is it?"

"A little past five."

"Sebastian will be out till noon. Good. Let's get in bed." He led her toward the bedroom.

"We'll have to think up another magazine," she said. "Even Sebastian's going to get suspicious if you keep calling about the *Saturday Evening Post*."

"How about *Hot Romance*?"

"Oh, I like that. Daddy absolutely frosted me at Granny's tonight. Do you think he has any idea about you and me?"

"How could he? We've been discreet."

"If you can call climbing up fire stairs discreet."

The bedroom was filling with soft predawn light as he removed her peignoir and dropped it on a chair. Then he pulled down the straps of her nightgown and began kissing her shoulders. She leaned her head back and closed her eyes as he began slowly fondling her breasts.

Outside, the rising sun was beginning to dissipate the fog, helped by a fresh wind that promised a lovely day. Dan Wilder, a redheaded cub reporter for the *Times-Dispatch*, emerged onto Montgomery Street and yawned. He had been at his desk all night working on a baseball article that was to run in Thursday's paper. The streets were mostly empty as he started walking toward his apartment. A Pierce-Arrow appeared and came roaring down Montgomery Street, zigzagging drunkenly. As it passed, Wilder saw it was filled with drunken men and women in formal dress. But drunkenness was nothing new in hard-drinking San Francisco.

It drank milk too, and just then Wilder spotted a horse-drawn milk wagon turning a corner.

The hands of the famous clock on the Ferry Building tower were at twelve past five. The minute hand was thirty-eight seconds into the thirteenth minute when it suddenly stopped.

"Oh, Jimmie, it feels so good . . . Oh, oh . . . Oh, God . . ."

Alma was, in Jimmie's phrase, a "noisy fuck." As he plowed into her, she writhed and moaned, her nails scratching his back and buttocks in a frenzy of sexual passion.

Suddenly the room started shaking and the air was filled with a strange howl that seemed almost like a roaring freight train. Jimmie stopped in mid-thrust, looking around. The chandelier above him was swaying crazily. The mirror over the bureau was swinging from side to side as if it were dancing.

"Don't stop!" Alma moaned. This was the wildest sex she had ever experienced.

The bed started sliding across the floor.

"Jesus . . ." Jimmie pulled out. "It's an earthquake . . ."

The whole building was swaying crazily. Outside their window, the heavy copper cornice on the roof shook loose and crashed down onto the sidewalk, killing the doorman and a horse.

Alma was screaming, and it wasn't from sex. She hung on to Jimmie as he tried to get off the bed. The noise became terrifyingly loud. Half the plaster ceiling, with its elaborate Victorian molding and rosettes, poured down, barely missing them and filling the room with plaster dust.

The hopping chandelier now fell on the bed, crashing on Alma's left arm and cutting her deeply as its Grecian-style bowl smashed. Above it, the cut electric wires angrily spat and sparked.

"We're going to die!" she was screaming, hanging on to Jimmie like a drowning person, smearing blood on his naked back. "We're going to die!"

Directly below them, Sebastian Brett snored drunkenly, oblivious of the fact that the Grand Hotel was breaking apart. Huge hunks of its brick facade were falling off. Suddenly the entire ceiling crashed down on him, crushing him instantly.

He never knew that his wife and her lover landed directly on top of him.

* * *

On Russian Hill, across town, another young couple, Chester Collingwood and Ellie Donovan, were making love when the quake hit. They held on to each other for fifteen seconds as their wood-frame house buckled and quaked.

Then the brick chimney caved in on top of them.

On Nob Hill, Titians, Rembrandts, and Manets swayed drunkenly in the picture gallery where, a few hours earlier, the cream of San Francisco had dined so elegantly. Now the stained-glass skylight running the length of the ceiling crashed down into a million shards as the ponderous limestone walls of the mansion began buckling.

On the second floor, Emma de Meyer Kinsolving Collingwood Levin sat up in bed. The great crystal chandelier she had imported from Prague was jiggling, its crystals tinkling and jingling weirdly over the earthquake's roar.

"David!" she screamed. Her husband sat up next to her and threw his arms around her.

The ceiling and chandelier thundered down on top of them, followed by parts of the roof as the entire mansion collapsed.

Dan Wilder was hanging on to a lamppost on Montgomery Street as the pavement buckled and dipped like a stone dragon. He watched a church steeple topple, followed by the church itself, collapsing like a crunched eggshell.

And then, thirty seconds after it started, it stopped.

"Jesus," he muttered. He let go of the lamppost. He took a few tentative steps, unsure whether the sidewalk was still solid, unsure whether the planet he had lived on for twenty-three years was still playing by the same ground rules. Then, almost maniacally, he started laughing. "Hey," he yelled. "I'm alive! I'm alive!"

He skipped a little jig of glee.

Ten seconds had elapsed. Now came the second shock, more violent than the first.

Dan Wilder's jig was interrupted as the entire front of the building he was standing before fell forward, crushing the life out of him.

By the waterfront, huge fissures opened, yawning ominously. Three-foot "waves" of pavement undulated through the streets. Power lines snapped, water mains burst, gas lines broke.

The second shock lasted twenty-five murderous seconds. And then the great earthquake, except for minor aftershocks, was over. The San Andreas Fault had moved northward. It had caused violent shifting in places within a fifty-mile radius, though the great city had taken the worst damage. Much of the waterfront was landfill. Chinatown was destroyed, and buildings in the poorer sections, where shoddy building materials and poor brickwork were notorious, collapsed like dominoes. A total of twenty-eight thousand buildings was destroyed.

But death was democratic: all the millionaire palaces on Nob Hill were destroyed except for one: the James Flood mansion catercorner from Emma.

By noon, as fire swept the city, turning the blue sky black with smoke, Can Do was climbing around the rubble of the mansion on Nob Hill he had served in for so many years.

"I don't believe," he kept saying to himself, shaking his head. "I don't believe."

Every few minutes he would stumble over a familiar object. A shard of a Chinese vase, a broken corner of a picture frame, a smashed French chair, a vermeil spoon. He didn't know what he was looking for, but something inside him refused to stop searching. Perhaps he was looking for his past.

And then he saw a hand sticking out of a pile of plaster, as if it were reaching for the sky. An old, elegant hand with a familiar band of gold on its fourth finger.

"Taitai!" Can Do whispered, kneeling before the hand in the rubble. Slowly he reached out and touched the cold fingers with his own. Tears began spilling from his eyes. "Taitai," he whispered again. "Why you leave Can Do?"

For Emma, David, Archer, Chester, Ellie, Sebastian, Dan Wilder, and perhaps as many as a thousand others—no one knows for sure how many—the glitter and the gold were dimmed forever.

40

"YOU sure as hell are lucky," said the fat man with the big cigar and the Tennessee accent. "Just plain, dumb-ass lucky. The whole goddamn Grand Hotel falls down while you're fuckin' on the top floor, and you climb out of it with nothin' but a broken wrist. And best of all, your girlfriend's husband gets killed when your bed falls on top of him. Now, if that ain't the goddamned luckiest thing that ever happened to anyone, I don't know what is!"

As General J. J. Channing began wheezing with laughter, his mountainous belly shook almost as violently as San Francisco had five days previously. Jimmie, his left arm in a sling, grinned sheepishly. They were in the saloon of J.J.'s yacht, cruising off Catalina Island.

"I guess I was pretty lucky," Jimmie admitted. "Alma told me it was the best sex she'd ever had."

The owner of the Los Angeles *Express* broke into louder guffaws and pounded his fat thighs as he rocked back and forth in his chair. "I'll bet! I'll just bet!" he wheezed. "Woo-ee, the poontang that shook San Francisco. Well, sir, I'll just bet she's not gonna forget that till the day she dies. But say, Jimmie, you lost a lotta relatives, you know that, son? Your family's been decimated, just decimated. And you know—and now, I don't want you takin' no offense at this—but don't it say somethin' peculiar 'bout God when he kills off a nice lady like your old granny and lets a mean sonuvabitch like you off with a broken wrist? Huh?"

Again Jimmie grinned. "Yes, I guess it does, J.J."

" 'Course, Wanda's got her own ideas about that. Anyway, it opens up quite an opportunity for you, don't it?"

"What do you mean?"

"Oh, come on, Jimmie, you're not usin' your head. Just tote up the score: your granny's gone, God bless her soul, an' that old Jew she was married to. Your Uncle Archer's gone. Your cousin Chester's gone. Your girlfriend's husband's gone. God done you quite a favor, didn't he? He killed off everybody in the Collingwood family except Curtis and Alma. It seems to me that if you married Alma and we got rid of Curtis,

354

you'd stand to inherit the whole goddamn shebang, wouldn't you? Especially since your granny didn't get a chance to change her will."

Jimmie was staring at him. "I don't know, J.J. I'm not sure what's in the will yet—or wills. San Francisco's just beginning to dig out. All I know is that the insurance claims are flooding into the Golden State Insurance Company."

"Yes indeed, I'm sure they are. But goddammit, son, you're still not usin' your head. I don't care what's in the wills. The point is, what was once a big powerful family is now a small powerful family. The power of runnin' the Collingwood Corporation, with its bank, its shipping company, its real-estate and insurance company, and, more to the point, its fourteen newspapers, is now concentrated in two people, unless there's somethin' unusual in the wills I don't know about. Alma and Curtis, they're the only survivin' children of Archer, right? And you and your three sisters and Alma and Curtis are the only survivin' grandchildren of Emma, right?"

"Right."

"Now, if you marry Alma and we get rid of Curtis, it seems to me that you are the natural person left to take over the company, right? That is, assumin' you'd want to take over the company, and only a fool wouldn't want to. Your Collingwood cousins are a lot richer than you, son."

"I never thought about taking it over," Jimmie said.

"Don't you think it's time you thought about it? Because if you was boss of the Los Angeles *Clarion* instead of Curtis, we could stop sweatin' about the *Clarion* blowin' the whistle on our sweet little real-estate deal, couldn't we? You beginnin' to see my point, Jimmie?"

He scratched a match and relit his cigar. The expression on Jimmie's face was the awed look of a man seeing the doors of the San Francisco Mint opening before him.

"But you keep saying 'if we got rid of Curtis.' How could we get rid of him?"

J. J. Channing's porcine eyes twinkled. "Why, the same way we got rid of the reporter. We murder him. And we'd be killin' two birds with one stone, Jimmie, 'cause I'll bet my bottom dollar Curtis has figured out you murdered Carl Klein."

A tall woman in a white skirt and blouse climbed down the ladder to the main deck. She opened the saloon door, standing in the doorway as the Pacific wind blew her snow-white hair. She had a handsome face with thick black eyebrows over steel blue eyes that had a fanatical intensity. The woman, who was almost six feet tall, looked at Jimmie and J.J. "I've just talked to Jee-zuz," announced the Reverend Wanda Wonder.

J.J. tapped his cigar in an ashtray made from the base of an artillery shell that had been fired in the Philippines during the Spanish-American War. J.J. had been made an honorary general by President McKinley for recruiting a platoon of American soldiers and paying their expenses for one month.

"What did Jesus have to say, honey?" J.J. asked.

Wanda Wonder pointed dramatically at Jimmie. "Jee-zuz said God destroyed San Francisco for its pride and its sins, its whores and its brothels, its greed and its lust. But most important, Jee-zuz said God destroyed San Francisco for the wealth of its Jews."

Jimmie's eyes widened.

General J. J. Channing got out of his chair and waddled to Wanda Wonder, planting a wet kiss on her cheek. "I'll say A-men to that, honey. And we got our friend Jimmie here, who's gonna take that wealth over for our side. Ain't that right, Jimmie?"

Jimmie nodded slowly, as if in a dream. "Yes, J.J.," he said.

"Hallelujah!" Wanda Wonder exclaimed, looking up at the cloudy sky over Catalina. "Did you hear that, Jee-zuz?" she cried. "All Emma Levin's money, all her power and her glow-ry, all—*all*—is coming to us. Praise the Lord!"

"Praise the Lord!" J.J. echoed, pinching Wanda's curvy bottom.

"Praise the Lord," Jimmie whispered.

My father's revenge! he was thinking. Th-th-this is muh-muh-my fah-father's revenge against the Cuh-Cuh-Collingwoods!

"It's just got to be a payoff!" said Detective Cliff Parker of the LAPD as he stirred his breakfast coffee in the kitchen of his Santa Monica bungalow.

His wife, Dorie, was frying eggs at the stove. "Honey, I agree with you," she said patiently. Her husband had gone over the subject endlessly the night before, like a dog chewing a bone. "Why else would Commissioner Murray tell you to stop investigating an unsolved murder?"

"He didn't even bother to come up with a halfway plausible reason. He just said, 'Parker, the Carl Klein murder is being taken over by the state police.' Period. Now, that's a bunch of hooey. There's no reason the state police should get involved with a local murder. And there's another thing—"

"I know. Curtis Collingwood knows more than he's letting on. You said all this last night."

Cliff sighed. "I'm sorry. But this has really gotten to me. Someone has paid off the police commissioner to cover up this murder."

"Obviously, it's Curtis Collingwood."

Cliff got up to refill his coffee cup from the pot on the stove. "Maybe," he said. "Maybe not. Klein was working on a story about the Owens Valley project, and—"

The phone rang. Cliff Parker put his cup on the table and went to the wall to take the receiver off the hook. "Hello?" A look of surprise came over his face as he listened. Then he said: "I'll be there."

He hung up and turned to his wife.

"That was Curtis Collingwood. He wants to see me in his office at ten this morning."

"I talked to Jee-zuz just an hour ago!" the Reverend Wanda Wonder cried from the pulpit of the small Church of Divine Meditation in downtown L.A. "I said, 'Jee-zuz, what are we going to do about this great national problem of sin?' And Jee-zuz said to me, 'Wanda, we're going to roll up our sleeves and go to work against sin. You have to work hard to get sin out of your soul, just the way you have to scrub hard to get your kitchen floor clean.' Jee-zuz said to me, 'Wanda, what good does it do you if you have a clean kitchen but a dirty soul?' So I say to all of you: Let's clean out our souls!"

"Amen!" cried the crowd of almost two hundred squeezed into the plain wooden church.

"Let's do spring cleaning in our hearts as well as our houses!"

"Amen!"

"Let's clean our sheets, air out our mattresses, straighten up our closets, and purify our souls!"

"Amen!"

"Let's put mothballs in our drawers and love in our hearts!"

"Amen!"

"Let's wash the curtains, wash the windows, and wash our souls!"

"Amen!"

"And then, when our souls are as clean as our houses, we can open our arms and our hearts and say, 'Jee-zuz, we'd like to invite you in for fellowship and prayer.' And if every American Christian did this, this great national problem of sin would go down the drain and America would enter into the Glow-ry Fellowship! Amen, praise the Lord!"

"Praise the Lord!"

"Now, as beloved Sister Harriet leads us in singing 'Rock of Ages,' our Glow-ry Fellowship ushers will pass the collection plates. And I beseech you to find it in your hearts to be generous. Remember: you're giving to Jee-zuz!"

Wanda, who was wearing flowing white robes, left the lectern and sat in a big wooden chair as beloved Sister Harriet began banging out "Rock of Ages" on the out-of-tune upright. The congregation, solid white and rather poorly dressed, began singing as the young men in the white suits passed the collection plates.

Curtis Collingwood, who had come in halfway through Wanda's "Spring Cleaning with Jesus" sermon, stood at the back of the church marveling at the zeal of the singing. Curtis thought Wanda's housewife imagery was ludicrous, but it was obvious from the way the money was piling up in the plates that she knew what she was doing.

He saw Jimmie Lopez come around the side of the church toward him. Jimmie, like Curtis, wore a black mourning band on his sleeve; his left arm was still in a sling. He came up to Curtis and said, "Thanks for coming."

"I wouldn't have missed Wanda for the world."

"Isn't she wonderful?"

"That's one word for it. You said on the phone J.J. wants to clear up Carl Klein's murder. What, exactly, does 'clear up' mean?"

"He wants to confess."

"You mean J.J. shot him?"

"That's right, and he feels terrible about it. Wanda finally convinced him the best thing to do was make a complete confession. She talked to Jesus, and he agreed. So J.J. called the police. Carlton Murray's outside waiting to drive us to the pier. J.J.'s on his yacht."

"Why is J.J. being so accommodating to me? This is a pretty hot story. I'd think he'd at least want to give it to one of his own reporters first."

"Jesus told Wanda that part of J.J.'s repentance had to be to let you scoop his own paper. After all, Carl Klein was your reporter."

Curtis stared at his cousin as the congregation sang the third verse of "Rock of Ages." "Jimmie, why is it Jesus always talks to Wanda Wonder and never talks to . . . well, me, for instance?"

"You'll have to ask Jesus."

"You're a bunch of lunatics. And if you think I'm going out to J.J.'s yacht alone, you must think I'm a lunatic too."

"You're going with the police."

"I have reason to believe Commissioner Murray is on J.J.'s payroll. So thanks for the invitation, but no thanks. I just talked to Jesus and he said, 'Get out of here while you're still in one piece.' Good night, Jimmie."

He let himself out through one of the church's double doors. It was a cool night. He was eyeing the two policemen standing in front of the church when he felt something hard press into his back.

"It's a gun," Jimmie said softly. "Don't make me use it. Get in Commissioner Murray's automobile."

*   *   *

It was nearly midnight when they disembarked from the motor launch and climbed the accommodation ladder hanging on the starboard side of General Channing's hundred-foot yacht. Curtis was followed by Jimmie, the two cops, and Police Commissioner Carlton Murray, a bloated man in a glen-plaid suit and a gray sweatstained hat. Murray had a cold and had sneezed constantly as the launch made the trip from the Santa Monica Amusement Pier through the mirrorlike Pacific to the yacht.

"Welcome aboard," J.J. said cheerily as Curtis stepped onto the main deck. "How are you, Curtis? It's been a long time. Say, I want to express my sincerest condolences for all the members of your family that got killed in the quake. That was a real shame."

"Why do I have this funny feeling that another member of my family is about to get killed?"

J.J. laughed. "Aw, hell, that's no way to talk. Say, it's a bit nippy out here. Let's go inside and have a little nip. Get it? Nippy—nip? God damn, I should be in vaudeville. Come on, fellows. By the way, did you all meet? 'Course, you know the commissioner, but these two fine-lookin' young officers of the law are Pete Hawkins and Bill Gray. Pete and Bill both are sharpshooters. Two of the best shots in L.A., the commissioner tells me. Well, now, let's go inside. How'd you like Wanda's sermon? Ain't she a pistol? Jesus talks to her so damned much, sometimes I wish she'd tell him to shut up."

Guffawing, he led them all inside the saloon.

"I let the crew all go ashore for a night off, so, Pete, you be the bartender," J.J. said, pointing to the small bar at one end of the room. Above it, a big fish tank had been built into the bulkhead, and it was filled with small and quite beautifully colored tropical fish. "Curtis, what'll it be? Whiskey? I've got some single-malt Scotch that'll make you weep with joy."

"J.J., cut the crap. What do you want?"

The fat publisher lit a cigar, eyeing his rival. "Well, now, if you want to skip the amenities, I'll tell you what I want. I want you to sign this letter—say, what did I do with it? I put it in one of my pockets. Oh, yeah, here it is. Let's see." He pulled a letter from a pocket of his rumpled brown jacket and unfolded it. "It's addressed to Commissioner Murray here and it says, 'Dear Commissioner: I hereby confess to the murder of Carl Klein, one of my reporters, whom I discovered in bed with my wife. I went crazy with rage and shot him in the head. Then I took his body to the beach, rowed it out in the ocean, and dumped it overboard. I can't live with my guilt any longer. By the time you receive this, I will have squared my accounts with God. It's the only way. Sincerely . . .' and that's where you'll sign."

"Well, you've got it all figured out, J.J. Congratulations. But before I sign, tell me what really happened. Who shot Carl?"

J.J. exchanged looks with Jimmie, who had perched himself on one of the bar stools, the gun still in his right hand. Pete Hawkins had gone behind the bar and was eating peanuts. Commissioner Murray was sitting in a chair, wiping his nose with a handkerchief. Bill Gray was leaning against the port bulkhead, his hand on his holster.

"Well, hell," J.J. said, "guess we're all friends here, ain't we? Jimmie, tell him."

"It was pretty simple. I sent him a note telling him to meet me at the amusement pier and I'd tell him what he wanted to know about the Valley Fund. I'd name names, the whole works. So we met and came out to J.J.'s yacht in the launch. Wanda had agreed to give me an alibi—"

"Why?" Curtis asked. "What's her involvement in all this?"

"Wanda Wonder's my girlfriend," J.J. said. "She may talk to Jesus, but she screws General J. J. Channing. Plus, she's invested a lot of her church's money in the Valley Fund. Wanda knows a good thing when she sees it."

"When we got to the yacht, I shot him," Jimmie went on. "We tied a weight to his leg and threw him overboard, but I guess we didn't tie it too well because his body floated ashore, as you know." Jimmie paused a moment, then said, "It was pretty much what we're going to do to you."

The silence that followed was broken only by the sound of Pete Hawkins crunching peanuts.

"You murderers," Curtis said softly. "You Jesus-quoting, cold-blooded murderers. You took a young man's life just to cover up a goddamned real-estate deal."

"Oh, it's more than that, Curtis," J.J. said. "Much more than just a deal. We're developing the whole damned San Fernando Valley. We're going to double the size of L.A. Just think of it. Ten years from now, L.A.'s going to be as big as New Orleans or Kansas City. And when Jimmie and I merge our two newspapers, we're going to have one of the most important papers in America."

"Oh, so Jimmie's taking over the *Clarion*?"

"Well, it kinda looks that way. There ain't gonna be too many Collingwoods around after you're gone, know what I mean?"

"Alma and I are getting married next month," Jimmie said, smiling. "We'll miss you at the wedding."

The door burst opened and Cliff Parker appeared. Bill Gray started to pull his gun from his holster, but Parker fired first, hitting his right arm. Two more policemen sprang into the room, guns drawn. Jimmie fired wildly at Parker. Three guns fired almost at once, hitting Jimmie in the chest. More shots. Pete Hawkins ducked behind the bar just in time. The fish tank shattered, sending water and tropical fish pouring onto the deck. By now a half-dozen cops were crouched in the saloon, holding revolvers in two-handed grips. General J. J. Channing, his face pasty with shock, had both hands in the air. Commissioner Carlton Murray yelled, "Who the hell authorized this?"

"I did," Curtis said. "Did you get the confession down?" he added to Parker.

"Every word," the detective said, holding up a notebook.

"I think the *Clarion*'s going to have an interesting lead story tomorrow."

"Curtis, we was only foolin'!" J.J. blurted. "It was just a joke."

"Some joke."

Curtis knelt beside Jimmie, who had toppled from his bar stool onto the deck. He was lying facedown, surrounded by flopping fish.

"We can make a deal," J.J. rasped. "Teddy Roosevelt's a friend of mine. I'll call the White House—"

"Shut up."

Curtis carefully turned Jimmie over on his back. He was still alive, barely. Blood was pouring from three bullet holes in his chest. He looked up at Curtis with glazing eyes.

"You won," he whispered. "The gringos won."

Then he shuddered and died.

The next day, the *Clarion*'s headline screamed:

> PUBLISHER OF EXPRESS INVOLVED IN MURDER PLOT!
> SHOOT-OUT ON POSH YACHT OFF CATALINA!
> COLLINGWOOD RELATIVE KILLED!
> POLICE COMMISSIONER IMPLICATED!
> WATER SCANDAL MAY COST TAXPAYERS MILLIONS!
> TEN TYCOONS INVOLVED IN REAL-ESTATE SWINDLE!
> HEROISM OF DETECTIVE PARKER!

"Jimmie!" Alma Brett sobbed as she swung her sledgehammer at her heroic statue of the Pioneer Woman. It crashed into a marble leg and chipped off a knee. "Jimmie! Oh, God, they've killed my Jimmie!"

She threw the sledgehammer on the floor. Crying hysterically, she ran to the small kitchen of the studio on her Burlingame estate. "I can't live without Jimmie," she screamed, grabbing a paring knife. Swiftly she slit her left wrist. As she saw the blood gush forth, though, she dropped the knife and ran to the phone, calling the main house.

"Lily, come quick!" she cried. "I've tried to kill myself!"
She hung up, grabbed a towel, and wrapped it around her wrist.

They buried Jimmie Lopez at the Calafía Ranch on a knoll overlooking the Pacific. Next to his grave were the graves of his father,
Juanito, and of his grandparents. After the brief ceremony Jimmie's
mother and three sisters stood by his tombstone for a few minutes, the
wind whipping their black veils and skirts. Then Curtis came over and
hugged his Aunt Star.

"I'm sorry," he said.

"He was a bad seed," Star said. "A scorpion. His father filled him
with hate when he was a child. Maybe it was my fault . . . who knows?
Anyway, maybe it's better this way. But so much death! Mother and
Archer and Chester and now Jimmie. Are we cursed?"

Curtis sighed. "I don't know. But I want to arrange a meeting of
those of us left. The lawyers want to set up a new sort of corporation
for the family. Granny's will has to be read, and with Father dead
. . . well, it's all a mess, but the lawyers are figuring things out."

"I guess you're the head of the family now," Star said.

"Yes, I suppose I am."

Curtis found himself looking at Alicia Lopez, and suddenly realized
he had been watching her all during the funeral. How sweet she is, he
thought. And how extremely beautiful.

"They say I'm one of the five richest women in the world," Arabella
Collingwood said as she walked around the Sienese pulpit her late
husband had bought in London three months before. "I suppose God
thinks that makes up for his taking away my husband and my son, but
if he does, he's wrong."

Curtis was with his mother in the Palo Alto warehouse his father
had bought ten years before. Everything in the warehouse—statues,
tapestries, armor, paintings, furniture—had been bought by Archer as
he chewed his way through the antiquarians of Europe, like some in-
satiable mouse. Arabella, dressed all in black, was a double heiress,
for the earthquake at one stroke had made her the recipient of Emma's
vast fortune and of Archer's as well. "And now, Alma," she went on.
"As if I didn't have enough woe, Alma tries to kill herself because of
Jimmie Lopez. Fortunately, she's incompetent. Oh, I know I'm sound-
ing bitter, but I can't help it. Thank God for you, my darling." She
held out her hand and Curtis took it.

"Well, there is some good news," he said. "Joel has started making
sentences."

His mother smiled sadly behind her black veil. "Such a sweet baby.
That is good news."

"And Betty thinks she's pregnant again."

"Oh?"

"She's going to the doctor today."

"Well, let's hope she is. The way this family's been almost destroyed, God knows we can use babies. Oh, Curtis, I miss your father so. He was the best husband in the world."

"Mother," Curtis said as tactfully as possible, "we all miss Father, but the accountants really want you to come to a decision about all this stuff he bought."

"Accountants," she sniffed. "I hate accountants."

"Yes, but the insurance alone on this warehouse is costing a hundred thousand dollars a year. Golden State has had to pay out over forty million dollars in earthquake and fire claims, and while the company's going to pull through, the accountants are trying to make every economy possible—"

His mother turned on him. "Economy? You're talking about a dream. This 'stuff,' as you call it, was your father's dream."

"I realize that, but it's totally impractical. I mean, what's anybody going to do with a pulpit?"

"What does anybody do with art? Art and things of beauty are perfectly useless, and yet they're perhaps the most valuable things in the world. Your father loved all this 'stuff,' just as I love my paintings. Poor Emma's paintings were destroyed, just as she was and so many others . . ." She fought back tears. "But Emma's dream of the museum mustn't be destroyed. I'll build it. And instead of her paintings, I'll put in mine and all your father's treasures. And it will all be perfectly useless, except it will give generations of Californians pleasure. And in the end, that may be the most useful thing of all. I suppose you think I'm a silly, spendthrift old woman?"

Curtis kissed her. "No," he said. "I think it's a wonderful idea."

General J. J. Channing was tried and convicted of being an accessory to a first-degree murder. He was sentenced to ten to thirty years, but because of his wealth and political connections, he served only ten months in San Quentin.

The giant aqueduct bringing the water from the Owens Valley to Los Angeles was to be completed six years later. It was considered an engineering feat comparable to the Great Wall of China.

Curtis Collingwood stood at the window of his twelfth-floor office in the Clarion Building, watching the rain pound Los Angeles below. Ironically, after such a great scandal caused by the lack of water in southern California, the rain that year came early and heavy: it was the first week of November.

" 'To all employees of the Collingwood Corporation,' " he began. Rose Markham, looking efficiently trim in a white blouse and gray skirt, sat in her usual chair taking dictation. " 'As the new chairman of the corporation, I wish to take this opportunity to thank all of you for your support in what has been a most difficult year for my family. And as a . . . a person, I want to thank you for your many letters expressing your sympathy for my most recent . . . personal loss . . .' "

He stopped. His secretary looked up. To her astonishment, her dynamic, aggressive boss was crying. "Mr. Collingwood, would you like me to come back . . .?"

He shook his head as he pulled a handkerchief from his pocket and wiped his eyes. Then he turned from the window and sat down at his desk. He looked at Rose with bloodshot eyes.

"Is my family cursed, Rose?" he asked hoarsely. "First the earthquake, then Jimmie Lopez, and then cancer?"

Betty's supposed pregnancy had turned out to be uterine cancer instead. She had died the previous week.

Rose's heart broke a little for this man she adored. "Sometimes bad things come in cycles," she said lamely.

"This has been some cycle." He blew his nose. "And now Joel has no mother. I've got to find him a mother, Rose. That kid has to grow up fine and strong. There's a lot riding on Joel. And I mean this entire company's future."

"I realize that."

He looked at her. "Have you thought about moving up to San Francisco, Rose?"

"Yes, sir. If you want me, of course I'll move."

"Well, since my father and my brother both are dead, I'm having to run the whole show myself, and that means San Francisco. Good. I'm glad you'll be with me, Rose. If I lost you too, well . . ."

He shrugged sadly. She looked at his slim, handsome face and wondered if perhaps he was thinking of her as . . . Don't get your hopes up, she told herself. But, my God, to be Mrs. Curtis Collingwood!

"What's that car?" Star Lopez asked, refilling her glass with gin. She was, as usual, in bed in the tower room of the ranch. Her daughter Alicia got up and walked to the rain-streaked curved windows. A red-and-black Great Arrow was pulling up in front of the house. Beyond, wind streaks scratched the choppy gray Pacific.

"It's Curtis!" Alicia exclaimed as she saw him emerge from the back seat.

"Curtis?" Her mother looked up from her gin and whispered, "I saw him eyeing you at Jimmie's funeral. And he was eyeing you again last week at Betty's service. Wouldn't that be the perfect ending?"

"Momma, what are you talking about?"

"I'm talking about your cousin, the best-looking, most eligible man in California. There's the doorbell! Get down there! And look pretty!"

Alicia hurried across the tower room. "Really, Momma, that gin is doing things to your imagination. Curtis couldn't be interested in me."

"Why not? What's wrong with you? Your blood's as good as his. Ask him to dinner. Tell Chinina to heat up the pot roast. And bring me a new pack of cigarettes."

Alicia shook her head as she closed the door behind her. All the same, she ran to the stairs and down them to the front hall. She nearly flung open the front door.

"Hello, Alicia."

Curtis had always seemed so distant to Alicia, so involved with business, so . . . rich. He was also nine years older. But on this rainy afternoon he looked surprisingly young and excited.

"I, uh, I was given two tickets to a new play," he was saying. "I wondered if you'd like to go with me. It's in San Francisco."

"San Francisco?"

"Well I'm moving up there, and I thought maybe you'd like to come up for a few days. The weather's been pretty rotten here, and you could stay with Mother."

"Come in, Curtis. I didn't mean to keep you standing on the porch. When are you going up?"

"Tomorrow morning. Mother's sending down the *Arabella*."

The private railroad car. She'd always wanted to see it.

"I'll have to ask Mother, but . . . well, yes, I'd love to go."

When Curtis returned to his car, he carried away Alicia's dazzling Spanish smile. She really is beautiful, he thought. She'd make a perfect mother for Joel, and not a bad wife for me.

The marriage would also bring the Calafía Ranch back to the Collingwoods.

·FIVE·

The Phantom
of Hollywood

41

AFTER Arabella Dawson Collingwood's fatal heart attack in 1909, her son Curtis became head of the sadly diminished Collingwood family. One of the richest men in the world, he and his new wife, Alicia, bought forty acres on the peninsula near Burlingame and decided to build themselves a home. Two years and several million dollars later, they moved into a forty-room Mediterranean-style villa overlooking San Francisco Bay. (Not far off, Arabella's museum went up on a splendid site also overlooking the bay.) The house, built of white stone with an orange tile roof, was imposing without being overwhelming. Tall cypress trees were planted, and Alicia, whose passion was gardening, began the planning of a garden that would take her years to complete and would become one of the wonders of California.

Meanwhile, the family lawyers, led by a brilliant young man named Lamont Vane, had been restructuring the enormous but somewhat ramshackle business empire Emma had built. The Golden State Insurance Company had survived the drain of the earthquake and fire claims, all of which were paid in full, and was now prospering as never before, thanks to the public's understandable nervousness about future quakes. Since the Pacific Bank and Trust Building on Montgomery Street had been destroyed, in 1908 a new thirty-story building on the same site was opened. Aggressively adding newspapers to his chain, Curtis was in a circulation war with William Randolph Hearst that benefited both press lords. In 1909 the Collingwood Corporation made a public stock offer of fifty million dollars. Though it was quickly bought up, this was Class B nonvoting stock. Control of the corporation was retained by the family, which owned the Class A voting stock. In 1910 *The Wall Street Journal* estimated the value of the Collingwood Corporation at over one billion dollars.

The heir apparent to all this, Joel de Meyer Collingwood, was an eight-year-old who liked playing with dolls.

"My son's a full-fledged, lily-blooded sissy!" Curtis spat the words across the dining table at his wife. "Do you know what he's collecting now? Masks!"

"Dear, it's three weeks to Halloween," Alicia replied. "All the kids are collecting masks."

"Gold masks with feathers?"

"He made that himself. He's terribly precocious, you know. And he showed me the white-and-gold costume he made for himself. It's a copy of one he saw in one of the books in the library . . . I believe some courtier at Versailles wore it to a ballet."

"My son is going to go trick-or-treating in a goddamned seventeenth-century ballet costume with a gold mask with goddamned feathers? Not on your life. I'll lock him up first. I tell you, Alicia, I'm fed to the teeth with Joel. He's inherited every bad gene in the family—and I include Betty's family! Her brother Gerald is a painter up in the Napa Valley and everyone knows he's a pansy. Well, my son is not going to be a pansy!"

"Curtis, he's only eight. He's a very sensitive, shy child with a great deal of imagination."

"Why do you always defend him?"

"Because I love him. And I know what it's like being shy. I had a terrible childhood with Mother boozing it up in her bedroom and Jimmie with his Mexican tarts out in the stable. It was hell, and I don't want that to happen to Joel just because he happens to be different."

"Different? He's weird. He doesn't like baseball. Who ever heard of a boy not liking baseball? You know what I'm going to do, Alicia? I'm going to make him like baseball."

"Oh, that's silly. How can you make anyone like a game?"

"I'm going to hire him a coach. I'm going to pay the coach to teach Joel how to pitch and bat and run bases. I'm going to put in a baseball diamond—"

"Not near my garden!"

"It'll be away from your garden. I'm going to buy Joel a uniform, and my son is going to play baseball."

Alicia rang the crystal bell. "I wish you luck. But knowing Joel, I think he'll be more interested in designing the uniform than wearing it."

Cheam, the English butler, entered the dining room and refilled the wineglasses. While he was pouring, Curtis sullenly cut his lamb chop and Alicia looked at the large yellow painting on the wall by a French artist named Matisse. After the disastrous loss of almost all his grandmother's art collection in the earthquake, Curtis had decided to uphold the family tradition and start a collection himself. Once he had started, he found to his surprise that he not only enjoyed collecting—he was consumed by it.

"Promise me one thing," Alicia said after Cheam had returned to the butler's pantry. "Don't be harsh with the child. Remember, he lost his mother. Try to meet him halfway. And don't expect miracles."

"I won't be harsh, but I'm going to be firm. It's for his own good, you know. No American male can possibly go through life not liking baseball."

He was a strange-looking child, almost gaunt, and tall for his age. He had thick brown hair, rather small blue eyes, and a long nose. He had inherited many of the good features of his handsome forebears, but they didn't quite seem to fit together. He was sitting on the floor of his bedroom playing with his toy theater when there was a knock at the door.

"Come in."

Curtis came in.

"Hello, Father."

Coming over to him, Curtis looked down at the miniature cardboard theater.

"What play are you putting on tonight, Joel?" he asked, trying to conceal his annoyance.

"It's not a play. It's an opera," Joel murmured as he continued to put his four-inch cutout figures on the stage.

"What opera is it?"

"*Carmen*. I designed all the costumes myself."

"Mmm. They're very colorful."

"Thank you, Father. It's taken me five nights to cut them out of the cardboard—of course, after I did my homework."

"I have no complaints about your homework, Joel. Your grades are excellent. But . . . Could you put that damned doll down and look at me?"

Joel pulled his hand back through the cardboard proscenium he had made himself and wordlessly looked up at his father. Curtis repressed a wild desire to step on the toy theater and all its actors and actresses.

"Joel, tomorrow after school there's a man named Mr. Reynolds who's going to come work with you for an hour."

"Who's Mr. Reynolds, Father?"

"He's the baseball coach at the Palo Alto High School. He's going to teach you how to play baseball."

Silence.

"You'll enjoy it, son. And you'll like Reynolds."

Silence. Joel's face had frozen.

Curtis knelt down to be more at his level.

"Joel," he said softly, "a boy should be playing baseball instead of playing with dolls. Don't you understand that?"

"If you say so, Father."

"Yes, I do say so."

Father and son stared into each other's eyes. Curtis was surprised by the stubbornness in his son's small blue eyes. Joel might play with dolls, but inside he was made of steel.

"Do you hate me?" Curtis whispered, genuinely curious.

Joel's mouth tightened, but he didn't reply.

"Answer me, Joel."

Silence.

"Answer me, damn you!"

Silence.

Curtis stood up, no longer able to control his temper. He pointed his finger at his child. "You'll play baseball," he said. "And you'll play it well. And you'll get rid of these damned dolls!"

He smashed his right foot down on the cardboard theater, flattening it and its tiny actors. Then he stormed out of the room, slamming the door.

Trembling, Joel slowly reached for the doll representing Carmen. She had been totally squashed.

Patiently, a strange look in his eyes, he began to reconstruct her.

"Look at him. It's useless."

Two weeks later, Curtis stood at the window of his library holding a cocktail as he looked out at the rear lawn. Next to the swimming pool, Joel was playing catch with Mr. Reynolds.

"What's useless?" asked Alicia, coming up beside him. She had, like her brother, Jimmie, inherited an intriguing blend of her father's dark good looks and Star's half-Manchu beauty.

"It's useless trying to teach Joel baseball. Look at him. He's got a glass arm. He'd be laughed out of the ball park. He hates the game, and he hates me for making him play it. I'm going to tell Reynolds to forget it. It's a waste of time."

"There are other things in life besides baseball."

"I know. I'll bet he's a whiz at crocheting."

"Darling, that's cruel."

"I know it's cruel, and I don't give a damn. My son's a pansy: don't you think that's cruel to me?"

"Curtis, you don't know—"

"Oh, I know. Maybe I'm wrong, but I doubt it. I'll tell you one thing: no goddamn pansy is going to run the Collingwood Corporation."

Alicia put her arm around her husband and kissed him. "Maybe this time you'll get a boy you like."

He looked at her in joyful surprise. "Oh, darling, please. Please give me a real son."

42

IN 1913 an event occurred that was to have as dramatic an effect on California as the Gold Rush sixty-four years before. Movie studios had opened a few years earlier: the New York Motion Picture Company had opened a studio in Edendale in 1909, which Mack Sennett took over in 1912. Vitagraph opened a studio in Santa Monica in 1911. But when Cecil B. De Mille came to L.A. to film *The Squaw Man* in order to escape the Patents Trust back east, a critical mass was attained and Hollywood was born—though few of the studios were actually located there at the time. Perhaps more accurately, the idea of Hollywood was born.

In 1916, as war raged halfway around the globe in Europe, Alicia and Curtis took their three children to the Calafía Ranch for the funeral services of Alicia's mother, Star, whose liver had finally given out. As her coffin descended into its grave between her husband, Juanito, and her son, Jimmie, Curtis' memory flashed back through her life. Star had been born during the Gold Rush and had lived through San Francisco's wildest era. It was all so respectable now, so tame. Chinatown, rebuilt after the earthquake, was now almost middle-class. The wild Barbary Coast had been outlawed. The colorful violence of Star's youth now seemed destined to be fodder for the silver screen.

After the funeral, the family boarded its private railroad car to go to L.A. for a few days. While Curtis was conferring with the management of the L.A. *Clarion*, Alicia took Joel and her two daughters to the Fox Studio at Sunset Boulevard and Western Avenue to watch a film being made. It was a "society" comedy called *The Countess Regrets*.

Now fourteen and almost six feet tall, Joel had been wearing thick glasses for the past two years to correct his severe myopia, and they made him look even stranger.

As he watched the camera turning and the silly comedy acted out, those myopic eyes behind the owllike lenses took on a look of intense, almost sexual excitement.

* * *

On a rainy autumn afternoon in 1920, the football team of exclusive St. Stephen's Academy in New Hampshire was scrimmaging with the Exeter team. The whistle was blown for halftime, and the St. Stephen's team ran off the muddy field to the benches.

"Water boy!" yelled Norman Hickby, the quarterback.

A tall, gangly, bespectacled senior in yellow foul-weather gear hurried up with a tin pail.

"Joel the Mole," commented Hickby, a husky six-footer destined for Dartmouth. He gave Joel a sneering leer as he took the ladle from the bucket and drank the water. Then he stuck the ladle back in.

"Thanks, Sister," he said.

As Joel stared at him, Hickby puckered his lips in a kiss, grinned, and sat on the bench.

An hour and a half later, the team was in the shower room of the Archer Collingwood Memorial Gymnasium, a gift of Joel's father. St. Stephen's had beaten Exeter, and the team was singing and yelling.

"Oh, oh, guys!" the left tackle called out. "Here's Sister! Don't drop your soap."

Joel, squinting without his glasses, came into the suddenly silent shower room. All eyes were on his skeletal, slightly stoop-shouldered body. He found a shower in the corner and turned it on.

"Woo-woo!" the right end called. "Ain't Sister cute!"

Catcalls and whistles echoed as Joel stepped under the shower head.

"Water girl!" the right tackle warbled. "Water girl! I'm *tho* thirsty, would you bring me a drink, thweetheart?"

"Did Daddy give the money for this gym so Sister could make out with the guys?"

Howls of laughter.

Joel soaped himself and said nothing.

"Sister," Norman Hickby said, coming to him and holding out a bar of soap. "Would you soap my back?"

More laughter. Joel looked at him, then turned away, facing the corner. Norman stepped up to him and jammed the bar of soap between his buttocks. "Bull's-eye!" he yelled, jumping back.

As the football team hooted and howled, Joel squeezed his eyes tightly shut and pulled the soap out of his butt.

That night, he was studying algebra in his small single room on the top floor of Dudley Hall when there was a knock on his door. Before he could say "Come in," the door opened. It was Norman Hickby in his pajamas. He closed the door and smiled.

"Hi, Joel," he said.

Joel's thick lenses turned on him. "What do you want?"

"Well," he said, crossing his arms and leaning against the door, "I just wanted to tell you I sort of admire you. You take a lot of shit from the guys and you never say anything back."

"Would it do any good if I did? They're all a bunch of dimwits."

"I suppose that includes me?"

"You said it, not I."

"Maybe they'd lay off you if you told them off. You know, they all think you're chickenshit."

Joel turned back to his studies. "Maybe I am. Maybe I don't give a damn what they think. Good night, Norman. I have an exam tomorrow."

Norman watched him a moment, then walked up behind him and put his hands on his bony shoulders. "I could protect you," he said softly, gently squeezing.

Joel put down his book. "Why would you do that?"

Norman leaned down and whispered in his ear: "If you'd be my girlfriend, Sister."

Joel froze. Then, from his throat came a howl so fierce and animallike that Norman let go and jumped back. Joel shot out of his chair and turned on the quarterback, trembling with rage.

"You disgusting pervert!" he screamed. He shot out his fist and smashed Hickby's nose so hard the quarterback stumbled backward over a wastebasket and onto the floor.

"Now, listen," Joel said, still trembling, "my father gives a lot of money to this school and he's got a lot of influence. If you ever touch me again, I'll tell my father and the headmaster, and they'll make sure you'll do nothing the rest of your life except fucking hairdressing! Now, get out!"

Norman Hickby, a look of terror on his Arrow Collar Man face, blood running from his nose, scrambled to his feet and flew out of the room.

On a warm summer morning in 1926, one of the five housemaids at the Collingwood mansion finished making Joel's bed. Charlene Miller was a pretty girl who had started working for the Collingwoods three weeks before. Already she had picked up a lot of gossip about the family from the staff. She knew that Mr. Joel, the only son, had just graduated from Yale. She knew his father didn't get along with him, and she knew why.

As Charlene dusted, she wondered about the many oddities in the big bedroom. Masks of all kinds hung on the walls: silver masks, wood masks, clown masks, spooky Halloween masks. Stuffed in chairs and seated on windowsills were all sorts of dolls: rag dolls, flapper dolls, porcelain dolls. An entire wall was lined with books on the theater: complete sets of Shakespeare, Ibsen, George Bernard Shaw, as well as current popular Broadway plays.

On the table before the big window overlooking the tennis courts rose a marvelous toy stage. Charlene paused to study it a moment. Two feet deep and four feet wide, it was a miniature set that one could look down on or stoop and peer through the proscenium with its real gold curtains. He sure must love plays, she thought as she reached down to pick up the toy actor dressed as Hamlet.

"Put that down!"

She jumped, releasing the toy, and whirled about. Joel was standing in the door.

"Please," he added more softly. He was wearing white flannel trousers and a blue-and-white-striped shirt, open at the neck. He's so tall and skinny, she thought, and so strange-looking with those thick glasses.

"I'm sorry, sir," she said. "I didn't mean to hurt nothing."

"I know. Your name is . . .?"

"Charlene, sir."

He softly closed the door, his weird eyes staring at her. "You're very pretty, Charlene."

"Thank you, sir."

He came to her slowly, pulling his wallet from his hip pocket. He took out fifty dollars and held it out to her. His hand was trembling.

"Would you . . .?" he whispered.

As she started to leave, he stepped sideways to block her. He pulled out fifty more dollars and held it up.

She looked at him curiously. "They say you don't like girls," she whispered.

"They're wrong," he whispered back, staring at her breasts.

She took the money from his hand, then started unbuttoning her uniform. "You'd better lock the door."

He held up the key. "I already did."

"If we get caught—"

"We won't. Do you think I'm ugly?"

She was stepping out of her uniform. "Oh, no, sir. You're not ugly. I think you're sort of cute."

He took a silver mask from the wall. "Have you seen the portraits of my great-grandparents downstairs?"

"Yes."

"Wasn't my great-grandmother beautiful?"

"Oh, yes. I could look at her for hours. And the senator was so handsome."

When she pulled her slip over her head, he peered through his thick lenses at her lush body.

"Compared to them, I'm ugly, wouldn't you say?"

"Well . . ."

He took off his glasses, put them on a table, and held the silver mask over his face. "Now," he whispered, "you can pretend that I'm as handsome as my great-grandfather. Fantasy is more powerful than reality. In fact, reality may *be* fantasy."

As he reached his hand out to touch one of her nipples, she whispered nervously, "You're like *The Phantom of the Opera*. I saw that movie. When Mary Philbin took off Lon Chaney's mask, I screamed."

"But his ugliness gave him a certain beauty, didn't it?"

"I don't know. Mr. Joel, I wish you'd take off that mask. It's sort of scary."

But Joel kept the mask on.

"The heir is here!" said one of the secretaries in the Pacific Bank Building on Montgomery Street.

"You mean Mr. Collingwood's son?" said another secretary, her lipstick smeared in a bee sting like Clara Bow's.

"Yes. It's the first time he's ever come here. Can you imagine? Being heir to all those millions and never once coming to see what it all looks like?"

"I've seen his photo in the rotogravure section. He's sort of nice-looking."

"Don't waste your time dreaming, Ginny. I hear he's one of"— she flipped her wrist limply—"those."

"No kidding?" She sighed. "What a waste."

As president and chief stockholder of the Collingwood Corporation, Curtis had an office that reflected his prestige. Like Emma's a half-century before, it was paneled and furnished with English antiques, for the idea that nothing was tonier than a London club still persisted. The main difference from Emma's office was the height: Curtis' was some twenty-five floors higher than his grandmother's, an idea that would have been inconceivable in the 1870's. But Emma would have been fascinated by the paintings on his walls: a cubist-period Picasso and a large Kandinsky. Her grandson had become one of the leading collectors of modern paintings in the West.

The door to his office opened and his secretary, Mrs. Gifford, led Joel in. Joel wore a dark blue suit that was conservative by anyone's standards, but, his father thought as he looked at him, he's still a strange-looking bird even in a banker's suit.

"Ah, Joel. You know Lamont, of course." He indicated Lamont

Vane standing by his desk. Lamont was a portly, balding man in a three-piece gray suit. "And I believe you know Miss Miller?"

Joel looked at Charlene, who was seated on a leather sofa. She was dressed nicely in a plain suit, and a small hat nestled in her brown curls. Joel nodded.

"I'll get right to the point," Curtis said. "As you know, Charlene is employed at our house as a maid. Yesterday she presented me with a letter from her doctor, a certain"—he checked the letter in his hand—"Dr. Mendenhall of Palo Alto, which confirms that Charlene is seven weeks pregnant. Charlene claims the father is you and is asking for a one-hundred-thousand-dollar trust fund for her child, or she will take the story to Willie Hearst. Of course, I realize it is highly improbable that you are the father, but Lamont felt we should ask you anyway."

Joel looked coolly at his father, who looked back with a slightly bemused air, as if to say: *You*? A father? Come on.

"It's true," Joel said.

His father's mouth dropped open. "It is?" he sputtered.

"Charlene's been my mistress for two months now, and neither of us has used birth-control devices. When she told me she was pregnant, I told her to ask you for a trust fund for the child. I'm giving her fifty thousand dollars myself, and I intend to take an active interest in the child throughout his or her life, including paying for a first-class education."

Charlene beamed. "Thank you, Joel."

Curtis was still staring at his son in amazement. Finally he turned to Lamont Vane. "In that case, Lamont, will you take care of the details?"

"Of course. Miss Miller, if you'll come to my office?"

Charlene stood up and followed Lamont across the room. As she passed Joel, she blew him a kiss. Then she looked at his father. "I know what you think about Joel," she said. "Oh, Mr. Collingwood, you're so wrong. He's terrific in bed. Good-bye . . . Granddaddy." Smiling, she left the office with Lamont, who closed the door.

Curtis put his face in his hands for almost a full minute. When he looked up, his eyes were red. "I . . ." He cleared his throat. "I owe you an apology, Joel."

"Why? Because all these years you've treated me like a freak?" Joel spoke quietly but with deadly intent. "Because you were ashamed of your only son? Because you thought I was a queer because I don't like baseball? What a narrow, provincial, Babbitt-y idea of manliness you have. Do you want to know the only real queer I've ever met? Norman Hickby, whom you used to cheer at St. Stephen's football games and who was voted the best athlete of the year. You've never taken any pride in anything I've done: I graduated summa cum laude from Yale, I can design sets and costumes—but that's all sissy stuff. Being sensitive and creative is sissy. Well, you owe me a thing or two, Father. You owe me for a rotten childhood. You owe me for all your contempt, which should have been love even if I was queer. You owe me for being a *shit*."

The last word was a shot. Curtis stiffened. He started to say something, then changed his mind. He got up from his desk, clasped his hands behind his back, and went to a window to look out. Joel thought he suddenly looked rather old. Finally Curtis turned. "Everything you say is true," he said. "I've misjudged you. To be frank, I hated you."

"I know."

"I prayed Alicia would give me another son, but she gave me daughters instead."

"I know. You're stuck with me. The girls don't give a damn about the business."

"Do you?"

"Perhaps. But you have to win my love, Father. You have to make up for the past. You have to give me what I want first."

"What do you want, Joel?"

"A movie studio."

For the second time his father gaped at him. "A movie studio?"

"Yes. I love the movies! You know I've always been fascinated with the theater, but movies are the future. I was the top student at the Yale Drama School, and I know I can make excellent, successful movies. Buy me a studio and finance me for six years—you owe me that much, at least. Give me till I'm thirty to do what I love. Then, whether I'm a success or a flop, I promise I'll come back here to San Francisco and learn the business from the ground up. You can have me for the rest of my life, but for six years, let me run a movie studio."

Curtis stared at his skinny, birdlike son. "Joel," he said, "you dumbfound me and I won't even pretend to understand you. But I've been given a son after all these years, and for that my heart is full of joy. You have a deal."

He crossed to Joel and hugged him.

For the first time since he was a baby, Joel Collingwood, the strange child, burst into tears.

Headline in *Variety*, September 20, 1926:

RITZ GLITZ HITS PIX BIZ!
Collingwood Scion Buys Pantages Studio!
Vows to Make "Classy" Films of "Quality and Beauty"!
Moguls Snicker.

43

TED Spaulding was driving his Model T Ford down a dusty Iowa road one summer day in 1928 when he saw a girl hitchhiker. Carrying a small suitcase, she wore a white dress that stopped above her knees, flapper-style. Never, Ted thought, had he seen such gorgeous legs in his life. As he drew closer and saw her face, his adrenaline started pumping.

"Hot damn, is this gonna be my lucky day?" he muttered as he pulled over and stopped.

"Where you goin'?" he called out the open window.

"Hollywood," the blond replied.

"Well, I'm not goin' that far, but I can take you into Des Moines."

The girl climbed in the front seat, and Ted threw the car into gear.

"So you're goin' to Hollywood? Gonna be a movie star?" said Ted, who had a friendly freckled face.

"That's right."

"What's your name, Miss Movie Star?"

"Dixie Davenport. Do you like it?"

"Dixie Davenport. Yeah, it has sort of a bouncy kinda rhythm to it, if you know what I mean. Is it your real name?"

"Of course not. I made it up."

"What's your real name?"

"None of your business."

"Okay. Where you from?"

"A little town outside Louisville, Kentucky. That's why I thought of 'Dixie.' "

Ted turned and grinned at her. "What made you think of 'Davenport'? Was you smoochin' with some guy on a sofa?"

She gave him a cool look with her big blue eyes. "Of course not. I was thinking of Davenport, Iowa."

"But you do smooch?"

"That's none of your business."

"Well, you're pretty enough to be a movie star. I read in the magazines that they do a lotta wild and wicked things out in Hollywood.

380

I guess you might say it's not virgin territory." Again he grinned at her.

"Don't be vulgar."

"If some big director or producer said he'd give you a part in a movie if you'd kiss him—or more—would you do it?"

"That's none of your business. And please keep your eyes on the road. I don't want to get killed."

"Say, you're a cool one on a hot day. And it sure is hot, ain't it?"

"Uh-huh."

"It's so hot you'd just kinda like to take off all your clothes and jump in a pool somewhere, wouldn't you? Don't that sound nice? A nice cool pool on your skin?"

"Uh-huh."

"I know where there's a pool. Wanna go?"

"What's your name?"

"Ted. Ted Spaulding."

"Ted, you're so obvious you're funny. Now, I'm not the type girl you think. And if I do anything wild and wicked, it's going to be in Hollywood where it'll do me some good, not with some red-haired hick who probably wouldn't know what to do if I did take my clothes off."

"Want to bet?"

"Oh? I suppose you're Rudolph Valentino resurrected."

"I know how to pleasure a woman real good."

She looked at him. He was about twenty, she figured, and nice-looking. He was wearing overalls and nothing else.

"Tell you what," he said. "It's three o'clock. There's a motel just outside Des Moines which we ought to get to in about an hour. I'll buy you dinner and pay for the motel. How about it?"

She didn't answer for almost a minute as the Model T bumped over the dusty road. Then she said: "Okay."

At five the next morning, as Ted lay snoring on his stomach in the rumpled bed of Cabin A at the Lazy Daze Motel, Dixie cautiously slipped out the other side and pulled on the white lace panties she had ordered through the Hollywood Love Nite catalog. Then she wriggled into her white dress and slipped on her white shoes. Watching Ted sleep, she went to the chair he'd draped his overalls on and felt for his wallet. She eased it out. The four tens and three singles she folded and stashed in her purse. Taking his car keys from the bed table, she picked up her suitcase and tiptoed to the door.

Two minutes later, Ted woke to the sound of a car starting. He raised his head and looked around sleepily. Through the gauzy curtains he saw his car pulling away from in front of the cabin.

"Hey!"

Galvanized, he jumped out of bed and ran to the window. His Model T was bumping onto the highway in front of the motel, heading west in the pink dawn.

"You bitch!" he yelled, running to the door and opening it, forgetting he had nothing on. "Come back with my car, you bitch!"

His car rolled out of sight.

"Shit!"

"Gentlemen, I've decided that Collingwood Studios' next production—and our first sound film—is going to be *Joan of Arc*."

Joel Collingwood, sitting at the head of the long table in his boardroom, had made the announcement in his usual quiet way. The reception of his announcement was so quiet, however, as to seem deadly.

"Joan of Arc?" repeated Chuck Rosen, Joel's vice-president in charge of finance. "You mean the saint?"

"That's right. It's one of the greatest stories of all time, and Joan is one of the great characters in history."

Rosen looked around the table at the eight others gathered. They looked as dumbfounded as he.

"Joel," he said, "when you hired me, you said you didn't want a yes-man. Okay, I'm going to be a no-man. I think Joan of Arc is a terrible idea for a movie. No, more than terrible: I think it's a lousy idea. That is, unless you want to continue to lose money, in which case it's a great idea. You've made three movies since you bought this studio, and all three have lost money. *The Lady with the Lamp* lost a fortune because no one in America gives a damn about some broad curing cholera in a war they never heard of."

"Florence Nightingale was hardly a broad, and I'm proud of that movie. It got wonderful reviews."

"Sure, from your old man's newspapers."

Joel's mouth tightened. "My father's newspapers do not give me any preferential treatment."

"Oh, come on, Joel, who're you kidding? Your father may tell his reviewers to write what they really think about your movies, but do they want to lose their jobs? And hey, I'm glad they give you great reviews. It's nice having twenty-nine newspapers all over the country in your pocket. But the audience still doesn't come. They didn't come to see Florence Nightingale, and they sure as hell won't come to see Joan of Arc. They want sex and violence, tits and tommy guns, whore and gore. They don't want no goddamn French saints."

Joel's tiny eyes, magnified by his thick lenses, bored into his finance man. "Nevertheless," he said in his thin voice, "they're going to get

Joan of Arc. I'm not Louis B. Mayer, Chuck. I'm not a businessman. I'm an artist. I want to create beautiful films, and if the audience doesn't like them, it's their loss, not mine."

Chuck shrugged. "It's your money."

"Exactly." Joel turned to Barry Marshall, his head of publicity. "Barry, I want you to help me find a girl to play Joan. I want to milk this for a lot of publicity. Call Wendy Fairfax at the *Clarion* and tell her I'm launching a search for the most beautiful, purest girl in America to play Saint Joan. We'll give Wendy the scoop and let her handle the story."

"The purest girl in America," Barry said thoughtfully. His was no easy job, since Collingwood Studios had quickly earned a reputation as a money-losing rich man's toy. "That's a nice angle. The purest girl in America. Yeah, I like that."

"Hold the bunch of grapes in front of your titties, honey. What's your name?"

"Dixie."

"Yeah, Dixie. Now, smile real pretty."

Dixie was posing naked, except for three strategically placed bunches of grapes, in a dingy photography studio on Hollywood Boulevard. She smiled as the photographer squeezed his bulb.

"That's great, Dixie. You've got a real talent for this. And I love your figure, honey. Let's try one without the grapes."

"You mean, you want to take me with nothing on?"

"That's the ticket, Trixie."

"Dixie."

"Sorry, Dixie. In the buff: titties, snatch, and all. Of course, I'll scratch the plate a little bit, make it look sort of blurry down there in the Grand Canyon. It'll be tasteful, you'll see."

"Mr. Evans, I don't pose in the nude."

The photographer ducked his head out from under the black cloth of his camera. "Look, sweetheart," he said, "don't you think it's a little late to be coy? I'll pay you ten dollars more to drop the grapes."

"Make it twenty."

George Evans hesitated. There was no doubt about it: Dixie Whatever-her-name-was oozed sex appeal. As a professional photographer who did pornography on the side, George had photographed dozens of gorgeous girls. Hollywood was filled with gorgeous girls. They came from all over the world, lured by the glamour and glitter of the movies.

But this girl was different. This girl had an aura . . .

"All right, twenty," he said.

Dixie Davenport put the grapes on a table and faced the camera, totally and gloriously nude.

* * *

"Well, Junior's done it again," Wendy Fairfax said as she entered the office of the publisher of the L.A. *Clarion*, Dexter Gray.

"Now what?" Dexter asked, leaning back in his swivel chair.

"The Boy Genius of Santa Monica Boulevard is going to make a movie about—are you ready for this one?—Joan of Arc."

"Jesus Christ."

"He'd be better off doing *Him*." Wendy perched on her boss's desk and reached for a cigarette. A sharp dresser, Wendy was the *Clarion*'s gossip columnist and was syndicated in all twenty-nine Collingwood newspapers. The readership of her daily column, called "Today in Hollywood," was estimated at four million. At thirty-six, Wendy was good-looking, powerful, and smart. She lit her cigarette and exhaled. "You talk to his father all the time," she said. "Doesn't he ever get tired of Junior blowing his money? I mean, I know the Collingwoods are worth zillions, but even so, the way that madman throws it off the ends of trains, you'd think Daddy'd get a teeny bit miffed."

"Curtis has never criticized Joel, at least to me," Dex Gray said. "I get the feeling he's made some sort of deal with the kid. But Joan of Arc? Whew! I can hear that turkey gobbling already."

"Uh-huh. And Barry Marshall tells me the Boy Genius is talking a million-dollar budget. Anyway, Joel's going on a big search to find the purest girl in America to play Joan."

"He can skip looking in L.A."

"Please, boss. Who could be purer than your glamorous gossip columnist?" She batted her big brown eyes. Wendy, a graduate of Vassar, had wanted to be an actress, but, failing that, had started her column instead and found it was a great deal more fun.

"As pure as the driven slush."

"Dorothy Parker you ain't, boss. So how about it? Shall we give it two pages with pictures?"

"Sure. It's better news than the Santa Ana wind," Dex Gray said. "Joan of Arc? My God."

Wendy was off his desk, heading for the door. "By the way, there is some news," she said. "Gil told me they've found another body up in the hills."

Dex Gray perked up. "Another prostie?"

"Yep. Throat slit, all beautifully butchered, Jack the Ripper-style. Welcome to sunny L.A."

Bob Crane was reading a western and listening to his radio when someone knocked on the door of his rented room on Van Ness Avenue. It was a hot night, his windows were open, and Bob was in his undershirt. Setting his Camel in a tin tray, he got up and went to the door. He was a wiry man with black hair and sharp, foxlike features. He opened the door. One of the sexiest blonds he had ever seen was standing in the hallway in her bathrobe.

"Hi," she said in a breathy voice, holding out a cup and giving him her prettiest smile. "I know it's late, but could I borrow some sugar? I ran out."

Crane couldn't take his eyes off her. "Uh, sure. Just a minute."

He crossed the room to a two-burner hot plate by the window. He picked up a box of sugar cubes and brought it back to the door. "All I've got are cubes. Is that okay?"

"Oh, sure. That's real kind of you. I'll pay you back tomorrow."

"That's all right. Are you new here?"

"Uh-huh. I rented the room across the hall. It seems like a nice boardinghouse."

"It's okay. You in the movies?"

"Well, I'm trying to be. I haven't had much luck yet. It's awfully hard breaking in."

He raised an eyebrow. "I wouldn't think you'd have much trouble."

"Well, thanks, that's sweet of you, but you don't know how many girls there are trying to do it."

"Yeah, I do know. I'm a cameraman."

Dixie's smile became even warmer. "Oh, yes, Miss Kendall, the landlady, mentioned that. She said you're such a nice tenant . . . This was after she gave me a long song and dance about not liking movie people."

"Well, you know how it is. Ten years ago, they had signs all over town saying, 'No movie people or dogs.' "

"Isn't that awful? You'd think we were all trash. Just because a few people are, doesn't mean we all are, does it?" She smiled slightly. "Well, I mustn't bother you anymore. So glad to meet you, Mr. . . . oh, we haven't met, have we?"

"Uh, Bob. Bob Crane."

"And I'm Dixie Davenport."

"Uh, what did you want the sugar for, Dixie?"

"I was making coffee."

"I've got some already made if you'd—"

Dixie lowered her voice. "Miss Kendall said we're not allowed in other tenants' rooms."

"What Miss Kendall doesn't know won't hurt her."

Dixie slipped into the room, giving him a smile that would have melted stainless steel. "I guess you're right, Bob."

*   *   *

The wind in the hills fluffed the girl's blond hair. Her naked body was sprawled in a ditch not far from Cahuenga Pass in the Hollywood Hills. Her throat had been slit and she had been partially disemboweled.

"Pretty, isn't it?" Cliff Parker asked. Now chief of detectives of the LAPD, he was the same man who had started his distinguished police career twenty-two years earlier by helping Curtis Collingwood solve the Carl Klein murder case on General Channing's yacht. Cliff and two other policemen gazed down at the butchered corpse as a police photographer snapped her from all angles. *Clarion* reporter Gil Amster and six others waited a few feet away to get a close look. "Any idea who she was?"

"We found her purse," Detective Brian Phillips answered. "Her name was Trudy Whitehead and she was a would-be actress turning tricks between bit parts. Same story as the other three. And we found the same calling card. With no fingerprints."

He held up a silver face mask.

"Hey, Chief!" Gil Amster yelled. "That means this is another Phantom murder."

Chief Parker looked back at the curly-haired reporter, who had coined the phrase "The Phantom of Hollywood" to describe the unknown murderer who left a mask as his trademark.

"Looks like," he said.

"Hot damn!"

The reporters were off and running to their cars to phone in the story.

The wind continued to ruffle Trudy Whitehead's dyed blond hair. Four years earlier, she had come to Hollywood from Montana to find stardom.

She was now with the stars.

44

WENDY FAIRFAX drove her Model J boat-tail Duesenberg speed-
ster through the lighted white-brick gateposts of 1141 Summit Drive in
Beverly Hills, a short way below Charlie Chaplin's mansion and Pick-
fair. The "Deuzie," which had set Wendy back ten thousand dollars,
was her passion: in car-mad L.A., the sleek convertible with its alu-
minum coachwork and its 265-hp, overhead-camshaft, straight-eight
engine was a show-stopper. She headed up the driveway toward the
Spanish-style mansion ahead of her. Fairhill had been built ten years
before by an orange-juice king, but was being rented by Joel Collingwood for the staggering sum of twenty-five hundred dollars a month.
Since Joel kept to himself, avoiding the Hollywood social swim, and
Wendy had never been inside Fairhill, she was looking forward to the
evening. She had interviewed him that morning about his search for
an unknown girl to play Joan of Arc and, rather to her surprise, he
had asked her to dinner. She had needed no prompting to accept.

She pulled up in front and got out. Dressed in a black Chanel, her
mouth a blaze of scarlet, her black hair cut in severe bangs just above
her brown eyes, she walked to the front door, flanked by elaborate
iron lanterns. As she waited, she looked over the grounds. Set on seven
acres were elaborate gardens and fountains softly illuminated in the
twilight. Wendy thought the place was magical, but then, Joel, the Boy
Genius, liked magic. Weren't movies magic?

The door was opened by Joel himself. He was wearing what had
become his trademark: white flannel slacks and an Italian silk shirt open
at the throat, with a sporty kerchief tied around his neck. He towered
above Wendy, looking down at her through his Coke-bottle lenses.
"Welcome to Fairhill," he said in his soft voice.

She entered the large entrance hall, taking in with a glance the
coffered wooden ceiling and diamond marble floor.

"I probably should have warned you," he continued, leading her
toward the living room, "I live on a rather odd diet. I'm a vegetarian
and I eat no fat at all—mostly salads and wheat and fruit. I hope you
don't mind."

"Not at all. I could stand to lose a few pounds." She stopped in surprise. The huge living room was totally empty. "Has something happened to the stock market I don't know about?"

"I beg your pardon?"

"Where's the furniture? Was it repossessed by the finance company?"

"Oh," he said vaguely, and she realized his mind was elsewhere. "When I rented the house, the furniture was all so ugly—department-store reproductions—that I put it all in a warehouse. And while my movies are losing money, I've taken sort of a vow of poverty."

She smiled. "Unusual for a Collingwood."

"Actually, the money I live on comes from someone who wasn't a Collingwood at all."

"Who was that?"

"There used to be a line of dresses called Countess Zita."

"Yes, I remember them when I was a kid."

"There actually was a Countess Zita, who lived with my great-great-grandfather, Felix de Meyer. Back then they caused a scandal because they never got married, mainly for religious reasons. When Felix died, he left Zita several million dollars. And when she died in 1910, she left her entire estate to me, which is what I live on. I know everyone in this town thinks I've got money to burn, but it's not exactly true. Besides, I like to live uncluttered."

"This is certainly uncluttered."

He grinned. "The clutter is in my head," he said, tapping his temple. "My movies are in my head. My movies are all that matter. There are some chairs in the kitchen. We can go there and talk."

He led her into another empty room. "This is the dining room," he said. "The table was ghastly."

"You have no servants?"

"No. I live very simply."

"Mind if I put this in my column?"

"Do you think anyone would be interested?"

"Are you kidding? You're a Collingwood. You sneeze and people are interested."

He paused at the door to the butler's pantry and scowled. "My father used to say that, and he was quoting his father. I guess a lot of people would like to be Collingwoods, but when I was a kid I used to pray when I went to sleep that I'd wake up someone else."

"Why?"

"Because my father hated me."

He swung open the door and led her through a butler's pantry into a large shiny kitchen where, at last, there was some furniture: a wooden table and four wooden chairs. Two places had been set at the table with Mexican plates and colored Mexican glasses.

"Would you like some wine?" Joel asked. "I get it from my father's bootlegger. It's a white Burgundy."

"Yes, thanks, I'd love some. Say, what are those masks?"

She had caught sight of the dozen or so masks hung around the kitchen walls. Some were silver, some gold, some sequined and feathered.

"Oh, I collect them," Joel said, opening the refrigerator and pulling out a bottle of wine. "I've always been fascinated by masks, ever since I was a kid. Maybe because I was never very happy with myself as a child, I wanted to hide behind masks and pretend I was someone else."

"Are you happy with yourself now?"

"Oh, yes. At least reasonably happy."

As he began uncorking the bottle, Wendy eyed the masks. Then she glanced at a rack of butcher knives near the sink. Then she saw Joel watching her with his strange eyes.

Wendy Fairfax suddenly experienced a sensation she had not expected on that balmy Beverly Hills evening: spine-tingling fear.

The head of a giant dog loomed over the entrance to Barkies' Sandwich Shop and its enormous paws flanked its sides. At eleven that night, Wendy pulled up in front of the popular hamburger joint on Sunset Boulevard, parked her Duesenberg, and hurried inside. Barkies' was one of many shops and stands going up in L.A. that looked like animals or windmills, giving the town its odd, hokey, movie fantasy look that already was eliciting snickers of derision from the sophisticated. Barkies' was also a favorite hangout for the press, and Gil Amster was seated at an end booth eating french fries drowned in catsup. Wendy slid into the seat opposite him.

"So, how was the Boy Wonder?" asked Gil, a good-looking native Angelino.

"Spooky. Also interesting. He's already interviewed over fifty girls to play Joan of Arc, but he hasn't found what he's looking for yet."

"If he's looking for a virgin, he'd better try North Dakota."

"What makes you think they've got 'em there?"

A pretty blond waitress came up. "Hi, Miss Fairfax. Want something?"

"God, yes. I'm starved. Bring me a medium cheeseburger, fries, and a Coke."

"Sure, Miss Fairfax."

"Got any movie work yet?"

"Oh, no, but I'm still trying."

"I now know why the Boy Genius is so skinny," Wendy continued after the waitress went to the counter. "Dinner was a monastic fast: bulgur wheat, salad, and strawberries."

"I'm glad I wasn't invited."

"He's strange. There's hardly any furniture in the place, which is huge. But, Gil, there's something even weirder."

"What?"

She leaned across the chrome-edged table and lowered her voice. "He collects masks."

Gil Amster frowned as he shoved the final french fry into his mouth. "What kind of masks?"

"All kinds. Face masks. Like your pal the Phantom."

Gil considered this, then shrugged. "So?"

"So? What if Joel Collingwood were a mass murderer? It would be the story of the century."

"Hey, baby, you're jumping to a few conclusions."

"Maybe, maybe not. There's a wacko streak a mile wide in the Collingwood family. Alicia Collingwood's brother, Jimmie, was a murderer and Curtis Collingwood's sister, Alma, is a certified nymphomaniac. Who's to say Joel isn't as nutty as they? He sure as hell isn't normal by my definition of the word."

Gil opened his third pack of Lucky Strikes for the day. "Are you serious?" he said, banging out a butt on his knuckle. "Do you really think Joel Collingwood is the Phantom of Hollywood?"

"I'm saying it's a possibility."

"Jesus Christ." He lit the cigarette. "It sure as hell would be a big story." He exhaled, sending a cloud of smoke up to the grease-stained ceiling. "I don't know if the Collingwood papers would print it, but it would be one helluva story. And wouldn't I love to smear a Collingwood with muck."

"Leave politics out of it."

"Why? They've got too much money, too much everything. Spread the wealth. It's what this country needs."

"Okay, okay, get off your socialist soapbox, you big lunk. Anyway, what are you going to do about it?"

Gil Amster thought a moment.

"Maybe I'll start watching Joel Collingwood."

"Bobby," Dixie Davenport purred, running her finger over the assistant cameraman's sharp nose, "do you think I could come watch you work one day? Since I can't seem to be hired to act in a movie, I'd love to at least watch one being made."

"Sure, baby," Crane said, lying next to her on his bed. For four nights in a row Dixie had tiptoed across the upstairs hall in the board-inghouse, making Bob very happy indeed. He ran his hand lovingly over her wonderful breasts. "But maybe I can do better than that. They're shooting a big French Revolution scene Thursday and need a lot of extras. I'll talk to Jeeter Smith—he's in charge of casting. How would you like to be a French peasant?"

"Oh, Bobby, that's so exciting! Oh, I just adore you!"

She was on top of him, kissing him fervently.

"Jesus, baby," he puffed, "if being an extra does this to you, what if you got a speaking part?"

She pushed her left breast into his face as she pressed her sex against his belly. "Just you wait and see," she whispered. "Just you wait and see."

"Who's the blond?" asked Willard Cornell, the director of *The Devil's Daughter*, the film about the French Revolution being shot at Paramount.

"Bob Crane's new girlfriend," Jeeter Smith replied. "He asked if I'd hire her."

"Christ, Jeeter, you know I don't like that."

"I know, but Bob's a good guy and, well, look at her."

"Yeah, I'm looking. She's fucking gorgeous. Jesus, with all the beautiful poontang out here, it's hard as hell to keep it in your pants."

"I know what you mean."

"Bring her over. Introduce me."

Jeeter made his way through the crowd of extras standing before a set representing the Bastille. The electricians were having some trouble with the lighting, and shooting had been delayed for a half-hour.

"Excuse me, Miss, uh . . ."

"Miss Davenport."

"Yes. Mr. Cornell, the director, wants to meet you."

"Oh." Smile. "With pleasure."

Dixie had pushed her breasts as far up into her peasant costume as she could, and she followed Jeeter through the crowd, her bosoms merrily bouncing. When they came up to Willard's canvas chair, Jeeter said, "Mr. Cornell, Miss Davenport."

Willard, a short, dumpy man in his fifties, inspected her. "If any French peasant had displayed as much bosom as you, Miss Davenport, I doubt it would have been the Bastille they stormed."

"The wardrobe lady told me to 'show it all.' "

"Uh-huh. You certainly follow instructions. Well, so much for historical accuracy. Do you have any acting experience?"

"No, sir. This is my first day. This is my first time in a studio, even, and it's *so* interesting."

"Huh. Well, you're a very pretty young girl, Miss Davenport, and I wish you luck."

"Thank you, Mr. Cornell."

The chief electrician came up. "We're set to go now, Mr. Cornell."

"Good. All right, places, everyone. We're going for a take." As Dixie hurried back onto the set, Cornell said to Jeeter, "Set up a screen test for that girl. I'd like to see if she can act."

"Right."

One of Hollywood's leading directors of historical films, Cornell knew Joel Collingwood was considering him to direct the lavishly budgeted *Joan of Arc.* He doubted that Dixie Davenport was the purest girl in America, but she was certainly one of the most beautiful. If the camera liked her, she just might possibly be the Joan of Arc Joel was looking for.

And if Willard brought Joel Joan of Arc, Joel could hardly refuse him the movie.

"Who is she?" Joel asked, awed. He was sitting in the screening room below his office with Willard Cornell. Before him a girl in a white robe was praying at an altar.

"Her name's Dixie Davenport," Willard replied, sucking his cigar.

Joel winced. "That could be changed. But she's extraordinary. Look at those eyes!"

"The camera really eats her up, doesn't it?"

"I've never seen such . . . sensuousness combined with such innocence. Has she ever acted before?"

"Nope. She was an extra on my set the other day. I spotted her and thought she might be exciting. I told her to pretend she was a mother praying for her child to recover from some crazy movie disease. That's all I said, and look at her. She's making it all up. I thought you should see it."

"Yes, and I won't forget this, Willard. What's her voice like?"

"Kind of breathy with a hint of a Southern accent, but she could be trained with a voice coach. I think she's a natural."

"I'm almost afraid to ask this, but . . . is she a virgin?"

The screen test came to an end and the projectionist turned up the lights before rewinding.

"No," Willard said, ashing his cigar in the stand-up tray. "She's shacked up with one of my assistant cameramen."

"Damn."

"Pardon me, Joel, but you're casting a movie, not looking for a sacrifice to the gods. How many virgins are there anymore? Virgins went out with Mary Pickford. You'd have better luck finding a unicorn."

Joel chewed nervously on his knuckle. He had already gotten so much publicity looking for the purest girl in America, it might be a disaster to cast someone a bit shopworn. And yet the girl had just the look he had been dreaming of.

"Run it again, Phil," he said to the projectionist.

The lights lowered and the girl with the luminous face again flickered onto the silver screen.

Gil Amster was nodding off at the wheel of his two-door Dodge. It was almost three in the morning, and Gil had been parked across the street from Joel's Summit Drive gateway since midnight. The vigil he had been keeping for the past two nights was wrecking his sleep schedule. He had begun to think this was all a crazy flight of fancy generated by a gossip columnist's pressure-cooker imagination.

A minute later, a light-blue Mercedes-Benz four-door sedan swung out of the twin brick gateposts and started down Summit. The headlights sweeping across Gil's face woke him up. He quickly checked his watch, then started his car. By the time he started moving, the blue Mercedes was almost out of sight. Gil floored his accelerator. Seeing the Mercedes turn right on Sunset Boulevard, he followed it.

But Gil's Dodge was no match for the Nürburg 460 of 1928, designed by the great Dr. Porsche himself and the last Mercedes-Benz to be built at Mannheim. Whoever was driving it took off. As Gil's speedometer strained to hit sixty-five, the Mercedes vanished in the night.

Randy Bates was climbing the hills in Benedict Canyon with his Boy Scout troop when he slipped down the side of a gully into a clump of brush. He was pushing himself up when he felt something stiff and cool. He looked down at a human arm. Screaming, he crawled out of the gully.

"Mr. Crawford, Mr. Crawford, there's a body down there!"

Jack Crawford, the scoutmaster, hurried over to the sobbing boy. "Randy, what's wrong?"

"There's a dead lady down there! She's been all cut up, and I *touched* her!"

As the other scouts filed to the edge of the gully, Mr. Crawford made his way down the slope. Parting the brush, he felt a hot rush of bile forcing its way up his throat.

Spilled on the ground was a pretty girl with light brown hair. She was naked except for her silk stockings and her left shoe, which was cocked half off at a crazy angle. Her throat had been cut and one of her breasts sliced off.

Resting on her stomach was a silver mask.

45

GIL AMSTER finished brushing his teeth in his Rexford Drive home in Beverly Hills. Entering the bedroom, he climbed in bed next to his wife, Wendy Fairfax, who retained her maiden name for her gossip column.

"God, I'm tired," Gil said. "Three nights watching Joel Collingwood's driveway has worn me out."

Wendy asked nervously, "What are you going to do, Gil?"

"The girl's name was Ellen Busby, and the best estimate of the time of her murder was around four this morning. By the way, she was a would-be movie star. Okay, Joel left his house at three this morning, so it's certainly conceivable he murdered the girl. Plus, he collects masks. None of which proves he's a murderer, but I'm certainly going to tell the police about it tomorrow."

"No!" Wendy almost shouted.

"Honey, I can't watch Joel Collingwood myself. I have a job. Let the police stake out his house."

"I knew this would happen. I could kill myself for telling you about the masks."

"What do you mean?"

"I realized after I told you, you can't say anything to the police about Joel Collingwood. In the first place, he's probably not the murderer. But more important, he's Curtis Collingwood's heir, and when Curtis Collingwood finds out you reported his son to the police—and he'll find out—he'll fire both of us. Worse than that, he'll blackball us from working for any other paper. Believe me, Collingwood can play rough. Neither of us would ever work again."

Gil stared at her in disbelief. "Honey, we're talking about murder. Forget what might happen to our jobs—"

"No, I won't forget! Curtis Collingwood likes me, he pays me thirty-five thousand a year, which is damned good money, and I'm becoming a power in this town. I'm not going to jeopardize that by spreading rumors about his son."

"But, Wendy, I'm a reporter!"

"You're also a husband and a father. Our first responsibility is to our children. Just forget I ever said anything about Joel Collingwood's masks. Just forget Joel Collingwood. And stay away from the police."

"I can't believe what I'm hearing."

"Well, believe."

"You're asking me to violate every principle I have as a reporter and a citizen."

"Forget principle! Gil, you and I are doing very nicely. We have good jobs we enjoy, we have a beautiful house, two beautiful daughters. We're not going to take on the Collingwood family! They're too powerful." She reached over and turned off her bed lamp. "End of conversation." She turned on her side, her back to her husband.

"No, it's not 'end of conversation.' "

"Gil, do you love me?"

"Of course I love you."

"Do you love your children?"

"Of course, but . . ."

"Then it's the end of the conversation. You're not going to the police."

"*You're* what's wrong with this country," her husband exclaimed angrily. "You let families like the Collingwoods get away with murder—literally, in this case—because you're afraid of them."

"You're damned right I'm afraid of them. Get off your soapbox, turn out your light, and if you don't like this country, don't vote for Hoover."

"I'd vote for Lenin before I'd vote for Hoover."

"Then vote for Lenin, but turn out your light."

Gil glared at her, started to say something else, then turned out his bed lamp. But, tired as he was, he didn't go to sleep. He knew Wendy was right, but principles were involved and he couldn't forget his principles and live with himself.

Or could he?

Dixie Davenport sat on the leather sofa in Joel Collingwood's reception room and wondered if the lightning she had dreamed of since she saw her first movie at age ten was about to strike. When Willard Cornell had told her Joel was considering her for Joan of Arc, she had thought at first it was some sort of bad joke. But then the phone call had come from Collingwood Studios, asking her to be there at ten the next morning. Was it a dream, possibly every pretty girl in America's dream, sitting in the office of a Hollywood producer?

"Mr. Collingwood will see you now," said the tall secretary in the polka-dot dress, who had just appeared in the door. Dixie stood up, giving a nervous tug to the skirt of her white dress. Some inner voice had told her to wear white. White was the color of brides, the color of innocence, perhaps even the color of French saints.

Dixie went into Joel's office, which overlooked Santa Monica Boulevard. The studio, built in a bastardized Mission style like so much of Los Angeles, had stucco walls on the outside, but inside the walls were heavy rough plaster. On these walls hung large framed photos of the stars of Joel's previous movies. But she wasn't looking at movie-star photos. She was looking at the producer. Joel was coming around his desk, his magnified eyes glued on the blond girl in the white dress.

"Miss Davenport? I'm Joel Collingwood."

"Hi."

He shook her hand. "Please sit down, Dixie. Would you like some coffee?"

"No, thanks. I'll take a Coke, if you have one."

Joel signaled his secretary and she left. He helped Dixie into a chair in front of his desk, then went around and sat down, facing her.

"Tell me about yourself, Dixie. By the way, is that your real name?"

"No. I made it up."

"What's your real name?"

"It's awful and ugly."

"I'd still like to know it."

"Beulah Snodgrass. See what I mean?"

"Mmm, I see why you changed it. Where are you from?"

"Kentucky. My father owns a gas station in a little town called Pine Grove. It's outside Louisville. He . . ."

"Yes?"

She bit her lip. "He's a drinker, and . . . oh, I shouldn't be telling you this."

"Why?"

"When your office phoned, I told myself to make up a decent background so you wouldn't think I'm cheap. After all, your family is so grand—"

"My family has had its share of people not so grand. There's a bank robber in my family, and a prostitute, not to mention a murderer. So don't be ashamed of your family, Dixie. It couldn't be much worse than mine."

She looked at him in surprise. "That's funny," she said. "I thought you'd be sorta stuck up, but you're not."

Joel smiled slightly. "I haven't got much to be stuck up about."

Miss Baird brought in the Coca-Cola, which she handed to Dixie. Then she left.

"You were saying about your father, Dixie?"

"We were poor. Awfully poor. My ma died when I was ten, and then my pa . . . well, when he drinks, he gets mean, and he used to beat me. He used to do other things too."

"Like what?"

She frowned. "I'd rather not talk about it. At any rate, everything was so ugly, and ever since I can remember, I used to ask myself, why me? Why can't I have something beautiful in my life? A beautiful dress, or something. And then I discovered the movies, and suddenly there was something beautiful in my life."

"And that's when you decided to come to Hollywood?"

She took a sip of the Coke. "Oh, not at first. But I kept looking in the mirror and I said: You're pretty, why not go where the pretty people go? And then, finally . . ." Again she hesitated.

"Finally what?"

"Oh, Mr. Collingwood, I shouldn't tell you this. You'll think—"

"I'll think you're honest if you tell me the truth, Dixie, and that could be important for both of us."

Tears welled in her blue eyes as she looked at him. "One night Pa got drunk and he came in my bedroom and . . . he tried to make love to me. My own father! And that's when I knew I had to leave."

She's fabulous, he was thinking. She's not only gorgeous and sexy, but there's a certain quality about her . . .

She opened her purse and pulled out a hanky, dabbing her eyes. "Well, now you know what I am, and it's not very nice. But I want beautiful things in my life, Mr. Collingwood. I want beautiful clothes and beautiful cars and houses, because everything in my life has been ugly."

"You may not believe this, Dixie," he said softly, "but my childhood was ugly too, and I used to dream about beautiful things. So maybe we can make beautiful things together."

He stood up. "The first thing I want to do is get some first-rate photographs of you. I'm going to turn you over to my chief makeup man, Ernie Lawson, and my costumier, Burt Karnovsky. They'll prepare you for a photo session this afternoon. It'll take a lot of time and you may think it's a big fuss, but believe me, good still photos are a must. I've got the best photographer in town coming over to shoot you, a man named George Evans, and . . ."

She didn't hear the rest. She wanted to scream. She had taken the gamble of telling the truth about her background, or almost the truth. She could feel the lightning sizzling around her, ready to strike. She could tell Joel Collingwood was impressed with her.

And now everything was going to be ruined, because of all the photographers in L.A., Joel had picked the man who had photographed her in the nude.

She had never seen such beautiful clothes in her life. She had spent an hour in makeup with Ernie Lawson, who had told her he had seldom worked on a face that needed less fixing. After another hour her hair had been done in a way she had never imagined for herself: parted in the middle, then straight down on both sides, ending in a soft inward roll that made her look positively glamorous. In Wardrobe, Burt Karnovsky and the wardrobe mistress searched through dozens of dresses, finally choosing a slinky silver lamé evening gown cut wide and low in front. The dress fitted her perfect figure well, but Brenda tightened it with clothespins in the back.

Then she was taken to George Evans.

A tall, thin man with a homely face and brown hair, he watched the vision of loveliness walking toward his camera and thought: Where have I seen her before?

"George, this is Dixie Davenport," Burt said. "Joel wants the works."

Photographer and model stared at each other. Now he knew who she was. "How are you, Miss Davenport?"

Dixie gave him a defiant smile. "Fine."

"The dress does wonders for you. My, my, yes indeed. Burt, do you want to leave us alone?"

"Sure."

"Now, Trixie—"

"Dixie."

"Oh, yes, excuse me. Dixie. I don't want to use any props"—he smiled slightly—"like grapes, for instance." Her eyes widened in fear. "I just want to concentrate on your face, because as you know, they say your face is your fortune out here. Though other parts of the body have been known to be photographed . . ." He paused until Burt had left the room. "Well, Dixie, you've come a long way since last we met. Joel Collingwood himself. You may just hit the jackpot."

"Do you still have those pictures?" she whispered.

"Oh, yes. I liked them so much, I put a very high price on them. Very high. Except I think the price has just gone higher."

"How much?"

"Well, you'd want the glass plates, and that would cost you dearly."

"I haven't got much money."

"I know that. But Joel Collingwood has all the money in the world. So right now, let's not talk price. After all, if he doesn't hire you, the plates aren't worth much, are they? But if he does hire you—if Dixie

Davenport plays Joan of Arc—what a laugh that would be. Those plates would be worth a fortune. So we'll wait. And meanwhile, it's in both our interests to make these pictures dazzle. So think beautiful, sweetie. Think real beautiful. We've come a long, long way from the grapes, hmm?''

As Joel stared at the proofs the next day, his heart pounded. She was radiant. He didn't care what her background was. The fact that she came from dirt, that her father had tried to rape her, gave her an earthiness that offset nicely her ethereal beauty. Hadn't Joan of Arc been a peasant girl, her bare feet stuck firmly in the mud of Domremy as her ears heard the voices of angels? Dixie's feet were in the muck of a rural gas station. Dixie Davenport—he'd have to change that name—he would turn her into a symbol of beauty. He had the money and power to create the perfect woman, the ultimate movie star.

At last Joel Collingwood had a live doll to play with.

Charlotte Collingwood, Joel's beautiful younger half-sister, neatly sliced off the top of her three-minute egg. "Who is this Laura Lord Joel's bringing to my engagement party?" she asked her parents. They were gathered in the breakfast room of the Burlingame mansion.

"I know," giggled her younger sister, Fiona. "I read about her in Wendy Fairfax's column. She's Joel's big discovery for the part of Joan of Arc. I saw her picture, too. She's real sexy."

"Fiona! What a horrible word," her mother said.

"Oh, Mumsie, really. You're still in the Dark Ages. There's nothing wrong with 'sexy.' Everybody's saying it."

"You're not 'everybody,' dear."

"I know," she sighed. "I'm a Collingwood. Bore, bore, bore."

"Fiona," her father said, "if you're so bored with your family, I'd be delighted to stop your allowance."

Fiona, a dark beauty like her mother, rolled her eyes. "Oh, rats. I take it back. Anyway, do you think this Laura Lord is Joel's girlfriend? Wouldn't that be the bees' knees?"

"Wendy Fairfax told Dex Gray," Curtis said, spreading Oxford marmalade on his toast as the butler poured coffee, "that her name used to be Dixie Davenport."

Fiona shrieked with laughter. "Oh, I love it! Dixie Davenport! That's so cheap, it's incredible!"

"Mumsie, is she going to be an embarrassment at my party?" Charlotte asked.

Alicia shot her husband a worried look. "I certainly hope not."

"Joel is spending a fortune on her," Curtis said. "Vocal coaches, diction lessons. He even hired an English actress down on her luck to teach her manners. So we may all be surprised."

"Oh, she'll be a real 'laid-y.' " Fiona giggled.

"Hollywood," Alicia sniffed, stirring her coffee. "Everyone's crazy for the movies, but if you ask me, they're ruining the morals of this country."

"Oh, Mumsie, you're such a fuddy-duddy," Fiona said. "I'd love to be a movie star. Do you think Joel would give me a part in one of his movies?"

"Over my dead body," Curtis said. "One child in the movie business is enough."

"Do you think Joel's movie will be sexy?"

"About Joan of Arc?" her mother said. "Well, hardly."

"The trouble with Joel's movies is that they're not sexy enough," Fiona went on. "That Florence Nightingale thing! Bore, bore, bore."

"The trouble with Joel's movies is," her father sighed, "that they lose money."

46

AT sixty-two, Mrs. Belgrave was an imposing grande dame of the old school who had acted on the London stage with Sir Henry Irving, the first actor in the history of England to receive a knighthood. Mrs. Belgrave still wore ankle-length dresses like Queen Mary and, again like the British monarch, carried herself with erect dignity.

"Now, my dear," she said to the newly baptized Laura Lord, "when you pick up your teacup, you also pick up the saucer. Like so."

They were sitting on Soundstage B at the Collingwood Studios, and a tea tray had been placed on an orange crate between them. As Mrs. Belgrave picked up her cup and saucer, Laura—who was still not sure she didn't prefer Dixie Davenport to the "classier" name Joel had dreamed up for her—mimicked her mentor's gesture exactly.

"Very good. And we *will* remember not to stick out our little finger, which is unspeakably vulgar and shows we really don't come from the best circles."

"But I don't, Mrs. Belgrave," Laura sighed. She found these etiquette lessons boring beyond belief. "My father owns a gas station."

"That doesn't matter, my dear. Mr. Collingwood wants you to feel at ease in any social situation, and that is why he has hired me. I will teach you things that refined people know as a matter of course. Now, to review this morning's lesson. We are at a dinner party. The footman—or waiter, as the case may be—serves us the fish course. Do we thank the footman?"

"Uh . . . no."

"And why not, pray?"

"Because service is to be assumed, and good servants should be invisible. Though it seems awfully mean, Mrs. Belgrave, not to say something, just to assume the poor guy isn't there. It's not very democratic."

"Being democratic has very little to do with successful dinner parties, my dear. And must we say 'guy'? It's a peculiarly unattractive word."

Laura sighed and repressed an intense urge to say "shit," which would have sent Mrs. Belgrave flying right out of the soundstage.

But she went along. She was going along with everything Joel was doing to her. She realized he was trying to mold her into something she was not—a lady—and she supposed it wasn't bad for her if she, in fact, did become a movie star. She had read enough fan magazines to know that the stars, with their incredible salaries and worldwide popularity, were becoming the new elite of Los Angeles, whatever their backgrounds. As the twentieth century neared its fourth decade, the entertainment industry was becoming increasingly important in the lives of everyone; movie stars were gaining the prestige that, a half-century earlier, had been reserved for titans of industry.

But Laura wasn't a star yet, and these etiquette lessons seemed somehow to be putting the cart before the horse. Yet Joel had insisted on them. She really didn't understand why.

She also wondered if he was ever going to make a pass at her. She wished he would. Rather to her surprise, she was finding the skinny, owl-eyed Joel Collingwood increasingly attractive.

"I'm so nervous," she said three days later as she sat beside Joel in his light blue Mercedes. They were heading up the Pacific Coast Highway for San Francisco.

"There's no need to be," he said, gripping the wheel with both thin hands. "My family is a little stuffy, but they're nice. You'll see. Now, let's review the cast of characters. My stepmother's name is . . . ?"

"Alicia. She's the former Alicia Lopez, and she's your father's cousin."

"That's right. And Father is . . . ?"

"Curtis Collingwood. His father was Archer Collingwood, who was killed in the earthquake with your great-grandparents."

"Excellent. And my two half-sisters?"

"Charlotte is twenty-two and engaged to her cousin Alistair Brett. And Fiona is nineteen and at Vassar."

"Bravo. Then there's Alistair's mother, who is . . . ?"

"Your Aunt Alma."

"You've learned your lines well."

"Do rich people always marry their cousins?"

Joel smiled. He found many of Laura's observations wonderfully insightful. "Well, I think rich people tend to stick with their own kind."

"Poor people stick with their own kind because they haven't got much choice. But when poor people marry their cousins, they have half-wit babies."

"Well, there are a lot of rich half-wits."

They drove awhile in silence.

"Mr. Collingwood, may I ask a question?"

"Sure. And why not call me Joel?"

"Okay, Joel. Why are you taking me all the way up here to meet your family?"

"My father has never been particularly enthusiastic about my being a film producer. He's had a policy with his newspapers to treat my movies as if I weren't a Collingwood because he doesn't want to be accused of favoritism, the way William Randolph Hearst plays up Marion Davies' movies just because she's his mistress. I'll admit that most of Father's reviewers like my films, or at least give me good reviews, but I suppose they worry about getting fired if they don't. Anyway, Barry Marshall is planning a massive publicity campaign to make you known all over the country as the girl who's going to play Joan of Arc—"

"What?"

"I said, you're going to play Joan of Arc."

"Oh, my God. Is it true? You're not kidding me? The part is mine?"

"Yes."

"Oh. I think I'm going to scream or faint or something. Why didn't you *tell* me?"

"I just did."

She reached over, threw her arms around him, and kissed his cheek. "Thank you. Thank you, thank you, thank you!"

"Watch out, I'm driving."

She released him.

"At any rate, I want my father to meet you and like you because I'm hoping he'll give up his policy of nonfavoritism about my movies and really throw his twenty-nine papers behind our campaign to make Laura Lord the best-known name in America after Charles Lindbergh."

"Oh, Mr. Collingwood, this is so exciting—"

"Joel."

"I mean, Joel." She smiled at him. "You're the only man I've ever known who's been good to me, and I really mean that. Every other man I've ever known has just wanted to use me."

"I'm using you in another way."

"But it's a beautiful way. Oh, Joel, you're the most beautiful thing that's ever happened to me."

Again he was silent, though she noticed his face looked rather strained, as if some emotional storm were going on inside his head. Then he said in his usual soft, unemotional tone, "I also want you to meet my family because someday you may be one of them."

That he had given her the part of Joan of Arc had floored her. But the suggestion that she might one day be Mrs. Joel Collingwood, one of the richest women in America, struck her with the force of a hurricane. Was this the real reason for the etiquette lessons, the voice coaches, the endless fittings, the hours with the hairdressers and cosmeticians? Was he molding not only a movie star but also the wife of his dreams?

"I don't know what to say," she whispered.

"Then say nothing."

Beulah Snodgrass of Pine Grove, Kentucky, stared out the windshield at the passing coastline of California.

But what she was seeing was a swirling galaxy of shooting stars, her wildest, most improbable dreams coming true.

Red Carter's Orchestra, featuring "The Smoothest Music West of the Rockies," segued into "He Loves and She Loves," the hit song from the new Gershwin musical, *Funny Face*, starring Fred and Adele Astaire, and the cream of San Francisco society glided over the temporary dance floor set up inside the gaily striped yellow-and-white tent on the Collingwoods' rear lawn. Six twelve-foot wooden torchères were posted around the tent, each crowned with a breathtaking explosion of white and pink flowers, all grown in Alicia's ten-acre garden. Candles glowed in hurricane lamps on the white-clothed tables as fifty waiters stood by, ready to begin serving the seven-course meal at ten. It was a balmy autumn evening, and a half-moon hung over San Francisco Bay completing the mood of romance.

"What a wonderful time to be alive," Charlotte Collingwood sighed, leaning her head on her fiancé's broad shoulder as they danced to the dreamy music. "I think I have to be the happiest girl in the world."

"And I'm the luckiest guy in the world," said Alistair Brett, the eldest child of Alma and Sebastian Brett. "You really are beautiful tonight, Charlotte."

"Who wouldn't be beautiful when you're as much in love as I am? And I love my ring!"

She took another look at her engagement ring, a Burmese ruby encircled with diamonds that Alistair had bought at Felix de Meyer, the jewelry store still owned by the family. She was wearing a pale blue Chanel evening gown that she had bought at the main de Meyer and Kinsolving store, still on Union Square fifty years after Emma had built it.

Alistair, who had long-jawed, Anglo-Saxon good looks, noticed a couple come out of the house onto the rear terrace. "Here's Mother," he said in a tone a few degrees above a snarl. "And Philippe. God, it's so embarrassing."

"Sweetie, don't be embarrassed. Aunt Alma likes young men. Everybody knows it."

"Yes, but does she have to marry them? It's as if she buys them. It's disgusting. He's twenty-four and she's practically sixty."

"Don't let her hear you say that. Anyway, he seems pleasant enough, and he's nice-looking and has a French title. Nothing to be embarrassed about. If you're looking for embarrassment, wait till we meet Laura Lord, née Dixie Davenport."

"Listen, I'm looking forward to meeting her! Where are they?"

"She and Joel are staying in town at the Mark Hopkins, so they may be a bit late."

"If she's as beautiful as her pictures, she must be a real knockout."

She gave him a lidded look. "Don't get too interested. I'm the only girl in your life tonight, remember?"

He smiled. "I like you when you're jealous."

The Marquise de Rochefort, the former Alma Collingwood Brett, sucked on her black lacquer cigarette holder and surveyed the party from the terrace. Alma, who was admitting to fifty (her exact age was a well-kept secret), was wearing a black bias-cut Vionnet gown she had bought on her annual trip to Paris. Looped around her throat were four ropes of pink Burmese pearls and one rope of Tahitian natural black pearls. All these were bound together by a diamond-and-emerald clasp, the huge cabochon emerald being one of Emma's famous stones that had been recovered from the rubble of her Nob Hill mansion. Curiously, of all Emma's treasures, her jewels were the few things that had survived the 1906 disaster, having been in a steel safe. Alma had inherited her grandmother's passion for jewels, as well as half the jewelry, and she now had one of the leading collections in America, valued for insurance purposes at fifty million dollars. With six art-deco diamond bracelets on one arm and four on the other, it was obvious she had no hesitancy in displaying it.

"It's such a perfect evening for a party," she said as Alicia and Curtis joined her on the terrace. Alicia, in a smart red silk Lanvin, was wearing the diamond-and-ruby necklace Curtis had given her on their tenth anniversary. "And Charlotte looks lovely."

"They're really a handsome young couple," Alicia said. "We're so pleased."

"Where's Joel and his tart?" Alma continued as her fifth husband, Philippe, Marquis de Rochefort, came up with two glasses of champagne.

"They should be here any minute," Curtis said.

"Well, I think it's rather *moche* of Joel to bring some Hollywood tramp to his own sister's engagement party. Thanks, darling." Alma took the champagne from Philippe, who winked at her French slang for "tacky." "But then, leave it to Joel to do the unusual. He certainly marches to his own drummer."

"I read he ees to turn a feelm about Jeanne d'Arc," Philippe said in mangled English. "Perhaps I can 'elp 'eem. I am descent from one of her friends, Gilles de Rais."

"The mass murderer and child molester," Alma said. "Really, darling, that's one ancestor I wouldn't brag about. Ah, I think they're here. My God, she *is* gorgeous."

They all turned. Emerging from the open French doors onto the tiled terrace was Joel, in a dinner jacket, and Laura. She was wearing a white silk dress with a silver sequin tulled net over the short skirt, the bodice cut low to display a wonderful bust. Her long, sensational legs terminated in white pumps with rhinestone buckles.

Jesus Christ, Curtis thought, now I see why he wants to make movies.

Joel brought Laura over to his family. "Mother, Dad, Aunt Alma: I'd like you to meet Laura Lord."

Laura smiled and extended her hand. "It's so kind of you to invite me, Mrs. Collingwood," she said in her best Mrs. Belgrave manner. "Joel has told me about your house. It's simply lovely."

Alicia shook her hand. "Thank you, Miss Lord. And this is my husband."

Laura turned to Curtis and her smile increased in wattage. "I'm so pleased to meet you, Mr. Collingwood."

She's the sexiest thing alive! Curtis thought as he shook her hand. And Joel is going to have her play Joan of Arc?

"Your mother's so beautiful," Laura said ten minutes later as she danced with Joel to "I'll See You Again." "And she seems so nice."

"She is nice. I love her a lot."

"And your Aunt Alma: I've never seen such jewels."

"Mmm. That emerald in her necklace belonged to a maharajah."

"Gosh. She seems a little chilly, though."

"She isn't in bed. She's a bit of a nymphomaniac."

"What's that?"

"She likes men, the younger the better. I think the Frenchman is her fifth husband—I lose count. Aunt Alma used to be a sculptress, but she gave up art for sex."

Laura snickered.

"Aunt Alma also had the distinction of crushing her first husband to death when the bed she was in with her lover collapsed during the big earthquake."

"You do have a nutty family."

"Rich people call us colorful."

" 'Rich people,' " Laura sighed. "I never thought I'd be at a party like this."

She felt Joel's hand on her back press more firmly. Their bodies moved closer together. I think he's finally making a pass, she thought. To think all this beauty might one day be mine, if I play my cards right. . . . Those goddamned nude photos! Why did I pose for them? Why?

But she knew why. She had been down to her last five dollars.

Joel had rented adjoining suites on the tenth floor of the Mark Hopkins, the new hotel on top of Nob Hill where once the turreted mansion of railroad tycoon Mark Hopkins had stood, only a block from the site of Emma's pseudo-French château. Laura was lying naked in her bed at four that morning, unable to sleep, her mind filled with memories of her fabulous evening at the Collingwoods'. All her life she had known people lived like that. They wore gorgeous clothes and slept in clean, sweet-smelling sheets like the ones she was in. Tonight she had seen it. She had seen the magic world of the very rich.

The door to Joel's suite opened and a crack of light spilled across the carpet onto her bed. She sat up, holding the sheet over her naked breasts. The door slowly opened wide. Joel was standing there in a silk bathrobe, silhouetted against the light from his living room. Silently he came in and walked to the bed. She looked at him as he stared at her through his thick lenses.

"I was proud of you tonight," he whispered, untying the silk belt of his red robe. "You behaved as if you belonged."

"I thought maybe I did belong, if only for one night. Thank you so much for taking me."

"My father was impressed with you. He told me he'll do everything in his power to help with your publicity campaign, and he has a lot of power."

"Gosh."

"Stop saying 'gosh.' It makes you sound like some gushy teenager. I'm going to make you the most beautiful, famous woman in the world. Your whole life is going to be a 'gosh.' "

He took off his glasses and put them on the bed table. Then he looked at her again.

"I love you, you know. I've never been in love before. It sort of frightens me, in a way."

"Why should love frighten you?"

"Because I'm terrified I'll be hurt by you."

"Oh, my dearest Joel, I would never, never hurt you. I told you you're the first man that's ever been kind to me."

He continued to squint at her with his small eyes. "Have you told me the truth about yourself?"

"Yes."

"I know there have been men in your life. I know about Bob Crane, the assistant cameraman at Paramount. I don't expect someone as beautiful as you to be a virgin. But have there been others?"

"Just . . . my father."

"You said he tried to make love to you. Did he?"

She closed her eyes. "He raped me."

"Good God."

"I was terrified. I thought maybe I'd have a baby, some sort of monster . . . but nothing happened." She opened her eyes. "That's why I had to leave home. I told him I never wanted to see him again."

"My poor Laura."

There were tears in her eyes. "That's why I love you," she whispered. "Don't you see? You've made my horrible, ugly life a thing of magic."

"Don't say you love me. You don't have to lie."

"But I do, Joel!"

"I know I'm strange and not handsome. I don't expect you to love me. Just let me love you, Laura. And never, never lie to me."

He took off his bathrobe and dropped it on the floor. She stared at his scrawny, nearly hairless body.

She lowered the sheet and turned it aside, revealing her own nakedness. Slowly he climbed on the bed and lowered himself on top of her. She opened her arms and took him into her as he kissed her with a passion that amazed her.

She had only sensed the love within him, because he was careful to hide his emotions behind a mask. But now the mask was off.

47

"THE Phantom murders have stopped," Gil Amster said as he sat on the counter stool next to Cliff Parker at Barkies' Sandwich Shop on Sunset. "You guys got any idea *why*?"

The chief of detectives, who was wearing a rumpled gray suit and gray hat, bit into his hamburger. "Maybe he got bored with the gore."

"Yeah. Or maybe he ran out of masks." Gil looked around. It was two-thirty in the afternoon, and the lunch crowd had thinned out. He turned back to Cliff and lowered his voice. "I sure would like to know if you have any leads."

"I'm sure you would, Gil." Cliff liked the reporter, but, as with all reporters, he kept a close mouth.

"I mean, you must have something."

Cliff chewed in silence.

The cute waitress named Thelma came to Gil. "Hi, Mr. Amster," she said. "The usual?"

"Yeah. Cheeseburger, fries, and a Coke."

"Okay." She scribbled the order on her pad.

"You're gonna turn into a cheeseburger someday," Cliff said. "Don't you ever eat anything else?"

"I eat tuna-fish salad on Fridays."

"You a Catholic?"

"Sort of."

"I didn't know that."

Gil was wrestling with his conscience, as well as with his reporter's hunger for inside information. The Phantom murders were the hottest story of the year, having pushed the impending presidential election from the headlines with ease. Dexter Gray was yelling for leads, and the maddening thing was that Gil *had* inside information but was afraid to use it.

"Look, Captain, what if *I* knew something about the case?"

Cliff looked at him. "What are you talking about?"

Gil pulled a pack of Luckies from his coat pocket and lit one. He

409

noticed the sweaty ring his fingers left on the cigarette paper. If Wendy found out . . .

"What if I had a piece of information that might help you guys out? Then would you let me know what's going on?"

"Cut the bullshit, Gil. If you know something, you have to tell me. You know that. Otherwise, I'll book you for withholding evidence."

"You have to give me your word you won't tell anybody where you got this," he whispered. "I mean, anybody. It could cost Wendy and me both our jobs."

Cliff studied him. "Yeah, I'll give my word," he finally said. "What is it?"

"There's a member of a very powerful family in this state who collects masks. Masks, get it? And I happen to know he left his house one hour before Ellen Busby was murdered, so it's possible he could have done it."

"Who are you talking about?"

"Joel Collingwood."

"Jesus Christ."

"He is sort of weird, you know."

"Yeah, I've heard. Christ, that brings back memories."

"You mean the Carl Klein murder?"

"Yeah."

"Maybe it runs in the family."

"I wonder. Anyway, thanks for the tip, Gil. And I can see why you're nervous about your jobs. Curtis Collingwood is no one to antagonize lightly. But since you've scratched my back, I'll scratch yours. We do have a lead on the murders."

Gil was like a piranha smelling blood. "What?"

"All five girls that were murdered had something in common."

"What?"

"I can't tell you."

"Do you have a suspect?"

"Yes."

"Is it . . . Joel Collingwood?"

"Here's your cheeseburger."

"His name is Ted Spaulding," Miss Baird said. "I gather he's a farmboy from Iowa. He's rather upset, Mr. Collingwood, and insists on seeing you."

"About what?" Joel asked.

"He says he wants to talk to you about Dixie Davenport."

Joel drummed his fingers on his desk. "Show him in."

A few moments later, Miss Baird returned with the tall, redheaded Iowan with the freckled face. He had on a badly fitting Montgomery Ward suit and was holding a straw hat in his hand. He looked nervously at Miss Baird as she left the office.

"My name's Joel Collingwood. I understand you have something you want to discuss about Miss Davenport?"

"You're danged tootin' I do!" he exclaimed, anger replacing his nervousness as he came to Joel's desk. "She's changed her name—now she's callin' herself Laura Lord. I seen her pictures in the papers and read all the stories. How she's gonna play Joan of Arc. Let me tell you something, Mr. Collingwood: you better get someone else, because Dixie Davenport is a thief and a whore!"

"A thief?"

"You're danged tootin'. She stole forty-three dollars outta my wallet and run off with my car. And now she's a big movie star—well, I say big deal! If she don't pay me back my money, I'm goin' to the police and she'll end up in the hoosegow, which is where that little slut belongs."

"Wait a minute. Where did this happen?"

"In the Lazy Daze Motel outside Des Moines about six months ago. I picked Dixie up . . . she was hitchhikin' to Hollywood to get into the movies, and God damn, I'll admit she was the sexiest thing I ever seen."

"Did you . . . did you make love with her?"

"Oh, yeah, and she's good in that department. She knows all the tricks, that's for sure. Listenin' to her brag, she's slept with half the men in America, which wouldn't surprise me none. Then, the next morning, that cheap piece of baggage takes all the cash outta my wallet, steals my car keys, and takes off with my Model T—which was paid up full!"

Joel's face had gone chalky. He thought a moment. "This is a serious charge, Mr. Spaulding. How do I know you're telling the truth? Laura's been getting a lot of publicity these past few weeks. How do I know you aren't just making this up to extort money out of me or her?"

"I'm no extortionist!" he yelled, shaking his straw hat at Joel. "And I'll tell you how well I know that little tramp: she's got a strawberry birthmark the size of a penny just above her you-know-what."

Joel winced. "You're telling the truth," he whispered. He opened a drawer of his desk and pulled out a big checkbook. "Would one thousand dollars be satisfactory, Mr. Spaulding?"

The farmboy gawked. "Well, the car wasn't worth that much. It had twenty thousand miles on it. I figure it was worth two hundred bucks, maybe."

"But you were inconvenienced, and you had to pay to come to California."

"Yeah, but I was figurin' to move out here one day anyways, the climate bein' so nice and all . . ."

"Still." Joel wrote the check, ripped it out, and extended it across the desk. Ted took it, read the figures, and gulped.

"Gosh, Mr. Collingwood, that's mighty decent of you. Thanks a lot. And . . . and I hope your movie's a hit."

"I hope so too. But I can see I'm going to have to have a little chat with my star."

"You tell her she ought to straighten herself out and that she's mighty lucky having a nice feller like you as a producer."

"Thank you."

Ted went to the office door, putting the check in his pocket. Just before leaving, he turned to Joel. "You wouldn't have a part in the movie for me, would you? I mean, maybe I could play some French farmer . . ."

"Leave your name and number with Miss Baird. We'll call you if there's an opening."

Ted's face lit up. "Gee, thanks. Hot damn!"

He practically danced out of the office.

On Rodeo Drive, Joel had rented Laura a Southern-plantation-style house set on a lot so small that barely ten feet separated the columned brick front terrace from the pretentious Tudor-style house to its right. Pink and white impatiens planted in garish profusion bordered the house and walk. Joel had rented the place furnished in *haute*-department-store-repro style, but when Laura had complained about the curtains in the living room, he gave her a ten-thousand-dollar decorating and household budget. He also gave her a fifty-thousand-dollar clothing allowance and sent her shopping with costumier Burt Karnovsky in tow to make sure what she bought was in keeping with the glamorous star image he was so expensively creating. For the expenses of the studio he had an annual five-million-dollar line of credit from the Pacific Bank and Trust guaranteed by his father. Thus, the expenses of building Laura into a star came under the heading of studio business, and since, when it came to his movies, Joel was a prodigious spender (or spendthrift, accountant Chuck Rosen moaned), he now pulled out all financial stops on the great movie-making pipe organ of his imagination. Nothing was too good for Laura: Vuitton luggage, custom-made shoes for her size-five feet, custom-made silk lingerie trimmed with lace made by an order of Belgian nuns, French soap for her marble bath. Joel made only one concession. Though her wardrobe was lavishly extensive, it was bought at wholesale at the Los Angeles branch of de Meyer and Kinsolving's. To cap it all, Joel bought her the ultimate in chic for the era: a four-door, tulipwood-bodied, 46-cv, eight-liter "Boulogne" model Hispano-Suiza. This automobile, built in Barcelona and given royal cachet by car-mad King Alfonso XIII of Spain, was the darling of the *richesse dorée* of five continents. It had inspired French author Pierre Frondaie to write a novel called *L'Homme à l'Hispano*, and played a starring role in that quintessentially twenties novel *The Green Hat*, in which author Michael Arlen described it, lovingly if curiously, as "a huge yellow insect that had dropped to earth from a butterfly civilization." Laura's Hispano was white, and with its famous *cigogne volante*, or flying stork chrome hood ornament, it set Joel back a whopping twelve thousand 1928 dollars. But in the car, chauffeured by her gray-uniformed Mexican driver, José, Laura truly looked like a movie star at a time when movie stars looked like . . . well, movie stars.

And she had yet to play anything in a movie higher than an extra in the Bastille scene of *The Devil's Daughter*. As Chuck Rosen surveyed the mounting bills in his office at Collingwood Studios, he literally groaned. "Joel's meshugge," he kept repeating to himself. "One-hundred-percent meshugge."

As Laura lounged in her marble bath, surrounded by huge bottles of Chanel No. 5, the perfume introduced by Coco Chanel eight years before, she had reason to believe that meeting him had been the equivalent of being handed Aladdin's lamp. When she rubbed him—which she did frequently, because Joel adored having his back massaged—all the fabulous resources of the enormous Collingwood fortune were at her disposal. And best of all, unlike film star Marion Davies, who had to satisfy the fumbling advances of sixty-five-year-old William Randolph Hearst to pay for her gilded existence, Laura had in Joel a young, ardent lover with whom she was, not without good reason, falling madly in love.

As she soaped her arm with her enormous sponge, the door to the bathroom slowly opened and a tall man in a silver mask appeared. Laura, like everyone else in California, had been devouring the headlines about the mysterious Phantom murderer, and when she saw the carving knife in his right hand, she screamed. He ran across the marble floor and placed the point of the knife against her throat. She froze with terror, her bulging eyes staring at the silver mask only inches above her face.

"Please," she whispered, "don't kill me."

"I told you never to lie to me," the man whispered, and she realized it was Joel. "You didn't tell me about Ted Spaulding."

"Who?"

"The farmer in Iowa whose car you stole. He came to the studio today and told me everything. You lied to me."

"I didn't lie. I just didn't tell you about it. And take away that knife before you hurt me."

"You've hurt me, just as I feared you would. I don't like being hurt."

She began to sob. "Please, Joel, I'm scared . . . please."

"Who else have you made love to?"

"No one. Take the knife away. And that mask, why are you wearing a mask?"

"I've devoted my life to you. I'm giving you everything. If you make a fool of me—"

"I won't!"

"What else should I know?"

"There's nothing . . . nothing!"

"Do you swear?"

"Yes, I swear! Please take the knife away, please."

She was almost hysterical. Slowly he removed the knife and straightened. Then he lifted the mask off his face, pulled his glasses from his pocket, and put them on. She was staring at him, still sobbing.

"Are you . . . are you the murderer? Are you the Phantom?"

"Of course not," he said. "But I thought it might be a dramatic way to impress upon you that I am really mad. Now, you've given your word to me there's nothing else in your background I should know about. I'll expect total honesty from you in the future."

"You scared me shitless!" she yelled as he started out of the bathroom. "You terrified me!"

He turned and gave her a cold look. "Good." And he left.

Trembling violently, she continued to sob. She wondered if he were perhaps a maniac. As close as she had come to Joel, she still knew little of what went on in his head, except that most of the time his mind seemed to be off in a dream world. Maybe he was seeing a Phantom movie in his head when he got the idea of terrorizing her with the mask and the knife, but maybe not. A mask and a knife were powerful and dangerous ways to frighten a girlfriend.

One thing she now realized with startling clarity: if learning about Ted Spaulding could arouse him to such demented behavior, what might he do if he ever saw George Evans' nude photographs?

"I've got to get them," she whispered. "I've got to."

* * *

The next morning, she took a taxi to the studio on Hollywood Boulevard, realizing that the last thing she wanted was to look like a movie star driving in a chauffeured Hispano-Suiza. Instead she put on a plain blue housedress, tied a kerchief around her blond hair, and put on sunglasses. The photography studio was in a small two-story white stucco building in the middle of a block that had seen better days. To the right was a bookstore in the rear of which one could peruse off-color books and magazines. Laura reflected that the juxtaposition of pornography supplier and retailer was convenient, if nothing else.

She paid the cabby, then hurried into the studio. She knew that Evans, a bachelor, lived alone on the second floor and that he had no assistants, doing everything himself, developing his plates in the rear darkroom. The small reception area in front had a few cheap chairs, a table with some out-of-date magazines, and a stub-filled ashtray. A wooden reception desk next to the door to the studio working area was empty, so she went to the door and rang a buzzer. After a moment it was opened by George.

"Ah, Miss Davenport." He smiled. "I mean, Miss Lord. Excuse me."

"I have to talk to you."

"Come in."

He stepped aside and she went into the studio where such a short time before, she had taken off her clothes in front of the hungry camera. Black electric lights stared blindly at a brick wall covered with a sheet against which George posed his subjects.

"Cigarette?"

"No, thanks."

He lit one, eyeing her. "So, what can I do for you?" he said, blowing out his match and dropping it on the floor.

"How much do you want for those pictures?"

He smiled. "I've been waiting for you, Miss Lord. I've been reading your publicity. It's been quite impressive, and casting you as Joan of Arc is, under the circumstances, an inspired move. I hear you've got a house on Rodeo Drive and tool around town in a Hispano-Suiza. Not bad. Joel Collingwood must be crazy about you."

"How much?"

He eyed her. "One million dollars," he finally said.

"That's crazy. One million for a dozen photographs?"

"One million."

"But I haven't got a million dollars."

"Get it from your rich boyfriend—slut."

The "slut" came out nasty.

"Don't you understand? I can't get it from him!"

"Why?"

"I just can't, that's all. You'll have to ask for something reasonable. I'll give you ten thousand dollars. I can borrow that on my car."

"One million."

"Please . . ."

"One million. And you've got till tomorrow to come up with it. Otherwise, I'll take the pictures to Joel. He'll pay a million for them."

"Please," she begged, starting to cry. "I have to have them. I'll pay you later . . . after the movie's made. I'll be worth a lot of money then."

"You're worth a lot of money now. Turn off the waterworks, my dear. You know the terms. A million by tomorrow. See you then, Miss Lord."

He blew smoke in her face.

"You bastard," she sniffed.

"No need to get personal. You know, you Hollywood types are all the same. You may get all gussied up in furs and jewels and drive around in swell cars, but underneath, you're all just a bunch of whores."

She slapped him, hard. His reaction startled her: he raised his hands to attack her. In another moment, though, he restrained himself. "Get out of here, whore," he whispered.

Still crying, she ran out into the sunshine of Hollywood Boulevard. A million dollars! As she paced down the sidewalk, she wildly considered her options. Could she borrow a million from Joel? But what could she tell him she needed it for? No, no, that was impossible. Could she go to Chuck Rosen, the studio accountant? But what could she tell him?

She stopped. Wiping her cheeks, she looked back at the studio.

Yes, that was it. Her only option. The only thing that could save her career and, possibly, her marriage to Joel Collingwood.

She'd have to steal the pictures.

Feeling a sense of relief, she hailed a cab.

Sitting in a light blue Mercedes across the street from the photography studio, a man was watching her.

It was Joel Collingwood.

At four-ten the next morning, a taxi slowed on Hollywood Boulevard.

"This is close enough," Laura said from the back seat. She handed a twenty-dollar bill to the driver. "You wait for me here, and there'll be another twenty for you."

"I'll wait till breakfast for you, sweetheart," the cabby said, giving her a wink. "But you know, this isn't the safest neighborhood in town."

"I can take care of myself. I don't know how long I'll be, but I don't think it should be more than a half-hour."

She let herself out of the cab. The street was nearly deserted, although in the next block she spotted a policeman. Hurrying between two buildings, she went to a rear alley and turned to the right. Since it was primarily a business district, there were few garbage cans, but a cat had found one to sleep on top of. Laura hurried down the alley thirty feet until she reached the rear of George Evans' studio.

There were three windows on the ground floor, one of which had been boarded up. Laura knew it was the darkroom. She set her bag on the ground and tried the first window. Locked. She tried the second. Locked. The alley was dimly lit by a distant bulb jutting from the top of a wooden pole. She opened her bag and fumbled around for a moment, then removed a black rubber suction cup and a glass cutter she had borrowed from the studio carpentry shop. She swiftly sliced a large square in the window and removed it with the suction cup, just as the studio carpenter had shown her. She reached in and unlocked the window. Then she shoved it open. Placing her bag through, she climbed in.

Inside the dark studio, she took a flashlight from her bag, turned it on, and moved the beam of light around the room. There stood the lights, tall black sentinels. The circle of light illuminated the sheet-covered wall in front of which she had posed nude. It found the prop cabinets, and she flickered it over the wax grapes she had held. Then a steel rack holding costume props sprang into view. Passing over a big nineteenth-century picture hat, Laura recalled seeing one of George's pictures in which the model had nothing on but the hat, its big bow tied prettily around her chin.

Finally the beam hit a cabinet Laura remembered. George still used glass plates—a cumbersome, outdated method but one that enabled the photographer to get portraits of startling clarity and texture. He stored the plates in that cabinet. Advancing cautiously to it, she pulled one of the many thin drawers, each holding a plate. The first held a picture of a nude girl sitting in a round hole in a wall, obviously meant to suggest a Chinese moon gate. Fake cherry blossoms framing the girl added to the tacky illusion of a romantic garden.

Laura kept rapidly opening and closing drawers until she found one of her own pictures. Sighing with relief, she took out one of her poses with the grapes. The other eleven plates were above the first.

Knowing the plates would be heavy, she had brought a mesh shopping bag to carry them in, with pieces of newspaper to separate them. It took her several minutes to pack them. Then she picked up the bag and aimed the flashlight at the window.

Until this moment she had worked at an even pace, keeping a cool head despite her tension. But now she hurried, and in so doing, tripped over the splayed legs of one of the tall steel lights. Over it keeled as she stumbled to the floor. The light hit with a terrific crash. Laura landed on the glass plates, smashing them also. Her intention had been to destroy them at home, knowing the noise would arouse George upstairs. Telling herself not to panic—but panicking nevertheless—she sprang to her feet to retrieve the flashlight that was rolling across the floor, its beam still on.

She had reached it and picked it up when she saw a pair of shoes. She backed up, running the light up the legs and torso of a tall man standing near the stairs. A man in a silver mask. A man holding a butcher knife in his right hand.

"Joel!" she cried, backing toward the window. "I had to get the pictures . . ." She started crying with fear. "But they're destroyed now. I tripped and fell on them . . . Look—"

"And that's your death warrant," whispered the man in the mask as he advanced toward her. "As long as the plates existed, they were worth money and you were safe. But now, you're just like all the other sluts I've photographed—"

"George?" she whispered, bewildered. "Are you George?"

"Yes, it's George. George the punisher. You must be punished for your immorality."

"You're crazy—"

"You whores of Hollywood have turned this peaceful town into Babylon and you must pay for your sins."

"Laura, get away!" yelled a man climbing through the window. She turned the light. To her amazement, it was Joel. As the masked man roared with rage and rushed at her with his knife, Joel ran and grabbed him. As Laura screamed, holding a jiggling flashlight beam on them, the two men wrestled. George, howling like a madman, thrust his knife into Joel's belly. Joel gasped as George pulled the knife out.

"Joel!" Laura screamed. He had doubled over, holding his stomach. She shone the beam on George. He was holding the knife high, its blood dripping on his silver mask.

"Whore of Babylon!" he cried. "Prepare to meet your doom!"

She continued to scream as he rushed at her. A shot fired from the window, then two more. Evans cried out, twirled halfway to his left, and pitched forward onto the floor. Men were climbing through the window. When she turned her light on them, she saw they were police.

"Joel!"

She knelt beside him. He was on his side, holding his stomach, from which blood was pouring.

"Someone call an ambulance," she cried. "Oh, my God . . . Joel, my darling."

"I'm sorry," he whispered. "I frightened you the other night. It was stupid and cruel of me—"

"Forget that! Why are you here?"

"I've been following you . . . to find out . . ."

His eyes closed.

"An ambulance is on the way," Cliff Parker announced, kneeling beside Laura. Someone flicked on the studio lights.

"Is he dead?" she whispered, staring at the blood.

"No, but he's lost a lot of blood. That lunatic really gored him."

"He can't die . . . he mustn't die."

Cliff Parker looked at the trembling blond. "You really love him, don't you?" he said, a note of surprise in his voice.

She turned to the detective, tears in her eyes. "He's the only man who's ever treated me like a lady," she whispered.

"We'd been staking out Evans for ten days from the bookstore next door," Cliff said an hour later as he and Laura waited in the hospital while the doctors operated on Joel. "So when you snuck into the alley this morning, we were really surprised."

"Why were you staking him out?"

"Several of the men on the force are, uh . . . Let's just say they collect dirty pictures. They told me that all five girls murdered by the Phantom had posed in the nude. I checked out a host of porno stores and tallied up that the photographer of all five was George Evans. Since it was a common link, we put him under surveillance. We set ourselves up next door, but for ten days he hasn't done anything except regular stuff like shopping and business appointments. It's possible he may have suspected we were watching him, I don't know. At any rate, you did us a great favor by forcing his hand tonight. Of course, you had a bit of a close shave."

"I had no idea George was crazy. Why did he put on the masks?"

"He loved the publicity he was getting, I suppose. He probably saw *The Phantom of the Opera* and decided he'd become the Phantom of Hollywood, which is exactly what happened. Life imitating the movies. I'll bet he read every word that was written about him, just the way Jack the Ripper did."

"But why? What was he trying to prove?"

"Evans' family owned a lemon grove on land that's now part of Universal Studios. Maybe that got him started as a movie hater."

"Yes, I remember he said something like 'You whores of Hollywood have turned this peaceful town into Babylon.' "

"Well, there you have it. There's a lot of people like him in this town, you know. The movies have put Hollywood and L.A. on the map, and the gossip columnists are turning it into Sin City, USA. But when I was a boy thirty years ago, Hollywood was just being developed by a Kansas City prohibitionist. It was a very strict place for years, and most Angelenos are still pretty straitlaced. George Evans decided to lash back. Of course, murdering actresses is a pretty extreme way of getting back at the film business."

One of Joel's doctors entered the waiting room. The smile on his face told the news. "He's going to be all right," he said. "The knife cut a part of his intestines, but we managed to stitch it together. He's going to have a lot of pain for the next couple of months, but I think he'll be around for a while."

"Oh, that's the best news!" Laura exclaimed, leaping from the sofa and giving the doctor a kiss on the cheek. The young man gulped and blushed.

"Uh, yes, um . . . are you Laura?"

"That's right."

"He told me just before we gave him the anesthesia that he, uh . . . loves you."

Laura Lord started weeping, but this time it wasn't from fear.

"I felt so guilty about what I'd done to you," Joel said the next day as Laura sat beside his bed in his private hospital room, holding his hand. "Putting on the mask and scaring you in the bathroom. It was a crazy thing to do, and I was afraid you'd think I am crazy, which I probably am, a little. But I'd never harm you, Laura. I just overreacted to what Ted Spaulding told me."

"You had reason to be angry with me," she said. "You were looking for the purest woman in America, and you got me, who's about as pure as mud."

"It doesn't matter," he continued in his weak voice. "But I was so ashamed of what I'd done, I wanted to apologize. But when I pulled up to your house, you were just getting in a taxi, which I couldn't understand for the life of me, since you've got the car. So I followed you to George's studio, and that didn't make sense to me either. So I started watching you. And the other night when you went back to the studio, I followed you again. Except I didn't know why you were going."

"Do you know now?" she interrupted.

"I have an idea."

"Then I'll tell you, because I want you to know. When I first came to Hollywood, I ran out of money fast and . . . I saw this ad in the *Clarion*. I'm sure you've seen them. 'Photographer looking for pretty models. Good pay . . .' You know. Well, I was desperate, so I went to the studio. It was George's and he wanted me to pose for him in the nude. And I did. The other day I went to buy them back, for obvious reasons, and he blackmailed me. He said he wanted a million dollars for them, and if I didn't give it to him, he'd take them to you and get the million out of you. I decided my only choice was to steal them. Of course, I had no idea he was the Phantom. And then you climbed through the window and got stabbed, so this whole thing is my fault, which I feel awful about. So don't you feel guilty. I'm the guilty one. I'm the rotten apple. It's some résumé, isn't it? I was raped by my father, I stole a car, I've slept with a lot of men, and I posed for dirty pictures. You don't come much lower than that. I think it's pretty obvious I'm not an especially good candidate to play Saint Joan. I've hurt you enough. I'm not going to ruin your movie too. Find someone who'd make a more convincing saint than me."

He studied her for a long time through his thick glasses.

"It's not your fault you were born poor," he finally said, "any more than it's my fault I was born rich. You had to struggle to overcome your poverty, and you looked at the world in a lot different way than I looked at it. I wanted you to be pure, and it drove me crazy when I found out you weren't. But who's pure in this nutty world? You read the ad for George Evans in the *Clarion*, my family's newspaper, so who am I to be holier than thou?" He shrugged slightly and added, "Besides, I love you, mud and all."

She laughed as she wiped her eyes.

"However, I do agree with you about Saint Joan of Arc. You're wrong to play her. Frankly, you're too sexy. I'm canceling the Joan of Arc project. You know, Laura, the reason I went into the movies in the first place was to make films of beauty. Perhaps Chuck Rosen's right. If no one goes to see them, what's the point? I've found a new script I want you to read. I think it may be just right for you."

"What's it called?"

He smiled slightly. *"Lady of the Night."*

"Oh, Joel . . ." She started laughing. "It sounds perfect for me."

"He went to see his daughter," Wendy Fairfax told Gil Amster as they sat in the corner booth at Barkies'. "I found out from Dex Gray. Joel Collingwood knocked up one of the family housemaids a couple of years ago, and she and his two-year-old illegitimate daughter live in a beachhouse at Santa Monica. The night you followed him, he had just gotten a call that his daughter was sick, and he drove to Santa Monica to see her."

"So much for my theory that Joel Collingwood was the Phantom."

"Well, it was my dumb idea. Anyway, thank God neither of us told anyone, especially the police."

"Yeah, I guess you're right."

Gil Amster decided that what his wife didn't know wouldn't hurt her.

The cute waitress came up to take their order. "The same, Mr. Amster?"

"Why not? Cheeseburger, fries, and a Coke."

"And you, Miss Fairfax? By the way, I got a job."

"No kidding? An acting job?"

"Yes, isn't it wonderful? Well, I'm an extra and I get killed in the first scene, but it's a big, splashy killing."

"That sounds exciting. What movie?"

"The new Joel Collingwood production, *Lady of the Night*, starring Laura Lord. Who knows? Dress extra today, movie star tomorrow. It happened to Laura Lord, it could happen to me."

"Absolutely," Wendy said, smiling. "Who knows? In Hollywood anything can happen. And I'll mention it in my column."

"Oh, would you? That would be swell!"

"But I don't know your name, honey."

"It's Thelma. Thelma Todd."

Blond Thelma Todd in fact went on to star in a number of movies, including *Monkey Business*, with the Marx Brothers, *Horse Feathers*, *Hips, Hips, Hooray* and *Bottoms Up*. On December 16, 1935, Thelma's body was found in her Packard convertible in the garage of the Pacific Palisades house she shared with her lover, director Roland West. The ignition switch was turned on, but the motor was dead. Thelma's clothes had been messed up and there was blood on her face, yet the grand jury handed in the odd verdict of "Death by monoxide poisoning."

The murder was never solved.

Headline in *Variety*, November 8, 1928:

UNKNOWN DOLL TO PLAY MOLL!
Laura Lord to Star in Gangland Film!
Joel Collingwood States Confidence in New Actress:
"She'll wow 'em!" he vows.

Lady of the Night, the story of a blond bombshell who is the girlfriend of a New York bootlegger whom she betrays to the police and who is wiped out in a hail of machine-gun bullets, was released in theaters all over America ten days after the stock-market crash of 1929. Curiously, Joel's timing couldn't have been better. Frightened by the crash, the public sought escape in the darkness of the movie palaces, and Laura Lord's sizzling, sexy performance delighted them. The film was a box-office smash, and Laura became a star overnight.

However, for Joel the triumph was Pyrrhic. His infatuation with films died as he realized that the public really did want tits and tommy guns instead of the beauty he had dreamed of. To his father's delight, Joel told him he was through with movies. He rented the studio to MGM for a fortune and returned to San Francisco to learn the family business.

In January 1930, rather to his family's dismay, Joel married Laura Lord. In June the same year, Laura gave birth to a son named Spencer. Those Collingwoods who were counting the months of her pregnancy sighed and said nothing.

In May 1933, in the very depths of the Depression, Curtis Collingwood died of a massive stroke. Joel became head of the Collingwood Corporation, and Laura, after five successful films, announced her retirement from the screen.

In 1936 Joel Collingwood announced the formation of the Collingwood Foundation, funded with fifty million dollars of Collingwood B, nonvoting stock. The foundation endowed the medical research of the Archer Collingwood Memorial Hospital. Joel, as philanthropic as his great-grandmother, Emma, also gave millions of his private fortune to charity and continued to support the Archer and Arabella Collingwood Museum of Fine Arts to which he gave his father's collection of impressionist and postimpressionist art. In memory of Zita, who had left him her millions, Joel established a million-dollar scholarship fund at Stanford University for needy children who showed outstanding talent in design.

Joel never learned to like baseball. Laura was never "accepted" by San Francisco society. They lived blissfully together until Joel's death from cancer in 1956.

Spencer Collingwood, twenty-six, a graduate of Princeton, inherited his father's fortune, which was estimated by *Time* magazine to be "in excess of $500,000,000." But at a meeting of the family in the Collingwood Building in San Francisco, Spencer announced that he had no interest in being actively involved with the running of the many businesses of the Collingwood Corporation, his true love being ranching. In a deal worked out by the family lawyers, Spencer was given fifty-percent personal ownership of the Calafia Ranch. Control of the Collingwood Corporation was given to Spencer's thirty-one-year-old cousin, the son of Alistair and Charlotte Brett: Harvard-educated Jeffrey Brett.

In 1960 Spencer Collingwood married a Los Angeles socialite named Sylvia DeWitt. The following year, Sylvia gave birth to a baby girl she and Spencer named Claudia.

In 1980, two years after Beulah Snodgrass/Dixie Davenport/Laura Lord Collingwood's death by an overdose of barbiturates (which was not called suicide even though Laura had developed a serious drinking problem after her husband's death), the Film Department of the Museum of Modern Art in New York held the first Laura Lord film retrospective. Her performance in *Lady of the Night* was hailed by the critics as a "classic."

True Gold:
The Value of Nothing

As the Boeing 747 slowly descended toward Los Angeles airport, Claudia Collingwood looked out the window of the first-class cabin at the purple smog that lay over the huge metropolis like a shroud. To the west, the sun setting over the Pacific was almost totally obscured.

"It has a weird sort of beauty, doesn't it?" remarked the middle-aged businessman sitting next to her. He had had desultory conversations with her during the long flight from New York. He had also drunk two bottles of an elegant 1980 Jordan Winery cabernet sauvignon.

"The smog?" Claudia asked. "You think it's beautiful?"

"It has the beauty of death," the man replied. Hearing him slur his words, she decided the wine must have hit him more than she had thought. "All those millions of cars down there on those clogged freeways, their exhaust pipes puffing, puffing, puffing . . . It'll never stop, you know. The smog'll get worse and worse until everybody chokes to death. And pfft! That's the end of California."

Claudia looked out the window again. The plane was now in the smog itself, and the lights of the city flickered out. The end of California.

It wasn't a very cheery thought to come home to.

"Daddy, I'm in Bel Air," she said on the phone two hours later.

"Welcome home, baby," said Spencer Collingwood, who was in his Quonset-hut garage a half-mile from the main house on the Calafía Ranch.

"I've rented a car and will drive down first thing in the morning. Have you given any thought to Jeffrey since I called you in Paris?"

"I sure have. That sneaky bastard, trying to sell the ranch off behind my back to a bunch of foreigners. To hell with him! And I've got a pretty good idea why he's trying to sell it, which I'll tell you about tomorrow. How's that Froggy husband of yours?"

"Daddy, I'm divorcing him."

"You're what?"

"I made up my mind on the plane. Talk about sneaky: he set me

427

up with Lord Northfield and Billie Ching, and I just can't trust him anymore. You were right, I made a mistake."

"Hallelujah! You mean you're coming home for good? No more France?"

"That's right."

"God damn, those are the sweetest words I've heard in a long time. No broken heart?"

"Well, a little broken heart. You know I was crazy about Guy, but he only cares about his château and his cognac. It took me two years to figure that out. Anyway, I'm hurting, but I'll survive—"

"Honey, you know how I hate to talk on the phone," he interrupted. "Besides, Mickey's signaling to me. I bought this great Porsche 926, and I'm going to give it its first run in the morning. So you get yourself down here tomorrow and we'll discuss the whole thing. Okay?"

"Okay, Daddy."

"Good night, sweetie. And again, welcome home. You've made your daddy a happy man."

He hung up. Claudia, who was sitting in bed, put the phone back on the bed table. She smiled slightly. Her father's one passion was sports cars, just as Guy's passion was his cognac.

Men, she thought, turning out the light and snuggling into the bed. For all their big talk, they're basically little boys with their toys.

Still, she wouldn't have minded having Guy next to her in bed . . . No! To hell with Guy.

Eighty miles to the south of Bel Air, Spencer and Mickey Carlisle, his mechanic, padlocked the double doors of the garage, then walked to their separate jeeps.

"The weather report's good," Mickey said.

"Yeah. I'll see you at seven, and we'll give it a spin."

Spencer got into his jeep and started driving to the ranch house. After catching sports-car fever twenty years before, he had built himself not only a fully equipped garage but also his own private 1.8-mile race course on a bluff overlooking the Pacific, a burst of self-indulgence only the very rich could afford. But despite the fact that he had inherited Joel Collingwood's enormous fortune and Laura Lord Collingwood's movie-star good looks, Spencer de Meyer Collingwood had never been a particularly happy man. Fortune had smiled on him so extravagantly at birth that he grew up inherently suspicious of people, as if someone might take something away from him. While he was young, his moodiness and suspicions were kept under control, and he led the more or less normal life of a rich man. But as he grew older, he spent more time on the ranch and less in Los Angeles and San Francisco. When his wife, Sylvia, died in a private-plane accident in 1974, he became even more reclusive, to the point that people began calling him "the hermit of Calafía."

Spencer was an almost rabid right-winger and gave millions to conservative causes; in right-wing Orange County, he fitted comfortably into the political landscape. On the other hand, he was a true conservative in the sense that he wished to conserve the beauties of southern California against the encroachments of civilization. He often spoke glowingly of his ancestor, the first Archer Collingwood, who had championed the cause of the Indians in the previous century, and said that Archer and Joe Thunder's philosophy of living with nature was the true gold of California. Twentieth-century man would have to change his ways, or nothing would be left for the twenty-first century except a huge dump. He used his enormous influence with the Collingwood Foundation to steer large amounts of money toward groups trying to save the planet from trashing itself into extinction. And his special enemy was developers, a word he pronounced with venom.

Parking his jeep in front, he headed into the ranch house. As usual, he ate by himself in the house that Star and Juanito had built almost nine decades before. His dinner of reheated stew was cooked and served by his only domestic servant, Ana, the wife of one of his Mexican ranch hands. Then he went into the library overlooking the Pacific, watched *Wheel of Fortune*, then climbed the dark wooden stairs to the tower room in which Star had drunk herself to death so many years before, and put himself to bed. The man who had everything led a dreary existence. If anyone wanted proof that money does not necessarily bring happiness, Spencer Collingwood, the cranky billionaire, was it.

At two that morning, a Range Rover containing four young Chinese drove down the beach and parked below Spencer's road course and garage. The men hopped out, climbed the bluff to the top, and ran to the garage. One of them, a professional locksmith, quickly picked the padlock on the doors. They hurried inside and turned their flashlights on the Porsche 926, which was on the hydraulic lift. They raised the car. Then the locksmith took a special diamond-edged saw from his tool kit, went under the car, and carefully began sawing the front steering linkage.

He sawed it just enough.

As the sun rose the next morning, a sea gull flew over the Calafía Ranch. Spread below him was a vast emptiness surrounded by the ever-growing towns, shopping centers, and development complexes of Orange County. A few citrus groves still existed on the ranch, but the fruit-growing activities had been curtailed by Spencer years earlier, and now most of the ranch was just barren land. At first glance, the drab brown expanse did not seem very inspiring, but the coastal stretch was actually a bloom of colors: warm ochers and creams alternated on the broken cliff faces with olive-greens, grays, and even masses of ashy rose. Cacti clung to the cliff walls in places. The sea gull knew that the long land line contained dozens of enchanting bays where the water on the sandy bars became a shimmering emerald green.

From the coast the land sloped gently upward for a few miles until it climbed into the hills. The land was neither pretty nor picturesque: rather, it had a stark grandeur. The sea gull, with its splendid eyesight, could see that the land teemed with wildlife. Ground squirrels scurried across trails or froze at signs of danger. Ground owls sat statue-still, only their heads slowly revolving like screws. Roadrunners raced uphill and down, almost as silly as their cartoon-character imitators. California quail everywhere, coyotes in the hills, wildcats, red foxes, a million tawny gray hares hopping through the chaparral, and, of course, rattlesnakes.

The sea gull swooped down over a shingled roof bristling with TV antennae. Before the sprawling Calafía ranch house, Spencer Colling-wood was climbing into his jeep to drive to the garage. The sea gull headed for the sea to feed. But as it approached the ocean, a terrible pain filled its belly. It cawed pitifully and went into a spinning dive. And then it smashed onto the rocky beach, dead.

It had not been shot.

Spencer put on his crash helmet and climbed into the white Porsche 926, which he and Mickey had rolled out of the garage onto the asphalt-composition track. Spencer closed the bubble top, signaled Mickey, and pushed the blue starter button. The Porsche roared to life.

"Good luck!" Mickey yelled as Spencer shifted into first.

It was a beautiful morning. The sun poured over the mostly tree-less, rather hilly land Spencer had chosen for his track, which looped around the countryside in a vaguely oval configuration. Spencer started north on the leg that bordered the ocean. Quickly he picked up speed: 60, 70, 80 . . . The finely tuned engine roared happily, the car handled beautifully. This is my best car yet, Spencer thought.

120, 130.

The car was a bullet. Spencer made the first curve and started on the eastern leg, practically flying over the little hills.

150, 160. Spencer was going south now, heading back toward the garage.

170, 175. Then he downshifted and brought the car to a halt beside Mickey.

"It's great!" he yelled after he opened the bubble top. "Hundred and seventy-five with no sweat. Let's turn up the turbo-boost to four bar and I'll try for two hundred."

"Roger."

Ten minutes later, Spencer started again. Again he went around the track, but this time he kept accelerating after he reached 175.

180, 190, 200.

"Wow!" he yelled to himself as the needle passed 200.

He was on the south leg of the track again, roaring toward the final curve, when he turned the steering wheel.

Nothing happened.

Spencer de Meyer Collingwood stared helplessly as the wall of the garage flew toward him. The Porsche 926 crashed into the garage at 200 miles per hour.

The fireball and its smoke were seen as far away as Long Beach.

"Claudia Collingwood?"

Claudia was at the hotel desk, paying her bill with her American Express card. Now she turned to see Harrison Ford, whom she had fallen in love with when she saw *Star Wars*. Except it wasn't Harrison Ford. It was a man who looked surprisingly like him, though he was a bit taller and his nose was sharper. He wore a conservative gray suit and a blue polka-dot tie.

"Yes?"

"I'm Arthur Stevens, your father's lawyer. Could I talk to you a moment?"

She retrieved her credit card and he led her across the lobby to an empty corner.

"There's been an accident," he said quietly. "Mickey Carlisle called me—he's your father's mechanic. Spencer was driving his Porsche and it went out of control."

"Is Daddy all right?"

"I'm afraid not. He crashed into the garage."

She winced. "Is he . . . ?"

The lawyer nodded. "The car blew up. I'm sorry."

Claudia thought of the difficult man she had had so many quarrels with over the years. Suddenly she remembered the pony he had given her when she was six and how carefully he had taught her to ride.

"Claudia?"

"Yes."

"Are you okay? I hate to break it to you like this."

"It's all right," she heard herself say.

"Mickey said you were coming down to the ranch today. I'm going down—would you like to go with me?"

She was in a daze. "Yes, thanks . . . Maybe that would be better . . . Let me finish checking out."

She could hardly see for the tears misting her vision as she went back to the desk. She felt a gnawing emptiness in her stomach, as if she hadn't eaten in days.

Suddenly she was the last Collingwood.

"You can't tell me this was an accident," she said an hour later as they crawled south on the San Diego Freeway in Arthur's silver Mercedes 380 SEL. An overturned trailer a mile ahead had almost choked the traffic to death.

"You can't tell me, either," Arthur said. "It's too damned coincidental. Besides, Spencer was a careful driver. He and Mickey had gone over that Porsche with a fine-tooth comb last night. But something tells me we'll never be able to prove anything, since the car was totally destroyed. Anyway, Mickey called the police, because he's as suspicious as we are. The cops dusted for fingerprints, but didn't find any except Mickey's and your father's."

"Did Daddy tell you about Lord Northfield and Billie Ching?"

"Yes."

"And how they threatened my husband?"

"Oh, yes. If it is murder, they're the prime suspects, though I doubt we could ever pin it on them. The Asians are taking over organized crime in this country, and there are plenty of Triad members in L.A. and San Francisco. Billie is a citizen of Hong Kong, and his bank launders drug money, which is brought into Hong Kong by the Triads, so the Triad bosses will gladly do him favors to keep him happy. All Billie has to do is make a phone call. An order is sent out to some goons in L.A. A crime is committed and no one can ever touch Billie. It's the perfect setup. Billie and Lord Northfield want your ranch. Your father was impossible to deal with, so . . ." He shrugged.

"And of course they think that I'll be so scared I'll do whatever they want."

"Are you scared?"

"You're damned right I'm scared, but I'm also mad. I'm sure as hell not going to be run off my ranch by some two-bit Hong Kong drug dealer."

Arthur smiled at her. "Hey, I like that. But Billie is hardly a two-bit operator. If the information I have is correct, Billie's bank launders billions of dollars of illegal drug money, and what better place to invest it than the Calafía Ranch, one hundred square miles sitting in the middle of the fastest-growing, richest county in America?"

"Do you think it's possible Billie might be thinking of using the ranch as a cover for drug operations?"

"I don't like to think it, but it's certainly possible. You've got all that coastline for boats, and you could land planes in the night. *Damn* this traffic!"

The Mercedes had slowed to a complete stop. Horns were honking.

"Daddy said on the phone last night that he knows—or knew—why my cousin Jeffrey Brett would want to sell the ranch. Do you have any idea what he was talking about?"

"Yes. Spencer thought Jeffrey was stealing money from the Collingwood Corporation."

Claudia stared at him. "But Jeffrey's the head of it."

"Exactly. Ever hear of insider trading? Last year Jeffrey called your father and tried to borrow twenty million dollars from him. Your father told him to go to hell."

"They never liked each other."

"The significant fact is the date of Jeffrey's call. It was two days after last year's stock-market crash. Spencer thought Jeffrey was heavy in the market and took a real bath. He hired a firm of accountants to audit the books. They haven't found anything yet, and they may not. But my gut feeling is that your father was right."

Claudia smiled grimly. "Yet one more high-class crook in the Collingwood family. Well, I'm not surprised. Daddy always said that Jeffrey was what Napoleon called Talleyrand."

"What was that?"

" 'Shit in a silk stocking.' "

"I like that."

She found herself staring at the exhaust pipes of the cars ahead in the traffic jam. She remembered the man on the plane. Exhaust pipes puffing, puffing, puffing. The end of California.

"It's not going to be the end," she suddenly said.

"What?"

"California. This man on the plane was saying that the smog would get worse until one day everyone would die and that would be the end of California. And Daddy gave millions to ecology groups. We all have to fight the smog and pollution just the way I have to fight Billie Ching and Nigel Northfield. I remember on Nigel's yacht that horrible woman, Perfume—"

"Billie's wife?"

"Yes, and Billie was saying America was through, a second-rate power, and we'd end up being a colony again because all the rich foreigners would buy America. Well, it's not going to happen! I owe it to all my ancestors who settled this state—even the crooks—to fight the rich foreigners. Billie Ching and Nigel are not going to get the Calafía Ranch!''

Arthur eyed the gorgeous blond sitting next to him. Her intensity impressed him. He had always heard that Claudia Collingwood was a spoiled rich girl who had flipped out for a French count. But there was more to her than that.

Claudia had the de Meyer steel in her.

In 1982, a sleek fifty-eight-story steel-and-glass skyscraper had been opened on Montgomery Street in San Francisco by Jeffrey Brett, who dedicated the new Collingwood Building to Emma, Archer, Scott, and Felix, whose names and dates were memorialized on a bronze plaque in the towering gray marble lobby. But the Collingwood Corporation had swollen to proportions that those nineteenth-century worthies could never have imagined. It now owned five television stations, eighty-nine newspapers, ten magazines, two publishing houses; it rented Joel's old Santa Monica Boulevard movie studio to a TV production company specializing in mind-deadening game shows; the Pacific Bank and Trust and the Golden State Insurance Company, with assets in the billions, owned vast tracts of real estate; the old Kinsolving Shipping Company that had started it all was, with a stunning lack of sentiment, sold off in the 1970's as a money loser and its millions reinvested in an airline, a paper company, a breakfast-cereal company, a drug company, and a Napa Valley vineyard. The vast corporation, like so many huge American companies, had spread its tentacles into everything. And controlling this empire from his luxurious office atop the Collingwood Building was sixty-four-year-old Jeffrey Brett.

Lawyers had long since taken control of the management of the colossal Collingwood fortune, and trusts had been set up to take advantage of every tax break and ensure that all the members of the by now far-flung family were independently wealthy. But the power remained in the male Collingwood line, and Spencer had inherited control from his father, Joel. But when Spencer announced in 1956 that he had no interest in running the corporation, this family tradition had been broken. In the ensuing deal the lawyers worked out, control of the corporation went to Spencer's cousin Jeffrey Brett, and half-interest in the ranch, Spencer's true love, was given to him and his heirs. Moreover, Spencer had no interest in the accoutrements of great wealth that had so fascinated his big-spending forebears. Art, jewels, palatial homes, vast entertainments, private railroad cars—they all bored him, and he sold all the luxuries he had inherited, including the Burlingame estate, to Jeffrey. Spencer retained plenty of gold, but the glitter went to the Brett side of the family.

Jeffrey had many advantages, besides the obvious one of being born the grandson of Alma Collingwood Brett. He was tall and good-looking. Daily workouts with his personal trainer in the executive gym on the fifty-seventh floor kept him trim. He had graduated fourth in his class at Harvard Business School. He had excellent taste, a great deal of personal charm, and spoke French and Spanish fluently. He was a good father to his three children and a reasonably faithful husband to his wife, Irene.

But he lacked two important things: soul and balls.

He was studying a financial report on KCOL-TV, the San Francisco station Joel had opened in 1949, when the phone call came through. His manicured hand picked up the phone.

"Yes?"

He listened a moment. His face turned pale. "Thank you."

He hung up. It had been one of the news editors at KCOL-TV informing him that Spencer Collingwood had been killed. Beads of sweat appeared on Jeffrey's patrician forehead.

One of the most powerful men in California—perhaps the most powerful—looked terrified.

Irene Brett held up the necklace with its six huge cabochon emeralds and three hundred diamonds, and drank in the beauty of the blazing stones. Irene had either inherited or bought all of what the family had come to call Emma's jewels, since Emma had begun the collection. However, Irene also owned jewels that had once belonged to Alma and Alicia, as well as Zita's Burmese rubies. Now she clasped the necklace around her neck. At fifty-seven, this patrician descendant of one of the Big Four railroad kings of the past century was an attractive, stylish dyed brunette whose dinner-party invitations were eagerly sought after.

Irene rose from the dressing table and ran her hands down her slim hips, straightening the scarlet Pauline Trigère evening gown. Irene's annual clothing budget was well over a quarter-million, and W had crowned her "Queen of the West Coast." Irene had glitter in spades.

"Do you think we have to go to Spencer's memorial service?" she asked as her husband entered the bedroom from his dressing room-bathroom complex, adjusting his black tie.

"I think I should, at least."

Irene came to him to help straighten the bow tie. "I don't see

why," she said. "He was such a ghastly man. He didn't invite us to the
ranch once in twenty years."

"But Claudia might be offended."

"So what?"

"By the way, I want everything to go especially smoothly tonight."

"Darling, you seem so nervous. Of course everything will go
smoothly. It always does, doesn't it? We have the best of everything.
We always have had, and we always will."

The best of everything, he thought. That summed up what he had
wanted out of life. But the price was turning out to be Faustian.

Perfume sat at the right of her host, Jeffrey Brett, and mentally
priced the dress Calista, Lady Northfield, was wearing.

"I like you dress," she said to Calista, sitting opposite her at the
dining table. "Zandra Rhodes?"

"Yes," Calista replied, knowing Perfume well enough to head her
off at the pass. "And yes, it was expensive."

"I bet," Perfume said, undaunted. She looked around the elegant
dining room, pricing everything in her mind.

"I like you rug," she said to Jeffrey, pointing to the flowered rug
under the table. "Aubusson, no? I bet that cost you plenty. Rug prices
go crazy lately. I bet you pay hundred fifty thousand buck, maybe
more."

Jeffrey stared at the gorgeous Hong Kong movie star poured into
a Geoffrey Beene. Jeffrey couldn't imagine anyone pricing a rug, or
anything else, out loud at a dinner party, particularly in the presence
of such illustrious cultural icons as Dr. Piers Walton, curator of the
Collingwood Museum of Fine Arts, and Mr. Wellington Truex, head
of the San Francisco Opera Board. Jeffrey had assembled some tony
people for Billie Ching and Lord Northfield, but Perfume was turning
the dinner into a flea market.

"It was expensive, yes," he said, taking his cue from Calista.

"I don't unnerstan you WASPs," Perfume sighed, although she
actually relished making people squirm with her pricing shtick. "You
get all uptight when I guess how much something cost. What's so wrong
'bout how much something cost? Bruce Willis get pay five million buck
to act in some dumb movie, and it big news on telly. But I say, 'Hey,
that beautiful Pauline Trigère dress you got on, Irene, I bet it cost you
five thousand buck,' and everybody think I vulgar and got no class.
Mind if I smoke? I know I'm not supposed to."

"Perhaps," said Mrs. Wellington Truex, who looked like Margaret
Dumont in a Marx Brothers movie, "everybody is correct in thinking
you are vulgar."

Perfume shot her a dirty look as the two white-jacketed waiters refilled the wineglasses with Corton-Charlemagne '73. "Okay, I vulgar, but then, whole country is vulgar. That's what America's all about: shopping."

"I think that's a bit of an overstatement," Irene said, appalled by Perfume and trying desperately to prevent the dinner party from turning into a bout of mud wrestling. "I like to think there is still a spiritual side to our national life."

"Yeah? Like what?"

"Our love of art, for instance."

Dr. Walton nodded agreement.

"Art?" Perfume asked, exhaling cigarette smoke. "Art's nothing but a money game, and museums is nothing but a way for rich people to look virtuous and get invited to the right parties."

Dr. Walton went into a coughing fit, and Mrs. Wellington Truex almost choked on her white Burgundy. Lord Northfield stifled a laugh.

"Then, of course," Irene continued rather desperately, "for many people there still is religion."

"Religion? Pooh," Perfume sniffed. "More people killed for religion in the past five thousand year than anything else. Religion gives me the creeps. When I hear you American politicians talk to God and having prayer breakfasts in White House, I wanna go hide somewhere."

Lord Northfield cut into his mahi-mahi, flown in from Hawaii that afternoon. "It seems we had a similar conversation last week on my yacht," he said. "America's goals, and all that. Your cousin Claudia was there, Jeffrey. If I recall, she made the fascinating observation that the best things in life are free, like air and water. But of course, clean air is becoming very expensive these days, and the bottled-water business is becoming so lucrative I'm thinking of buying into it myself. I can envision in twenty years going to a restaurant and being handed not only a *carte des vins* but a *carte des eaux* as well, with vintage years like Evian 1964 or San Pellegrino 1996."

"Sure," Perfume said. "Nothing free anymore. And everything is for sale. By the way, I'm crazy 'bout that necklace, Irene. That some gorgeous piece of jewelry, and those emeralds! Wow! I bet they cost a bundle!"

Irene smiled her most patrician smile. "They didn't cost me anything, Mrs. Ching. My husband inherited them from his grandmother."

Snotty bitch, Perfume thought. But she won't be so snotty when Billie and Nigel get through with that wimpy husband of hers.

"Did you murder Spencer?" Jeffrey whispered an hour later. The cultural icons and their wives had left, and Jeffrey had led Nigel and Billie Ching into his paneled library for cigars and brandy.

"Murder Spencer?" Billie asked, sipping his Remy Martin. "Really, Jeffrey, what a tacky idea. Why in the world would you think we murdered Spencer Collingwood?"

"Because when you called me from the yacht, you said you were going to deal with Spencer your way. And then when they called me today and told me Spencer was dead, I . . ." He gulped.

"I don't think it's very friendly to assume 'my' way is murder," Billie said. "That casts definite aspersions on my character, wouldn't you say, Nigel?"

Nigel was examining a Fabergé thermometer, one of Jeffrey's collection of the Russian jeweler's objets d'art. "Definitely, Billie. Jeffrey, I think you've gone too far. You should apologize. We are legitimate businessmen, after all. Businessmen to whom, I might add, you owe eighty million dollars."

Trembling and sweating, Jeffrey felt his Ivy League cool completely draining away. In fact, he looked like a trapped rat. "I'm cooperating with you, Nigel. Hell, both of you know I want to get rid of the ranch. But I never dreamed you'd murder Spencer!"

"There's that word again," Billie said. "Really, Nigel, if Jeffrey keeps this up, we may have to do something to him . . . or one of his family perhaps."

Jeffrey stared at him. "Are you threatening me?" he whispered.

Billie's moon face remained impassive. "Jeffrey, if anyone in this room is a criminal, it's you. Let me review the situation. Last year you were gambling heavily in the bull market, using a false front to cover your stock maneuvers because you were using your insider information as CEO of the Collingwood Corporation to gamble against your own company's stock."

"That is very serious, Jeffrey," Nigel said, running his finger over a malachite picture frame holding a photo of the last tsar of Russia. "A serious felony. It could get you time in a federal prison."

"Even worse," Billie continued, "You had put up stock of the Collingwood Foundation, of which you are chairman, as margin to buy more stocks on the markets."

"Using stock of a charitable foundation is very bad, Jeffrey," Nigel noted. "This is not only illegal and spectacularly greedy, it's also non-U."

"Then came October 19, the crash, and you were caught with your trousers down. You were wiped out in a day. You were desperate for cash, and you didn't dare go to a bank—even your own bank—because of your criminal activities."

"You went to Spencer to borrow some of what you owed, which was a stupid mistake," Nigel said. "You should have known he wouldn't lend you anything, and you merely aroused his suspicions."

"When he turned you down, you came to us. We lent you the eighty million you needed."

"We, as they say, 'saved your ass.' "

"Ergo, dear Jeffrey, it is you who are the criminal, not us. We can prove what you did. Even if we had arranged Spencer's death, you could never prove it. So you will continue to do what we tell you. Is that perfectly clear?"

Jeffrey tossed down the rest of his cognac, eyeing the two well-dressed snakes. "Yes," he whispered.

"Good. Now, we are going to give Claudia one more chance to behave reasonably. As you know, a memorial service is being held for Spencer tomorrow at the ranch. You, as a grieving relative, will of course attend."

"I have never been so embarrassed as I was by that ghastly Perfume woman," Irene said, seated at her dressing table brushing her hair. She was in a nightgown, but Jeffrey, who had just come upstairs, was still in his dinner jacket, holding a brandy snifter and leaning against the bedroom door. "I almost died when she said art is just a money game, a way for people to get invited to the right parties. Really! And with Dr. Walton there! Amelia Truex said to me as she left that she thought the woman must have been raised in a bordello. And pricing everything as if we were some sort of bazaar—" In her mirror she saw her husband tilt his head crazily. "Darling, are you all right?"

He dropped the snifter and slid down the door, collapsing on the floor.

"Jeffrey!" Irene jumped up and ran to his side. "Dear God, you're drunk! Is that what you've been doing downstairs?"

"I had a little nightcap," he slurred, his eyes closed.

"Jeffrey Brett, you haven't gotten drunk in twenty years, not since Harvard beat Princeton by a field goal. Now, get up and I'll put you to bed—"

"I'm 'fraid, Irene," he whispered. " 'Fraid."

"Afraid? Of what?"

"Of them."

"Who? Billie Ching? Lord Northfield? Who? Speak to me!"

But Jeffrey had passed out. As his drunken snores rumbled out of his half-open mouth, Irene straightened.

"Well, you'll just have to sleep on the floor," she announced firmly. "I'm not going to drag you to your bed, and I hope you have a monumental hangover in the morning."

She turned out the lights, went to her bed, and climbed in. As she turned out her bed lamp, she repeated to herself, "Afraid? How very strange."

*   *   *

Claudia watched the California quail dart across the path in front of her. It was dawn the day of her father's memorial service. Since there had been literally nothing left of Spencer after the crash of his Porsche, the necessity of funeral arrangements was obviated, but the sudden disappearance of her father from the planet without even a good-bye left her sad and empty. Though she disliked funeral homes and open caskets, she wished she could have seen him one more time. Memorial services were the trend in death these days, but they were somehow unsatisfying. She wondered if the Victorians' wallowing in the trappings of funerary grief, so mocked by succeeding generations, might not have been somehow healthier after all.

She strolled down the path from the ranch house to the beach. The sky was pinkening and a cool breeze was blowing in from the ocean. She had walked this beach many times as a girl. Now, as then, the rhythmic slapping of the surf soothed her.

She thought of Arthur Stevens. He had been unexpectedly nice— unexpected in that one didn't think of high-powered lawyers as thought- ful human beings. He had asked her if she would like him to spend the night at the ranch house, and she had quickly said yes: the thought of being alone in the house under the circumstances had been unpleasant. They had cooked dinner together and enjoyed each other's company. She found him strong, smart, and extremely . . . reassuring. Yes, that was the word. She liked having him around.

He was also, she had to admit, one of the sexiest men she had ever met. She was not unhappy when he informed her his wife had run off with his personal trainer.

As she walked down the beach, she looked at the ranch she loved, this land that she now had to fight to save. But how? If Jeffrey sided with Lord Northfield and Billie Ching, what options did she have?

It was then she saw ahead of her an elderly woman with gray hair. She was kneeling by a dead sea gull.

"Good morning," Claudia said, coming up to her.

"Good morning."

"What happened to the sea gull?"

"It was killed, poor thing. I've seen a lot of them die lately. There's a landfill near Camp Pendleton that many of the gulls go to. They'll eat anything, you know. And sometimes they get poisoned from the garbage. God knows what's in those dumps."

Even before my family, Claudia thought, staring down at the dead sea gull, there were the Indians. And before them, the birds and the animals. A bird might not seem important, but in the last analysis, was there anything more important?

Suddenly she knew what she had to do.

"Thank you," she said to the old woman as she started running up the beach.

"Thanks for what?" the lady cried, surprised.

But Claudia didn't answer. She had to find Arthur. She knew he had gone out a half-hour earlier for his run, and she had suggested her father's race course as a terrific jogging place. She had not wanted to see the garage where Spencer had met his death, which was why she hadn't run with Arthur, but now it didn't matter. She knew how to avenge Spencer's death. She'd need Arthur's help, though.

Fifteen minutes later, she climbed up the bluff to the racetrack. It was growing hot, and she was panting and sweaty. She saw Arthur coming toward her in the distance. She started running in his direction, waving her hand. When they reached each other, Arthur stopped, though continuing to run in place to keep his pulse up. Carrying two eight-pound weights in his hands, he was wearing nothing but his running shorts and shoes. While she caught her breath, she admired his sweaty, muscular torso.

"Arthur . . ." puff, puff, ". . . I know what I want to do with the ranch. That is, if you think it will work . . ."

The memorial service was short and lightly attended, because the recluse had had few friends. Afterward a procession of seven automobiles filed back to the ranch house, where Ana had prepared a light lunch of salads and white wine. Most of the guests were ranch hands, and Claudia reflected that they had been as close to her father as anyone. It was an odd finale for a family that had been known for its lavish entertainments and social cachet.

To Claudia's surprise, Jeffrey flew down from San Francisco in his private jet for the service. She hadn't seen her cousin for years, but thought that time had treated him well, although he looked a bit wobbly. Jeffrey was suffering the monumental hangover Irene had wished on him. However, after several glasses of wine he seemed to recover his equilibrium.

"I'd like to talk to you later," he said, coming over to Claudia. "After the others have gone."

"Of course. Is it business?"

"Well, family business."

"Then, if you don't mind, I'll have Arthur with me. He's representing me now."

"Oh." Jeffrey's bloodshot eyes looked at Arthur, who was wearing a well-tailored dark blue suit.

Damn, Jeffrey thought. That makes things ten times worse. That Arthur's one tough son of a bitch.

"I know this is an awkward time to bring up business," Jeffrey said an hour later as he, Claudia, and Arthur convened in the rather battered library of the house. "But since we are all together, I thought I should take the opportunity to bring up the ranch. Billie Ching and Lord Northfield have contacted me with their two-billion-dollar offer. Of course, I haven't indicated to them whether I would accept it—"

"Would you?" Claudia interrupted.

"Well, I certainly would consider it. It's a handsome offer, and Billie and Nigel are top-drawer developers. They told me they'd shown you their model and you'd been impressed."

"Yes, I was. But if the ranch is to be developed, why wouldn't we do it? We have the financial resources with the Pacific Bank and the insurance company, and if we did it, we could do it the way we wanted."

"Yes, of course, that's true. But while your father was alive, developing was out of the question. And now our plate is so full with other projects, it would be years before we could start on the ranch. Billie and Nigel are ready to move ahead now, and they're offering a damned good price in cash. We all will do extremely well, and it won't cost us a nickel of our own money."

Claudia went to the old-fashioned wooden mantel lined with family photographs, including a studio pose of Emma sometime around the turn of the century. Claudia looked at the photos a moment, then turned to Jeffrey.

"So you'd let the ranch go, just like that?" She snapped her fingers. "Forget the family tradition, forget the family, sell out to a bunch of rich foreigners?"

"The Calafía Ranch has been only a part of our family tradition, Claudia."

"But a big part. You have no sentimental attachment to it at all? It's just a real-estate deal?"

He shrugged. "I can't truthfully say I have any sentimental attachment to it, no."

"It's just like the Kinsolving Shipping Line? It was losing money, so sell it."

"Claudia, you have to be practical. I'm as sentimental as the next person, but times change. We can't afford to be strangled by the past. The dead are dead: the world belongs to the living."

"So much for Memorial Day. Well, the fact is, Jeffrey, no one is going to develop the Calafía Ranch. Neither Billie and Nigel nor us nor anyone else. I've decided to give the ranch to the State of California."

Jeffrey stared at her. "I assume you're joking," he said.

"Not at all. The ranch is going to remain just as it is forever. It will be open to the public to camp in—but only on horseback or on foot. No cars will be allowed on the ranch. There aren't going to be any shopping malls, any fast-food stands, no theme parks or multiplex movie houses, no landfills, no garbage—and certainly no gambling casinos. There's going to be nothing. Because by leaving it natural and untouched, we leave it unpolluted and clean. And that is the greatest gift the Collingwood family can give to the State of California, which has given a lot to the Collingwood family."

"I don't believe this," Jeffrey sputtered. "You're giving away a billion dollars?"

Claudia smiled. "Yes. It's a rather magnificent gesture, isn't it? Very much in the family tradition. But I have two trust funds with enough money in them for seven lifetimes, and I'm no pig—unlike certain of my relatives. This is what my father wanted, and somehow I think this is what my ancestors would have wanted, wherever they are. You say the world belongs to the living, but I don't believe that. We have a debt to the past and an obligation to the future. And our obligation to the future is to stop trashing this planet."

Jeffrey stood up. "You're as crazy as your father," he said.

"Maybe Daddy wasn't so crazy."

"He was a nut. I hate to disappoint you, Claudia, but the disposition of the ranch doesn't rest in your hands alone. I represent the rest of the family, and—"

"Excuse me, Jeffrey, but we're way ahead of you. Read it to him, Arthur, please."

Arthur pulled a paper from his jacket pocket. "When Claudia told me her decision this morning, I faxed my office for a copy of the agreement Spencer made with you and the rest of the family back in 1956. Paragraph Eight reads"—he unfolded the paper—" 'In return for the undersigned, Spencer Collingwood's, relinquishing of executive control of the Collingwood Corporation, the undersigned, Jeffrey Brett, agrees not only to grant Spencer Collingwood and his heirs and assigns fifty-percent personal ownership of said ranch, but also to grant Spencer Collingwood and his heirs and assigns veto power over the disposition of said ranch. Furthermore, the other contracting parties—i.e., the rest of the Collingwood family owning Class A shares of Collingwood Corporation stock—cannot prevent Spencer Collingwood or his heirs and assigns from disposing of said ranch in any way they see fit.' "

He folded the paper and smiled.

"You're making a terrible mistake," Jeffrey said hoarsely. "I beg of you to reconsider. The ranch can be developed in a way to protect the ecology . . ."

"No," Claudia said. "My mind's made up. It was made up for me this morning, when I realized even the sea gulls are being poisoned. There's going to be no development. The ranch is going to stay forever natural, and maybe that will help the ozone layer a bit, not to mention the greenhouse effect. Jeffrey, to be brutally blunt, you've betrayed the family." She looked at her watch. "I heard the weather report. They say there's a possibility of thunderstorms. You may want to get your jet back to San Francisco before—"

"I get the hint, Claudia. With all your wonderful talk about saving the planet and family tradition, you're causing a rift that may tear this family apart. Think about that when you think about your goddamn ozone layer. Meanwhile, my lawyers have their work cut out for them. Something tells me we're all going to be seeing a lot of each other in court for the next ten years." Giving Arthur an icy look, he stormed out.

For a moment Claudia didn't budge. Then she turned to Arthur. "Can his lawyers stop us?" she asked.

"I'm sure they'll try. They'll probably argue that the 1956 agreement never contemplated giving the ranch away and that the rest of the family is being unfairly deprived of income. On the other hand, since you can veto anything they could do with the ranch, the ultimate power is still in your hands. Somewhere down the line they'd probably settle, particularly if we can work out some favorable tax arrangements with the state."

"Have I done the right thing?" she asked nervously.

"You've done a wonderful thing," he said. "I've never admired anyone so much in my life."

She turned to look again at the photos on the mantel. "I think," she finally said, "Emma would approve."

The private 727 with "Perfume" painted on the nose eased down onto the single runway jutting like a knife into Kowloon Bay. Billie Ching and Perfume stepped out of the jet into the steamy haze of Kai Tak Airport in Hong Kong. After a perfunctory check with a waiting customs minion, the two walked to their helicopter, which lifted off, flying them over Victoria Harbor and then Hong Kong Island. Twenty minutes later, the copter settled onto the pad behind Billie's mansion overlooking Repulse Bay. The house, which had been built in the early thirties by a Chinese import-export magnate, looked very properly British colonial. Built of stucco, it had a tiled roof and was surrounded by porches and verandas. As several houseboys unloaded Perfume's Bottega Veneta luggage, Billie went into the house to his air-conditioned

office. He sat at his desk, picked up his phone, and punched a number.
"It's Billie," he said after a moment. "Initiate phase two."

"This is one of my favorite restaurants," Arthur said two nights
later as he led Claudia into the crowded Chinois on Main, Wolfgang
Puck's Santa Monica restaurant.

"Do you eat out a lot?"

"Yes, since Katie left. I'm not a bad cook, but . . . well, I like to
get out of the house. I get a little lonely."

They were shown to a table near the copper-domed kitchen.

"May I order for you?" Arthur asked. "I think I could order
something you'd like."

"Of course."

"I'll have the grilled salmon with cilantro sauce and black and gold
noodles," he told the waiter. "And she'll have the lobster risotto with
deep-fried spinach. And a bottle of the Mondavi Fumé Blanc."

"It sounds fattening," she said as the waiter left.

"It really isn't."

"Tell me about Katie."

He toyed with a spoon a moment. "She's quite beautiful. We met
at UCLA and I fell in love after about ten minutes. We were married
after I got out of law school. She wanted to be an actress . . . I mean,
she was really very serious about it."

"Was she good?"

"I suppose. But the movie business is so unpredictable. I mean,
why do some people become stars and other people never click?"

Claudia smiled. "My grandmother, Laura Lord, became a star with
a lot of help from my grandfather."

"Oh, sure, connections help."

"Connections? It was sex."

Arthur smiled. "Well, maybe. Katie's got a lot of sex appeal too.
Anyway, she was in a couple of movies and did some episodes for
Moonlighting. But it never seemed to happen for her. It hurt her a lot.
And then one day she took off with my personal trainer. They live in
Venice now and she's heavily into yoga."

"Any kids?"

"Gilbert. He's ten. He's a real sweet kid who lives on his
skateboard."

"I'd love to meet him."

"Would you like to drop by the house after dinner? I'm only a
little way from your hotel. Gil will be there."

"I'd love to."

The waiter brought the bottle of wine. As Arthur swirled his glass

and sniffed the bouquet, she had an odd sense of déjà vu. Suddenly
she realized why.

She had felt just this way during that first dreamy lunch with Guy
at the Château de Soubise two years before.

"Do you like Rachmaninoff?" he said an hour and a half later as
he turned his Mercedes off Stone Canyon Road into his driveway.

"I adore Rachmaninoff."

"Then you're a romantic, like me."

"You fell in love with Katie in ten minutes, but I fell in love with
Guy in five."

He smiled. "And look how we both ended up. Come on."

The house was a handsome California version of a New England-
style home, although it was made of whitewashed bricks instead of
clapboard.

"I like your house," she said as they paused at the front door.

"Thanks. I bought it last year. I call it Mortgage Manor. I'm putting
in a tennis court." He unlocked the door and went inside to turn on
lights. With the lights also came the opening strains of Rachmaninoff's
third piano concerto.

"Horowitz," he said as Claudia came in. "Make yourself at home.
I'll go get Gil."

She stepped down into a capacious living room. Three electronic
sculptures on the walls were blinking, casting flashes on two huge striped
paintings in Day-Glo colors. The house was very contemporary, which
was not her favorite style; but it was in good taste.

"Hi."

She turned and saw a boy standing in a doorway. With his father's
features, he was a beautiful child.

"I'm Gilbert," he said. "My dad said to tell you he's getting some
wine. And he was right."

"Right about what?"

"He said you look like Princess Di."

"Why, thank you."

"But that you're a lot smarter."

Claudia burst into laughter.

"Gilbert, you talk too much," Arthur said, coming up behind him.
He was carrying two pale green wineglasses. "We'll have a quick nightcap, then I'll take you to the hotel. What do you think of Gilbert?"

"I think he's very handsome and very nice."

"I'm not, really," Gilbert said. "I'm really a brat."

"His words, not mine." Arthur gave her one of the glasses. "Here's
to Calafía State Park," he said, touching his glass to hers.

"Oh, no. It's going to be called Collingwood State Park."

"Fine by me. Cheers."

They looked into each other's eyes as they sipped the wine. I wonder, she thought, if it's smart to sleep with one's lawyer. I mean, if he asks.

At six thirty the next morning, she put on her jogging clothes, tied her Reeboks, then left the hotel grounds to start a two-mile run. She headed south on Stone Canyon Road, then turned right on Bellagio Road, and ran by the grounds of the Bel Air Country Club. The road was virtually empty.

She had run her first half-mile when a gray Toyota motored up behind her. Suddenly it shot ahead and gunned for Claudia. Two seconds before she was hit, she became aware of her danger and tried to run off the road.

But the car hit her and she was sent flying almost twenty feet, landing in a bush.

The Toyota, driven by an Asian, never stopped.

Jeffrey Brett was running scared. The news of Claudia's near-fatal "accident"—which he knew it wasn't—had jolted him into a state of panic. Arthur had phoned him that Claudia had survived the car attack but that she was in Cedars-Sinai Hospital with a broken hip, a broken right leg, two broken ribs, whiplash, multiple contusions, and—most ominously—she was in a coma. The doctors gave her a good chance for survival, but they were more guarded about the coma. She had received a severe blow on the back of the head, and there was a distinct possibility she might never regain consciousness.

Jeffrey paced to one of the window walls of his vast office. Fifty-eight floors below, San Francisco was spread before him. He could see Rincon Hill, where one hundred and forty years before, Scott Kinsolving had built his wooden mansion and received his new bride, Emma. Rincon Hill was now the western terminus of the Oakland Bay Bridge. He could see Nob Hill, where Emma and Archer had built their pseudo-Renaissance palace. A twenty-story hotel now stood on the site.

Claudia had said he was betraying the family. God knows, it had had its fair share of crooks and lowlifes, Slade and Loretta Dawson being prime examples of the breed, but now the Collingwoods were like the Rockefellers, Mellons, Fords, and Duponts. Surrounded by the halo of good works, they were as close to royalty as one could get in America, above suspicion.

But they were not above the law. Jeffrey pulled a handkerchief

from his pocket and wiped his brow. Claudia was right: he had betrayed
the family, and he might have to pay for it with that most unthinkable
of horrors for a Collingwood: prison. All because of such an old, familiar flaw: greed.

One of the richest men in America, he had an income in excess
of five million dollars a year, and yet he had been spending over seven
million a year. One spectacular year he had spent nine million. There
were the girls, of course. Bedding Irene was like bedding an Eskimo
Pie, and he had played around: high-class call girls, even a few daughters
of family friends. Being a Collingwood was sexy: girls were moths
around the flame of class, celebrity, wealth.

But the girls hadn't chewed up his fortune. There were the cars,
the yacht, the private jet. Jeffrey had inherited the family mania for
art, and he had spent well over thirty million on art over the years.
Irene's jewels and clothes, the mansion in Burlingame, the pied-à-terre
in Trump Tower in New York, the château in Normandy, the chalet
in Gstaad, the estate in Maui. The glitter had eaten up the gold.

Playing the market had seemed an almost foolproof way to beat
the game. How simple to buy and sell your own company stock when
you knew every move the company was going to make. It was a money
machine. How did he know the goddamn market was going to crash?

"Mr. Brett," said the voice over the intercom, "Mr. Stevens is
here to see you."

He quickly returned to his desk. "Send him in."

He sat down heavily. Well, here it was. The final shoot-out at the
Collingwood Corral. Jeffrey had no doubt that Arthur had figured it
all out. The sound of his voice on the phone had been lethal.

He looked around his office he was so proud of. The furniture was
prime modern with classic overtones: a triumphant mix of contemporary
pieces with choice antiques, including two magnificently ugly Chinese
war gods flanking the stainless steel doors. The colors of the walls that
weren't glass were subdued heliotropes with violet trim. The office had
been done by John Saladino, and everything was the best. Two Mon-
drians, one of which had set Jeffrey back a staggering $11 million, and
three Klees paid obeisance to the Great God Contemporary Art. The
setting for the shootout was Haute CEO. No office in America, Jeffrey
reflected, was classier.

The stainless-steel doors opened and Arthur came in, glancing at
the life-size Ming Dynasty war gods on either side. The doors closed.
Arthur walked across the soft violet carpet to Jeffrey's English Regency
desk with its columned corners.

"Slade Dawson," Arthur said. "I spent twelve hours studying Collingwood stock transactions for the past two years, and I finally figured
it out. You're Slade Dawson."

Jeffrey's face was ashen. "I couldn't understand why Spencer's accountants didn't spot it."

"Spencer's accountants don't know the Collingwood family history the way I do. You picked the name of one of your less savory ancestors to cover up your insider trading. Slade Dawson was trading Collingwood stock and doing damned well until October 19. Then he took one of the great baths of the century. Who bailed you out? Billie Ching and Lord Northfield?"

"Yes."

"I'm taking this to the SEC and the California prosecuting attorney, so if you want to fight it, you'd better get your attorneys in here fast."

"I'm not going to fight it." Jeffrey sounded tired. "I did it. I betrayed the family. But I swear to you, Arthur, I had no idea they would murder Spencer or try to murder Claudia. I'm a crook, but I'm no murderer."

Arthur studied his frightened face. "Yes, I believe that, Jeffrey. Frankly, you don't have the balls to murder. But you're going to do time, Jeffrey. If you cooperate with the state and help us indict Billie and Nigel, you ought to be able to get a reduced sentence."

Jeffrey stood up. "You'll never prove anything against Billie and Nigel. No way. They're too clever. And if I turned against them, God knows what they'd do to one of my kids. No, there's only one way out for me, Arthur. And I have no intention of spending even one night in prison."

In one motion he picked up a steel-and-leather Barcelona chair and smashed it against the glass wall behind his desk. The double-pane window shattered. The office was suddenly filled with a roaring wind.

"Jeffrey! For Chrissake!"

Arthur raced around the desk. Jeffrey had thrown down the chair and was standing in front of the gaping hole, looking fifty-eight floors down, the wind whipping his suit and his hair. He hesitated just long enough for Arthur to grab his right arm.

"Let me go!" he screamed.

"Get back!"

"I won't go to any goddamn prison!"

The two men wrestled before the shattered window. Arthur managed to tackle Jeffrey and they rolled back and forth on the floor, beating each other. Then Arthur found himself at the edge of the window, his head sticking outside the building, the wind pounding his ears. Arthur had a fear of heights, and for one sickening second he swiveled his head and looked down at Montgomery Street. The cars were tiny ants.

Then he felt Jeffrey push off him.

"Tell Claudia I'm sorry!" he yelled. And then he dived out the window. Arthur saw Jeffrey sail over him, his eyes shut tight, his mouth open in a scream.

The scream died away like a lonesome train whistle.

And then silence.

She looks like Sleeping Beauty, Arthur thought as he sat by her bed in the private hospital room. He gently took her right hand.

"You have to fight it, Claudia," he said softly. "The doctors say your brain has to heal itself, there's nothing they can do. It's been three days now. Please wake up."

She was breathing deeply, her eyes shut. Her brain waves and heartbeat were monitored, and they beeped peacefully on the green screen by her bed. An I.V. tube slithered into her left nostril.

"You've got to wake up," Arthur continued. The doctor had told him of a theory that coma victims could hear voices even if they didn't react. There were cases on record where people had been talked out of a coma. Arthur thought it was worth trying. "We all need you, Claudia. You're the last Collingwood. Jeffrey's dead, and Irene is selling Emma's jewels to pay back Billie Ching and Nigel. She and the rest of the family have agreed to giving the ranch to the state, so it's all over. Billie and Nigel are through. We beat them, Claudia, so please, please wake up."

Claudia didn't move a muscle.

"I don't know if you can hear me," he continued, "but I have a selfish reason for wanting you to wake up, and it's not only that you're a pretty important client to me." He wiped his eyes. "God, is that a klutzy way of saying it. You see, I've fallen in love with you. I know this is probably some crazy pipe dream on my part, but what can I say? I think you're terrific. I also think you're gorgeous and I would love to make love to you. And Gilbert thinks you're great. Okay, so here I go again. I fell for Katie in ten minutes, but with you it was only, like, two. So anyway, if you can hear me, I'm like, you know, nuts about you."

The door opened and a nurse appeared. "How is she?" she whispered, coming in.

He shrugged. "The same. I don't know. I'm getting depressed."

The nurse went to the other side of the bed. "It takes time," she said. "I'm going to bathe her now, Mr. Stevens."

Arthur stood up, looking at the Sleeping Beauty.

"Good night, Claudia. I'll be back tomorrow. And remember what I said: you have to fight."

"You're a good friend," the nurse said.

"Yeah. And I'd like to be more than a friend," he sighed.

He was waiting at the elevator down the hall when he heard the nurse.

"Mr. Stevens!"

She was running toward him, waving. "She's awake! She just said a word!"

"What?"

"She said, 'Emma.' Who's Emma?"

Arthur was laughing as he ran back toward Claudia's room.

"A pretty terrific gal!"

Two months later, he held her in his arms as he carefully stepped down into his swimming pool. She had finally been released from the hospital, her right leg out of its cast, a pin in her hip, the cuts and bruises healed. He had brought her home to his house, arranged around-the-clock private nurses, and every morning took her into his pool to help her exercise her legs. Rachmaninoff's "Rhapsody on a Theme of Paganini" played softly from the poolside speakers.

"You know, you're getting to be a habit," she said, smiling, her arms around his neck.

"I hope it's not a bad habit."

"Hardly. You've been wonderful to me. Above and beyond the duties of expensive lawyer. I really owe you so much, Arthur."

"I got a fax from Maître Legrand."

"Guy's lawyer? Now what?"

"There're no problems. Apparently Guy's going to marry the widow next door to the château."

"Madame Valmont? Oh, that's perfect!"

"Why?"

"She owns sixty hectares Guy's always lusted for. She'd never sell, but now that she's a widow, Guy's marrying her to get the land."

"Well, as the yuppies say, real estate is life. You can start your kicks now."

They were neck-deep in the water. He held her as her long legs started slowly kicking beneath the water.

"I had the oddest dream last night," she said.

"What?"

"I dreamed I was back in the hospital and you were sitting beside my bed. And you said . . . let me see: what was it? You said, 'I've fallen in love with you. I know this is probably some crazy pipe dream on my part, but what can I say? I think you're terrific!' "

He stared at her. "That's no dream. That really happened. I did say that! You mean, you were awake and didn't tell me?"

She shrugged, giving him a sphingine smile. "Who knows? But if you don't kiss me soon, I think I'm going to be very unhappy. You know, we Collingwood women have always had a soft spot for good-looking guys."

He brought his mouth to hers. She stopped kicking as they kissed. Suddenly Claudia Collingwood felt very happy indeed.